CHILD of the
WILDERNESS

Missy Priest

PAGE PUBLISHING, INC.
New York, NY

First originally published by Page Publishing, Inc. 2015

ISBN 978-1-68213-454-2 (pbk)
ISBN 978-1-68213-455-9 (digital)

Printed in the United States of America

CHAPTER 1

1976

The night was particularly cold and dark for the first part of spring in East Texas, especially cold for the farmhouse that was shelter for the children who lived there. Sara was only sixteen and had been supporting her little sister, Saline, thirteen, and baby brother, Jody, two, for the two years leading up to this point.

The house had no central heat, heaters, or fireplaces. The limited supply of blankets was well used.

Sara knew that her mother and her new husband were both drunk and stoned. Her new stepfather was only twenty-one years old and, in general, married their mother as a means to try to get closer to both Sara and her sister. But both young girls were armed with the knowledge that only comes with the benefit of experience having lived with the former husband of their mother—another mean drunk who thrived on the terror he caused to the children in their family.

Sara listened as the two drunks got louder and louder, knowing that her two siblings could never sleep through what was happening. She prayed that both would fall into a drunken stupor rather than escalate into the violence that had become intolerable. She prayed that God would give her the strength to be able to protect her young siblings again.

There was milk in the refrigerator and little else. Sara had not worked that day, so she had not been able to bring food home for the three of them. But somehow her mother and her husband managed to supply themselves with booze, drugs, and cigarettes. They all three were hungry, cold, and afraid. After two years in Texas, however, they had a way to escape when things got too bad to be in the house. Sara and Saline had prepared a place for them in the old barn out back. They had hidden blankets and padded it with the stuffing of an old mattress so they would not have to sleep on the hard floor.

There were four bedrooms in the old farmhouse, yet the three young siblings slept together for the love and security it provided. The two sisters would pull a heavy dresser to block the door, just in case Oscar, their stepfather, would attempt to get into the room. Beating at his hand happened from time to time, but because of their mother's abusive previous husband, they stayed together to keep each other from being molested. So far, it had worked.

Although older than Saline, Sara was much smaller in stature than her sister. They shared the same mother but had different fathers. When Sara knew trouble was coming, she would have Saline take little Jody to the prepared place in the barn, and she would join them when she was sure they were safe. It was going to be one of those nights. She hated to send her siblings out of the house to the barn, leaving what little shelter the cold farmhouse provided. And the misting rain made it that much colder.

"Take Jody to the barn, Saline. I will stay and get the milk and join you in a minute. And hurry, you don't want to get to wet," Sara said.

Saline didn't want to leave her older sister alone in the house, but she obeyed.

Saline and Jody went out the window to go to the barn, then Sara went as quietly as she could to the kitchen to get the milk. She turned no lights on and was as silent as a mouse. But then behind her, a light turned on.

"What do you think you are doing?" Oscar asked, walking toward her. Oscar was about seventy pounds heavier than Sara, but in his drunken state, she knew that he would be clumsy in his movements.

"I was just getting a glass of water, is all," Sara said, trying hard to control the fear in her voice. She could smell the all too familiar odor of too many cigarettes, alcohol, and pot all combined. It sickened her. To let him touch her was not an option. She knew that she would not get any protection from her mother. Her mother had never protected her children from harm; it was up to Sara to protect herself and her younger siblings from yet another monster.

Oscar stepped toward Sara, and she didn't move, didn't even try to step back. She knew that her stepfather's reflexes were slowed from all the drinking and drugs. She was counting on that. Another step forward. Sara tightened her grip on the bat that was hidden there just in case. Her reflexes, along with her fear, sprung before he could reach her. She struck the side of Oscar's head before he knew what was happening. He fell to his knees but quite unexpectedly grabbed Sara as he fell.

Sara had expected the blow to knock him out for the night, and once again she would be able to escape, but now he had her. She screamed and started fighting. Only one blow from Oscar, striking her, and she was down. The blow struck her like an iron pot. She closed her eyes to the stench of him. Then he fell on top of her, not seeing what it was that had made him stop his pursuit of her. Then her eyes opened, and she saw her younger sister stood above her.

Saline stood holding the bat that Sara had dropped when their evil stepfather had attacked. Quickly, she climbed out from under him and saw active bleeding from his head, but she couldn't stop to see if he was alive or dead; she had to hurry. She got the precious milk from the refrigerator and took her little sister's hand, and they hurried, not stopping, to the barn.

When she knew that both of her siblings were safe once again, Sara got on her knees and thanked God for her sister and brother being with her. But her silent prayers to God this night were different from what she usually showed her younger siblings.

"Dear God, I have had faith so long. I am sorry for my persistent prayers, but I am so tired and hungry and scared, and I know you see us here. Please let someone help us. We feel forgotten by this world. Jesus, please help us. In your name, once again I stand before

God. Give me the strength to protect those I love. Amen." She concluded and got in the little corner to spend the rest of the cold night trying to comfort the other two children.

Sara and Saline huddled together and once more made sure their little brother got his milk; only then could they lay down and rest. They put their heads down and only then rested.

Neither young woman knew that the very next day would be the day that God would, indeed, deliver to them the kindness that they had waited for so long. Real rest was something that neither girl had ever known, but they now had waited for God to deliver them from the nightmare that was their lives.

The next morning, still huddled in the corner, the children had woken up, and Sara went to work. At the little café on Interstate 20, Sara made sure that her friend put enough food aside so she could take it home to feed her little sister and brother. But as always, first, Mary had made sure Sara herself had eaten a full meal and drunk a glass of milk that she had made.

At five feet six inches tall, Mary knew that Sara had arrived at her current weight of only 104 pounds by giving most of the food she collected to her family, so Mary made sure that the young girl also took care of herself to eat so that her younger siblings could continue to have food.

Mary herself was only five years older than Sara. Yet like her, she had had to grow up at an early age. But unlike Mary, Sara was not what anyone would call callous toward other people. Yet at the same time, if a man touched Sara in passing, it would send her crying to the kitchen, scared to death for her life.

Mary knew Sara's family and knew her mother was a real piece of work—a woman so shameful and self-centered she would offer any of her children to the highest bidder to feed herself and her addictions.

Mary's own two children were her life and the life of that of her husbands, so much so that if anyone ever touched a hair on their heads, she knew that they would have to do so over her own dead body first. And so when her young protégée would come in as she was today, with bruises that she could not cover, on her arms and face, it angered Mary to the point that she had to do something.

After having known Sara for just over a year, she took the liberty of finding just the right person that could possibly do something about not only Sara but her sister and her brother as well.

Her search came in the form of a middle-aged man named John Byers.

John Byers was everything that Texas stood for. His and his family's success and fame were everything that Texas stood for. But as powerful of a man as he was, his blue eyes reflected warmth. His wife, three sons, and friends were ever present at his side when he would come in the little café, and she had noticed that the eldest boy's attention had caught the notice of Sara. Unfortunately, Sara's attention was usually set on other things. But Scott Byers, the eldest son, had told Mary he would like to meet the thin yet very sweet girl that seemed unusually mature and find out something other than little things about her.

On that day, before Sara had arrived at the little café to work her usual very long shifts of over twelve hours, John Byers had come in to get his morning coffee before he went about starting everyone on the vast workings of the one of the largest ranches in the country, then be off to Dallas to check on the oil empire that he regarded as the "way he supported his livestock habit," when Mary approached him.

"Ms. Mary, where is your young partner?" he asked, knowing she had something on her mind.

"She had another physical encounter from that stepdad of hers again," she answered, then saw his brows rise.

He hated to see the young lady come in with long sleeves to try and cover the bruises he had seen on her.

She could read his thoughts, and she had met Sara's stepfather few years before.

"Have you seen her this morning?" he asked.

"Yes," Mary answered. "She never complains. But she has tried to safeguard her little sister and baby brother by the three of them sleeping in the falling-down barn on their place because their stepfather once again was drunk."

"They slept in a barn?" he said, looking up from the stack of papers in front of him. "It was freezing last night. Are you sure of this, Mary?"

"Yes. I saw her emerging this morning when I tried to pick her up for work. But she is walking in. Please don't let her know that I said something," Mary said and hurried to the kitchen.

Mr. Byers looked above his paper at the young woman who came in the door with her long dark-red hair down as opposed to being in a ponytail as usual, ready for work. When she brought his coffee out, she tried to let the hair cover only the latest swollen eye that had deep bruising already apparent. He knew it to be something that would be present for some time to come. And he knew there were likely broken bones and other bruises that he couldn't see.

When she returned a few minutes later to refill his coffee cup, just about the time, the front door to the café opened for his sons. He placed his hand on hers to ask her her name.

The panic of the young woman's next movement brought everyone to their feet and, of course, Mary from the kitchen.

She threw that glass decanter that held the coffee pot and narrowly missed Mr. Byers's head. Then Sara took off toward the kitchen, looking for cover. But instead of the kitchen and Mary, Sara ran straight into the arms of Scott Byers. Mr. Byers's eldest son, then, was only five years Sara's senior.

For a moment, everything seemed to stop as Scott looked down into the glowing emerald-green eyes of the fair-faced, red-haired little beauty. Then Scott's own anger had to halt as the little creature in front of his eyes seemed to roll back, and she collapsed.

Mary really didn't know what to do when she saw Sara begin to fall to the floor, momentarily cradled in the strong arms of the kind yet fierce young man she had known all her life. Mary knew that Scott had been trying to meet Sara and could not have arranged things to happen any better.

Mary brought a cool rag out to dampen Sara's face, and Scott, who had eased Sara to the floor, sat there with her in his arms and wiped her face and talked to her as one would a fearful little animal that had been injured and discarded in the road.

Scott pushed her hair back and used the damp rag to try to revive her while he had her securely, so maybe she would not be afraid. John Byers looked at the two on the floor and the ranch hands that had come in with his son and motioned for them to leave the pair alone to their own devices, to try to possibly make the young girl a little less alarmed.

Yes, this was a problem that John Byers could handle silently, knowing that this was something left to ranch hands, and the bastard who had hurt the obviously injured, as did the ranch hands. Decent people didn't harm young women, who also happened to be children at the same time. Yes, this problem would not be one that would not be reoffended as long as he lived and could take care of it so easily.

When Mary had come from the kitchen, he smiled and cocked an eyebrow, and the silent communication was taken as a binding contract that these children would forever be in the appropriate hands.

After a few minutes, Mary walked upon the two, who were still on the floor. She asked Scott if all was well. Sara, who seemed to be emerging out of a deep sleep, looked up into his blue eyes that seemed to be trying to tell her as he would a young calf that she didn't have to worry about her surroundings and that all was being taken care of. Noting her surroundings, then seeing that Mary was not far away, her eyes started to mist.

"Don't worry, my beauty. No one is going to hurt you," Scott said.

"Mary," she said, trying to see where her friend was.

"She is right here," he said. "I am Scott Byers. What is your name?" he asked and wiped a tear that had started to make its way down her face. "You are a little pale," Scott said tenderly and continued to wipe her face.

"What happened?" she asked, never taking her green eyes off the man that held her.

"I have wanted to meet you, my little beauty, and you seemed to walk into my arms," Scott said, not willing to let her go as easily as she arrived. "What happened? Who has hurt you so much?" he asked, knowing full well the answer, as Mary had been telling him for months. He knew all too well not to trust the common gossip to tell him everything he needed to know about the fragile young woman he had taken an interest in over a year before. He had known her stepfather for most of his worthless life. He was a drunken bully who loved to pick on women and small animals rather than take on a more worthy person.

John Byers saw this as a splendid time to make introductions to the young girl child. "Young lady, I am John Byers," he said to the young girl. "I didn't mean to alarm you a moment ago. I just wanted to ask if this was a school uniform that I see you wearing so frequently," he asked.

Sara frowned a little bit and saw the decal on the front of the private-school uniform that she had worn while she attended a school in Wales, over in the UK, since she was five years old.

"Yes, sir," she answered in a voice that was barely heard.

Then kneeling down, he asked where that might be. The answer would take a family such as the Byers family years to completely comprehend.

The answer would take them from the beautiful countryside of East Texas, across this continent, to a land of kingdoms complete with castles and palaces and the like, to the world of another kind of wealth and power that people in this country didn't know existed in anything but storybooks.

"Really?" Mr. Byers said. "Son, I believe that your momma would like to hear about this place from her," his father said, which turned the question back to Sara.

"Oh, sir. I am sorry," Sara said and attempted to rise, causing her to become dizzy.

"Don't you worry, my dear. Our son will provide you means of transport. It is the least I could do for scaring you like I did," he said, making Sara feel foolish. He reached out and touched delicately her soft, pale cheek that was indeed the result of the bastard he knew from before. "Fear not, little angel. We have a way to deal with such as this, where they don't make a child fear even friends reaching out. We will deal with him, and my Allison will get you and yours strong again. Son, make sure she knows the directions."

"Yes, sir. I believe I will deliver them personally," Scott said softly.

"Mary, my Allison wanted to make sure that you are still coming this weekend to the BBQ," Mr. Byers said.

"We wouldn't miss it," Mary said and smiled. *Yes,* she thought, *this couldn't have gone better if I had planned it.* And that was the end and the beginning.

Sara had walked to work early that morning, the mile it took to go from her mother's little country house to the café. Mary knew that she frequently had to walk that far up the busy interstate highway that brought with it every kind of human in the world that should make the young girl be fearful of it. Yet the demon that was living right there in her mother's house was worse than anything else that could happen any place. She had to provide the means by which she supported her sister and brother so her siblings would have a roof over their heads, and no, the barn was not what this kind man had meant.

For Sara, to trust was not something she could just let herself do. She knew what bad men and monsters were, and it terrified her to trust without running things by her sister, Saline, first. Her sister was usually her common sense. But this man had all but forced a promise, and the silent prayer that was offered up seemed almost like the answer she had waited a lifetime to hear, if only...Then her silent, unheard response seemed almost too good to be true—if only?

She heard her own reply, "Yes, sir," which brought on smiles from throughout the café.

"Good," he said, rising. "Son, make sure the young lady has all she needs."

"Yes, sir," Scott said, looking at the beautiful face that seemed to be appraising the young man's responses to his father, and the other people that walked from the café, and Scott Byers to deal in whatever way he deemed appropriate for the young woman on the floor.

"Don't worry, my little beauty, no one will ever hurt you or anything you love again," Scott said and gave her a smile only meant to give her the faith she seemed to be lacking in one so young. "I will see you when you finish tonight."

Then all at once, Sara knew that this was indeed the moment God had promised her when her heart had stopped half of her lifetime ago. Faith had finally provided her the reward she had always dreamed of, and she hoped that the wait was finally over. Then her consciousness left her, and all at once, after the years of desperation and despair, she was asleep.

Nearly a full twenty-four hours later, Sara opened her eyes to an off-white room that was completely different from the farmhouse or the little café. Then she realized that she was in a room that she didn't know. Not far from her sat a woman sitting, who seemed to be sewing on something in her hands.

Sara made the attempt to rise from the warm and comfortable bed that she thought to be so soft she really didn't want to rise.

The woman looked up from her sewing and placed it on a small wooden table. She looked at Sara and picked up a cup that had a straw in it.

"Saline," Sara said, looking for her sister.

"You sister and brother are both well, my dear," the woman said and walked to a door and called someone that must have been on the other side of it to bring something for her to eat. "My name is Allison Byers. I believe you have met my husband and our sons. They told me of you and your brother and sister and would not let them wait to bring you to me. I have always wanted a little girl, but I never imagined her having such beautifully displayed eyes as yours. Tell me, does your mother have the beautifully displayed eyes the color of yours, or your father, perhaps?" Allison asked.

Sara looked to the woman who had asked the questions.

"I only asked because both your brother's and sister's eyes are different than yours," she asked.

"I don't know." She knew that what she had been called her entire life was a bastard, so named for her unknown father, whom she didn't have a clue who. The woman saw her despair. She sat on the side of the bed and picked up the school jacket.

"John has told me that you were not raised here."

"No. My mother is from here. I was in school in the UK for seven years. I really never knew very much about anything, except being there and moving here when I was fourteen. If I didn't work, I don't think Momma would let me live in the house at all," Sara said.

"How long have you been back?" Allison asked.

"Just over two years," Sara said.

"Is it very different over there?" she asked.

"Women are not raised to be anything but ladies over there—different languages, social graces, how to act in society. Not things that really apply to real life I have found out the hard way."

"My dear, most people are still very socially conscious. If they say that they are not, they are lying," Allison Byers said.

"I learned to read in French and in Welsh, but I am having problems in English. I have not gone to school here because of not being able to read well in English. I had been introduced at court, but I could not read in English. That seems strange now," Sara said.

"You speak quite well. I am sure that you do better in English than you believe."

"Saline teaches me at night. She is so smart. She learned to speak in French so we could keep in touch by writing letters to each other. She can do anything, so it is more important that I am able to work so she can stay in school for now," Sara said.

"I believe that you put too much on yourself. Did you say something about legal problems?" Allison asked.

"No, ma'am," Sara answered.

"I thought I heard you say court," Allison asked.

"I went to school with several ladies, duchesses, and a few other nobles. To be introduced at court at twelve means you are taking your place with the nobles. My stepdad then had an uncle who was a duke in Germany. I had to be educated in case I ever met them," Sara said.

"You know things beyond your years. I hope that we get a chance to talk further at supper. Why don't you see if you're feeling a little more rested, and we will eat soon," Allison said.

"Thank you, ma'am, you are very kind," she said.

Allison left the room, and Sara made quick work of pulling her heavy hair back. She picked up her jacket. She made sure that her wool skirt had held its pleats. She wore the school uniform because she had never liked wearing pants. She had always dressed like every other girl at school. The uniform was equalizing, and she had always liked it. But she knew that people here found it odd that she wore a skirt all the time.

She did hope this nice lady didn't think that she was stupid. Why did she rattle on and talk to her? It had been so long since she had talked to anyone except Mary or Saline. Her life in the UK had always seemed so fulfilling at the time. Now she found that most of her education was lost. When Sara had first come to Texas to live, it was so much like the countryside in Wales had been. She loved Texas so much that she just knew that if she told anyone, she would have to move or something.

She walked to the window to see where she was. She already knew she was in a different place. She looked outside and saw people with purposeful movement outside. There were many horses, dogs, cows, etc., all moving around as though they all knew what they were supposed to be doing.

Never, since she was a child, had she ever truly felt safe. She had consoled herself since she was eight with the knowledge that some-day, if she remained faithful to God and did what her heart told her to do, a man would come and find her. He would love her forever, and she would love him. Now for the first time, she had believed it could be true. She didn't want to be naive, but something was keep-ing her from feeling like she had to run from this place. She said a silent prayer then paid closer attention to the activity outside.

There were many people outside. All seemed to have a pur-pose in what they were doing. Then there were teenagers who were outside. Some were working, and the younger end of them looked like they were doing chores. No one was afraid. No one seemed to be running from anyone. Then there were several horses that were running up.

Sara was a country girl, but she had never been on a cattle ranch. She had seen them in Westerns, but that was about it. The riders came up and walked to the house. She heard a heavy door open and close, then men's voices.

She turned back to the window and looked out. Even with horses running up, no one ever seemed to hurry. Then she saw Saline. She was holding Jody's hand. She was laughing at something that Sara could not see. Saline rarely smiled. Between being hungry, not getting enough sleep and being terrified, and ultimately having to commit battery on their stepfather time and time again had taken their toll on both of the young girls' lives.

A knock on the open door startled Sara. "I am sorry. I didn't mean to scare you. May I come in?" Scott Byers asked.

"Yes," she said.

Scott walked directly over to her and gently put a hand on her face, where the bruises were so in contrast to her fair skin. Sara didn't move, didn't blink, and Scott noticed that she also was holding her breath.

"You look more rested. Are you hungry?" he asked, knowing in order to talk, she had to breathe. "Sara, I really need you to breathe," he said.

Sara took a breath but did not take her eyes off him.

"That's better. It is a few minutes before supper. Do you like horses?" he asked.

"I love horses," she said. She was making a conscious effort not to hold her breath.

"You you know how to ride?" he asked.

"Of course," she said. "Where are we going?"

"To unsaddle my horse," he said. "I am not going to ever hurt you, Sara."

Again, silence. Scott knew from some kids that he had known growing up that children of abuse were not quick to give their trust.

When they went out the door, all the people that had been around seemed to disappear. It was just Sara and Scott. Sara remembered the promise. She remembered how she felt when she knew that someday, she would not have to fear for her life.

When they were to where the horses were, Scott untied his horse and wasted no time getting in the saddle. Then he reached down and took Sara's hand and said he was going to help her get up in the saddle. He had thought of swinging her up behind him, then remembered the skirt she was wearing. He pulled her up in front of him. Instead of putting her leg over to the other side, she was sitting sideways. He put an arm around her and began the half-mile trip to the horse barn.

"Are you okay?" he asked.

She nodded. He could not see her face to try to figure out what she was thinking. "This is our family ranch. My grandparents on both sides owned all the land around here. My daddy was an only child. So the land went from them to my parents, and then there was oil on part of the place, and it just kept growing from there. Daddy didn't consider himself a 'wildcatter,' just lucky, according to him," he said. "Where are you from, Sara?"

"Wales. It is in the UK," she said.

"You were born in Wales?" he asked, knowing the answer.

"No. California. But I only lived there until I was 5," she said.

"And you went from California to Wales? I don't think I have ever heard of that. Did you have relatives there, or maybe it was where your mother went to school?" Scott was well versed on how to keep a conversation going.

"No. She has never been there. She is a Cherokee Indian from Texas," she said.

"Who took you to Wales the first time?" he asked.

"They took me to the airport, and I boarded a plane. I went from there to New York and had to change planes. A lady on the plane made sure that I got to where I was going. I got on the plane and went to sleep. When I woke up, I was in London. I didn't know what to do when I got there. But someone saw me and asked if I was Sara Lyn and told me I was to go with them," she said.

"How did you know you could trust them?" he asked. The thought of leaving a five-year-old on a plane alone angered him.

"I didn't. But they took me to a big car, and we drove to Wales. I lived there either eleven or twelve months a year. If I was not supposed to go home at Christmas or in the summer, I went to Bath and stayed with my friend and her parents. She was a lady. Her father was a member of the House of Lords in London. We had great fun together. But one time I didn't get to see Saline for nearly two years," she said.

"Didn't you miss your parents?" he asked.

Silence.

"I taught Saline to speak French so we could write letters to each other," she said.

"Why didn't you write them in English?" he asked.

Silence.

"At five, you learned to speak French?" he asked.

"And Welsh, yes. My class was the French class," she said.

"So you speak two other languages?" he asked.

"Yes," she said.

He took notice in regard to how she sat on the saddle. This girl was no stranger to riding a horse, although how she stayed in the saddle sitting like she was was a complete mystery.

They arrived at the horse barn. Scott swung off the horse easily and put his hands on Sara's waist to help her down. She had intensity in her eyes.

"You do know that if you try to jump off my horse, you will likely break your leg," he asked. He noticed she was protective of her right side but said nothing.

As she had done so many times at school, she put her hands on his shoulders and then said thank you to Scott. Although he wanted to know everything that there was to know about the pale young woman, he didn't ask any more questions about her past.

She put her head against the horse's neck and seemed to enjoy the smell and warmth of the horse. Normally, Scott was the only person who could handle Champ. He didn't like most people. But he seemed to like Sara. Scott began to pull on the cinches to be able to remove the saddle.

"What is his name?" she asked.

"Champ," he said. "A few years ago, I used him as my project when I was in high school. When he won his first-place ribbon, it seemed only right that I name him that."

"You have been out of school for a long time?" she asked.

"I graduated from high school when I was sixteen. I was moved ahead a couple of times. I graduated from SMU nearly a year ago with a degree in agriculture and business. I am twenty-one years old," he said.

"You must learn quite easily," she said.

"What grade are you in, Sara?" he asked.

"I had to drop out. I have to take care of my sister and brother. Saline is very smart. I learn from her at night," she said.

"You seem pretty smart yourself," he said.

"Learning here is different. I mean, I went to a private girls' school. You don't learn things that are important, I have found," she said with a soft British accent she tried to hide.

"Here it is the three *R*s—reading, writing, and arithmetic. Of course, a little history and such never hurt," he said, smiling. "Don't let the saddle hit you as I pull it off." He pulled the saddle off and put it on the saw horse, then took a brush and started brushing the horse down.

Sara looked around the horse barn. She actually turned and looked behind her, leaving Scott to brush the tall horse. He was making a little progress.

"Would you look on that shelf and hand me the liniment?" Scott asked.

Sara looked to where he gestured. There were a few bottles that all had different names. She went and began to try to pronounce the names on the bottles. She picked up the first bottle that started with an *l*. Then she handed it to Scott.

"This isn't liniment," Scott said, looking at the bottle.

Sara turned her back and went back to the bottles. She picked up another bottle and did her best to sound out the word and picked up the bottle.

"Sorry," she said.

"No problem. Can you put this one back? It is an antibiotic," he said.

With just a little small talk while he tended the horse, Scott finished and put the horse in a stall with fresh water and sweet-smelling hay. Scott removed the headstall and left his horse happily eating. He looked around and didn't see Sara. He could hear her soft voice talking to one of the horses from outside the stall. He stayed and listened for a minute.

"Who are you? You don't have to be afraid." She knelt down in front of a horse she didn't know. She put her hand up to the mighty animal. The horse, whose ears were back and whose eyes were wide, had been a gift to his father not long before. His papers said that he was a King Ranch registered quarter horse. Many of the Byerses' horses were from the famous King Ranch in the hill country.

Scott saw the way she was with the horses. She had no fear of the nervous very large horse in the stall. Scott knew if the horse attempted to harm her, there would be no way to intervene. He continued calm under her hand. Then she stood slowly. She stroked his neck like she had Scott's horse. Turning her back to Scott, she looked around the barn until she saw a horse that was the most beautiful animal she had ever seen.

"They are all such pretty horses," Sara said.

"So you like horses," Scott said.

"Yes, of course. We used to ride every morning and every night. Do you know that there were some of us who would tie out reins in a knot and put them on the horse's neck, then kick the horse? It felt like we were flying. We would just close our eyes and fly across the pasture. Guess that sounds rather silly, doesn't it?" Sara said, blushing.

"It doesn't sound silly at all to me. Would you like to go for a ride after supper?" Scott asked.

"What about Saline and Jody? Who will be watching them? Does Momma know where we are? She will be angry if she does not get my paycheck," Sara said.

"My daddy took care of that. And you will be returning to school," Scott said.

"I can't go to school here. I can't." She stopped.

"You can't what? I know that you are smart. And that you work hard. You will be fine," Scott said.

"Scott. I can't read well in English. I was taught to read in French and Welsh, but not English," she said.

"Then I guess we will have to have you taught. My parents really like you. They cannot tolerate what your stepfather does to you. You have friends now, Sara. You, Saline, and Jody, no one will ever hurt you again."

"You have but just met me. I am just a waitress. If you saw what I am, you would throw me out with the trash. But my job, I work more than full time. The owner will not understand," Sara said.

"Actually, Sara, he does. You see, my father owns the little café. Across the interstate, there is another of his businesses. It is a livestock auction. There is a sale every Saturday," Scott explained. "And now, my angel, I think that it is time that we get to the house for supper. Momma does not like it if we are late," Scott said and opened his pickup truck door for Sara. "And I think that Momma may have a surprise for you," he said.

"For me? Why would she have something for me? She doesn't even know me," she said.

"Don't worry, Sara. I just think she likes having some girls around here. I don't have any sisters."

In Sara's mind, if someone did something nice for her, they expected something in return.

"There is no hidden agenda, Sara. My momma just really likes you," he said as they drove up to the house. They went into the back door, to the dining room. Scott went to the bathroom to wash up a little.

Sara went to the room that she had been staying in to wash her hands and brush her hair. She wished that she could do like Saline and Jody had been doing—laughing and talking to people. But they entrusted their safety to her. Sara was so afraid, but of what? Not of this family, but what about when they were gone? They would be back within reach of Oscar. Sara just could not take that anymore. Before she knew it, she was crying silently. She quietly pushed the bathroom door closed and sat in the corner and cried her heart out. What would she tell her sister and brother when they had to go back?

There was a knock on the door. "Sara, are you okay?" Sara could not catch her breath to answer.

Scott opened the bathroom door and walked in cautiously so as not to invade her privacy. He saw Sara crying on the floor in the corner with her knees pulled tightly to her chest. "Sara, my love, what is upsetting you? Did I say something wrong?" he asked, searching her face for answers.

She shook her head no.

Then, just out of reflex, he pulled her into his arms. She was a little stiff at first, but then she relaxed her body. When she was able to say something, she did so in one or two words at a time.

"I just don't want for us to go back," Sara said and began crying anew. She was panting, struggling for breath. Her little exertion had caused a thin layer of sweat on her forehead. Her skin was quite warm to touch, yet she shivered as though frozen.

"Who said you were going to have to go?"

She didn't respond.

"Has anyone even brought it up?"

Sara looked at the floor and shook her head no.

"Maybe this seems too silly to say out loud, but I fell in love with you when I looked into your eyes. I imagined children with your emerald eyes. I don't understand. Why do you think you will have to leave? Look at me, Sara. Won't you please look at me?" he asked gently.

Her face had tears that continued to roll down her cheeks.

"None of you ever have to leave here. Daddy has lots of friends who are trying to make sure that it is so. With that, there will be an arrest warrant for Oscar. You, Saline, and Jody are going to be with us, unless you don't wish to be."

"There is no place I would rather be. I have just always tried to be happy, and it is to be taken away," she said.

"You and I are going to be married in a couple of years, if you want to marry me," he said.

"Will you still love me then?" she asked.

"Even more than I do now. I know you are young, and you don't know feelings very well, but I wish nothing more than for you to fall in love with me the way I have with you," he said and kissed her forehead. "Now, why don't you get ready for bed? I will explain that you are quite tired. And I will bring us up some supper, and we can eat and watch some TV together. Does that sound good?" he asked.

"Thank you, Scott. I have never been in love before, but every time I see you, I get butterflies," she said and blushed.

On impulse, Scott kissed her softly on the lips. When he pulled away, the soft look on her face was loving.

"I feel like I am going to faint."

"I am here, angel. I won't let anything happen."

After a couple of minutes, she felt better. "Wash your face and relax. It is going to be cool tonight, so wear a warm gown, and I will be up in a bit," he said and went back downstairs to the dining room.

"Sara is a little tired. Would it be okay if I brought her a tray in a little bit, Momma?" he asked.

"Of course, do you think that she would mind if I spoke to her for a moment before you bring her supper?" she asked.

"Not a problem. I think that she was going to take a bath before I bring her supper," Scott said.

Everyone sat eating supper for a few more minutes. Saline was talking to Scott's younger brothers, and all were laughing. Jody was sitting in John's lap and eating anything that was put to him.

With everyone so occupied, Allison picked up the little bundle she had been working on for the last couple of nights. It was a full-cut brown skirt with large pockets in the front with a tiny waist. The skirt reached her knees. Then she had bought her a sweater of pink cashmere that went well with the skirt. And she had enclosed a brand-new London Fog coat in a burgundy color to match her own hair. She was so excited to be buying things for the girls. And even buying little duds for Jody was a delight. But so far, she had not been able to get Sara off the ranch for one reason or another. But tomorrow would be their day.

She was expecting Sara to be dressed, but what she saw on her back when she entered silently was beyond imagining. There were too many bruises to count, and cuts, some deeper than others. The backs of her legs were enough to bring tears to Allison's eyes. She went out of the bathroom as silently as she had entered. She left Sara's room and walked to Scott's room and threw herself down on the bed and cried. She cried for this child that had taken so many licks so her siblings would not have to suffer as she Sara did.

Scott walked by his room and saw his mother lying there crying. He put down the tray and went in. "Momma, are you okay?"

"Oh, son, that poor little thing has been through so much that I had not even thought about. Her back and her legs have so many welts that are still bruised and angry looking. Her legs had where someone had used a belt hard enough to draw blood. I didn't let her know I was even there. I didn't want to embarrass her."

Scott hugged his mother and said, "Why don't you stay here for a few minutes, and when she is in bed and we are eating, why don't you come in and join us? Dry your eyes, Mom, and I will see you in a minute. I love you, Momma," Scott said and walked out the door with the heavy tray and was heading to Sara's room.

Allison Byers was so proud of her eldest son. He was a true man of honor, quite like his father.

Sara did as Scott requested and put on the very warm gown. "Scott, you did come back," she said.

"I told you that I would," he said as Sara brushed her wet hair. He then pulled down her side of the bed so she could eat her supper and stay warm at the same time.

"When Momma makes a tray, she puts enough on it for one hundred people," he said.

"I thought I heard her a few minutes ago, but when I turned, no one was there. Ghosts, I guess. I was really glad that she didn't come in at that second," Sara said.

"Why is that?" he asked.

"I guess I am just shy," she said, wanting to drop the subject.

Scott started looking at a place on the back of Sara's gown. With her long heavy hair parted and pulled in front of her, he could see bruises on her neck; he would then look back at what he was eating, only to look at the back of her gown again.

"What do you keep looking at, Scott? You have been looking at something every couple of minutes," she asked.

"You have a tag sticking out of your gown that keeps getting my attention," he said.

"If it is bothering you that much, pull it off. I can't reach it," she said, trusting Scott completely.

Scott looked at the trusting girl and hoped she still trusted him after what he was going to do. She put her plate down and pulled her hair out of the way. Scott grabbed the tag and too roughly pulled the tag and the back of the gown with it. What his mother said was true.

"Sara, I am sorry. The material was so fragile." She began to back away from Scott. "I should have let Momma pull it out. I didn't mean to tear your gown. I will go and get you another and send Momma in here," he said and was out in a minute.

A moment passed and Allison came into the room. Sara really didn't know what to think of the people who seemed to care for her and her siblings. Her instincts and her faith were clashing at each other—her instincts from a terror-filled life versus her faith in God. She had asked God for help, and from out of nowhere, there were people who cared about her.

Allison had another nightgown and was intent on helping her change.

"My dear, what has happened to you?" Allison said in a voice that indicated that she was concerned.

Sara's ever tired eyes looked up at the woman. "My mother does little to interfere with our latest stepfather. But really, it is not as bad as it seems," she said, obviously ashamed.

"I would really like it if you would see my brother in town," Allison said. "He is a doctor and will never hurt you or force you to do anything you don't want to. You have some of these that are open and angry looking. Would you mind if I treated them before they become infected?"

"For you I will," she said.

"You want to take care of your brother and sister, so you really need to be up to the challenge. I know. I have three sons and countless foster children that I love," Allison said.

"Thank you for everything," Sara said, her green eyes looking directly into Allison's soul for a brief instant before she looked away.

Scott returned after a moment, and they proceeded to have their supper. Saline and Jody came in to say good night to their big sister. He noticed that when she hugged Jody, she flinched, something that he had not seen her do before. It concerned him greatly, but he knew that tomorrow his uncle Alex would see her and set things to right.

Scott went to sleep in the chair next to Sara's bed. Sara fought sleep as long as she dared then looked to Scott, and for the first time, she felt safe. She slept through the night without a nightmare.

The next morning, Saline was off to school. Maria St. Claire, a friend of the family, whose husband was also John and Allison's adopted son, had decided to watch Jody, and Allison and Sara were on their way to town.

Sara could not help but watch the people in the small town for signs of her mother or Oscar. She hoped that her mother would just forget about them, but she knew that as the days went, they were going to be missing their weekend money for their "quality party time."

She was outwardly afraid of what someone could do to her, but no one could imagine the emotional toll that life was taking on someone so young.

Allison had faith, however, that her brother, who was always kind and seemed to care about every living thing from the moment he was born, might just be able to help just a little.

Allison made sure and kept the conversation light and free-flowing while driving into town. She and her older brother Alex had always been close. They saw each other, somehow, several times a week for one thing or another.

Sara was to go in immediately when she got there, and Alex would come in and find out a little about the young girl that she had come to admire so. He then went back and introduced himself and talked to her as he drew some blood and asked her about her life in general. He noted a different accent to her voice and thought she was merely either from England or from Ireland and had just moved to Texas.

She told him little about where she was from and did tell him about how she had come to have faith so strong. "I had rheumatic fever when I was eight. I came home from school that summer with a fever. My throat was sore, but my mother had three other kids besides me at that time and thought it was just a cold. One night I got taken to the hospital in the middle of the night because I couldn't breathe. That night, I was put in a Catholic hospital in Southern California and was moved a few weeks later to Children's Hospital. I had had a chest tube for several weeks and was getting no better. The reason they sent me out was that I was dying. My sac around my heart was filling with fluid, and I needed a specialized cardiologist to help me. I arrived what was considered to be too late. They had started pumping on my chest before I arrived. The doctor put a tube to drain the fluid, but I didn't respond. I could hear them talking, and then the pain stopped, and I was in a warm place with a feeling like what one would feel when they are loved very much. I will never forget that feeling," she said and smiled a little at the memory. "The doctors gave up, and I knew that I was going to meet God. But I knew that I had other things to do in my life and that if I did as he had told me to, I would be loved in life by someone very special, and that for eternity, I would be with him. So I returned. My stepdad was sitting on the side of the bed. I don't really know why, because he never really cared for me. And I guess I must have groaned. He fell off the bed and was clawing for the door.

"The doctors and nurses came back into the room. I started telling them what happened, and the cardiologist said that I had been dead for over a half hour and had come back. That his only answer after hearing what I said was that I was a miracle. He wrote about it in *The New England Journal of Medicine* in August of 1968. He kept track of me all over the world, until I move here," she said.

Alex had read something like this a few years ago, and now the little girl of eight years ago was sitting in front of him, telling him what happened. He hoped that she didn't notice the hairs on the back of his neck standing. She showed him the scar on her right side where the large-bore chest tube had been inserted. Because of how long it was in, and the tetracycline that had been added to it several times, the scar was very angry. She confessed to have pericarditis a few times.

Her serene look made him know that she could not tell him a lie and almost made him feel that she could see into his soul. She let him listen to her heart and lungs and didn't move away until she heard the door open behind her. She was startled, and the sudden noise left her trembling for the rest of the visit. Before she left, he had x-rays done, and she went back to Allison, who had waited the entire time in the waiting room. Allison said she was going to tell her brother that they were leaving and would be back momentarily.

"Alex, is she well?" she asked.

"I wish I could say one thing that was well with that child," he said.

"She has three broken ribs on one side and one cracked on the other. She has bruises and contusions all over her body. I am going to say that she has been malnourished for at least two years. There are no broken bones in her face from what I think must be the last assault, but it will take time for the swelling to go down. The swelling on her back and chest concern me greatly," he said, sitting heavily in his office chair. He began to write prescriptions.

"What else is there, Alex? We have really started to love her in the few days she has been with us," Allison said.

"I can see as you could love her, Ally. I have only spent about an hour with her, and she is a rare jewel. Those eyes are rare and very beautiful. But she is not well. She had rheumatic fever as a child, with every complication you can imagine. I seem to remember reading about her years ago. I know, just by looking at her, she is profoundly anemic. I didn't want to press her too hard. She is very easily alarmed," he said.

"Believe me, that much we all already knew. She has nightmares that would awaken the dead," Allison explained to her brother.

"I didn't press very much on the exam part because I could tell she was afraid, but I did draw blood. That will likely tell me what I don't already know. I am going to write some prescriptions for you to pick up for her. There is something for pain that I know that she must be in, and a mild tranquilizer for her to take a couple of times a day, and something to help her sleep. With that, she needs vitamins and iron. Those may upset her stomach, so I will give her something for that as well. I am also going to start her on two antibiotics to see if we can get a handle on that fever. She is a poster child for pneumonia to happen. For now, all the food she will eat, a safe environment, and patience. She has no reserve left, and depending on what I find in her blood work in a few hours, she may have to come back here. Her right lung is so scarred that she literally does not have room for air. With that said, with the broken ribs, she could easily have pneumonia. I just can't see it through the other trauma her chest has been through on a regular x-ray," he said. "Does her family have any idea where she is?"

"No, absolutely not. We even pulled her sister out of the school in the town they are closer to and put her in the one here in town and switched her last name to ours for the remainder of the school year. There is always someone from the ranch at the school, just in case anyone starts looking for her," Allison said. "Will Sara be okay, Alex?"

"I don't know. I will call her cardiologist and see what medicine she is supposed to be taking and see if he believes she still needs it. Only time will tell. She is a pretty sick girl. She is going to need lots of rest. From the look of her, she hasn't slept in years. Should she survive, we are not talking about a few weeks, but months to years. I will call and let you know about the lab results," he said.

With that, Allison and Sara left the clinic. For the first time in her life, Sara was letting in the pain and exhaustion from all the work, fear, and abuse in. When she sat in the car, she thought she would never be able to rise again.

"I thought that we could have lunch and maybe do some shopping," Allison said and looked to Sara. "Sara," she said, shaking her gently. "Sara."

Sara sank in the seat of the car, having felt spent from being left in a room with a man she didn't know.

Allison felt her forehead and found she had a little fever. "Sara, I was thinking that we could go and get something to eat, or go back to the ranch and you could rest, what would you prefer, my dear?"

Sara looked up at the kind woman. She saw concern, sympathy, and something that she didn't know when seen on the face of someone she had known for so short amount of a time. She wanted to please this woman. "Can we eat in town? I know that you have to get tired of cooking for everyone, and if you need to go shopping, that would be quite nice. I have never been, and would like to see," she said.

"Are you sure you are feeling up to it?" Allison asked.

"Yes, of course," Sara said. She took a shallow breath because of the pain it caused when she would take a deep breath. She would do anything for her or her family. She owed them a great deal.

"What do you say we go to a different town? I know that you must know some people around here, so we will go someplace else so you don't have to worry," Allison said.

"That sounds lovely, ma'am," Sara said.

"I will leave your prescriptions at the pharmacy, and we will pick them up when we return," Allison said.

Allison drove to a town about twenty miles away. It had been so long since Sara had been any place that she looked out the window to see what it was like.

"Tell me more about yourself," she asked.

"There is not much to tell. I was born in California and went to school in the UK from the time I was five and until I was twelve. When I was fourteen, I moved here," Sara said.

"Did you like school in Wales and in England?"

"Oh yes. I truly loved being in a girls' school. Did you know that the last time that I came home, the family of a school chum wanted me to stay with them?" Sara said.

"Really? Were you tempted?" Allison asked.

"I could not stay. Saline needed me. Her letters were quite disturbing. The headmaster intercepted one of her letters and decided that I should stay. It was hard to say no," Sara said, wiping a tear from her eye. "My best friend, Lady Lauren Dickerson, was like a twin sister, and her parents wanted me to stay. I wanted to stay and would have if Saline was there."

"I don't know very much about private school. I went to public school."

"All of us were little girls together. My best friend was like me. She was a lady. Her father was a duke and a lord. One year I was not to go back to the States for Christmas, and her family took me home with them. They are from Bath. It is on the east coast of England. The snow was so heavy and beautiful. I wish you could see," Sara said.

"How old were you?" Allison asked.

"I had just turned seven. I was born in November, so they gave me a surprise party. I never had a birthday party before," Sara said with a little smile on her lips for an instant. "I loved school and my friends, but I loved my sister more. So I had to go back to California.

But when I was twelve, I was sent back from school and..." Sara stopped, not realizing that she was saying more than she should.

"Did you misbehave?" Allison asked.

"Excuse me, mum?" Sara asked.

"Why would your school send you home?" Allison asked.

Sara looked troubled, then abruptly asked if Allison would mind stopping for a moment.

Allison pulled the car onto the shoulder. Sara got out of the car quickly. She fell to her knees, gasping for air.

Allison quickly got out of the driver's side and went to Sara. "My dear, are you okay?" she asked.

"Mum, I am just out of breath," she said, gasping.

Allison rubbed her back softly. "Sara, if there is something that is troubling you, maybe you should get it off your chest, and you will feel better," Allison said.

"Mum, there are things that I would love to tell someone. But I can't place that burden on you. That is too great a burden to carry," Sara said.

"Well, let's get you off the ground and think of better things then," Allison said.

Sara got up and dusted her knees off. "I am sorry. I didn't mean any disrespect," Sara said.

Maternal instincts took Allison over, and she pulled Sara to her and held her tight. At first, Sara was stiff, and then, quite unexpectedly, Sara put her arms around Allison.

Allison stroked her hair, and then she held Sara's face in her hands. "There is nothing in your past that is going to scare me. What scares me is you keeping it inside. It is just not good for you."

Both got back in the car. They drove to a restaurant, and Allison parked the car. They were seated and given menus.

"What will you be ordering, Sara? I promise you that the food is very good here," Allison said.

"Do they have soup?" Sara asked.

"Soup, do you mean before the meal?"

"At school, we frequently had soup and hard bread, accompanied by a glass of milk," Sara smiled at the memory.

"I believe that you can have soup instead of salad before the meal. Don't you want something more filling?" Allison asked.

"Yes, mum, of course," Sara said, looking at the menu.

The waitress came, and Allison ordered and ordered something for Sara as well.

"Where are you from, little miss?" the waitress asked.

"California," Sara said softly with her head down. She knew that there was still bruising on her face and did her best to conceal it.

"I have known people from California, and they sound nothing like you. I figure you to be from England," the waitress said.

"My daughter went to a boarding school in England for most of her life. But now she is back in Texas for good," Allison said.

"You have a sweet accent," the waitress said.

Sara smiled a little at her.

The pair ate their lunch, Sara never forgetting her table manners. Then they did some shopping. Come to find out, Allison did most of the shopping at a high-end store for Sara and her siblings. She bought Sara several skirts and all the things that went with them. When Sara asked about a petticoat, they went to a bridal store and bought some pretty petticoats.

When they finished shopping, Sara looked a little worse for wear, so Allison drove back to town to pick up Sara's prescriptions and then to the ranch. Sara was falling asleep until they hit a pothole and startled her.

"I am sorry. I think that I must have gotten tired today. I don't know what is wrong with me. I usually work all the time and don't get nearly so much time away," Sara said. "I suppose I have gotten lazy."

"When we get home, I believe it would be good if you rested for a while before supper," Allison said.

"I will help you make supper or set the table if you like. It just doesn't feel right not doing anything," Sara said.

"Sara. My brother said that you are going to have to take it easy for a while. Plenty of rest, plenty to eat, and it just makes me feel good knowing that I can help a little. Now, you need to get some rest, and we will come and get you for supper. But first, you need to take these," Allison said, walking into the kitchen and getting Sara some water.

"What are these for?" she asked.

"You have some vitamins and iron and something for pain. Did you know that you have four broken ribs? You need to take care that one of those ribs does not do further harm." Allison handed Sara five tablets and a glass of water. Sara took the medication as Allison had asked.

"What of Saline and Jody?"

"Saline should be home from school soon, and Jody is with Maria. Do you think you can rest for me?" Allison asked.

"Yes, mum, I will do my best," Sara said, sitting on the bed, removing her shoes.

The medicine made Sara start to feel sleepy. She put her head on her pillow and thought of waiting for Saline and Jody to come in. But the effects of the medicine were too potent, and soon, she was sound asleep.

Over the next few days, Saline and Jody began to feel what it must be like to have a normal home. They played and laughed and acted more like children. During that same time, Sara rested, took her medication as she was told, and did her best to feel safe.

She and Scott talked often when he got off work. She was falling in love with him, and she knew it.

One night, the pair was walking in the area around the house. The weather was beginning to get warmer. Sara was wearing one of the skirts that Allison had gotten for her. She had to admit that it was cooler to wear the cotton skirts that Allison had bought for her than the wool uniform skirt.

They were walking arm in arm in the moonlight. "Are you starting to feel more relaxed, Sara?"

"I think I am. Your mom makes sure that I take the medicine that your uncle gave me. I think that has something to do with it," Sara said.

"I am so glad that you are here with us. Can I show you something?" Scott asked.

"Of course," she answered.

Scott urged her toward his truck and opened the door. Sara got in, and they drove across a large open pasture.

"Let's get out for a minute," he asked.

Sara looked around the rise in the pasture. "This is the most beautiful place I have ever seen," Sara said, taking in the view.

"I am glad. They start building our house later this week. I just thought that you should see where we would live when we married," Scott said.

"Scott, why do you want me? I am not much," she said.

"The first time I saw you, I knew that you are the one I wanted for the rest of my life. If you love me," Scott said.

"Scott, there are things that you don't know about me, terrible things," she said.

Scott walked to the back of his truck and let the tailgate down and motioned for Sara to sit. "There is nothing that you could tell me that would change my mind. Even though you are young, you take responsibility for so much," Scott said.

Sara searched his face and saw nothing threatening, and his words were sincere. Sara looked at the sky. It was late afternoon, and the stars were just starting to come out. She had to trust someone, and if Scott really wanted to marry her, he had to know.

"After my older brother was born, my mother had affairs with several men. When she got pregnant with me, my stepdad knew that he was not my father. From the time I was born, he referred to me as the bastard. My brothers and sisters are all blue-eyed blondes like him. My mother is a Native American with black hair and eyes. From the start, I had red curly hair and green eyes, and my build is much smaller. My stepdad hated me from the start. So when I was five, he sent me away to school so no one had to see me," Sara said.

"But that was not your burden to carry."

"He was abusive. You don't know the horrible things that happened. When I was twelve, I had been in school for three months and was sent home," Sara said, taking a deep breath and closing her eyes.

"I had never done anything wrong in my life, but it was discovered that I was expecting his baby. At the same time, I found out that he was hurting Saline as well. She was but nine years old, and he was her real father."

Scott's blood was boiling. He had never met this man, and he knew that he could kill him with his own two hands; he looked to Sara, noting that she had tears rolling down her face. "What happened to the child, Sara?" he asked.

"It was 1972, before *Roe v. Wade*. But he found someone in downtown Los Angeles and took me there. I thought that they were going to kill me. I don't know what they did with the baby after I was gone. It was not big enough to survive. Momma told me that he just left it for the rats. I know that I will burn in hell for that. But I had to help Saline," Sara said and suddenly started to cry openly. "I couldn't always protect her from him, but I tried so hard. But I have been able to protect her since we moved here so far."

Scott took her in his arms, feeling her trembling. "Does that animal ever come back here?"

"He hasn't for over a year. I didn't care that I had to work, just so long as we never have to see him. He is cruel in his very soul," Sara said. Then suddenly she sat up. "Scott, I didn't mean to tell you that. I have never told anyone that before. He said that if I ever told anyone, he would kill me."

Scott pulled her back to him and stroked her hair. "Have no fear, my angel, I will never tell a soul. You are safe with me. No one will ever hurt you again," Scott said and held her close. Tears streamed down his face. He knew that there was something terrible in her past; the nightmares that were so violent told him that. "Can you remember when he started hurting you?"

"It was the year before I started school," she said.

My God, he thought. *She was only four years old.*

"I don't blame you if you don't want me around now," Sara said.

"I told you, Sara, there is nothing that you could tell me to make me love you less. Do you believe in fate?" he asked.

"I believe in faith," she answered.

"So do I, and I believe that we are supposed to be together, but that is only if you love me," Scott said.

Sara pulled herself up to face Scott. She saw truth in his eyes. "I know that I am young, and I don't know very much about anything that makes a difference. But I prayed the night before I met you that he would help us. Then the very next day, I saw your face. I have never been in love. I have never even dated. But, I think I love you."

"You believe in God?" Scott asked.

"Yes, of course. I was baptized into the Church of England when I was six. That is the Episcopal Church here. But I have not been able to go since I got back to the States. I don't even know if there is one in town," she said.

"Would you like to go to church?' he asked.

"I would love to go to church. I miss it very much. My step-father is an atheist and would burn my prayer book when I would come home."

They found themselves enveloped in the quiet calm of the evening.

"You haven't said what you think of this place," Scott asked.

"I think that it is perfect," Sara said.

"Do you think about kids?" Scott asked.

"I want lots of kids. I want to prove that you can have lots of kids and be good to all of them. And if there is a child who needs a home, I want to be able to help them as well," she answered.

"It sounds like we will need a very large house."

"A large house would be great, but if it is not large, if there is enough love, size won't matter. And I want to be a nurse. I promised God that I would take care of people," she said.

"My job will be to provide you with everything that you need," Scott said tenderly.

Then it happened. Scott's blue eyes perfectly met Sara's green eyes. Sara had never kissed anyone because she wanted to. Their faces moved closer and closer until their lips touched, at first tenderly, then with a hunger that both of them felt.

When their lips parted, their eyes stayed locked on each other. "I love you, Sara, and nothing will ever change that."

"I love you, Scott," Sara answered, a little winded.

"I think that we had better get back to the house. I am sure Momma has likely got supper ready for everyone," he said.

He put his hands up to help her off the tailgate, and his hand landed on what was obviously a broken rib. Sara flinched. "I am sorry. I didn't mean to hurt you. Are you okay?"

"Yes, I am just a little sore," Sara said.

Scott walked with Sara to the driver's side of the truck and let her get in. Together, they drove back to the house.

Sara had a feeling that she had never had before. She knew that Saline and Jody loved her, but this was different. Someone who didn't have to love her indeed loved her. And she loved him. She really felt safe, and if it was just for today, she would enjoy it. She hoped that she had not told Scott too much, but he had to know if he really loved her.

They drove to the house, not saying anything in particular and just seemed happy to be in each other's company.

When they arrived at the house, Sara turned to Scott. "Please don't tell anyone that we kissed. I know how rumors can start, and I have never kissed anyone before," she said and blushed.

"Your secret is safe with me. Shall we get some supper?"

Sara merely nodded. They entered the house, and everyone had assembled. When Saline and Jody saw Sara, they ran to her. She picked up Jody but had a look of pain. Then they all sat.

Allison had made chicken and dumplings and had some hard bread to go with it. She had fixed other things as well, but Sara was mainly interested in the soup. Everyone was talking about something. It was an environment Sara had never been in. She didn't talk, just enjoyed the family atmosphere.

Sara and Saline helped clear the table, then most of the family migrated toward the family room. Sara was tired and just wanted to take a hot bath and to lie down. She realized that those two things were things that she had not been able to do in recent years, and so she received them as a special privilege.

Allison seemed to know her feelings and told her she would be along in a minute. Sara walked to her room and started running the bathwater.

"Momma, I can't go into detail, but the abuse started when she was four years old. It likely wouldn't be a bad idea to have Uncle Alex check for things that she could have gotten through any kind of abuse. You can't imagine what she has gone through. But I swore I wouldn't tell anyone more."

"Alex is already checking for anything she could have gotten. And he already has her on antibiotics. He believes, with time and a safe environment and plenty to eat, she will be well. We can do that. I am already in love with all three of them," Allison answered.

"Momma, when she turns eighteen, I am going to marry Sara. So I need to start building our house," Scott said.

Allison was stunned but happy with his choice. She smiled and got Sara's medicine bottles and left him to give Sara her medicine.

Sara was up to her neck in hot water. Every ache she had in her body seemed to be abating. She knew that she dare not stay too long. She felt like if she did, she would melt into the water and not be able to get out. So she got up out of the water and saw that there was a fresh gown that was left out for her. She pulled on the fresh, warm gown and walked back into the bedroom. For the first time since she had arrived, she looked at her surroundings. For the first time in a very long time, she had her own room and her own bathroom. She opened and closed her eyes as if expecting for it all to disappear. Then she wrapped her arms around herself and gently lay back on the bed. She took great care in not putting too much pressure on the painful places that still plagued her, but they were improving.

Allison entered the room where Sara was and made sure that all was well.

"Yes, ma'am. I am fine," Sara said.

"I have your medicine for you." Then Allison noticed that her cheeks were flushed. She felt her forehead and noted that she had some fever.

"I just got out of a hot bath and feel much better than I did earlier," she said in a way that Allison knew from raising her own children. When the boys wanted to do something when she knew that they were not feeling their best, they would act like they actually felt better than they did.

She smiled to herself, knowing that with everything that this girl had been through, she still had those things that made her the same young girl as other girls her age.

"Are you having chills?" Allison asked.

"Yes, ma'am," she said simply. "I think that I am just a little cold."

"Then, why don't I get you another blanket while you get into bed?" she said. When she left the room, the phone rang. She picked up, glad to hear Alex's voice on the other end.

"Allison. Sara likely would do better in a hospital right now," he said. "She is in bad shape."

"Momma!" came a yell from Sara's room.

Allison raced down the hall to find Sara shivering so violently that she could not talk.

"Momma, what is wrong with her? She seemed okay earlier," Scott said.

"Scott, stay with her for just a minute, and I will be right back." Allison walked in a quick pace to the family room where the family was.

"John, may I speak with you for a minute?" she said and turned her back on the rest of those assembled in the room.

"Is there a problem?" John Byers asked of his wife, knowing the answer.

"John, do you think Maria would want to sit with the children for a while?" she asked.

"Of course, I will give her a call," he answered. He knew that his wife didn't ever overreact to such situations.

"I don't know what to tell the children about their sister, John. Alex said to bring her right into the hospital. He is afraid for her life," Allison said.

"Sweetheart, you call Maria, and I will get the car. Ask Maria if she would mind telling the children that their sister is asleep and not to awaken her," he said.

"Good idea. Alex didn't say what was wrong, but it is serious." Allison said and went to the phone.

John went and got the car and fairly ran back into the house. A few seconds later, Maria came in.

Scott picked up a shivering Sara, taking care to wrap her in the blanket.

"Allison. Would you mind calling when you know something?" Maria asked.

"You know that I will," she said, hugging Maria. With that, the four of them hurried to the small hospital in town to meet Alex.

CHAPTER 2

Growing Trust

D r. Alex Carmichael waited in the emergency room of the hospital for his newest patient. He prayed that the young girl would be strong enough to pull through. Allison had always wanted to have her own girl, and now she had Sara. He knew that it was more complicated than that but also knew that his brother-in-law had a lot of pull in Texas. But first, they had to get Sara well.

He saw John's car pull in and opened the back door and picked Sara up. "I had already given her the medicine, Alex, so she is sleepy," Allison said.

Alex had told the nurse what he wanted done when Sara arrived. She was taken to a patient room, and the nurse and a nurse's aide began to get her set in the room so he could talk to the concerned family.

"She has pneumonia, Allison. I would imagine the broken ribs kept her from breathing deep, causing the pneumonia. She is also critically anemic, and her little body has been so starved that she has no reserve left," he said. The nurse came out of the room and reported her vital signs to him.

"Start an IV of normal saline, and I will be in shortly," he said.

"I hope that she will be able to stay here until she is well, but she may have to be moved to a larger hospital," he said.

"But she will make it, won't she?" Scott asked.

"I am sorry, son, but I don't know. But I will not leave her until I know that she is stable." Alex put a hand on the young man's shoulder. "John, we likely need to be calling the sheriff about this. Her mother allowing that son of a bitch to harm her own children…" he trailed off.

"Do everything for her. If she needs to transfer, make it happen. Allison and I have filed for temporary custody of the children, and her mother does not know where they are for now," John said.

"No one from here will say a thing, you have my word. I need to have a look at her. Give me a few minutes with her," he said and went into the room.

"Sara," Alex said gently. "It is Allison's brother, Alex."

Sara opened her eyes. "Uncle Alex," she said weakly.

"That's right. You are a pretty sick young lady. I hope you don't mind staying in town for a few days so we can get you well," he said.

"What about Momma?" she asked.

"She will never know that you are here. You are completely safe here," he said.

"I am so cold," she said and fell gently against the pillows.

Alex told the nurse to put an oxygen mask on her. He drew more blood for additional lab work. He and the nurse stayed in the room for nearly two hours before he stepped back out to talk to his sister and her family. He also saw the sheriff was sitting with them.

"Sheriff, I hope that you came here with arresting the people who did this to that child," he said.

"John and Allison have filled me in. Is Sara able to give me a statement?" he asked.

"It will likely be a few days. Right now, she is too weak. And it will be a few days before she is out of the woods," Alex said.

"Uncle Alex, I am going in to sit with her, okay?" Scott said.

"Go ahead, son," he said, trying not to let Scott know how concerned he was.

"I think that you should know that her family has been to the county sheriff's department and the police department in the town closest to their farm. So far, they have no idea that she is here. No one outside of myself knows where she and her siblings are," the sheriff said.

"We would really appreciate it if it stays that way until we can find a way to keep them legally," John said.

"I will do everything I can, John," the sheriff said.

"I believe it would be better to question the young lady tomorrow, just to give her a chance," Alex suggested. Everyone nodded in agreement.

It was a long night for the entire Byers family. Sara's fever continued to rise. Her pulse was rapid, her breathing shallow and rapid. She began to toss and flail in the bed. Then the delirium began. When the nurse would come in to take her vital signs, she would flail against what she perceived as a forced movement. Her strength was failing. At 2:00 am, Alex knew that he was going to have to transfer her to a larger facility that was better equipped. It was then that he began to think that she might not be able to pull through.

"Uncle Alex. Is Sara going to live?" Scott asked.

Alex had always respected his nephew's direct way of getting to the point. He could see that young Scott had come to care deeply for Sara and didn't want to hurt him. "I honestly don't know, son. She has been mistreated for so long, her little body is weak. I know that there are other things besides the pneumonia that are plaguing her, but I don't know her full history."

Scott walked to window and looked out at the dark night. Sara had trusted him with a secret, and he didn't know if it would help to let his uncle know. With only the best intentions intended, Scott began to tell of the abuse that she received from the time she was born.

"Her stepfather began abusing her when she was four. He regarded her as a bastard. She was the product of an affair her mother had. From that time, she was treated with no regard," Scott said.

Alex could see the tears that began to fall down Scott's face, but he continued to look out the window. "She was beaten, locked in closets for days at a time, sexually abused, and anything else you can imagine. Then at age five, she was sent to Wales to a private school for young ladies. She would be there for months to years at a time with no visits from her family." Scott stopped for a moment to collect his thoughts. He dropped his head and shook it unconsciously and continued.

"Her stepfather did not just keep her for himself, he would…" Scott took a breath. "He would share her with his customers. When she was twelve, she became pregnant. It was discovered when she was sent back to school in England. A family offered to adopt her and take care of her, but she was worried about her sister. Her father had started abusing his own daughter. So she went back to try to protect her sister and was taken to an illegal abortion clinic. I don't know how much damage was done. I don't know if it has anything to do with what is happening now, but I thought you should know," he said and stopped.

"Scott, nothing that you have told me will be written down or told. But that knowledge might help me to help her. And as God as my witness, I will do everything possible to save her. I will go in to check on her. Why don't you rest up for a little while?" Alex said to Scott.

Scott continued to look out the window.

Alex went to the room to find Sara continuing to flail in the bed. He took a vial out of his pocket and injected a tranquilizer in her IV. He felt like he was invading her privacy in the most intimate way possible, but someone had to help. When she stilled, he asked his nurse to come in the room with instruments he would need for a pelvic exam. What he discovered, to say the least, was shocking. She had indeed be pregnant before, likely pretty far into her second trimester. The butcher who had ended the pregnancy had no regard for the life of the young girl. She had a very painful case of pelvic inflammatory disease. Antibiotics would cure the infection, but there would be no way to tell how much scarring there would be.

After a few more minor procedures, he asked the nurse to tell Scott he could come back into the room. He would not be going home that night. Alex didn't want to send her to a larger hospital with strangers unless it was absolutely necessary. Her reaction to strangers would be counterproductive.

After the sedation wore off, she continued to talk in her sleep, sometimes in English and sometimes in French. Her fever broke the first time at about 6:00 am. The sweat drenched her entire body to the point that her gown and bed had to be changed several times.

Scott assisted, treating her as he would a china doll. He never asked his uncle about what he had discovered and any further opinions. He knew that he would let him know what he needed to know.

Allison Byers arrived back at the hospital right after dropping Saline at school. "How is she doing, Alex?" she asked, looking at the tired, sad eyes of her brother.

He walked over to his sister and gave her a hug. "I would like to have five minutes alone with the son of a bitch that hurt her," he said.

"Is she still running such a fever?"

"It finally broke at about six this morning. She has a number of problems, and she is weak," he said.

"Did you find more?" she asked.

"I am sorry, sis. I can't discuss it with you," Alex said.

Allison knew that Alex never broke a confidence and didn't press him. "Is Scott still here?"

"He is in the room with her. He has never left her side. Did you know that she speaks French fluently?" he asked. "She was delirious last night, and part of the time, she spoke French."

"Is she awake now?"

"Off and on. I don't know what has kept her going like she has. But we will get her well," he said, kissing his sister's forehead. He gave a weak smile and was off to see his other patients.

Allison entered Sara's room and found her in a fresh clean bed. Scott, on the other hand, looked a little worse for wear. "How did she do last night, son?" Allison whispered.

"She broke her fever a couple of hours ago. We had to change her bed twice because of the sweat," Scott said.

Scott had never been the person to care for the sick humans. Like most young men, he tended to let the women have the tasks of helping with such things as sponging, changing beds and gown, etc. She had no doubt that he loved her with all his heart. She also knew that though she was not really familiar with someone loving her just because, she saw in the last few days what John called the look.

Growing up and only being regarded as the bastard her entire life and traveling alone to foreign countries at five years old made Allison take a pause. Now there were people she could count on, so maybe she could know just a little about being their baby girl.

"Has she been talking to you all night?" she asked.

"No. She has been delirious and talking out of her head. Do Saline and Jody know where she is?" Scott asked.

"I have told Saline but didn't go into detail. She was worried, but I told her that her sister would be home before very long. That seemed to satisfy her. I took her to school and told her I would pick her up," Allison explained.

Sara's eyes opened, and she tried to think of where she might be. Her whole body hurt. She was afraid to move as this might bring more pain.

"Sara, are you okay?" Scott whispered.

"Scott. Where am I? I don't feel very well," she said.

"You are in the hospital here in town. You have pneumonia," Scott said.

"What about Saline and Jody?" she asked.

"They are at the ranch and are both fine," Scott answered. "Now we just have to get you well so you can go home."

Sara appeared puzzled at his response. Home? Was he sending her back to Momma and Oscar? Scott seemed to see her despair.

"Everyone cannot wait for you to get back. But Uncle Alex said you would have to be here for several days," Scott said.

"Sara, my dear, I was so worried when we brought you in. I will not keep you. I just wanted to see you for a few minutes," Allison said.

"Thank you," was all she could say.

"Scott, we brought your truck to town for you. You should really get some rest too, son."

"I will, Momma," he said. With that, Allison left the room.

"So, my angel, how are you feeling this morning? You scared us last night," Scott said.

"I didn't mean to make you worry. I am sorry," Sara said.

The door opened, and Alex walked into the room. He looked tired yet seemed pleased for some reason. "Sara, it looks like you will be staying with us for a few days at least. You are a pretty sick girl."

She attempted to sit up and was immediately dizzy.

"Now, young lady, you are going to have to take it slow. You need to rest and eat as much as you can. You are at least twenty-five pounds underweight. Then there is the fever that you have been running. I should have sent you to a larger hospital last night, but I really wanted to keep an eye on you myself," Alex said.

"But why?" she asked.

Alex waited for a moment before he answered, "Would it be okay if Sara and I talked for a few minutes alone?"

When Allison and Scott left the room, Alex sat on the bed beside Sara and picked up her hand. "Sara, the only thing we want to do is to get you well and protect you. No one will ever hurt you again. I hope that you believe that," Alex said.

"Will Mrs. Byers take care of Saline and Jody?" she asked.

"Of course she will. And before you ask, you will be going home to John and Allison's ranch. You have friends now that want what is best for you," he said.

Without warning, Sara coughed. The pain that resulted brought tears to her eyes. Alex picked up a pillow and showed Sara how to hold it against her ribs to splint them.

"Can you tell me how your ribs got broken?" he asked.

Sara looked away. Alex knew that most children of abuse had misplaced shame. He gently took his finger and touched her cheek, turning her face back to him. "It takes a very hard blow in someone so young to break ribs."

"He was going to hurt Saline. I couldn't let him do that. He hit me once, and I fell on the ground. Then he started kicking me. He was wearing working shoes with steel toes," she said.

"When did this happen?" he asked.

"I don't know exactly, two or three weeks ago maybe," she said.

"And you have been working in this condition?" Alex asked.

"I didn't have a choice. I am the only one who works. I have to feed my family," she said.

"Sara, you are barely sixteen years old. No one your age should have to be the one to support their family. And I don't know of anyone who could work with four broken ribs." Alex took his stethoscope and listened to her heart and lungs. "Are you talking about your mother's husband?"

"Yes, sir," she said.

"I know how painful this must be, but I need to ask you a few more questions. Is that okay?"

"Yes, sir," she said, her eyes showing fear at what the questions could be.

"Has he ever raped you or your sister?" he asked.

"No," she said in a whisper.

"Have you ever been raped?" he asked.

Tears filled her eyes, and she said nothing.

"This is important, honey. I know that it is hard to talk about, but I just want to help," Alex said.

Sara's eyes appeared like green liquid orbs. She seemed to search his face for a sign that she could trust him.

"Yes," she said and closed her eyes at the word.

"Was it someone you knew, or a stranger?" he asked.

The shattered look on her face told him that she had been living a life in hell. "Did Scott tell you?" she asked.

"Tell me what?" he asked. "Scott has not told me anything. If Scott gives someone his word, he will not break it. I am a doctor, and I could tell that you had a terrible secret. But, Sara, it is important to know that it was not your fault," he said. "But I need to know who did that to you."

Sara took a shallow breath before speaking. Having to work to support her family had kept her ahead of the nightmares. Now everything had caught up with her, and she thought the feeling would surely kill her. "Saline's dad and his friends. They hurt Saline too. I tried to protect her, but I couldn't. But we did keep him from raping us."

"What about your mother? Didn't she try to help?" he asked.

"Never, she was even there when…" Sara said and trailed off. "Ask Scott."

"Ask Scott what?" Alex asked.

"He knows, just ask him," she said. She turned away from him and pulled her knees nearly to her chest and silently sobbed.

Alex knew that she was not going to say anything further. "For now, you need to get some rest. No one will hurt you here. I will ask your nurse to give you something for that cough. Is there anything else that you might need?" he asked.

"No, sir," Sara said. Then as Alex was walking to the door, she said, "Thank you."

"You are very welcome," he said and was out of the room.

He closed the door and stood with his back to the wall and closed his eyes. He had to talk to Scott but wanted to catch his breath before he did.

"Uncle Alex. Is Sara doing better?" Scott asked.

"About the same. I just had to talk to her. And she told me a lot and said for me to ask you," Alex said, putting an arm around Scott's shoulder. "Allison, I think she would really like to see you."

Alex and Scott walked to a private room to talk about the timid young girl. The reality was not a pretty one. The two men combined their information to give them a general idea of what Sara's life must have been like.

"Scott, we have to call the authorities about this. That animal that her mother married needs to answer for what he has done," Alex said.

"Daddy is trying to get temporary custody of the three of them. This may help," Scott said.

Alex picked up the phone and called the county sheriff. Afterward, they waited a few minutes until the sheriff came into the office.

Both men stood and shook hands with Sheriff Randy Oakley.

"Doc, do you think the young lady is credible?" he asked.

"I have no doubt. Her exam showed the most horrible abuse that I have ever seen," Alex explained.

"There is something that I have to insist on. And that is that the three of them remain with my family. We will fight for them," Scott said.

"That won't be a problem, Scott. Does her mother know where they are right now?" he asked.

"No," Scott said.

"Scott, your parents are willing to take all three of these children into your home? Are you sure?" the sheriff asked.

"Absolutely. My mother is in the room with Sara, if you would like to ask her."

"Then, let's go and talk to the young lady. Her name is Sara Alexander, and she is sixteen?" he asked.

"Yes," Scott said as they approached her room.

Alex knocked then opened the door, and the trio entered.

"Sara," Alex said, "this is Sheriff Oakley. He is going to help us make sure that your stepfather never hurt you or your siblings again. Do you think you can talk to him for a minute?"

"No. No. I can't do that," Sara said in a panic. She pushed the cover off herself and got out of the bed and pressed herself against the wall. "Please, I can't do that. You don't know what Momma will do."

"Sara, honey, you need to get back into bed," Allison said calmly.

"No. I have to get Saline and Jody and get away from here. I can't go there again," Sara said.

"Go where, Sara? You're not making sense," Scott said.

"Momma told me that if I didn't work, and if I talked to the law, she would send me and Saline back to California. We can't go back there. We just can't. I would rather die than go back. Please, just leave us alone." Sara was hysterical by then and slid to the floor in the far corner of the room. She faced the corner and cried hysterically.

Sheriff Oakley had seen abuse victims before, but this was one of the worst. He had to make something good happen for this family.

Scott went to Sara and held her to him.

"I have to protect Saline and Jody. Saline has already tried to kill herself once in California, and I can't let that happen again." Then she sobbed like a baby who had been hurt.

There was not a dry eye in the room. The sheriff wanted to make it known that he was on her side, so he knelt down. "Sara, I am on your side. You will not be going any place except here and back to the Byerses ranch. John and Allison care and are fighting to get custody of you three. But I need to get some information regarding who hurt you so he can be arrested and put in prison. Do you think you can help me with that?" Randy asked.

"What do you need to know?" Sara asked, continuing to cry.

"First, let's get you back into bed," Alex said.

On trembling legs, Sara stood, and Scott helped her to lie down in the bed.

"Who has beaten you so?" Randy asked.

"Oscar Redding, my momma's husband," she said, snubbing and trying to catch her breath.

"Has your mother beaten you as well?"

"No," she said simply. "Oscar is the cat's claw."

"What does she do when Oscar hurts you?" Randy asked.

"Nothing. She says that Saline and I encourage him. But it is not true. We stay as far away from him as possible. But they get drunk or stoned, and he comes after us," Sara said and took a breath. "I even made a place for us to be safe in the barn."

"You have stayed in a barn?" the sheriff asked.

"There was no place else. I didn't know what else to do," Sara said and began to cough, leaving her breathless.

"I believe that is enough questions for now," Alex said. "Sara is very ill and needs rest."

With that, everyone except Allison left the room. When in the hall, the men began to talk about what would happen next. Certainly, Oscar would be arrested, and the sooner, the better.

"Is there any way for him to be arrested without her mother finding out where they are?' Scott asked.

"For the time being, but there will have to be a trial, and the two girls will have to testify. And their mother has been to the sheriff's department to report them missing," Randy said.

"I would imagine that she ran out of money for drugs and cigarettes," Scott said.

"I can put off their mother knowing where they are for a few days. Will that give your parents time to get custody of them?" Randy asked.

"I believe so. I just hope that we can keep anyone from telling her mother where they are," Scott said.

"No one from here will let her know," Alex said, and the others all agreed.

"Is her sister going to the same school as before?" the sheriff asked.

"No, we pulled her out and put her in Bethany Woods Academy. One of us takes her to school and picks her up every day. And her last name is listed as Byers, not Alexander," Scott said.

"Alex, did you take pictures of the bruising and any other evidence that may be present?" Randy asked.

"She was unconscious for a few hours when she first came in, so I collected what evidence I could. There are various stages of bruising over about 75 percent of her body, but the broken bones and the healing bones are self-evident," Alex answered. "There are angry-looking abrasions and some other open wounds you will see as well. And keep in mind that she is five feet six inches tall and weighs only ninety-six pounds. That was after she had been at my sister's house for a few days and had food to eat. No telling how much she weighed before that. The starvation is affecting her ability to recover from pneumonia. She may not be able to survive.

"She is supposed to take medication for a heart condition that she has not had since she moved here two years ago. She has a condition called pericarditis, which resulted from a crippling case of rheumatic fever that was the result of her so-called parents ignoring the fact that she had strep throat. I am going to see if I can get hold of her cardiologist from eight years ago and if he remembers her and try to get her records," Alex said.

"It sounds as though you have taken a keen interest in this girl, Alex," Randy said. "I am glad that your sister wants this girl. It seems like she needed someone who could afford to take an interest."

Alex could not really say what it was about the way Randy had made the comment that angered him. "Do you remember what you were doing when you were sixteen Randy? I do. And you were not the sole support for your thirteen-year-old sister and two-year-old brother. If not for the love she has for the other two, she would have been dead a long time ago. And keep in mind that this all happened in the county where you are the sheriff."

Alex's words hit Randy in the heart. "Makes you think, doesn't it? You are supposed to protect, and I am supposed to keep them healthy," Alex said, shouldering part of the burden. "We owe her."

"You're right. Let's get it right. I will need a full physical accounting, if you don't mind. Then I will have what I need to pick up Oscar Redding today," Randy said.

Everyone nodded.

"You may want to talk with Mary Reynolds. She worked with Sara at the café. She knows her better than anyone else," Scott said.

"I'll do that, thanks." With that, the sheriff was off.

Alex and Scott reentered Sara's room. Allison sat in a chair at the bedside, holding her hand.

"Are you feeling a little better, my angel?" Scott asked softly.

Sara looked to Scott. "Why is everyone being so nice? You are all going through so much trouble."

"We all love you," Allison said.

The medication that Alex had ordered was beginning to take effect. "Please don't let Momma send us back."

"No one is sending you any place," Scott said and wiped a tear from her cheek.

"No one has ever treated me like all of you have." She was having trouble keeping her eyes open. "I love all of you too," she said then floated off to sleep.

When they were sure that she would likely rest for a few hours, Allison told Scott that he likely needed to go back to the ranch and rest and shower. She knew that he needed to be distracted for a little while.

Scott took his mother's advice, kissed her cheek, and left for a few hours.

That same day, at the farmhouse, Sara's mother, Joan, and her latest husband, Oscar, were becoming more and more agitated. They had no idea where Sara, Saline, or Jody were. But more importantly, they had run out of money to support their collective habits.

"Damn it, I knew that I should have chained them to the wall. Those bitches have a beating coming," Oscar said, rubbing a fading bruise on his cheek. "I thought they didn't know anyone in Texas."

"They don't, at least not anyone who would be able to hide them," Joan said.

"And even if Sara ran away, that does not say where the other two are," he shouted.

"Remember, I was not the last one to see them. You were," Joan said. "And without Sara to bring in money, it looks like you will have to get a job."

Oscar picked up a chair from the kitchen and threw it across the room. He had never gone so long without having his beer. And since he was fifteen, his father made sure he had his Valium. Now there was nothing. His hands shook constantly, his head throbbed, and he had spent three days vomiting from the withdrawal of the stream of narcotics he had taken for so long; and all this because of those damn kids. Oscar had never had to work before. His mother made excuses for him, and his father was just tired of him and would give him drugs to make him stay away. Now that was over.

Oscar felt cheated. He had married Joan Alexander as a means to get closer to her two daughters, Saline and Sara. It was the perfect arrangement for him. Sara worked and supported them, and there was Saline. Both girls were real beauties yet looked completely different from each other—Sara with burgundy hair, green eyes, and fair skin; and Saline with blond hair, bright blue eyes, and clear complexion. Their mother was beautiful as well, nearly six feet tall. Her Indian heritage showed with her black hair and eyes and olive skin. Oscar felt like he had walked into his own paradise.

It was not his fault that he didn't deal well with rejection. He could not hold any kind of a job because of his temper, so he had to rely on either his parents or a third party to make his living. And he needed his "medicine" to control his temper. And if one pill made him feel mellow, then five would make him feel even better. Life had just not been fair to him as he saw it.

Those kids should have been glad to have him around. Having been left alone with their mother, with no one to protect them, he felt like they should be grateful to him. But time and time again, they had rejected him and even acted embarrassed by him. For nearly two years, since he had known them. He just knew he would have his chance with one of them. But those two girls constantly had each other's backs. The longer his yearning went unsatisfied, the more intense it seemed to be. When they came back home, and they would, the rules would change.

"One of us is going to have to get some work, likely you," Joan said.

"I don't need to work. My nerves are too bad. Just wait, they will come back, and then things will get back to normal," Oscar said.

A knock on the door interrupted his ranting. Oscar opened the door and saw the sheriff's deputy.

"I am from the sheriff's office, may I come in?" he asked.

"What do you want? Have you found my kids yet?" Joan asked.

"Are you Oscar and Joan Redding?" he asked.

"Yes," Joan answered.

"I am Sheriff Randy Oakley, and Mr. Redding, you are under arrest for the willful assault and battery of Sara and Saline Alexander. You have the right to remain silent. Anything you say can and will be used against you in a court of law. You have the right to an attorney and to have one for questioning. Do you understand these rights?" he asked, putting the first cuff on Oscar's wrist.

Oscar realized what was about to happen and swung his self around to resist. Joan rose from the couch to protest as well. The second deputy stepped into the house, and both were easily restrained. The couple was placed in the back of the car while Randy looked toward the barn. He walked to the falling-down barn and walked in that general direction.

When Randy got to the barn, he pulled up the tin panel that Sara had told him about and crawled in. He had to turn his flashlight on to see in the small dark room. The ten-by-ten room was a little more than a lean-to. The tin walls and roof did little to stop the cold from entering. The dirt floor was primitive. As Sara had said, she had taken what blankets she could, and some old hay, and padded the floor as best she could. Then he saw the small cooler they kept to hold the milk for Jody. Randy lifted the lid and found that there was still some milk. It was true, all of what he had been told. A young girl forced to fend for her brother and sister. He picked up the cooler and the blankets from the floor and handed them to the other deputy, who in turn put them in an evidence bag. Then he crawled out.

To think of how cold a winter it was a few months ago and the children sleeping there. He would make sure and send someone to take pictures of how life was for the three youngsters that would sway a jury.

Randy also wanted to make sure and get a search warrant to look in the house for other signs of abuse. Such things as drug paraphernalia were all collected and labeled. He hated people who abused children. In this case, this animal broke bones.

He walked back to the car, and they left and headed to the sheriff's department. Both were booked on various charges.

Joan kept screaming that she wanted to see her children and how they would lie to anyone to get what they wanted. Oscar told the arresting officer to call his father, that he would get him out. Both were told that they would get their phone call and to shut up.

When allowed to make their phone calls, Oscar called his father, who agreed to get him an attorney. Joan made an unusual phone call, to her ex-husband.

"Henry, I think that you would want to talk to me about this," she said.

"Why would I want to talk to you about anything?" Henry said.

"It seems that the kids have been in touch with the authorities. Sara has told the sheriff about what you did to her," Joan said.

"And that affects me how?" he asked.

"I am quite sure that she has told what you and your friends did to her and Saline. All I have to do is verify what they said, and you may have federal agents on your front porch," she said.

"What do you want, you bitch?" he asked.

"I want a good attorney and enough money to have a good living," she said.

"I want those girls sent back out here so I can keep control of them."

"I don't even know where they are. No one will tell me. And I can't possibly find them in here," Joan said.

"I will be there tomorrow and bring you money. Keep your mouth shut," Henry said and then hung up the phone.

The thought of returning to Texas was not in Henry Alexander's plans. When he had returned to California over two years before, he never intended on returning. When he left, his son Tommy, eighteen, and Sophie, ten, went with him, his plan, never to see the other three of them again.

Now, because of that bastard stepdaughter, he would have to show them who is the boss and what the consequences would be for such behavior as they had done. He would put the fear of hell in each of their minds and then never have to see them again. Having to pay Joan was an irritation in and of itself. Although he had several fortunes, to give any to that whore irritated him.

Henry called his travel agent and got a roundtrip ticket to Dallas. He would have his mother keep an eye on Sophie for the next couple of days. He would give those girls the surprise of their lives.

When Sara awoke, Allison was sitting by her bed and appeared to be hemming something. Sara remembered where she was and the happenings of earlier that day. She prayed that what the Byers family found out about her past would not change their opinion of her.

"Ma'am, what time is it?" Sara asked.

"It is about three in the afternoon. You have had a good rest. How are you feeling?" she asked.

"Is it okay if I go to the bathroom?" Sara asked timidly.

"Of course, let me help you," Allison said.

Allison helped Sara to sit on the side of the bed and get her bearings and then stand up. She was dizzy for only a moment but steadied herself by holding on to the IV pole and allowing Mrs. Byers to assist her. When she was to the bathroom, Allison gave her some privacy. After emptying her bladder, she stood and washed her hands and face. Then she looked in the mirror. What did Scott see in her? She didn't understand it. Still present were the fading bruises Oscar had put there. But not wanting to ponder the question for fear of fainting, she opened the bathroom door and walked out.

She went to the window and looked out at the cool spring day. The grass was so green, the trees were growing fresh leaves, and people were either walking from place to place or driving. Normal activity, what must it be like?

"Baby, don't you think you should lie back down?" Allison asked.

Without question, Sara, leaning heavily on the IV stand, walked back to the bed and lay back down. Just the small but necessary trip had spent her energy. Every injured place on her body seemed to cry out in pain. But more over, she thought that she was quite hungry.

"Before I came up here today, Maria brought me a huge bowl of potato soup and some hard bread for us to eat. I have just been waiting for you wake up so we could enjoy it together. Now, let me fluff up those pillows for you," Allison said and made it where Sara could eat in the bed without difficulty.

"Thank you, ma'am, and please thank Maria for me. It smells heavenly," Sara said as Allison placed the bowl of hot soup and a glass of milk on her over the bed table.

"I remember you telling me that you liked to eat soup. And as I have not eaten lunch as yet, would you mind if I ate with you?" Allison asked.

"No, of course not," Sara said.

"I am sorry that I am so much trouble for you. But it has been nice to talk to someone who cared," Sara said, tasting the hot savory soup. It tasted like very rich potato soup. "This is some of the best soup I have ever eaten."

"I am glad that you like it. I can see how having hot soup at night with a glass of milk would make little girls feel full and sleepy. What kinds of soup did you used to have?" Allison asked.

"A bunch of different kinds—lamb stew, beef vegetable, corn chowder, potato soup, and others. They were all very good. I know that it sounds silly, but it made me feel loved being able to sleep so well. I guess that is why I continue to like eating soup at night," Sara said.

"It sounds like it was comforting," she said.

"It was. I wish I knew how to cook and had something to make soup out of. I would even try making bread from scratch," Sara said. She laid her head back on the pillow and took a breath, flinching a little because of the ribs. Then seeing the worried look on Allison's face, she willed herself to continue. "I always told Saline about how comforting hot soup was at night, but we never had enough to make soup, even if I knew how to cook."

"Well, I have always wanted a little girl to teach to cook and sew and all the things mothers and daughters do. When you are well, maybe we can do some of that together. What do you think?" Allison asked.

Sara almost looked excited about someone wanting her. "Would you really want me around? I mean, you have a family and a house to take care of. Why would you want to teach me?"

"All of us have come to love the three of you since you have come into our lives, and we just can't imagine life without you in our home," Allison answered.

"Thank you, ma'am, I have come to love all of you too," she said.

The pair sat and finished their soup. It was more than Allison had ever seen Sara eat.

Sara wanted to make this kind lady happy, as she had made her feel happy and secure. When she was finished, she laid her head back on the pillow. She knew that she had fever again but hated to complain.

Allison, having raised multiple children, knew that her flushed cheeks likely meant her fever was back. She excused herself and walked out and told the nurse.

For over a week, Sara remained in the hospital. Occasionally, at night they would bring Saline and Jody to visit. Jody would sit beside her on the bed, and Saline would tell her the happenings of their time both in school and on the ranch. She loved seeing both of them so happy. God had indeed intervened on their behalf.

"Ma'am, would you mind if I went to church?" Sara asked.

"Of course not. I don't think that you need to go today, but after you get home, that will be fine. What church do you attend?"

"I have not gone to church since I lived here because I was always working, but I attend the Episcopal Church. I hope that is not a problem," Sara said.

"We have an Episcopal Church in town. It is no problem at all. I have never been there, but the way I see it is that we all worship the same God. I would love to attend with you if you don't mind," Allison said.

"Do you have a church that you already attend?" Sara asked.

"The Church of Christ, but I am glad to attend services with you at St. Justin's," Allison said.

"I would really love that," Sara said with a little excitement in her voice.

"Then it is settled. When you are well, the following, Sunday we will go to St. Justin's."

Both continued to eat their soup, Sara only leaving a small amount when she was full. Then the two engaged in small talk. The nurse came in and gave Sara her medicine, and that didn't interrupt.

When it was later in the afternoon, Scott entered the room to find both Sara and Allison napping. Scott smiled. He was so glad that his mother had taken on the role of lioness with Sara.

Allison Byers had always been a proper Southern lady, but there was the exception of when she thought something was threatening anyone she loved; she could be fierce.

Scott walked over to his mom and kissed her forehead. She immediately opened her eyes and saw her son. Sara awakened when she heard the activity.

Scott walked around the bed and picked up Sara's hand, kissing the back of it. "How is my angel?"

"I fell asleep. What time is it?" she asked.

"It is nearly five in the afternoon. How are you feeling, Sara?" Scott asked.

"I think I am better. I ate all my soup that Maria sent to me. I hope that I get to go ho—" she paused, "I hope that I get to be discharged."

"According to Uncle Alex, he is thinking of your going home tomorrow. With the understanding that you will take it easy, eat well, and allow yourself to recover," Scott answered.

"Are Saline and Jody still okay?" she asked.

"Both are fine. I don't believe that you will ever be able to separate Daddy from Jody. They go everywhere together. Daddy took him to the cattle auction yesterday, and he was thrilled."

"I thought that Maria watched him," Sara said. "He is not in the way, is he?"

"Of course not, and Saline is making exceptional grades in school. She is still getting used to wearing a private school uniform," Scott said.

"She has never had to wear a uniform before. Where they went to school, they got to wear everyday clothes," Sara said. "I always liked uniforms better."

"What else do you like?" Scott asked.

"Silly things," she said.

"What kind of silly things?"

"I have already told you that I love to ride horses, and side saddle at that. When I go places, like church, I like to wear hats, and if it is cold, I used to like to wear capes," she said.

"Are you talking about like Batman and Superman?" Scott asked.

Sara gave him a strange look. He understood by now that her strange looks were the same as his mother raising the room when displeased. "No. They are not the same."

"Why would you prefer a cape to a coat?" he asked.

"A cape covers you from the hood down to your ankle. That makes them very warm. I used to have a cape when we first arrived, but I used it to cover our place in the tack room. That left me without a jacket, but I have never really needed one. Saline had one, but we used it to keep Jody warm. He didn't have one because babies grow really fast, I have found," she said with her head down.

Scott knew what "their place" meant. He knew that it made her feel shame when she thought of the only "safe place" she could find was the tack room.

"That sounds reasonable. Do you know how to drive?" he asked.

"Yes. I learned to drive when I was about ten. And I learned on a three on the column," Sara said.

"Did you learn to drive here, or in the UK?"

"Here. We used to take trips to the desert when I was young, and we were turned loose with motorbikes and a Toyota jeep. All of us taught ourselves," Sara said.

"Your parents didn't drive with you?" he asked.

"No. Saline learned to drive before I did. She taught me. She is a great teacher. We would usually drive the jeep together rather than ride the motorbikes," she said.

"Motorcycles, not motorbikes," he said.

"I have a lot to learn still about things here."

"You are doing fine. How are you feeling today?" Scott asked.

"I am feeling much better. Has Uncle Alex said when I get to leave here? Your mother said I could attend church in town," Sara said. She then let her head fall back on the pillow. "I am not used to feeling tired so much."

"Maybe you should," Scott said.

"Should what?" she asked. Her face was drained of color with just them talking easily to each other.

"Let yourself rest when you feel tired," he said with an air of seriousness in his voice.

Sara didn't answer immediately. "I can't do that," she said and looked away. Usually that meant she would not talk any further, but Scott had gotten to where he could pull her back.

He took his finger and gently turned her head back to him.

"Would you really like to attend church?" he asked.

"I have missed going to church so much. But I still recite mass every day and say prayers every night," she said.

Scott decided that he would have to accompany Sara as well as his mother. "Have you got your driver's license yet?"

"I got a hardship license last year for the times that Momma and Oscar were too drunk to drive Saline to school," she answered.

"Speaking of your momma and Oscar, they were arrested a few hours ago and are in the county lockup. According to the sheriff's deputy, Oscar was bawling like a baby by the time he got there," Scott said.

"What happens when they get out?" she asked.

"Nothing that will affect you and the others. Daddy and Momma have got emergency custody of the three of you. You will not be going back to live with your mother," he said.

Sara put her head back and closed her eyes. Could it be true? Did she never have to worry about Momma and Oscar anymore? Never worry about going hungry or being cold again? "Thank you, God," she whispered. "Breathe." But it was loud enough to where Scott could hear.

Scott smiled at Sara, and Sara at him. Maybe dreams did come true. They spent the rest of the evening talking about pleasant things. The concern for her fatigue still bothered him.

The following morning, about the same time Sara was being discharged from the hospital, a plane was arriving at DFW airport from Los Angeles.

Lord Henry Alexander was not looking forward to being in Texas again. His plan this time was to get his bitch of a former wife out of jail and to let those two girls know what would happen if they decided to start talking.

He rented a luxury car and was on his way to the small town that he had left his former wife and three brats two years before. The town was about an hour east of Dallas. He took Interstate 20 first to the farmhouse and then to the sheriff's department.

He found his wife to be held on fifty-thousand-dollar bond. He spoke with the officials at the jail, found a bail bondsman, and had Joan out within a couple of hours.

"Are you not going to get my husband out?" she asked.

"Hell no, I am not wasting money on him. And if you want a ride back to the farm, you will shut the hell up and get in," Henry said. "I am going to go back in and file a missing persons report."

"I have already done that, and no one seems to have found them," Joan said.

"Someone will tell me," Henry said and slammed the door.

Inside, he went to the desk and insisted on speaking to the sheriff. A few minutes later, he was across the desk from Sheriff Randy Oakley.

"My wife told me that my kids have run away. I will make it worth your time if you could tell me if you have heard anything regarding them," Henry said.

Randy looked at the man. Yes, this man was a bully. He had absolutely no doubt that he also abused his children. "Yes, I know where they are."

"Then let me know so I can get my kids. They need to be taught better than to run away," Henry said.

"I believe they are in a good place now. You don't have to worry about such things. After all, you have not given them a thought in over two years," Randy said.

"You son of a bitch, they are my kids, and I want them. And there is no hillbilly bastard going to keep them from me," Henry said.

"In Texas, we are not referred to as hillbillies. We are referred to as rednecks," Randy said and leaned back in his chair. "And my responsibilities are to those children. I will not let them be hurt any further."

"I am their father. I have that right," he said.

"And you deserted them. So if I were you, I would get the hell out of my office before I decide to render charges against you."

"I will happily leave. Right after you tell me where my kids are," Henry said and stood to walk around Randy's desk. Randy stayed seated.

The sheriff's smug posture angered Henry, so he reached down by the scrap of the neck and lifted Randy out of the chair and put him against the wall in a threatening manner.

Before becoming the sheriff, Randy had been an army ranger. He knew how to take care of himself. So when it only took a few seconds for him to free himself and to pin the stupid ass, it took Henry by surprise.

"Now you have bought yourself a day or two in jail," Randy said and cuffed the man. He proceeded to read him his rights and half drag him out of his office, where he was assisted by two other officers.

"You need to place this animal under arrest for assaulting a cop. I will write it up," Randy said.

"We will take care of it, sir." The two officers took Henry down the hall to booking. Randy sat back down at his desk and made a phone call.

Joan had waited in the car for over an hour before she went back inside to find out what had happened to Henry.

"He has been taken into custody," the receptionist said. "He will not be getting out today."

"Well, I need to talk to him. He has the keys to the car," she said.

The receptionist was checking in the contents of Henry Alexander's pockets and saw the keys. She picked them up and gave them to the woman. Joan took the keys and left.

When she got home, she looked in her former husband's suitcase, and there she found his wallet, complete with cash and credit cards. She no longer thought of her husband or kids. In her mind, she had struck gold. From her years of being married to Henry, she knew well how to use a credit card. With Henry now in jail with no means to get himself out, Joan decided to go shopping. "Thank you, Henry," she said and was out the door.

The following morning, Sara was released from the hospital, with the understanding that she would take it easy for the next couple of weeks and follow up with Uncle Alex in a few days. Alex didn't like that Sara was still so easily fatigued but hoped that with time, rest, and all the love in the world, she would improve.

Sara was so happy to have a place to go home to, at least for a little while. She knew that Saline would be in school by now. They went in through the kitchen door and immediately saw John and Allison sitting at the table, talking. They rose when they saw Scott and Sara walk in.

"Welcome home, my dear," Allison said.

"Thank you. It is good to be here," Sara said.

Mr. Byers walked over and kissed Sara's cheek. "I have some good news for you, young lady," he said.

"What is that, sir?" she asked.

"Come over and let's sit and we will talk," he said.

With the four of them seated at the table, John Byers started to speak. "I have been talking to some people for the last few days. The sheriff, our attorney, and the family court judge. And I am glad to be able to tell you that custody of you, Saline, and Jody has been given to Allison and me," he said.

"Really?" Sara said. "We get to stay?"

"Unless you have someplace you would rather be," John said and smiled at the young girl.

Sara was out of her chair before anyone thought about it. Quite out of character for Sara, she ran around the table to John and hugged his neck. She clung to him for a minute. "Thank you. Thank you so much for caring," she said through tears. Then she went to Allison and hugged her.

"I have been functioning as an adult for so long. I will have to learn to be someone's daughter," Sara said.

"From this point on, you are our baby girl," John said.

"I am older than Saline. I have never been the baby."

"I told you, Sara. We have fallen in love with you," Allison said. "And you are our baby girl. Understand?"

"This isn't a dream?" she asked, taking a step back.

"No. This is as real as it gets," Scott said. "I promised you that no one would ever hurt you again."

"Does Saline know yet?" she asked.

"She is very happy," Allison said. "I believe that little Jody is too young to know what is going on."

Sara sat back at the table beside Scott. "I hope that you never get tired of us."

"Never happen," everyone said at once. At that, the phone rang. John got up from the table and answered.

"John, it is Randy. We have a little problem," he said.

"What's that?" he asked.

"I have someone here that we need to talk about. Do you think that you and Scott could come to town?" he asked.

"Sure. Who do you have?" John asked.

"Henry Alexander. He has been detained since yesterday," Randy said.

John was silent for a moment. "We will be in in a few minutes," he said and hung up the phone.

"Scotty, I think it is time for us to get to work," John said.

Scott knew that something was wrong. "I am ready. I will see you tonight Sara, Momma."

Both men grabbed their hats and were out the door.

"Daddy, what is going on?" he asked.

"It seems as though Henry Alexander is in the county lockup," John said.

"What?" Scott asked. "Why is he in Texas?"

"Randy said he is looking for the kids," John told his son.

"Are we going to see him?" Scott asked.

"Absolutely," John said as they got in the truck and took off for town.

Back in the kitchen, Allison wondered what it was that made Scott and John leave the house so suddenly. She was glad that Sara seemed to be so thrilled that she didn't seem to notice.

"Can I help you today?" Sara asked.

"You are supposed to be taking it easy for the next few weeks," Allison said.

"I can help a little, can't I?" Sara asked.

Allison could see that her young protégé wanted in earnest to show how grateful for her she was. But Allison also knew that she didn't need to overdo.

"I will be starting lunch in a little while. Why don't you go in the family room for a little while, and I will let you know. Sound okay?" Allison asked.

"Yes, ma'am," Sara said. "First, I had better change out of my gown and put some clothes on." She stood too quickly causing her to become dizzy and had to steady herself.

"Good idea," Allison said.

John and Scott arrived at the sheriff's department and went inside. Randy looked up from his computer and saw John and Scott. He picked the phone up and called lockup and asked that they take Henry Alexander to the interview room.

"John, Scott," Randy said, shaking hands with each. "Sorry about bringing you up here like this, but I figured you would want to know."

"Did you find out why he was here?" John asked.

"Evidently, when we arrested the kids' mother, she called her ex-husband to bail her out. Twelve hours later, he was here and did indeed bail her out," he said.

"Why is he currently locked up?" Scott asked.

"After he paid the bail on Mrs. Redding, he came back inside to ask me about the kids. I simply told him that they were in good hands and I would not let him know where they are. He took a swing at me, and I arrested him."

"He didn't pay his own bail?" John said.

"He must have left his wallet in his car because he doesn't have it with him now, and the kids' mother left in his rental car. I haven't seen her since she was released yesterday," Randy answered with a grin on his face. "Let's go see if he has settled down yet."

When the trio walked into the interview room, they saw a very irate man that looked like he was about to explode.

"It is about time you got here, you son of a bitch. What did you do, bring me a lawyer?" he yelled.

"Sit down, Mr. Alexander," Randy said in such a way that he immediately sat down.

John and Scott looked immediately into the coldest eyes they had ever seen. His eyes were a powder blue that made them think of Nazi Germany. He looked to be about six feet tall with broad shoulders.

"Just who the hell are you two? More hillbillies?" Henry Alexander said.

"We prefer to be called rednecks," Scott said. "And what do they call bastards like you in California who brutalize and abandon their children? Or a grown man who has sex with his own daughter and stepdaughter when they are only four years old?"

Henry said nothing but rather he stood and slugged Scott in the jaw. "You need to learn some manners, kid."

Scott smiled and grabbed Alexander and buried his fist in the man's face, and then just for general purposes, raised his knee as hard as he could. "What's the matter, not used to someone who hits back?" He watched as he slid to the floor then went back and took his chair.

Randy seemed to be amused. "Mr. Alexander seems to lack manners and control of his emotions."

"I want him arrested," he demanded.

"Sorry, self-defense is not against the law. Now are you going to take a seat by yourself, or do you need handcuffs?" Randy said. "John, I find people from California to be a little light on their feet."

"Who are they?" Henry demanded.

"I am John Byers. This is my son Scott," John said.

Henry knew the name Byers from someplace but couldn't place it just now. "I am waiting for an attorney. I don't suppose either of you would happen to be an attorney, would you?"

"No," John said. "I am the man who has complete custody of your children."

"That is not possible. Where are my kids?" he demanded.

"That is none of your business. I would suggest that you get your ass on a plane before you manage to get yourself hurt," John said.

"What he is saying, Mr. Alexander, is that your stepdaughter gave a statement regarding your treatment of both she and her sister before you abandoned them. So I am now charging you with willful battery, among other things, of children. And let me tell you, the state of Texas would love nothing more than to castrate you and put you in Huntsville for the rest of your life," Randy said. "So you need to stand up please." At that, Randy told him he was under arrest and read him his rights.

"You can't take anything that bastard says as true. She has fantasies. She lies," he said.

"In the weeks that I have known her, there is one thing she does not do, and that is lie. And before opening your mouth again, she has been to a doctor that gave us all the information we needed," John said.

"That bitch has never been anything but trouble. Just let me talk to her. I will get things straightened out," he said.

"What will you do? Put her in front of a bulldozer and try to bury her? Or maybe you will put her in a shoe closet for days? If I ever see you again, I will kill you, and in Texas, for it to be murder, you have to have a body," Scott said.

"No. You will never see or talk to her again. Ya know, I have always wanted to know just exactly what kind of a chicken shit beats on a child. She has broken bones that are years old. There is no doubt of what you have put those children through," John said. "Randy, would you mind getting him out of my sight?"

"Yes, sir," Randy said, pushing his prisoner.

"Wait. I want to see my attorney. You have no idea who you are dealing with. When my attorney gets finished with you, I will own whatever little shack you claim to own."

"Hold up a minute," Scott said. "You bring every attorney that you choose. There are 150,000 acres of property close by here. Make any attempt to come near Sara, Saline, or Jody and you will be buried on it."

"I will have those brats back before the end of the week," he said. "You will find that I am Lord Henry Alexander. The proximate heir to the Duke of Hamburg. That means I have diplomatic immunity, so uncuff me."

"You have no ID, no passport, and no lawyer here as yet. You are going to the general population. They will teach child molesters how to play choo-choo in no time. Come on, Alexander, let's see if we can find a public defender that can stomach you," Randy said.

"I want to call my own attorney," he said.

"You will get a phone call after you are booked," Randy said, and they left the room.

Outside of the room, Henry could not contain his rage. No one treated him like this. His uncle was a German duke for God's sake. Henry had been born there, and now he was in "no place" Texas, being treated like a criminal.

"I don't know who that bastard thinks he is, but I will show him."

"John Byers is the richest man in Texas. He is the founder and owner of Byers Oil and Natural Gas, along with the largest ranch in East Texas. And if he sets his mind on something, he reaches his goal—100 percent of the time. As does his son," Randy said. "You are screwed. Now move."

There was no more talk. Randy turned Henry Alexander over to the people in booking and said he still had his one phone call. Randy informed the booking officer that the charges were assault of a law officer, battery of a child causing great bodily harm, and long-term incest. The small room was crowded with offenders waiting to begin the booking process. With that in mind, Randy made a point of saying it where people could hear him. He knew that even though the man that had been arrested didn't like being caught, they hated child molesters. He smiled as he walked back to the room where Scott and John Byers waited for him.

"John, Scott, thank you for coming up here this morning. But I thought it necessary that you know both that he is here and what he looks like," Randy said.

"We really appreciate that man being in custody. That man is a monster," John said.

"Scott, I don't think that I have ever seen you fight anyone quite like that. Good job."

"I just wish I could have given him what he really deserved," Scott answered.

Randy grinned a little. "I think that between now and tomorrow, he may learn what it is like to be afraid. I had better get back to work. I will be talking with you later." Randy concluded and shook both John's and Scott's hands and was off.

John and Scott walked to the truck and headed back to the ranch. For a few minutes, neither spoke. Then not knowing what Scott was thinking, John spoke first.

"He can't hurt Sara from where he is, son."

"I know that, Daddy. That is not what worries me," Scott said.

"Then what is it, son?"

"We both know that bastard is in town. Part of me wants to keep it from Sara, but again, she has bared her soul to me. To all of us for that matter. So how can I keep from her the fact that he is here? She trusts us, and in keeping a secret from her, it would be lying," Scott said.

"Scotty, Sara is wise beyond her years. She trusts you completely. If it were me in such a situation, I believe that I would let her know. Think about it. If it was to get back to her somehow and you withheld it from her, what would that do to her trust of others?" John said. "Besides, knowing that he is in the county lockup and not able to get to her may actually help her."

Scott sat and thought for a few minutes.

CHAPTER 3

God's Promise

Gradually, Sara began to move around more. She watched her siblings run and play with both the family and the other people's children that lived and worked on the ranch. This was a happy place. She was going to be as much help as she was allowed.

Each day she felt stronger. She followed Allison's advice regarding rest and, as a result, was getting stronger and stronger. Sara would ask Allison what she could do to help frequently. Allison was always glad to give the young woman instructions.

Saline and Sara were both much help to Allison. Each seemed so grateful that they would do anything for any member of the family. The two girls were everything that Allison thought a daughter would be.

Little Jody was thriving in his new environment. His eyes stayed bright, and his cheeks were now pink and chubby.

The Byers family could not remember a time when the three newest members were not with them.

Scott's two younger brothers, Riley, sixteen, and Colton, twelve, were getting used to living in a house with girls. All of John and Allison's boys had been raised to respect women, and little Jody was a constant source of entertainment.

Slowly but surely, the kids seemed to relax and act as though they had always lived there. Although easily alarmed, Sara was coming around. She watched people interacting with each other and wondered if she would ever be able to as they did.

A few days after Sara returned from the hospital, Scott took her by the hand and said he needed to talk to her. They walked down the hall to Scott's room and sat in the chairs by the window.

"Is there something wrong? Have I done something wrong, Scott? I really didn't mean to if I did," Sara said.

"No, of course you haven't done anything wrong. Everyone here loves you, including me. It is something else completely," Scott said.

"What is wrong, Scott? Do we have to leave?" she asked.

"Absolutely not, but I will tell you." He took a breath and continued. "A few days ago, your mother and Oscar were arrested. And somehow, with that, your stepfather, Henry Alexander, came out here."

Sara's eyes widened, and she stood and threatened to bolt from the room. "I have to get out of here. He will kill me and take Saline and Jody. I can't let that happen," she said with tears in her eyes.

"Sara, baby. Sit back down. He is in the county lockup. He assaulted the sheriff and was locked up a few days ago. Sheriff Oakley is also keeping him locked up because of what he did to you and Saline," Scott said.

"He will get out. He always does. He will come and get us. You don't know what he will do. He will bury me alive, he almost did that once," she said, bordering on hysteria.

"He is not getting out of jail, Sara. We will protect you, I promise," Scott said.

Sara's eyes were wide. She was completely shaken by the news. He reached out and took her hands and found that she was trembling violently. He took her into his arms and held her tight.

"He will kill me. He will bury me alive. Then I can't save Saline and Jody. He will hurt you and your family, and I can't let that happen," she said. "We will be separated forever."

"He is not going to hurt anyone. We will protect the three of you. Please believe me, Sara. I love you more than my own life, and I won't let him hurt any of you." he said, attempting to reassure her.

Her panic continued. "Where are Jody and Saline? Saline has already tried to kill herself once. I can't lose my sister. I promised her that I would not let her get hurt again," she said, running for the door. "And Jody, he is just a baby. Oh god, I can't believe he is back." Her eyes continued wide, her breathing rapid and shallow, then, all at once, stopped. She was on the ground.

Scott ran to her. He didn't know what had happened. "Momma, Daddy, help!" he yelled.

"Dear lord, son, what happened?" his mother asked.

"I don't know what that monster did to her, but he has all but destroyed her," Scott said, gently lifting Sara from the floor. "Can you call Uncle Alex, Momma?"

With that, Allison was out the door.

"I told her about that bastard being in jail here, and she got hysterical. She said that he would bury her alive. And she believes it in her soul. I am afraid for her, Daddy. I don't know what to do," Scott said. He laid her on his bed and got a blanket from the end of the bed and covered her.

"Son, she has lived a life that we will never completely understand. We just have to make her feel safe and keep that bastard away from her. And just maybe have him put in prison for what he has done. That might help her in the long run," John said.

"Was I right to tell her, Daddy?" Scott asked his father as he stroked Sara's cheek.

"Do you think it would have been better to find out from someone else?" John said.

"I see your point. But I feel like I hurt her."

John stayed but said nothing.

Sara's eyes opened slowly. Her eyes fixed on Scott. "Did I have another bad dream?' Sara asked.

"I am afraid it was not a dream. But we won't let anything happen to you. I just wanted you to hear it from me first," Scott said.

Her silence was even more terrifying than her screams in the night.

"You are safe here, baby girl," John said. "Trust me," he said and walked from the room.

Sara sat up on the side of the bed. She looked lost. Why had he come back? He had done everything possible to hurt all of them. Sending her away to school for so many years, then abusing her and Saline, and finally abandoning them. She was so glad when he never came back, and now her worse fear had returned.

"He is in the county lockup right now," Scott said, sitting down beside Sara and taking her hand.

"He was put in jail before, but he got out. He always knows someone so he can get out," she said.

"But this is Texas. And you don't mess with Texas or Texans," he said. Scott said and put a protective arm over Sara's shoulders.

"Please don't tell Saline. She is so young. And she is as happy right now as I have ever seen her," she said.

Scott smiled warmly at Sara. She was so concerned about her young sister and considered her to be so much younger than herself. She wanted to shield her from something that could hurt her, even if that meant Sara would have to carry the extra burden herself.

"Don't worry. We won't be telling her. And you are right, she is very happy. And I want you to remember something as well," Scott said.

"What is that?" she asked.

"This is your home now, and you are only sixteen. I would really like for you to be happy as well," Scott said.

"But you have done so much already," she said.

"Sara, you are brave and courageous and have been everything to Saline and Jody for so long. Now it is time for someone to take care of you."

Sara's eyes searched Scott's face for any sign that he would change his mind or was being insincere. She saw nothing but truth in his blue eyes, and something else that she wanted to believe was love. "Thank you, Scott. And I am sorry that I fainted," she said.

"You have fainted a few times. Have you always fainted like that?" he asked.

"Since I had rheumatic fever," she said. "It makes me feel so stupid."

"Do you know if something is wrong?" he asked.

"I know that there is, but I don't know what exactly. I have a scar around my heart that keeps it small. I don't know what that means, but someday I will," she said.

Scott was concerned. His grandfather had died of heart failure a couple of years before. He hoped that was not what was wrong with Sara. He looked up and saw Uncle Alex.

"Have you been scaring people today, young lady?" he said good-naturedly.

"I didn't mean to. I just got scared and fainted," she said.

Alex had heard what she had told Scott but didn't want to let her know. He had been reading about her case in medical journals. He had even thought about calling her former cardiologist. "How do you feel now?" he asked.

"I am better. Really," she said.

"I believe you are. Just remember what I said about taking it easy," he said and patted her shoulder.

"Thank you, Uncle Alex," she said.

Alex could not help but smile. He walked up the hall to the family room where Allison and John waited to find out what he thought could be wrong.

"What do you think, Alex?" John asked.

"I believe I am going to go back to the clinic and give her cardiologist a call. And I will let you know what I discover," Alex said and was out the door. "I believe she has what she needs right here for now. And just to let you know, if you need someone to castrate those two bastards, let me know," he said, walking out.

When Alex got back to the clinic, he used the information that he had gotten from Sara to locate the cardiologist who treated her eight years before. It did not take long between looking up the article in the medical journal and having his name to find him.

Dr. Steven Quinton was a world-famous cardiologist/cardio-vascular surgeon. Although he was an adult cardiologist, he also treated children when necessary. His phone number was not difficult to obtain.

He dialed the office number and identified himself and who he was calling about, then requested to speak with Dr. Quinton or to have him call. The receptionist was polite and asked him to hold for only a moment.

"Dr. Quinton here. Did I hear correctly that you wanted to talk about Sara Lyn Alexander?" he asked.

"Yes, that is correct," Alex said. "I am from Texas, and I have recently started treating her. She is having some problems that I believe may be related to when she had rheumatic fever as a child."

"Sara is alive?" he asked.

"Yes, of course. Why do you ask?"

"I had followed her care, or tried to for the first four years after she had spent the summer in the hospital. I even went to Wales, to the school she attended, a few times at the request of the school. After the last time I saw her in Wales, her mother told me she had died," he said.

"She told you what?" Alex said.

"I didn't believe it of course, but she had been taken out of school, and I could never get in touch with her family again," he said. "The family that wanted her in the UK was looking for her as well. They are royals and put a great deal of time, money, and worry looking for her for the last two years. Sara was adopted by them, which made her a royal as well."

"I have heard her stepdad is a real piece of work?" Alex said.

"He is very hard to forget. Did she tell you that he and Sara's mother basically dropped her at the hospital, dying, and left for three days to Las Vegas?" Dr. Quinton said. "She was in critical condition for over six weeks. If not for her grandmother, she would have been alone most of the time. But that is all past. How is she doing now?"

Alex quickly explained the clinical problems and the home environment that she had lived in until a month ago when his sister's family had taken her out. "Now she concerns me because when she gets stressed, she faints."

"Sara was to have continued to take medication until she was a young adult, the reason being because she has a pericardial peel. Her heart becomes restricted and literally cannot pump effectively, so if stressed and her blood pressure rises even slightly, she faints. She also did have frequent bouts of pericarditis. Left untreated, it would be agony for her. She was on Indocin for the first four years after she was hospitalized and should continue to take it. Eventually, she will require a pericardiotomy, but at eight years old, radical surgery like that would have hindered her development. Knowing that one day, the surgery would be able to be done much easier made me wait," Dr. Quinton said.

"You must have become attached to Sara."

"The poor little thing was not unlike a child of the wilderness. Yet, she had the warmest heart and oldest soul I have ever known. Do you know that after she was pronounced dead, that when she returned to us, she could tell you the names of everyone in the rooms? I had fallen down in my own religion when I was in medical school, and when she told me what she had experienced, well, I have seldom missed a service in church again. She affected everyone in that room the same way. Everyone in that room still works in Children's Hospital in Los Angeles, so I can say that with certainty," he said.

"I have read your articles regarding her. She is still very warm. She has been living back here with her mother and a new stepfather. Either one works, so at fourteen Sara started to work to support her little sister and brother. She never complains. When I had her in the hospital for well over a week, she had four broken ribs, just to name part of the problems. She expected nothing from anyone for her, but it warms your soul to see the look in those green orbs when something is given to her."

Alex took a breath then continued. "She has so much to overcome. I am just looking for the best way to start, I suppose."

"Would you mind if I came out and saw her for myself? I wouldn't be there to misput anyone, just to see her well," Dr. Quinton said.

"I was really hoping that you would say that. Could you bring any records that would be good to have out here please?" Alex asked.

"Absolutely, I will be on a plane to Dallas tomorrow, if you wouldn't mind picking me up," he said.

"Call me with your arrival time," Alex said. Then the two exchanged information and went on about their day.

Sara made a very conscious decision. She had always had faith, and there had been nothing to tell her that she could not trust the Byers family, so she was going to put herself at ease and live.

As promised, when Sara was feeling better, Scott, Allison, and Sara went to town on Sunday, to St. Justin's Episcopal Church. The chapel was smaller than the one that Sara had attended while in school, but the people there smiled when they walked in.

People walked up to both Allison and Scott and began talking. Sara knew from being in a small town that most of the people knew one another from someplace. While they were talking, Sara walked to the chapel. She dipped her fingers in the water provided and crossed herself and then walked and curtsied before sitting down. She then knelt down, crossed herself again and began to pray.

Scott watched her as she walked in and was now praying. When she was at last seated, Scott and Allison walked in to join her. The music started, and the services were underway. Sara sang, prayed, followed, and had the entire service memorized without ever having picked up the prayer book.

When the service was over, members of the congregation began to introduce themselves to Sara. When she could finally put two words together, people realized she was from some place other than Texas. But where she was from intrigued them even more. She told one woman who asked that she had been baptized into the Church of England when she was six. Others heard what the soft-spoken young woman was saying and turned to listen. She attempted to answer their questions as well as she could. But after a few minutes, Allison said that her brother would have her hide if she let Sara get too tired. But then she assured them she would be there every Sunday from now on.

Sara looked into the faces of the people and saw warm smiles and twinkling eyes. She smiled pensively, trying to fit in with the kind people.

When they arrived back at the car, Scott opened the car doors for both Sara and his mother, then went around to the driver's side and got behind the wheel.

"Did you have a nice time Sara?" Allison asked.

"Yes, I did. It has been four years since I have gotten to go to church, and I have really missed it. Thank you for taking me," she said.

"As it turns out, I knew most everyone there. But I have lived here all my life," Allison said.

"It must be nice to know people so well," she answered.

"It won't take you long before you know everyone in town. That is just the way things are in a small town," Allison said.

"I will do my best," Sara said.

The following morning, Allison got Saline off to school, and Maria was watching Jody for a little while. Allison told Sara that Alex wanted her to come in so he could check her progress.

Sara had dressed and brushed her hair and was ready to go quickly. She loved talking to Allison. What must it be like to have a mother who loves you this much? Sara would ask herself frequently.

Sara felt so blessed that the Byers family had found them. It felt like she now had a real mother, father, brothers, and friends that all cared about her.

Allison, like Sara, felt much the same way. Everyone felt like it was not a chance thing that brought the three desperate children to the ranch, but rather something had been an act of God. And Allison could not help but to pet and spoil them. She loved buying and making clothes for both girls. And little Jody also got toddler toys.

The hope was that with the love and security in a tightly knit family, that much of the damage that had been done by their raising could be reversed.

They pulled in to the clinic and went in the back way.

"Good morning, Allison, Sara," Uncle Alex said when he walked in. Another man was with him. Sara lifted her eyes to see who else was there.

"Dr. Quinton? When did you come here?" Sara said and smiled at him. "It has been so long. I didn't think you would remember who I am."

"How could I forget the young lady who made me reopen my eyes to faith?" he said, walking over and hugging Sara warmly.

Even with the doubt that she had for most people, she had always trusted Dr. Quinton, even when it hurt. She felt like he was a God-given man selected for her.

"Your parents told me that you had died a couple of years ago. I didn't believe it, but I couldn't find out anything further. But Dr. Carmichael called and said that you were here," he said.

"Who?" she asked.

Everyone looked at her for a moment, then Uncle Alex spoke. "I don't think that Sara knows my last name."

"No, sir. They said you were Uncle Alex," she said and blushed a little bit. Everyone laughed for a moment.

"How have you been feeling since I saw you last?" Dr. Quinton asked.

"I have had some problems, I guess," she said.

"I hope that you don't mind that I have been talking to Dr.— Uncle Alex. He was most concerned about you when he called, and I was only too glad to come to see how you are. At least I didn't need my passport this time," he smiled. "Your mother has not had you on any of the medicine that you were to be taking?"

"No, sir. She said that I was no longer sick, and we couldn't afford it," she said, looking at her feet.

"Have you had any problems with your chest hurting or feeling dizzy?" he asked.

"Yes, sir," she answered. "But Ms. Allison's family has been very kind and has taken care of me."

"I can see that. I am glad to hear it," he said.

Allison was amused at being called Ms. Allison. But now that she thought of it, she had not heard Sara call her anything but mum.

"You came to Texas just for me?" she said.

"I wanted to see you for myself and assure myself that you are indeed alive."

"I am alive. I don't know why they would say that I had died. But they likely wish that I had," she said softly.

"And we plan to make sure she stays with us for a very long time," Allison said.

They talked for a few more minutes, and Dr. Quinton listened to her and asked if there was a place where he could order a cardiac workup. Sara looked a little panic-stricken.

"No," she said all at once.

"What is it, Sara?" Allison asked.

"I know what he is talking about. I have been through enough trouble. I don't want to go through all of that again," she said.

"It is not as much as all of that. In the last few years, there have been new trends in cardiac medicine, and it is not like it was. I promise," Dr. Quinton said.

"May we please just go now?" Sara said, her Welsh accent easily heard and easily separated from what most people would call an English accent.

"Sara, Dr. Quinton has come all this way. Are you sure that you want to leave so quickly?" Allison asked.

"It is all right, Allison. I will be here for a couple of weeks. There is time," Dr. Quinton said and smiled. "Can we talk later, Sara?"

"Yes. Yes, of course," Sara said and was out of the room.

When the two women were in the car on the way to the ranch, Sara apologized for having been so rude. She hated the thought that she might have hurt people who were trying to help her. She has had so many surprises lately, things that she hadn't imagined coming to pass. She just needed to mentally catch up. Then, with the upsetting emotions, her blood pressure began to rise, and the dizziness that preceded fainting started. She closed her eyes to try to overcome the feeling.

"You don't have to worry, my dear. You are human, and you need time to process everything that is going on around you," Allison said, giving her hand a squeeze.

"Mum, have you ever felt like the entire weight of the world is on your shoulders?" she said, so breathless that Allison thought she would die in the front seat of her car. "I know that God never would have given me more than I could do, but sometimes it all just hits me so fast that it terrifies me. In some ways, it was easier in the UK, because the daily routine was constantly slower," she asked.

Allison had been fortunate her entire life. She had loving parents, a loving brother, and went on to have a loving husband. She was indeed a very blessed woman.

Allison pulled off on the side of the road and hoped that she would be able to say the right thing. "Sara, you have survived a life that would make most grown people falter. I know that it has not been easy. Yet, because you followed your heart and kept the faith that has guided you, you, Saline, and Jody are now safe and loved and cherished." She added, "And your brother and sister know that no matter what happens in this life, that you will always put yourself between danger and them. You no longer have to bear that weight alone is what I am trying to say. God brought us together. Remember that, okay?"

Tears ran down Sara's face. Allison's words had indeed taken the weight off her shoulders. "Thank you, mum," she said. "Do you think that Uncle Alex and Dr. Quinton will still want to talk to me?"

"It wouldn't surprise me if they are waiting just for you," she said and turned the car around and went back to the clinic.

Joan had spent no telling how many tens of thousands of dollars in padding her life for as long as possible. In addition to taking large amounts of money, she bought clothes, cigarettes, and beer and saw four different doctors to make sure that she had plenty of prescription drugs. After she had been on her spending spree for two days, she got bold and used Henry's American Express and bought herself a 1976 Grand Marquis. She even got so bold as to pay the small farmhouse off. All the while, as she shopped, it never occurred to her to buy things like food, blankets, or heaters. She knew that eventually, Henry would be out. And in the time, they would come up a plan regarding what to do regarding those two girls. Then again, there was Jody. She wanted Jody back. Joan knew that if something happened to Henry or Tommy, there would be Jody to take the place of the duke of Hamburg. As long as she had Jody, she had her foot in the door to Henry's family. And she really needed that. Jody would one day be her way out.

When she returned home from her shopping trip, she brought everything that she had bought into the house. For the drugs and booze, she had made a place where they were easily hidden in the back of the closet. There had been a loose board. So she made the opening large enough to where she could put the prescription medication in and the cash that she had collected thus far. She would have to find other hiding places, but as long as she had her house to herself, that would not be difficult.

About then, she heard the front door burst open. She didn't know which of the two angry men would be released first, but she had no desire to wait around to find out. After making sure that the secret hiding place in the closet was completely undetected, she went to the front of the house.

"Glad to hear your daddy still wants to bail you out of jail. I must say it took him some time," she said, going over to the coffee pot and poured herself a hot cup of coffee.

"How in the hell did you manage to get out so fast?" Oscar demanded.

"Henry does not want any of his past made public knowledge out here. Along with the fact that I still have his car, credit cards, everything you could think of to make us more secure. I may well bail him out in a day or two, but I still have some shopping to do."

"He also wants to know where those brats are," Oscar said to his wife.

"How am I supposed to know? I have not seen them for weeks. I can't think of anyone who would help them. If Sara would just send her part in supporting this place, I would just assume her to be gone. But her kidnapping my other two children is a disgrace."

"I believe that the sheriff knows where they are. As a matter of fact, I know that they know where they are," Oscar said.

"How could they possibly know that?" Joan asked.

"When your ex came out here, he demanded to know where they are. He smiled and said that he would not tell, only that the children were well and very happy," Oscar said.

"They are my kids. I deserve to get them back, or at least my day in court."

"I don't think that these are the kind of people that you want to take on, Joan. They make Henry Alexander look like a small lamb," Oscar said.

"How so?" she asked.

"For one thing, they own much of the state of Texas. They are not the kind of people that I would line myself up against. Another thing is that they are in both oil and natural gas. I don't know how they have come to know them, but they are firmly planted in the Byers family. They even have custody of the kids."

"That can't be true, because I didn't relinquish custody," she said.

"This doesn't have to be a bad thing. You said you have plenty put back from Henry's cash, credit cards, and checks to last us for years," Oscar said.

"Oh, and I just remembered something else that I made sure and took care of, even though it did take me all day long." She quickly explained that she had gotten enough drugs to last them into the next millennium.

"How did you manage that? You don't work, and that working daughter of yours that you promised to me has not turned up."

"We don't need Sara for any of this. She was just another mouth to feed. I went to several doctors today who were only too happy to give me all the meds I needed," Joan boasted.

"Do you know what happened to me when I was locked up in that place? Those sons of bitches. And the guards turned a blind eye. That bitch has a lot to answer for as far as I am concerned," Oscar said.

"You have no way to get to her or the other two for that matter. They have the law and that family on their side. They would kill you if you got close to any of them, if I understand correctly. Besides, we have all we need, so just enjoy it. But because I hate the idea of breaking a promise to you, I might be able to make this work to our advantage," Joan said, opening a beer and taking a few pills.

But Oscar's anger was far from spent. There would come a time when he would have his way with both of those bitches. "What do you have in mind?"

"Make them pay for the kids if they want them that bad. Certainly people like that would rather pay than go to court," she said.

"Brilliant," Oscar said.

Back at the clinic, Sara was nervous but doing as she should. Dr. Quinton assured her. "Sara, have I ever lied to you before, even in the hard times?" he asked.

"No, sir," she answered.

"And I have no reason to start. I know that you have been hurt in the past by the same people who should love and cherish you. But you are my own personal miracle, and I want nothing but the best for you."

Sara searched his face for truth and found nothing but truth. "Okay," she said. "But if something happens to me, please see that Saline and Jody are safe."

"Sara, baby, all of you will be taken care of from now on," Allison said, pulling her into her arms.

"What do you want me to do?" Sara asked Dr. Quinton.

"I have made arrangements to transfer you to Baylor in Dallas. You will only have to be there a few days. And you will be in the high-security part, so there will be no possible way for anyone to get to you," he said.

"When am I supposed to go?" she asked.

"Immediately, I am worried about your heart," Dr. Quinton said.

Sara had tears in her eyes. She didn't want to leave. She was afraid that they wouldn't want her back.

"But my sister and my brother," she said.

"Sara, I promise you on my life that we will keep them safe and happy until you return," Allison said, pleading.

Sara knew this kind woman would keep her word. For that matter, the entire family would do anything to keep their word. "You have been so good and kind to us that there is nothing I would not do for any of you."

With so much fear in her, she had still had the faith that had taken her through the darkest places that there could ever be and reluctantly agreed.

"How long will I have to be there?" she asked.

"I will get you back just as quickly as I can," Dr. Quinton said.

"Okay" she said.

"Then, what do you say that we start going that way? They are actually expecting you," he said, urging her to the door.

Sara was led to the car like a lamb to slaughter, but she knew that she could trust these people, even still said a silent player.

An hour later, Scott, Sara, and Allison arrived at Baylor University Medical Center. When she was being admitted, the hurried activity around her was making her anxious. Blood was drawn, an IV started, and tests begun.

It was after the CAT scan, a test that was new to her, that Dr. Quinton came to her and said that he found what had been causing her to faint. When she was eight, she had had a buildup of fluid around her heart, literally crushing the life out of her. Because of the medication that was given to save her life at that time, it had caused her sac around her heart to become stiff, thus unable to stretch. Because of the trauma she had been through, fluid had collected around her heart, and when stressed, her heart function was reduced. A condition called cardiac tamponade. It was not as serious as before, but a few cc's needed to be removed to allow her heart to beat more easily.

Sara remembered the procedure from before. But what she really remembered was that during that procedure, she had died. But Dr. Quinton wanted to perform the procedure, a pericardiocentesis, immediately.

"Okay. May Scott stay with me?" she asked. She was so afraid, and just a little comfort during the painful procedure would help.

"If Scott is up to it, it will be fine," he said.

"If Sara can go through it, I can be there," he said, giving her hand a squeeze.

Dr. Quinton wasted no time in ordering the necessary supplies. He also ordered another IV started just in case it was needed. As Sara's blood pressure was low, he had to hold off in sedating her, so she would be awake throughout the entire procedure.

"Scott, I have never exposed myself before. Please don't think less of me," she said.

Scott could tell she was scared to death. As the technicians, nurses, and doctors filed in, Sara's anxiety grew. Soon, she had a sheen apparent on her forehead.

"Are you ready, Sara?" Dr. Quinton asked.

Sara merely nodded.

"Okay, we've been here before. Little stick and burn," he said as he injected the space between her ribcages. Sara made an involuntary cry.

"I am sorry, baby. That will help what is next. I need a four-inch needle with lidocaine," he said to the nurse.

When Scott saw the needle, he was terrified. He could only imagine what Sara must be feeling.

"Here we go," he said. Scott squeezed Sara's hand, more for his own comfort than hers.

Inch by inch as he inserted the needle, the perspiration grew on Sara's forehead.

"I have to inject something directly in for the pericarditis, Sara, and it is going to hurt," he said.

"Scott, I am going to die," she said at the same time that the monitor screamed, and Scott didn't know what was happening. Then Sara's eyes rolled back, and she was unresponsive.

Scott was terrified. "Sara, talk to me. Don't leave me. They are going to take care of you," he cried.

"Her heart rate has dropped, and I have to get that fluid off. Not to mention the pain she is in. Give me a minute."

Scott picked up Sara's rosary and began to pray, something he had learned from her that gave her comfort. He would give his life for her, yet he felt so helpless. As Dr. Quinton pulled the fluid out of Sara's pericardial sac, which relieved the congestion that was causing many of the young woman's recent problems. Her parents knew that she would be prone to infections and should have taken care to keep her healthy. He had told them she would have to be handled with kid gloves until she was in her late teens to early twenties. Obviously, no one was listening. A loving and caring family had come into her life, and between them and him, she would survive and find the happiness she so deserved.

Medication was given when Sara's blood pressure and had rebounded and stabilized. Then she was given Demerol to help with the pain. He would leave the drain a few hours until he established what had caused the excess fluid. Then, with time, antibiotics, and all the love that was now around her, she would recover.

It was early evening before Sara awoke a little sore but better able to breathe. The impending doom that she had felt a few hours ago was no longer present.

And there, sitting in the chair beside her was Scott. The worry on his face made him look beyond his years. His intense blue eyes were but loving. But there was something else in his face.

"Is everything okay, Scott?" she asked.

"I am sorry, Sara," he said with tears in his eyes.

"Sorry for what?" she said, sounding a little hoarse.

"I would never have wanted you brought here to be in such pain. And I couldn't help you."

"Scott, the problem with my heart has existed for half of my life. You didn't do it. And even if you did, as far as I can see, the first time that I fainted, it was the best thing that happened to me," she said.

His questioning look needed no words.

"It brought me to you, and I thank God for that. If you still want me, we will likely have children, and there is pain involved with that as well. But think of the joy that that pain brings in and of itself," she said, taking a breath.

"I love you. I will always love you. We were raised in two countries thousands of miles apart, and we found each other. I believe it is clear that we were meant to be here."

Scott moved to the bed and slowly and gently, taking care with the IVs and the monitoring lines, pulled her to him. He still held the rosary that Sara so cherished. He looked toward heaven and whispered a silent prayer, thanking God for delivering this beautiful, pure-hearted angel to him.

"Sara Lyn Byers, get used to your new name, my angel. I didn't know anyone could love someone as much as you love people around you, and I promise you, you will have everything in life you could ever wish for." And then he cupped her face with his hands and kissed her, a kiss that sealed them for life.

From the door, Dr. Quinton felt like he was trespassing on their privacy, but the tender moment was so heartfelt by each that he just wanted to know that it ended well. He knew what Scott was feeling when he looked up toward heaven and really, in his heart and soul, knew that someone else was watching over them.

Dr. Quinton and his wife had been married over thirty years until her death the year before, and as much as they wanted children, they were never able to have them. She had been a pediatric nurse to fill that need, and he spent much time at Children's Hospital. They were so happy together, and his life since her death had been so empty. Maybe he needed a change.

He waited until after Scott had let his patient lie back on the bed before he entered the room.

"So, are you feeling better?" he asked, taking her hand.

"Yes, sir. I am hungry. Do you think I could have some soup?" she asked.

"I think Maria has made a couple of different kinds of soup that are in your refrigerator. One of them smelled so good I didn't think there would be enough left to send to you," Scott said.

"What kind is it?" she asked.

"Bacon, potato, and cheese, I think," Scott answered.

"Can I eat now, Dr. Quinton?" she asked.

"Absolutely, and you are ordered to put on as much weight as possible to look as radiant as you can in that wedding dress," he said.

"Am I going to be okay?" she asked.

"I will know for certain in the morning, but it looks very good tonight."

For the remainder of the eight days stay in the hospital, there were some things that were difficult. Sara could feel herself feeling well. Then she found herself feeling something that was a gift indeed. She felt happy.

CHAPTER 4

Saline's Story

From that time, a couple of months prior that, Sara's Prince Charming had come and taken her and their little brother, Jody, out of the cold, brutal life that they had lived. Things had become fun, full, loving, and lasting.

In the months and years before Scott Byers and his family had come into their lives, Saline had begun to trust the God that Sara had talked to, prayed to, and begged forgiveness to for anything that she thought she may have done wrong.

That very cold April night after surviving a solid two weeks of their stepfather, Oscar, her big sister, Sara, was black and blue and in a great deal of pain. Saline knew that at night after she thought that she and little Jody were asleep, Sara Lyn would cry her heart out. Not wailing, but in silent heart-wrenching sobs, because she knew that she was dying, physically, bit by tiny bit and was afraid what would come of the two she loved more as a mother would love her children.

Sara had known of dying as a child of eight being pronounced dead and coming back to life after meeting God. Every day they were together when she was home from her school in the UK, Sara would speak of Jesus and a god that loved them, even after the worst beatings.

Saline, at the age of thirteen, had blossomed into a stunning beauty. Her long thick yellow-blond hair hung to her waist. She was already two inches taller than her big sister, and because Sara gave them more food from the little café so she could help more with Jody, she ate. But she had become so nervous. Her stomach was upset, and it hurt all the time. Saline had her father's blue eyes, height, and build. Her sister's stature was not as big, likely because she had been sick much of her childhood with rheumatic fever.

Now at night, her skin felt hot all the time, but she shivered in the cold. She was pale, and her green eyes appeared to swim inside of the sockets.

That morning, Mary had come to the barn, and when Sara didn't wake up, she shook her because she thought she had died. As Sara dressed herself then checked Jody, Saline told Mary that she was dying. She had prayed for so long on her knees that she thought she had fallen asleep in that position.

But Saline respected her sister's private thoughts and would not let her lose any dignity because she cried in the dark. She always told Saline she would be there, and yes, Saline had known what it was like to give up hope. One day, before they left California, she had run into busy rush-hour traffic. It was only because Sara had thrown herself into her sister and saved her life that she was still there to date.

"Don't worry, Saline. I think today your big sister's God will be answering." They left.

Then, a couple of hours later, the tall cowboy, complete with cowboy hat and boots, had pulled the tin back and told Saline and Jody to get in the truck. Once inside, he took off his coat and put it on the two children. "I am Scott Byers, and you don't live here anymore."

"Wait," Saline had screamed and jumped out of the rolling truck. She ran to the barn and pulled a much-worn bag out, then ran back to the truck and got warm. She felt years of old ice seeming to melt off her. Only then did she notice this man looked a little disheveled, and his knuckles were already swelling and bleeding.

She took his hand. "You're hurt." She seemed to be looking into his soul. He was almost embarrassed when the thirteen-year-old Saline smiled a radiant smile and then began to laugh. The two teenage girls were so young to be functioning in such a responsible manner. "Are you Prince Charming?" Saline asked.

He looked confused.

"Mary said Prince Charming was coming from Sara's god today. But don't get me wrong, sir. If you hurt my sister, I will beat the shit out of you and make you eat it." Her beautiful face took on a fierce mother lion mode.

Scott liked her immediately. "Well, Miss Bad Ass, you sound nothing like your sister. Come to think of it, you don't look much like her."

"We have different dads. Sara is a bastard. Does not know who her dad is. My dad told her to remember she was a bastard and never to forget it," she said.

"You may say you are going to kick the shit out of me, and may do it. But if I ever hear you refer to my future wife as a bastard again," he said, pulling off the road, "I will personally turn you over my knee and not stop whipping your ass until you blush. Now stop threatening me and act like a lady. And haven't you learned anything in boarding school about the way a lady talks?"

"I went to private school in California. We are spoiled degenerates, not like Sara, who is the real deal. She went to school with royalty and was even presented at court at twelve." Saline bragged of her sister.

"What was she in trouble for?" he asked.

"Not in court, dummy, at court. You know, the queen's court. If you're going to be her prince, you need to learn a few things. My dad is the sole nephew in a German line of nobility. Sara can tell you about my family all the way back to the seventeen hundreds. She speaks fluent Welsh and French, even learned to read and write in both, but I have to teach her to read English at night. She is a little behind in her studies in the last few months, but she is very smart and very proper, and don't you forget it," Saline said and stuck her nose in the air. Then she started sniffing. "What is that smell?"

"Cow crap, Lady Saline, I have to work on the ranch today. I will have to drop you off with my mom. She can handle you. And my momma is a lady too. She and Daddy own half of the state of Texas, so you had better lose the attitude and behave. My momma has had a ranching oilman for a husband and raised three sons. So she can and will handle a delicate little creampuff like you," he said, thinking how different two sisters could be.

"I am helping raise a two-year-old and help Sara fight off that son of a bitch Oscar, so I don't have need of a babysitter. Anyone who raises a hand to me or mine will be sorry for it."

Scott knew he had gotten through, but the young girl was tough to a fault and had all the bull and bravado of a young Texas woman.

"No one in my family has ever hurt anyone. But she will fill your mouth up with hot sauce or soap if you don't act like a lady, and not a bar room hussy," Scott said.

Saline never lost eye contact but seemed to be rethinking her options, and she took a breath. "Okay. Since you are to be my brother, tell me about yourself. And by the way, I am a sophomore in high school because I always make As. So please don't treat me like a baby. I speak German, French, and Latin and am currently trying to learn Chinese for amusement. I don't like living in the country, so I read a great deal."

"Well, Lady Smarty Pants, I graduated high school at sixteen and never made a B and graduated SMU at nineteen, with degrees in business and agriculture. I have owned my own property, cows, and oil since I was fifteen, and I suppose, if my father is the king of Texas, I am its prince," he quipped back. "So when you're not reading or changing diapers, what else do you like to do?"

Saline had the same sadness when approached about such things as her sister.

"Sorry, honey, I am heartily like you, I am afraid, competitive by nature. Seriously, what else do you like to do?" he asked.

"I can't do anything. I have to help Sara, and I am not complaining. She has saved me so many times, and now she is sick, hurt inside, and I think she is dying. The last two weeks, Oscar has gone even more nuts. He attempts to become even more perverted than usual. She fell one night a couple of weeks ago when he started. He was wearing steel-toed boots he found in the closet. He said he could use those to keep us in line," she said with tears in her eyes. "She gave me Jody and told me to put him in a little pen we have outside that we put him in while we help each other. I put him in and ran back, and she was on the ground. The sound of her ribs breaking made me sick," she said, shaking her head. "I only hit him twice with my bat. If I didn't have to get Sara out of there, I would have just kept up until I knew he was dead. She could hardly breathe. She coughed up blood for a week. But she made me swear not to tell Mary what happened and went to work the next day." Jody saw her distress and began to fret. "Go back to the farm please. I forgot Jody's bottle."

"We will be at the ranch in a few minutes. That boy looks like he could eat beef, so we will get rid of that bottle." Scott reached over and took the toddler and put him in his lap. Jody was quickly laughing at the new game and forgot he was hungry for the final few minutes to the ranch.

"Momma will have breakfast ready when you get there and will get you used to your new home. Tell me more about what ails your sister."

"Sara was sick when she was younger. She is supposed to take medicine, but Momma won't let her get it. She had, ah, well, I forgot the name for right now. We were up late and—never mind that. She has never been well. Last night, her skin was so hot, and she shivered after she finished talking to her god, and we said amen. It is something that my sister likes to do, and don't make fun of her. She died when she was eight for twelve whole minutes, and she met this god, and he told her to have faith, always, even when it hurt." She started to cry. "Now she is dying, and I don't know what to do. But she does. She is supposed to be a nurse someday."

Scott put a protective arm around her and pulled her close. "No one is dying on my ranch. And my uncle is a doctor. I promise, honey. Does your supersister like to do anything?" he asked.

"She doesn't read well because she didn't get to learn English. Dad wouldn't let her. She loves music, piano, and dancing. And in England, she went to church—Mass, they call it—every day. But she couldn't here. My dad is an atheist. He thinks he is the mightiest thing anyplace, and we should worship him. I hate him. If I would have been, I would have made him sorry for ever touching us. He already two inches taller than her big sister, and because Sara gave them more food from the little café so she could help more with Jody, she ate. But she had become so nervous. Her stomach was upset, and it hurt all the time. Saline had her father's blue eyes, height, and build. Her sister's stature was not as big, likely because she had been sick much of her childhood with rheumatic fever.

Now at night, her skin felt hot all the time, but she shivered in the cold. She was pale, and her green eyes appeared to swim inside of the sockets.

That morning, Mary had come to the barn, and when Sara didn't wake up, she shook her because she thought she had died. As Sara dressed herself then checked Jody, Saline told Mary that she was dying. She had prayed for so long on her knees that she thought she had fallen asleep in that position.

But Saline respected her sister's private thoughts and would not let her lose any dignity because she cried in the dark. She always told Saline she would be there, and yes, Saline had known what it was like to give up hope. One day, before they left California, she had run into busy rush-hour traffic. It was only because Sara had thrown herself into her sister and saved her life that she was still there to date.

"Don't worry, Saline. I think today your big sister's God will be answering." They left.

Then, a couple of hours later, the tall cowboy, complete with cowboy hat and boots, had pulled the tin back and told Saline and Jody to get in the truck. Once inside, he took off his coat and put it on the two children. "I am Scott Byers, and you don't live here anymore."

"Wait," Saline had screamed and jumped out of the rolling truck. She ran to the barn and pulled a much-worn bag out, then ran back to the truck and got warm. She felt years of old ice seeming to melt off her. Only then did she notice this man looked a little disheveled, and his knuckles were already swelling and bleeding.

She took his hand. "You're hurt." She seemed to be looking into his soul. He was almost embarrassed when the thirteen-year-old Saline smiled a radiant smile and then began to laugh. The two teenage girls were so young to be functioning in such a responsible manner. "Are you Prince Charming?" Saline asked.

He looked confused.

"Mary said Prince Charming was coming from Sara's god today. But don't get me wrong, sir. If you hurt my sister, I will beat the shit out of you and make you eat it." Her beautiful face took on a fierce mother lion mode.

Scott liked her immediately. "Well, Miss Bad Ass, you sound nothing like your sister. Come to think of it, you don't look much like her."

"We have different dads. Sara is a bastard. Does not know who her dad is. My dad told her to remember she was a bastard and never to forget it," she said.

"You may say you are going to kick the shit out of me, and may do it. But if I ever hear you refer to my future wife as a bastard again," he said, pulling off the road, "I will personally turn you over my knee and not stop whipping your ass until you blush. Now stop threatening me and act like a lady. And haven't you learned anything in boarding school about the way a lady talks?"

"I went to private school in California. We are spoiled degenerates, not like Sara, who is the real deal. She went to school with royalty and was even presented at court at twelve." Saline bragged of her sister.

"What was she in trouble for?" he asked.

"Not in court, dummy, at court. You know, the queen's court. If you're going to be her prince, you need to learn a few things. My dad is the sole nephew in a German line of nobility. Sara can tell you about my family all the way back to the seventeen hundreds. She speaks fluent Welsh and French, even learned to read and write in both, but I have to teach her to read English at night. She is a little behind in her studies in the last few months, but she is very smart and very proper, and don't you forget it," Saline said and stuck her nose in the air. Then she started sniffing. "What is that smell?"

"Cow crap, Lady Saline, I have to work on the ranch today. I will have to drop you off with my mom. She can handle you. And my momma is a lady too. She and Daddy own half of the state of Texas, so you had better lose the attitude and behave. My momma has had a ranching oilman for a husband and raised three sons. So she can and will handle a delicate little creampuff like you," he said, thinking how different two sisters could be.

"I am helping raise a two-year-old and help Sara fight off that son of a bitch Oscar, so I don't have need of a babysitter. Anyone who raises a hand to me or mine will be sorry for it."

Scott knew he had gotten through, but the young girl was tough to a fault and had all the bull and bravado of a young Texas woman.

"No one in my family has ever hurt anyone. But she will fill your mouth up with hot sauce or soap if you don't act like a lady, and not a bar room hussy," Scott said.

Saline never lost eye contact but seemed to be rethinking her options, and she took a breath. "Okay. Since you are to be my brother, tell me about yourself. And by the way, I am a sophomore in high school because I always make As. So please don't treat me like a baby. I speak German, French, and Latin and am currently trying to learn Chinese for amusement. I don't like living in the country, so I read a great deal."

"Well, Lady Smarty Pants, I graduated high school at sixteen and never made a B and graduated SMU at nineteen, with degrees in business and agriculture. I have owned my own property, cows, and oil since I was fifteen, and I suppose, if my father is the king of Texas, I am its prince," he quipped back. "So when you're not reading or changing diapers, what else do you like to do?"

Saline had the same sadness when approached about such things as her sister.

"Sorry, honey, I am heartily like you, I am afraid, competitive by nature. Seriously, what else do you like to do?" he asked.

"I can't do anything. I have to help Sara, and I am not complaining. She has saved me so many times, and now she is sick, hurt inside, and I think she is dying. The last two weeks, Oscar has gone even more nuts. He attempts to become even more perverted than usual. She fell one night a couple of weeks ago when he started. He was wearing steel-toed boots he found in the closet. He said he could use those to keep us in line," she said with tears in her eyes. "She gave me Jody and told me to put him in a little pen we have outside that we put him in while we help each other. I put him in and ran back, and she was on the ground. The sound of her ribs breaking made me sick," she said, shaking her head. "I only hit him twice with my bat. If I didn't have to get Sara out of there, I would have just kept up until I knew he was dead. She could hardly breathe. She coughed up blood for a week. But she made me swear not to tell Mary what happened and went to work the next day." Jody saw her distress and began to fret. "Go back to the farm please. I forgot Jody's bottle."

"We will be at the ranch in a few minutes. That boy looks like he could eat beef, so we will get rid of that bottle." Scott reached over and took the toddler and put him in his lap. Jody was quickly laughing at the new game and forgot he was hungry for the final few minutes to the ranch.

"Momma will have breakfast ready when you get there and will get you used to your new home. Tell me more about what ails your sister."

"Sara was sick when she was younger. She is supposed to take medicine, but Momma won't let her get it. She had, ah, well, I forgot the name for right now. We were up late and—never mind that. She has never been well. Last night, her skin was so hot, and she shivered after she finished talking to her god, and we said amen. It is something that my sister likes to do, and don't make fun of her. She died when she was eight for twelve whole minutes, and she met this god, and he told her to have faith, always, even when it hurt." She started to cry. "Now she is dying, and I don't know what to do. But she does. She is supposed to be a nurse someday."

Scott put a protective arm around her and pulled her close. "No one is dying on my ranch. And my uncle is a doctor. I promise, honey. Does your supersister like to do anything?" he asked.

"She doesn't read well because she didn't get to learn English. Dad wouldn't let her. She loves music, piano, and dancing. And in England, she went to church—Mass, they call it—every day. But she couldn't here. My dad is an atheist. He thinks he is the mightiest thing anyplace, and we should worship him. I hate him. If I would have been, I would have made him sorry for ever touching us. He is entitled, and don't think he does not know it. He believes the greatest leader in the world is Adolf Hitler. And he knew everyone in law enforcement in California. Before we moved here, he had hurt us both, real—anyway, she rode her bike all the way to downtown Los Angeles from our North Downey mansion and went to Parker Center. She had to get us help. She nearly died after what he did when she came home early from school. And yes, I wanted to die. But Sara said I would go to hell forever. Must be like California, I guess," she quipped.

"You have never been to church?" he asked.

"Dad didn't believe in God. He burned so many of Sara's prayer books and rosaries I lost count. He would hurt her, and she would get on her knees right in front of him, and say that God loved her and she would never forget it. He knew how to make it hurt, but she still talked to her god. He couldn't take that away. Before she came home, Lord and Lady Dickerson tried to keep here there, but I had sent a letter, and I wish I would never have told. Oh, you have me talking about. Damn, I hate myself sometimes," she said, obviously shaken.

"Well, I don't, and my momma has always wanted sweet girls, and not just boys. So I guess Sara's God answered her prayers too. Know this, little sister, no one will ever hurt a hair on your pretty head again. So if you want anything, just ask, and try to behave," he said.

"What road is this?" she asked.

"I guess you would call this our driveway," he said.

"I am really not ignorant. And I know what it is like to be worshipped by classmates who want to live like me. And Sara's friend Karen and her brother Richard, he played the piano. They would help Sara and me when we would run over to their parents' house at night when Dad was drunk and Momma was drunk, or their perverted friends would come over. She would run for cover when she saw Richard. Or if he was just in the room, she would look like a spooky cat. But he knew. He was nice for an old man like you," she said.

Scott nearly swallowed his front teeth. In his early twenties, he was not exactly old.

"One time without thinking, Karen was brushing some leaves out of Sara's hair, and Richard just felt her hair and she saw him in the mirror touching her. And she ran into a wall, and it knocked her completely out," she said.

"Knocked her out? What did this Richard do to her?" he shouted.

"Man, woe little Joe, that is who Sara says she wants to marry. Richard would never hurt us. Too many people know who he is, so don't go busting knuckles on him. And don't hurt his hands. He needs them for his work," she said with authority."

"Who are these older people?" he asked.

"You don't know Karen and Richard Carpenter? "Top of the World." They are singers, and he and Paul Williams write lots of them. They used to visit Sara when they were performing in the UK. Even took her back to school a couple of times," she said.

"Of course I know who they are. They are close to thirty, not older. But you're just a kid," he said then yelped as she pinched a plug out of his arm.

"I have warned you. You may be bigger, but if you mess with me, calling me a kid, I will wait until you go to sleep, like Oscar, and pull out my soft ball bat. Shit, I left it in the floor," she said.

He stopped the truck and told her, "Yeah, found it. It is in the back of the truck. I'll have to get you a new one," he said, casting a glance, warning her to behave again, and picked up Jody.

For once, Saline didn't say anything when she saw her bat in two pieces with what looked like blood on the handle. As they walked in the door, she whispered to where only he could hear him, "Only you could break my bat to get a wife."

He swatted her good-naturedly and told her that was for his arm. She smiled and pranced in.

"Momma, we're here," he yelled.

"My god, just because I slept in the barn doesn't mean you have to act like an ass," Saline said.

All Scott could do with this one was hope to God that she didn't talk that way to his momma. He walked over to the refrigerator, taking out the hot sauce and putting it on the table, prompting Saline to closing her mouth.

Allison Byers was not like anyone she had ever met. "Momma, you may want me to take this one back," he said.

"Nonsense. I never threw you back. Hello, baby, I am Allison Byers. Scott is my oldest son. Our other two are more like wild animals now. Their daddy put them to clean out the barn because they messed up the breakfast table this morning. Riley is sixteen, and Colton is twelve," she said.

"I am Saline Catherine Victoria Alexander. Sara calls me Saline. I am thirteen. I am a sophomore," she said.

Allison recognized the same intelligent look that her husband and eldest son had in her. She also knew the girl looked like she could try hard to chew her up and spit her out. Likely, she should be grateful she was like that. Her sister appeared exhausted mentally, physically, and emotionally and completely broken.

Allison had grown up in the country and helped her brother in his clinic in town. She took care of animals and people and knew when they had given up on life, and you had to work with them if they were to survive. She hoped she was not too late.

"And who is this?" she said, taking the little toddler, who smelled food and wanted it.

"I left his bottle in the barn—house—this morning," She said, hoping Scott would not correct her. "He is hungry."

"How old is he? He looks a little old for a bottle." She wished she hadn't of said it. Sara was doing the best she could with what she had, and likely so was her sister.

"He is two. How old are they when they eat food? Momma never tells me anything. And Oscar sure as hell doesn't know," she said and bit her lip as she saw the hot sauce.

"No doubt Scott has been filling your head with horror stories. But as you can tell from the broken glass and turned-over furniture, we don't really hurt kids. We just try to work it out with them. And you are far too pretty to be mean as a boy," she said.

Scott saw Saline start to rise with that, and once again she rethought it. "You can't overwork my sister or myself, mam. We may be just poor girls now, but we are not nothing, and don't forget that." Saline held her gaze for a minute, and then her look softened at the woman. "Sorry, Mrs. Byers," she said, shaking her head. "I guess it has been too long since I had to use manners. Sara is nothing like me. Don't hold me against her. It is just hard, sometimes."

This one would take a different approach. She was upset and hated with an iron that glowed red. Having seen bruises on her the same but less in number than Sara's, she couldn't blame her. Mary had told her. But Saline was not to be taken, looked over, or ignored. She hated people like she loved them.

"My dear, my son has likely been goading you all the way over here. Go wash your hands, Scott, and show Saline her home and let her do the same. I will take care of Jody and get him fed," she said.

"Yes, mam," he said and placed his hand firmly over Saline's mouth.

She was about to wail Scott's hand away, but then Allison said, "There is plenty of shit to shovel if the two of you start fighting."

Saline started laughing so loud that she walked into a man without seeing who he was. She was about to say something, and Scott replaced his hand. "Saline, quit wiggling. This is my daddy that you were fixing to use that foul machine on."

Saline turned on her heel and firmly slapped his cheek. "Well-mannered young men do not grab ladies. Now, sirs, are you going to show me where I am supposed to be? Obviously, this hopping jack ass is too much of a bully to do so. I am Saline. I am Sara's sister," Saline said.

John watched the standoff. He had no idea how to deal with the intense blond girl with blue eyes that was so much different from her sister. He thought Scott may have robbed the wrong barn. This girl was the most beautiful girl he had likely ever seen, and she was still young. "Right this way, young lady. You're a little spitfire, aren't you? Guess you might be wondering about how you came to be here. Well, I meant only to inquire if your sister was okay this morning, and I alarmed her, and she turned around and ran into my son and fainted," he said kindly.

She turned around to see Scott standing there. "You sick son of a bitch, you hurt my sister," was all she said before she clubbed him in the nose, knocking him to the ground. Then she jumped on him.

Allison heard the commotion and came running, with Jody, who hopped on top of his sister, who was trying to claw Scott's eyes out. Jody thought it was a game.

John reached down and easily grabbed the young girl, having just come back from separating his younger sons a few minutes earlier. "Allison, what the hell is with these kids this morning? Scott looks like he's been in a fight, but surely not with a girl?"

Saline stomped his toe. He had been around a ranch for too long and was expecting her to stomp his toe, so he broadened his stance. "Well, this is a sweet one," John said, picking her up and walking outside, depositing her in the water trough. "When you cool off, wash your hands and face and eat your breakfast before you get any meaner. And keep it down. Your sister is asleep on the other side of the house, and if you have woken her up, you will face me. Do you have a problem with that?" he asked. "Good. Then get cleaned up. My Allison has prepared your breakfast, and she gets mean when it gets cold," he said and then walked into the house.

"John, what did you do with that poor thing?" she asked.

"Threw her in the water trough. She started a fight with Scott."

Scott had walked over the freezer to get some ice. "Daddy, you always said not to hit a girl, but she's mean."

"Son, I would imagine the other one would ice down your nose if she were awake. But I believe this one broke your nose. Maybe she will be the one to keep Colton in line. For God's sake, son, wash your hands. Is he still alive?" John asked.

"Yes, they haven't torn the barn down yet," Allison said.

"Son, you still don't hit even that girl, or I will tell every man on this ranch who it was that broke your nose," he said.

"Hell, Daddy. I am an honest man. I am putting up warning pictures warning men not to let this happen to them." The three of them laughed and watched Jody in the first throes of solid food.

When Saline came back in, she very sedately asked about her sister.

"As I told you, little miss. She is asleep, and my brother-in-law is going to check in on her. No one on this ranch will hurt any of you, lie to you, or starve you. That is a promise I make to well over five hundred employees that have been with me since I was my son's age. You are welcome here and are encouraged to make it your home. But I have two brawling boys, and I don't need any more hornets buzzing around me, understood?"

She looked the man in the eyes and saw nothing there to be wary of. "Sir, I have lived the most of my life afraid, lonely, and the last few years, cold, hungry, and on two hours of sleep in a barn. My sister is weak, and someone has to watch over her. I apologize if I overreacted," she said.

"I know you better than you know me. I have known Mary her entire life, and she has worked for me since she was ten. I have known of you since Sara started working in my café two years ago. And as my son has told you, no one, and I mean no one, is ever going to hurt you including yourself," he said.

Saline sat but continued to watch warily. This girl had an awareness about her that belonged to men in their eighties. Nothing got by her.

"Okay. I am not a child. I can carry my weight," she said.

"You're a little stubborn, but I can deal with that, but you've got at least twenty miles in any direction that belongs to me, and there is not room for that chip on your shoulder. You are hungry. You have better eat before you get in any more trouble or fall on your face because you are too bullheaded to eat. And if you do the latter, we will laugh," he said.

The young girl gritted her teeth, picked up her fork, and continued to look him in the eye. Then the Mexican standoff was over, and she ate. A few minutes later, Jody looked like he was going to take a nap, and Saline felt satisfied and knew if she lay down, she would sleep as well. But first, "Can I see my sister?"

"Of course, you can. Let's go," Scott said.

They walked to the room where Sara was sound asleep. She had not woken up for several hours. Saline seemed satisfied that she was okay.

"Do you want to see your room?" he asked.

"We are not staying on the same room?" she said.

"We have a huge house and lots of rooms with their own bathrooms. And knowing that you don't know us, Daddy had locks put on the doors if you like, so you will feel secure about getting a good night's sleep," he said.

"She can fly. She used to all the time. I could watch her for hours," Saline said.

"Fly? What do you mean?" he asked.

"Sara is a natural dancer. She could ballet dance, but usually it is shorter dancers who got the best parts. But Sara used to be so light on her feet she would just fly. When she had to move back to California, my dad put her in a public school. For PE, she chose dancing, because she was already an expert. If there is any music that she hears, her feet will move to the music with such grace—either wearing those terrible shoes, barefooted, or ballroom dancing in heels, complete with lifts, being tossed in the air.

"She hasn't danced in a very long time. No matter how bad, she seemed to get a joy out of that and talking about church, singing to God. Her voice and her soul lift, and it were as though she was one of his angels in heaven. I wish I could know that peace," she said.

"You will, Saline. Don't give up. And Sara will be well and happy again as well. I promise. Do you believe in love at first sight?" he asked.

"I don't believe in very much anymore, except her love. She could have stayed and lived with her best friends' family, but she came back for me. Our mother does not even want us. She just wants us to provide her with a living," she said.

Again, he put a protective arm on her shoulder. She reminded him of his horse when he first rode him. He needed an experienced rider that was sure of himself at all times. Like Champ, he could tell she wanted to bolt and run but was smart enough to wait and see.

"I have waited for her to notice that I thought she was who I wanted forever. And this morning, she ran right into my arms. I would never hurt her. I caught her before she hit the floor. Her hair and eyes are rare. She will never be the kind of beauty you are. But I saw how hurt and broken she was. Daddy had planned to bring all of you here to us later this week. Through Mary, we know that monster Oscar and your mother. Oscar is going to jail later in the week. Everything is filed," he said.

"And you believe in her god? And your parents?" she said.

"With every fiber of my being, from the first time I saw a calf's eyes open and see the world, or a seed to turn into grass that feeds the cows, every time I was hurt, I knew that God had not let me get hurt any more than my parents would. But he would be there with me in my darkest hour and bring things back to right. When my little sister died a few days after she was born four years ago, my mother nearly died as well." Scott's eyes moistened. "My parents were so sad for two years, but they never lost faith. Then, Sara went to work for Daddy. She was Mary's special pet. Daddy made sure she took good care of your sister, and it took time to get y'all legally away. And by the way, your precious bat was sacrificed this morning to make that monster really miss a part of himself that he would dearly try out on you but never did. He will walk and talk differently for a couple of weeks. But you are a lady and didn't hear that from me.

"The three of you made my momma and daddy happy again, so I know that you were hand-delivered by God to them, and you will know that forever.

"Now, you will find Momma has bought you everything you could ever need, and she believes you should rest as well. Okay?" Then he looked down at her hand and frowned. "Saline, you broke your finger on my face." Quite in his nature, he kissed her finger and said he would be back in a few seconds with ice.

Saline sat down on the bed. She was dumbfounded. Could God really have done this? Softly she said, "God, if you are there, don't let this be a lie. Amen."

Scott put the ice on her hand, and she was asleep before her head hit the pillow.

Scott walked to the family room where his parents were. Jody was in the nursery that Allison had lovingly prepared for him, complete with baby monitors.

"She was asleep before I left the room. She broke her finger while breaking my nose. I brought her some ice," Scott said.

"Scott, did you learn anything about how those children came to be so ill cared for?" Allison asked.

Scott walked into the room and fell into a chair. "Some," Scott said simply and then continued. "They were both abused by Saline's father. She didn't say specifically, but her manner when she almost said a few things," he took a breath, "I believe that both she and Sara were physically abused and raped by Saline's father."

Allison gasped. "Dear lord, I was afraid of that."

"And Saline has tried to kill herself while in California. She ran out into rush-hour traffic. If Sara wouldn't have knocked her out of the way, she would have been killed. I believe that Saline survives for her sister.

"Sara puts herself between Oscar and the other two constantly. And when Sara was twelve, she returned from school in the UK to help her sister."

"That little thing would get herself hurt so her sister and brother would not get hurt?" John said. "She is tiny."

"She also believes her sister is dying, and the only reason she has hung on this long is for her brother and sister. And Sara has to be on medicine for her heart and hasn't been for over two years. I don't fault the attitude that she has taken," Scott said. "But I am angry at the people who have robbed that little girl of her childhood. That made her not want to live."

The sound of an animal-like scream rang through the massive house. Scott and his parents were on their feet, running toward the sound. The scream came from Sara's room.

When they arrived, Saline was already there, trying to talk to Sara.

"Sara, it was a dream. We are okay. Please, Sara, you are going to hurt yourself," Saline pleaded.

Sara continued to scream.

"I am here, Sara. Please wake up."

Then, Sara was in a corner. "Don't hurt us. We didn't do anything wrong. We didn't tell." Then she slid down the wall and wrapped her arms around herself. She was shaking so violently that one would have thought she would have fallen apart.

"Stop! Stop please!" Sara screamed, her sightless eyes taking in nothing but the nightmare she had.

"Sara, it is only a dream. Please wake up," Saline said.

"Saline, what happened?" Allison asked.

"Sara has nightmares. I just have to wake her up. It is not some place we haven't been before," Saline said.

"Saline, let me try please," Scott said.

With a little hesitation, Saline let Scott close to Sara. "Angel, baby, it is Scott." His voice was soft. "You are safe. Can you look at me?"

Sara's skin was hot, and her body soaked. "Run on, Saline, take Jody. Momma, can you bring me a cool washrag?" he asked.

Allison went to Sara's bathroom and was back in an instant.

He sat on the floor with Sara and washed her face with a cool rag. Her eyes were so wide.

Riley and Colton also ran into the room, thinking someone was being murdered. Both were stopped short when they saw Saline. Saline's looked to be older than her thirteen years and was the most beautiful girl they had ever seen.

In Sara's room, she had still not woken up from the demon that was haunting her. Gradually, Scott pulled her into his arms and began to talk softly into her ear as he stroked her hair and cooled her face. Without ever having woken up, cradled in Scott's arms, she relaxed.

Scott gently stood with Sara in his arms and put her back on her bed. As he moved his arm from under her ribs, she groaned, and her face contorted for a moment. Scott could feel where her ribs were broken. He pulled the bottom of the back of her blouse up and saw that it was bruised beyond anything he had ever seen. She moved a little, and he replaced her blouse then took the bed cover and pulled it up over her.

Scott put his hand to her forehead and discovered that Saline was indeed correct; she had high fever. There was no telling how many injuries she had sustained. He was glad his uncle would be looking in on her.

After leaving Sara's room, confident that Scott only wanted to help, Saline went back to her room and sat on the bed. She was so worried about everything of the last few days—people she didn't know, a new place, and her sister, who had always been her hero. Years ago, when Sara had seen death and returned, she thought she would die with her.

Saline had always been stoic, a born fighter. And Sara had always been the one who protected her both from her father and herself. She could not bear losing her sister. They were so close. She had learned French, so she could communicate with her in letters. Even had the letters mailed to her best friend's house so they would be undetected by her dad. That act had caused both of them grief, but it was worth it because they had each other.

The horrors of her life suddenly rolled over her. Her body ached, her hand hurt, and she was so tired that she thought she would die. But she couldn't sleep from worrying so about Sara. Quite like Sara, she never cried. To show anyone that they had the better of them had never been an option. But thirteen-year-old Saline knew that their choices were limited: chance going to authorities and being separated from each other, go back to California, or stay in Texas and take their chances. Saline shivered at the thought.

The day before, they had been so hungry that they had diluted Jody's milk to have more volume, so at least he could eat. Both girls had become very familiar with doing without. It was a fact of their lives. It was nothing to have a refrigerator half full of beer and no food.

Before she knew it, tears had begun to pour down her cheeks. She didn't know if she could trust these people. She didn't know what to look for as far as trusting people. She remembered as a young child when her father would have parties, the actors that she had seen on the TV and thought must be such nice people were nothing but drug addicts and child molesters. Nothing made anyone richer than booze, drugs, and providing little girls as play things.

Karen, Richard, and their parents had provided a safe place from time to time. Since that time, there had been no one who seemed to care. The so-called churchgoing people did nothing but refer to them as white trash because of their mother's conduct.

Saline let herself fall over on the soft, warm bed and buried her face in a pillow and began to cry. The world was just too real. Kids at school, their biggest worry was what they were going to wear from day to day. What would it be like to have that kind of life?

Then, she heard someone come in the room. Saline bolted upright and saw Allison Byers walking toward her.

"Is Sara okay?" Saline said, trying hard not to let her voice crack.

"She is sleeping peacefully again. Scott is sitting with her right now. I promise you. He would never do anything to hurt her," she said and took a seat on the bed beside Saline.

"I know that you have had to watch after each other for a very long time and that you are going to have trouble trusting anyone, but, Saline, I have known of you for over two years. We have done everything to make a life for you because we want you. I wish we could have taken you from that life earlier. We want you as part of our family." With that, she reached and wiped the tears that continued to roll down the young girl's cheeks. "That is only if you want to be here."

Feeling a huge weight being lifted off her shoulders for the first time in her life, Saline looked into the eyes of the gentle woman who spoke. Then, completely out of character, Saline all but threw herself into the kind woman's arms and sobbed.

Allison held her as she shed so many years of tears she could not imagine. She began to rock to and fro with her and stroked her hair. She whispered reassurances to her and let her cry.

About an hour later, Saline was spent from crying. She pulled away from Allison for a moment. "I am sorry, Mrs. Byers. I didn't mean to act like a baby. I don't usually cry, but I am so worried about my sister."

"Saline, you have nothing to be sorry for. You love your sister and brother. Do you think that you can rest little before we eat lunch?" she asked.

Saline nodded. In truth, she thought she was going to pass out from emotional exhaustion.

Allison got up and went into the bathroom and wet a washrag then returned to Saline. She washed her face and then hugged her again and kissed her forehead. "We will come and get you when lunch is ready. There is a warm gown in the bathroom if you want to get out of those wet clothes. Okay?" she said.

Saline nodded. "Mam?" she asked.

"Yes, baby."

"Do really want us to be here from now on?" Saline asked.

"There is nothing on this earth that I want more. Get some rest," Allison said and out the door.

Saline was overwhelmed by fatigue. She went to the bathroom and pulled off the damp clothes she had been wearing. She quickly washed the scent of the barn off herself. Saline had been having abdominal pain for over three years, and suddenly it was feeling worse than before. Everything was so real now. She walked to the bed and lay down, feeling like she could sleep for a month. She lay back on the pillow and held another pillow to her chest and was in a dreamless sleep within seconds.

In what seemed like seconds but was actually two hours, Allison returned to awaken Saline for lunch. Allison showed her the closet that held new clothes for her. It was like a dream looking at the new clothes. Saline picked up the sleeve of one of the sweaters and smelled the new smell deep in her nose.

"You can change and put on some clothes if you like. Do the clothes suit you?" Allison asked.

"They are too beautiful to touch. I feel so dirty," Saline said, looking at the oversized tub. "How long is it until lunch?" she asked.

"About twenty minutes. Would you like to take a bath? I have some bath salts and bubble bath," Allison said, starting to run the water.

The impulse of the moment overtook Saline. A hot bath in a big bathtub was too tempting. She pulled her gown over her head.

Allison gasped at the marks on the young girl. Saline pulled the gown up against her as though she were ashamed of herself.

"Saline, baby, I am sorry. You have done nothing wrong," Allison said, walking over to her. She looked only at her beautiful face. "May I ask a favor?"

"Yes, mam. You have been so kind," Saline said with tears streaming down her face.

"My brother is a doctor. Will you let him have a look at you? I assure you that I have only the best intentions in mind. I will be with you if you like." Allison waited for her to answer.

It was a big step for Saline, a man to touch her. She lost count of how many men had touched her. She couldn't believe her own words when she heard herself answer. "Okay."

Allison hugged her close, careful not to touch any of the places that she had seen. "I will come and knock on the door when it is time to eat. Okay?"

"Yes, mam," Saline said. As quickly as Allison was out of the room, Saline was in the tub. She took a washrag and scrubbed herself until her skin stung. She scrubbed as though she wanted to take away the marks that labeled her as an abused child. Then she washed her thick blond hair and scratched until she knew that every bit of the dirt floor of the barn was gone. Then she lay in the tub of hot water and soaked for a minute.

Allison had left the room, and instead of going back to the kitchen, she went to her and John's room. She closed the door and went over to their bed and threw herself down and cried. She was heaving so loud that Riley heard her in the hall.

"Momma. Are you okay?" he asked.

"I am okay, son. I will be down in a minute," she said through the door.

Riley was concerned but went to the dining room to see if his father was there as yet.

"Daddy, I think you need to go see about Momma. She is in y'all's room, crying," Riley said and went to the stove to make sure nothing was in danger of burning.

John was up from the table and went upstairs to see about Allison. "Allison, what's wrong, darlin'?"

"John, those animals who hurt those children need killing. Saline wanted to take a hot bath before she ate. She pulled her gown off, and I couldn't help but gasp. If Sara is that black and blue, I don't know how she can survive. We have to keep them safe, John. I had no idea how cruel life had been to them," Allison said and began to cry harder.

John held his wife as she cried. He had never seen her so emotionally distraught about anyone she had just met. The last time he had seen her so upset was after the loss of their daughter.

"Alex will be here after a while. He will help," he said.

"I asked Saline if she would let Alex look at her. She did that thing where she was staring you in the eye for a few seconds. But she did agree, but only if I am with her. I am afraid for them, John," she said.

"Allison, honey. We will give them everything that they need and all the love in the world. And God help any of those people if they were to come here. Now you need to wash your face and check on Saline, and we will have a good lunch. Okay?" he said.

Allison smiled up at her husband. "Okay."

With that, John left the room and went back to the dining room.

Allison did as she had told Saline she would and knocked on the door.

"Just a minute. I am getting dressed," Saline said. She had decided on putting on a pair of slacks, a turtleneck to hide the bruises, and the soft sweater she had seen earlier. When she had started looking through the walk-in closet, she saw everything she could possibly need.

Saline's hair was still soaked, which made her feel even colder. She needed to find a hairbrush to brush it out. She opened the door and went into the bedroom, where Allison was waiting for her.

Saline quickly brushed her hair and braided it for the time being. "May I check on Sara before lunch?"

"Yes, of course," Allison said and then turned to face Saline for a quick moment. "I am sorry if I embarrassed you earlier. I really didn't mean to."

"Not a problem. At school, in gym, the girls don't apologize about pointing and staring," Saline said.

She followed Allison to Sara's room and showed her that her sister was still sleeping and that she would eat when she woke up. In the dining room, Scott, Colton, Riley, and John were seated at the table, along with the ranch foreman.

Saline had always looked more mature for her age, so when she entered, everyone looked up and saw the extremely beautiful young girl that looked to be closer to twenty than thirteen. Each man stood when Allison and Saline entered.

"Everyone, this is Saline. Saline, these are our younger sons, Riley and Colton, and this is our ranch foreman, Ray. Please be seated, my dear," Allison said.

Riley and Colton stared, mouths agape.

"Boys, I think you need to be doing less staring and more eating," John said to his sons.

Allison took the liberty of fixing a plate for Saline to try to merely ease her into eating at the table with a bunch of men and boys. John held Jody in his lap as the little boy worked on eating a chicken leg. He would give him bites of beans and potatoes, and he had a sippy cup of milk.

Saline saw that Jody was happy with his position at the table.

"Please forgive our younger sons, Saline. It is not often that they sit at the table with a beautiful young lady," John said.

"It's okay. I almost never sit at a table to eat," Saline said without thinking. She thought of how they generally ate, huddled in the corner of the barn. "Where is Sara?" she asked, changing the subject.

"She is still asleep. My brother said that she likely needed sleep now as bad as anything. But she has not had any more nightmares," Allison said. "When she wakes up, there will be something for her to eat, and someone is always sitting in the room with her. Maria is in there right now."

"Thank you," Saline said and began to eat.

"On Monday we need to go to Evermore School and get you enrolled so you don't miss any days," Allison said.

"I don't go to Evermore. I go to public school," she said.

"We realize that. But for safety reasons, we have pulled you out of the school you were attending and switched schools and your last name to keep you well hidden and safe," John said. "Did you have the same school uniform as your sister?"

"No, we didn't wear uniforms. She was in boarding school. We went home every day from school," Saline said.

"I have the paperwork if you want to take some electives or continue as you were. It will be a little different, but not too much," Allison said.

"What kind of a school is Evermore School? It is not church school, is it?" she asked.

"No. It is a private school," Allison said.

"Do they have to wear uniforms?" she asked.

"I believe that they do."

"I don't like to wear dresses. I have never liked to wear dresses. The boys at school always are pulling your skirt up," Saline said.

"I don't think that you have to worry about that. It is an all-girls school, and the uniforms are nothing like your sister's. And there are also pants that can be worn. And this school will keep you safe. So isn't that worth it?" Allison asked.

Saline nodded and then began to daydream. What would it be like to sleep all night with a full stomach and wake up and get to eat? She was feeling better already. "I can do that," she told Allison. "But, Mrs. Byers, how long is this going to last? What if next week or next year you decided you don't want us? Then we have to go back to the farm, and Momma and Oscar will be angry, and we will be cold and hungry again. I don't think Sara can last much longer."

"First, we have gone to great lengths to make sure that you are able to be here forever, and we will never change our minds. Second, there will always be someone at the school keeping an eye on you to keep you safe. Someone will take you to and from school. We have left nothing to chance. This is as real as it gets," Allison assured.

"Sara is very sick. What if something happens to her?" Saline asked.

"Sara is going to get better," Scott said.

"When Sara wakes up, we are taking her to the doctor to help her. You are not alone anymore. Everything has been considered," John said.

"Sara was supposed to take heart medicine for a long time and see a heart doctor. But that stopped when we moved back here," Saline said.

"Do you remember the name of the heart doctor?" Scott asked.

"Yes, Dr. Steven Quinton in Los Angeles. He even went to her school to see her from time to time. He called her his miracle patient," Saline said.

"I will make sure that Alex knows who he is. Now, young lady, you need to eat your lunch before it gets cold," Allison said.

Saline had no idea what she was eating. She just knew it was hot and tasted good. And the thought of getting to sit at a table like most children did was a big plus. In no time, she had cleaned her plate.

Jody was sitting in Scott's lap, eating everything in front of him. He was happy and even laughing. Saline didn't feel anything threatening from anyone in the room. "May I have another one of those?" she asked.

"You can have as much as you want," Allison said, passing her the potatoes.

"Thank you," she said in return.

When the meal was finished, John and the man at the table and his sons left out the door. Allison started clearing the table. Not really knowing what was expected of her, Saline began to help Allison clear the table. Allison didn't make a fuss about it but seemed to appreciate her action. When the kitchen and dining room were clean once again, Allison went to the freezer and looked inside.

"Is there anything that you like to eat? I am a pretty good cook and would be glad to make something you want," Allison said.

"Anything tastes good to me. I am not picky. Sara likes soup," Saline answered.

"Soup?"

"Where she went to school, they had soup and hard bread for supper every night. She said it made her feel loved for some reason," Saline said.

"I will remember that," Allison said and smiled. In that moment, Saline made decision. They had to trust someone, and so far, these people seemed to care.

Time passed, and Sara had been in first the small hospital and then spent over a week in the hospital in Dallas. Dr. Quinton even came to take care of her.

Saline liked Uncle Alex. When he came over, he set her broken finger and splinted it. Now Jody was thriving, and even though she had to wear a uniform to an all-girls school, she still loved learning.

Today was the day that Sara was to come home from the hospital. *Home*—that was a word that she never would have thought would have meaning. The Byers family had been good to them. Even when she and Colton had a disagreement, they didn't hurt them, but they did have to pull weeds from the garden for an entire afternoon.

There was plenty to eat, her own bathroom, and clothes that fit. But more than that, the family seemed to really care about her.

Scott was nothing like her own older brother. He would kid with her, but never in a bad way. She finally felt like she had a place that they all belonged, for now.

As Saline had promised Allison, she went to the clinic to have a complete physical. Uncle Alex had already seen to Sara, so nothing about Saline was going to be any kind of a surprise, nothing new anyway.

Alex started out asking questions and then pointed questions about her past. Saline answered his questions and did well at controlling her voice, but her body shook. She could not control the trembling. He listened to her heart and her lungs. Then he opened the back of her gown and saw what Allison had told him about.

There were a large variety of bruises in various stages of healing. She also had what looked to be healed brands.

"What made these circular marks on your back and the backs of your legs?" he asked.

"A cigarette lighter from a car, my dad liked to treat us like we were animals."

"I need you to lie flat for me," he said and put a sheet over her so she was never completely exposed. He saw the same circular burns on Saline's breasts. He couldn't imagine the pain involved. He noticed that Saline was starting to get tense as he examined her breasts. She put her hand on her lower abdomen. Uncle Alex then examined her abdomen. She had so many that were extremely painful. "Have you ever had a pelvic exam before Saline?" he asked.

"I don't know," was the first thing that came in her head, but in truth, she had been examined by someone once at her grandmother's request.

"Do you want me to tell you what I am doing?" Alex asked.

"No. But tell Mrs. Byers later," she said directly.

Alex knew she had been examined before, knew exactly what he would find, or at least basically, and likely because she didn't want to hear the results, didn't want to hear it.

Alex kept having to remind himself that the young lady was only thirteen years old. But when he started the exam, he realized age didn't say much about the way the young girl had been treated before she arrived in Texas. Alex did the necessary procedures and then told Saline where everything was and to get dressed.

"Dr. Carmichael?" Saline said. Alex paused at the door. Allison was already outside the door, so he pushed the door too.

"Yes, Saline."

"My grandma took me to the doctor when I was nine. She didn't want what happened to Sara to happen to me, so she wanted to get me birth control pills," Saline said. "Her doctor said it was not necessary. I would never be able to have kids. I was too damaged. And with the surgery that I had, I really was not a girl anymore," she said about the time that thunder clapped overhead. "Isn't it a beautiful day? We used to get thrown out of the house on cold, rainy weather in California. We learned to appreciate cloud bursts. To Sara, it was not as cold as she was used to in Wales. Of all things, Daddy was afraid of the rain. It became our favorite kind of weather.

"We were not bad girls, Dr. Carmichael. Early we thought we were, so both of us began to do things around the house, everything nanny said, bring Momma her medicine. But we found there were no rules to live by. It had little to do with us. We just so happened to be there. Soon he had every man on his crew who wanted to advance in status to bring their kids to the house for him. I would never bring any friends home from school, because I knew what would happen.

"He knew how to put a hurt on you. He could shove your arm right out of the socket by putting it behind you, and he would tell us we knew the magic words to stop it. We would die before we said them, and sometimes we welcomed the thought. Sometimes I welcomed it so much that I decided I had lived my last day. I had gone to school ahead of Sara so it would be over before she got there. There is nothing that will stand between me and safety with Sara around. She ran and pushed me out of the way and broke her arm in the process. Sara was a tennis player. That ended when she broke her arm. But she said tennis is just something that helped her pass the time; she couldn't live without me. If I had to choose a mother, it would be her.

"I like you, Dr. Carmichael. I have never said that to anyone I did not know well. Just don't let any of this be a lie," Saline concluded.

"Can you turn to face me Saline?" he asked.

Saline turned toward him.

"All of us are your friends. For all intents and purposes, you were born into a new family. You have made my sister's family very happy just knowing that they had two new daughters and a new son. That is how we all see it. You don't have to believe me. Mark St. Clair, Maria's husband, his father worked for John when Mark was in junior high. He and Scott have always been best friends. He rode out to the pasture one day and didn't come in. When we found him, he had died. John and Allison adopted Mark. Talk to him. I hope that is how you will come to see it. You don't have to be afraid of any of us. No one will hurt you. Call me Uncle Alex please," he said.

Saline looked at him for a long moment then closed her eyes to the tears. "Terror is like a runaway train, Dr. Carmichael. You can't stop it," she said in a very low voice that made the hair on the back of his neck stand on ends. "You just can't stop it."

Alex smiled at the beautiful young lady. She wanted so much to believe in something good. Her intensity was well beyond her years. "I will see you in a few minutes."

When he was out of the room, Saline thought she would collapse. She wanted to believe in these people. "God, if you are there, I asked again that this not be a lie. If it is not, thank you. Amen."

Outside the room, Alex stood and spoke. "I can't believe the difference in the two girls. Yet they are so close you cannot emotionally separate them. But one is so calm and loving and uses her own body as a barrier for her young siblings. The other uses violence and hates anyone who threatens them. But I believe that if you can get through to Saline, she could love the same way she hates."

"You saw what she did to Scott. And the way she stared down John, I couldn't believe it," Allison said.

"If it is the way she stared me down a minute ago, I know what you mean. This is important though. If something happened to hurt her one more time, it would break her. For God's sake, we have to keep them safe. Then there is the physical part. She will never have children. She had a hysterectomy when she was nine. The rat bastard who did it said that she was not even a girl anymore. It kills me to think of what she has been through to arrive where she is. And to think, someone took away her chances of a family before she was nine years old. I just need five minutes alone with that Alexander bastard with a scalpel. Amy, could you draw blood on her for everything?" he asked as Amy went to the room.

"Sure, Alex. No problem. And the architect wants to talk to you," she said.

"Thanks." He then turned back to Allison. "Making this place so much bigger is a pain in the ass," he said as he walked around the contractor's equipment. He then knocked on the exam room door. Saline said to come in.

"May I ask a couple more questions, Saline?"

"Yes, sir. Shoot," she said.

"What would give your family diplomatic immunity in the United States?" he asked.

"My dad is the proximate heir to a line of nobility in Hamburg, Germany. Why? Is he here? He would be the first person my mother would call in a jam," Saline said.

"He is in the county lockup. I tell you that not to upset you, but because I will never lie to you," Alex said.

"Good. Let the son of a bitch out. I will kill him myself," Saline said with the fierceness of a mother lion. "He comes near one of us. I am not a kid anymore. I will kill him."

Alex didn't doubt her words. "Saline, you go home to my sister and brother-in-law's ranch. No idiot in their right mind is going to take on five hundred armed cowboys. They don't have diplomatic immunity, just a quarter of a million acres to bury his body. And have no doubt, they would do it. And John would do it for them."

"But what about us? My sister can't sleep for the nightmares that she has. Jody is just a baby," she said.

"Saline, y'all belong to us now. Everyone on our ranch would take up arms to protect you," Allison said.

"What if the people from Hamburg try to take us away?" Saline said.

"Those sons of bitches have had two years to do that. Now you belong to us, and I welcome that rat bastard to come on my property. I will kill him myself. And for the record, I won't bury him. I will leave him for the buzzards," Allison said.

Saline had heard lies from adults her entire life. She knew a lie before it ever crossed the lips of the person telling it. Her heart swelled at the thought of so many standing up for them. In the last few weeks, on the ranch and at school, people smiled when they waved at her. And not with the usual looks that she got from men, but genuine looks of kindness.

She and Colton had locked horns a couple of times, and as they had told her, no one laid a hand on her. But they both got to pull weeds out of Mrs. Byers's vegetable garden.

"May I ask a question?" Saline asked.

"Yes, of course," Alex said.

"From the time I was born until we moved here, I knew that we were wealthy. But money means nothing to me or Sara. If we had to live out of a cardboard house but had enough to eat, were warm, and not afraid, we would have been happy. That wealth that we grew up with was of no comfort.

"If I hadn't of sent a letter to Sara when she was at Lord and Lady Dickerson's estate in Bath, she could have just stayed there. They had already adopted her. She came back for me. Lauren was their daughter and Sara's best friend. I swear we did nothing to ever lead anyone on, like my dad said we did.

"Why would you go to the trouble of standing up for three kids that were considered white trash until a few weeks ago?" Saline said.

Allison walked over to the young girl. "Your mother and father are white trash. You and your sister and brother have never been. Sara works, and the two of you take care of a toddler. And, young lady, I will never hear you ever refer to yourself as trash. Understood?"

For a few seconds, years of ice began to melt from Saline's heart. "Understood," she said and threw her arms around Allison. "Thank you," she said before she began to cry.

Allison smoothed her hair and held her the same way.

Alex smiled down at his sister. She had gotten through. No more need be said. Alex left the room and wrote prescriptions for Saline for various problems she had. One problem was two cracked ribs that had to be very painful. When Alex ordered x-rays, he discovered she also had some problems with her neck. Saline had severe scarring that was discovered in her pelvic exam. He didn't tell Saline what he saw as she already seemed to know. The scarring appeared to be from having been repeatedly being burned by something. Alex knew she had to be in a lot of pain from a very severe case of pelvic inflammatory disease.

Alex had to wait for the labs to come back before he knew the extent of her medical problems. He told Allison he would call in a couple of days with the test results. Saline broke away from Allison for a moment.

"Uncle Alex," she said and walked over to him. "Thank you for caring," she said and hugged him.

"You're family, honey, I will always care," he said.

CHAPTER 5

When Love Hurts

Henry was finally released from the county lockup and was escorted to the Dallas Fort Worth airport. He was given instructions that if he returned to the county, it would be to his own peril. He had assaulted a citizen and a police officer.

But Henry knew something that they didn't know. He was the nephew of a German duke, an aristocrat whose sole existence was to keep a pure line. So as he had been born in Germany to a German, he had diplomatic immunity. He would go back to California, but only to make sure all was well with his other children, Tommy and Sophie, but then would return. He could not trust that slut that he had been married to keep her mouth shut. He had lived in the United States most of his life, true, but most of the time, he traveled and had business to tend to.

The most elaborate stars and other celebrities in California attended the pool parties that he would have. He loved his California lifestyle. He welcomed various people from law enforcement, because you never know when you're going to need a little legal help, and of course, people in politics. All were all too willing to befriend a man that would one day be a duke.

On the plane back to California, he remembered what Sara had done that caused a stir in his perfect life. He considered his wife and daughter more property than anything else, and they were treated as such. But Sara broke the rules. She had ridden to Parker Center in downtown LA and told a detective that he had been abusing herself and her sister. The detective made a report and the following day came to his north Downey mansion. Henry knew it had to be Sara; she would do anything for her sister.

He had not been home that morning, but when he returned and found out from Joan what had happened and that the police were looking for him, he grabbed up both girls and took them to a friend's job site and threw Sara into a hole that was to be a swimming pool and then started the bull dozer. Inch by inch the mountain of dirt got closer and closer to covering Sara, and Saline screamed hysterically, begging him to stop. When at the last possible moment he did, he beat both girls nearly to death and then arranged to move both them and their slut of a mother to Texas to the small farm that they owned there. With that, the charges went away.

He had spent over a week in the county lockup of a small town in Texas with every kind of human waste imaginable, and it angered him to think about it. With that sheriff announcing that he was a child molester, he had spent that time being assaulted time and again by the inmates. He would make those girls pay for what they had done.

He had to find out about this family that had the three kids, and he would get them back so as to shut them up.

When Sara returned home from the hospital this time, it was really like she was coming home. For weeks, the Byers had done everything possible to let them know that this was now their home. With the soreness subsiding and feeling better than she had in what seemed like years, there was an eagerness to start some sort of a normal life.

As Sara and Scott pulled into the parking area, both Saline and Jody ran outside to greet her, closely followed by Allison, John, Riley, and Colton. Everyone took their turn hugging her warmly.

John appraised the young lady and noted that she had started to gain some much needed weight. She had color in her cheeks, and the bruising was completely gone. He hugged her and stroked her cheek. "You look beautiful, baby girl," he said.

"Thank you, sir, I would not be here without all of you. Thank you," she said again.

It was nearing suppertime, so everyone went in the vast yet warm house. Sara saw Saline in the kitchen helping Allison with supper. She offered to help, but Allison reminded her of what both Uncle Alex and Dr. Quinton had told her.

It would take time and much rest for her to regain her strength. Sara went to her room and looked through the bag that she had from the hospital. She hadn't been able to find her rosary, and she looked through everything for it.

"Is this what you are looking for?" Scott said from the doorway.

"Where did you find it, Scott?" she asked.

"On your table at the hospital. When Dr. Quinton put the tube in your heart, I picked it up and did my own talking to God. It has not left my side since," he said, holding it out to Sara.

Sara smiled a radiant smile at the man she had fallen in love with. "When I left England the last time, Lady Dickerson gave it to me. Her daughter and I were best friends from the first day I arrived at school," she said when she saw it in Scott's hand. She walked over to him and closed his hand around it. "You keep it. You have done so much for me. I want you to have it."

"I will always keep them with me then. How does it feel to be home?" he asked, walking toward her.

"Wonderful," she beamed at him.

"Let me give you a proper greeting," he said and took her in his arms. He looked into her eyes and kissed her warmly. "I am so glad you are home. Are you up to eating in the dining room tonight?" he asked.

"Yes, of course. I want to see everyone. Jody and Saline look so happy now. And I know it has only been a few weeks, but your brothers seem like my own family, as do Momma and Poppa," she said, referring of course to Scott's parents.

It didn't feel right calling them by their first or last name, and Allison had invited her to call them as she would parents, so she did. Both John and Allison were the perfect parents to them.

"I can't believe the change in Saline since she came here. She somehow seems so much younger than she did before. She smiles and laughs and just seems to enjoy everything," Sara said.

Scott smiled, remembering that first day. Since then, she had settled down and had begun to help Allison around the house. There had been a couple of dust-ups between her and Colton, but the two seemed to care for each other much like brother and sister. Riley took her to school every morning and thought she was the most beautiful thing she had ever seen.

"Now, there is something we need to start on. You will be taking it easy for a couple of months, so it is the perfect time to work on reading and such. It will help pass the time and help when you want to go to school or take your GED," he said.

"Who is going to teach me?" she asked.

"All of us. We have obtained books that will help you get everything from French to English. And one day, you said you want to be a nurse, so you are getting a head start," he said. "And I even speak French."

"But everyone is so busy, except me of course," she said.

"That is why we will all be helping," he said.

With that, he saw a light in her eyes. "Are you happy, my love?"

"It is as it was promised. Everything is falling in place. I am so happy," she said.

"Then I think we had better head down to supper," he said.

In the dining room, everyone was taking their place at the table. Jody had a high chair now and was thriving. He ate nearly everything put in front of him.

Allison, knowing Sara's love of soup, always tried to have some fixed. The meal smelled heavenly, and after everyone was seated, it was time to eat.

Saline was happy to have her sister back and looking better than she could ever remember. Since she had been enrolled in school, she had done exceptionally well. Everyone could see why she had been moved ahead a couple of years.

Allison and John were glad that they made the decision to put the Saline in an all-girls school. Saline was such a breathtaking beauty and was more developed than other girls her age. They hated to think what high school boys would think of her.

Regardless of how she felt about starting school there, Saline was so glad to be there. She had new friends and plenty of activities to keep her busy. She had even started to love outdoor activities. She would accompany Riley and Colton to the pasture to feed the livestock and even go fishing.

She could not believe how hard every member of the Byers family worked. With all their wealth and prominence, they were just like what had to be a normal family. She had learned to appreciate the thousands of acres that insulated the main house from the road to town. She was happy every morning she woke up on the ranch. She loved her new family and hoped they would always want her.

The next weeks were a turning point in the lives of everyone on the ranch. Saline finished the tenth grade with honors. Her fourteenth birthday was the month following the end of school. She was given a birthday party with her new friends from school and the people of the ranch, who had also fallen in love with the newest additions to their home.

Jody was now running from place to place rather than walking. His language skills were growing every day, as was he physically.

There were other toddlers who lived on the ranch with their parents who worked the ranch, and Jody was right at home with every one of them.

All three of the Byers sons welcomed the new additions to their household.

Dr. Quinton had decided to move his practice to Dallas after spending two weeks on staff at Baylor. He had no family to speak of in California, and Baylor had made him a great deal if he would move to Dallas. He was glad to know that he already had his first patient in Texas.

Sara got stronger every day. She was glad she knew the doctors that she was to see who were treating her. She grew strong enough so as she and Scott could ride horses in the evenings. Scott had found her one of the more gentle mares in the horse barn. He was going to keep his eye out for a more suitable horse in time.

She was a very good rider. She was completely at home on a horse, and the horses responded to her touch. Each day, the couple grew closer.

From time to time, Scott would take her for rides on the ranch to feed the cattle and would even go with him to see the progress of their house. One afternoon in early July, Scott decided to see if Sara was ready to get off the ranch for something besides trip to the doctor.

"What did you have in mind?" Sara asked.

"How about something like a movie and going to eat?" he asked.

Sara knew that she was safe with Scott anywhere or anytime. "I would love to. I have never been on a date before."

Scott thought for a minute about her turning seventeen in only a few months. Most girls started dating at fifteen. But Sara really didn't care about a social life when she was responsible for her brother and sister.

"How about going to the movies after church on Sunday and then getting supper afterward?" he said.

Sara smiled at him. "I can't wait."

About that same time, Joan and Oscar Redding had discovered that their habits were more expensive than first thought. Along with that were the attorney fees for each, Oscar for two counts of assault of a minor, and Joan for assault of a peace officer. At first they wanted the attorney that the county would be providing until they found that they would likely have to serve some time in jail, so they got their own attorney.

So one of them had to go to work. As Joan had no previous work skills whatsoever, it was decided by her that it would be Oscar. So he took a job as a mechanic in the Ford house about thirty miles from the farm. He didn't like the drive, having to be sober to work, or what he got paid. Then there was the thought that Joan got to stay home all day long and do whatever she wanted.

He knew that she had money hidden someplace that she didn't tell him about, and he had done his best to find it, but to no avail. He also knew that Henry Alexander was coming to Texas and lurking about from time to time.

Henry had to keep his visits to Texas short because he had been told not to enter the county again. He knew from Joan that Henry worried about his reputation as he was to take his uncle's place in Germany one day. At that point, he would have the riches of the world at his disposal. But until that time, he was supposed to keep his name in a positive light.

Henry also knew that because of his divorce and recent arrest, his name was in the papers for all the wrong reasons. Henry had been threatened to lose his succession if he didn't stay out of the press. His precious title would go directly to Tommy in that case. He had to be getting desperate to find those two girls.

Oscar had been told by a couple of people that they were well concealed and he would never find them. He considered himself smarter that Henry Alexander. He had started looking for them in the schools within fifty miles of the school that Saline had been in. Oscar's mother was the secretary of the high school that Saline had gone to, so she helped him look in every school around.

When Oscar had told his mother that he wanted the girls to come home because they needed their mother, she fooled herself into believing her son. So far they had been unable to find her.

In the weeks and months since the kids disappeared, Sara had not shown up at work. She didn't have a car, and he had followed Mary home enough to know that she was not at her house. But Mary did know where they were. The one time that Oscar did try to extract something from Mary, she had kicked him so hard that he threw up in the middle of the café. Mary even taunted him, in that she would know that he was following her, and she drove one time until he ran out of gas.

One Friday, he went to work and was passing the grocery store in town and saw someone with the same color of dark red hair as Sara. But there was something different about the girl. She was wearing nice clothes and was laughing with a middle-aged woman as though one of them had told a good joke. They appeared to be mother and daughter, so he stopped the car and continued to watch them. They had disappeared into the grocery store, so Oscar went in as well. It only took a couple of minutes before he found them.

Over the last months since they had been gone, something had changed about her. She had gained a little weight, which gave her a curvier figure. Her eyes that were previously sunken and sad were now full of life and happiness. The clothes both were wearing were well fitted and expensive.

Oscar didn't know the other woman, but it was obvious that Sara trusted her. They were talking then Sara went a couple of rows over. It looked like she had to pick something up that they had missed. While she was alone, Oscar took that opportunity to approach his stepdaughter.

"So here you are," he said.

Sara, who was paying too much attention to what she was doing, was struck momentarily dumb at hearing Oscar's voice. "Get away from me," she said.

"Your mother has been looking for you. I had to go to work because you are off running around with people you don't know," he said.

"I owe you no explanation. We are happy and loved now, and do not plan on seeing any of you again," she said.

"I need to talk to you. Did you know that some son of a bitch beat me to where I could hardly move for several days? And I am out on bail because of something you said that I did?" he said.

"That sounds like you need a lawyer, not me. Please leave me alone. I need to go back," she said, beginning to panic a little.

"You bitch! Do you know what happened to me when I was put in jail for a few days? It was all because of you," he said, grabbing her arm.

Sara began to struggle to get free of him. "Stop! Help!" she yelled. "Leave me alone."

Oscar attempted to cover her mouth. Sara bit his hand and continued to struggle to achieve her freedom. Oscar immediately struck Sara hard across the face and then shoved her so that she tripped in the middle of the aisle of the store.

Sara continued to yell for help, and people began to rally to where the sound was coming from. Sara was on the ground only a moment before she was up and moving away from him. She looked and saw some cooking utensils then grabbed a meat hammer. Oscar grabbed her and once again knocked her in the face. Sara recoiled and hit him with the coarse end of the meat hammer on the side of his face. In return, Oscar balled his fists and slugged her as hard as he could in the stomach.

Sara struggled to catch her breath. People were coming to her aide. Sara still had the meat hammer. She waited until Oscar was close enough to touch her and struck him with the fierceness of a mother lion. She struck him on the side of the knee, knowing that she would likely cause damage. As she swung the hammer, she thought of her, Jody, and Saline being so cold and hungry and afraid of them sleeping in a falling-down barn to keep Oscar from raping them.

When the meat hammer hit its mark, Oscar collapsed. "You filthy bitch, I will kill you!" he yelled.

People looked at the scene that was in front of them. A grown man had attacked a much smaller girl.

"That bitch assaulted me. I want her arrested," he yelled.

Sara, still dizzy from the assault, picked up the meat hammer and went to where he was lying on the floor. She saw the people who had seen part of what happened and nodded their heads at her. Two men went to where Oscar was as Sara approached. She also saw Allison running toward her.

In her proper English accent, she spoke to him, "You are on probation for assault of a minor. Now you have done so again with many witnesses as to what happened," she said.

"You stupid bitch, you have crippled me," he said.

"Now you get to go back to jail as you have violated your probation. All those men in the county lockup knowing that you have harmed a minor girl have a special fondness for people like you. So I have to ask, who is the bitch is now?" she said and got up, staggering to Allison.

"I am sorry I made such a fuss, Momma. He grabbed me and tried to take me out of here," she said, beginning to cry. "I could never bear to leave our new home and family."

"You did well, baby girl. And you are right. He is going to jail now," she said, looking toward the two police officers who approached Oscar.

As they began to handcuff him and read him his rights, Oscar said, "What about her? Why don't you arrest her?"

"Self-defense is not a crime," one said and roughly took him out of the store and into the waiting police car.

As they drove toward the jail, Allison said, "We can come back and do this later."

"No, Momma. I am okay. We can finish now. I don't have to be afraid of him now. So let's not make it bigger than it is. Okay?" Sara said.

"Are you sure you are up to it?" she asked, noting that Sara's left eye was starting to swell. "Tell you what. I will finish, and you can wait in the car. It would make me feel better." She pulled out her keys so as Sara could start the car and turn on the air conditioner and lock the doors.

"Okay," Sara said then whispered, "I hope I didn't embarrass you." Then they walked out of the store to the car.

When they returned home, Jody and Saline were in the family room. Saline was playing with her baby brother.

When Oscar didn't come home that night, Joan thought that he had likely gotten drunk and slept it off in the car, but there was the phone call that came where Oscar wanted her to try to bail him out only to arrive and discover that he was being held without bail.

"You did what?" Joan yelled.

"I found Sara with some woman at the grocery store in Terrell. They were walking in at the time," he said.

"Who is the woman she was with?" Joan asked.

"Allison Carmichael Byers. She is as untouchable as you get," he said.

"She has kidnapped my children. I don't think that makes her better than me. I will have those kids back home before tonight," Joan said.

"No. You won't. You have lost. Sara looks better that ever. She is wearing expensive clothes and looks happy," Oscar said.

"What are you talking about? That girl has never been the type to show that she was happy. I will find her and bring her back to the farm where she can go back to work. Where are Jody and Saline?" she asked.

"I didn't see them, and she didn't say," he said. "You have to find a way to get me out of here. I have not had my medicine today and spent most of last night throwing up."

Joan knew that he was not talking about prescription drugs so much as his recreational stash. "I believe they call that withdrawal. And I doubt they will call that a medical emergency to get you out of there."

"You don't understand. I am in the general population. These people are animals," he pleaded.

"There is nothing I can do, Oscar. But I will be back. If possible, I will try to bring you something," she said and left.

At supper the following night at the Byerses' home, everyone seemed relaxed and talking about just about everything. The previous night, Sara was slightly shaken regarding what happened, but after supper, she and Scott had gone riding, and it seemed to clear her head.

"Here comes the next Clint Eastwood," Riley said when Sara and Scott entered the room. "Daddy, I think we could all quit any work and sell Sara's line. 'Who's the bitch now?'"

Everyone including Sara laughed at the comment. Riley and Colton had heard what Sara had told her latest stepfather the following day. Gossip like that in a small town was a big form of entertainment.

Sara didn't know what made her bold enough to say something so unladylike, but the phrase got attention. As for her fighting back, she could not let herself be taken back.

After supper was finished, Scott still had some work to do regarding the oil business. Sara and Saline helped Allison with the kitchen, and the three of them talked.

"Oh, Sara, I have something of yours that was in my bag in my room," Saline said.

When they were finished in the kitchen, Sara followed Saline to her room. Saline gave her her ballet slippers.

Now she was in the huge hay barn that was only half full. She had a tape player that she asked if she could borrow. Saline had some of the tapes that Sara had loved to dance to. She started the music and was immediately pulled into the theme to *Swan Lake*.

She had tied the satin ribbons very tightly around her ankles, and as she had not danced in a very long time, she didn't know how long she would be dancing. She had pulled her heavy hair into a high ponytail. Her full-cut skirt added to the dramatic effect of the dance.

She had been in the barn for over an hour when Scott had gone to her room to see if she wanted to go for a ride. Saline told her that she had seen her go to the hay barn.

Scott heard the music before he even went in. He didn't want to interrupt, yet he wanted to see what Saline had told him about months ago. When he silently crept into the barn and saw his future wife, it took his breath away. Scott had never seen ballet dancing before. It was more beautiful than he could ever have imagined.

After the music stopped, Scott walked into view. "I didn't know that you liked to dance," Scott said.

"I had almost forgotten how," she said, using the back of her hand to wipe perspiration from her face. Scott handed her his handkerchief.

"All evidence to the contrary," he said then walked over to the radio and turned it to a country channel. "May I have this dance?" he said.

In no time she was in his arms, floating with him. It was pure intoxication. When the music stopped, they were still holding each other. Sara stood on her toes and kissed Scott lovingly.

"I didn't know you could dance," she said as her arms went around his neck.

"I don't do it very often. But we can change that if you want. But in case you ever want to use it, the garage is air-conditioned. It is pretty hot this time of the year for dancing in the barn," he said and kissed her again.

"Let's go for a ride," Scott said, and they walked to his truck. "I wanted for you to see how much progress they are making with the house."

It had only been a few weeks since she had been there, and she was amazed to find that it was nearly completed.

"It is so big, Scott. And it is just like I dreamed it would be," she said.

"It is time that you had a look at the inside of our house," he said.

As he opened the front door and turned on the lights, Sara could not believe what she was seeing. He must have been listening to every word that she ever spoke. They had entered into a huge room that was very rustic. It was built around a fireplace that was in the middle of the room. There was already some furniture in the room. The carpeting was plush and brown, adding to the look of the beautiful room. They went up two steps and turned right. There were six bedrooms, each with a private bathroom. They went to the left of the steps, and there was a door at the very end of the hall.

"I told them to decorate this one like a lady would like it. I believe you will like it," he said and opened the door.

The master bedroom was just what Scott said. She loved the room, complete with a sitting area and beautiful cherry furniture. There was a small room just off the master bedroom. She looked to Scott to find out what it was.

"A nursery. We wouldn't want our babies on the other side of the house until they get a little bigger," he said.

Sara looked in the bathroom complete with a very large garden tub. And there was an oversized walk-in closet.

"Scott, it is perfect. I can't believe how perfect it is. Do we really have to wait to get married? I am so in love with you," she said.

"I have been in love with you since the first time I saw you over two years ago," he said.

Sara walked back into the bedroom from the bathroom and went to the window to see what she could see when she looked out— the beautiful pasture complete with cattle grazing.

"I am so happy, Scott," she said, walking over to him. Her arms went around his neck, and then her hands began to feel him arms, his face, his neck, and his chest. She unsnapped his Western shirt. She ran her hands through the hair on his chest. She had never done this before, and her hands trembled. She was hoping that he didn't think her too forward.

When her hands reached his hips, she looked up to Scott. "Scott, I have never done this before, like, ah, I mean, I want you so much. Can you help me?"

He looked in her eyes. Yes, he was going to marry her as soon as possible. He was experienced as a compassionate lover. Not that he was a playboy at any time, but rather women had tended to throw themselves at him when they found out who he was.

He took his hands and pulled the ponytail holder from her hair, letting it cascade down her back. Then he walked over to the king-sized bed, and together they pulled the cover down. He then completely turned his attention to Sara.

He began to unbutton her blouse that was all but see-through because of the perspiration from her dancing. Then he pulled the tail of the blouse from her waistband. He again looked up at her face, to see if she was afraid, but the look she had was one of innocence and wonder.

He then took great care in unbuttoning her skirt and let it fall. He also pushed down the elastic waistband of the petticoat. She stood before him, in her bra and panties. Her waist was tiny and gave way to round hips. Her breasts were full and wanting.

Sara unbuckled Scott's belt and then his pants. Scott stepped out of his pants and shook his shirt off. She kissed his chest and then his back and then returned to face him, and they kissed deeply. Scott used his tongue to explore the depths of her mouth. Then he reached around her and undid her bra. He placed his hands on her firm breasts and could feel she had goose bumps.

He had no idea what the bastards had done to her earlier in her life, but he knew absolutely that she had never been this far with any other man. He pushed her panties down, and they fell to the floor. Then he put his mouth on one breast and began to suckle it gently.

Sara could feel her knees get weak. Almost as if he were reading her mind, Scott picked her up gently and placed her head on one of the pillows of the king-sized bed. They continued to explore each other. Scott used his hand to further explore her body. He massaged the inside of her thighs, and she ran her fingers through his hair then began to move her hand further. She ran her hand down his buttocks and down his leg then his manhood. Scott began to moan. Scott knew that she needed to be ready for him, so as she was not afraid.

At last Scott was inside her. He kissed her and massaged her breast until she thought she would explode with desire. When at last they had had their release, both lay in each other's arms.

"I promise you, I didn't plan this. But I did plan on this." He took her left hand and slipped a ring on it. The center stone was a perfect two-carat emerald cut diamond; the sides were emeralds, the same color as her eyes. "I want to love and cherish you until the day that I die. Momma and Daddy said we could marry the day after you turn seventeen, as they have guardianship of you. But only if that is what you want."

"You have read my mind," she said. "But, Scott, what if I can't have kids?"

"We will have kids, I promise you. It is either that, or we will have to put hay in all those bedrooms," he said. He hated to tell her that the doctor had determined that she would be able to have kids. But he would let her be surprised when she got pregnant the first time.

"When we do then, would you mind if we leave it up to God how many we have and when we have them?" she asked.

"That is fine with me. I love kids," he said. "Do you still want to go to nursing school?"

"Yes, of course. If you don't mind having a nurse in the family," she said.

They stayed in that room for a while longer and pretty well made plans for their future.

"May I ask one more opinion?" Sara asked.

"I don't know. You have been going beyond your limit lately," he said in fun. "Anything, you name it."

"Who should I ask to give me away? Your dad is filling in as my dad. Uncle Alex has been so nice to me, and Dr. Quinton saved my life," she asked. "I can likely not ask your dad as he is getting me for a daughter-in-law, so it would seem strange giving away to get."

"Well, I happen to know that Dr. Quinton has said something about it, and Uncle Alex and he discussed it, and they decided on Dr. Quinton," Scott said.

"Oh, thank goodness. I didn't want to hurt anyone's feelings," she said.

"You have not even seen the best part of the house yet. The kitchen is every woman's dream. Get dressed, and we will have a quick look before we go back to the house," he said. "Did you know you are the most beautiful thing I have ever seen?"

Sara blushed and finished dressing.

That Sunday, Sara and Scott stayed after church to talk to the priest at St. Justin's. They wanted to ask him to marry them, and for a date that the church was available. As it turned out, the day after Sara turned seventeen was open, and on a Saturday, so that day fit perfectly into everyone's schedule. The date would be November 5 at 1:00 pm.

Sara asked Mary to be her maid of honor and Saline to be her bridesmaid. Little Jody would be the ring bearer. It was four months until the big day.

Saline started back to school in August and was doing very well. Sara was learning to read from everyone in the family, and little Jody was a happy, growing three-year-old.

Scott had his younger brothers and Maria's husband, Mark, as his groomsmen. His mother helped Sara with everything, and the women at St. Justin's all pitched in to make the first wedding in the chapel one to remember.

The people of the ranch, who had helped so much with both the protection and care of the three newest members, were invited of course, and Maria was also asked personally by Sara to be a bridesmaid, as she had helped her so much with Jody. The two women had become fast friends in the time since they had come to the ranch.

During the day, Saline went to school, Allison and Sara did things around the house and talked about the big day, and Scott and John went to work either on the ranch or to Byers Oil in Dallas. It was a busy time of the year on the ranch, getting ready for winter.

Sara continued to maintain good health, taking the medication that Dr. Quinton had prescribed for her.

In early September, while Saline was in school, a knock came on the front door of the Byers house. Sara was in the living room with Jody. John and Scott were in Dallas, Allison was in town, Colton was at school, but Riley had stayed home with a cold. Sara got up and went to the door. She opened it and could not believe her eyes.

"Momma, what are you doing here?" she asked.

"I could ask you the same thing. Aren't you glad to see your mother?" she asked, obviously amused at having taken Sara by surprise. "I am glad that you seem to be well, but I have not missed you," she said honestly. "Well, I have missed my children. Just like I miss my husband, especially now," she said.

"Oscar is where he belongs. He has spent the last two years beating on all of us. You may not have minded getting beaten up, but Saline and I did mind," Sara said.

"Are you not going to invite me in?" Joan said.

"No, I am not. You are not welcome here, Momma. If you would have wanted us there, we wouldn't have spent the last two years of our lives afraid," Sara said.

"Well, it is nice to know that having rich friends has made you talk back to your mother. Well," Joan said, walking past Sara and taking a seat on the couch, "I am here to tell you that I really need my husband and children at home, especially now, unless you want our baby girl to be born with no father, like you. And of course, who would keep Oscar away from her? Should it be a girl, that is."

"What?" Sara said.

"Oscar and I are going to have a daughter this winter. I really think he does not need to be in prison for that. Do you?" Joan questioned.

"It does not matter what I think. There is way too much evidence against him for him not to be found guilty," Sara said.

"If that is so, then you, Saline, and Jody should come home."

"We are at home. We no longer belong to you. We have a home here," Sara said.

"And what did you have to give these people to take you? You know that Saline's father could give you everything," Joan said.

"He never gave me anything. Now you need to leave here, now. I never want to see you again. You are here to get someone to pay your way. I don't do that anymore," Sara said, picking up Jody.

"Sara, is everything okay?" Riley asked, stepping into the living room. "You heard the lady, get out."

"I am here to take my children home," she said, reaching for Jody.

"No. You are not taking Jody. He is too young to protect himself from you, and he does not even know who you are," Sara said, holding Jody tight. Jody began to fuss, afraid of what the strange lady was doing. He put his chubby arms around Sara's neck and said, "Momma."

Joan knew it was Sara he was referring to. Joan grabbed Jody's wrist and pulled, causing him to fall to the ground.

"You cold-blooded bitch," Riley said, pushing her against the wall. Sara picked up a crying Jody. Joan had pulled him hard enough to where he fell hard on the floor, hitting his head on the table on the way down. "My daddy told me to never hit a woman, but I think he would make an exception this one time."

"Riley, no. Momma, get out of here before I call the sheriff," Sara said.

"I won't leave here without my son," she said, taking a step toward him. Sara put herself between her mother and Jody.

"Get out of this house." They heard and saw Maria standing there holding a shotgun on Joan. "All I have to do is yell, and there will be a half dozen very strong ranch hands in here before you have time to turn around. Now, leave, and don't think about touching Jody."

Joan went to the door. "I will be back," she said and left.

Jody was in Sara's loving arms and began seizing. "Maria, what do I do?" she pleaded.

"We have to take him to town, to the doctor. Riley, are you well enough to get my car?" she asked.

"Yes, mam," he said and was out the door. He returned a few moments later and said, "Let's go."

"No, Riley, you need to stay so you can tell your mother what happened and come with her. And call your uncle and tell him we are coming," Maria said.

Little Jody continued to seize. When they were nearly to Uncle Alex's office, he went limp. "Jody," she said. "Jody, wake up. Maria, he is not breathing," Sara said.

Maria ran inside and got Alex. Alex ran to the car to see the small child.

"Please, Uncle Alex, do something," Sara pleaded.

Taking the child from her arms, he ran him back to the clinic. He asked Maria to take Sara to his office.

In the exam room, he looked at the little boy's eyes and noted that his right pupil was blown. But even more ominous was that he was not breathing. He instructed his nurse to start mouth-to-mouth resuscitation. He knew that there would not be a good outcome from this. He could see the area on his head where something had hit him or he had hit something.

Alex tried to save little Jody for well over an hour but was unable to because of the damage the bleeding had caused in his brain.

He had to tell Maria and Sara that Jody had not made it. He walked into his office and saw the two sitting together.

"Sara," he said.

"She knows," Maria said. He saw that the two young women were holding hands.

Alex had known Maria her entire life. She was a very religious woman. Her entire family was Catholic. It actually didn't surprise him that she knew, although he couldn't say why.

"May I see him?" she asked.

"Yes, of course," Alex said, leading her to the exam room where he had left little Jody with the nurse.

The nurse had taken Jody's little body and wrapped him in a white sheet, as nurses are trained to do.

Sara walked over to Jody and lovingly picked him up, as she had done every day of his all-too-short life. She kissed his little his head. "I am sorry," she said. Then sat with his little body and silently wept.

"Maria, what happened?" he whispered.

"Sara's mother came to the ranch today. She was trying to take the baby from Sara's arms. He hit the table," she said. "Alex, the last thing he said and did was put his arms around Sara's neck and said 'Momma,'" she said and cried.

Maria's explanation made complete sense when he saw that his right arm was pulled from its socket.

"Are you sure that is what happened?" he asked.

"Yes. Riley was home from school, sick, and saw the whole thing," she said. "He stayed behind to let the family know."

It was not long until the family arrived to a silent room with a younger-looking Sara holding the now dead little Jody. Tears streamed down her cheeks, but she never made a sound.

The sheriff arrived as well, but in the end, as much as the family and the sheriff wanted her to pay for her crime, it was a tragic accident. But because of the emotional impact for everyone involved, he picked up Joan and arrested her for trespassing.

When the funeral home arrived, Sara kissed his forehead and then handed him to them and went to the door, stopping to thank everyone, and said that she was sorry because there would be a horrible circus starting. No one understood what she was talking about, and she did not say a word on the way home.

As hard as the death of their brother hit Sara, Saline was furious at how her parents never loved him that he was merely a spare. She told everyone that if they didn't take her to her mother, she would walk. Alex had gone to the ranch after he left the clinic and after her agonizing for several hours, Alex had to give her a strong tranquilizer. She finally fell asleep, spent in the arms of her sister, who still had not uttered a single word.

At the sheriff's department, Joan was ranting and raving regarding her arrest. No one had told her anything except she was to spend the night in jail for trespassing.

When Randy returned to tell her about her youngest child, he found her ranting and raving disgustingly. She was telling the world that she needed things to be easier because of her condition; after all, she was having a baby this winter.

He finally got so disgusted and angered he decided to see what kind of a reaction she had to her son's death.

"Did you know that your interference at the ranch today resulted in your having killed your son?" he said.

"Oh, he just fell. Sara picked him up the second he hit the floor," she said.

"But before he hit the floor, he hit the table. And he is indeed dead," he said. "But the funeral arrangements will be handled by his guardians."

She was still not convinced. "Then you will have to let his father attend the funeral. And of course, you will have to contact the people in Germany so he will be given a funeral becoming a member of the German aristocracy," she said.

"Out of the question. That smug bastard comes to this county and he will be arrested. The rest of the crap you were talking about regarding Germany, I have seen how well Germany takes care of 'its own.' So I say again, the funeral will be a private one, and none of you will be attending," he said and dropped a copy of the *Tyler* paper that had the accident on the front page. "Take this filth to her cell."

Randy could still hear her but didn't turn around. When he returned to his office, he called the ranch, and John answered.

"John, how much have you found out about anything concerning the kids and Germany?"

"It seems that there is some of that that is real. It seems that Saline's father is the next in line to be a duke of something. And Saline kept calling Jody the spare. But if I am not mistaken, all those kids were born in California," John said, a little confused.

"I found out something regarding how they can be German. It seems that you are German not by being born there but by bloodline. Evidently, there are two sons, the oldest who lives with his father, and Jody. His mother seems to think that Germany has a right to his burial," Randy said.

"Over my dead body! No one interfered when those people did nothing about what was happening to these kids. Now it is our job. We love all three of them," he said. "Are you going to allow Jody's father back for the funeral?" John asked.

"No, of course not. When will the funeral be?" he asked.

"Day after tomorrow. The service will be at St. Justin's, and he will be buried here, in our family plot. I have never used my position for anything, but I will for this," John said.

"I hear ya. I will see you at the funeral," he said.

When Saline began to awaken, her sadness took hold. Everyone on the ranch had come to the main house to say how sorry they were. Jody had become a fast favorite with everyone. Now the entire ranch shared in the grief. John had told everyone to take a few days off and invited them to join them at the private service.

The day of the funeral, four of the ranch hands came to the house and told John that they would be happy to watch over the church during the funeral, as they thought there would be trouble.

"Are you sure you want to do that?" he asked.

All four nodded.

"Then could each one of you put a gun in your trucks, just in case?" he asked.

"We already have, sir," said Mark, Maria's husband.

"Thank you all. It is going to be a very long day," John said.

The Byers family, both old and new, arrived at the church early. There were people who were already there that none of the family knew. But they were not allowed close to the family.

Inside the church, the tiny casket that held the child was open. With Jody in the casket were some of his favorite toys. He looked to be napping. There were so many flowers that the majority had to be kept in the fellowship hall. Over one hundred people from the ranch were in attendance, along with members of the church and family friends. It had not been announced where the funeral would be, but people close to the family knew that that was where Sara and Scott went to church.

The music started and people sat. On the first row sat John and Allison, with Saline between them. Scott sat by his mother, with Sara at his side and Riley and Colton on her other side.

Father Keith started the service.

"We are gathered here today to say good-bye to this special little boy, Jody Alexander Byers. He was born in California just over three years ago and died three days ago. He leaves behind him two very courageous young ladies, his sisters Saline, fourteen, and Sara, sixteen. Since Jody's birth, it was these two young women who loved and protected him every day of his young life, along with a family who has adopted the three children, John and Allison Byers. And of course, other members of his family from his new life, who loved, protected, and ultimately will miss Jody."

The priest continued with comforting passages that were read to them. Comforting music and prayers were said.

As the funeral was being conducted, Mark and three other people from the ranch kept a watchful eye open for anyone who tried to enter who didn't belong. They saw some people who stayed back until the family went into the chapel. Mark approached them and asked for ID.

The men who tried to enter told him to stand aside. The four armed men pulled guns out and told the men with strange accents to leave, or they would shoot. One man took one more step and heard the sound of the guns being cocked. At that, they left. All throughout the service, either Joan Redding or Henry Alexander never showed up.

When services were concluded, the people inside were invited to the ranch for the graveside service, and to the house later.

No one from the service had a dry eye. Everyone from the funeral was at the ranch for the graveside service.

It was a busy afternoon. Saline was comforted by knowing that so many people loved Jody and that he would be buried not far from her.

Sara had appreciated everyone's kind words but excused herself and went to her room. She sat on the bed, slipped her shoes off, and cried. After a time, she started to get up and go back to where people were assembled, but she could not bring herself to.

She changed her clothes and went to the stables. She wanted to clear her head before she talked to anyone else.

In no time, she had put a saddle on the mare that Scott had given to her. She walked her out of the barn and cantered off to the pasture. Some of the people from the ranch saw her riding away.

Sara rode a half mile away to her and Scott's house. A few weeks earlier, she had been so happy. She was planning her wedding, and Jody was supposed to be there. She still wanted to get married, but would she be able to? She walked to the kitchen to get some water.

She looked around the beautiful kitchen that was hers. The appliances were brand-new. The wooden cabinets were just as she had wanted them. She hoped that she would be as good a cook as Allison Byers was someday.

Sara had a little wave of nausea. She sat down for a minute and closed her eyes.

"Sara, are you okay?" Scott asked.

"Scott, how did you know where I was?" she asked.

"I just had a feeling. Are you okay?" he asked again, sitting down beside her. "You haven't eaten anything in days. You don't want to make yourself sick."

She started crying. Scott took her into his arms. "It is okay to be upset, Sara. We have all suffered a huge loss and will never be the same."

"It is something different. I had started to dream about a day in the near future when Jody would be playing with children of ours. It seemed so much like it could happen," she said. "I know that Jody has been so happy here for the last months, and I know that he is in a better place now. It was just, I wanted that so much," she said.

"Baby, we all did. We all loved Jody very much," he said. "A few years ago, Momma and Daddy were expecting a baby. There were complications, and Momma nearly died. The baby, our baby sister, died. I never thought I would ever see them happy again. Then you, Saline, and Jody came into our lives, and all of us found happiness again. I know that it does not seem like it now, and everyone is sad now, but one day, I promise you, we will be happy again."

Sara had never thought about there being something like that in Scott's past. He had his share of pain as well.

"Do you think we should postpone the wedding?" she asked.

"I don't think so. It is not for a couple of months, and I believe it will be just what we need. But I will understand if you need some time," he said.

"I don't need some time, Scott. I just don't know how everyone else will see it," she said. "But, Scott, Jody had been so happy, and she came in and he died afraid. He was holding my neck so tight when she reached for him. Everything we all went through and I couldn't protect him. She found us. I tried so hard and couldn't hold on to him. He was so much comfort after, after, my own child. Oh my god, he is gone. He helped me so much, and now he is gone." Sara was heaving so hard she could not catch her breath. And then she stopped.

She hadn't fainted in several months. He picked her up and carried her to the master bedroom. He laid her down, putting her head on the pillow. He then walked around the bed and pulled her into his arms. He held her close, still careful not to press too hard on bones that were still healing. She had not eaten in days. She watched after Saline every minute, thus didn't sleep. The woman/child that he loved so and could hardly wait to marry never bore her soul in such a way.

Scott and everyone close to Sara knew that Jody regarded her as his mother, not his sister. He had helped her to survive. His hatred of Joan Redding, Henry Alexander, and Oscar Redding almost overtook him. Then he looked down at the sleeping beauty he held close. He remembered a time a little over four years ago when his baby sister was born and Allison nearly died. Sara was feeling the same loss as his mother had felt.

Scott continued to hold Sara until she awakened from fainting. He frequently checked her pulse and breathing. She just needs a little nap, he reasoned. After two hours, the sun was beginning to set, and Sara awakened slowly.

"Did you have a good rest, baby girl?" he asked.

"Oh, Scott, I am sorry. I shouldn't have behaved that way," she said, closing her eyes.

"Some things are better when they are on the outside and not making you sick on the inside," he said then continued, "Right now we are going home, and you are going to eat something. Keep in mind you are still recovering from many things that Uncle Alex and Uncle Steven said would likely take a few years to overcome."

"So, baby girl, let's go home before they start to worry," Scott said.

"Home, that sounds like a good place."

"I believe that everyone is already looking forward to it, and maybe that is the thing to make us all happy again." At that, still holding her, Scott closed his eyes and said a prayer that he was right.

CHAPTER 6

The Circus

The circus that Sara had spoken of began the next morning. The people whom Mark had kept from entering the church showed up on the ranch. They demanded to speak with the Alexander children, saying he was a member of their family.

The man who claimed to be their uncle was about sixty, with salt-and-pepper hair that was neatly cut, dressed in an expensive three-piece suit that was very dark gray and well fitted to his tall height of six feet eleven inches, with the same cold blue eyes as Henry Alexander.

Sara and Saline were inside not far away from the front door, so they could hear the interaction of the two.

"I am only going to say this once. These three children spent over two years that no one seemed to care where they were or what happened. And now, you people show up. Just exactly who do you think that you are?" John said.

"I am their uncle," the man said with a very thick German accent, "the duke of Hamburg," he said, seeing Saline inside. "Saline, Sara Lyn, come along," he commanded, making both girls freeze in place.

"Do you think I am impressed? These kids now are our responsibility, and everyone on this ranch will risk their lives to make sure that no one takes them anywhere. There is nothing a cowboy likes better than to mix it up from time to time. I would imagine a prissy duke such as you would make it interesting. It is nearly twenty miles to get off this ranch. You have twenty minutes to get off of my land," he said.

"Not without my nieces and my nephew's body," was all he managed to say. John put his fist in the man's face and then threw him from the porch. "If you come back on this ranch, I will kill you. Saline and Sara belong to my wife and myself now. Get that through you skull. Mention the name of John Byers here in Texas, and not many don't know who I am." John concluded the man on the rear, causing everyone around to laugh.

"Thank you, sir," Sara said.

He walked over and hugged the young lady he had come to love like a daughter. Saline stood nearby, and he had no doubt that she had heard what the people out front had said.

"Will you really fight for us? We won't have to leave?" Saline asked. "I don't know what difference it makes anymore. Momma is going to kill all of us, one way or another," Saline said.

"I won't hear you talk like that. No one is leaving here. I promise you. We will take care of things, and no one will come on this ranch unless they are supposed to be here. When I told you this is your home, I meant always," John said.

"Just not Jody?" Saline said. John could tell that she was just barely hanging in there.

"I know how you are feeling right now. Like you will never be happy again, and the sadness will never go away. I don't attend services like I should, but I work with the land. And I believe that God is out there. He knew that y'all needed just a little help and that we needed something to make us happy again. I know that we were all the answer to one another's prayers. And Ms. Saline," he said, putting an arm across each girl's shoulder and pulled them close, "you have trouble believing that, but think about how dark it can be at night or the cold in the winter. The world is darker right now because of our loss, but tomorrow the sun will come up, and after the coldest day in winter, the grass will turn green and baby calves will be born.

"The hurt you know now will get a little easier to bear every day, and you will remember Jody's little laugh, his silly little dance, or just the way he smiles in his sleep. For the last few months of his life, he was a happy little boy. He had not only your love but the love of every person on this ranch. He was not hungry or cold. He had hundreds of people who watched after him. That is what you have to remember. Okay?" he said.

"Yes, sir, Daddy," Saline said. "I wish that you would have been our daddy—always."

"Well, I am now, so those people had better remember it."

Joan Redding came to the ranch that same day. It was about the same time of day as it had been when she had been there before, so she thought it would just be Sara there again.

Joan was starting to get a little desperate as she was running out of money, cigarettes, and drugs. Oscar continued to be in the county jail, and it was starting to look like she was going to have to either find a way to get those girls back to the farm or, for the first time in her life, go to work.

She got to the front door and once again knocked on the door. It took longer this time for the door to be answered, but as before, it was Sara who answered. She looked like she had been crying for days, but that was not what stuck out. Rather it was the two-carat center stone on the ring finger of her left hand.

"Who the hell gave you that?" her mother said, taking her hand, attempting to examine the ring closer.

"None of your business," she said, pulling her hand back. "You need to leave now," Sara said with an edge in her voice that Joan had never heard out of her eldest daughter.

"It is time for you to quit playing in someone else's house. I can only imagine what one would have to do to get something like that," she said. But her attempt at taunting her daughter brought her a door coming toward her face, and she narrowly caught it before it was closed. She pushed it back open.

"Momma, you have to leave. You didn't want us, but this time, there was someone who did. Now you need to leave before someone finds you here," Sara said.

"I am not leaving without you girls," she said, grabbing Sara's wrist and pulling her out the door.

Involuntarily, she screamed. Her mother stood a full six feet tall, six inches taller than her daughter, and she had very broad shoulders, and partially due to the drugs, she was stronger. "We have to see if that cow at the restaurant will give you your job back."

"Let her go." She heard a man's voice from behind her.

"Just who the hell are you?" she asked, not releasing her grip on Sara's wrist. "I am her mother, and I am taking her home."

"Before you proceed, I would look around you," the man said.

Joan looked around and saw that there were people all around. Sara's terrified scream was something that they had not heard in a few months. And with the funeral only a day before, the family and people of the ranch were staying closer to the house as a means of both support and protection.

"This is my daughter!" she yelled. "I am Joan Alexander Redding."

"You are the whore who killed Jody," Saline said from the porch.

"Honey, go on back inside. I will be right back in," Allison said, walking directly to Sara.

Joan had never seen Saline listen to anyone so easily.

"Let her go this minute."

"Who are you?" Joan demanded.

"I am the woman who took your place. My husband and I are Sara and Saline's guardians," she said and physically peeled the woman's fingers off Sara's wrist.

"Why is my daughter here? And I demand to know who she is marrying!" Joan yelled.

"She is marrying me. Now you need to leave. You come near these girls again and you will be spending some quality time with the piece of trash you call your husband," Scott said.

Joan got a wicked grin about her. "Well, sonny, she has to come home to go back to work. I can't work as I am expecting a baby in a few months."

"Then I would suggest you pull whoever you have stuck up there out and get a job," Scott said. "Now you have twenty minutes to get off our land, and if you come back, you will be arrested. And if you ever touch my future wife again, I will kill you."

"You act like you are getting something pure. Well, let me tell—" she started but was cut off by being grabbed by her shirt and being shoved backward, causing her to fall. The move had not come from Scott, but from his mother. Then John was there.

"You heard my son, get off this ranch and never come back," John said. "Mark, make sure she is off here in the twenty minutes that Scott gave her, if you don't mind."

"My pleasure, sir," Mark said. "You heard the man, bitch. Move it or I will throw you off here."

Joan was not left with a choice. "Just a thought, the duke is here and wants to see his nieces. If you argue with his grace, you will lose. He is staying at the farm," she said and drove back down the driveway.

Back in the house, Scott saw that Sara was not worse for wear, but she did have a glow about her when she saw his eyes on her.

He whispered in her ear, "You had better stop looking at me like that or I will disgrace us here in the living room," he said, smiling.

Sara smiled up at him.

Allison told Saline that she needed help in the kitchen, moreover to keep her brain occupied and not think too much on her mother's visit.

Phone calls from local law enforcement had started that morning. Randy told him that some people from Germany may be trying to cause problems. He didn't know how a man from Germany who had not been involved in the kids' lives to that point could possibly cause any problems.

John knew that people from different countries living in the US could assert or at least try to assert diplomatic immunity. Even if that were the case, Sara and Saline had both been born in the United States. Above and beyond that, the court had given him and his wife guardianship permanently. No one could remove them, not even some duke from Germany.

John smiled to himself when he flexed his hand and remembered why it ached a little. That prissy duke was not expecting someone to do anything except be in awe of him. He could not respect a king who ignored children to the point they were, much less a duke whom he had never heard of.

Just in case there were any further problems, John had asked that everyone keep a firearm with them and to stay close to the house. He also had people watching the entrances to the ranch. Unless accompanied by John, Allison, or Scott, the sisters knew that they needed to stay close to the house.

Many vehicles attempted to enter the ranch uninvited; two even drove on without stopping, only to find they would have a tire blown out. Absolutely nothing was left to chance.

Having lost a child four years before, John knew how important it was not to get back to work too soon. Knowing how everyone had felt about little Jody, he told them they were welcome to stay close to home for the week, and they would start back fresh the following week. John had come to know that by respecting the people who worked for him at a time when they were vulnerable, that he got that same respect back.

He would not let anyone take advantage of anyone who worked on the ranch when they were vulnerable, and the people on the ranch took care of the family the same way.

The ranch had always functioned like a small town. Everyone knew everyone. That meant that everyone knew who was married and who had kids; everyone knew everyone's name. Most had worked for John for most of their lives. Some had been friends of Scott's when he was in high school or college and had started to work on the ranch later. Each family who worked on the ranch had their own house to live in. They paid no rent but paid their own utilities. If they took an interest in owning their own ranch, John would help them get started.

When John and Allison had lost their daughter, every woman on the ranch made sure that Allison had assistance for several weeks and fixed meals and stayed with her, something that they had learned from her when they had fallen on hard times. It had become an extended family of people all working and helping one another.

Saline had to return to school the following week. She, like everyone, was still upset but was comforted by the fact that so many people could help her remember him. She loved school and learning things on her accelerated level. There were no boys around her to taunt her, so she slipped easily back into the routine.

Saline had come to love and respect everyone on the ranch. John and Allison Byers were the parents she had seen her friends have in California. She was glad to help around the house and even in the garden. Before, she hated living in the country; now she could not ever imagine living in the city. From the first time she saw a tomato growing, she was hooked. Then Riley had taken her to the pasture to see if a cow had had her calf. She had had the calf but died soon after. Riley asked if Saline wanted to try to raise it on a bottle.

It only took her a couple of days to get the hang of feeding a seventy-five-pound calf a bottle, but now Ginger, the straw-colored heifer calf with white hoofs, followed her around like a puppy. She took her responsibility to her calf very seriously.

Allison was also teaching her to cook and sew. She had seen her while making a skirt for Sara, and she took interest. She could already make simple things, like skirts or shorts.

She thought of her own mother, who had never taught her anything, except possibly how to get loaded. For the first eleven years of her life, she would go to school and come home to a stoned mother. They were looked after by their nanny during the week. Then she thought about what her dad had done to her nanny when she had reported what he was doing to Saline and Sara. He and two of the people from his crew had beaten her to death in front of the two young girls, thrown her in a hole in the desert, and left.

Then her dad would be home on the weekends. Saline played softball but rode her bike to get there.

Then after moving to Texas, their mother had let the first use-less piece of trash she found drunk at a bar on the lake move into her bed. When Joan's divorce was final, a few days later, she married Oscar. It didn't matter to her that he was nearly twenty years younger and didn't work. But Saline and Sara had decided that he was not going to hurt them the way that her father had. It had worked, but not for lack of his having tried.

Saline remembered seeing the bat in the back of Scott's pickup. She smiled at the thought of Oscar having to answer for what he had done. She wished her own father would have had to answer for everything he had done.

Their new home was so different from either of the ones she had ever known. The only meal that her mother had ever cooked was supper, and that was because her father told her to. Allison fixed three meals a day every day. Her brother Tommy was not at all like the guys that she lived in the house with. Tommy was verbally abusive and physically abusive when he was left in charge of his younger sisters. Colton and Riley were kind and seemed like nice people. They were sweet and maybe a little intimidated by her being a natural beauty. Saline had never really processed the fact that she was pretty. She had always seen herself as damaged. Never letting anyone close enough was her way of not taking a chance on them seeing that she was. Riley was nice to talk to. They would feed the cattle and talk about school or cows or anything else that was different for her. He had even taken her fishing a couple of times. When she caught her first fish, it was so exciting. He didn't tell her it was just a small fish.

Riley never moved fast around her or made a move without her knowing what he was doing. He was an amazing friend. And Riley also would talk to her about a couple of the girls he dated. Saline had always been somewhat of a tomboy, so when Riley would ask her if she wanted to go with him, she would.

Riley knew some of Saline's past and thought of her as a sister and would never do anything inappropriate. There had never been any young man that she had trusted before. She would talk with him about part of her life in California and about how cute Jody was from the time he was born. Sometimes she would cry; sometimes she would just talk about him. Riley knew that it was helping her, because slowly, she began to smile again.

She and Colton got along most of the time as well. However, from time to time, both of their tempers would flare, and they would get into trouble. But as she had been told since coming to the ranch, no one ever hurt her. They would get put to work doing something until it was thought that they would decide it was fitting not to fight.

One night, right before Saline was going to bed, Sara went into her room. "Can I talk to you for a minute, sis?" Sara asked.

"Sure, Sara, come on in," Saline said.

Sara walked over to where Saline was already in bed. She wrapped her arms around her sister and kissed her cheek. "I just wanted to ask you something. Are you still okay with me getting married in a couple of weeks?"

"Of course, I am Sara. You and Scott are so happy together. And you love each other so much. I hope that I can have that one day."

"You will. You are the most beautiful girl in the world. You are so smart. Any man would be so lucky to have you. But until then, you have two devoted parents who love you, and three new brothers who would give their lives for you. And then there is me," Sara said.

"I am so happy that you are well, Sara. I thought the night before we came here that you would die. I couldn't bear losing you," she said, hugging her sister.

"And I could never bear losing you. So you are okay with us living in our new house and you living here?" Sara asked.

"Yeah, I love them. They are all so good to us. Momma is teaching me to cook and sew, and Riley and Colton are teaching me to fish. And I have my calf that I have to take care of. Ginger needs me to be here. And we will see each other every day. I am just so glad that you are my sister. I have been the luckiest girl in the world to have you. I have the only sister in the world that would have come home to save me. You have always been here for me, and I love you, and now Scott and I know that you will be happy," Saline said.

"Thank you, Saline. I will always be here. I thank God for you every day. Know that," she said.

"I think I am starting to," Saline said.

While Sara was in Saline's room, Scott heard her voice and followed it. He listened for a moment outside Saline's room and smiled to himself.

He knew from the first he loved Sara, but he didn't know if they were going to be able to get through to Saline, especially since Jody's death. But what had brought the three children to the ranch had made them all grow closer with each passing day.

He could not wait until he and Sara were man and wife. He even told her that he had a surprise for her after the wedding. So Sara decided that she would give him something to look forward to as well.

A few days before the wedding, Scott and Sara took their marriage license to the bank, and Scott opened a Mr. and Mrs. account so Sara would never have to ask for anything; she would be able to take care of things on her own after a while.

Then he gave her the duplicate copy to his lockbox key while he was there.

While in town, Sara looked at all the people who waved at Scott just by seeing his truck. It was amazing how anyone could know so many people. They stopped at a local diner and had lunch in town for a change. People would come over to inquire as to his family, and Scott would introduce his soon-to-be wife. People usually responded by shaking her hand or kissing her cheek.

One lady came over and enthusiastically hugged Scott. He pulled her back gently and introduced Sara. "We will be married at St. Justin's on Saturday."

"What? I had hoped that you hadn't been around because you were preparing to marry me," the woman said.

"Diana, we have discussed that a million times. Sara and I have been in love since the first time we met. And last I heard, you were married to George Allen," Scott said.

"We are getting divorced."

"I am sorry to hear that. I hope that in time you will find someone who makes you happy," Scott added.

The woman stood. "Like I ever will be able to with you married," she said and stomped off.

"What was that about?" Sara asked.

"Oh, that was Diana. When we were in sixth grade. She planned our lives together. Then she grew up to date everyone in town, before she decided she wanted to plan the rest of our lives again. She has been calling me since I graduated college," he said.

"I guess she is not getting the point, is she?" she said.

"Well, the last few months, I have been spending every second I could with you. It is the first time I even thought about her. When she is in her nineties, she will still be too loose for me," Scott said. "I prefer quiet ones who just stand back and worship me."

"I know that I do, and I hope that I don't embarrass you," she said, her eyes adoring.

"Never happen. I am actually jealous of the way that men look at you," he said.

"What! No one would ever look at me. I am a redheaded stepchild. Isn't that supposed to be something people don't like? I promise I don't try to draw attention to myself," she said.

Scott didn't think about how she would perceive men looking at her and was sorry he said that. "Sweetheart, you are a beautiful lady. You eyes look like rare gems, and I have never met anyone with eyes that color. You hair is like a glass of burgundy, setting in the sun, sparkling its brilliance, and there is so much of it. I didn't know where the shape of your face came from until your mother was at the ranch. It is a pitiful shame that she lives her life the way she does. She had to have been pretty at one time. And you have her Indian cheekbones and thick hair," he concluded.

Sara was devouring him with her eyes. Her smile was warm. She just could not believe but at the same time knew that it would last forever. Scott leaned over and kissed her softly. Sara blushed immediately.

"Is something wrong?" he asked.

"I have just never been kissed in public before," she said and ducked her head a little.

"Baby girl, you have all my love and respect, but you never seem to surprise me about your innocence," he said. "Remember, at the wedding, the grand finally is that you and I will kiss in front of a captive audience. We could practice if you like."

Sara didn't understand that, but let it go. She continued to blush until she thought her cheeks were on fire.

As they were about to leave, Sara asked if they could go by St. Justin's on the way home. Of course, he said yes. But they still had stops to make on the way.

They went to a furniture store so Sara could pick out some more of the furniture for the house. The owner of the family-owned store had furniture brought in just so she would have her choice. He actually was not surprised when she picked out mostly oak furniture from a place called Abrant, in Fort Worth. The room she was thinking about was the family room, and the furniture she picked was perfect.

Then they looked at furniture for the dining room and had a choice of two beautiful tables: an oval oak table that would seat six, and the second, a rectangular table that would seat eight. Then they were shown that there were two extended ends that simply slid out from under the top of the table and doubled the number it would sit.

"I think the larger one. What do you think, Scott?" she said, looking up at him.

"I was hoping that was the one you would like," he said.

"We will have to have someplace for all of our children to sit," she said.

"Scott," came a feminine voice from a few feet away. "I thought that was you. What are you doing in a furniture store?"

"Ordering flowers," he said, kidding the woman that he had gone to school with. "Teresa, this is my soon-to-be wife, Sara Lyn. We are going to be married on Saturday. Sara, this is my dear friend Teresa. We went to high school together." The two women shook hands in a friendly manner.

There was something about this lady that Sara liked.

"Congratulations you two," she said and hugged them both. "I hope that you will be as happy as Ed and I are. Did you know that we have two sons now?"

"I knew that you had one. I have been kept pretty busy here lately, but I promise to keep up better in the future. The wedding is at St. Justin's this Saturday at 1:00 pm, and you and your family are most definitely invited," he said.

"Sara, are you from around here?" she asked.

"Not originally. But yes, for the last three years, I have lived not far from here," she answered and of course blushed.

"Unless I miss my guess, you are from England," she said.

"I went to a boarding school in England when I was younger," she said.

"I am fascinated. I love hearing about England, all that royalty stuff. Would you like to have lunch tomorrow?" she asked.

Sara looked up at Scott. "You are working tomorrow, are you not?"

"Yes, my love, but she is asking you. I believe she would love to," Scott said.

"Is she blushing?" Teresa asked.

Sara looked down at her feet.

"I can hardly wait until tomorrow. I promise, Sara, I don't bite, and I would love to get to know you," Teresa said warmly.

Sara looked up and saw her eyes. She saw nothing to alarm her. "Do you think your mum can give me a ride?"

"Don't worry. What time would you like her here?"

"How about eleven thirty?" Teresa asked.

Sara nodded, and Teresa excused herself.

"Scott, you don't know if your mom is free. She has been so busy with the wedding," she said.

"Don't worry about it," he said and kissed her cheek. They finished in the furniture store and made a few more stops, then stopped at St. Justin's as requested.

As always, he got out and put his hand up to her. They entered the church, and Sara curtsied then sat. Then she was down on her knees, praying.

Scott always watched when she prayed. If she was troubled, when she started praying, she was more relaxed when she finished. He looked around the sanctuary and saw that it was beginning to look like their wedding was close. It was Thursday, so only two more days. He thought dreamingly.

"What do you think? Does it look too feminine?" Sara asked.

He looked at the burgundy carpet that went down the aisle that had been put out for their ceremony, and the silk bunting in burgundy and emerald green, the two colors that she had selected, and he knew that the green was for him. But both colors together looked like they were always supposed to be there. "It is beautiful. Like you," he said and kissed her.

"I am glad that you like it. But there is no way that you will see the dress before you should," she said.

"I hope that they have found enough roses," he said.

"All those roses are so expensive, Scott. It is so extravagant," she said. "Can I tell you something else I would like to do some day?"

"Of course."

"I would like to join the Red Cross and volunteer, after I become a nurse. You know, for disasters and things like that. What do you think?" she asked.

"I think that they would be lucky to have you," he said. "Your heart is always so open to people. I love you so much and pray you know that."

"I promise you, Scott, I am going to make you the happiest man in the world," she said. "I hope I am not defiled. My mum has always said no one could love me because I am. What does *defiled* mean?"

"First, I am already the happiest man in the world since the day that you ran into my arms," he said. "Second, you are not defiled. Your mother is defiled. It means that you have become what you have been around. And I assure you, you are the kindest, most thoughtful woman I have ever known, and it is an honor to live in your world."

"Well, it took me a couple of days longer, but I am also the happiest woman in the world," she said.

"Let's go home. What do you say?" he asked with a little devilish smile.

She smiled back up at him. "Let's go." And hand in hand they went back to the truck. They drove to their home first and stayed and looked at the room where some of the furniture would go. The furniture that Scott had bought before Sara had seen it, he had listened to her so much that he knew what she wanted. And so the furniture they got today would match perfectly.

They went to the bedroom and looked at the beautiful room. "Looks like Momma and Maria have been here," Scott said.

"I can't believe how much more beautiful they have made everything," Sara said of the perfectly matching curtains and bedspread. The room was so perfect.

"I believe she and Maria may have a few more surprises. They have been listening to everything you say for months now. So unless you want to ruin every surprise, I think we should go to the house," Scott said.

"Okay" she said, yawning.

She looked exhausted. He noticed her nodding off the ride to the main house.

They drove to the house and found it was nearly suppertime.

"I will see if Momma needs some help," Sara said, going to the kitchen. She was walking there when John stopped her in the hallway.

"I have been looking for you, Sara. Did you and Scott get everything taken care of?" he asked.

"Yes, sir, of course," she said.

"Well, as all the women have taken to picking out the things for wedding gifts, Uncle Alex, Dr. Quinton, the boys, and I decided that we wanted to get a present just for you," he said.

"Oh, Poppa, you don't have to do that. You have given us so much. And you gave us a family. There is nothing else that is necessary," she said.

"And you gave us our happiness back, both you and your sister, and of course, little Jody, God rest his soul," he said as Sara crossed herself. "And this isn't that much, but you have to close your eyes and take my hand."

Without hesitation, she did. He began walking toward the very back of the giant mansion. He opened the door and told her to step down. They positioned her and told her to open her eyes.

Sara looked up and saw a burgundy Jeep Cherokee with a huge emerald green ribbon around it. "Is that for me?"

"It is all yours, Sara Lyn Byers," he said and hugged her.

She hugged him back and whispered in his ear, "Thank you, sir. I love all of you so much." Then she broke down and cried.

John was expecting many things, but not tears. The other members from around the SUV walked over to see what the holdup was.

Uncle Alex came over and hugged her.

"Thank you, Uncle Alex. I love it," she said.

Then Dr. Quinton came over, with the boys, and they all shared hugs. "We thought as you like to drive in the pastures, this would work better for you than a car," they said.

"We were going to wait until after the wedding, but Scott said you were having lunch with Teresa Priest tomorrow," Riley said.

"Yes, I am, yes. Scott you knew about this?" she said.

Now she knew why he was not worried about transportation.

"Thank all of you. I hope that I am worth it." She barely got that out before she started crying hard. She was so embarrassed that she fled inside. The men were dumbstruck.

Scott started to follow, but his father said it was likely just because the wedding was less than forty-eight hours away. He saw the logic in that and left her to herself.

In her room, Sara felt silly for having cried. She hated that she had to wait to give Scott his wedding present, but it had to be after the wedding and not one second before. It had been a long wonderful day, and she went into the bathroom and washed her face and hands then brushed her hair. She sat down on the bed to catch her breath. She wanted to go down and drive the new jeep. She could drive to town tomorrow. She arose, feeling much better, and went down to do just that.

The following day, Sara got up and dressed in a dress that she Allison and Maria had picked out. She could never be one of those women who bought everything in sight, but it was nice to go and look at things with the two women she loved so. This dress was royal blue, with long sleeves. The cuffs, collar, and belt were black; the dress was fitted at the waist, with a skirt that flared. As the day was cold, she got her coat out as well. Then she reached up and picked out a royal blue hat with a medium brim around it. At the back, it had a small arrangement of blue and white flowers and a silk band around it. She pulled her shoes out and put them on.

Allison walked into the bathroom to see if she was ready to go. She knew she would want to know if she looked okay. And Allison had no doubt, she would look perfect.

"Oh, Sara, you look beautiful. That dress really brings every good feature out. Are you ready to go?" she asked.

"Yes, mam, and you are welcome to come as well," she said.

"Oh, no, the flowers are arriving at the church in a little while, and we have to start putting them out. It is also supposed to be a beautiful day for a wedding, just maybe a little bit cold. It may even snow tonight," she said.

"Wouldn't it be beautiful if a little snow were on the ground?" Sara said, dreamy.

Allison had never seen the young woman dreamy before. "Yes, it would, and the ground is cold enough to stick for a little while, without affecting the driving. You go on and have a good time. You will love Teresa. She and Scott were buddies in junior high and high school. She is a bit of a tomboy."

"Okay," Sara said. "Do you want me to come by the church and help?"

"Oh no, we have the women from here, Mary, and the women from the church," she said. "You just have a good time."

And Sara was off.

When she drove off, Allison called Teresa and told her that she was on her way and to keep her busy for a while if she didn't mind.

"Not a worry, Allison, Scott has already told me. Does she have any idea about the surprise?" she asked.

"No."

"Great! I will see you tomorrow," she said.

Sara arrived in town about thirty minutes later. She was nervous about meeting someone new but had been assured by both Scott and Allison that she was a nice person. Sara yawned while in the jeep. She was not getting enough sleep in the last couple of weeks. Between the wedding, the people from Germany calling, and avoiding her mother, there just were not enough hours in the day to sleep.

She arrived at the furniture store, where she was supposed to meet Teresa Priest, and went in. She walked to the desk and told the lady who she was and why she was there. Teresa walked in a couple of minutes later.

"Oh, Sara, you look just like I always thought someone from England would look. And that is no insult. You look beautiful," she said.

"Thank you, you look beautiful as well. Are we having lunch here in town?" she asked.

"Oh no, I made reservations in Tyler. Will that be okay?" Teresa asked.

Sara had not been so far away in at least two years. She really hoped she could trust this lady. "Yes, that sounds good," she said. "I have not been far from ho—I mean, the ranch—in a long time."

"Really? I go shopping a lot. And I don't like to go to Dallas. So I just go to Tyler," she said. "May I ask you something?" she asked.

"Of course."

"How did you come to go to school in England? I am fascinated by things like royalty and castles and palaces. And here in Texas, we just don't have much of that," Teresa asked.

"I was born in 1959 in a very upper-class area of Los Angeles. When I was to start school in 1965, it was when they were having riots in Los Angeles and they were going to start forcing immigration, even into the private sects, so my stepfather sent me to Wales to a private school," she said.

"You already had a stepfather by the time you were six?" she asked.

"Five," Sara said. "I was born late in 1959."

"So you're the oldest child in your family?"

Sara was feeling a little claustrophobic but tried to maintain control. "No, I have a brother that is two years older than I."

"Your mother works fast," she said.

"You have no idea," Sara said under her breath.

"Excuse me," she said.

"Oh, nothing, I was thinking of something I have to remember later, is all," Sara said.

"I made reservations at a restaurant that serves the best seafood you have ever eaten," Teresa said as she pulled into a very tall building.

"Have you ever been to England?" Sara asked.

"As a matter of fact, I went a couple of months ago. It was the first time I had ever been. I enjoyed myself. Tell me, have you been to any of the royal residencies?" she asked.

"Well, yes. But I didn't go on any tours or anything."

"Why not? I saw Buckingham Palace, and it was really beautiful," Teresa said.

"I have been to Buckingham Palace when I was twelve. Our school went as part of our training," Sara said.

"And she was so nervous when she was presented I thought I would have to catch her." Sara heard behind her.

She turned and saw Lady Lauren Dickerson. "Lauren," Sara said, standing and throwing her arms around her. "It is so good to see you. How did you know I was in Texas?"

"Mrs. Priest told us," she said.

"Us?" Sara said. Then she looked behind Lauren to see her parents standing with her. The same people who tried to help her the last time she was in England. "Lord and Lady Dickerson? Oh my, you have not changed a bit."

"Sara, you are beautiful," Lady Dickerson said and hugged her tight. She remembered what she looked like the last time she had seen her and thanked God that she looked so well.

"Lord Dickerson, I am so glad you came," she said.

"Sara, you will never know how hard we looked for you. The loss of a child does not compare with anything I have ever known," he said.

"Oh, Lauren, I never thought I would ever see you again," Sara said.

"When I thought you had died, I thought I would die too," Lauren said, embracing her friend like she would never let her go.

Teresa stood back and watched as the four reacquainted themselves for a few moments. Their titles were formal, but they were very familiar with one another.

"My dear, it is a pleasure and an absolute gift to see you here. Your stepfather wrote us that you had died, and until we spoke to your future husband, we knew no differently. Had we known, we would have been here," Lord Dickerson said, then kissing Sara's cheek.

"I am so sorry. I didn't know. I would have written if I would have known," she said and began to cry.

"Sara, you never cry," Lauren said.

"Please, let us sit and get you some water," Lady Dickerson said.

"I am so sorry. I have not been getting very much sleep lately, and our baby brother just died a few weeks ago, and I suppose I am just in a basket," Sara said.

"In a basket?" Teresa asked.

"Is that not a saying?" Sara said.

"Oh, a basket case," Teresa said, putting a hand over Sara's. "And you are not a basket case. You are about to get married. And if it will help you to relax, you are already technically married, as you already have your marriage license."

"Thank you, Teresa. I had never thought of that," Sara said. "Excuse me, I am being rude. Do you already know who Teresa is then?'

"Yes, of course my dear. After we talked to your husband to be, Mrs. Priest came to show us how much better you have been doing and to invite us to your wedding. And if you would like her to be, she brought Lauren her dress to have fitted," Lady Dickerson said.

"Really. Lauren, are you really here to be in my wedding?" Sara asked.

"Of course, I am. I have missed you, Sara. You were always my best friend. When I thought you had died, I had to change schools. I was so sad. But you look so well. Oh, Sara, do you remember the Christmas and the summer you spent at our house in Bath?" Lauren asked.

"How could I ever forget? Those were some of the only happy memories I have. That is until the Byers family found us." Lauren and Sara looked at each other a second and hugged each other again.

"I think that we had better order," Teresa said. "I don't' think that the people in the restaurant would appreciate us standing here talking. And, Sara, Scott told me to make sure you eat something."

Everyone took their seats and looked at the menu. When the waiter returned, everyone ordered. Salads and soup were brought, and the five of them talked throughout the entire meal.

After the meal, they were sipping coffee. "Have you got a place to stay as yet? I don't want to miss a minute with you before the wedding," Sara said.

"As a matter of fact, your Scott has invited us to stay at his father's house," Lord Dickerson said. "And as Lauren is part of the bridal party, I thought that would give you a little bit of time to catch up."

"That is so wonderful," Sara said. "Thank you, Teresa, for helping get them here."

"Well, it is my pleasure. I have never been in the presence of three ladies and a lord before," she said. "Shall we go to the car?'

"Yes, of course," Sara said.

Lord Dickerson sat in the front seat, and the two old friends and Lauren's mother sat in the back of the luxury car.

"Teresa, when we were nine, we went to Caernarfon, Wales, from our school in Borehamwood to see Prince Charles crowned as the Prince of Wales. We were standing in line with the other girls from our school that included several ladies, princesses, etc. Sara had brought back a book from Disneyland about Cinderella and her Prince Charming and thought that Prince Charles would look like the one in book," Lauren explained. "He was right in front of us, shaking hands with all of us from Meadow Park, and when he took

Sara's hand, she said, 'You are not a prince. You don't look like the one in the book.' He smiled at her, and she kept looking at him like she wanted him to go get the real prince."

"So what happened?" Teresa asked.

"Charles wasn't going to walk away with her not believing he was the prince, so he turned and said, 'Mummy, do you mind?' And Her Majesty came across the small road. Sara looked at her and did a very proper curtsey with Charles still holding her hand. When she looked back up, the queen told her she had the most beautiful eyes she had ever seen. Then, satisfied that Charles was indeed the Prince of Wales, she did another very proper curtsey and apologized. He just winked and continued. I already knew Charles. He is our cousin."

"What did you do?" Teresa asked.

"I couldn't do anything. I was laughing too hard," Lauren said, causing everyone to laugh.

"Well, Sara, here we are. I hope that I didn't keep you too long," Teresa said, smiling, and then stepped out of the car. "I am taking the Dickersons to the ranch. Would you like Lauren to ride with you?"

"Absolutely," Sara said. "I will see you at the ranch?" she said to Teresa.

"I will be right behind you," Teresa said and got back into the car.

Sara and Lauren got into the jeep and sat for a minute. "I never thought I would see you again, Sara. I have missed you so much," Lauren said, taking Sara's hand for a moment.

"I have missed you too. I spent nearly three years now going nonstop, but that is not an excuse. I was so ashamed about what that man did to me. I promise, I didn't know that he told you that I had died. I am so sorry," Sara said. "But as it turned out, Saline tried to kill herself a few months after I returned. I have so much to talk to you about. How are you doing?"

"I am still doing about the same as usual," she said.

"How is your leg? I noticed you no longer have a limp at all," Sara asked.

"It is great. When I got this lighter-weight prosthetic, I felt like I could run a million miles with it. About the only thing I can't do with it is swim. Sometimes, when I am not thinking about it, I will find myself scratching it," Lauren said and laughed a little, then continued, "I can't believe that when I first found out I had cancer, I just wanted to die. But thanks to you, I am here eight years later."

"Nonsense, I didn't do anything, I was just there," Sara said.

"But you had been so sick you nearly died. Then it took you years before you could do as you once had. If not for being able to talk to my best friend and you to give me faith, I don't think I could have made it. I mean, I lost my hair and my leg, then the chemotherapy made me so sick. I am so glad that the last time we said good-bye that I had hair that was several inches long. And I still can't believe that you cut off so much of your own hair and gave it to Mummy. I thought she would swallow her eyeballs. At least I didn't look like a lightbulb any longer."

"No matter how bad, you always listened. I don't know how I would have made it without you. I really loved those Christmases we spent with your parents. And the summer in Bath, we had such a great time. Even in school, our picnics in the middle of the night. Seems like a million years ago, in someone else's life," Sara said.

"You look so happy now. I am glad you found someone you love. Is he really as great as he sounds?" Lauren asked.

"Better. His whole family is. They have been so good to us. I think that they loved our baby brother as much as we did. He is buried on their ranch, in the family plot. But he spent the last few months of his life healthy, happy, and so loved. Saline and I, before we came here, spent two years of pure hell. And there was no one. The man that Momma had married this time is only five years older than I am, and if he would have had his way, he would have raped both Saline and me. But we learned and stayed together. He is in jail now, thank God. Guess what! I said something you wouldn't believe," Sara said.

"Do you mean out of character?"

"Yes," Sara said and told her about the incident at the grocery store. When she finished, they were pulling up to the main house. They had to wait a few minutes to get out of the jeep as they were both laughing so hard they were weak.

When Teresa pulled up beside them, Lord Dickerson got out of the car and walked over to the passenger side and opened the door and heard the girls' laughter.

"Oh, Daddy." She laughed. "Sara finally did something out of character. You will have to get her to tell you." She then leaned over to Sara and whispered, "Who's the bitch now?" Both laughed anew.

The three in Teresa's car were so happy to see the two girls enjoying themselves. Between Sara's bad parents, poor health a few years ago, and Lauren's having aggressive cancer that took two years to recover, both seemed to grow up quicker. They had been best friends since the first day they started Meadow Park Academy. But now they were laughing like children.

Teresa, Sara, and the Dickersons went into the house. Allison had just gotten back from town and was starting supper.

Sara brought the party into the kitchen of the Byers mansion and made introductions.

"Momma, this is Lord George and Lady Frances Dickerson and their daughter, Lady Lauren Dickerson. This is the best mother in the world, Allison Byers, and my little sister, Lady Saline Alexander," Sara said.

Allison stepped forward and put her hand out. "George, Frances, and Lauren, it is so nice to meet you in person at last. How was your trip over?"

"Very good, thank you. This is a beautiful home, Allison. I have always wanted to come here to Texas but am usually kept in England for one thing or another," George said.

"It feels like we may get a little bit of snow tonight. But there will be no ice. Wouldn't that make the day beautiful?" Allison said. "I apologize. I believe that I am even more excited about the wedding than the kids are. We have all boys, and I never thought I would get to plan a wedding."

"Oh, George, John asked me to tell you where he is when you get here. Saline, baby, would you mind taking Lord Dickerson to Daddy?" Allison asked.

"Yes, mam, Momma," she said and led Lord Dickerson to the family room where John, Mark, Scott, and the boys were.

"Daddy, Momma asked me to bring Lord Dickerson to you," Saline said. Then she turned to Lord Dickerson. "Sir, I personally wanted to tell you thank you for caring about what happened to my sister. She used to speak very well of you and your family," she said and put her hand out.

"The friendship is mutual, young lady." George smiled and put his hand out, shaking hers. "And you are most welcome. Your sister loves you very much. She missed you while she was in England."

"Thank you, sir," Saline said and smiled at him and then returned to the kitchen.

"John, it is so good to finally meet you. George Dickerson," he said, shaking John's hand.

"Good to meet you, George. This is my son Scott and our other sons, Riley and Colton. And this is our foster son and geologist Mark St. Clair." All shook hands. "These are the groomsmen, I believe, my Allison calls them."

"I thought coming in here would be a way of not being in the middle of the ladies as they converse about the wedding," George said.

"Good move," came from most of the men in the room.

Back in the kitchen, everyone was talking and cooking. Frances had donned an apron and was assisting the other ladies.

Aunt Mary, Uncle Alex's wife, had come in and was introduced to the people she didn't know.

"Sara, my darling, I believe Uncle Alex is looking for you. I think he went into where the men are hiding from us," Aunt Mary said. "Are you ready for tomorrow?"

"Yes, mam," Sara said and then involuntarily yawned. "Oh, lord. Please excuse me. I haven't been getting much rest in the last bit."

"Baby, why don't you go and take a nap? It will be a while before supper, and you want to be rested for tomorrow," Allison said.

"Yes, mam. I think that I will," Sara said and then left, going in the direction of the family room on the other side of the house.

"Uncle Alex, Aunt Mary said you wanted to see me," Sara said.

Alex came across the room to where Sara was. "Yes, I just wanted to see if you were getting enough rest. You look a little tired," he asked.

"I didn't realize I was so tired," she said, yawning again. "I am going to lie down before supper."

"Good idea. Steve will be here for supper. And I brought you something so you can rest tonight," he said and gave her the bottle of medication.

"Thank you, Uncle Alex. I will see you at supper," she said and kissed his cheek.

Sara walked to her room. She was tired but smiled to herself, thinking about the secret that she was keeping. But no one else could know before Scott, so she would have to be careful.

When she got to her room she closed the door softly and walked into the bathroom. A hot bath sounded like just what she needed. She ran the bathwater and put some very fragrant bubble bath that Allison had bought her in the water. She got a warm gown and panties, then pulled her dress off and placed it on a hanger. Then she pulled her stockings off and continued to get undressed until she was naked and at last eased into the water.

She was so happy now. She never would have thought that she could be so happy. She still thought frequently of Jody, and she still missed him terribly. She kept fresh flowers on his grave and talked to him daily. She knew that he was in a place where he would never hurt again, and he would be there waiting for her one day.

She relaxed for a few minutes in the water. She was so happy to see the Dickersons again. She never even thought they would want to see her again. But then thought of how close they were a few years ago. Then she thought of how she would feel if she would have found out that something happened to one of them. Then she started crying again. Taking some deep breaths and telling herself that she really needed to stop or she was going to give herself away, she lie down and fell asleep.

A couple of hours later, when Allison came to Sara's door, she found her sound asleep. The young woman that she had come to love and admire seemed even younger than her seventeen years that she had just turned that day. She had not mentioned it being her birthday and likely would not. She had never brought celebration upon herself and likely had not even thought of the date.

Allison knew that her entire life had not been about dates or who she was, but rather what she was as a provider and as a loving sister. If her son would have asked to marry a woman of eighteen, likely they would have denied the request. But this young woman had been functioning in an adult world since she was a young child. She had crossed the Atlantic a dozen times, alone since she was five, and went to school and learned two languages without having a parent or guardian accompanying her. She came home to raise two younger siblings and was willing to give her life for them. How many people twice her age would be willing to do so?

"Sara baby, are you hungry?" she asked.

Sara awoke from a deep sleep and opened her eyes, rubbing them. "What time is it?" she asked.

"It is suppertime. Do you think you can eat?" she asked.

"Oh, of course," she said it with her English accent still evident, but somehow it seemed so familiar and comforting even to the Texans who were leery of outsiders. Texas had accepted her. And tomorrow, everyone would know who and what she was.

"Do you want a tray brought, or do you want to come to the table?" she asked.

"I will eat at the table. I will be dressed in a minute," she said.

A few minutes later, everyone was assembled for supper. Excitement was in the air rather than the sadness of the few weeks prior. Sara and Scott were seated side by side and had eyes only for each other. The Byers family and guests beamed at the couple. The Dickersons were pleased that the young lady so regarded as a child was indeed alive and well and, at last, happy.

After supper, Scott and Sara went outside for a few minutes and said good night, but only until the morning.

"My angel, I promise you a happy life, and I will be here with you forever," he said.

"And I will be here with you. What if my family shows up, intent on trouble?" she asked.

"Just know. They won't." They kissed and parted their last time for the night, for the rest of them would be together.

CHAPTER 7

The Wedding

Early the following morning, Sara awoke to the first rays of sunlight that came through the window. She stretched and got out of bed. She looked at her reflection in the mirror and said to her, "It is your wedding day."

Happiness flooded over her. Today and every day from here on she would be with the man she loved more than her own life. Her excitement was overtaking her, so she decided before breakfast, she would go for a walk. So she walked to the closet and dressed in a heavy skirt and sweater and put on heavy stockings. Allison had bought her some knee-high riding boots a few weeks before, so she decided them perfect for her purposes.

As soon as she was dressed, she went to the nearest outside door and silently went out. When she turned and looked at the new day before her, she saw a blanket of fresh snow covered the ground. But the sun was coming, and there were only scattered fluffy white clouds in an otherwise blue sky. The air was cold, definitely well below freezing, so Sara buttoned her coat then began walking in the direction of the horse barn.

As she walked, she began to think of the day ahead, and soon, she was fairly dancing across the snow-covered yard. When she came to the three-foot split rail fence, she raced toward it and, putting her hand on the fence post, very acrobatically flew over the fence, twisting in the air. Then she continued making her way to the barn and went in.

Up at the house, Scott had awakened early as well. He was looking out the window before he got dressed for his wedding day and walked over to the window and saw that it had snowed. Regardless, the day was perfect.

Scott heard footsteps coming up the hall and turned to find his father coming in.

"Good morning, Daddy," Scott said.

"Morning, son, ready for your wedding day?" he asked.

"You bet. I think that Sara is already providing the entertainment. Evidently, she woke up early and is going to say good morning to Champ. Take a look," Scott told his father.

John walked over and began watching the young woman in the yard. She was prancing like a Tennessee walker. When she approached the fence, he thought she would slow and use the gate. Then he saw her speed up and leaped gracefully over the low fence and kept going.

"Well, I guess I don't need to ask if she is nervous. I am no palm reader, but judging on the two of you and what I know about both of you, you both will have a long and, for the most part, happy life," John said, putting a hand on his son's shoulder.

"Daddy, I think that having girls around so close is making you go soft," Scott said.

"Strange, that's what your momma just said last night." He grinned. "Better make sure she is not late for breakfast," he said, walking down the hall to the dining room.

"John, are the kids starting to wake up yet?" Allison asked.

"I know that Scott and Sara are. I just saw Sara skipping across the yard to the barn," he said.

"I thought she might sleep in this morning. She has a long day."

John walked up behind his wife and put his arms around her. "So do you, my dear," he said in her ear. "And I happen to know that you were up much later than they were."

"And so were you, but you seem to be going strong," she said, turning in his arms. "And you were up quite early."

"You wanton woman, what will you do when I fall asleep during the wedding?" he whispered.

"I will make you remember," she said, kissing his cheek, and then continued on making breakfast.

A few minutes later, Saline and Lauren were looking for Sara.

"I believe she got up early and went down to the horse barn to say good morning to Champ. I have never seen her look so happy. Scott has gone down there as well.

"Would the two of you mind if I asked you to go and get them for breakfast?" Allison said.

"Not at all, Momma, we will be right back," Saline said.

"Wait a minute, I am going," Colton said.

"Why would you want to go, Colton?" Allison asked.

"I don't want them to get lost," he said sheepishly.

"Okay. But you had better behave," Saline said.

The two kids started toward the barn.

"Race you," Saline said then took off running.

"Hey, wait up," Colton said.

"Nope, I like to see you lose."

Colton ran as fast as he could to show her up. When Saline disappeared around the side of the barn, Colton thought he had lost. When he got there, Saline bombed him with snowballs. She was laughing at his being caught off guard.

"You look like such a dork," Saline said, continuing to laugh.

"Do I?" he said, walking over to where she was becoming weak from laughing. Colton picked Saline up and took her outside. He got to a pretty deep area of snow and dropped her in it. And then took a few steps back.

"Oh man, you look like a snow bunny. Don't mess with boys, we always win," Colton said, laughing.

With that, Saline began to cry then turned out of the barn and ran.

"Saline, I didn't mean it. I was just kidding, but you are just a girl," was all he had the time to say. Saline had stepped outside, picked up a bunch of snow, and got up on top of the low roof. So Colton was easily taken by surprise.

"Truce, you win, but now we have to find our brother and sister," Colton said.

"You have found us," Scott said from the hay loft. "We were just having a good time watching you," Scott said, coming out of the hay. "Let's eat, I am starving. Race y'all to the house," Scott said, and everyone started running. Everyone in the house was watching the five of them running to the house. Sara, not known for her speed, was of course in last place.

"Momma, have you seen the snow?" Colton asked.

"Yes, son I saw that," Allison said, knowing it was as she had hoped it would be. "Everyone, it is time to eat," she said.

Everyone from the house began to take their seats. As usual, Scott and Sara were side by side. Talk was merry during the meal.

"Lauren, did your dress fit just as well? I am glad one of the dresses will be functional as to other events you could wear it to," Sara said.

Lauren looked to her friend. She knew part of the hell that Sara had spent her life trying to survive and had made it. But she could tell that her friend had ghosts in her closet and likely would for years to come.

Scott was a one of a kind sort of a man. He had eyes for only Sara.

"Lauren, what do you think of Texas?" Sara asked her friend.

"It is so big and open. This area is much like you would find as your own kingdom." She grinned.

"I don't think that King Poppa would like that to get out," Sara said and then blushed. Then everyone in the room laughed.

"It is going to be a busy day today, mostly for the women. So we had all better start getting things done," Allison said. Everyone seemed to rise from the table and go do their separate things that they had to do.

Lauren, Saline, Sara, and Maria were on the way to Sara's room for the last-minute fittings of the beautiful gown. Allison cleared away the breakfast dishes and placed them in the dishwasher and was then on her way to Sara's room. She walked into the room and was swept up in the spirit of the situation.

Lady Dickerson was the first to speak to everyone. "What are you planning on doing with your hair, my dear?" she asked.

"I thought I would wear it down. It has lots of curls in it," Sara said.

"It will be beautiful. May I take a few strands and do something a little different?" she asked.

"Yes, mam, of course," she said.

Then the door was closed, and the sound of laughing and talking emulated from the door. The men went on about their business.

Back in Sara's room, there was constant activity. Things were going a bit slow due to the fact that Sara was shy. She knew that she had scars that were still angry looking and didn't want anyone else to see if at all possible. She kept her back as close as possible to the wall.

When it was time for the stylist to do her hair, Sara sat in the chair and let the stylist brush and roll the ends of her hair. Sara's only recommendation was that it be worn down and look natural.

"You have the thickest hair that I believe I have ever seen. And the color is just beautiful. If you were lost in a crowd, people would be able to find you because of the unusual color," the stylist said. She rolled the ends of Sara's hair and then brushed it to a high gloss. When she was happy with the way that it looked, she took a very loose fitting net and placed over Sara's head to keep her hair from being blown before the wedding.

Very little makeup was added, because she had a beautiful complexion. Eye makeup was added to make her eyes completely sparkle.

Then it was time to begin the process of putting on her underclothing first, which Sara did by herself in the bathroom. Then there was the very full floor-length petticoat to be contended with. Sara's slender waist made dressing her like dressing a doll.

Still, even though she knew the people in the room, she didn't want to show any marks that could be on her body.

Then Lady Dickerson gasped. She saw a six-inch angry-looking scar on her back.

Allison took her aside and told her that although the children had been living there for months, there were still some old injuries that had not healed and that she wished she would not make her feel self-conscious.

"Oh, Allison, I am sorry," she whispered. "I in truth had no idea. There will be not one more word out of my mouth regarding it. Dear God, she saved my baby's life. Why didn't we look harder for her? I will never forgive myself," she whispered and then recovered herself.

"Okay, Sara, here come the boobs," her sister said. "What you need to do is hold on to the bedstead and suck in." Sara did as she was told.

"Oh my goodness, I am not that fat. It is okay if I breathe?" Sara said.

"I think that we can loosen that a little. Her waist is quite small." In between putting on a layer of underclothes, Sara was given a bite of food with a little drink.

Then at 12:15 pm, it was time to put on the beautiful gown that had been picked out by Allison, Maria, and Saline. All agreed that it was the most beautiful dress that they had ever seen.

The neckline was rounded and modestly low in front. The sleeves were sheer and ivory in color and buttoned at the cuffs. On her shoulders were two bows that fit completely on her shoulder. The empire waist made Sara's already tiny waist look even smaller. Yet the curve of her hips could be seen no matter what Sara wore. Then there was a surprise that she had not been expecting.

Lady Dickerson brought in a heavy box and put it on the bed. "Sara, everyone wants to look like princess on her special day. Since you came into our lives, you have made us feel like royalty. Well, I guess we are royalty. What I mean to say is that you are selfless and honorable, and whatever part our of family you can be, you are more than welcome."

It was then that Lady Dickerson opened the jeweled case. "As you know, it is the tradition for royalty to wear a tiara that is handed down from generation to generation. Although Lauren will one day wear this, she wanted this to be what is borrowed for your wedding for good luck. I hope it will make you feel as beautiful as it did me," she said and arranged the tiara and her veil on her head. After they arranged the ten-foot silk train, she looked in the mirror and could not believe the transformation.

Allison then approached her and handed her a baby-blue hand-kerchief. "Something blue, my girl. My mother gave it to me on my wedding day. I pray it brings you as much happiness as it has us," she said and kissed her cheeks.

Tears fell from Sara's eyes. She had never known the love of a mother until this day. Now she had two. "Now don't mess up your makeup, not that you need that much."

"Oh, Sara, you look so happy. I never thought we would ever know what it was like to live normally and be loved. I want you to know, Sara, that I have prayed every night since we came here. I never really thought that someone watched over us, now I do. I love you, Sara, more than you will ever know. That day that you pushed me out of the way of that car, I really wanted to die. Now I know that God has a purpose for me," Saline said to her sister.

"I thank God every day for you, Saline." The two sisters embraced.

"I think we are keeping someone waiting," Saline said.

The snow didn't keep people from attending the wedding. The Byers family was known all over Texas and the surrounding states as very wealthy and very generous people. Sara had never expected such fanfare, but she attributed it to the Byers family and not herself. After all, the only people who really knew her were the people at the ranch and her sister.

"My beautiful miracle," Dr. Quinton said, looking at Sara. The music began, and Mary, Maria, Lauren, and Saline made their way down the aisle to the altar, and then the time-honored "Bridal Chorus" began.

As there are typically as many groomsmen as bridesmaids, Scott and Uncle Alex agreed that as Dr. Quinton was to accompany Sara, that he would be a groomsman.

"I think this is our song," Dr. Quinton said. Sara smiled radiantly up at him.

Between the heavy train and the very snug-fitting bodice, Sara was fatigued by the time she arrived at the altar. Then she looked up at Scott, and tears filled her eyes. She used the hankie that Allison had given her a few minutes before. She thought about all the people who had made this day happen, and tears continued to fall.

Scott thought it odd that this woman who was so stoic and self-reliant be reduced to tears. She had been acting emotional for the last several days. Then he thought of prewedding nerves. Throughout the service, Sara never openly cried, but tears never stopped running down her face. When at last the priest pronounced them husband and wife, they kissed and the people in the congregation stood and applauded the new couple. Sara blushed and put her head against Scott's shoulder.

"May the happiness of this day that has been brought to two people from different worlds together enrich all who receive them together in the name of the Lord, amen."

The couple knelt together in prayer and then rose as man and wife. They were given their first Mass as husband and wife.

Lady Dickerson approached her and made a small slit in Sara's veil so the tiara she wore showed through, sparkling in the sunlight.

With tears streaming down her face, Sara thanked Lady Dickerson and hugged her close.

"The day is just beginning, my love," he said.

She looked at him in wonder. When the recessional started, it took all four bridesmaids to turn the train. They walked a happily married new couple, arm in arm. Smiles greeted them the entire way down the aisle.

Before they walked outside, Scott pulled a burgundy floor-length cape and placed it around her shoulders. "It is a little cold out there," he said. Scott had remembered what Sara had said regarding wearing capes, so he had one made for her.

Sara looked up, questioning. Then the doors opened. The look on Sara's face showed all the shock in the world. Horse-drawn carriages were lined up for the honored guests.

Scott and an attendant assisted Sara in climbing in the carriage, complete with the long train and the cape. The red cape gave her a regal look, and the tiara made her look like nothing less than royalty. Scott sat beside her and put his arm around her and pulled her close. The other carriages that carried the rest of the family and close friends began to roll. Sara felt like she was in a fairy tale.

In small towns, where everyone knows everyone, when the town street is blocked off for any reason, people want to see. So people braved the cold weather to see the new couple and were surprised at her familiarity. To some she looked to be familiar but could not know from where. Her beautiful burgundy hair almost matched the floor-length cape. Her green eyes sparkled in the cold winter's air. People waved, and Sara waved to the people as well.

They were driven by carriage to a meeting hall on the square about a mile away. When the newlyweds entered, they were introduced, and the reception began, complete with music and dancing. The opening waltz was slow, and Scott and Sara had only eyes for each other.

"Were you surprised, my love?" Scott asked.

"You know that I was. I don't know how you did all this, and I didn't know a thing about it. I thought Saline would have said something about it."

"I think it kept her mind off Jody. And she loved every bit of it," Scott said.

"Well, I have a bit of a surprise, not as big as all this. But I hope that you will be pleased," she said.

"I don't think that there is much about you I don't know," he teased.

"What about a baby?" she said.

"Sure, we can leave the party early," he said and smiled.

"We won't have to do anything. I am pregnant," Sara said and waited for his response.

"Really? That would mean that one time?" Scott said and picked her up and spun her around. "I can't wait to tell Momma and Daddy."

"Will they think less of me because we got the cart before the horse?" she asked. "I don't want them to think of me as a tart." Her eyes began to mist.

"Is that why you have been crying so easily? Baby girl, I was born six months after my parents married."

"These silly hormones, I just can't get hold of them sometimes. Do you think that we should tell them tonight?" she asked.

"Unless I miss my guess, it is going to be obvious in a couple of weeks. Have you been sick or anything like that?"

"Just sleepy all the time," she said.

"Wait, you haven't been to the doctor?" he asked.

"No. Not yet."

"Well, Mrs. Byers, this is the happiest day of my life," Scott said, kissing his new wife passionately. "We will celebrate further later."

"I don't suppose I could impose a dance with the bride, could I?" Uncle Alex asked.

"You may indeed. Sara, why don't you let Uncle Alex in on your surprise?" Scott said.

"What have you two been cooking up over here?" he asked.

"I was just giving Scott his surprise," Sara said sweetly.

"And what would that be?"

Sara blushed and ducked her head a little. "It seems we jumped the gun a little. Please don't think badly of me. It was only one time, and it was the night Scott asked me to marry him."

"Sara, you don't have to explain anything to me. I could tell the first time I saw you together you loved each other. Have you seen a doctor yet?" he asked.

She looked at the floor and shook her head.

"Baby girl, with your past history, and your recent problems with your heart, don't you think you should?" he asked tenderly.

Alex hugged her close for the slow dance. Sara could not see the look of concern on his face.

After a couple of hours of dancing, Sara was starting to feel the weight of the heavy gown and tiara. She asked Scott if it would be okay if they sat down for a few minutes.

They went to the table that had been prepared for them and sat down. Scott helped himself to a glass of champagne, and Sara asked for a glass of iced tea.

"That man said he was your friend from Austin. Who is he?" Sara asked.

Scott saw the man and waved. "He is the governor. He didn't tell you?"

"No," she said.

She had not noticed among the well-wishers, where everyone in the state was welcome, people were taking pictures.

Scott stood to talk to a few well-wishers. When he turned back to Sara, she was sound asleep with her head resting on her hand.

Scott stood with his father and uncle when he looked over at his bride. "My bride, the born party animal," he said, and they all got a chuckle out of it. "Daddy, I guess it is a good time to tell you that I found out a couple of hours ago that you are going to be a grandfather."

John Byers's chest swelled with pride. He thought about how she had been so weepy and didn't have much of an appetite. John hugged his son and called Allison over to let her know of her impending status.

"Oh, son, I could not be more delighted," she said, thinking about the loss of little Jody not so long ago.

"I believe she would be more forthcoming if she could stay awake," Scott said, looking over at his wife.

"Poor little thing. She has no idea that people are taking her picture, and she is sleeping right through it. You might want to take her home, son," Allison said.

"I believe you are right, Momma. It will take us an hour to get through the people as it is," he said and went to get her cape and asked the carriage driver to come around.

Lauren came over to the table and started talking to Sara only a few minutes before she realized she was fast asleep. "Sara," she said, startling the bride to the point of falling off her hand. "I can't believe you are asleep at your own wedding party."

Shaking her head a little, she apologized and told her that she had a secret to her oldest friend. "I am afraid I am going to have a baby," she said.

"Really!" Lauren said. "Does Scott know?"

"I told him a couple of hours ago. I was so afraid I would give myself away before the wedding because I kept on crying and falling asleep. We were only together once, and it was not planned at all. We were looking at our house one night in the summer, and it happened. Do you think people will think that I am a tart?" Sara asked.

"Are you kidding? Does anyone here look like they are judging you? They are happy that the most eligible bachelor in Texas has taken a bride. I am so happy for you, Sara," she said.

"Oh, Lauren, I am so glad you are here." She felt her head and realized that she still had her mother's tiara on with her veil. "Does your mum want this back now?"

"Oh no, she wants you to wear it until after everything is over with. She thought of you quite like a daughter while we were in school. And believe me, I am not in a hurry to walk down the aisle myself. And Scott seems to be a love," Lauren said.

"He is. I looked up, and he was there, and suddenly life was as God promised," she said.

"I know that your life has been difficult, and you had to grow up faster than I did, but you having found your Prince Charming perchance is just a miracle," Lauren said.

"I know it is. And seeing you again is a miracle in and of itself."

"I was so afraid that you had died. That monster deserves to be thrown to the wolves. I say that, and someplace down the bloodline we are related. I believe Mum and Dad are talking to his family in Germany regarding him, and Dad usually tends to get people to listen," Lauren assured her.

Sara was so glad that Lauren was in Texas. She and her parents had always made her feel like family and that she was wanted.

"Well, Lady Lauren, I think that I need to take my little party pooper home so she can rest. She will be needing lots of that, I am sure she has told you," Scott said.

"Will I see you tomorrow?' she asked.

"You won't be going on a honeymoon?" Lauren asked.

"Sara elected to wait and have a honeymoon at a slower time of the year for us," Scott said.

"Will you come to our house tomorrow?" Sara asked.

"Sure. We will be here for a few more days, and Mummy has grown quite attached to your new mother-in-law. Until tomorrow," she said, hugging her friend. Then all the single women gathered for the throwing of the bouquet, which was caught by Lauren.

Scott and Sara began making their way to the door, saying good night to well-wishers. The number of people present made it take an hour longer to get to their carriage. When they were seated, they took the carriage around the town square a couple of times and then back to the church in the carriage.

"I didn't mean to fall asleep, Scott. I can't seem to keep myself awake lately," she said.

"You don't owe me any apologies, my dear. After all, it is I who caused your fatigue," he said. "Daddy and Momma are thrilled, by the way. I expect Momma to start making baby clothes tonight."

She cuddled closer to Scott both to be nearer to him and to keep warm.

"Was our wedding everything I promised?"

"It was like a fairy tale come true. I hope the honeymoon does not end when we get home," she said.

"That is when the honeymoon begins," he said and kissed her.

When they arrived back to the church, they got into Sara's jeep. They drove back to their house to spend their first night in their new home.

When they arrived, Scott picked Sara up and carried her gown, tiara, and cape over the threshold. When he gently set her down, he kissed her deeply, wanting.

"Welcome home," he whispered.

"Welcome home to you too," Sara said. "Can we get something to drink? I am dying of thirst."

"I believe we have some champagne in the kitchen, and of course, we have tea in the fridge," he said.

"I am only seventeen. I don't think I am supposed to drink champagne," Sara said.

"We are home, married, and I said it is okay for just a little," Scott said.

"Okay. Just a little," she said.

"I will pour you an extra cold glass of the best French champagne, and I will run an extra warm bubble bath, and we can relax," he said.

"Sounds like a dream, but I am afraid it is going to take me forever to get out of this dress."

"Don't worry, I will help," Scott said and winked.

Sara smiled and picked up the glasses. Scott got the bottle of champagne, and they met in the bedroom. Scott started the water in the oversized bathtub and then walked back into the dressing room where Sara had already removed her shoes and was sipping champagne.

Scott walked behind her and took a drink from his glass, then set to the work of undoing the buttons on the back of the beautiful gown. He breathed softly on the back of her neck, giving her shivers that traveled down her spine. He would kiss her skin every time he undid a button. He took his time, bit by bit, taking in the beauty of his bride—her tiny waist, her rounded hips, her green eyes that searched his face in wonder. She continued to sip the bubbling beverage and was feeling quite relaxed and aroused.

When the gown was removed, Sara turned to Scott and began to do as he had done her, removing his clothes slowly and using her lips and her moist tongue to enhance the effect. She was not a practiced lover, but as Scott's accomplished student in the art, he thought he would go mad while she teased.

When he was nude, his manhood in full display, he began to remove her petticoat but first unfastened her stockings from their garters and kissed her inner thigh. Sara gasped when he started. He removed her petticoat and began to suckle her breast through her chemise. It only took a small tug to remove her panties, and then he began to massage her moistened womanhood. He pulled her chemise over her head and kissed her breasts, down her stomach, and down farther, a feeling she had never had before. Her back arched, and she moaned, not wanting the feeling to ever stop. At that point, he picked her up and got into the hot bath with her. The hot water further enhanced the feeling, her entire body in erotic spasms that felt like they came from deep within her. When she could take no more, Scott entered her, and within minutes, both of them exploded in a burst of sensual sensations, clinging to each other until they subsided.

When they were spent from the day, the night, the hot water, and the champagne, they got out of the tub and the air in the room was cool. So they rushed to the big soft bed that awaited them. Each wearing only the clothes God had given them, they went to sleep, only to awaken again and again to the yearning of their bodies.

Sara slept later than usual, but Scott made sure she was awake for church. The entire family attended church together. Scott and Sara returned home and spent the entire day together. Scott insisted that she nap when she felt sleepy and even napped with her a couple of times. The pleasure of just watching her sleep and feeling her in his arms were a gift.

As she slept early in the afternoon, he saw that she smiled in her sleep. "Sara Lyn Byers," he whispered. "I will cherish you every second of our lives together. I love you." He placed his hand low on her abdomen, wondering if their child would look likes its mother. She still had fading scars—some medical and some abuse. "I will protect you with every fiber of my being." He then gently kissed her abdomen and laid his head on it.

In her sleep, she put her hand on his head and smiled.

Scott had no doubt that this girl had been sent to him for safekeeping, and he intended on keeping his end of the bargain. They slept in each other's arms until the sun rose.

The following day, Scott was to go to work, and the ladies had things they had planned to do as well. Scott could think of no happier place on the world than the Byers ranch.

As Scott had always done, he was up with the sun, but Sara still slept. The air in the room was cool, so he looked through some of her things and got one of her warm gowns and slipped it over her head. In her sleep, she snuggled his hand. She looked so sweet and innocent. He leaned down and kissed her forehead. She continued to sleep.

He then slipped on a pair of jeans and went to the kitchen and called the main house. His father answered.

"Daddy, what have we got going today?" he asked.

"Are you and your little bride planning a day of it?" he asked.

"No. She knows it is a busy time of the year and said we could do something later. I think she is eager to set up household. I believe they call that nesting," he answered.

"Is she awake this early?" John asked.

"No, she is fast asleep. Frankly, I don't know how she was able to function as long as she did in that dress. As pretty as it is, it must weigh fifty pounds. But she was something, wasn't she, Daddy?"

"She glowed. People who didn't know her kept asking if her hair and eyes were really the color they are. I assured them that they are."

"I hope that we didn't disappoint you and Momma regarding the baby," Scott said.

"Son, the two of you have been living under the same roof for months and obviously are in love. And either of you are made of stone. I don't consider myself one of those hens who matchmake, but after seeing the way you looked at her for the last two years and the way that she looked at you that day in the café, I just had a feeling," he said.

"But frankly, Daddy, it was only one time on the night I asked her to marry me, in July," Scott said.

"You make me proud, son," John teased. "You take after your old man. I'll be over in about an hour. I think that your momma, Lady Dickerson, and Maria are making the two of you some breakfast to bring over then. And, son, you may want to prepare Sara that she made the front page of the *Dallas Morning News*."

"What?"

"'Young millionaire oilman marries German nobility.' It mentions Lord and Lady Dickerson, Lauren, and everyone else. I don't know who sent a cameraman to take pictures. But the biggest one is a picture of the two of you in the carriage when you left the reception. Right next to it is a picture of Sara asleep at the table."

"You don't suppose that duke that you slugged months ago had a photographer following her, do you? Sara is my wife now, and Saline my sister-in-law, and no one—I don't care who they are—will ever get close enough to hurt them again. Tell Momma to hurry with the breakfast. I am hungry as a bear," he said and replaced the phone on the hook. He then walked into the closet and got a Western shirt and put it on and proceeded to put his belt on and put his things in his pockets.

He went over to the bed and shook Sara a little. Her eyes opened slowly, and she looked over at him.

"It wasn't a dream. You're still here." She smiled.

"You can't get rid of me now. We are going to have visitors in a little bit. Do you want to get dressed or have breakfast in bed?" he asked.

Sara threw the cover off. "I have spent way too much time in bed. I want to look well, not sick. Do you want to dance?" she asked, twirling in front of him. Then she walked into the dressing room and got a skirt, petticoat, stockings, and sweater on in record time then went to the kitchen and got the tea pitcher out of the refrigerator. "Can I ask something while we are alone?" she said, taking a little bit of a serious tone.

"Sure. You can ask me anything."

"Am I any different, ah…" she didn't know how to ask.

"You are perfect. I would almost say that you were healed by God. And I will never ever want any other woman, because I got you," he said in a tone that mirrored her seriousness.

"Thank you," she said, kissing him sweetly.

"I thought you wanted to dance," he said, turning on the radio. "Tell me, Mrs. Byers, what is your favorite kind of dance?"

"Completely depends on mood. I had almost forgotten how much I loved to dance," she said.

Scott took her in his arms, and they began to move to the music. They were still dancing when the breakfast party arrived. They could see in the window that the two were dancing. They opened the kitchen door and walked in with some heavenly smelling food.

Sara stopped dancing when she smelled the food. "I am starving. Thank you for bringing something to eat. I am still in the process of learning to cook," she said and continued, "Lady Dickerson, I have your tiara in the dressing room. I didn't let anything happen to it."

"Sara, I was not afraid that you would. It was my pleasure to have you wear it and look so beautiful in it," Lady Dickerson said.

"I think that the two of you will want to look at the Dallas paper this morning, and the Houston paper, *Tyler*, well, you will get the picture," John said.

Scott picked up the paper and looked at the two pictures displayed on the front page. One was a picture of them as a couple at the church following the wedding. Sara looked up at Scott rather than at the camera. The second one was a picture of Sara sitting at the bridal table, fast asleep. The story of the wedding started and continued on page 4, with even more pictures of the couple, the Dickersons, Saline and Lauren, and John and Allison, just to name a few.

Sara walked over to look at the paper with Scott and saw herself asleep on the front page. "Who took this? Why are we on the front page of the paper? I know that others must have gotten married."

"The article mentions the joining of the most eligible bachelor in Texas having married a German noblewoman. And everyone of importance is mentioned. I believe that your uncle may have had something to do with this. There is no one else I can think of," John said.

"Will these cause problems?" Sara asked.

"Likely, reporters will want to talk to you and take your picture for a while."

"Why? A year ago, no one really cared what happened to us and did nothing to help us, and now they want to talk to us? I won't do it," Sara said, obviously upset.

"You don't have to, baby girl, but that does not mean that they won't follow you every place you go, snapping your picture the whole while," Scott said.

"We are a family that is in the news frequently, and with that comes the inconvenience of publicity from time to time. But it will pass," John said. "Then you will be just another housewife."

"Do you think that anyone will recognize me without the wedding dress and tiara?" Sara asked.

"I would like to say no, but your beautiful burgundy hair is easily recognized," Lady Dickerson said. "But, Sara, remember at Meadow Park, they taught all of you young ladies that in some cases, you will have to deal with the press every day. And it is the way in which you handle yourself that determines who you are."

"Lady Dickerson, our little church in town is nothing compared to the Abbey, but I would love it if you would join us in church this morning," Sara said.

"We would love to be there, and we're hoping you would ask," she said.

Everyone in the room spent the next hour talking about the wedding, the ranch, and of course, the baby. Lord and Lady Dickerson were as John and Allison. They felt like they were becoming grandparents as well, and in a big way, they were. After the meal was finished, everyone went back to the main house to dress for church.

The entire family joined the new couple in going to church including Riley and Colton. Mark and Maria were both Catholic, but the Episcopal Church was much like the Catholic Church, so both attended as members of the family.

When the large party arrived, they were immediately surrounded by a large group of reporters.

"Lady Sara, did you have your uncle to attend the wedding?"

"No. He was not invited," Sara answered.

"What about your mother and father?"

"They also were not invited because of a family matter. They are dangerous. You can see that recently they were both in jail for things they had done," Sara said.

"Lord Dickerson, what makes a British lord come to a German lady's wedding?"

"Sara and our daughter, Lauren, went to school together in Wales. And for the record, Sara Lyn Dickerson Byers was presented at court at Buckingham Palace when she was twelve," George answered.

"My wife is the second cousin to Her Majesty the Queen. At twelve, Lady Sara had spent most of her life in Wales and England because her birth family abandoned her and never visited. That meant she became a young child in need of love. We adopted her, and it was never contested. Here is a copy of the paperwork. Now if you will excuse us, we don't want to be late for Mass."

Sara looked up at Lord Dickerson. "Thank ,you Lord Dickerson. I have missed you so much, sir."

"You have been ours since you were nine years old. Lauren had your hair, and we had you. So don't you think you could call me Poppa?"

"Thank you, Poppa and Mummy," Sara said.

The large party entered the sanctuary that still had the carpet, bunting, and flowers from the previous day. The smell of the flowers was intoxicating. When they were all seated in three rows, Sara walked to the front of the church and knelt at the altar. There were several others doing the same.

"Frances, why did Sara go to the altar?" Allison asked her new friend.

"Unction. If someone is sick or in need of personal prayers, the priest approaches each and gives a personal prayer and blessing. I would say she is asking a blessing for the baby," she whispered.

"What a beautiful thing. If Sara is feeling anxious or sad or just unsure of anything, she is always better after church," Allison said.

"She and Lauren are both deeply religious. The priest in Wales said both were in the chapel daily. When Sara was baptized into the Church of England, she was baptized as Sara Lyn Dickerson. Those animals in California never contested it, so the law says she is ours."

"I thank God for y'all, Frances," Allison said, taking her new friend's hand.

"And I thank God for you as well. Now we will be grandparents together," Frances said.

The organ began to play; Sara went back to her place beside Scott. Together as a whole family, they prayed, sang, and listened to scripture. Sara was happier than she had ever been.

Saline had begun to believe what Sara had taught her her entire life. She wanted to join the church and wanted to discuss with Father Ron as to how she would do that.

Saline lingered behind the rest of the people so she would be the last person to talk to the priest. She just wanted to get instructions, which Father Ron was happy to give her, telling her also that they would talk further later.

The entire family made sure they were all together before walking outside. Well-wishers spoke to the new couple and greeted the rest of the family to St. Justin's.

When the front doors opened, there was a virtual sea of reporters.

"Well, baby girl, I think we will have to make a run for it," Scott said, smiling.

"I think walking briskly will be better for a girl in my condition," she said, smiling radiantly at her husband.

Then from nowhere was a face from her past that was too overwhelming to deal with.

"So, my little bastard is married. Unfortunately, you are only seventeen," Lord Henry Alexander said and grabbed her upper arm for a second.

Sara's panicked took over, her eyes rolled back, and she fainted. Dr. Quinton, who had been immediately behind her, put his arms out so she fell into them rather the ground. With Sara in his arms, he saw Lord Henry and was taken aback with the hatred that burned for him.

"John, take her back inside," Steve said and handed a limp Sara to him. Steve was the first to respond to Lord Henry.

"You filthy son of a bitch, if something happens to her, I will kill you myself," he said, taking hold of Lord Henry around the throat and forcing him to the ground.

"What the hell do you care? You were just her doctor," Lord Henry said.

"Could someone please call the sheriff?" Steve said.

Then Saline was there. She saw her sister being carried back into the church. She wanted to know who hurt her sister immediately. Then she was looking into the coldest eyes she had ever known. Lord Henry was still on the ground, and Saline attacked him. Saline pulled both knees up and landed with her full weight on Lord Henry's crotch. She then used her fists several well-placed times before Alex reached down and pulled her off her father. Saline continued to swing her fists, but only hit air.

"Honey, go back inside and check on your sister. Okay?" Alex said to the beautiful young woman. Saline resisted.

"I wanted to give him what he gave to us. He was an expert on inflicting pain and humiliation. Let him see how it feels," Saline said, preparing to attack again.

"Ms. Byers, I thought you wanted to become a member of our church. Let's go back inside and talk about what it is you want to be a member of. And your sister is asking for you," Father Ron said, putting his hand out to her.

She looked back at her father and spat in his face. She took Father Ron's hand. "I choose faith. Please get me started, Father," she said, straightening her skirt. "I will never live without faith again." Saline finished, and she and Father Ron walked back to the church.

The reporters continued to take pictures of every person who could possibly be a person of interest. Henry remained on the ground, curled in a ball due to the beating he received from his daughter.

"Those people have kidnapped my children. When the law gets here, I will be taking my children home to California."

Saline continued to walk sedately with the priest.

Lord Dickerson cleared his throat and requested attention of the reporters. "I am Lord George Dickerson from London, England. Sara Lyn Dickerson-Byers and our daughter attended the same private school in Wales for seven years. When she had not been home for two years, she was adopted legally by my wife and me.

"Lord Henry Alexander abandoned the children that he abused nearly three years ago, leaving them here in Texas to starve. Through that act, he lost the right to be his children's father. He told everyone who cared about them that they had died. Our family, which is very powerful, and the Byers family here in Texas, that is also powerful, have adopted the girls and saved their lives.

"Witnesses who are present to testify to that effect are Dr. Alex Carmichael, Dr. Steven Quinton, and Sheriff Randy Oakley. He may try to say that he has diplomatic immunity, but imagine him trying to exert that after he has let his young children starve to death.

"Then there is his uncle who is also here. His Grace Joseph Alexander of Hamburg is one of the wealthiest men in the world. He did not intervene on the children's behalf. Please join me as a decent human being in saying that we will not tolerate him any longer. Thank you," George said and briskly walked back to the church.

Inside the church, Sara had awakened. When she saw the people around her, she knew that she hadn't been dreaming when she saw her stepfather approach her.

"You are safe, baby girl. He can't hurt you," Scott said.

"Can we go home? I never want to leave our house again," she said as a fearful tear started down her cheek.

"You don't think you should go to the hospital here in town first?" Scott asked. "Remember, we need to look after the baby also."

"I am fine, really. It was just shocking to see him," Sara said. Scott helped her to stand. "I want to go home. They can't go there, can they, since Poppa owns the place, right?"

"That's right," Scott said and smiled at him. "Riley has pulled the jeep around to the side entrance. Let's hurry and get you in the jeep and then home," he said. Then the crowd moved around out front of the chapel to act as a decoy of sorts. Scott and Sara made a clean getaway.

"Can I take a nap on the way home? I am so sleepy I can hardly keep my eyes open," she said, nodding off.

Scott knew the effects of pregnancy on a woman. In Sara's case, her body told her she needed rest, and the suggestion was too powerful to ignore. "You can nap. And I am afraid I have to insist on us taking a long nap after we have had lunch at the main house. Okay?" he said. But Sara was already asleep.

When everyone returned to the main house, Allison had smoked a brisket. She started it the night before on low heat so it would be tender.

Father Ron had taken such care with Saline since she made the decision to have faith in something much greater than her father. Six months earlier, she knew that she wouldn't have stopped until she had killed or castrated him.

Now she had a father that loved her, the right kind of love between a father and daughter. She had a second father who was showing her the way to God. She also had a mother who loved and wanted her, complete with more friends and family than she ever thought possible. Saline rode back to the ranch with Riley, Colton, and Lauren. Everyone had unwound by the time they were home. Most of the ladies went to the kitchen to put lunch on the table; the men went to the family room where George and John played pool. Sara had gone to Scott's old room. It was now their room since they were married.

She took her cape and shoes off and lay down on the bed. The room was a little cool, so she reached down and covered herself with her cape and was asleep.

When lunch was ready, she didn't awaken. Scott saw how she was sleeping so sound he didn't awaken her. She could eat when she woke up.

In the dining room, conversation was free flowing, both about the wedding and reception, passing around the pictures of everyone and everything. And of course, what the ladies would love to have seen happen to Lord Henry for showing up at the church.

All at once, the dreaded scream. Everyone was on their feet, running upstairs to Scott's room. She was in the corner and didn't awaken. Parents, both old and new, sisters, brothers, and friends—they all went to try to keep her from hurting herself in the violence of the nightmare.

"Oh no," Frances said. She was the first one to get to her. "Baby Sara, Mummy is here. Wake up for Mummy. Everything is okay," she said and pulled her into her arms. "You have Scott who is worried right here. You have two mummies and two poppas to protect you. He will never get that close again." She held her and started rocking her.

"Run, Saline!" she screamed again and again. Frances continued to rock back and forth.

"Are you okay, Frances?" Allison asked, seeing the tears that streamed down her new friend's face.

"Absolutely. It is part of the little girl we tried so hard to help. She has nightmares. Likely you already know that. You have to be careful of the stairs. In our home in Bath, she ran and fell down them. A friend of ours says these are not dreams. They are called flashbacks. She didn't react when it happened, and to her it is just happening," she said and held the young girl tightly. "Oh my god, what has happened to our little girl when we couldn't find you?" she said and sobbed as she held Sara.

"Here, Frances, let me," Scott said. Scott picked up his wife, knowing this was part of the package he married. "Sara, it is time to wake up. You have to eat so the baby will grow. We have to go back to our house and open some more wedding presents."

Everyone else walked from the room and slowly made their way back to the dining room.

The silence in the room was deafening for a few moments. Saline finally stood. "Momma, I am going for a walk. The four of you need to talk," she said and walked over to Frances and whispered something in her ear. She then walked out the kitchen door.

"Frances. What is it?" Allison asked. "Please."

"I think you know the biggest part, but I don't believe you know very much about Saline's father." Frances took a breath and spoke. "Lord Henry was raised by his mother from the time he was six years old. His father was to take the duke's place one day. His death put Lord Henry as the next in line to head the aristocracy."

"Not to seem ignorant, but is there a difference between the aristocracy and royalty?" Allison asked.

"Germany is a republic, but the aristocracy is the old families of extraordinary wealth that survived World War II. In order to keep Hamburg its duke, they have to have a bloodline that lives up to the expectations of the people," Frances explained. "The people of Hamburg know that the aristocracy is closely related to most of the royal families in Europe.

"Royals are those who are born into royalty or marry royalty or both. We were both from such a family. And down the line, we are also related to Lord Henry, because in the 1800s, Queen Victoria married a German prince. Aristocrats will have their daughters marry a royal for the position. Although it is not that simple, that is the biggest part of it."

"But Sara is not of German blood," Allison said.

"His Grace is not aware of that. He is the one who sent Sara to Meadow Park to be educated, as was indicated," Frances explained. "Joan Redding had an affair after the birth of their first son and conceived Sara. He had intended on divorcing her, so she became pregnant, knowing the duke would never let them divorce with her pregnant."

"Henry hated Sara just for the fact that she existed. He beat her from the time she was in diapers. Starved her, locked her in everything you can imagine, humiliated her by whatever means he could use, and made sure that no one knew she existed. If friends came to their home, she was locked away. The only person allowed to see her was the other children's grandmother, Henry's mother," George said.

"No kids came over to play with her?" Allison said.

"No one really knew she existed. Even His Grace has never seen her. He had the other three kids to only refer to her as the bastard. Lady Catherine tried to have her removed from the home and raise her even though they were not technically related. She saw firsthand what Henry was doing to her," George said.

"Who is that, Lady Catherine, I mean?" John asked.

"Henry's mother," Frances said. "One time, she took both Sara and Saline all the way to New York City. Sara had gotten sick, and Catherine was not leaving Saline in the house to be used as a bargaining tool," Frances said.

"Did she change her mind?" Allison asked. Frances closed her eyes to the memory.

"No, she would never have sent them back. In New York, Catherine called when they arrived. The plan was for her to fly to London with both girls, and we would take both of them to our home in Bath. It is not actually in Bath, but a few miles from there. But before she could think of putting Sara on a plane, she needed to go to the doctor. She went to a hospital in New York, thinking that would be the fastest way to get her seen. In that time someone must have followed them, because Henry showed up at the airport when they were about to board. But rather than let them board, he forced them, because of his status, to be allowed take his children.

"What he did and had done for two solid days was inhuman. His mother nearly died. Sara and Saline were beaten almost to death, and he raped both girls and allowed the three men who had assisted him to take turns to have them as they would for those two days. A week later, Sara was taken to the hospital because she had rheumatic fever and nearly died several times. Henry and his wife went to Las Vegas for a few days when they dropped Sara off in the emergency room," Lord Dickerson said. "On one of his visits to Sara in Wales, we invited him to our apartment in London. He recanted the condition that Sara was in the first time he saw her. She weighed only thirty-two pounds.

"The next time we saw her two months later, it took her weeks before she spoke, and then we discovered Lauren had cancer. We decided that both girls should be taken out of school and tutored at home.

"Watching my two babies heal each other was something I will never forget. The agony that the two of them overcame was nothing shy of a miracle. Sara was terrified of men. Not just men she didn't know, but all men. That includes George, our sons, and even Dr. Quinton." Frances got up and walked to the window and looked out at the activity. "When it was the usual time to send Sara home for Christmas, she would still run and hide if she saw a man come in the room. We did not let her go home that year. Putting her on a plane would have finished her off, and we just could not do it."

"He was never charged?" John yelled.

"As Henry said then, he has diplomatic immunity. He cannot be charged, and if he were, he would be released. Even after he tortured and killed the family nanny," George said.

"He has killed people before?" Allison asked.

"About that same time he beat the kids' nanny to death, even allowed the older boy, Thomas, to take part. He is as big an animal as the rest of them," Frances said. "Lauren, Lady Eugenia, and I are the only people who could get close to her for a while."

"Lady Eugenia?" Allison asked.

"She was the girls' tutor the year they were out of school. She had been an instructor in Wales and had volunteered to take leave to be with them. She knew Sara better than any adult. She even had Sara and Lauren moved to a room that joined hers because of the nightmares that Sara had. She gave Sara a little book and told her to write things that happened to her. She never read it until Sara told her it was okay to do so. It helped her so much that it was not something she carried. When the girls went back to school, Lady Eugenia went back with them."

"Is the girls' grandmother still living?" Allison asked.

"So far as I know. She looks after the girls' younger sister, Sophie. In speaking with her, she says that Henry has left her alone. His uncle has been threatening Henry because of all the negative attention he and Thomas have been getting.

"He knows that Sara is married. It is only a matter of time before he knows she is expecting a baby, making her a perfect person to take his place," Frances concluded.

"Over my dead body." They heard Scott say. "Sara is my wife now. Momma and Daddy have custody of her, as do the two of you. Any of that bunch gets close to her again, I will kill them. They have done all the damage they will ever do to her and Saline."

"George and Frances are just getting us caught up, Scott. You may want to listen, son. Some things are hard to hear," Allison said.

"There is nothing that I have not heard from Sara. Before we married, she wanted to make sure that I knew what I was getting. She was afraid that no one would want her if they knew about her past," Scott said. "And she is awake and will be in here in a minute."

"Does she know she had a nightmare?" Allison asked.

"Yes. She doesn't remember anything though. She never does," Scott said. He walked over to his place at the table and took a drink of his tea.

"She asked me if she and I could go to the grocery store tomorrow," Allison said.

"That should be fine. Take a couple of the hands with you, or have them follow you there and back. Lord Henry is in the county jail for a couple of days. Then he will be sent back to California.

Randy has someone constantly watching the others that were with them," John said.

"I don't doubt anything you say, John, so please don't get me wrong when I ask, are you sure you can keep them safe?" Frances asked.

"I can keep them safe from that trash getting their hands on them again. The reporters are a different story. But I have found that you can learn to function around reporters," John said.

"And the girls don't leave here alone for a while. Saline always has someone with her, and Sara hardly leaves here. She does want to go grocery shopping tomorrow morning, but I will be with her," Allison said.

"I believe there will be safety in numbers, so I would love to accompany you as well," Frances said.

"I would like that," Allison said.

"Will I be able to go to the grocery store?" she asked.

"You remember, you and I have been to the grocery store before without incident. As a matter of fact, you likely will need to go grocery shopping today so you have things to cook. Why don't we go together?" Allison said.

"I would love to accompany you as well," Lady Dickerson said.

"We want to go to," Lauren and Saline said almost in unison.

"Okay," Sara said. "But the people in town have only seen me one time that they know of, and they may not even know who I am without all the finery."

"I hope that is the way of it. But all the same, there is safety in numbers," Allison said.

"Mummy, I need you to go with me the first time anyway. I don't have a clue what to buy. And I have learned much from watching you cook, but do you think it would cost too much to also buy a cookbook? One with big letters and lots of pictures," Sara said.

"Sara, my love, we opened an account not so long ago so you will have no need to worry about money," Scott said.

"Okay," Sara said, a little unsure about spending money.

In her life, she had spent seven years in a girls' school and didn't have to concern herself with money. Then she spent the years since she had returned in poverty. She had never had money that she could spend without worrying if there would be enough. She had never been to the grocery store to buy a bill of groceries. She knew that her life was new, and she had much to learn, but it was not anything she couldn't learn. She just didn't want to take advantage.

Mummy Byers had given her everything that a girl could ever want or need. From clothes to gowns all the way down to feminine hygiene products. She never asked for more. Now she would be able to go to town and shop as she pleased. But it was so new. She hoped that she didn't take advantage.

Then something happened that she could not explain. It was almost like she had tiny wings fluttering in her abdomen. She put her hand on her tummy and smiled a little.

"Sara, is anything wrong?" Allison asked.

"No, nothing at all. I just had this feeling that I can't explain right here," she said.

"Did it hurt?" Scott asked.

"Not at all, it was just a strange feeling," she said with her hand on her tummy that was just becoming noticeable. She smiled at the sensation.

"Do you need to sit down, baby?" Scott asked, worried at she was feeling.

"No. I don't think so." Then she started using her fingers as if counting. Judging from the only time she and Scott had made love, she was four months along. "I think I was just feeling him move the first time."

"Judging from the look on her face, son, there is nothing to worry about. Why don't we eat some breakfast?" Allison suggested.

They took the prepared basket of food to the kitchen and placed the food on the counter, buffet style.

When they were all seated in the living room, John and Scott decided it would be a good time to leave the women to their own devices and for them to go to the office in Dallas. They knew that the people who reported to them were completely competent, but knew also that the oil business, like the ranch, needed attention.

When they arrived, the people in the office were surprised to see Scott. Most had been at the wedding and the reception.

"Sara is such a cute little thing. I don't think that I have ever seen anyone with quite that color of hair before, but it is very becoming. Normally, redheads are freckled and such," Scott's secretary, Geneva, said. It was known that she had had an infatuation with Scott for a couple of years, but Scott had never liked dating people from the office. Everyone at Byers Oil knew their jobs well; thus, to date a valued employee was not productive for the company or the employee.

"Her beautiful hair was the second thing I noticed about her," he said.

"What was the first thing?" Geneva asked, thinking that it had to be something sexually related.

"Her eyes, they are emerald green. You can't help but notice them. They seem to glow," Scott said.

"Oh. I really didn't notice her eyes," she said. Scott picked up some resentment in her voice. He knew of Geneva's attraction to him, but she was in her mid thirties and worked for the company. So he just let it slide.

"Have I got any messages?" Scott asked.

"Several. You take off a few days, and they really start to stack up. I thought about calling you about a couple of them," she said.

Scott looked through the messages and found nothing that was urgent. There were several letters of congratulations, rescheduled meetings, and a few he had to call. But nothing that was urgent. He then went into his office to make some calls and do some paperwork. He and his father had planned on having a business lunch at 1:00 pm, and he was never late. He didn't want to start out his married life by being late.

For months Scott had had a pet project that he had brought up to his father, one that would propel the company into a worldwide oil company and that was to purchase a refinery. In the last few weeks, one had become available, and that was what their meeting was concerning.

Since the energy crisis in 1972, Byers Oil was looking for ways to improve the oil supply in the United States. Refining their own oil instead of selling it to others would get rid of the middle man and thus save money.

John had a big stack of work to do as well. John Byers was an exceptionally organized man. In addition, he knew who his friends were, and he watched out for the people who watched out for him. It had always worked for him in his family, the ranch, and the oil company. He also made a point of hiring people he could trust when his back was turned. When they proved themselves trustworthy, he would give bonuses, and to some, shares of the company as an extra incentive. His employees, he liked to regard as friends and trusted them more than most people in his position. He was in no way, shape, or form a snob. He dined with the people that worked for him and asked them to do nothing that he would not do himself.

With his position as both a rancher and an oilman, he attended the cattle baron's ball and the oilman's ball in Dallas county and the county of which they lived. The events were quite formal and festive, and the entire family took part. But there were hundreds who also attended the balls. They were lavish affairs where the wives wore their best ball gowns and jewelry.

"Mr. Byers, it is almost time for you and Scott to go to lunch," his secretary said.

"Is my son ready to go as well?" he asked.

"Yes, sir. He is waiting for you," she answered.

"Thank you, Judy."

"Sir, may I tell you how I enjoyed the wedding Saturday? I have not met Sara formally as yet, but she is very beautiful. I hope that they have a lifetime of happiness, sir," she said.

Judy had been with the company since before Scott was born. She had always been John's secretary and knew how to handle the office.

"Thank you, Judy. We are all very happy for both of them."

"I didn't catch her older sister's name."

"Saline. She has several names, but Saline is her first name, and she is two and a half years younger than Sara," John said. "Everyone thinks that Saline is older."

"Really? I must say that both of them are extraordinary beauties, but Saline is the most beautiful lady of any age that I have ever seen." Judy knew some of the background of the two girls but didn't like to probe. "The two of you have a good lunch," she said and went back to her desk.

John and Scott took the elevator to the thirty-fifth floor to the Oil Barons Restaurant. It was a private restaurant that requires you to be in the oil business to enter. They were taken to a waiting table where they met with their banker and their attorney. The four men were seated. Everyone ordered and pulled out the business that they had waited for months to conclude.

Contracts were signed, and every detail gone over completely. "I believe that the press has already gotten wind of this," the attorney said.

"I didn't want to say anything to them until the papers were signed and we took over. Would you mind setting up a press conference for about five this afternoon? Will you both be available?" Scott asked.

"We cleared our schedules for today knowing how big this is," the banker said. "And congratulations on your marriage, Scott. We were not able to make the wedding, but I am glad you are happy."

"Thank you, Art, Sara and I are very happy. She was a little concerned about the pictures on the front page of the paper this morning."

"I saw that," Sam said. "You are going to be making headlines for weeks when the press knows of the refinery."

Different people from the restaurant began to come to their table to talk to Scott about the wedding and the pictures on the front of the paper.

"Is she really a royal?" a woman asked.

"Her uncle is a duke in Germany, but she does not associate with him. She would really prefer if you didn't bring it up," Scott said and then wished he hadn't.

When it was clear that they were not going to be able to complete their business in the restaurant, they went back down to the offices.

A few minutes before five, they went downstairs to meet the press and announce the refinery. Scott gave a brief statement and took questions.

"Mr. Byers, do you think that having a refinery will help to ease the energy crisis we keep hearing about?" one asked.

"Yes. I know that it will," Scott said.

"Whose idea was the refinery?" another asked.

"The idea was brought to me by my son," John said. "And I could not help but agree with him, I am proud to say," John said.

"Is the announcement of the refinery in any way related to your marriage to a German noblewoman?"

"No, of course not. One has nothing to do with the other," Scott said.

"Is the new Mrs. Byers from Germany?"

"No. She was born in California but was sent to the UK to be educated with she was five. She returned when she was twelve. She is considered to be a citizen not only of the United States but of the UK and Germany as well," Scott said.

"Is she going to be giving us a statement today?"

"No, she is at home taking care of our house and visiting with friends," Scott said.

The questions continued to come, both about the refinery and the wedding. After about a half hour, they concluded.

Around noon at the ranch, the women left to go into town. Allison, Frances, Sara, Saline, and Lauren were in Allison's town car. Conversation flowed easily among the ladies.

"Sara, George and I would like to invite you and Scott to come to our home in England when things slow down for him here," Frances said.

"Thank you, Lady Dickerson. I am sure that we will," Sara said.

They arrived at the grocery store completely undetected. Allison got a shopping cart, as did Sara. Allison had an idea of what she was going to need to get started as a housewife. Not only with buying food, but cleaning supplies and such. By the time they were finished, they had to start a third shopping cart.

Before they got to the checkout stand, Sara asked Allison what she had to do to write a check.

"Oh, dear, I had not thought of you not knowing how to use them. Don't worry, I will help you," Allison said.

When she had finished writing it, Sara felt like she had taken last rites into womanhood. She smiled at everyone in her party. They walked out of the store into a crowd of over one hundred people, including reporters. All of the women were dumbstruck.

"Lady Dickerson, is Sara Alexander related to you?"

"Her name is Sara Lyn Byers, and yes, we are a very close family," she answered.

"We have heard many conflicting reports about something that happened between her uncle and a member of the Byers family. Could you clear that up please?"

"No," Sara said. "I don't know who the people who trespassed on the ranch were. I do know that they were too uncouth to be anyone of any titled person I know. I had never met any of them."

"Is it true that aside from your sister that none of your family was invited to your wedding?"

"Yes, that is correct. I had not seen any of them in years, and though we had lived with our mother until a few months ago, she is a woman of very low moral character," Sara answered.

"So you ran away from home and left your mother?"

"You crazy bitch!" Saline yelled. "My sister has never left anyone."

"Saline," Sara said softly. "It is quite all right. My little sister is easily upset at the mention of our mother's name as a victim. Our mother was directly responsible for…" Sara's eyes began to tear and she took a breath, "our baby brother's death. Saline and I took care of him all the days of his life. We saved him so many times, and our mothers' selfish unthinking act took him away from us."

"So you ran away?"

"No," Sara whispered. She seemed to be looking for a safe place for a minute.

"She never ran. She is the bravest, most honorable young woman I have ever known. The night before Sara, her little sister, and baby brother were taken away, it was cold and raining. And staying in the house was not safe. Their mother would not protect them from her drunken, out-of-his-mind newest husband.

"She had broken bones in her face, four ribs, starved them, and her mother would not let her buy the heart medicine she had taken since she was eight, so she was dying. She had not slept, eaten, or felt safe most of her life. She stayed in the house, all 106 pounds of her, and gave her siblings time to get to the safety of a falling-down barn. The next morning, she walked to work to provide food for her family and collapsed in the arms of the man she married.

"No one from any place tried to keep them from harm. So we took them from that. Germany forgot them. Their mother is a gutter rat, and any person who thinks that they will call either of these girls anything will answer to me," Allison said.

"And whom would we be quoting?"

"Mrs. John Byers," Allison said. "My husband and I filed the paperwork and now have custody of the two of them. We won't stand back and watch one more thing happen to our girls, and that includes them being slandered in the press. Now, we have things to do. Please excuse us," Allison asked that the young man who was pushing her shopping cart to follow her.

She also made sure that their little shopping party stayed intact.

When they were all in the car, Saline began to rant. It seemed so strange to Allison that the young girl was so well behaved at the ranch; just a little push in the wrong direction made her become violent. Saline was indeed the strong sister, but her temper and youth made her dangerous to herself. It worried Allison what would happen if someone approached her and her sister or the family was not there.

After months at the ranch, the two girls seemed undone by the comments of a few nosey reporters.

"Don't worry, Sara, this was your first time with reporters, and you did well," Lauren said to her friend.

"Saline, are you okay, sis?" Sara said.

"I would still like to go back and strangle that bitch with her microphone cord," she said.

"I would love to have seen it, but likely it would not have been a good idea," Sara whispered.

Sara sat back in the seat and put her hand on her belly. She laid her head back and closed her eyes briefly. She was so sleepy. The press throwing questions at her had gone to the back of her mind. The way that she felt here lately, a nap always seemed to help just about anything. Before she knew it, she was asleep.

CHAPTER 8

A New Life

Allison, Frances, Lauren, and Saline talked for most of the ride home. Allison was worried that Sara had fallen back into the dark place that she had been in several months ago when she was so terrified yet functioned. She looked into her rearview mirror and saw Sara with her head resting against the back of the seat, sound asleep.

"I don't think that we have to worry about the way the bride is worrying about what just happened," Allison said.

The other ladies looked to Sara and laughed quietly.

"I can't believe she can just go to sleep after something so unsettling," Lauren said.

"But I believe she needs the rest, for both her and the baby. After what happened when she was twelve, she really needs this baby," Saline said and looked to see if anyone was going to question her. Saline didn't know who knew about what she was talking about. When no one said anything she let the entire subject drop.

When Saline was certain that her sister was sound asleep, the rest of the women continued to chat, although in hushed voices.

"Has she made an appointment to see a doctor about the baby?" Frances asked.

"My brother Alex has made an appointment for her in Tyler for day after tomorrow. Alex knows that there may be some problems, so he found the very best," Allison said.

"I can hardly wait to be an aunt. And with us living so close, I can see the baby every day," Saline said with all the excitement in the world in her voice.

"I do hope that we can find out her date of confinement. I would love to be here for the birth," Frances said.

"Mummy, I don't have to worry about school for several months. If it is quite all right with Sara and Scott, and of course the Byers family, I would love to stay with Sara until she has the baby. Will that be okay, Mummy?" Lauren asked.

Frances thought of years before when Sara pushed Lauren so much when she had cancer. She had been willing to shave her own head so Lauren didn't feel so alone. Lauren had told her not to. And as Sara had said, she would stay with her until she was well, which included not going home at Christmastime one year.

When they thought Sara had died, the family had been grief-stricken for years. Frances believed that if not for her friendship, her daughter may have died.

"I believe that would be a very good idea, Lauren. Watching the interactions of the three of you in the last couple days has been a treat. And thank you, all of you, for your generous hospitality.

"George has to leave in a few days, business things, but with your permission, I would like to stay just a little longer to reacquaint myself with someone I thought I had l lost forever," Frances said.

"I was hoping that you would say that," Allison said. She had never met anyone from overseas before, but had made fast friends with Frances and her family. Through long conversations, she had discovered that Frances was a second cousin to the queen of England. She was such an important lady, yet so giving. The cousin that Frances had spoken of reminded her very much of Allison. Both women were wives, mothers, were stern, and had their own empires to see to.

To Frances and George, this had been a real vacation. Aside from the news people at the grocery store, everything else had gone well.

The following day, Sara was to go see Uncle Alex. She knew that she needed a doctor to deliver the baby, but the thought of a man touching her in such an intimate way scared her. The Byers family had been so kind to her that she hated to disappoint them, so she had agreed to go.

That night, Sara tried hard to show Scott that everything was going well. But the harder she tried, the more he could see something was wrong. It was her first time to cook in her new kitchen, and she wanted everything to be perfect. Momma Byers had helped so much in telling her what she needed to have in the house.

Since she had gotten home, she had tried to shake off the press conference outside the grocery store. She had decided to tell the people nothing but the truth, and yet they wanted more. In the end, she didn't know what to say. She thanked God over and over that Allison had been there. Never before had she had someone to stand up for her like she had.

"Did Uncle Alex find a doctor to deliver the baby?" he asked.

"Yes. He is in Tyler. His name is William Chambers," she said.

"Did you set an appointment?" he asked.

"Uncle Alex did. I am supposed to go in day after tomorrow. I don't want to go, Scott. I would rather deliver at home than to go to some strange man I don't know," she said.

"I don't really think that is something you would want to do. Remember Pulling Calf 101?" he said.

"Yes. That is just about how much I don't want to go to a doctor like that," she said.

"Having babies is painful. Have you thought of that?" he asked and then nearly swallowed his tongue when the words were out. Sara just looked at him.

"What if he can tell what happened before?" She stopped herself.

"I doubt that moron a few years ago was even a doctor. And that was nothing you did wrong. Our baby has nothing to do with that." He could see he was getting no place. "What about if I go with you?"

"You have to go to work. You just had the refinery deal finalized," she said.

"Baby girl, there is nothing more important to me than you. Tell you what. Daddy assumed that you and I would be gone a couple of weeks on a honeymoon. How about if we go see this doctor together and then we will go and have lunch and do some shopping. You are going to need some clothes to let our child grow. Not to mention things for the nursery."

"Are you sure? I don't think this is a man's province," she said.

"Well, let's just change the rules a little. What time do you have to be there?" he asked.

"Ten a.m.," she said.

"Good, that will give us time for shopping and the most expensive lunch money can buy," he said.

"Okay," Sara answered in a manner of a lamb being led to slaughter.

Scott knew that he was not going to score any points until the visit was over, and she was not afraid. So he stopped talking and helped her finish making the meal, and they sat down to eat.

"You learn fast. This is good, what is it?" he asked.

"Lasagna, I found it in the cookbook I just got," she said.

"Momma is a great cook, but I don't think she has ever tried Italian," he said.

Sara smiled. It was their first meal that she had fixed; she was so glad she had done well. She was determined that they were not going to have to eat easy things like hot dogs until she learned to cook.

They talked about other things including family, the refinery, and horses. Then she told him about Lady Dickerson and Lauren staying for a while longer.

"I could tell she and Mom got along well. Lauren is welcome to stay here. I think we can find a place to put her," he teased, gesturing toward their very large home.

"Lauren says she is giving us time alone and is happy to stay at the main house. Besides, I think that she and Saline really love each other as well."

"I like Lauren's way of thinking." He smiled, leaning over and kissing Sara thoroughly.

Sara was anxious about the doctor's visit. But she knew that the life inside of her was precious, and with her medical background, it was necessary.

She was up early on the day to go and see Dr. Chambers. She showered and got dressed in a lovely full skirt and matching sweater, then pulled on stockings and her dress boots. She brushed her hair to a high gloss and got her coat out of the closet.

Scott had dressed like usual in his good jeans and Western shirt and then pulled on his good pair of boots that he wore to the office, and topped all that with his hat.

They drove to Tyler, and Sara rarely spoke. He hoped it would not be as bad for her as she thought. When they arrived, they got out of the jeep and checked in. Uncle Alex had sent her complete records so they didn't have the usual mountain of paperwork.

When the nurse came and called Sara, he thought she was going to bolt and run, but she stood to walk in along with Scott.

"Sir, you can wait here," the nurse said.

"I prefer to stay with my wife. She is a little nervous," Scott said.

"Sir, it is office policy that only the patient is to go in," she said, tapping her pen on the file she carried with Sara's name on it.

"There is no question as to whether I stay with my wife. Sara is my wife, and she wants me to be there."

"Your wife is a grown woman and needs to take responsibility for herself," she said.

Scott took a breath. For a moment, the nurse thought she had won but then, "Tell us where we need to be. Mrs. Byers is expecting a baby, and standing idle with you running your head is not doing her any good."

The nurse's mouth formed a fine, grim line of defeat. "I will let Dr. Chambers know that you are here and then you can go back where you belong," she said and led them to an exam room. "You

216

need to take everything off and put this on," she said, about half throwing a gown at Sara.

"Thank you for your hospitality," Scott answered. After the door closed, Scott assisted his wife to change. Her hands were shaking so hard she could barely manage the buttons. When she was seated, a knock came at the door, and entered a man in his fifties, with a kind, smiling face.

"Mrs. Byers, I am Dr. Chambers. Rumor has it one of us is going to be a mother," he said.

"Yes, sir," she said, blushing.

"Well, tell me about yourself," he said.

Sara looked at Scott and was speechless.

"My wife is a little nervous. Maybe I can help. I am Scott Byers," he said, extending his hand.

The doctor took his hand and shook it. "Very nice to meet you both. First things first. Do you know when your last period was?" he asked.

"The last part of June, I forgot the date," she said.

"I can guess pretty close," Dr. Chamber said. "How much did you weigh before you were pregnant?"

"She weighed about 110 pounds. She has been trying to put on weight for the last few months," Scott said.

"It says here that you are five feet six inches tall. Let's see what the scale says," he said, putting his hand out to assist her to stand. Her eyes widened a little.

"Here, baby girl, let me help you," Scott said.

She had not stepped on a scale in months. She had no idea how much she weighed.

"One hundred nineteen pounds, and you are a little over four months pregnant. Your due date is around April 2. Now have a seat again, and we will see how everything looks," he said.

Sara did as requested. Dr. Chambers pulled out the table so the exam table was longer and she was lying flat. He had some electronic instrument in his had he had picked up from the counter. "This will feel a little cold, but it will not hurt."

"What are you doing?" Sara asked as he rolled the instrument on her low abdomen.

He removed his ear pieces and gave them to Sara. "What is that?" she asked, listening to what sounds like something underwater and looking at the screen.

"That is your baby," Dr. Chambers said and looked at the picture that the sounds were picking up. "You are having a son in a few months." He point to what appeared to be a third leg. Scott knew immediately what he was referring to.

Sara forgot her anxiety as she listened to the sound of her son in her belly. Every movement, the doctor reflected kindness, not so different from Uncle Alex. Sara was lost in dreams of the start of a family with Scott. Tears of happiness filled her eyes and down her cheeks. Her smile was radiant.

After the exam part was finished, he asked more questions, then he gave her directions. "You are very young, but you are healthy and it is my job to keep you that way, and I will. So I refuse to have you to worry.

"What you do need to think about is putting on more weight and getting plenty of rest. Drink plenty of fluids, and take vitamins. Your baby is perfectly developed and needs to gain weight. Any morning sickness?" he asked.

"No, I am just sleepy all the time," she said.

"You have had rheumatic fever?' he asked.

"Yes, sir, when I was eight," she said.

He picked up the chart and saw that she had scarring on her heart. "Do you take any medicine?"

"Medicine to keep my heart from beating too fast. Dr. Quinton says I have a scar on my heart, so it can't get bigger. Sometimes I have to take medicine if my chest hurts," she said.

His face took on a concerned look. "First, continue to take your Lanoxin, just like you are doing. But don't think about taking the other. If your chest hurts, call me. Are you talking about Dr. Stephen Quinton, the cardiologist from California?" he asked.

She didn't say anything.

"Yes. That is her cardiologist. He has moved back here and is on staff at Baylor," Scott said.

"Is our baby going to be born alive?" she asked, fear-filled because of his concern.

"I am going to make sure of it. I will also make sure Dr. Quinton has privileges at St. Mary's. I look forward to meeting him.

"I am afraid I will have to be serious for a minute. Your heart can't expand right now, so I am afraid we need to limit your activities—nothing that requires very much exertion. That means jogging, horseback riding, swimming. I think you can figure out what from there. Take at least three to four naps a day. You may do things around the house, but don't push it. Church is fine, and if you go shopping, make sure you are not alone," he continued on telling her how and what to do and what to expect. Then he said it was okay to get dressed.

On his way out of the exam room, he tapped Scott's shoulder lightly. "Baby girl, I will be right back, are you okay?"

"We are fine." She smiled. She was still thinking about her baby boy, and it was now real to her.

"Dr. Chambers, is there a problem?"

"Not so far. I have drawn the usual blood to send. But rheumatic fever is nothing to play with. It is the cold and flu season. If she gets a sore throat, call me. If a sore throat turns out to be strep throat, she will need antibiotics early. And she needs to see me every two weeks to keep a very close eye on her," he said.

"She will be here. And thank you for being so kind with her. She is afraid of everything," Scott said.

"Don't let her know this, but Alex and I are friends and only want the best possible care for Sara. He has told me about her. I will take care of her. I give you my word," he said and was off.

A few seconds later, Sara appeared in the doorway, and they left the doctor's office. When they walked to the jeep, from out of nowhere, there were bulbs popping and questions being asked. Scott took Sara's elbow and urged her back into the doctor's office.

"I am going to get the jeep and pull it closer," he said and fairly ran out to get to it. He turned the key and pulled it into gear. When he was within ten feet of the door, he got out and helped Sara from the door to the jeep. Both just waved without ever saying one word to the press.

"Dr. Chambers. Why did you break office policy like that?" Gina, his nurse, asked.

"You have never taken care of someone like her before. She is going to take kid gloves and patience, period."

"We have seen patients that are as young as fourteen. She is seventeen, hardly a novelty," Gina said.

"Have you ever taken care of royalty? I haven't. And I don't know if you noticed while you were stating all the rules, but the little thing was scared to death. She has a bad history, and you did not help by scaring her," he said, scolding her.

"You baby her now, and she will never be able to grow up," Gina answered.

"Tell me, Gina. Could you handle that?" he asked, gesturing out the front window.

"Who are they?" she said about all the people around Scott and Sara.

"The press. Mrs. Byers is the niece of a German duke and was educated in the same school as other royalty," he said.

"She is *that* Sara Byers?" Gina asked.

"The one and only. So the next time she is here, you show respect. And if anyone from this office talks to the press about her, they are fired," he said and went into the next room.

Gina watched as the young couple navigated their way through the people who seemed to be charging them. "Respect?" she whispered. "They deserve a medal of valor."

Gina had always believed that it was essential for doctors and nurses to keep a professional distance from their patients, but in this instant, she could almost feel the shy girl's distress. Gina decided that the next time that they have an appointment, she would tell them to come to the employee entrance at the back; that could help.

Sara was a little more relaxed after the appointment at Dr. Chambers's. Scott had not stopped smiling since he had found out he was going to have a son.

"Do you want to keep it a secret what the baby is?" Scott asked.

"Are you kidding? I would blow up. Have you got any names you have been thinking about?" she asked.

"John Austin Byers; it is Daddy's name. What do you think?" he asked.

"Perfect," she said, taking his hand and putting her head on his shoulder. "Where are we going to lunch?" she asked.

"Do you like seafood?" he asked.

"I love seafood. I haven't got to eat it in years, but I love it," she said.

"How about Red Lobster? I would suggest the East Texas Cattle Barons or Oil Barons clubs, but everyone there knows who I am and will likely swamp us. I would rather have you to myself. Unless you want to go there," he said.

"Not this trip. I rather want you to myself as well."

Scott looked down into her face and saw that she was absolutely radiant. "Do you think they have clam chowder?"

"If they don't, I will tell them to make it," he jested. "What kind of seafood do you like?"

"Everything except squid and mussels. I love crab and everything else."

"I usually end up on the surf and turf."

"I would think no less. I also like steaks with seafood. But like I said, it has been a while since I have gotten to eat them," she said. "Momma was always trying to get me to drink white wine with my seafood, but I don't like alcohol."

They arrived at Red Lobster and were seated, as requested, in a corner booth. Scott also asked the waitress not to let anyone know if they start asking about them as a couple. They were, after all, a unique-looking couple. They ordered and continued to have mostly small talk and of course about the baby. Scott was glad to see Sara enjoying herself so completely. As noon approached, the restaurant started getting crowded.

A woman came over to their table and asked if they were Scott and Sara Byers as they were finishing their lunch.

"Yes, mam, but we really don't want a bunch of people to know that we are here," Scott explained.

"I completely understand. That is why I came over. There are reporters who know you are here and have been running a camera for the last few minutes. I just thought you may want to know," she said and turned to walk away.

"Please wait," Sara asked and stood, with the woman between her and the camera. "What is your name?"

"I am Miranda Edwards," she answered.

"Thank you," Sara said and then touched her arm softly. "Truly, thank you."

She smiled, feeling like she had really done something for the couple.

Sara turned back to Scott and retook her seat beside her husband. "Do you think that people will get tired of following us around after a little while?"

"I think that as long as we don't provoke any gossip, they will get tired of me marrying royalty and you marrying the most eligible bachelor in Texas," Scott said with a twinkle in his eyes.

"But I am not really royalty. Last year I was just poor white trash according to whispers that I would hear."

"You have never been trash!" Scott said with a little edge in his voice. "I have heard from people who thought you had died. That was the reason no one was looking for any of you," Scott said. Then he saw out of the corner of his eye, people moving slowly toward them. "I believe it is time for us to move on. What do you think?"

"I am right behind you," she answered.

"Then you are in the wrong place." He clasped her hand in his and pulled her to his left side. "I always want you at my side, not my backside." He smiled.

"Then I will always be here," she said.

They walked from the restaurant to the jeep, through the people popping pictures and asking questions around them. Scott opened Sara's door and firmly closed it when she was inside. They drove slowly and turned on the highway.

When Scott was sure no one was following them, they went to the mall for shopping. They went to two high-end department stores and stayed shopping for about two hours. Both decided they had better head back to the ranch, to their family awaiting news of the pregnancy and the health of the mom-to-be.

Most of the family had stayed close to the house that day, just for the purpose of finding out firsthand any information. So it was not a surprise that they stopped at the main house before they went to their house.

When they entered through the kitchen, Allison and John were sitting at the dining table, talking, mostly small talk to pass the time until they had news of the health of its newest members. When neither Scott nor Sara was smiling when they entered, both thought the worst-case scenario. Sara had been through so much that everyone was only cautiously optimistic.

They walked over to the table, and Sara sat with Scott behind her, standing. "Momma, Daddy," he said, reaching in his pocket and pulling a picture from the pocket over his heart. He handed it to his father.

"What is this, son?" he father asked, looking at the strange picture.

"His name is John Austin Byers, your 100 percent healthy grandson, whose birthday is sometime around the first of April," Scott said, and then his and Sara's smiles threatened to cause permanent damage to their faces.

Allison fairly screamed with joy, hugging each of the children. John stood and shook hands with his son, hugging him, and then kissed Sara's cheek.

"What about Sara?" Allison asked.

"She has to take it a lot little easier, but she is well and getting stronger. But no strenuous activities, gain a little weight, and take three to four naps a day. Because of her recent illness, she will be going to the doctor every two weeks, but that is about it," Scott said.

"Scott took me to eat seafood. I think I may have gained five pounds at the restaurant," Sara said.

Everyone laughed with them. "Where is everyone?" Scott asked.
"I believe nearly everyone on the ranch is in the den," John said.
"What do you say, baby girl? You ready to tell our world?"
"I have been ready for hours," she said.

When they walked in, silence filled the room. "I would like to introduce, John Austin Byers, the second, our perfectly healthy son," Scott said.

Cheers, hugs, and handshakes filled the room. Saline, Lauren, Mary, and Maria giggled like schoolgirls. Then the room heard a whole new sound, the sound of Sara giggling joyously. Everyone was proud. They had been through so much to bring them to this point. But everyone had agreed that they would wait for the big celebration after the baby was born.

After a time, they decided that Sara needed a little rest and went to their own house.

It was a joyous time on the ranch. The holiday season was just around the corner, and they had gotten good news.

Before long it was Thanksgiving Day. Everyone on the ranch was invited to the main house to celebrate, or they could celebrate privately in their own homes.

In the south, it is an unspoken rule that if a woman attends a meal, they bring a course. As there were over two hundred people in the house, it was a huge meal.

The ranch hands set up the tables in the huge formal dining room that had been built as part of the main house for just such occasions.

The Byers family liked to have the people present on Thanksgiving, because they made the ranch possible. Each ranch hand got their Christmas bonuses at that time so they could start their Christmas shopping as soon as they wanted.

It was a relaxed family atmosphere, and everyone present enjoyed themselves completely. It seemed like so much time had passed since the wedding, but it had only been a few weeks. But the difference in that stage of pregnancy spoke for itself. Her tiny waist from the wedding had taken on the physique of a very pregnant young lady. She had seen Dr. Chambers for the second time and had gained two pounds.

The change in Gina's attitude was easily felt. As they were leaving, she told them about the entrance that they used for the office that they could use. Both were thankful, as the reporters seemed to come from everywhere, especially when they had seen the couple emerge from the doctor's office the first time.

When obviously she had started to show, two weeks later, Scott addressed the issue. The growing group of reporters called him anything from Sir Scott to Your Majesty. He smiled and didn't correct.

"Is it true that you are expecting a baby?" someone asked.

"Yes, I am," she said simply.

"When is the baby due?' another asked.

"A little ahead of schedule," Sara said.

"Is that why you married so young?"

"No. I didn't even know we were having a baby until at the reception. I don't know how she managed to keep that from everyone. Absolutely, no one, except her knew. I still don't know how I missed that," he said, winking at Sara. "But at least the good news is that I can still tell when a cow is going to calve."

Everyone got a good laugh.

"Your Grace, did you have morning sickness?"

"My name is Sara Byers. And no, I have just been sleepy. I believe people saw that I fell asleep at the reception," Sara said.

"Now, we really need to return to the ranch," Scott said, and he and Sara left.

That night, every channel reported about the Texas royalty that was expecting a baby and had the commentary that they had answered.

After Thanksgiving, it was the season of Advent in the Episcopal Church, the time of year when a young couple traveled across the desert to give birth to the Messiah. The only happy holidays that she had ever had were those that she stayed in the UK for. Now she and

Saline had a happy home. She hoped that her mother was well in her pregnancy but rationalized that she had six living children, so it was not a mystery for her.

In truth, she had no idea when her mother was even due. She said in the winter, but not when. She prayed for her mother to be well and have a healthy child, but there was no way that she was going to visit with her.

But if she thought too much about it, it would start bothering her, and she didn't need that.

In the weeks before Christmas, various different shopping parties went out to purchase Christmas presents for everyone on their individual lists. With the exception of a cool day every few days, it was starting out to be a very cold fall leading into winter.

A few days after Thanksgiving, Scott surprised Sara by bringing home a Christmas tree. He told her that since he got the tree, she could decide on what sort of ornaments to use. With that, Sara took great care in decorating the tree. She bought multicolored lights, then bought red and gold garland. When she was checking out, she saw some metal individual ornaments in several Christmas shapes. She thought for a second about something that would make this Christmas special. A keepsake—she would get an ornament for each person on her list and put a name and the year on it. Then she picked up one that said "Our first Christmas." That would be the first ornament, and every year she would get a new one and add to it. Next year she would have to get one for their baby's first Christmas.

With the things that she had already gotten, both for friends and family, not to mention the things for the tree, she was feeling a little guilty for having spent so much. But it was the birthday of the king, and he, after all, gave his life for them.

The Sundays before the Nativity, several members of the family would accompany Scott and Sara to church. Saline, who referred to the Lord as Sara's God, rarely missed a Sunday. Lauren, of course, always attended. She and Sara, when in school, attended services whenever the doors were open.

There were people who attended services to get closer to someone in the news but didn't learn anything that a newspaper or TV crew would want to know.

The entire family attended services on Christmas Eve. John, who had never attended services at St. Justin's, smiled when the services were over, saying that he felt like he had just gone to the gym to go to church.

The doctor had told Sara that she really needed to get more rest. She had been to the doctor a few days before Christmas and had lost half a pound. Dr. Chambers didn't scold, only told her that the baby was very well, but the mommy needs rest.

John had said that he would really rather if she and Scott would wait until later in the morning to come to the house. He said that Allison had Lauren and Saline to assist her, so they needed to have some time together, because next year they would have a baby to look after.

Sara thought on the way home that she would never sleep that night because the idea of having a loving husband and family to look forward to would keep her awake. Scott seemed to sense her quandary, so when they got home, he made a fire in both the living room and their bedroom. He wanted to make sure that they had the cozy warmth of the fire that Sara seemed to enjoy so much.

When they crawled into bed, Scott decided to find out about the more pleasant parts of Sara's mostly dark past.

"Tell me about Wales," he said.

"Wales? Why?" she asked.

"You hear about England and Scotland all the time on the news, but never Wales."

Sara leaned back against him and could almost picture the landscape. "It never really gets warm there, and it rains and snows all year round. But after you have been there a few weeks, and your knees callous a little bit, you come to love it," she said, taking a breath. "School was in the country, much like here. I used to sit in front of the fire downstairs after I thought everyone had gone to bed and dream about a life in the country forever and never having to return to California.

"After I had been in school a couple of years, I looked over my shoulder and saw Lady Eugenie, my elocution and deportment teacher, standing on the stairs. She didn't say anything, so I looked back at the fire," Sara said, turning her face up to look into Scott's face. "Sometimes I thought I could see that someone would love me someday.

"I went to her class the next day, and she asked if she could talk to me. She said she knew that there were things that happened that I needed to find an escape from. She had a little book that she handed me with no writing in it. She asked if I would like to write the things down while I sat before the fire so I wouldn't have to worry about them. And she said she would not read it unless I asked her to. She even said she would keep it in her desk so no one would come across it." Sara smiled. "No one had ever given me anything they didn't have to before."

"What about at Christmas?" Scott asked.

"If I went to California, there were always boxes under the tree with my name on them, but they were empty. It really didn't matter to me, because I didn't need anything there except Saline.

"Then Lauren would always bring me something from her family. The card was always signed, 'We love you, Mummy Frances and Poppa George,'" she said and got quiet.

"Did you write in the little book?" Scott asked.

"I did. So much so that I wrote on every page. I told Lady Eugenie that I didn't care if she read it. Sometimes she would come and get me to take walks with her in the spring and summer. There are mountains and rolling hills in the part of Wales were we were. Meadow Park is in the country. I don't know if I mentioned that. When the wild flowers and the heather would start to come out and the fields turned green, I would have to wash my white wool sox every night from running when we would go on our walks. She was like you, she listened a lot. I hadn't thought about her in a long time.

"Did I tell you the valley that was below us had a river through it? Someday I want to go back there just to see if she is still there.

"She taught me to curtsy properly, for court," she said.

"Tell me what that means," Scott asked.

"It will sound silly to you. You are smart and know all those things that you really need to know," she said.

"I like silly," he whispered. "I believe that while you were there, maybe God thought you needed some silly."

Sara smiled up at him and then snuggled back against him. "When we turned twelve, we knew that we were to go to Buckingham Palace, where Her Majesty, the Queen, was, and our name would be called, then we'd walk a few steps forward and curtsy to her. She's a nice lady. She would smile as we would do our duty. And we would be real members of the queen's court."

"Who is it who gets to do that?" Scott asked.

"Noblewomen, members of noble families from different countries. They didn't know that I was not really one of them. You have to have your best set of manners when presented. I was introduced as Lady Sara Lyn Dickerson. Strange, because I have never even been to Germany, and I never want to go," she said.

"Why?"

"What if I get there and then they looked at me and know? Sir Henry says they will take one look at me and send me to the gas chambers with the other six million bastards they already killed," Sara said with eyes wide.

"He is wrong. You are the most beautiful thing I have ever seen. And if this were Wales or England, I would be the next king of the ranch and you my queen," Scott said.

Sara didn't say anything, but she smiled.

"Does it get as cold there as here?"

"Much, much colder, especially in the fall and winter. We would always have lots of snow. But I never had a warm pair of arms that wanted me until a few months ago," she said.

"How did you and Lauren meet?" he asked.

"The first day that we were there, Lauren was running around and saw me sitting by the fire. I had been put on a plane the day before, then arrived in London, and then driven to school. I was so sleepy that I fell asleep sitting cross-legged before the fire. Lauren didn't make fun of me. She just sat beside me until I woke up and saw her there. She told me that she was Lady Lauren Dickerson. And I told her who I was, and we were friends from then on.

"When I was eight and was sick for one whole summer in California, in the hospital, she wrote me at least weekly. We had to write in French because I didn't know how to write in English at the time. Lady Dickerson would take pictures to send me.

"Both of us took dance and music and such, so we were always together for all but a month of the year. The following year, we were playing on the same team in cricket, and Lauren tripped over a rock and broke her leg. That is when they found she had cancer. Lady Dickerson got permission from the head mistress to take me out of school to be with Lauren, and we were tutored.

"She went through so much, and she still lost her leg. She thought that she was going to die all the time. Her hair fell out, and she cried so much that I took the scissors and cut about two feet off my hair and put a rubber band around it and asked Lady Dickerson if she would make Lauren a wig and make her feel better," Sara said.

"How much hair did you have left?" he asked.

"Depended on where you looked. I didn't do a very good job cutting it. When her lady's maid got done, it was fashioned and went to about my shoulders, and it was so curly without the weight that I told Lauren not to lose her new wig because I didn't like short hair," Sara said, smiling. "She laughed and told me I looked like Shirley Temple. It was so good to hear her laugh again. Her lady's maid did my hair every morning and even fashioned it like Shirley Temple."

"Did she get her wig?"

"Yes, of course. That is why I gave it to her. She wrapped her arms around me and squeezed so tight. I stayed with them for nearly a year before we went back. I taught Lauren to walk again. Then, one day, I got our tap shoes and said we were going to dance. Lauren is the best tap dancer you have ever seen. It took a couple of weeks to get her to where she got the hang of it, but she dances better now than before. And you brought them back into my life. I love you, Scott," Sara said and began kissing him thoroughly.

Scott ran his hands through her hair, and soon they were enjoying the pleasures of each other's bodies. Scott was restrained because he didn't want to hurt Sara or their son, but both thoroughly enjoyed their first Christmas Eve together. They fell asleep in front of the fire, in each other's arms.

Christmas morning at Joan Redding's farm, the house was cold. Yes, Joan had bought heaters for the farmhouse, but she completely forgot to call the gas company. Oscar had been released from his four-month stay in jail to finish his term on probation. He had taken a job cleaning up an auto repair shop and hated the thought of being away from his fix. After several months not receiving anything for his nerves, he was intent on securing enough to keep him feeling good. But try as he would, he still made only minimum wage, and that barely paid the bills. Now, he was stuck in a cold house without the means to fill the gas tank or money to even get beer.

"You are going to work some overtime," Joan said. "I can't work right now. I am carrying your kid."

"My nerves can't take any more of this. Why didn't you just get rid of that kid? Do you even know when you are going to have it so you can get you a job?" he asked, looking at his wife. His normally tall, thin wife now looked so misshapen. Her abdomen made her look like a freak. Her eyes seemed to be bugged because of her sobriety. He couldn't think about touching her at all.

"All you had to do is bring those girls home, and things would have been back to normal if you would have taken Sara when you saw her. You didn't have to have any conversations with her." Joan laughed out loud. "The thought that she kicked your ass is laughable. You deserved to go to jail."

"You had better stop talking. I can't control myself when I get mad like that. I will go crazy if you don't stop," he said.

"You are worthless," Joan said, walking away.

"Don't you walk away from me. I am your husband," he yelled.

"Husband?" Joan said, turning back to him, laughing. "From what I understand, you made several men a good wife."

"Stop, you bitch," he yelled.

"Maybe your problem all along is that you prefer to be with a man. Yeah, I can see that." She laughed. "My husband the choo-choo," she added for further effect.

"You're one to talk, you whore!" he yelled.

Joan slapped him, and that was it. Oscar lost his head and slugged her square in the face.

Joan Redding was very well versed in the art of being attacked by a man. She got up and used her very long, thick fingernails and scratched his face and neck so deep that it started to bleed immediately.

After a few minutes, Oscar, unable to make her beg for mercy, used his fist and slugged her in the abdomen as hard as he could, prompting her water to break. He froze when he saw the sight; he screamed like a little girl.

When Joan felt the first contraction, she also started yelling. She knew that she needed to get to a hospital. She needed her spinal block and a slug of Demerol.

Oscar got her to the old Pinto and drove the twelve miles into town to the small hospital. Joan had never been in labor without having a spinal and given pain medication.

Alex Carmichael was in the hospital when she arrived. When Oscar told him their names, he knew who they were and what they had done. He remembered little Jody's lifeless body and how hard it had been on his two older sisters and his sisters' family. Now this woman, who cared so little for her children, was here to have yet another child. He saw the swelling in her face from what looked like a recent blow. He also saw what looked like claw marks on her husband's face that were starting to clot.

"I am eight months pregnant, and my water broke. I need a spinal and some Demerol," Joan said.

"How many times have you had a baby?" Alex asked.

"This is number 7. I need some drugs. I am in agony," she said.

Alex rolled his eyes at his nurse and asked that she get her to a room. Amy did as requested. She had worked for Dr. Carmichael for twelve years, and she respected him. He had delivered hundreds of babies in the small clinic. That is, the uncomplicated pregnancies.

He would send the complicated pregnancies to Dallas or Tyler. He thought of how far along Sara was now.

Alex had planned on being at the ranch by lunchtime, but an emergency had come in, and he had to get it taken care of before he left to go to the ranch. Now he didn't know yet how long this would take. He waited a few minutes for his nurse to help the woman change into a hospital gown and settle her in bed so he could examine her.

Alex knocked on the door and then entered the hospital room. "I am Dr. Alex Carmichael. Who is your doctor?" he asked.

"I have not been to the doctor as yet," she answered.

"Yet?" Alex questioned. "When exactly where you planning on going? Looks like you are fixing to pop."

"Well, my damned daughter and her sister ran away from home, and my older daughter is the one who makes us a living. I couldn't afford to go to the doctor," she said. "I need a spinal block. I am in pain."

Alex controlled his anger toward her for the moment. "I need to do an exam to see how far in labor you are," he said. Amy helped her to lie back and raise her knees. "You are only dilated to a two. It will be a few hours until time to deliver."

"Well? What about a spinal?" she barked.

"Mrs. Redding, I am not an OB doctor. I am county doctor that delivers babies. I will give you some Demerol every couple of hours, and then you will deliver," he said.

"I will die of this before I deliver. My water is broke, and I am in pain," she said.

"Amy, get 25 mg of Demerol for her. IM. I need to listen to the baby now, to make sure it is okay," he said.

"This is my seventh kid, it is okay. What about me?" she said.

"I still need to listen to the baby," he said, putting the stethoscope on her abdomen. He could not hear the baby. "Amy, bring me the Doppler please," he said to her across the narrow hall.

She returned a moment later with a shot of Demerol and the Doppler. She asked that Joan roll to her side and gave her the strong medication. Then, she assisted her back to her back again so the doctor could listen to the baby.

Alex put the jelly on her belly and further listened to the baby. He could not hear the baby.

"Has the baby been active in the last few days?" he asked.

"Haven't really paid attention. This is my seventh, and when you have had that many, you just don't pay as close of attention as the first," she said.

"I am not hearing the heartbeat, is why I am asking. How did your water break?" he asked.

A pain came, and Joan began to complain. "Just giving me a shot is not going to work. I have never gone through labor without a spinal."

"I have told you that I don't do spinals. Did you hear me regarding your child?" he asked.

"I am not deaf. If there is something wrong with it, I will just have another one," she said.

"Mrs. Redding, you are forty-two years old. Who says that there will be another one?" he asked her. "Did something happen to cause your water to break?"

"My husband and I had a disagreement," she said.

"Then he hit you hard enough to break your water?" Alex asked.

"He recently didn't have enough money to buy his medications, and he has been nervous. He didn't mean anything by it," she said. "Can he come in?"

"Are you sure that is what you want? Do you plan on telling him that his child will be dead when it is born?" Alex asked.

"Na," Joan said. "I will surprise him."

Alex hated this woman already. Her lack of emotion told him she was likely pathological. She only cared that she got drugs. And if she cared so little for a child she was carrying, he could only imagine what she thought of her daughters.

Alex stepped from the room and told Oscar he could go in the room. "I will check on her, but it will be several hours before she delivers," he said.

"Dr. Carmichael, I need something for my nerves. I can't handle this without something for my nerves," Oscar said.

His manner made Alex angry. He didn't ask about his wife and child, but only for drugs. He didn't smell alcohol on him and figured that without Sara living and working at the café, there wasn't enough money for things like beer.

"What is it that you usually take?" he asked.

"About thirty of valium and something for pain. She scratched me," he said.

"You need pain medicine for a scratch? I am not giving such a dose of anything. Amy, would you get him some aspirin please? I will be back in a little while to check on your wife. Do you think I need to stay in case he starts getting violent?" he said and walked over to Amy.

Amy had worked for Alex since she became a nurse. She knew him to be very overly protective of the employees. "You go to Allison's and tell everyone hello for me. And if you remember, bring me a doggy bag."

Alex nodded and asked that they call if there is a problem. "I am going to Allison's house. Would you call me if she progresses before I return?" he asked.

"I will be fine, you know I will, Alex. Say hello to Allison and her family. Tell them I will be out tomorrow," she said.

"I will. I will bring some food back when I return," he said.

Amy smiled and told him to have a good time.

At the main house, Scott and Sara arrived to the smell of delicious food that was about to be served—turkey, ham, and all the trimmings. They went to the family room and said hello to the family, then Sara went to the kitchen to see if she could help. There were three tables that had been set to sit as many people who arrived.

Lauren and Saline had been assisting with the meal. Maria, who was like a big sister to Sara and Saline, had become a trusted friend to Sara. So much so that Sara had asked if she would be her baby's godmother. Maria, of course, being Catholic herself, knew what she was asking. She was thrilled to be the godmother to the newest addition to the family.

Sara had wanted to ask Lauren to be the godmother, but she was not going to be eighteen until the following June and agreed this time Maria was the best choice.

Maria's husband, Mark, and their children always ate at the main house on Christmas. Mark's father had worked on the ranch, and Mark had been raised there. One day, when Mark was nine, John had to tell him that his father had been riding in the pasture to check on the herd and had had a heart attack. Before they could get him to the hospital, he had died. John had insisted that he move to the main house and finish high school as his father had wanted. He then went to Texas A&M University and majored in agriculture and geology. When he graduated, he asked John if he needed a geologist for the oil company. Mark went on to discover oil wells all over Texas.

John had named the wells that Mark had located after their founder and even gave him 50 percent of the proceeds of the well. John also gave Mark two hundred acres to build his house when he got ready.

A few months later, Mark had met Maria. She was the daughter of an attorney in the town closest to the Byers ranch and his wife, a Mexican American woman. Maria had the best characteristics of both. Her long hair was darkest brown and very thick. Like her father, she had hazel eyes that at times seemed to be bright blue and then at other times green. Her build was perfect in Mark's eyes. She was five fee four inches tall, with an hourglass figure. Her smile was perfect, looking like she had had years of braces, but in reality, she never had.

At twenty-two years old, Maria was a beautiful woman. She loved her life on the ranch. She helped Allison when she needed help around the house and was friends with every woman who lived on the ranch. She and Mark had two small children: Oliver, four years old, and Martin, two years old. Both Mark and Maria wanted a big family and were off to a good start. Both of the children were in the family room with the men. They had gotten their presents from Santa Claus this morning, and then Maria had started cooking in their house, before they left for the main house.

Sara had wanted Scott to pick out the godfather. She didn't know very many people and thought that Scott would come up with the most likely person. When he picked Mark, Sara was pleased. It was the perfect selection.

At the main house at lunchtime, Christmas dinner was served. Everyone was in the holiday spirit. For everyone, it was a different holiday than the last two Christmases had been. Saline and Sara had a family that loved them now, and they were not hungry, cold, or scared anymore. Nothing would ever take the place of Jody. The hole that he left in everyone's hearts could never be filled. But talking about memories of him helped everyone to deal with his loss.

John said grace and said out loud what a miracle they had in their house. The two girls had been saved from a life of further abuse, and each thanked God for their new family and friends.

Everyone in the huge dining room was chatting about pleasant things. The men talked about the ranch and their work, and the women were busy thinking about the newest addition to the ranch. Aside from the women in the family, and Maria, there were only a couple of dozen women on the ranch. In general, men would start to work on the ranch and marry later when they had decided to stay working on the ranch.

Working on the ranch was a man's work. Although there were some things, such as raising a baby calf on a bottle like Saline was doing, but there was little else. Some of the women would have their own gardens to grow their own produce, and of course, they were housewives. Some worked at jobs that took them off the ranch, and others chose to attend college, but the heavy work was for the men to do.

After the meal had started, Uncle Alex walked in. "Sorry to be late, sis. I had a patient come in at the last minute that needed attention," he said.

"Not a problem. We have plenty," Allison said to her brother. Alex sat down near John in case he had to let him know about the girls' mother.

"John," Uncle Alex whispered. "I need to give you and Scott some information right quick," he said.

John rose and tapped Scott's shoulder. The three of them walked back to the family room. "What's up, Alex?" John asked.

"The patient who came in at the last minute was the girls' mother. Looks like she and that husband of hers had been fighting. She is in labor right now, and the baby is dead. I don't know how long it has been that way," he said.

"You left her there alone?" Scott asked.

"I have three nurses that are there, along with a nurse's aide. They will call me when the baby gets close," he said. "That husband of hers is there as well. Like I said, there is evidence that they had a pretty good fight.

"Do I tell Sara and Saline about their mother and the baby?" he asked.

"Not just yet. Wait until their mother has delivered the baby. When she is okay, then we can tell her. I don't want the girls to feel like they need to be with her," John said. "Agreed?"

Both Alex and Scott agreed. Then they went back to the dining room where someone had turned on Christmas music. Everyone was talking and laughing. When the meal was finished, the ladies started clearing the table. Sara started helping as well but was stopped by John, reminding her about his grandson. She stopped helping and followed everyone to the family room to rest until the rest of the family finished.

"Baby girl, it will be a little while before they are done with the kitchen, so why don't you catch yourself a nap?" Scott suggested.

"I believe I will. I feel like I could sleep for a week," Sara said softly and rubbed her chest without thinking.

"Is your chest bothering you, Sara?" Alex asked, but Sara didn't hear him. He thought about following her but knew how much she wanted this baby. If something were wrong, she would mention it, he decided.

He then thought about calling the clinic to see how Sara's mother was doing. He was just about to pick up the phone when it rang. He picked it up because he was closest to it.

"Byers residence," he answered.

"Dr. Carmichael, I believe you need to come to the clinic immediately," a male voice said.

"What is wrong? And who am I speaking with?" he asked.

"I am Sergeant Johnson of the city police. One of your patients' husbands attacked your nurse and stole the controlled medications from the clinic," he said.

"Your nurse Amy has a broken arm, and I believe a concussion. She needs to have her arm set and for you to have a look," he said.

"I will be right there," Alex said, slamming the phone down.

"Alex, what is wrong?" John asked, walking over to where he was standing.

"Oscar Redding attacked my nurse. She is hurt. He also stole the narcotics from the drug cabinet. I have some patients who need those medications. Damn him. His wife is in labor, and he steals the drugs she needs," Alex said.

John had only seen his brother-in-law angry a couple of times. When he got angry, John knew that he shouldn't be alone. "Let's go," John said.

The two men went to the door closest to where they were. Scott was told what was going on, but no one else.

"Well, now I get to deal with that crazy wife of his and tell her that her husband is the reason that she will have to go cold turkey for her labor. If not for my other patients, I would almost be glad it happened that way," Alex said.

"What about your other patients? What do you do about them?" John asked.

"After I am done with the police, I will make a request out to an area hospital for possible supplies that we will need until the area supplier comes back," Alex explained. "I do have medications left in the treatment room that he had no way of knowing about, so that will help."

Alex and John arrived at the clinic to the sound of a loud scream and the liberal use of profanities. They went inside and one of the other nurses was doing her best to care for Joan Redding.

"Mrs. Redding, calm down," Alex said with his voice raised.

"I am in pain. I want my pain medicine and my spinal block," she demanded.

"Then you are out of luck. Your husband stole the hospital supply of medications and left. So it looks like you will be going natural. He also attacked my nurse, and I have to go see her now," he said, leaving the room.

Down the hall, in the treatment was Amy. She was holding her broken arm. Alex reached down and picked up his medical bag. Fortunately, Oscar didn't know about the medications he kept in his bag. He gave Amy an injection and waited for it to take effect.

"I didn't mean it to happen, Dr. Carmichael. I told him that the medications were for the patients and not him. Then he came up behind me. I tried so hard to fight him off. I don't know where he went, and then I heard a door close," she said, her voice sounding heavy.

"Don't worry. I will get that bone set before you know it."

With expert efficiency, Alex closed the break and placed a cast on it, then elevated it on a pillow, and then he went to the room down the hall that was making the most noise.

"Mrs. Redding, you seem to be having a problem," Alex said.

"Of course I am, you son of a bitch. I am in labor. I am in agony. Why are you not doing anything about that?" she yelled.

"The fact of the matter is that I would do something about the pain you are in, but your husband stole all the narcotics from the lockup, then broke the nurse's arm. So until the morning, I have no medications to give you," Alex said.

"What! I need to change hospitals then. I will die like this," she yelled.

"Believe it or not, hundreds of years before doctors got involved in childbirth, women had them just fine. As will you. Judging on where you are now, I would say it will be about five hours," Alex said and flipped off his gloves.

"I want a second opinion," she said.

"In a small town like this, a second opinion is something you don't have the luxury of," he said and left the room.

Fortunately for him, the hospital had been built years before, and the rooms were all but sound tight. He could go down to his office and relax for a while. He needed to stay close as to keep an eye on Amy for a while. And although he didn't care for the woman, she would be giving birth to a dead baby in a matter of hours. He didn't know how she would take that.

Another thing on his mind was that Oscar had on hand now a large amount of narcotics. If he had overdosed, he would be brought in dead or overdosed. If he were to come in to see his wife, forgetting the fact that he had stolen drugs and assaulted a nurse, he would be arrested.

Police would be around close until he was found. Alex felt comfortable that Oscar would turn up soon.

He took that time to call the ranch. "Scott, I am going to stay in town for a while," he said.

"How is Amy?"

"She had a broken arm and a concussion, but she will be fine."

"How about the girls' mother?" Scott asked.

"She will be delivering a dead baby. I think she is either too stoned to care or just doesn't care. All she can rant about is how much pain she is in," Alex said. "This is your first Christmas together, make sure the girls are having a good time," Alex said.

"Will do, call me if any more happens," Scott said and hung the phone up.

Back in the family room, the mood was festive. Gifts were exchanged, including gifts that had been sent from London. One very special gift was a coat and matching hat in Allison's favorite color, rose. But Frances had added something different. She had the color created and called it Allison's Rose.

She also sent clothes for Saline and Lauren and some beautiful maternity clothes for Sara.

By late evening, everyone was beginning to feel a little spent. Scott and Sara decided to go back to their own house, and just about everyone else decided to take a nap.

On the way back to their house, Sara noticed that Scott was a bit distracted. "Is something wrong, Scott?" she asked.

"Just have something on my mind," he said.

"What is it? I am going to worry until I know what it is," she said.

And Scott knew that to be true of his wife. "Can we get inside first?"

"Of course," she said, and they entered the house through the kitchen entrance.

They sat down in front of the fire, and he looked at his wife. He hated to have to break bad news to her, but knew he must. "Oscar brought your mother to the clinic earlier. Evidently, they had been fighting, and your mother's water burst. She has been is labor ever since. But there is more. She has not been to a doctor before today, and Alex discovered that the baby didn't have a heartbeat. He is certain the baby is dead," Scott said and waited for what had to be a very emotional answer. But rather, Sara fell to her knees, crossed herself, and began to pray. Prayers accompanied by silent tears for yet another lost sibling. "Can I go to see her?" Sara whispered.

"I will take you myself. Daddy and Uncle Alex are already there. Do you want Saline to know yet?" Scott asked.

"No. Not yet if that is okay. She is having such a nice holiday, and I wouldn't want to ruin it for her," Sara said, much like the older sister she had always been to her.

"But, Sara, for you and for our child, you mustn't stay long and tire yourself. She will be delivering in the next couple of hours, and Uncle Alex will be there with her. After the baby is born would be a better time for you to visit. Okay?" he asked.

"I want nothing but to see that she is recovering, no more. Then to be treated like a queen for the final months before our child is born. I promise. Nothing means more to me than that," Sara said.

"We will leave when Alex calls. Why don't you try to catch a little nap before then? We don't know just how long it will be, but I will awaken you the moment he calls," he assured her.

"Why are you so good to me?" Sara asked honestly.

"Because I waited for you all my life, and now there are three of us. Did that sound too corny?" he asked, smiling at her.

"Just corny enough, and I am a little tired. Will you lie down with me until I go to sleep?" she asked.

"Of course, I will," he said, taking her into his arms in front of the fire. She was asleep in seconds. It worried Scott somewhat that Sara got tired so easily but thought it the effects of pregnancy.

Two hours later, the phone rang. A few things had happened: the first being that Oscar had come back to the clinic due to a wrong combination of drugs and would be in custody there until he was medically cleared. He had been given Narcan, a medication to reverse the effect of any narcotics he had taken, so he was angry at everyone for the time being, and Joan was about an hour from delivering the baby.

Sara stood for a moment and got very dizzy, almost to the point of throwing up. That had never happened before. She had a pounding headache that had started several hours before and thought it must be stress.

"Do you need to lie back down, baby girl?" Scott asked.

"No. I think I need to see how Momma is doing," she said.

"Let me get your heavy cape. It is quite cold outside, and I don't think you want to catch cold," Scott said, pulling the cape tightly around her and kissing her cheek.

"What would I do without you?" she said, looking adoringly at him. While Scott was getting his own coat, Sara looked at herself in the mirror. She had changed into one of the beautiful maternity dresses that Lady Dickerson had sent her. It was a beautiful royal blue with a white collar and wrist cuffs. Then to make it just a little more maternal, it had two tiny cradles on the white collar. The material was very soft, likely silk, and had a petticoat in the dress.

When Scott approached again, her thoughts changed to thinking about him, anything to keep her from thinking about her mother.

"What have I told you about those little looks of yours?" he asked.

She smiled radiantly at him and put her arms around his neck. "That you love them," she said, then kissed him.

"Everything else you have told me about them is amiss to me about it. But I will try to remember it later," she whispered.

"I believe I would rather you forget it later. I love you," he said, wrapping her snuggly in the floor-length wrap.

When they were in the jeep, Sara started thinking about the events of the day. It had been such a wonderful Christmas. "Do you think that your family liked the gifts we gave them?"

"I believe that they loved them, especially the personalized ornaments that I have no doubt will become an annual thing, and a beautiful thought," Scott said.

"I feel for my momma," Sara said, deep in thought.

"I am surprised to hear you say that."

"I am not stupid about her. Just knowing that she is going to give birth to a dead baby makes me think," she said. "Maybe the baby is better off being with God from the start rather than being hers first." Sara rubbed her expanding belly affectionately. "No matter how many kids we have, they will always be wanted and loved. And I hope that we are blessed with ten of them." She smiled.

"Well, I promise to keep you with all the babies you could ever want," he said, winking at her.

With the life that she had had from the moment they had met, she could have been so cold about her abusive mother. But she was almost innocent and very warm. She loved everything.

They pulled in at the clinic, and Scott came around to Sara's side and opened her door. Sara looked up at Scott. "I am scared, Scott."

"I am right here, baby girl. I won't let anything happen," he said, putting his arm around her. They walked in the clinic. Right away they could tell there was a lot of activity.

"I need some pain medicine. I just had a baby and am in pain," Joan Redding said.

"You were just given pain medicine a few minutes ago, Mrs. Redding. Just give it time to work," the nurse said patiently.

"You people killed my baby and then put me through agony afterward," she said.

"Mum, they had nothing to do with the death of your baby," Sara said gently, placing a gentle hand on her mothers' arm.

"No, but you did. You left, and there was no money for any-thing," Joan said.

"We had to leave, Mum, you were letting him kill us," Sara said.

Joan looked Sara up and down and missed nothing. "You think you are better than I am? You're just a whore yourself out for more."

"Mum, Scott and I are married. We married right after I turned seventeen. I was even able to keep a secret from everyone before the wedding. And that is that I am pregnant. Scott didn't even know," she said.

"If you would have stayed home like you should have, we may have still had Jody and this baby," she said dryly, with no emotion in her voice at all.

"The biggest difference in your daughter and you is that she will love our children. She loves and raised both Saline and Jody, and you didn't care what happened to them. At least Sara and Saline are happy now. You need not ever worry about them," Scott said.

"You sorry bastard, you can't take my kids," Joan said. "How am I supposed to make it?"

"Do like the rest of the people in the world, get a job," Scott said.

Joan's tone changed. "Sara, I have to recover from having lost my child. I have never even gotten to properly grieve from the loss of Jody. I still can imagine him running and playing in the yard at the farm, not dead in a grave. I need my oldest girl at home, with me. And while I am here, I would love it if you would take me to my son's grave," Joan said, taking Sara's hand in her own. Sara's eyes began to tear.

Scott knew immediately what she was trying to do.

"Take your hand off my wife," Scott said.

"She is my daughter. I will touch her wherever and whenever I want. It is none of your business," she said, suddenly grabbing Sara's arm more painfully.

Sara pulled her wrist back, rubbing it as though it had been burnt. She looked at her mother as if she had just seen her for the first time. She had always seen her mother as the victim of men, but now she knew that she was something worse than she had ever thought. She used everything and everyone in her life. Tears began to roll down her pale face. She appeared as a child with a broken heart.

"Sara he is not part of our family. Your marriage does not exist because you are not old enough to give consent. That means that your baby will be like no more than you, a bastard." Joan seethed.

"No," Sara whispered and then ran from the room.

Scott walked over to the woman who looked thrilled in her effect of her daughter. "My parents are considered both girls' parents now, and Sara was given in marriage to me by her legal guardian, my father. You are not part of Sara or Saline's lives any longer. Come near them again and I will kill you," he said, leaving the room. He could still hear her with her sick laugh.

Scott looked around the clinic and then felt a chill and saw the side door cracked. He went to it and found Sara kneeling on the ground, crying her heart out. There were no words he could say to make her feel better. Rather he put his arms around her and picked her up and carried her to the jeep and buckled her in then got in on the driver's side. She pulled her cape closer to her and sobbed silently. Scott said nothing, letting her have her cry.

When she seemed to have caught her breath, she asked the question that he knew was coming. "Scott, will our little boy be a bastard?" she asked softly.

Scott took her hand in his and kissed the back of it. "No. Not in any meaning of the word. The king of the world came into being much in the same way, remember? Scott said. "According to my beliefs, you and I became one that very first time. I had asked to you marry me, and you said yes, and we sealed the bond by the most pure and holy act of love that you can perform. Our hearts and souls were open to each other, and we created another being in that act—our son. It was the most perfect wedding gift you could have given to me," he said as he pulled the car near the kitchen door.

"When I found out, did I act ashamed or angry?" he asked. "I was so proud and happy and completely blessed, so much so that the first people that I told were our son's grandparents." He kissed her gently. "Wipe that word from your vocabulary, little one. There has never been a more wanted or more perfectly timed being in this world. Now, why don't you run inside and I will park the jeep?" he said.

She nodded with a little more certainty about her.

As she entered the house, the house was a little cool to her. She decided to light a fire and sat down beside it and rubbed her arms briskly. She still wore her wrap because she felt so cold.

"Sara, what are you doing down there?" he asked.

"I am just a bit cold, and I am sure it is just stress, but my head has been aching today," she said.

"I am sure it is fine as well, but why don't we call Dr. Chambers to let him know?" he suggested. She nodded, hating to bother the kind doctor but worried about their son.

Scott left the room to call Dr. Chambers. "Bill, sorry for the late hour, but I am calling about my wife, Sara Byers. She has just had a very emotionally traumatic incident and says her head hurts. I have seen her rubbing it and standing slowly as if to get balance most of the day." Scott went further to explain the events of the day and the very happy Christmas they had had until a couple of hours before.

"Scott, I think I need to give Steve a call and see what he thinks," Dr. Chambers said.

"Shouldn't be too hard to find. He has been at the main house all day," he said and gave the number to him.

CHAPTER 9

John Austin Byers

It had been six weeks since Christmas, and with that, quite a few changes. Sara had a cold that turned out to be strep throat. She had spent two weeks in St. Mary's, clearing up the infection, and she required a pericardiocentesis before it was all said and done. She had lots of visitors in the hospital. Mary, Saline, Lauren, Maria, and Allison, just to name a few, made sure that one of them was always with her. And Scott would be there when he would come in from work. John would also stop by from time to time.

In those two weeks, Sara was exhausted, likely from fever and the third trimester of pregnancy. She did everything she was told. She took her medicine and rested, and no matter how she felt, she ate well.

The day before she was to be released, she was asleep on the chaise lounge in her room when someone walked in. She didn't rouse to start, but when she heard the words, "So this is how royalty is treated." Her eyes opened wide. She saw standing there in her room, her mother and Henry Alexander. The first thing she thought was, *Why are they together?* Then she thought, *Why are they here?*

"Get out of here or I will call the nurse," Sara said, placing a protective hand on her abdomen.

"I just came to see about my first grandchild. Do we know what it is yet?" Henry asked.

"You know it is not your grandchild, Lord Henry. You have told me that often enough," she said.

"Yes, but it seems that since you are married to a very respectable man and is having his child, your uncle would like to meet both of you. He is in Texas, you know. He wants to see his successor and heir," Henry said.

"Please leave," Sara stood and yelled.

"But we are your family."

"Lord Henry, you don't know the meaning of the word. Now I want you both out. And I have met His Grace. He was asked to leave as well. Now you need to leave," Sara said.

Henry had never heard his stepdaughter with such confidence in her voice before. Something had changed. Henry approached her, and Sara did the only thing she could do. She pulled the call light out of the wall, making an immediate signal for personnel to enter the room.

Then the monitoring equipment started to alarm. Sara could feel her chest start to ache and sat down, her hand once again holding her very pregnant tummy.

"Who are you?" the nurse asked. Sara had been in the hospital nearly two weeks, and no one had ever gotten her so upset before. "Sara, you need to get back into bed. And you need to get out of here."

"We are her parents. We deserve to be here," Henry said. Then the door opened again, and Henry was face-to-face with someone he never thought he would see again. "What the hell are you doing here?" Henry said.

"I am her cardiologist, and you need to get out of this room," he said, shoving Henry through the door roughly. He shoved him against the wall and put his forearm at Henry's throat. "All those years you told me she had died, only to find her a few years later alive and now, thanks to loving people, healthy. And you don't get her back."

While still having Henry pinned against the wall, he told the nurse to get security up to the floor. When security arrived, they took both Henry and Joan off the floor to the security office to find out what the situation was. Dr. Quinton went back in to check on his patient. "Are we doing okay in here?" he asked.

She was breathing very hard and fast, eyes wide. "How did they get here? What did they want? Do they have Saline? Don't let them have my child. Please don't let them come back." She kept backing into a corner and was barely coherent.

"Get her some Valium please," he said softly to the nurse.

"Don't let them hurt our baby. They want to take us away," she said. The monitor continued to sound loudly as though her heart were about to explode.

"No one is going to take you away, Sara. I am here. No one will take you away. I give you my word. But you have to settle down a little so the baby does not get here too soon," he said. Seeing that she slowed her breathing to his words, he continued to talk softly to her.

Sara fell to her knees with her hand on her chest. "I don't think he is going to get here, Scott."

Dr. Quinton gently lifted Sara and laid her on the bed. He applied oxygen; Sara's eyes began to roll back. "Sara, I need you to stay with me. It is Dr. Quinton. You used to call me Dr. Heart when you were a little girl. Your nurse is giving you something to help you to relax. Don't worry, it won't hurt your baby. He is fine. We need to get your blood pressure down right now." He continued to talk to her and soothe her as he could.

It took a rapid amount of medical activity to settle the young mother down. Her blood pressure was so high it made her eyes look like they would surely pop out of their sockets.

When Dr. Chambers entered the room, he was concerned about both mother and child, but it didn't take but a few minutes to get Sara settled, and her blood pressure under control. Not long after, Scott arrived with Allison and Saline.

"Sara, baby girl, did he hurt you?" he asked. Sara barely opened her eyes to his voice. She was hearing but felt too spent to speak. Dr. Chambers urged Scott and Allison outside, leaving Saline with her sister and the nurse that remained.

"I believe that if Sara stays stable and calms down, she should go home tomorrow for her own good. The ranch and her home provide her the security in knowing that there are people around. There will be a nurse with her at home, and I know that there will always be someone with her. So as long as her blood pressure returns to normal, and she takes her medicine to keep her calm, I believe the ranch would be the best place for her."

Everyone seemed to agree. "If one of you wanted to stay the night tonight, you could take her home early in the morning," Dr. Chambers said.

"I would love to stay. I brought my sewing anyway," Allison said.

"Will you be okay, Momma?" Scott asked.

"Of course, how many times have I sat up with you at night when you were not feeling well, young man?" Allison said to her eldest son.

"I remember, Momma. And I have no doubt you will spend your fair share of time rocking Austin," Scott said.

"I am already planning on it. I will stay here tonight. I will call if anything happens."

"I am going to visit with my wife for a few minutes," Scott said and went into the room. Saline stepped out for some privacy.

"Scott, I didn't even know they were here. I just woke up, and they were there. I was so afraid. Did I hurt the baby?" she asked.

"No, both of you are fine. And unless something happens tonight, you get to go home in the morning. Would you feel better being at the ranch?" he asked.

"Oh yes, Scott. There is no place I would rather be," she said, a little breathless. "Dr. Chambers says this is a big baby. I think he is trying to grow into my lungs."

"Momma is going to stay with you tonight, and there is going to be a guard outside the door and a plain-clothes guard at the nurses' station at all times to keep you safe," Scot told her.

"What about Mum and Lord Henry?" she asked.

"I know they are with security, but I wanted to come in and see you instead. Let the authorities contend with them," Scott said, sitting on the bed and taking her in his arms. "It is getting hard to get my arms around you. I am rather jealous of our son getting to be so close all the time."

Sara lay onto him and felt his warmth. "Tomorrow we get to be in our bed, in our house, just the two of us."

"I forgot to tell you that part of your going home is that you will have a full-time nurse until the baby is born. It is a precaution, because you have a history of heart problems. And you will be on bed rest except for going to the bathroom," he said.

"Okay," she said. "I don't exactly feel like running about the fields right now, so I will just look out the windows at them," she said.

"Oh, and Saline wants to give you something. Can I ask her to come in?" he asked.

"Yes, of course."

"Saline, did you have something for your sister?" Scott asked.

Saline walked over to her sister and gave her an envelope.

"What is it?" she asked.

"Your diploma. You passed your GED," Saline said.

"Really? I didn't think that there was any way that I had passed," she said, looking at the official-looking paper.

"So now you are a wife, soon-to-be mom, and a high school graduate," Saline said.

"I have everyone to thank, for teaching me to read and every-thing. I can't believe I really passed. Now there will be nothing in the way of being a nurse." She smiled. "I don't mean to be ungracious, but would it be okay if I take a nap. I am so sleepy," she said.

"You go to sleep, baby girl, and when you wake up tomorrow, you get to go home," he said and kissed his wife good night. "See you tomorrow."

"I love you, Scott. Thank you, Saline, for everything. I am not stupid anymore," she said, smiling.

Both Saline and Scott smiled at each other. Allison came back in the room. She bid her husband and sister good night and was given a sedative by her nurse. Allison took a seat in a comfortable recliner and began talking about things at home, people they loved, and of course, the baby. Before long, they both fell asleep.

Earlier, right after being taken to the security office, Henry and Joan waited to find out what the powers that be would be likely to want to do with them. But being the players that they had always been, they had planned very well. On this trip to Texas, Henry had brought his eldest son, Tommy, with him as his backup plan. He told Tommy that if he saw that security had come and gotten them, he was to wait ten minutes and call the hospital operator from a phone booth and tell them there was a bomb. That would easily send the lax security officers looking for something that was not there, and he and Joan would just walk out the front door.

The only pitfall to this was that he would have to tell his uncle, who was waiting at a nearby hotel, that he would not be presented with his "niece" and soon-to-be-born nephew. He was sure that they would be able to do something to make up for that, but just what at this point was unknown.

When the code gray was called, it alarmed the hospital staff that there was the potential for a bomb on the hospital site. And as planned, in the commotion, they walked right out of the hospital.

Tommy had walked back into the hospital to see what kind commotion he had caused with his phone call. He stood in the hospital lobby and saw people running from place to place, looking for possible places a bomb could have been placed. It completely amused him so much that he took a seat to admire his handiwork for a little while. Then he saw something curious. A beautiful tall blond girl in a school uniform had walked to the gift shop. She talked to the lady in the shop about a gift to buy for her sister, who was expecting a baby in a few weeks. The lady picked a basket with a big blue ribbon on it and arranged it with a bear and some assorted baby things, not to mention a nursing gown for her sister, as she knew she would be breastfeeding her son. She paid the lady and told her what room to deliver it to and thanked her very much for what she had done.

No doubt, the beautiful girl was his little sister Saline. She walked over to the front doors as if waiting for someone, and when he saw no one, he went up behind her and said, "Walk," and he took her arm firmly. Saline started as always to fight her way out of the hold, but Tommy whispered in her ear that if she didn't walk, he would have Sara and her baby killed. She walked blindly to a waiting car in the parking lot. In the car, his mother and father waited.

"Look what I found," he said, roughly shoving Saline in the backseat.

"You stupid bastard, they will kill you for this."

Tommy slapped her hard across the face for her comment.

"You son of a bitch," she said and flew into him, grabbing a hold of his crotch and squeezing it until she felt something pop. Then Tommy was throwing up in the backseat. Saline took those few seconds and jumped out of the slow-moving car. She picked herself off the ground and ran hard back to the main entrance to warn Scott and Momma Allison of his threat.

Henry put the car into park and ran after his daughter. She was about to put her hand on the door when he grabbed her by the hair and threw her to the ground, using his fists on her face until he had her attention. "You will come with me," he said.

Saline merely spat in his face. He jerked her to her feet. She fought with everything she had, but he took her by the wrist and threw her hard into the wall, breaking her wrist and knocking her out cold. He leaned down to pick up the now-not-so-pretty blond in the torn and bloodied uniform, when two very strong hands grabbed him from behind.

He turned to see the angry eyes of John Byers bearing into him. With him were two very tall young men. "I told you that if you ever messed with either of our girls again, what I would do. Mark, Paul, could you please escort this trash to the truck and tie him in the back of it, and wait for me to come back? I won't be long," he said.

"We will be waiting, John," Mark said.

Henry started to attempt to escape. Then he felt something sharp in his ribs. "I would just assume to run you through as look at you, just give me a reason. Now walk."

Henry did as he was told. And when he arrived at the truck, he was literally hogtied in the bed of the truck, chained to the hitch, and gagged. He was then covered with hay. "Have a nice ride."

John had never considered Saline delicate. He knew she would try to fight her way out of hell if she were there. To see the tall, strong, beautiful young woman that he had come to love as his own daughter broke his heart. He yelled inside the hospital for help, and an orderly and a nurse came running. They applied a neck brace to Saline's neck and loaded her on a stretcher and took her inside. While she was in x-ray, he called Scott, who was just leaving Sara's room, when the nurse caught him. He explained what had just happened, and Scott joined him, waiting to hear from the doctor how badly Saline may be injured.

"I would imagine that alarm that went off had something to do with him, as a means of leaving the hospital," Scott said.

"I believe you may be right. Alexander will not be going any-place tonight. Mark and Paul have him tied up in the back of the truck. I think it is time that we dealt with him." Scott merely nodded in unspoken agreement.

When the ER doctor came out, he said that she may have a skull fracture and some bleeding in the brain, but they were going to try to control it without surgery. Her right arm was broken in two places, and she had three facial bones broken. Aside from that, it was bumps and bruises. He would know more in the morning and would call immediately if anything changed.

John and Scott then walked straight to the president and CEO of the hospital and straight into the office. He was sitting behind his desk.

"My name is John Byers. Among other things, I own the Byers ranch, and Byers Oil out of Dallas. Right now I will write this hospital a check for one million dollars if they can assure me that three of this family's members in this hospital will be protected. My name is on one wing of this hospital. I believe that I can afford to ask for protection for my family," John said.

"Why do you think that your family needs protection?" the CEO asked.

"Two people intent on harming our daughter-in-law entered her room and attempted to abduct her. Then, a few minutes later, the same people abducted our daughter and assaulted her. She is currently in a coma, and we are waiting to see what other damage has been done. This is a hospital for God's sake. People should be about to have solace here and feel safe. I have no doubt that they are the people who called in the bomb threat in an attempt to get to the girls, and I want security stepped up, or I will withdraw all support that I pay to this hospital immediately."

The CEO picked up the phone and called security. "Pay close attention. We have had two people nearly abducted in the last hour. I need a blanket of security immediately on two patients. Complete with name Jane Does listed, and they both need to be moved to any open ICU room. Their names are…"

"Sara Lyn Byers and Saline Byers," John said. "And my wife Allison Byers is staying with Sara tonight."

"Sara, Saline, and Allison Byers. Allison Byers is staying in the room with Sara Byers tonight. And I believe the bomb threat to be a hoax. Continue to keep looking at anything suspicious. Keep these women safe. Understood?" he said. "Call in whoever you need to. There are members of the sheriff's department who have agreed to assist, so give them a call. Thanks," he said and hung up the phone. He then got up and walked around the desk. "Take me to the young lady who was abducted please."

John and Scott went back to the ER to the place they last saw Saline. "I need to see my daughter, Saline Byers."

The nurse at the desk looked at the board then said, "I am sorry, sir, there is only one visitor at a time and her brother is in with her."

"Her brother! Oh god," Scott said.

"Open the door now," the CEO insisted. The pneumatic door swung open, and the three men heard her long before they saw her.

She was screaming hysterically, and they found her standing on the stretcher throwing anything she could find within her reach. Then they saw the young man that was unmistakably Saline's brother. He was tall, muscular, and had the same hair color and eyes. He had his hand firmly on her wrist.

"What the hell do you think you are doing?" Scott yelled.

"She is my sister, and I have a right be here," he said.

"Unhand her," Scott said with his voice lowered. "Now."

Tommy unhanded Saline's wrist and then took a step back.

John walked over to Saline, who was still hysterical. "Saline, honey, come to Poppa. We won't let them hurt you again," he said and put his hand up to her, the gentle hand that had never hurt her. "Just look at me, baby."

With her hands shaking violently and her arm bleeding because she had pulled out her IV, she put her hand out to John. He sat down on the stretcher beside her and held her tightly and stroked her hair.

"He wants to take me away again, Poppa. Daddy wanted to hurt me again. I couldn't do it. I can't live like this anymore. I can't be his whore anymore. He wants to bury me and Sara alive. Just let me die so I don't have to go through that anymore." Saline broke from John for an instant and found herself in the corner of the exam room. "Sara. Tommy is coming to get you. I have to get to my sister and nephew. They can't take another of her babies. It would kill her." Her eyes were darting, the swelling in her face making seeing distorted. Saline had never cried for herself. She had never spoken from heart so clearly.

"Son, get that animal out of here," he said. "Saline, baby, Poppa is here. This man is the CEO of the hospital and assures us that you will be safe here," John said, stroking her hair.

Tommy was a football player and was well muscled and had about forty pounds on Scott. "You heard my daddy, get out," he said, shoving him toward the door. When he was in the hall, Scott followed him as he walked, then he turned and balled up his left hand and attempted to slug Scott. Scott had anticipated the move, so he easily sidestepped him, and he hit a pipe instead.

"That had to hurt," Scott mused, infuriating Tommy further.

"You little prick, I will kill you." The CEO attempted to intervene, but Scott put his hand up.

"Let's take this outside, and you can have your shot," Scott said and looked back at the CEO and winked.

They walked out the pneumatic door that led to the ambulance bays. Then Tommy once again attempted to swing at Scott and once again missed. In haste Tommy once again swung a weak swing with his injured left hand. Scott rubbed his jaw. "You picked the wrong man for that." And Scott utilized his moves he had spent years perfecting. Using mostly his legs, he would strike so quickly and with so much force that his opponent fell.

"Now know this, you ever come near those two girls again, I will finish the job," Scott said and went back into the hospital. The CEO looked once more at Tommy Alexander, who was struggling to stand. When he walked in, he requested that security have him photographed and escorted from the hospital. And to call the police and have him arrested for assaulting and attempting to abduct a minor.

Scott went back to Saline's room where she had been sedated, but she continued to cry.

"Daddy, is she okay?" Scott asked.

"She will be, son. She will be here for a couple of days," he said as he continued to hold the frightened girl's hand.

"Why don't you go home, Daddy? I will stay here for a while to make sure that everything is well," Scott said, really not wanting to get too far from his wife.

"I may for a while. I have some pressing business to take care of. I will let your momma know where you are," he said. "But not Sara."

After a couple of hours, Saline seemed to be settling down a little. Her beautiful face was bruised and disfigured, and he knew she had to be in terrible pain.

"Saline, do you need something for pain?" he asked.

"Not if I am going to get hooked on it," she said.

"Don't be silly. If you take pain medicine only when you are in pain, you are taking it like you should. Let me call your nurse," he said.

"Please don't leave me alone," she pleaded.

"I am not going anywhere," Scott said and pressed the button then told the nurse that Saline needed something for pain.

A few minutes later, a nurse came in with a medicine cup of pills in it and a replacement IV bag. She helped Saline to sit as she took the medicine. "I am going to be moving you upstairs in a few minutes. The doctor wants to keep an eye on you for a couple of days. But you don't have to worry about anyone bothering you. You are entered as a Jane Doe and are going to be in a VIP unit. There will be guards there to keep an eye out as well," the young nurse said.

"Thank you," was all Saline could think of to say.

"It must be nice to be from such a rich family. My mom and dad both work just to pay the bills."

"Are they happy?" Saline asked.

"Yes, of course."

"That is worth more than all the money in the world," Saline said.

"Can you remember what happened to you?" the nurse asked.

Saline turned her head away before she answered, "Yes, from the first time it happened. Sometimes you think being dead has to be better. Then days like today, you know it would be better," she said.

"But it will get better," the nurse said.

"Saline, no one will get close to you again," Scott said.

Saline didn't respond anymore. After months of her tougher than life bravado, there was nothing left. Silent tears went down her face, but she didn't make a sound.

Scott knew that in her short life she had been let down way too many times to give a second chance easily, possibly never. But they had to try. At present, she was in pain and scared out of her mind. Talking to her would only make her loose what little self-control she had.

When the nurse was ready to leave the room, he asked her to call Sara's room and requested that his mother come to Saline's room and he would sit with Sara. His mother had the patience and motherly love that she needed so badly.

John Byers believed in justice. If it could not be obtained through the courts, there was what he and many men of his time called Western justice. Diplomatic immunity, be damned.

Scott had waited until the next morning to tell Sara about Saline. He had called when she was asleep to keep up with how she was doing.

She was physically okay but terrified. Allison had suggested to the doctor that she go home to the ranch and that a nurse was staying there with their daughter-in-law, who was being discharged. She also explained a little about her past and that she found safety and security at the ranch. She also let him know that her brother was a doctor, who lived nearby. The doctor finally agreed and gave her a list to give to the nurse. He wrote the necessary prescriptions and gave them to Allison with a follow-up appointment. The doctor then wrote the order for discharge. Allison walked back to Saline's room.

"Baby, the doctor said that you can come home to the ranch this morning rather than tomorrow. Do you feel like going, or do you want to stay another night?" she asked.

Saline had tears in her eyes. "If I leave this room, they will know where I am."

"We will take you with armed guards downstairs to the car, and no one will get to you. I promise you. Your Henry is not a problem anymore, and your brother is in the hospital and under arrest. And your mother would never try anything on her own," Allison told her.

Then she remembered something Scott had told her about God. "Scott told me a few months ago that God is like parents. He does not make them get hurt but is there to help them when they do. Is that really true?" she asked.

"Yes, absolutely," she answered quickly. "He was with me when I lost my baby girl."

"I must really love all of you, because I think that I am starting to believe," Saline said. "I really would love to go home."

Allison hugged the young girl warmly then took a brush and gently brushed her hair so as not to cause pain on the bruised areas. Allison picked up a gown and warm robe and slippers for her to change into from the hospital gift shop.

There was a knock on the door, and it opened. "Momma, is Saline going to get to come home today?"

"Yes, son, she is getting dressed now."

"Is my sister okay?" Sara asked the nurse who pushed the wheelchair.

"She is going home today, baby girl," Scott said. "She is just putting on her clothes."

"Thank God. Are you sure Henry won't be looking for us?" she asked.

"Certain," Scott asked.

The way that Scott had said what he did, she didn't question why. She didn't want details, just that he was gone. Just then, the baby seemed to move in such a way that even the nurse and Scott could see.

"Wow, I think he is ready to go home as well," the nurse said.

"I know he is. I can't wait until I am holding him and being wheeled out," she said, smiling.

Scott had heard of the way pregnancy affects women and knew that she was feeling her hormones lately. He would see her just sitting, holding her tummy, and smiling as if dreaming of the life inside her. Then, Saline's door opened, and she was being carried in another wheelchair.

Sara looked to her sister and seemed to assess the damage their brother had done. "I'm sorry. I wasn't there."

"If you would have been there, there would be no Austin in a couple of weeks. Besides, you have been hogging the attention for months, I need a little more," she said, giving her sister an assuring smile.

Two nurses wheeled the two young ladies to the car. They both got in the backseat, leaving Scott and Allison to get in the front. The drive home was filled with chatter from all. The drive home took about forty minutes.

Scott dropped off Sara at their own house, assuring her that she needed to rest, and someone would be down in a little bit.

The nurse was not supposed to start until the next day, so as Scott had to go to the office that day, there were several volunteers to check on his wife for the day.

Saline had a built-in support group living under the same roof. Allison seemed to know when she needed something, and Riley and Colton made frequent rounds to tell her new happenings in the home even though she had only been gone a couple of days.

"I know I look like a monster right now, but the bruising will go away, and I will look normal again," she said.

"Scott said that he put a world of hurt on your brother. And Daddy made sure that you didn't have to worry about your dad again," Riley told her.

Both of the younger Byers boys had taken an immediate liking and close friendship to Saline. Never had she ever shown fear of anything. And for Riley, she was very good when taken to town on a night out, to make the girls from his school jealous. Either Riley or Saline had any romantic notions, but they had formed a very close bond that had to resemble the love siblings have for one another.

"What do you mean?" she asked.

"I don't know if I should be telling you this, but Scott saw Tommy in the same room you were in the emergency room, so he dragged him outside where he practiced a few of his martial arts skills on him. He beat the holy hell out of him. But don't tell Sara. I don't think she likes hearing about such things," he said.

"You're right, she doesn't. So I won't tell her if you give me details. And what happened to my dad? Did he kill him? I hope so. I want to spit on his grave," she said.

"Daddy wouldn't kill him. Not so soon. He just had him relocated taken to Central America and took his passport and left him there with no money or ID. He spoke with some officials, and I don't think he will be back for a while. I believe Mark and Paul gave him an attitude adjustment too," he explained. "And when they threw him off the plane, he was buck naked."

Even though it hurt to laugh, Saline had to hold some sore spots to do so. "By the time he finds his way back here, I don't think he will remember English, much less us."

Both of them talked and laughed for a little while, and Riley said that he had needed to see to some stock. The weather was very cold, and it threatened to snow. On his way to the pasture, he stopped to check on Sara. She was sitting in front of the fire and watching the TV. She started to rise when she saw him come in, but he motioned for her to stay seated. He walked over and hugged her warmly.

"How is my number one nephew and his momma today?" he asked.

"We are fine. I am just feeling a little heavy these days," she said.

"You look much better. I am glad you are home," he said. "Sara, can I ask you something? You don't have to answer if you don't want to."

"Of course," she said. "Wait just a minute. My water is boiling. I am making some tea," she said.

He stood and put a hand out to her to help her up.

"Thank you. I am not very good at getting up," she said, and they went to the kitchen.

"I don't really know how to ask."

"Just ask. I am usually good at answering." She smiled.

"Well, you and I are about the same age. I will graduate in May," he said.

"Yes, I know and I will be there," she said.

"You have not been to school with people your own age since you were fourteen. You have supported a family. You protected Saline and Jody. I just can't imagine what gave you, I mean, I don't know. How did you know what to do? Did you ever miss being with people your own age? Or going on dates or anything like that?" he asked.

She finished making the pitcher of tea and poured herself a glass. "We have never really talked much. I usually try to hide from people rather than talk to them. You do know what happened the day we came here, don't you?" she asked.

"I knew y'all were coming that week, but I don't know why you had come early," he said.

Riley never liked to pry into anyone's secrets, but as he was about to be out of high school and had someone so close to his age, yet from a different background, he broke character and asked.

"Saline and I have different fathers. So her father sent me away to a school in Wales and then England. He hated me about as much as a body could hate. He even put me in the French class to further hinder my learning. But when Saline started school in California, she was a very fast learner. By the time she was seven, she was teaching me to read and write in English. I taught her French. That way we could stay in touch.

"Her dad always referred to me as the bastard. Both my older brother and younger sisters knew that. Anyway, the abuse that I can remember started when I was four, maybe younger. Sometimes I would return to school and be," she stopped and took a breath, "like I was when I came here." She continued talking, telling him though not in detail about the abuse, frequently stopping to ask if he really wanted to hear what she was saying. He kept telling her to continue.

"Saline wrote me a letter when I was twelve, telling me he was hurting her too, and I had to return to her. My best friend's family offered to keep me and raise me as their own, under the circumstances. Lord and Lady Dickerson and their daughter, Lauren, begged. They had taken me out of school for two weeks before I returned to California and really tried to convince me. But I had to protect Saline. It was the hardest thing I ever did—leaving Lauren. Then when Henry left us here, I was fourteen and Saline was only eleven. It was in the middle of winter. He divorced Momma and left us with no means of support, so in order to eat and all, I found a job. I guess I have always been able to pull it together in a pinch, especially for Saline," she said.

"Wow. I wish Daddy and Scott would have killed them both," he said. "But why did those people take you out of school? I mean…" he didn't know how to continue.

"Lauren had cancer and lost part of her leg when she was about eight. She had to have chemotherapy for about a year, and I lived with them and even taught Lauren how to walk and tap dance again. I had been sick the previous summer and was still recovering, so they had us both tutored. When Lauren lost her hair, I went into the bathroom and cut off nearly two feet of my own hair and asked Lady Dickerson to make her a wig. She did. She hugged me so tight I thought I would break. We were so close. Well, you know Lauren, why am I rambling on so? When will she be back?" she asked.

"Day after tomorrow, keep going," he said.

"They knew what Henry was like through what he did to me." With that, she stared at the fire for a minute.

Lauren had told him quite a bit about her life but left out much.

"I can't believe I am talking about this again," she said, walking to the fire. She rubbed her belly and kept talking. "I never saw what the future would be when I returned. There were still things out there I didn't know could happen. A private girls' school in the country has a way of isolating you. We didn't watch TV or anything. We played, went to church, studied, and all such. Then I would go back and change into something else. It seems so strange now."

"I think I can guess, but why did they take you out of school?" he asked, standing beside her at the fire and adding a few logs for her.

She shook her head and thought about just walking away. Then she looked to Riley. She knew, quite like Scott, he would never tell a secret, but what was he thinking? One day, if he found out from someone else, what would he think?

"Scott is the only other person whom I have ever told this to. I thought it would kill me to tell him. I couldn't even tell Uncle Alex. I told him to ask Scott. But you are my brother now, and an adult, and I hope I can trust you with this. I was pregnant with my stepdad's child," she said with tears just starting down her face. She maintained her stare at the fire.

Riley's face was also streaming tears. "What happened to the baby?" he asked, thinking that Jody may have been hers.

Sara looked up at him briefly then back at the fire. Then she sat back down as if exhausted. "I didn't know how bad anything could be. One night Momma and Henry took me to downtown Los Angeles. They told me I had to go to the doctor. It was dark and cold, and I could hear rats. It was there that they aborted the baby. I screamed the entire time. I thought I was being killed, slowly. I was tied up with my mother staring at me and smiling the entire time.

"When it was over, they threw me in the backseat and took me back to their house. My step-grandma came by the next day and saw what had happened, she took me to her doctor, though I don't remember it and tried to help. She took care of me for a few days before she had to return me. Grandma Catherine always treated me like I was her granddaughter.

"He didn't want anything to do with me after that. But there was Saline. And try as I would, I could not save her. Not until we were back here. I kept Oscar from ever hurting us like that.

"I fell in love with Scott and really didn't know what the feeling was. To be told by someone that they love you, you have to wonder what they would think if they saw your soul. I didn't seek him out or anything like that. I hope that you—"

"Don't ever say that," he said. "I had seen you so many times at the café and knew that was not what you had in mind. We all knew that. That son of a bitch never should have laid a hand on either of you. You were so young. I just can't imagine what you had been through. You have my love and respect. I could never hold anything against you or Saline. I had thought something completely different, and now it is so stupid," he said.

"What is that?" she asked, sniffing.

"I thought somehow that Jody might be yours. Not because you would ever encourage anything like that, but because I thought that someone had hurt you like you said. I hope I don't offend you by that," he said.

"Momma was expecting Jody at the time. It was so hard when he was born." She cried for a minute, and Riley sat and held her hand. "But when she brought him home, I fell in love with him. I think it helped ease the pain a little. I could not blame an innocent baby for what his dad had done to me. I couldn't believe anyone would ever look at me, much less want me, except Saline," she said.

Riley looked up at her and saw she was a little pale. "I think that you should lie down for a little bit. Aren't you supposed to take something about now?" he asked.

"It is on the counter."

Riley walked over and gave her the medicine. At that moment, Sara reminded him very much of his mother after the loss of his sister. She hadn't been the same until three abused children needed someone as badly as all she had needed them. He had seen what such a loss could do to a woman. She took the medicine. He put his hand out to her and she started to get up and closed her eyes and sat back down.

"Wait a minute please," she said and closed her eyes.

"Is everything okay? I didn't mean to pry, Sara. I really didn't," he said.

"No. I knew one day you would likely find out. My mother is good at telling people things like that, so I am glad I told you first. Austin is moving around like he is running a race. Okay," she said, extending her hand. She stood up, and they walked to the bedroom.

"I feel foolish. I am moving so slowly."

"I don't know how you are moving as fast as you are," he said. He knelt in front of her. I swear I will never tell a soul."

She gently touched his cheek with one finger for a second. "Thank you. I have never had a man as a friend," she said and lay back on the pillows and turned to her side.

"Will you be okay for a little bit?" he asked.

She smiled at him. "I will be fine," she said and dozed off.

Riley thought how young she looked. Then he picked up a blanket from the end of the bed and covered her so she would not catch a chill.

He walked from the house silently and got in his truck. He vowed, much like Saline, he would protect both of his new sisters for the rest of their lives. He worked feeding cattle through lunch and had to pull a calf later in the afternoon. When he was driving from the pasture, he saw that Scott was home, so he kept on driving to the main house for supper.

Three weeks passed. Saline was healing well and going to school and not taking part in PE because of her ribs.

Lauren had returned from England as scheduled and, like everyone else, was awaiting the arrival of the baby. Lady Dickerson, or Frances, as she wanted to be called, had returned with Lauren, and she, Maria, Mary, and Allison had given Sara a baby shower. It was a complete surprise to Sara, and she was so grateful for the dozens of ladies who attended.

Besides the doctor, Sara's only other outside activity was going to church.

Then one morning toward the end of March, Sara and Lauren had been talking since Scott went to work. Her nurse hadn't arrived as yet, so Lauren was keeping an eye out. Sara's back had started to bother her the night before, so she was trying to move around and stretch some, but with no luck.

"Are you supposed to walk so much?" Lauren finally asked.

"My back is killing me. Don't ask silly questions," she said with an edge Lauren had never heard before. "Oh."

"What is it? Oh lord. Sara, your water just broke!" she yelled.

"Oh god!" she yelled and doubled over. "Help. Oh god, Lauren, don't leave. God, it hurts," she said for about a minute, then it subsided. "Call Scott. He should be at the main house."

John answered, "Hello."

"John. This is Lauren. Is Scott there?" she asked.

"I think everyone but you girls are here. Alex is even here for lunch," he said. Then he heard Sara in the background. "Honey, is something wrong?"

"No, not wrong, just a little early. Get down here and bring whoever you think necessary. They didn't train us to be midwives," she said and hung up.

Dr. Quinton was even there with Uncle Alex. He had come down to check on a couple of patients he saw at the clinic in town and, of course, to check on Sara.

"I believe Sara is in labor," he yelled. "Come on, let's get down there. I could hear her in the background!" he yelled. So everyone loaded into three vehicles and started to Scott and Sara's house.

Scott got out of his truck and ran to the house when he heard Sara scream.

"Lauren, how long has she been in labor?" he asked.

"She has had a backache all morning, but her water broke, and she started having pains every couple of minutes," she said.

"Her back?" Alex said. "Oh dear, how long has her back been bothering her?'

"Since last night," Scott said.

"Then I think that she needs to lie down for a minute," Alex said. "Allison, could you get my bag?"

Allison ran to his car and came back with his bag.

"Don't we need to go to the hospital?" she asked and then screamed again.

"Let's take a look first," he said, helping her to lie down. In less than thirty seconds, Alex informed them there was no time that the baby could be born on the way.

"No. It just started. Is he okay?"

"He is fine, Sara. But you need to listen to me. The backache was labor pains. The baby's head is just pressing on your back. When your water broke, the pains likely just moved to the front," he said.

"No shit!" she said, starting to have another contraction. "How long will it take? Oh, please don't leave. I didn't mean to say that. It hurts, Uncle Alex."

"I know, honey. Let me take your blood pressure, and then I will give you something for that," he said.

Dr. Quinton walked in the room. "What do you think, Alex?" he asked.

"I believe she is going to be delivering here. Can you give me a hand? And ask Maria if she minds coming in, and Scott," he asked.

"Help me, Uncle Alex. Can Scott and Lauren stay with me?" she asked, breathing hard.

"Is your chest bothering you at all?" he asked.

"Not much," she said.

"Before I give you something, you need to listen. This is a big baby, so you will have to work hard to get him here. I won't leave you. I promise you. Okay?" he said.

"Okay. I know how to work hard," she answered. "This is different. I need to push," she said.

"No. Not yet," he said.

"I can't help it!" she screamed.

"She's right," he said as she fell on the pillows after the effort.

For nearly two hours, the family could hear Sara's cries and the urgings of the others in the room.

"How much longer?" Lauren kept asking.

Riley and Colton, having never known of a woman giving birth at home, also worried. John, Allison, Mary, and Frances had different worries. Hands would check in by the back door rather than the front now to disturb the delivery.

Then finally the cry. John Austin Byers was in the world. Uncle Alex handed the baby to Maria after he looked him over, and Maria, having been a lay midwife, knew just what to do. She cleaned him and wrapped him in a warm blanket and handed him to Scott, who was sitting in the middle of the bed, wiping Sara's face. Scott put him close where Sara could see him.

She put her hand on his, and they seemed to look into each other's eyes for a minute. Sara took his hand and counted his fingers. "Could you call your parents and tell them that he is here?" she said weakly.

"Go on, Scott. I think your dad will break the door down if he doesn't hear something. But come right back," Uncle Alex said. He worked on Sara another half hour or so, with the assistance of Dr. Quinton. Dr. Quinton couldn't hide his emotions, feeling much as a father would when seeing his child in distress.

Lauren wiped Sara's face with a cold cloth. "He is just beautiful, Sara. I am so glad I was here for this."

Scott stepped outside the room, to the anxious faces of the family. "Momma, Daddy, here is your grandson, John Austin Byers," Scott said.

Allison gently took her first grandson and looked at the beautiful baby. He had a head of thick dark hair, and his eyes were open, seeming to take in the world. "He is beautiful, son," she said. "What about Sara?"

"He asked me to come back after I brought the baby out. I will let you know in a minute," he said.

When Scott was back in the room, he told Sara how much the family already loved the newest addition.

"Can I hold him?" she asked.

"Not quite yet. I am giving you some fluids. He will weigh nearly nine pounds, so you are going to be sore," he said, trying to manage the bleeding from a tear from the large baby. "Just a few more minutes."

"Is anything wrong?" Scott asked.

"Just a little tear, I am sewing it up now. Then we will need to change the bed, and she can hold him. And young lady, if you ever scare me like that again, I will have your hide," he said.

"Scare you. I thought it took longer. Am I going to the hospital?" she asked.

"I really don't want to move you just yet. So I think you will be staying here," he said.

Alex picked up Sara as Maria changed the bed and put warm blankets down. She helped Sara into a fresh gown, and then she lay again.

"Can I see him now?" she asked.

"Just for a few minutes," he said, opening the door.

"John, as you're the one holding him, would you mind if your daughter-in-law sees her baby for a minute?"

John Byers walked into the room and proudly placed the baby in his mother's waiting arms. The others who had waited so long also came into the room. "Baby girl, you have made me the proudest man in Texas. You did good."

"Thank you," she said, holding their son, kissing his head. She cuddled him close. She placed her cheek on the top of his head, and they both lapsed into a peaceful sleep.

Alex put a finger to his lips and urged the family out of the room. When they were back in the living room down the hall from the new parents and baby, he spoke to them, "She is weak, but I believe she is fine. Her blood pressure is low, but she lost a lot of blood, and she will be sore for a while. The baby is perfect. I gave her something for pain and to help her rest before y'all came in, so she will sleep for a little while. She has chosen to breastfeed him and will likely awaken when he cries the first time. You should be proud of all of them. They are a beautiful young family," he said. Then he went back in and checked on her again.

Austin slept for about an hour and was ready for his first feeding. Sara awoke quickly and began talking to little Austin. Scott had dozed off beside her, and for just a few minutes, they were alone as a family.

Sara turned to her side and untied her gown. She instinctively let the hungry tot nuzzle her breast and begin to receive milk. Then she began to softly sing to him. Austin placed a hand on Sara's breast and looked up at his mother, only a few inches from his face. The love that swept over her was like a plague. Their eyes met in the magic of feeding and singing, and Sara fell in love all over again. There were no thoughts of the long pregnancy or labor, just the sweet face of John Austin Byers.

Sara was so involved in the baby that she didn't hear the door open and people walking in at the sound of the baby's cry. John, Allison, Saline, Lauren, and Riley stood in awe as she interacted with her new son.

"You are named after your granddaddy. Momma almost hit him in the head with a coffee pot, but she didn't hurt him. Your daddy is asleep right now. And no one will ever hurt you. You will always be loved and cherished."

"Sara, who are you talking to?" Scott said, rising up from his nap. "Oh, Sara! He is beautiful." He turned his head with tears of joy in his eyes and saw his family. "Momma, Daddy, everyone, look at our son. He is already hungry."

"It is okay if they want to come closer. It is not anything they won't see later," Sara said as the family came closer. "What do all of you think?" she asked.

John walked over to Sara, Scott hanging closely over her shoulder, watching his son having his first meal. Allison snapped a picture. The moment was etched in the memory of the entire family forever. John placed his hand on Sara's forehead and smiled. His daughter, he thought. She is indeed a miracle. He knelt down so they looked into each other's eyes. "Baby girl, I am so proud of you," was all he could say.

She smiled. "I am real hungry. Do you think I could get some soup in a minute?" she asked.

"I believe Frances is making some soup and anything else you could eat right now," Allison said.

"Tell Uncle Alex and Dr. Quinton I am sorry for changing their day," she said.

"Tell them yourself, they are still here," Allison said.

Austin had gone to sleep, and Sara didn't really know what came next, so Allison asked if she could burp him. Sara agreed and retied her gown. She attempted to sit up but found it difficult.

Maria was quickly at her side. "Let me help you."

After she was propped up with pillows, she spoke to Allison. "Momma, could you take him to the window and open the curtains please," she asked.

"Why?" she questioned.

Sara appeared out of breath, so Lauren spoke, "It is a Welsh custom, that when a baby is born, to show him to the light. They taught us that in school."

"What a wonderful thought." She opened the curtain to the fading yet beautiful sunlight of the very early spring day. Then Allison handed Austin to Saline, who was sitting on the bed beside her sister.

"Oh my god," she whispered. "He was just inside you, and now I am holding him. He is so soft. Hi, Austin," she said. "I am your Aunt Saline, and I love you so much," she said happily to the sleeping child.

Sara looked around the room and saw the smiling faces and lowered voices, so as not to wake up the sleeping baby. She felt the love and warmth of family and close friends. She was still feeling the effects of the medication a couple of hours ago. About the time she thought she was drifting off, Lady Frances Dickerson brought in some heavenly smelling soup. She carefully placed a tray on Sara's lap. The thick beef stew with vegetables was just what she needed. The crusty sour dough bread had just been baked. There was a tall glass of iced tea waiting for her, and as it had been in school, there was also a dessert.

"Thank you, La—I mean, Frances. I am starving," she said, tasting the hot soup. "It is lovely," she said and continued to eat. "I am so tired."

"You should be. Alex said that Austin weighs nine pounds. He is a big baby. It's a lot of work to get them here," Frances said.

"I can't wait until he has sisters and brothers. They will all be so happy," she said as she looked at her son still being held by Saline.

"I have made a very large amount of beef stew if anyone else is hungry." With that statement, several of those in the room went to eat.

"Scott, have you eaten anything today?" Sara asked.

"I have been in here since I got home. And come to think of it, I think I am as hungry as you are. Would you mind if I went to get some supper and come back?" he asked.

"Go ahead," she said, putting more soup in her mouth.

In the kitchen, everyone had begun eating. Conversation revolved around the miracle that they had all just witnessed. Uncle Alex left for a little while to check on the patients in the clinic, Dr. Quinton riding with him. Maria was staying close by in case her friend had any problems. After eating, Riley, Colton, Lauren, and Saline left for a little while, telling everyone they would be back in a while.

Scott had done as he said and gotten a tray and come back. Austin's cradle had been brought in and put beside their bed for ease.

After they had eaten and were content, Sara asked Scott if he would help her to the bathroom for a minute. He came around the bed and pulled the cover back. She eased her legs off the side of the bed. She really didn't know what to expect. For all she knew, she would fall apart when she stood. When she stood, she used the posture she had been using while carrying the heavy baby and lost her balance. Scott laughed a bit and supported her so she could get her balance. They walked slowly to the bathroom.

"I believe that there is anything you might need in here. Maria is very smart about things like this," he said. When he was sure she was okay for a minute, he opened the bedroom door and asked if one of the ladies in the room would help him with the bed. Allison, Frances, and Maria were in the room quickly.

"Where is Sara?" they asked.

"She needed to use the bathroom. I helped her, and she is changing. Are you okay, baby girl?" he asked at the door.

"I am fine. I will be ready in a minute," she said.

When she was finished, she called Scott, and he assisted her back to bed. The ladies had stayed just in case.

"I never thought you would want to get up so quickly," Frances said. "You just had the baby a couple of hours ago."

"I believe it was that or wet the bed," Sara said, smiling at her. "And Scott was practically carrying me." She had changed her gown and panties and done all the things a woman who has had a baby would. "Now I think I could sleep for a week, or at least until he wakes up."

Scott stayed close by her. There would someone there through the night with them just in case there was a problem. But as it turned out, she had no problem aside from a little discomfort. She slept and fed her new child for the night. Tomorrow the sun would come up, and all would be well.

CHAPTER 10

Peace for a While

For the first weeks after little Austin was born, he thrived. As Alex had delivered him, Sara and Scott decided that he didn't need a pediatrician, and Uncle Alex was to care for his first grandnephew. Austin was a happy baby and thrived on Sara's breast milk. His weight at birth had been about nine and a half pounds as best they could tell from the bathroom scale and was already approaching ten pounds.

Sara's recovery was slower due to it being her first time to deliver and delivering such a big baby. She didn't complain about her chest bothering her, but Scott would see her holding her right side when she thought no one was looking.

It concerned Scott because he knew that she had always held her heart, on her left side. Now, it was her right side. He had seen the angry scar on her right side that she said had been from a long-term chest tube when she was young. He would see her tired and ask her, and she would just reply that she was tired.

Scott had gone back to work in Dallas. The refinery, which had been his idea, was now in full production. Everyone was happy and relieved that it was finally a part of Byers Oil. He also had his usual work with both the gas and oil companies and insisted on not hiring anyone to run the business part of the refinery as yet as he wanted to get his feet wet with it.

As such, there were frequent calls down to the gulf to check on progress, not to mention a few overnight trips to personally monitor progress.

Lauren and Saline would stay with Sara on such nights.

Lauren was so excited for Sara, but there was a little sadness that she had for herself from time to time that Sara would see.

"Lauren," Sara said. "You don't resent me, do you?" Sara asked.

"How could I ever resent you? I have to admit. I think about never being able to have children of my own and get sad, but I wasn't even supposed to be alive right now," Lauren said. She knew the strong chemotherapy would sterilize her when she grew up. "You helped me to make it through having cancer so I could be here now."

"I didn't do anything. I was just there," Sara said.

"The way that you are always there for people you care about."

Sara had been thinking about something for the last few days, and when Maria had been down, she had discussed it with her. She said she would understand if she wanted Lauren to be the godmother to little Austin rather than her. She told her that she had no doubt that there would be other children, and she wouldn't mind having that honor with one of the others. Sara had hugged her and thanked her and promised her that she would have others, and she would no doubt be the godmother.

"I want to ask you something, but I don't want you to feel like it is something you have to do," Sara said, watching as her friend held Austin.

"Just ask," she said.

"Would you want to be Austin's godmother? Think about it. You would always have him in your life. I know that we live pretty far apart, but—"

"I will take the plane," Lauren interrupted. "I was so hoping you would ask. And I will always be here for him. I am so glad we found each other again," she said, the two of them embracing. "Who is going to be the godfather?" she asked.

"Maria's husband, Mark. He has been Scott's best friend since they were born. I never in a million years thought there could be a place like this."

"Do you think Mark will be a good godfather? He is catholic and attends services nearly every week," Sara asked.

"I think he is perfect. He is a good father to his little boys. I am so happy for you," she said.

"Why don't we start supper? You can help me read the cookbook," Sara said.

"What are you going to make?"

"I am going to try to make this," Sara said, pointing to the beef stroganoff on the page. "It has mushrooms, beef strips, and thick gravy, and you pour it over rice."

"It sounds very good. You are making me hungry," Lauren said.

"Why don't you stay and eat with us? You have not tried my cooking yet. It won't be as good as Allison's cooking, but you can tell me how I am doing," Sara said.

"I would love to. I can visit my godson longer," she said. "Oh, could you hold him for a second? I have something to show you," she said, handing Austin back to Sara, and then left the room for a moment.

Sara took a moment and laid the now sleeping Austin in his smaller bed that she kept in the kitchen. Then she started reading the recipe.

"What do you think?" Lauren said, walking back in the kitchen, wearing the wig that her mother had made with the hair that Sara had provided.

Sara started giggling at the sight of the natural blond Lauren wearing the auburn wig. Then Lauren started laughing at the sound of her friend's long-lost laughing. She had laughed on Christmas, but nothing like now. Both of them laughed so hard that Lauren noticed that Sara had started holding her right side. After a few more minutes of laughing, they started on supper.

"When is the christening going to be?" Lauren asked.

"Next Saturday, at noon," Sara answered. "I was thinking it would just be a small intimate service, but there are the ladies from church who call and ask about it. They want to be there. I hope that we can to this without a lot of fanfare."

"I would just plan on fanfare. But we can handle it. Are you feeling okay, Sara?" Lauren asked.

"I am still a little sore. Especially, my, uh, sit-down spot. And I am tired. But that is true with most mummies with new babes, isn't it?" she said.

"Do most new mummies hold their ribs when no one is looking? How long have you had pleurisy?" Lauren asked, remembering back to when she had known Sara as a child and would hold herself the same way, yet wanting to go out and play with the other young ladies.

"I just noticed it three days ago. But Austin is just nine days old, and I want to breastfeed him for at least six weeks. If I take the medicine, I can't breastfeed him," she said.

"I know. Do you have a fever?" she asked, feeling her friends' forehead.

"I don't think so. I did for the first few days. But I think that is because of the baby."

"You don't have one now. But I know it has to hurt," she said.

"When I saw Dr. Chambers a few days ago, he gave me Tylenol No. 3 and said to take one or two if I needed them. He said they won't hurt Austin. I have been taking them, but only at night. I don't like taking them all the time," she said.

"Sara. You and I both know how easily you can get sick with pleurisy if you are not able to breathe properly," she said, sounding a little motherly, a tone she had taken on when they were children when she knew that Sara was getting sick and didn't tell anyone.

"I know. But I just want to be a new mother—a normal new mother. Not one with a crazy family, or who is sick. Just a new mother like any other mummy. Please don't let Scott know yet, or Uncle Alex," she pleaded.

Lauren looked at her friend. "I am going to be here every day. If you so much as sneeze, and I am going to practice breathing with you during the day."

"I don't want to do anything that takes me away from Austin. I promise I am taking care of myself," she said.

As they had talked, they had put together the meal that they were planning. When it was simmering, they turned it down low and covered it. Austin woke up, and they walked into the den to feed him.

"I have been here several hours, and you haven't taken a nap or lay down. Why don't you lie down, and I will finish supper?" Lauren said. "And where is that medicine?"

"It is in the cabinet above the second sink in our bathroom," Sara said. "Would it be okay if I lie down in here, boss lady?" she asked, actually glad to lie down for a bit.

"I suppose," Lauren said, giving Sara her tea and two tablets. She then pulled the blanket off the couch and put it on the floor. She also had brought a couple of pillows from the bed.

She held a fussy Austin as Sara prepared herself to feed him. When Austin was nursing and Sara lay down, Lauren went to check on supper and set the table. She then put the water on to make the rice.

When she checked on the pair a few minutes later, Sara had turned over so she could easily change breasts, and mother and child were asleep. Lauren picked up another blanket and covered Sara. She then picked up Austin and turned the lights down.

"Well, big fellow. I believe you need to burp before you go back to sleep. Did you know I am going to be your godmother? We are both very blessed to have an angel for a mummy and a friend. Now you need to burp or I won't let you sleep," she said about the time Austin burped loudly. "Well done, young man. Now I can let you nap, and you won't have a tummy ache," she said.

Lauren turned to walk to the bedroom and saw Scott had been listening to her.

"Love the new hairdo. I nearly kissed you, because I thought you were Sara," he said, smiling.

"Well, you could kiss my cheek. After all, I am to be your son's godmother," she said.

Scott smiled and kissed her cheek. "Would you like me to put him down?"

"I don't know. You won't wake him, will you?" Lauren asked, smiling as she said it.

"I give you my word. I won't wake him," he said.

When he came back, he asked where Sara was.

"She wanted to lie down in the den as to be able to smell supper cooking," Lauren said, pulling him a little farther from the den so Sara couldn't hear them. "Have you noticed her pressing on her right side?" Lauren asked.

"Yes, but I didn't know what it was. She has always grabbed her left side, over her heart. Does this have something to do with the scar?" he asked.

"She has pleurisy. It is from the same thing. I gave her some pain medicine so she can do deep breathing exercises when she awakens," she said.

Scott looked at the young woman, who knew his wife so well. "Thank you. I did not know that," he said.

"She does not want to stop breastfeeding Austin, but if she started running a fever, you may want to ask Uncle Alex about it," she said. "I told her I would be here every day if that is okay, just to make sure. If she does not breathe because of it, she will get pneumonia," she said seriously.

"She had pneumonia when she first came here. Wow. They have been here for a year today. I had not realized that until this moment. I should have reminded Momma," he said.

"She remembered. She is bringing a celebration cake down later to surprise both Sara and Saline. She was talking earlier today, after Saline had gone to school about how last year at this time, she had three sons. She said now she also has three daughters and a grandson. She was so sweet as to include me," Lauren said. "I love her too. She is the best spare mum in the world. And Mum and she are best of friends. They write and talk a few times a week."

"I knew that she had fallen in love with your entire family. She believes it is an act of God that we were all brought together," Scott said.

"Please don't let Sara know that I had mentioned the pleurisy. I have never told a secret. Until she was nearly thirteen, we had no secrets. I knew about what her stepfather and his friends did. I hated him so much at one time I had to pray for my own soul," she said.

Scott walked over and looked in the den and saw that Sara was sleeping peacefully. He held his fingers to his lips to show Lauren she was still sleeping. She went into the kitchen and stirred supper and turned the heat off and drained the rice. She then put both in serving dishes and covered them. She and Scott continued to talk.

"Did she have nightmares then as well?" he asked.

"Oh yes. Lady Eugenie asked if I wanted to take a room with her if she moved her closer to hers. I did, of course. When she would wake up in the other room, she would wake several young ladies. Sometimes it would take me several minutes to quiet her. Does she still have the nightmares?" she asked.

"Yes. Not so much since Austin was born, but she has been tired and she tries not to show, but she is still very weak. If she were to get pneumonia again, I don't know what she would do. I will talk to Uncle Alex if we get a moment. There will be other children to nurse. He had told us last year that it would likely take her years to recover. I cherish her with all my soul. I never want her to go through what she did last year again," he said.

"Amen," Lauren said simply. "I have the table set, and I believe supper is finished, if you needed to take a shower or anything."

"I believe I will. I have been in meetings all day and just finished checking on Champ. I will be back in a little bit," he said, going to their room.

Lauren took a seat at the bar and watched the smaller TV that was there. She had discovered reruns of a show called *I Love Lucy* and loved it. She relaxed and thought of the little family that she had directed all day. How she would miss everyone when she had to go home, but she hoped she could put it off for a while more.

Scott had finished with Champ and gone back to the house for supper. Sara never napped for very long at a time.

He walked in to hear Lauren and Sara talking. Austin was still sleeping in their room, so the trio was able to talk. Each would check on him every little bit. The meal was unhurried, each knowing that Austin would let them know when he was hungry and that Sara had to eat plenty to keep her milk coming in.

After the meal was finished, Sara started clearing the dishes. "Baby girl, I believe the mother of my son is still recovering from having a very large baby. Lauren and I will get the dishes," Scott said in a manner that didn't leave any room for question. Sara went to their room and stretched out on their bed. She and Lauren had been talking most of the day.

It was so good having Lauren so close to her. Sometimes it seemed like nothing had changed at all. But then she would think of all that had changed. They had been through so much together. When it had been discovered that Lauren had bone cancer, Sara had been there with her for over a year. Lord Dickerson had paid for a private tutor for the girls so they wouldn't fall behind in their studies.

In truth, Sara was not up to being back to school full time when she had returned. She had only been out of the hospital for three days when she had returned. She was not able to climb the stairs to get to the dorm rooms, so when Lauren had broken her leg not long after school had started, the Dickersons brought both girls home, Lauren to be treated for cancer, and Sara to help recover further. They slept in the same room at the Dickersons' estate. Each girl requested to share a room in the beautiful sprawling mansion.

Most mornings, either Sara had awakened to Lauren having been up most of the night throwing up, or Lauren would wake up because Sara was having nightmares. At times, when Lauren wanted to give up fighting cancer, Sara was always there, making her want to live again. And when Sara would be so afraid of things her sister would write her, Lauren was there for her to give her courage.

Lauren was at her lowest when she lost her leg and then found out she would also have to have chemotherapy and would lose her hair. But when Sara cut two feet of her own hair off and gave it to Lady Dickerson, asking her to have a wig made for Lauren, it encouraged the young girl to try that much harder.

Then there were the times when Sara would have chest pain. The Dickersons knew the cardiologist who had taken care of their charge and called him directly. Sometimes he would adjust her medication, and at other times he would fly to England to see her. Only one time did she have fluid to reoccur, for which she had to have it drained.

Through that year, the two sick girls helped each other to get better and ultimately survive.

Now they were together again. Sara had always been able to talk to Lauren about anything. Things that Saline would be too young to know, she would talk to Lauren about.

In the afternoons, when she returned from school, Saline always stopped first to see her sister and baby Austin. It was a happy time that the two girls had never been able to completely enjoy.

The following afternoon, when Saline returned from school, the entire family and a good many of the people who lived and worked at the ranch came to Scott and Sara's house. Allison and Frances had made a special supper complete with a cake marking one year since they had come to be part of the Byers family.

Sara was in the bedroom lying on her side, nursing little Austin when people began to arrive. Saline and Lauren were sitting on the bed, and the three of them were chatting away. Sara's chest had been hurting for several days, but she didn't want to let anyone know. The joy of getting to feed little Austin so naturally was one of the most precious experiences she had ever had. The only thing that worried her was that it hurt over her right side where she had had the chest tube for so long.

She had also noticed that she ran out of breath more easily. She was going to nurse Austin for at least one more week before she told Uncle Alex. That would mean that Austin had all the immunities that he needed from her.

When Allison and Frances arrived to see the three young ladies talking in the middle of the bed, Sara was just finishing up feeding Austin. Frances took the baby to burp him, and Sara put her clothes back in place.

"Are you feeling okay, Sara?" Allison asked.

"Yes, mam. I am quite fine."

Still not convinced, she put her hand to her forehead and discovered that Sara had a good bit of fever.

"How long have you had a fever?" Allison asked.

"I had not thought about it. I think I need to be drinking more water and juice, is all," she said.

Allison decided to mention it to Alex when he arrived. He was in town in the clinic at that moment. Allison had always felt lucky to have a doctor just a few moments away. The part of the ranch that had belonged to her family, Alex had built a beautiful house. He only managed about two hundred acres for his own cattle as his patients kept him busy enough. His own three sons were grown, and like him, they had started to medical school. He would have been proud of whatever they did. All were level-headed young men. They ranged in ages from twenty-nine to thirty-five.

When John and Scott got in from Dallas, followed by his brothers, the ranch hands were also there when the three young girls emerged from the bedroom. Both Sara and Saline were surprised by the party. Lauren had known but hadn't said anything. After Sara, Lauren, and Scott had eaten supper, Scott went out to tend to some chores on the ranch. He about half felt like he was neglecting the ranch since establishing the refinery but was assured time and again that he was not.

Talk was light, mostly about Austin, the ranch, and happy things.

Sara tended toward staying in a fixed position because she didn't want anyone to think her unwell. But when Austin cried, she got up to check on him. She swayed a little and held her right side then continued the walk to their bedroom. She went to Austin's cradle and picked him up. "And just what is wrong with my little cowboy? You can't be hungry because I just fed you an hour ago." She then checked his diaper and found the cause of his fussing. She began changing the dirty diaper.

"How long has your right side been bothering you like this?" Dr. Quinton's voice came from the doorway. Sara turned to see his all-knowing eyes on her.

Sara put her head down and answered, "A few days."

"Why didn't you say something, honey?" he asked.

"It is not so bad. I just wanted to keep nursing Austin, and if I have to take medicine, I won't be able to," she rationalized.

"Maybe it won't come to that. Have you ever thought it could be a muscle you pulled when you delivered?" he said, trying to give her hope.

"It's not," she said, shaking her head. "But I want just one more week. You can't imagine the feeling that it gives you when he suckles and has a gentle hand on your breast. And our eyes meet, and it seems like he is reading my mind. I have never been so happy. Is that asking too much?" she asked, looking up at him.

"It is not asking too much at all. You have always been your happiest when you are giving, and to give to your baby in such a way, I can only imagine. But I can tell just by looking at you that you have a fever, and you wouldn't want to give that to him. But I will tell you what. Tomorrow, why don't you come to the clinic and have a chest film and let's see what it is," he said.

"I think I know what it is, and I can't bear it," she said, looking into the precious face that she loved so much. "And he is to be christened in two days. Can't it wait until then?" she asked.

Dr. Quinton knew what her faith meant to her. And against his better judgment, he agreed to wait to do anything further, just yet.

Sara knew he was serious yet still wanted to feed Austin naturally. She knew it was best for the baby, and when their faces were so close, it was almost like they were one. But, she also agreed with Uncle Alex he had never lied to her and her sister.

"But it could be that I can keep nursing, couldn't it?" she said with hope in her eyes,

Dr. Quinton hated to lie to the young mother and had promised her at one time that he never would lie to her. "Honey, you have a fever, and your right side hurts. I know that you want what is best for your son, but what if you have something that can be given through your breast milk?" he said. "Why don't I give you some antibiotics for a couple of days and see if it helps. Then you will be able to be at his christening like you have planned."

"Will you be there?" she asked.

"Of course, I will," he said and left Sara and the baby to their devices.

Saline had begun to grow into her own completely different personality from her sister. She had seen Allison plant tomatoes, cantaloupes, and other items of produce. She quickly became very well versed in growing things, as well as cooking, sewing, and riding horses. She often saddled her horse and rode to the cemetery and placed flowers on Jody's grave. And since Sara hadn't been able to ride for the last few months, she even rode Bunny for her.

Scott had found a pretty Arabian mare that was spirited yet gentle. She was almost a blue black with three white stockinged feet and a blazed face. Saline even used Sara's sidesaddle to ride her horse. It took her a while to get used to the sidesaddle, but she was able to maneuver quite well after a time. She and Riley would go for long rides on days they didn't have anything to do. They talked a lot about just about anything, including about Riley's girlfriend.

Saline had met the young lady who was the same age as Riley. Her father was an attorney and her mother a secretary. They had met in town a few weeks prior and had started dating not long after that. Riley had dated several girls, but never for more than a week or two. But now, with Saline's coaching, he was in the longest relationship he had ever had.

Amy Washington liked to ride horses, go to the movies, and eat pizza and was completely fascinated by the newest additions to the Byers family. She asked the usual questions that most people asked about them—about their German father being a royal, leaving both girls royals as well. Saline had given him permission to answer her questions honestly. Saline could tell she really liked Riley, for himself, and not for the family he was a part of.

He had even invited her to the christening. She had accepted the invitation.

By the day of the christening, everyone was up with the sun. Little Austin even seemed to be a little excited about what was happening that day. He was not two weeks old. Sara continued to breastfeed him, and taking antibiotics seemed to be making her feel much better.

Since having Austin, Sara's weight was staying above 125. She looked much better and felt better than she had in the recent past.

On Saturday morning, when she awoke, the baby was still asleep, and she thought about how good a hot bath sounded. She checked to see if someone else was in the house and found Saline had been there for the last little while. She was sitting in the den, waiting for her sister to awaken.

Saline knew that the baby woke up every two to three hours to nurse, so decided to let her sister sleep rather than wake her up to let her know she was there.

"Good morning, sleepy head," Saline said.

Sara yawned involuntarily and returned the good morning. "I don't suppose you would want to do me a huge favor, would you?" she asked.

"And just what would that be?"

"I want to take a nice hot bath. I have only been taking showers since before Austin was born," Sara said.

"No problem. Maybe he will wake up, and we can spend some quality time together before the christening. Take your time," Saline said, hoping her nephew would awaken.

Saline had awakened before anyone at the main house, so she dressed for the christening and hurried to Scott and Sara's house. She loved spending time with Austin. He helped to fill the void that Jody's death had left. He also kept her from thinking so much about her father and brother's attempts to abduct her just a few weeks before. And today would be his first trip off the ranch. She was determined to keep her eyes wide open for anyone that looked out of place.

She had looked in her closet for the right thing to wear that morning. She had been given a dress from Lady Dickerson for Christmas that looked perfect. The dress was powder blue, the same blue as her eyes. She had also sent her a matching hat and coat. The dress was silk and went to just above her knees. The silk dress was perfectly fitted to Saline's outstanding figure. It was also made for a young lady Saline's age, so as not to be dowdy.

Saline had never worn a hat before, but for this occasion, she had decided to see if she even looked good wearing a hat. If not, she could always take it off. She had rolled the ends of her waist-length golden hair then brushed it to a high gloss, pulling the sides back in a hair clip then put on the hat.

The bruising to her face had been completely gone for weeks, and she was as breathtakingly beautiful as she had ever been. When she was satisfied with how she looked, she put her coat and shoes on and left the main house for Sara's house. Saline had never had to try to outdress anyone. She would have looked good in rags and, before the last year, had proven it.

All the girls at the public school in town resented to exceedingly beautiful, off-the-chart intelligent thirteen-year-old sophomore. Her clothes then had been old, and because like Sara she had lost so much weight, her clothes didn't fit well. The boys at school all noticed her and most flirted with her openly. But Saline didn't respond to either the girls who were jealous of her or the boys that would give their right arms for a date with her. She wanted nothing to do with the boys in school, and the majority of the girls were silly and immature, even though they were older that she was.

Saline didn't have a pair of powder-blue heels but did have cream-colored shoes and white shoes. After only looking at each once, she settled on the white ones.

Saline heard Austin begin to move in his cradle, so she went in to pick him up before he could start to cry. He was awake but not fussy as yet. She picked him up and got his pacifier so Sara could relax in the tub.

She gave little Austin his morning bath and then put his diaper and a sleeper back on him. She didn't know what Sara had planned to dress him in, so she had just pulled out the first thing she saw. She then went into the den, to a rocking chair, and began talking to her nephew, the kind of silly talk that most people did to babies.

After a little while, Scott came in the kitchen door to see if Sara was awake yet and found Saline. Not long after that, Sara came out of the bathroom, feeling like a new woman. She was not dressed as yet because she had decided to feed Austin first just in case he spit up on her. She then handed Austin back to Saline to burp so she could dress.

She went to her dressing room and looked at the dresses she had to choose from, before deciding on a silk burgundy dress that had buttons down to the waist. It had long sleeves, and as usual, the skirt was flowing. She had already put on her petticoat and stockings before she went into her closet to find which dress to wear, so it only took a moment to put her dress on. She also wore a pair of black designer heels that Allison had bought for her a few months before. Then she brushed her hair and picked out a hat that matched the dress in color and had soft plumage on the back.

When she stepped back into the den where Saline and Scott were, she found that the whole family had come over and brought breakfast for everyone before they went to the church.

"May I tell everyone something before we attend the christening?" Sara asked.

Her words spoken to everyone as groups made people want to listen, as she never spoke but to a person or two at a time.

"I don't know if you know this, but every time there is a service, there is also Mass for the entire congregation. I hope that won't take too long for all of you," she said then ducked her head. She expected everyone to walk out. When everyone stayed, she was happy. She knew they wanted to be there, so there was no more conversation.

Later on, when they arrived at the church, everyone was surprised how many people were in attendance. No one, with the exception of family and close friends, both on the ranch and church, knew what was taking place at the church that day.

"So much for the element of surprise," Scott said at the usual circus that life had become lately. He leaned back into the jeep and told Sara to make sure and cover Austin's face before they walked in.

As they walked in, Scott held tight to their son, and Sara stayed close to him. On the inside, the music had started, and people were seating themselves. Then all the people in the congregation stood as Father Ron entered, and the service began.

When called, Scott, Sara, Austin, Lauren, and Mark stood. Scott held Austin then handed him to Lauren. Austin had woken up but was quiet, as though he knew what his role was. It was a happy occasion.

It had only been a little over a year since the wealthy East Texas family had saved three children from hell. The two that remained were happy at last. Fears on this day were far from anyone's minds. God was in charge, and everyone had faith that all was well.

When the service was concluded, there were many more people that were outside than before. The press had gotten wind that there may be a sighting of the new baby and were present to bring the pictures as proof to the news.

"My lady, how old is the baby now?" one asked.

"He is two weeks old today," Sara said without correcting the man for referring her as my lady.

"Have you named him as yet?"

"Yes. His name is John Austin Byers, after his grandfather," she answered.

"Were you and, what would you call your husband?" another asked.

"Scott. Obviously," she said with a questioning look. "He didn't change his name when he became a father."

"I meant to ask what his title is."

"Mr. Scott Byers," she said. She didn't know what the reporter was asking her. "He is also the vice president of Byers Oil in Dallas, if that is what you are asking."

"You are being serious?"

"Of course," she answered.

"That was not what I was asking. You are related to royalty. Does that not make him royalty as well?"

"No," Sara answered, then just held the reporter's look.

When it was clear that she intended to not answer the question any more thoroughly, another question came.

"Has your uncle seen the baby as yet?"

"Uncle Alex delivered him," Sara answered. "We didn't get to make it to Tyler to have him, so he had to deliver him rather than my doctor in Tyler."

"I am talking about your uncle, the duke."

"Oh. No. And other than a possible picture of him, I would never allow it," she answered.

"What about your mother and father? Have they gotten to see him yet?"

"Absolutely not, and it is time for me to feed our son, and I prefer not to have an audience. Please excuse me," Sara said then began walking toward her jeep. More questions came, but she kept walking, accompanied by the family.

When she was safely buckled in and the door closed, Scott began to walk to the driver's side.

"Mr. Byers, why is your wife set on not including her mother and father in her life and the life of their grandson?"

"Until just over a year ago, they had proven themselves completely unfit as both human beings and parents. When my wife and her siblings came to the ranch, she had been forced to quit school so she could make enough to try and feed and provide shelter for her brother and sister. Her 'mother and father,' as you call them, are both drug addicts and alcoholics. They lost the right to be in Sara or Saline's lives. That is all I have to say," he said and got into the jeep. He looked over and saw that Sara had already begun to feed Austin. She knew how to nurse Austin without exposing herself by putting a receiving blanket over her shoulder.

The reporters continued to snap pictures even though Sara was no longer answering questions.

"How you holding up?" he asked her.

"Irritated, but I am trying not to think about it. Austin knows when I get irritated, and he gets irritated," Sara answered.

Scott started the jeep, and soon they were on the way home.

"Is there a pizza place in town?" she asked.

"A what?"

"I have been craving a pizza for ages," she answered.

"There is one about fifteen miles from here, if you don't mind the drive," Scott told her.

"I don't mind. Do you like pizza?"

"I love pizza. We may be the only married people in the world who didn't go out for pizza while they were dating," he said, making a U-turn to drive to another town. "I am glad we are setting that to right. God knows what would have happened if you wouldn't have mentioned it," Scott said, winking at her.

Sara laughed at his words. She finished with Austin's feeding, burped him, then put him back in his carrier.

When they arrived at the pizza place, Scott came around and opened the door for Sara to get out.

"Do you think any of the reporters from the church would have followed us?" she asked.

"I haven't noticed any. So let's eat. Austin will likely sleep right through it."

So the little family walked in to the smell of Italian spices and baking crust. They looked at the menu for only a moment before Scott ordered what they had agreed on.

There was a TV on so diners could watch it while they were eating, if they liked. The restaurant was about half full of customers, so they hoped that they looked like any other family who had stopped for lunch.

Sara had taken her hat off and left it in the jeep so as not to be so easily noticed.

The waitress came back with their drink orders and noticed the dress Sara was wearing. "That is a beautiful dress you are wearing. Is there a special occasion?" she asked.

"Our son's christening was a little while ago," Sara answered.

The waitress leaned over to see the sleeping baby. "He is beautiful. What is his name?" she asked.

"Austin," Scott answered.

"Well, Austin," she said to the sleeping baby, "is this your first time for pizza?"

"It is. I haven't had pizza in years. My husband is treating my craving," Sara said.

"Where are you from, sweetie? You don't sound much like you are from here," she said.

"I went to school in the UK," Sara answered.

"My goodness! I have never met anyone from another country before. I have lived in this town my entire life. Are you from the UK as well, sir?" she asked. The waitress was so friendly that they couldn't help but enjoy the conversation.

"No. I have lived about thirty miles from here my entire life," Scott answered.

The waitress looked up at the TV at something curious. "Do you want to see something curious? I have never commented on the clothes someone is wearing before, and not long after I noticed your dress, there is already someone else wearing it."

"In here?" Sara asked.

"No. Up on the TV set. She is still on, look."

They all three looked at the picture.

"Mam, I think I can make your day if you can keep a secret," Sara said. The waitress nodded. "That is me."

"Really?" the waitress said, taking care to notice the faces of the people, not just the clothes. "If I am not the biggest dunce in the world."

"Please don't mention it to anyone," Sara asked.

"Don't worry, sweetie. I told you I can keep a secret. Why are you on TV?"

"What is your name?" Sara asked.

"Angela, Angela Wells."

"I am Sara Byers, and this is my husband, Scott. I guess we are a little famous," Sara said and explained a fraction for the woman. She listened with earnest as Sara spoke.

"Well, I tell you what. Looks like those people in the press have put you through enough for one day. I will be back with a nice hot pizza in a couple of minutes. And I will seat people a little farther away so you can have some privacy. How is that?" Angela asked.

"Sounds perfect, and if you are due a lunch break anytime soon, please join us," Scott said.

1CHILD OF THE WILDERNESS

"I believe I will. I never take advantage of owning this place."
She smiled.

When she returned, she sat down with the little family, and
together they talked and ate.

They learned that Angela had worked in the pizza place since
she was a teenager and had become the manager a few years ago
and only in the last two years was able to buy it. Together with her
husband, they had turned it into an excellent pizza parlor. They had
three teenage children. All of whom worked there.

"You don't look much older than my middle child," she said.

"I am seventeen," Sara said. "And this is the best pizza I have
ever eaten."

"Thank you. My pizzas are an art form," Angela said. Then she
rose. "I had better get back to work. If you ever need a pizza delivered, just call and ask for me, and I will deliver if you like. It must be
quite difficult to get around with so many people trying to monop-
olize you. And I give you my word. I don't ever abuse my customers,
bad for business."

"Thank you. We will be calling," Scott said. "For now, I believe
I had better start home. It has only been two weeks since Sara had
our son, and she needs some rest," Scott said, giving Angela his business card. "And may I say, if you ever need anything, please feel free
to call."

When they had paid and were on their way out, Angela could
not imagine two people so young being put through so much just
to go from place to place. She continued to listen to the TV and the
background according to some news jockey. She felt lucky for the
life that she had as opposed to being on TV like that. She then went
back to work.

"Momma, who was that girl with the gorgeous dress and husband?" her daughter asked.

"They are the people on the news, just look," she said, pointing
at the TV.

The young girl looked at the TV in wonder. "Why didn't you
tell me there were famous people here?" she asked.

"According to what they said while we were eating, what is on the TV happens to them every time they are in public, Becky. I rather felt sorry for them and did my best to keep them hidden."

"You ate lunch with famous people, Momma?" she asked.

"They invited me to. I just couldn't refuse. They are a sweet couple. And their baby is only two weeks old." The mother and daughter continued to discuss the couple as Sara and Scott, with Austin still sleeping, headed home.

Sara already planned on feeding Austin after she had changed clothes and taking a short nap. It had been a wonderful day, with the exception of the reporters. It seemed like every day now a new blessing presented itself.

As planned, they arrived home, and Sara did as she had planned, and Scott had some things to do and said he would be back later. Sara had a peacefulness that she had never known before. She was happy and content and blessed. She and Austin curled up and slept.

Henry had finally gotten home only a week before. He had spent the last weeks going through pure hell. He could not believe that some field hands had taken him to such a place as Peru. People would not loan you money for a phone call, much less food.

Then he finally got back to California and found that Tommy had only been released from the county jail and was staying with his mother at that falling-down farmhouse. He had to have his son flown home and find another way to get those girls back. His uncle said that unless he had an heir besides Tommy, his inheritance would no longer exist. Lord Alexander and Tommy had spent way too much time making asses of them on the news and in every paper in the world. Sara and Saline were the only members of his family fit to be named as a successor.

Henry looked at the TV set and saw the news report with that bastard stepdaughter of his. His uncle had no idea that there was not a drop of German blood in her veins.

What the duke saw was a lovely, well-mannered young lady, who had already married well and had the next generation started.

Damn! he thought. Every time his stepdaughter belched, they were on the news and on every channel. He would go back, and he would throw them in a crate if he had to, and that included Sara's baby son. His pride was on the line, and he would not let two teenage girls ruin what he had always planned on being his.

Saline was by far one of the most beautiful girls he had ever seen. There was no man who could not be drawn to her beauty. She looked like a textbook picture of everything that was German— tall, perfect build, with a first-class brain to complete the package. Though what a woman could do with a brain besides spend money was a different story.

For most people from the aristocracy and royalty, the hope was to better themselves through marriage. Saline was beautiful and single. A news story from a few months before showed Saline laughing with Sara and her friend from school, Lady Lauren Dickerson. He couldn't believe Joan had screwed up things for him so badly, and from over a thousand miles away at that.

The thought of his future depending on his ex-wife's bastard child made him angry enough to kill for. The only thing she had ever been good for was his bodily pleasure. She was smaller by far than his three children.

In theory, he should have left Saline alone as a little girl. But even as a very young little girl, one could see the beauty that the girl would one day be. His youngest daughter, Sophie, was a beauty as well, but not in comparison to Saline.

Sara and Saline, though raised half a world apart, were closer to each other than a set of twins. Time and again, Sara would do her best to come between him and Saline; when she rode her bicycle to Parker Center in downtown Los Angeles, that was it. He moved three of his children and his slut for a wife to Texas. Years before, he had bought land in Texas as a place to go to get away. Or as it were, a place to get rid of something.

For now, he was going to think of his next move. Let those girls and their new family relax. Just a few months were all he needed.

On Joan Redding's farm, both Joan and Oscar were working their respective jobs. Joan had refused to press charges, claiming that the loss of their baby was a terrible tragedy. For the time being, Oscar was out on bail, pending charges of assault and battery of Dr. Carmichael's nurse. Dr. Carmichael had done everything possible to assure that he would be in the county lockup until his trial. He was facing prison time for the assault not only of Amy but also of Joan's two daughters.

For now, Oscar continued to work in the repair shop, continued to hate his job, yet worked it on the chance he would be able to put back enough to at least buy a beer.

Joan had started working at a cap factory close to the farm, doing piecework. The more visors she could make, the more money she made. The job required her to work ten to twelve hours a day, five to six days a week with no overtime pay. Over one hundred women worked in the factory. Most of them would be working there for the rest of their lives. Most were high school dropouts and had half a dozen kids. But having never seen the lives that other people had, they were content to live their lives in the factory, raising their kids and cooking their husbands' meals.

In Joan's mind, she was better than all of them. So she rarely spoke to any of them. Besides that, the machines were so loud that if one were to want to talk, they had to shout to be heard.

While she sewed her caps, she thought about how nice it would be to have Saline and Sara working in the cap factory instead of her. How in this world did Sara end up married to a man whose family owned a good portion of Texas? She had thought about Scott Byers, how he had talked to her at the clinic in town. He didn't have to know that she really didn't want another brat. Most people felt sorry for a woman whose child had been born dead. But Scott Byers telling her that she, Sara and Saline's mother, could never see her flesh and blood was too much. The thought of her being a grandmother made her crazy. When the rare occasion came where she could go bar hopping on the weekends, she sure didn't want anyone to know that at the age of forty-two, she had a grandchild. The kid was two weeks old for heaven's sake, and she still didn't know the sex of the kid. She tried to shrug off her anger and turned on the TV. It was early evening on Saturday, and the first thing she saw was her two daughters with their so-called new family walking out of a church. Sara was holding their child and smiling. When the questions began, Joan became more and more irate with each response. She could see Saline not far from her sister and the rest of that family that had stolen her livelihood.

Then, when Sara said that she would never be allowed near their son and that their son was named after her husband's father, she could feel her self-control getting the best of her. But she had to bide her time. Henry would be coming back to Texas. Being with Henry would be the way to make it back into his family of German royals.

"Just wait, you whores," she said to the two sisters who smiled for the cameras and everyone else. "Just wait. Next time." She didn't continue. She would wait for Henry and see.

CHAPTER 11

Months had flown by since Austin's birth. He was growing by leaps and bounds. In late May, Riley had graduated with honors from high school. He had multiple scholarships to anywhere he wanted to go. He chose SMU due to their standing as an excellent law school.

He had discussed with his parents his thoughts of finishing law school and working for the oil company. John of course was proud to have another of his sons working in the family business. Like Scott, Riley's idea was to go to school and drive to commute rather than live in a dorm.

At the same time, Saline was finishing up her junior year and looked forward to being a senior at the ripe old age of sixteen. Saline now loved the girls' school where she had been attending since the Byers family had found them. Although she occasionally thought about what it would be like to meet a boy and fall in love, yet she would not find a boy while in school.

The girls at school had fallen into two groups concerning her. Most were her friends, but there were the rare few that envied her beauty and her brains. Saline saw her beauty as being what had caused her dad to abuse her. Like most victims of abuse, she spent part of the time blaming herself, though there was always someone there to change her mind.

She thought of how happy everyone had been at the wedding, on Christmas, and of course, at Austin's birth. She was not jealous of her sister but saw her as what she wanted to be.

That summer, she, Allison, and Maria had planted a huge common garden. They planted tomatoes, onions, watermelons, etc. Allison had taught her the value of fresh produce versus that grown in a hot house.

Her calf that Riley had given her the year before was now grazing in the pasture with the other cattle. Just to make sure they knew the calf, Riley notched the calf's right ear.

On her sixteenth birthday, John and Allison had surprised her with buying her a jeep similar to Sara's. She had known how to drive from ten. Now she could do it legally.

Before they had come to the ranch, it had been over two years since she had gone swimming. They didn't have a pool in Texas, and she refused to swim in something that had a mud bottom. Now, even though there was a swimming pool at both the main house and Scott and Sara's house, Saline preferred swimming in the creek that Riley and Colton had shown her. The water in the creek was shaded and cool, perfect for those one-hundred-degree days. They would start out sitting in inner tubes and let the current take them downstream about a half mile and walk back up.

Of course, she learned those things you had to be careful for when living in the country, such as wasps, bees, snakes, wild hogs, and skunks.

The only thing that concerned a few was that she always seemed to be on guard since the attack at the hospital. By the time school had started up again, it had been over six months.

If she happened to be in her room and someone walked by, she would be staring at herself in the mirror. It was as though the wounds from childhood had been hiding and had come out during the attack.

When asked if there was something wrong, she could always say no. The hope was that with time and security, she would improve.

In late August, she started her senior year. In addition to her high school courses, a few college courses were offered. She took a college English course and applied mathematics. And of course, she made all As. Grades were never a problem for Saline. It was trying to figure out what she wanted to do with the rest of her life. She had lived most of her life just surviving from day to day; there were no thoughts of the future, for two reasons: (1) if you were thinking about the future, you may not hear danger approaching, and (2) if you looked into the future and thought about it happening forever, you would give up on life.

Much of Saline's free time was spent with her nephew. She and Sara would put Austin in a stroller and walk to the cemetery and place fresh flowers on Jody's grave almost daily. Attending church was now something Saline did for herself. She was now learning something after Sara had learned it.

Lauren had returned to England after Saline's graduation, with the promise that they would stay in close contact. Each family had invited the other to visit each other often.

When it had come time to decide on college, Lauren had requested to attend college in Texas. She had stayed in England for just over two months and returned. Lauren decided to attend the University of Texas at Tyler. Her major changed from day to day. Her hope was to be inspired.

Saline also decided to attend with Lauren. They took several of the same courses. There was always someone from the ranch that was there keeping an eye on them for safety reasons.

Scott was very busy from the late spring until the holidays then things began to slow for just a little while. As the refinery began to form a routine, it was simpler to manage.

He and Sara loved each other more every day. Austin always seemed to be doing something to talk about for the house. Scott never thought about loving anything more than his wife and son. On Thanksgiving night, that theory was challenged. Sara told him that she was once again pregnant. The baby was due in late May. Her health had improved, and she was feeling good. The picture of two children playing in the den was one of her favorite mental pictures.

As yet, the late fall and early winter had been very mild as compared to the previous year. But if there is one thing to remember about Texas; it is, if you don't like the weather, wait five minutes.

Just after the first of the year, Sara and Maria were sitting in the den of Sara's house. Maria, like Sara, was also expecting a baby. Both were trying to teach themselves to crochet to make baby clothes and blankets. Maria's younger son and Austin were napping. They had been awake all morning. So when they had finished lunch, they were ready for a nap.

The front doorbell rang, so Sara got up to answer. She opened the front door and could not believe her eyes. Lord Henry shoved the door open before she could say anything. Maria heard the noise and went to see what was happening.

"Get out of this house before I call the sheriff," Maria said.

"If there is one thing that I learned from before, it is that we are at least thirty miles from town, and no matter how fast, we will be gone before anyone can stop us," he said.

"No one from this house is going anyplace with you. Now leave my home," Sara shouted.

"That stupid son of a bitch thought he was so funny sending me to Peru and dumping me there. I wonder what he is going to think when his namesake and his mother are gone," he said.

"You didn't want me and never did. Now leave," Sara said again.

In one fluid movement, he caught Maria by the hair then put a knife to her throat. "Go get the baby, or I cut her throat."

"Don't do it, Sara," Maria said.

Sara looked from Maria to Henry then back again. She slowly started across the den.

"No, Sara. Don't do it," she pleaded.

"He has diplomatic immunity. He can kill us both and get away with it," Sara said. "Why would you even want me? You have hated me since I was conceived."

"Give me the phone. You are the last person on earth that I would want. But my uncle knows nothing about what you are, and he has all but disowned me and Tommy. That leaves you girls, and you already have a son," he said. Sara did as told. "Now you have sixty seconds to get the kid before I slit her throat," he said, seething.

"Okay. Just don't hurt her," Sara said and turned toward their room.

When she had returned, she stood in the doorway and would not move closer. She held tight to the little bundle wrapped in a blanket.

"No, don't do it, Sara. For God's sake, please don't do it."

"Shut up, woman. Bring me the kid."

"Let her go. Then I will bring him to you," Sara said.

"This is not a game. Bring him to me." He then shoved Maria to the floor. He then pulled a gun from his back waistband. "Bring him here or I kill her now."

"No," Sara said. "If you want him, you come get him."

He cocked the gun and aimed it at Maria's terrified form. But Sara stood firm. If he wanted Austin, he would have to go and get him.

Outside, toward the barn, there was the usual activity that went on in the seasons that cattle had to be fed. It was cold but not brutal, and the sun hadn't shined in over a week—a depressing winter's day.

The ranch hands moved around doing various purposeful tasks.

John and his three sons were among those feeding cattle. Everyone was talking while they loaded the pickups with feed and hay. But even with the wind, the talking, and the sounds of the barn, everyone heard the gunshots. The shots rang from the direction of Scott's house.

"Dear God, no!" Scott yelled. Then he got in his truck and drove the short distance and saw a car parked by the front door. "Sara, Sara," he yelled, nearly knocking the heavy front door off the hinges as he threw it open.

He saw Maria on the floor of the den, covering her head. Then he saw Lord Henry Alexander and Sara. Lord Henry was stretched out on the floor, dead. Sara was sitting on her feet. The bundle she was holding had two holes in it. He could see the sleeve of her sweater red with blood.

"Austin," he whispered, tears forming in his eyes as he got closer to Sara and his son.

With her right hand, Sara held the bundle. In her left, she held the revolver that Scott kept in his nightstand. Scott attempted to pull Austin from Sara. When he pulled the receiving blanket from her, he saw the pillow that it had covered.

Sara's finger was still on the trigger, the double-action revolver cocked. "Give me the gun, baby girl," Scott said gently. But try as he did, he couldn't get her hand off the gun. "Everyone had better move out of the way."

Maria looked up to the motion and heard the familiar voices in the room, Mark close by her side. "Sara. Where is she? Lord Henry has taken her and the baby. She was standing there with Austin."

"Sweetheart, Sara is right over there, but something is wrong with her. She wasn't holding the baby, it was a pillow," Mark said. "Are you okay for a minute? Sweetheart, are you bleeding?"

"Yes, of course," she said. "I am fine."

"Mark, I can't get this gun from her," Scott said.

John had located the phone and called both the sheriff and Allison.

"Okay, I have my finger behind the trigger, so it won't fire," Scott said.

Before long, sirens seemed to come from every direction. John and Riley turned Lord Henry from being facedown to his back. In his right hand was a freshly fired pistol. The mortal wound to his midchest had killed him before he hit the floor. But it would be for the coroner to decide what happened after he had evidently forced his way in.

John placed the semiautomatic weapon in his waist to give to Randy when he arrived.

When he did arrive, he had no doubt that what action had taken place was well over, so neither he nor any of the rest of the law officials had guns drawn. Five of the ranch hands had a man tied up from the driver's seat of the car. The sheriff's deputies put him in the backseat of one of the cruisers.

"Scott, what is happening with Sara?" he asked.

"She seems to be stuck," Scott said. "I have my finger in the trigger, so it won't fire the other five bullets. Unless I break her fingers, I don't know how I will get it out of her hand. And it looks like a bullet has grazed her arm."

"Did she say what happened?" he asked.

"She has not said one word," Mark said. "Where are the boys?"

Maria bolted for the nursery. The boys were not there. "Help, I can't find that babies," Maria cried.

Several people, including Allison, deputies, and ranch hands hurried to the room where Maria was looking frantically for the missing tots.

"Everyone, be quiet for a minute," Allison said. "I hear whimpering." She followed the sound to Scott and Sara's closet. She opened the door, and there sat two scared little baby boys. "Here they are. They are fine," she said, picking them up and handing Maria hers, and kept little Austin.

When they came back to the den, everyone was relieved at finding the boys.

"Where did you find them, Maria?" Mark asked.

"That animal was going to take Sara and Austin. He threatened to slit my throat if Sara didn't get the baby and go to him. He had a knife to my throat, see. Then he pointed a gun at my head. I was so scared," she said, raising her chin, revealing a flesh wound. "He shoved me, and I don't know anything until I saw you. She hid the babies in the closet so he wouldn't find them," she said, holding her son tight. "She saved us all." The words caused everyone to frown for only a split second. She would always put everyone else before herself. She had spent her life with the mentality that everyone else was more important, more worthy of love than she.

"He was just holding a knife?" Randy asked.

"No. He had this in his right hand. When we turned him over, we found it. He was dead when everyone got here," John said. "It has been fired."

About that time, Sara's grip on the gun weakened, and she fell to her right side. "Let's get her to her room," Randy said.

Scott picked up his wife. As bad as her stepfather was, if someone was selected to kill him, it would not be his wife. She would not be able to forgive herself under any circumstances. But he was sure that to everyone present, if she hadn't done what she had done, he would have killed her.

As it was, with Maria not seeing and Henry dead, the only person who could fill in the details was Sara.

"Son, what happened?" Allison asked.

"Henry apparently came on the ranch with someone else and walked right up to the front door. According to Maria, he rang the bell, and Sara opened the door, and he muscled his way over both of them. He put a knife to Maria's throat and was drawing blood. At some point before Sara returned, he had a gun," Scott told his mother.

"She has a bullet wound. Grazed her right arm, is all," Randy said. Then he turned to his deputies. "Look in the wall that was behind her. You should be able to find the bullet."

The deputies went back up the hall as instructed.

Scott went over to where Sara was lying. He took her hand then closed his eyes.

"Is something wrong, Scott?" John asked.

"This is going to get ugly, Daddy," Scott said. "Who is the guy who was in the car?"

"A man with a thick German accent was escorted to the barn until we see what Randy wants to do," John said.

Sara's eyes suddenly flew open. "What happened?" she asked without moving. "Austin. Where is he?"

"The babies are fine. We found them where you put them, in our closet," Scott said.

"What about Maria?" she asked.

"She was a little shaken up, but she is okay." John answered.

"What about Lord Henry?" she asked. "My arm burns."

307

"It was grazed by a bullet. Do you remember what happened, Sara?" Randy asked.

"He was going to kill Maria. Then take me and Austin to Germany," she said.

"Why were you holding the gun with your left hand? You are right handed," Scott said.

"I had to make him think I had Austin. If I would have held him with my left hand, he would have thought I was pulling something. He kept telling me to come to him. I felt like I was frozen." She took a breath then continued, "He reached behind him and pulled out a gun. I pulled the gun from under the blanket and pointed it at him. I told him to leave my house. He pointed his gun at me. I heard a loud sound. Something hit my head," she said, rubbing a place on her forehead.

Allison pushed her bangs back and could see she had a golf-ball-sized goose egg on her forehead. It had already started to turn black.

"Call my brother and tell him about the bump on her head and see what he says to do. And Maria's neck also could use a few stitches," Allison directed John.

"I believe that other than the bump on her head, shock is why you couldn't get that gun out of her hand."

"Did I hit him?" she asked. "Is he hurt?"

"Sara, he hit you, and you hit him," Scott said. "It was self-defense. And you were protecting Maria and the boys."

"Could you tell who shot first?" Randy asked.

"No. I am sorry, I don't know," she answered then suddenly thought a moment longer. "He is dead, isn't he? Is that why no one will answer?"

Maria walked into the room, over to where Sara was. "Oh, Sara," she said, hugging her friend tightly. "You saved my life and the lives of our children. I can never tell you how grateful I am."

"Does Saline know?" she asked.

"She has not home from school as yet. She should be here soon," Allison said.

"Am I in trouble?" Sara asked.

"No, of course not. You shot him in self-defense. And keep in mind, Sara, that if it would have been the baby you were holding, he would have killed you both," Randy said.

"Will it be all right if I call my priest in a bit?" she asked.

"I will call him myself," Randy said. "If y'all don't mind staying back here for a few minutes, I will show the medical examiner in and get everyone cleared out."

"May I see what I did? It may help me to remember," Sara asked.

"I see no harm in that, just not too close," Scott said. He took Sara by the hand, and together they went toward the den.

After they had left the bedroom, John asked Maria if she would mind calling her daddy in a little bit, letting him know what had happened. Maria merely nodded.

When Scott, Sara, and the others arrived at the place in the family room where he was covered on the floor, one of the deputies pulled the cover down to reveal Henry Alexander's face.

Sara looked down at the man who had haunted her for as long as she had lived. She crossed herself and closed her eyes tightly for a moment. She didn't have any idea what would happen to her for having killed him. But somehow it didn't matter. Had she been actually holding Austin, he would have shot him. He had threatened Maria. Sara and Saline had suffered cruelly at his hand. Now he lay at her feet, dead. She prayed God would forgive her for having killed a man.

She crouched down and stared down at him for a few seconds longer. She hoped that Saline would not hold it against her. Then she stood again. "Please get this filth out of our house," she said. "Thank you."

"Excuse me, may I keep you for a moment longer? Do you think you are up to it?" the coroner asked.

"Are you sure that is necessary?" Scott asked.

"I believe I could answer a lot of questions, if she wouldn't mind," he said softly.

"It is quite all right, Scott. I don't mind if it will help," Sara said. "What would you like to know?"

"Could you show me where you were standing please?" he asked. Sara did as asked. "And how were you standing?"

He asked a few more questions then seemed to have all the conclusions he needed.

"I can tell you that if you wouldn't have turned like you had, you would have been seriously injured. And that he fired first."

"How can you possibly know that?" Randy asked.

"I don't need the autopsy to know that when Mrs. Byers shot, he was instantly paralyzed from the neck down. He could not have pulled the trigger as he would have to do to have shot second," he said.

"Thank you for letting us know," John said. "That helps a great deal."

She then walked to the kitchen, followed Randy and Scott.

"This is the man that was in your stepfather's car waiting for him. I would highly urge you to tell us what brought you here today," Randy said.

"This is Alexander family business," the man said.

"Shut up!" Sara said. "You people act like you own the world. You are nothing but garbage." She took a breath then continued. "Did you come here to kidnap myself and our son?"

"We came to take you to Hamburg so your son can meet his uncle. You need to assume the responsibility that you have been avoiding," he said.

"I don't have an uncle from Hamburg. Neither does our son or my sister," Sara said. "Who am I addressing?"

"I am private secretary to His Grace," he said.

"Does this mean that you have ceased to have a name?" Sara asked.

"I am Sir Thomas Ivan Schumann," he answered.

"You were willing to resort to kidnapping to achieve your goal?" Randy asked.

"Lady Alexander and her son are considered property of the German people. As such, they are expected to do as requested. As is her younger sister. In order for His Grace to recognize your marriage, you will have to request his permission to marry," the secretary said.

John, Randy, and Scott were ready to kill the man, but Sara put her hand up and spoke to the man again. "There is no one named Alexander on this ranch. My name is Sara Lyn Byers. Our son is

John Austin Byers, and my sister is Saline Byers. If you get to looking further, you will notice that Lord Henry is not my biological father.

"Hamburg was willing, not so long ago, to let us starve to death and live in inhuman conditions. So if you don't mind," Sara said, taking steps forward until she was within a few inches from him. Then she spit in his face. "Take him that."

"You are spoiled and selfish. He paid for your education in the UK. For you to say that you are not your father's is an act of defiance that I can only assume you learned from you new family," he started. That was interrupted by Sara slapping him.

"My family here has taught me that there are decent people who are willing to stand up for people that they don't know well, that you can be loved for no reason.

"Tell me about being spoiled and selfish when you have to live in a barn to keep your brother and sister safe from harm. You know nothing about the family that you serve. I can also tell you that you are trespassing here, and you need to leave here and never come back," Sara said then turned her back on Sir Thomas.

"You have not seen the last of your family," he said.

"Yes, I have. Now leave," she said.

"I will be leaving here and returning to our embassy. I am sure it will not take long to convince the government here that it will be in the best interest of all involved for you to return with me," he said.

Sara said nothing.

"Do you hear me?" he asked and took a step toward her. "Look at me."

Sara closed her eyes and continued to say nothing. It was not until her eyes rolled back that Scott realized she had held her breath. Something he had not seen her do in over a year. Scott was immediately at her side.

John went to Sir Thomas and had him by the front of the shirt and slammed him up against the wall. "You dumb son of a bitch. You Germans just don't learn. The custody of the two girls you speak of belongs to myself and my wife. As Sara is now eighteen and married, she can make her own decisions, and I believe unless you are too stupid to listen, she has. Now I believe that you confessed your intention to kidnap our daughter-in-law and grandson," John said and looked toward Randy. Randy nodded in agreement. "So you are now under arrest. And there are several people who are witnesses to that fact. And in Texas, that carries with it the death penalty."

Randy began to read him his rights and was interrupted.

"Unhand me, you stupid fool," Sir Thomas demanded. "I am here at the request of His Grace and Lord Henry. You have no legal standing to come between myself and members of the German aristocracy."

"No legal standing?" Randy questioned. "Let me show you something." Randy practically dragged Sir Thomas to the den. "Come back here and you will be next. Welcome to Texas. We have ways to enforce the laws when it comes to people like you. Hands on your head."

"I have done nothing wrong. You cannot arrest me," Sir Thomas said.

"You are trespassing on private land. Any law broken during the commission of a crime makes that person liable for any other crime. That can mean that this would be felony murder. And in Texas ,it takes about eight months to enforce the death penalty," Randy said and fairly threw the man into the front yard.

About thirty minutes later, the members of law enforcement and the people from the coroner left the ranch. Sara had woken up a few minutes after that. She was concerned about what Sir Thomas had said.

Father Keith had arrived and was talking to Sara. He could see that she was mentally struggling with the thought of having killed a man.

"Do you believe that I will be forgiven for having killed Lord Henry?" she asked.

"Of course I do. The Bible tells us that you have the right to defend you and yours. And think for a moment. Have you ever fired a gun before?" he asked.

"No, of course not. I had never even picked one up until today. I used to watch *Bonanza* and hoped that you fired the kinds of guns the same way," she said.

Father Keith smiled to himself. "So you picked up a gun and wrapped a pillow in a blanket while moving two babies into the closet. Then you kept your head together while you ordered him out of the house."

"I begged him to just leave. When I saw the gun he was holding, I didn't think he would shoot. I heard shots and felt my arm burning. That is all I can remember," Sara said. She continued to talk with the priest for a little while longer, then he was off to return to the church in town.

Saline arrived home about three thirty that afternoon. When she didn't find anyone at the main house, she raced to her sister and brother-in-law's house.

"Sara!" she yelled from the side door at the kitchen.

"I am here," Sara yelled back, running toward her sister's voice. Sara and Saline found each other's arms. Saline didn't yet know what had happened but was glad to be home.

Saline had no idea what could have happened but knew it had to be pretty bad. There were over fifty people in and around the house. She didn't know what to think.

"What happened? Is everyone okay?" she asked. Then she shrieked at the stain on the carpet where Lord Henry had been.

"Saline, I didn't mean to do it. He was going to kill Maria. Then kidnap Austin and me. I killed him," Sara said.

"Who?" Saline asked.

"Henry."

"He was here! No, he can't just come here like that," Saline said.

"I killed him, Saline," Sara said.

"Are you sure?" she said, looking at her sister for only a second. "Of course, you are sure. What I meant to ask…It doesn't matter what I am thinking."

"I am sorry, Saline," Sara whispered.

"Sorry? Sara, he came here to take you and Austin away from us. He was no better than a rabid animal. You have done nothing to be sorry for. And there will be no flowers sent from me to his funeral," she told her sister.

For the next few days, there were many people who attempted to enter the ranch, but none got through the gates.

The press had camped out to try to get anyone from the ranch to talk to them, but it didn't matter if people were arriving or leaving; no one stopped.

Lord Henry's body was flown to Hamburg for a state burial. Phone calls from Germany would come to the house, but none made it through. The wintertime activity kept most who lived at the ranch busy.

Scott and John went to the office in the mornings and would come home in the evening. There would be reporters, but either of them had anything to say.

Joan had gotten wind of what was happening when Henry hadn't returned to the farm with Sara and her kid. Then she saw a TV bulletin regarding a shooting. She made it her business to be on the news, talking to the reporters, telling "the real story" of the shooting of Lord Henry Alexander. She would see vehicles leaving and entering the ranch, but none so much as gave her the time of day.

Joan became even angrier with her eldest daughter as the days went by. She had what Henry had agreed to give her for assisting him to get back in his uncle's good graces again. And after his death, she had his credit cards and was working on how much money she could get together before someone realized what she was doing.

Oscar was even home now but spent most of his time stoned or drunk. He had even taken care not to raise a hand to anyone, as after having spent a few months in jail without his precious drugs for his nerves, his beer, and his cigarettes, he had no desire to go back.

Joan was now angry at Sara because neither she nor any of the rest of her new family would pay any attention to her, even if she stepped in the road when they were arriving or departing.

On day 5, two days before Henry's funeral, she changed her plan.

Joan was outside of the Byers ranch, and a reporter approached her. Joan had taken care to brush her long black hair and pulled the front of it out of her face, revealing her high cheekbones and olive complexion. She had applied just enough makeup to accent her beautiful darkest brown eyes.

Joan had always been an exceptional, natural beauty. But with just a touch of makeup would cause heads to turn.

She dressed carefully, and when she was satisfied that she had the look that would get the most attention, she left out the door and to the luxury car she had bought the year before. She then drove to the entrance of the ranch.

When she got out of the car, she made sure that she had used the corner of her fingernail to bring a mist of tears to her eyes, giving her a sympathetic look. The reporters approached her; she used a tissue she had in her hand to dab her eyes.

"Mrs. Alexander-Redding, have you come to see your daughters this morning?" a reporter asked.

"Yes, I have begged our daughter to please allow me to pass so I may meet our grandson. He is nearly a year old, and I have never even seen him with the exception of on the TV," she said.

"Has your daughter told you when you will be able to see your grandchild?"

Again she dabbed her eyes. "She will not even take my calls. I am afraid that my eldest daughter has turned out to be a very selfish young woman, and she has turned our daughter Saline against us.

"My former husband was so desperate to see his grandson, who is the heir to a line of nobles in Germany, that he risked all just to be able to talk to her. When he arrived, she invited him into their house and shot him," she said, turning her face from the crowd of reporters that was growing in size. "I never thought of our daughter as a killer, but I guess you just never know," she said.

"Your daughter killed her father? What about the law? Have they not come to arrest her?"

"No. When you live on a huge cattle ranch and are as wealthy as this family is, law means very little. And should they happen to get in the way, they can always be bought," Joan added.

"Will you be attending your former husband's funeral in Hamburg?"

"Yes. I will be accompanying our older son and our youngest daughter. Tommy is now twenty, and Sophie is twelve. They have not been out in public as yet because of how they are mourning their father. We will be leaving late tonight. We fly out of DFW," she said.

"Are your other two daughters also attending their father's funeral?"

"I wish that I knew. It would be lovely for us to take the fourteen-hour plane ride to catch up and finally meet our grandson. That is something the Lord Henry wanted with all his heart," Joan said, dabbing her eyes further. "I am sorry to be so emotional. I am afraid that the last two years have been emotionally traumatizing for me. First with our girls running away and taking our baby boy Jody with them, then Jody's death from a tragic fall a few months later, and then the stillbirth of our precious little baby boy on Christmas Day just a few months following Jody's death."

The reporters were having a field day with all the stories that Joan was telling.

"I was not even allowed to attend Jody's funeral. Then a few months after that, I was kept from even going to town on the day Sara married. I can only hope that one day Sara will open her eyes and see what she is throwing away. You will have to excuse me," Joan said, turning to go to her car.

While her back was turned to reporters, everything seemed to stand still. No one was talking, and then all at once, pictures were being taken, and questions began again. But something was wrong, because everyone was walking away from her.

"Sheriff Oakley, is it true that Lady Alexander murdered her father?"

"No. As a matter of fact, I have letter from the coroner, who states that Mr. Alexander had shot and hit Mrs. Byers in the arm. He also hit the wall behind her. And we know this because when Mrs. Byers fired, it severed his spine.

"This is the sequence of events that happened on that morning. Both Mrs. Byers and her dear friend Mrs. St. Claire were letting their toddler boys have a play day, while they visited. There was a knock on the front door. When the door was opened, Mr. Alexander forced his way in the house and took Mrs. St. Claire by the hair and held a knife to her throat.

"We know that he held a knife to her throat because he drew blood. He told Mrs. Byers to get her son and return in sixty seconds or he would kill Maria.

"When she had returned, she held her little bundle in her right arm and stood twenty feet from him and said he could let Maria go now. They exchanged words, and he pulled a gun and now threatened to shoot Maria if she didn't come to him.

"She stood firm and said for him to come to her. He then pointed the gun at Mrs. Byers. She had gotten her husband's gun from the nightstand and had it hidden under the blankets. She pulled it out and told him to leave her house. He fired twice, one bullet hitting her in the arm, the other went into the blanket that held the baby." He listened as the people gasped.

"Fortunately, Sara had the presence of mind to hide the toddler boys in the closet and wrap a pillow up in receiving blankets. Otherwise, that bastard would have killed an innocent baby. So in answer to the posed question regarding murder; self-defense is not murder," Randy concluded.

"I forgot to mention this, Maria St. Claire and her family are lifetime close friends of the Byers family. Her father and mother are both attorneys here locally. Charges will be pressed if any untruth regarding anyone one here decides to print it."

Joan took that opportunity to approach the sheriff. "Since you are so worried about the law, my children are still being held by those people, and they need to attend their father's funeral. Saline is still a minor, and I am her mother."

"A cat would be a better mother," Randy said. "And if you come near any member of this family, I will personally put you in jail."

The cocky smirk of the sheriff angered Joan. He was able to get close to her two girls, not that she even cared about seeing them. But Saline was related to money, and Sara had married it. It angered Joan even further that she was now considered to be a grandmother. She was in her early forties and capable of having more children if she liked.

Joan also thought as she watched the sheriff get in the car and drive in the gates that she only had a narrow window of time to get what she could out of the situation.

Texas during the winter was someplace between cold and cool. When Joan and Henry had taken Tommy, Saline, and Sophie to meet Henry's uncle a few years earlier, it had been in the winter. Winters in Hamburg, or any part of Germany for that matter, were frigid.

Joan ignored the reporters' questions and went back to the car. She knew that she had to go back to the farm and pack a suitcase. She was to meet Tommy and Sophie's plane at DFW, and they were to fly on the same plane that carried the body of her former husband. She dreaded listening to Oscar's whining when she got back to the farm. He thought he should be able to go as well. He was Joan's husband now.

Joan had told Oscar that the only reason she was to attend was because she was the kids' mother.

"Besides, you wouldn't like being around the kind of upper class that they are. You would most likely get mad and try to bitch-slap them and get yourself thrown in a German jail. And I don't have time to get you the kind of clothes you would need," Joan concluded.

Oscar felt humiliated as he stood there and listened to her run her head for a moment longer before he spoke.

"How in the world was it that you convinced Sara and Saline to go to Germany with you? Oh yes, and the baby, you know, your grandchild," Oscar asked.

"They will not be going. I have no way to get to them. That no good sheriff has it in for me," she said.

"At least leave me the car. I hate having to drive that old car of mine. You won't need it," Oscar said.

"Until I got that car, you contented yourself with your car, so you can keep driving it. I am the one with the brains enough to do what is necessary to get that car for myself. You would likely have one of your fits and wreck it," Joan said.

Oscar thought about her leaving the luxury car loaded with all the options that were known to man. She had to keep in Joan's good graces for now. Perhaps after she returned from Germany, she would secure enough to get him a new car. He further thought of the two Alexander children who would be coming to live at the farm. Sophie was nearly thirteen now and nearly as beautiful as Saline, with the same yellow blond hair and blue eyes. If she was anything like Saline, she would be well developed for her age. He thought about that while Joan kept taunting him about his not getting to go to Germany.

"And who knows, with his wife dead, maybe the kids' uncle will look in my direction since his wife is now dead," she said.

"You are married to me," he said.

"A circumstance I could change at any time."

"And I could kill you before you leave if you don't stop talking like the slut you are," he said.

Joan picked up her suitcase, full of the new clothes she had just bought, and put it in the backseat of the car. She had already locked her overnight bag that had her medicine and half of her money. She had left money enough so as Oscar would have food, and if he also worked, he would have enough for his addictions.

Joan had learned early in life that things didn't have to be unpleasant. There was always something you could take to make you feel better. Her life was all about her closest buddies: opiates, Valium, Halcion, cigarettes, and of course, plenty of booze to wash it all down.

She hoped that Tommy and Sophie didn't give her too much trouble. Tommy, quite like his father, didn't care anything about family but rather about the lifelong comfort that he had been promised as his father's heir.

Joan was shocked when word had come that she was also expected to come to Germany. She could not wait until she was there. She didn't like the climate, but she loved being around people with aristocratic backgrounds. They didn't care who they had to walk over to stay rich. Although she had never really cared for her former husband's uncle, she did like what he stood for: money and lots of it.

She got in the car and left for the airport. Since the death of his father, all Tommy could think about was he was next in line to carry on the family name. Tommy and Joan spoke from time to time but were not what anyone would call close. But when it came to money, they could form a bond that would benefit them both.

She arrived at the airport and went to the gate that they were to arrive. She sat and looked out the window. She was impatient. She wanted to get her children and board the plane that the duke sent for them. She was prepared for the long flight. First, she would talk to her Tommy and make sure that they were on the same page, then she would take her pills, along with the drinks that were served by the people in the luxury plane, and have her own party. She really hadn't thought that much about Sophie.

She knew that the duke would make sure that Sophie would be raised by her only living parent. Of course, she would agree, but what she did when she returned was her own business.

Sophie had always been rebellious, even as a little girl. The flight had arrived, and the people continued to file off. She had not seen Sophie in over three years. She had seen Tommy only briefly when they attempted to abduct Saline from the hospital.

She saw Tommy first; his blond hair and blue eyes were inimitable. With his tall powerful build, she had never thought about Sara's husband being able to overtake him.

"Tommy. How was your flight?" she said and approached her son.

"Long," he said, approaching his mother in an awkward embrace. "What happened to Dad?"

"Where is Sophie?" Joan asked.

"I am right here," she said,

Joan looked to see her daughter. She had grown tall, nearly six feet tall. Like her father, her eyes were blue, and she had long straight blond hair. Quite like her sister Saline, she was a head-turner.

"What happened to my dad?" she asked.

"He was shot," Joan said.

"Who shot him, I believe, is more the question," Tommy said.

"Sara shot him," Joan said.

"Sara? She doesn't even know how to hold a gun. Where did this happen? Is she in jail?" Tommy asked.

"No, she is not in jail. He went to her house and attempted to take her and her son. It is a long story. When we board the other plane, I will explain further," she said.

The trio walked across the airport to the private terminal where they were told to board.

Unlike that flight that they had just come off of, this plane had been sent just for the three of them and the cargo it carried.

The three of them boarded and found comfortable seats situated close together. When the plane began to taxi, Joan began telling them what had happened to their father.

"I don't know what happened regarding your dad and your uncle, but I do know that it had become very important that your uncle wanted Sara and her son brought to him. That task was not easily accomplished as you well know, Tommy," Joan said.

"Dad went to her house?" he said.

"Your dad and your uncle's secretary. I don't know what happened exactly, but it ended in Henry shooting Sara, and Sara shooting and killing Henry. It was ruled as self-defense. He was holding a knife to her friend's throat," she said.

"She was not arrested?" Sophie said. "She killed our father."

"When you are a member of that family, you can get away with almost anything. In your dad's case, he had been thrown off that ranch more than once, and in truth, he should have known better."

"She is getting away with the murder of our father because of who she is married to. Do these people know that we are German aristocrats? That means we have diplomatic immunity," Sophie ranted.

"It does not matter. It was self-defense. There was a witness," Joan said.

"We will see what happens when we get to Hamburg," Sophie said.

"Neither Saline or Sara are going to be at the funeral. Both will be staying in Texas. They want no part of the circus that will happen in Germany," Joan said.

"Whose idea was that? Theirs or their new family's?" Tommy said.

"I didn't ask. The pure fact is that they will not be there. Have either of you talked to your uncle?" Joan asked, trying to change the subject.

"I did. He said that he wanted all of us to be present at the state funeral. I haven't called and let him know that Saline and Sara would not be attending. Sara is not traveling right now because she is expecting her second child. Saline refuses to leave the ranch," Tommy said. "There is no way that bitch should have gotten away from me a few months ago."

"I am Victoria. I will be your server and attend to anything that you might need. As soon as we reach cruising altitude, I will begin serving drinks and meals."

"So what do we tell your uncle regarding Sara and Saline not showing up?" Joan asked.

"I don't know why he even wants to see them. He wants an heir and a spare. He has me and Sophie. What more can he want?" Tommy said.

"I agree with you completely," Joan said.

The plane continued to rise to cruising altitude and everyone in the cabin began to move around. The meals and drinks were served, and the three family members began eating and talking at the same time.

"I will kill Sara for killing our dad. She just killed him because she didn't have a dad," Sophie spouted.

"It was self-defense, or were you not listening? He shot her first, dummy," Tommy said.

"It does not matter. She didn't have to kill him. She just wants his place in the family," Sophie said.

"She wants nothing to do with the German side of the family. She and Saline have a family now. As far as anything else, they want nothing of it," Joan said. "So it looks like it is up to the two of you to find your place in the family."

"Sophie is far too young, so it looks like I am next in line. So I win," Tommy said.

The two continued to bicker, and Joan decided to take her medicine so she could relax for the several hours' flight. She was shown where they were to sleep, so Joan washed up, rolled her hair, and took enough medicine to see her thorough the night. She called Oscar and told him where his ration was because she knew he would be needing it, and she then said good night.

Her last thoughts before drifting off to sleep were of living in castles and palaces and traveling to many such places for the rest of her life. She found herself if a very welcome relaxing sleep.

Joan woke up a few hours later to the sounds of Sophie and Tommy fighting. When the flight attendant came over to her, she asked if they had been fighting all night.

"Yes, mam. They have. We are still a few hours from our destination. Would you care for some breakfast?" the polite young woman asked in her German accent.

"Yes, thank you," Joan said then stood and walked to where Tommy and Sophie were.

"You two need to separate and shut up. You have done nothing but fight since we boarded. You are already in hot water with your uncle, Tommy. Do you want to be in further? We need to talk about this. Keep in mind that they have newspapers in Hamburg as well. When you meet your uncle this time, you need to be a gentleman, and even you, Sophie, need to be a lady. He does not care about your being able to play football and the like. He wants to know your knowledge of Germany and of Europe. Please tell me you know something about both places," Joan said.

"Don't worry. I graduated from that school Dad had me in. I speak German, Russian, and Italian. I know the history of all the European countries and all the other bullshit that they think that I need to know," Tommy said.

"Did you bring the appropriate clothes for the funeral?" she asked.

"I thought that we could do some shopping and find something there. Surely to God they have malls there," Sophie said.

"What is he going to say when he discovers that Sara and Saline have not shown up for the funeral?" Tommy asked.

"Hopefully he will be glad enough to see the two of you and completely that he will forget the other two," she said.

"Fat chance he expects the entire family to be present. It is in fact a state funeral. People from all over the world will be in attendance," Tommy said.

"And do you really think that would include the woman that killed your dad?"

"I believe they would want her to be accountable for her actions," Tommy said.

"From what I understand, it was self-defense. After all, he did break into her house and threaten harm unless she and his grandson came with him. And he fired first," Joan said.

"That is only what the papers say. They were not going up against that family. And if she were innocent, why is she not coming along to clear her name?"

"I haven't seen you showing up on her doorstep to question her about who shot whom first," Joan said,

"Are you calling me a coward?" Tommy said, standing.

"No. I am giving you credit for common sense. Sara and Saline are in the custody of the Byers family. Sara is married to the eldest son. That family owns over half of Texas—gas, oil, natural gas, and cattle—they are not a family you want to get on their bad side," Joan said.

"She killed my father," Tommy said with clinched teeth.

"And you have spent the last five years making an ass of yourself. How do you know that your uncle won't disown you the moment he lays eyes on you?" Joan asked.

Tommy seemed to give her words some thought. Tommy knew that they were not members of a royal family but members of the German elite—a wealth he was not willing to give up on. The Alexander name went back centuries and stood for property and more money than he could even imagine.

"I am of German blood. That means something. I am the next heir. That means I am the next duke of Hamburg with Dad now dead. I am the rightful heir. I am sure that my uncle will see everything in me that he would expect to see in the next duke," Tommy said. "Thomas, the duke of Hamburg. It has a great ring to it."

"Tommy, you are way too much like your father. All you can think of is your own greatness. You have no idea what it is like to live in Germany and have people constantly around you. Your sister actually shocked me in her ability to talk to reporters, and did you see her wedding? The entire town was involved. The Texas governor attended. She was indeed like royalty. And I hear she is to have another child. The family she has married into is one of the wealthiest in the world. That family is likely worth more than any German family," Joan said.

"What do I care for a bastard sister? So she has married a family from Texas. I am the nephew of a German duke." Then there was silence for a few moments. Joan knew the faults that had been identified by the German relatives. She hoped that his uncle would come to know his nephew and they would be close. They had only met a few times during their lives. In only a few hours, they would be meeting face-to-face, and God only would know what would happen.

For the first few nights after having shot and killed her stepfather, Sara did not sleep. Austin was never far from her. The thought of anyone ever trying to take their precious baby was her worst nightmare. Maria and Sara formed a closer bond than they ever had. Each of them having babies that would be born within a few weeks of each other was exciting. Sara did her best to think of their family, but from time to time, the picture of Henry lying dead in the floor would enter her mind.

One morning, Sara and Maria both needed to pick up a few things from town. They decided to take Maria's car, because Sara's Grand Cherokee was more easily noticed. They left Allison and Saline watching the babies while they were gone. The press had given up the pursuit of Sara in favor of the death of Lord Henry, so no one really thought about her and Maria going into town as anything but a good idea.

They arrived in town and saw a storefront that was full of baby items that they just had to stop to look at it. Each made selections and brought them to the car. Then they went to buy materials and patterns for maternity clothes that they would make. Then they finally had a few things to pick up from the grocery store. Sara was the first to check out and Maria behind her. That would give time to put her items in the car before Maria arrived.

But something was wrong. Sara's cart was turned over, and she was nowhere in sight. The young man who had pushed her cart was sitting on the ground, shaking his head.

Maria immediately went to the first person she could find and told them that she thought that her friend had been taken. In minutes, there were scores of people who were from local law enforcement and local branches of the FBI looking for Sara. It took about an hour to get her picture to airports and the bus terminals. Maria was frantic. Guilt had immediately swept over her. Just a few days before, Sara had saved them all.

When the family arrived at the grocery store, Maria was beside herself. Allison was trying to calm Maria, reminding her that she had her own child to think about.

"What happened, Maria?" Allison asked calmly.

"We were just shopping. There were not reporters or anyone else, because we took my car. And we were careful to look for anything unusual. I am so sorry, Allison."

"Maria, you have done nothing wrong. Now I need you to relax a little before your own baby gets in trouble. We will find Sara, and she will be well." She hugged the young woman she had known her entire life.

When Uncle Alex came, he wasted no time in taking her to the clinic to sedate her for a little while until things could be worked out.

"Randy, has anyone stepped forward to say that they saw anything?" Allison asked.

"There were several people who saw a struggle from across the parking lot. They couldn't recognize anyone, except Sara of course. Her hair is hard not to notice. The young man pushing the cart was struck over the head and didn't see them. No one will hurt her, Allison. They know how valuable she is to everyone here," Randy said.

"I know that, Randy, but what will we have to do to get her back? She has had too many health problems in the past that are addressed on a regular basis," she explained. More and more family members arrived. They were frozen as to what to do. Saline and Austin were kept under heavy guard at the ranch.

About an hour after her being kidnapped, Sara felt herself being put into the seat of a plane. Only then were her hands untied and her eyes uncovered. In front of her sat a man she had only seen a handful of times in her life. "I am sorry we had to obtain you this way, my niece," he said in a gentle voice.

"You are not my uncle. Lord Henry should have told you that," Sara said.

"He said that you had a bad attitude and were hard to control. That is why I had you sent to school abroad. That is where the story changes somewhat." He watched her eyes; they missed nothing. She was tense, so tense that it worried him. She was obviously pregnant. About four months, he thought.

He reached out a hand toward her to calm her. "Don't you touch me." Sara had her seatbelt undone and was out of the seat.

"Sara, you need to settle yourself. You are going to hurt yourself or your baby," he said.

"I want to go home. My son needs me."

"We only want to take you to your father's funeral."

"He is not my father. Ask my mother, she will tell you. He tried to kill me and my son, and I killed him. Now take me home."

"You will be returned home after your father is laid to rest," he said.

Sara said nothing.

"Tell me about yourself," he asked.

Sara said nothing.

"I am not the devil. I am your uncle, the duke," he said.

Sara continued to be silent, looking out the window.

"The proper thing to do would be to respond," he said.

"I am familiar with what is proper, sir. I also know it not right to kidnap someone. Now take me home and I will talk to you all the way there. Otherwise, I have nothing to say." She then looked out the window into nowhere.

"Sara, it is a very long flight. With your father now dead and your brother in more trouble than he can ever get out of, you are the next heir. And with your having a good marriage and a son and another baby on the way, you are the perfect person to take my place, although that will likely be a long time. Does that not make coming to Germany a little more desirable?" he said and touched her hand.

Sara pulled it away immediately. "Is that what you people think? There is nothing in any part of Germany I am part of. Did Lord Henry not ever tell you that I am not even his child? Did the red hair and green eyes not tell you something? The man that I shot was not my father in any way, shape, or form. He beat me, raped me, and took me to a butcher in downtown LA to have his child removed from me when I was twelve. Check with Lord and Lady Dickerson in England. They knew all about it. And everyone else at the school that I was sent to so no one would know that my mother had strayed. He hated me from the moment I was born and was willing to kill me to take our son." She stopped and attempted to catch her breath. She could feel her chest begin to tighten, and a fine sheen of sweat was on her face. "I am not your niece. I am the lady who killed your nephew. I need to go home."

"Sara, what is wrong?" the duke asked.

"Take me home. Please. I need Dr. Quinton," she said, holding her chest. She stayed in her seat and pushed away any hands that came toward her. "Scott, I need Dr. Quinton," was the last thing she said before she lapsed into unconsciousness.

"Dr. Forbes, you are needed. Lady Sara is unwell."

The doctor looked at the young woman who looked to be about four months pregnant. But the hand on her chest worried him more. "What did she say?"

"Something about a Dr. Quinton."

"The cardiologist? I need to talk to him, immediately," the doctor said.

"Are you sure?" the duke asked.

"Would you like the young lady to survive?" he said.

The duke spoke with the pilots to try to make a call to a member of the Byers family to find out about the young woman who was currently having difficulty.

It only took a few minutes before they were talking to Dr. Quinton, who just so happened to be at the ranch, waiting and worrying with the rest of the family.

"Dr. Quinton, I am His Grace's physician, Dr. Forbes. Lady Sara has had some difficulty and clutched her chest and fell."

"She has a history of rheumatic fever and has frequent pericarditis and pericardial effusions. She is also pregnant. She needs a hospital. Where are you close to?"

"We are flying over England at present."

"You need to make an emergency landing and get her to the closest hospital to the airport, if you want to save her," Dr. Quinton said.

The duke gave the instructions and requested an ambulance at the airport.

By the time they were on the ground, the ambulance was ready. Sara was still unresponsive. The duke rode in the ambulance with his niece.

Hours later, things had changed. Sara started to awaken in a white room with a nurse at her side. Her throat was dry, but she managed to ask for water.

"I am so glad to see you awake, my lady," she said, giving Sara a drink.

"Where am I?" she asked.

"You are in St. Thomas Hospital in London," the nurse answered.

"My baby…is my baby well?" Sara asked.

"Yes, my lady. Fine and strong, but your heart gave us a scare. But you will be well in a few days. Your uncle has not left your side." Sara turned to see the same German man that had been on the plane.

"Please don't leave me alone with him. He has kidnapped me from my family in Texas," Sara said.

"I won't be leaving you alone with him, my lady. There is a lady Dickerson who would like to see you."

"Please, send her in, and call my family," Sara asked.

"I already have, mam. Lady Dickerson, she would like to see you," the nurse said and opened the door for her.

"Sara, thank God you are doing better and safe. When we heard you had been abducted, it was the longest hours of our lives. Your family is on the way over at present," Lady Dickerson said.

"Why is he still here?" Sara asked.

"I believe he has something he would like to tell you, and he will be gone."

Wanting him away from her as soon as possible, she turned to him, almost afraid of what he would say. "What do you want of me?" she asked.

The duke rose, his face had the look of worry for the young girl who had been through so much. "Sara, I honestly sent you to school in Wales because your parents said you were a problem child, but the reports I got from school were of a well-behaved young lady that did very well. I didn't put the part with Lord Henry together until you said it on the plane. From deep in my heart, I am so sorry for what you went through, yet of all of you children, you are the most qualified to be the next successor to the title. But that will not be for a number of years. All I ask is that you think on it, and there will be no pressure from anyone," he said.

"You believe me then?" she said.

"With what all I have heard from others, I can believe no other. But even though you have no German blood, you have all of what it takes to be a German duchess. A duchess named by a duke gives you that right. I do hope you will think about it before you decide." He nodded to both Sara and Lady Dickerson and left the room. Sara felt a huge weight lifted off her shoulders. She laid her head back on her pillow and relaxed. It was like a nightmare had ended.

"Are you quite all right, Sara?" she asked.

"I just think for the first time I am free, and I am happy and free." Sara put her head down again and was in a peaceful sleep.

Sara spent another twelve hours before the doctor would say that it was okay for the young mother to travel the long distance home. It was twelve hours by plane, and the idea of her sitting in a fixed position for twelve hours seemed like it was inviting trouble. Lady Dickerson said that he needed to leave it to her and everything would be fine. The doctor, trusting the noblewoman, agreed to let the young lady be discharged.

"Are you going to be flying back with me? Are you even sure that you can get a flight on such short notice?" Sara asked.

"It will be tomorrow afternoon before we leave, but we will be staying in the city rather than going back out to our house," she said.

"To a hotel?" Sara said.

"No. To an apartment I use in the city when I am here. And it is quite cold, so I have picked you up a few things so you won't catch a chill," Lady Dickerson said. "Your uncle asked me to give you this when he was gone. It was his wife's before she died and wanted you to have it. And though you have no real feelings for him, I believe that he is, in his heart, sorry for the actions of your stepfather."

"Why are you being so nice to me? You have always been nice to me," Sara said. She nodded that she would accept the gift as it was given. She opened the heavy box with the help of her friend and gasped. It was an emerald and diamond tiara and an emerald and diamond ring. At the bottom was a picture of the wife he had lost wearing both. A tear escaped her eye because she knew that it was really over.

"Because we thought we had lost you again and are so grateful that we got you back. Now let's get you dressed, and we will be out of here."

"You will get no argument from me," Sara said. She was up and dressed in a pretty frilly maternity dress that Frances had picked up for her, complete with matching shoes, hat, and coat.

The nurse brought the wheelchair for Sara, and she sat down. Then the nurse told her that she was expected to take it easy as the doctor had explained. And no emotional upsets. She was wheeled to the front door to the Rolls-Royce that waited for them. When Sara stood and thanked the nurse, she saw the duke appeared again. She turned to get into the car before he could get to her, but pregnancy had slowed her. "Sara, remember what I said. You are most welcome to Hamburg anytime," he said then kissed her cheek.

His touch was gentle, and unlike Lord Henry, he smelled fresh and clean.

Sara merely smiled, nodded to him, and disappeared into the luxury car with Frances. "Where are we going?" she asked.

"Kensington Palace. We have an apartment there," Frances answered.

When they arrived and the gates opened and they were driven inside, they went to the place near where Sara supposed her apartment was. When they entered, the door was opened by a uniformed man. Sara smiled up at him, and he winked down at her. They walked down the wide hall with red and gold carpet and ample portraits and mirrors everywhere all richly displayed.

Sara saw a man walking toward them, who appeared to be deep in thought in what he was looking at in his hands. When they were a few feet away, Lady Dickerson stopped, curtsied, and then greeted Prince Charles. Sara also curtsied but said nothing. Sara stayed behind Frances as they spoke.

"And who is this?" he asked.

"This is a very dear friend of our daughters. They went to school together in Wales and then in England. Lady Sara Lyn Byers," she said.

"Very nice to meet you young lady," he said, extending a hand.

Sara extended a trembling hand and again curtsied.

"She has had a very long day, sir, and needs to get some rest. She has a flight tomorrow afternoon."

"And where might you be flying to?" he asked.

"Texas," Sara said in her soft, still completely evident English accent.

"Well, my lady, I do hope that you will be coming home soon," Charles said.

"Thank you, Your Royal Highness," she returned simply. He looked at the girl again, thinking there was something familiar about her, but didn't hold them up further. He went on down to his apartment and turned on the news of the day and continued to go through his papers. Then he heard reference to the duke of Hamburg, and it made him think of the name of Alexander. He would call down to his cousin's apartment later and talk with her.

Sara was led into a very large living room that was both elegant and homey. She yawned and looked around the room and saw a lady there.

"I am sorry. I didn't mean to startle you. You must be Lady Sara that Lady Dickerson has told me about. May I show you to your room?" Sara looked over her shoulder to see Frances giving her the go-ahead.

"I am Leda, your lady's maid. If you need anything, please ring."

"May I have a glass of milk?" Sara asked.

"Immediately, mam, then may I suggest that you take a little nap? Unless I miss my guess, you are expecting and need rest," she said as she pulled the bed down and pulled out a warm gown. "I will be right back with your milk." When the door closed, Sara slipped out of her dress and stockings and put them over a chair and sat on the bed. She stretched out then turned over on her side. She was nearly asleep when Leda came back.

"Your milk, My Lady. Is there anything else I can get you?"

"No, mam, thank you so much."

"I will wake you for supper in a little while." With that, Sara finished her milk and lay down and was asleep in no time.

Frances had walked back down the hall to Charles's apartment.

"I hope I am not disturbing. I thought you may be wondering about my little charge. She is the niece of the German duke who decided to abduct her as a means to get her to go to Germany. She had some medical problems on the plane and had to land here."

"Was it her father who was killed this past week?" Charles asked.

"Yes, it was. But she will not be attending his funeral. She is going back home. Lord Henry, her stepfather, attempted to shoot

Sara, and she shot him. She is terrified of just about everything right now. Your mother has allowed me to take one of the royal flights to take her home to their family," Frances said.

"Please tell me more," Charles said, urging her to sit, and they began to talk for a while. Charles was astonished at what he heard. His heart went out to the little thing.

"Will the two of you dine with me here this evening?" he asked.

"Of course, she is a little shy."

"I will not push anything, don't worry."

"Then, I will see you at supper," she said, rising, kissing Charles's cheek.

After a couple of hours of rest in the unthreatening atmosphere, Sara awoke refreshed. She was ready to go home. But she knew she had to wait a day. She looked over and saw Frances nearby.

"Is it time for supper, Frances?" Sara asked.

"Yes, it is. You are just in time. Did you have a good nap?" she asked.

"Yes. I feel so much better. I was so afraid when I was on the plane with that terrible man, that I would never see anyone I love again. I guess he didn't turn out to be such a terrible man when I told him what his nephew was really like. Does that make me a bad person?" Sara asked.

"No, that is what makes you better than your mother, her husbands, and most of your siblings. You are special. I put out a lovely dress for dinner. I thought we could eat with a few people about your age that live here in Kensington Palace. Okay?"

"I would do anything for you, you know that," Sara said.

"I have put you some fresh clothes out, let me know when you are ready," Lady Dickerson said.

"May I call Scott first?" she asked.

"Oh, didn't I tell you that he is having supper here?" she said as Scott came from around the door.

Sara began to cry as she went to Scott, and they embraced. "I was so afraid I would never see you again and our family and baby. How is my Austin?"

"He is only three days older than when you were taken. And he misses his momma very much. Are you okay? Did he try to hurt you?" Scott asked, with the entire concern showing on his face.

"He didn't hurt me. I got angry on the plane when he started telling me how grateful I should be, and I guess I got in such a state that I held my breath, and you likely know what happened from there. But he listened. He is not trying to force me to do anything anymore. He realizes I am not his niece by blood but says that I have all the qualities of a duchess," she said.

"I am so glad that I have you again. And no matter what country you are ever in, you will always be my baby girl," he said, kissing her softly.

"Let's go to eat," Sara said.

They followed Frances to the dining room and found there to be a few people there.

"Scott and Sara Byers, these are two of my cousins, Charles and Andrew, and another cousin, Christina, and her daughter Philipa."

Scott shook hands with those present. Sara curtsied as she had always been trained.

"Nice to meet you all," Sara said.

"Nice to meet both of you as well," Christina said.

Each took their seats, and supper was on the table. There were servers there in case it was needed. Everyone started eating and kept conversation light. When the meal was concluded, everyone went to a sitting room for tea. Scott and Sara stayed very close to each other.

"How is our newest member treating his momma?" he asked.

"He is keeping me hungry all the time. And he is glad that we are going home tomorrow," she said.

"Are you sure you want to leave here? I mean, this is quite a place," he asked.

"I have been in places like this before. But our home is the best place in the world," Sara said.

Sara and the other ladies were handed a small glass of something that looked like juice. The men were drinking what looked to be scotch. Sara took a drink of the warm drink and felt warm all the way to her toes. She could feel herself relax a little. After a few minutes, she finished the little glass, and the same man brought her another. Scott was talking to Charles and Andrew, just a few feet away. Frances called her over to talk to her and Philipa.

"You look like you are feeling better since Scott got here. He and my cousins are discussing the countryside of Scotland versus the countryside of Texas. They could be at that for hours. Charles is passionate about the country," Frances said.

"Scott is just as passionate about Texas. He told my younger sister Saline when they were having a disagreement that she might be a lady, but his dad was the king of Texas, and that made him a prince," Sara said, and the three of them laughed.

Then the thought of Scott standing, talking to two princes as equals became funny. She started to giggle. She took another sip of sherry.

"What are you laughing about, Sara?" Philipa asked.

"The thought of Scott being Prince Scott, Pillfa, I mean, Philipa," she corrected and then started to giggle again.

The three women continued talking in lively fashion. Scott had never seen Sara so active in a social setting with people she had not met before. Her skin glowed, her eyes shined, then he noticed that she had a sherry glass in her hand. He smiled because he knew that she had no idea that she was drinking sherry. He then turned back to the men he had been talking to.

"I have to tell you, gentlemen, I have the best of two worlds in her," Scott said.

"How is that, Scott?" Andrew asked.

"I married a woman with the intelligence at fourteen to raise her own brother and sister. Yet she had always been taught before that at the finest schools in the UK, from what I understand. She is tough enough to protect her family yet knows so little of the world in general that she is an innocent," Scott said.

"And she is beautiful. She has the most beautiful eyes I have ever seen," Charles said. "She is the young lady with the book from Wales."

Scott remembered the story Lauren had told them. "The one and only."

"And all that hair," Andrew added.

"Yet, she does not realize she is drinking sherry and is becoming intoxicated, because she never has been. So I had better bid you each good night. And please feel free to join us at the ranch at your first free moment," Scott said, shaking hands with each and walking over to his wife.

"Incredible people. I have never met anyone from Texas that I am aware of. But if any more of them are like these two people, they are exceptional people," Andrew said.

"From what I understand from Frances, their family owns about half the state and is in oil and gas, but is highly respected in raising cattle and horses. She is very fond of all of them. And Sara went to school with Lauren most of her life. She is part of the Alexander family from Hamburg. She is from a very distinguished family in her own right, then she married into the Byers family," Charles said.

"She looks younger than I am," Andrew said.

"I believe you two are the same age."

Andrew and Charles looked toward the couple who had eyes for only each other. Each having the look of being mature beyond their years, and both so happy that there was nothing in life aside from their son at home they could ever need. Happiness like that could never be bought. Scott took her glass and kissed her forehead. He asked the man who was tending to the room for something, and the man smiled and walked away momentarily and came back and gave Sara a glass of water.

"May I ask one question before you retire?" Andrew asked.

"Of course, anything you like, Your Royal Highness," Scott said.

"I know the two of you didn't grow up together. So how does a German lady born in California and raised here meet an oilman and rancher from Texas?" he asked.

"I threw a coffee pot at his father's head and turned to run and ran right into him," Sara said in all seriousness. Everyone laughed.

But when she held her look, they knew that she was not kidding.

"Charles, I do believe I need to tell Mummy to send me to Texas for a time." Andrew smiled. "Good night, Sara."

"Good night, Andrew," she said and was led away by Scott.

When Sara and Scott were in their room, those remaining began to ask questions about the couple. Normally, when people from their station in life met, the conversation was stayed and unmoving, with little or no emotion. But this was a different sort of situation.

"I am not sure I understand how this came about, Frances. I thought Lauren's friend had died a few years ago," Charles said.

"There were things that happened in California when Sara returned when she was twelve. We begged her not to return to the situation, but in her mind, she was the only person to protect her sister. She was ten at that time and had already attempted suicide once by running into traffic. Sara ran out blindly and pushed her out of the way. Lord Henry Alexander was a monster, a sick, sadistic monster with all the money and power in the world," Frances said bitterly.

"But Texas is hundreds of miles from there," Andrew said.

"He took Sara, Saline, their infant brother, and mother and left them on a small farm in Texas that he owned with no means of support. Sara worked to support the entire family alone and took care of her sister and brother herself," Frances said, careful not to tell too much.

"But their mother, why didn't she work?" Charles asked. "She didn't protect them?"

"Never, she remarried a man only five years older than Sara. They were both addicted to drugs and alcohol. When she would pass out, the new stepdad would go after the girls. But both girls had each other's best interest in mind. Sara made a place in a falling-down barn to keep them safe."

"A barn, so he never found them," Andrew said.

"He never molested them, thank God. But the day that Sara told you she had met the Byers family, the incident with the coffee pot in the café, she had a high fever. She has a condition with her heart that her mother would not let her have the medicine for. Her stepdad had beaten her so badly that the side of her face had broken bones. She had been working for two weeks with four broken ribs. She only weighed one hundred pounds. Her entire body was black and blue, yet that night, according to her sister, she was on her knees praying for God's help, trying to give them faith to survive.

Like Lauren, she is deeply religious. She was baptized in Wales in the church and attended services every time the doors were open. Her family was atheist, except her. That she is able to sit at the table, even with the two of you is a big step for her," Frances said. "At eight, she had a bad case of strep throat when she returned home for a summer visit. They didn't get her treated. It turned into rheumatic fever. At one point, she was pronounced dead for twelve minutes. To hear her speak of what she saw when that happened lets you see a pure soul that regardless of how bad someone hurts her, she never ever hated, including when her mother pulled her little brother out of her arms, causing his death two years ago."

"The people who helped them, what sort of people are they?" Charles asked.

Frances smiled at the thought of her family's new friends. "The best. I don't mean that they are wealthy, although they are. They are fair, faithful, and honest. You have never met people like them before. They own the largest ranch in East Texas and have over two hundred people who live on the ranch that are treated as close as family. They have their own houses. Some even have been given their own part of the ranch. It is the most incredible place I have ever seen."

"Much like Balmoral, sounds to me," Charles said.

"Very much, but something more. Everyone from the ranch and the oil company are invited to both Thanksgiving and Christmas dinner. And there is no one, man or woman, who would not put up a gun to protect anyone who resides on the ranch. The family would also bear arms to protect the people who work for them. They are not violent people. Everything is always done according to the law. That is the only way that John Byers would have it."

"If the father disliked his daughters so much, why did he go to where Sara was to kill her?" Andrew asked.

"Lord Henry's uncle took him out of the succession when he was arrested for kidnapping and assaulting Saline. He had lost custody of the girls the previous year, but because she is legally German by blood, he and his son attempted to take her back to Germany. She fought with her brother in the backseat of the car and jumped out while it was still rolling. They hurt her pretty badly. But she got away. Mr. Byers came between Lord Henry and Saline and had Henry taken to Central America and took his passport.

"Henry then waited over six months and showed up at Sara and Scott's house. She and a close friend and their babies were making baby clothes together, both are pregnant. He held a knife to Maria's throat and told Sara to get her son and go with him or he would kill her. Sara knew that he had diplomatic immunity and would likely get away with it, so she went back and got a baby blanket and a pillow. She also remembered that Scott kept a pistol in his nightstand. She took both of the sleepy toddlers and put them in the closet in their room and closed the door and went back to Maria. She hid the gun. He threw Maria to the floor and pulled a gun out, and using her left hand, Sara pulled Scott's gun out and told him to leave. We don't know why he shot Sara. He shot twice, hitting her once in the pillow that he thought was the baby, and the other creased her right arm. Only then she fired Scott's gun only once and hit him in the chest."

"Did she say that was what happened?" Andrew asked.

"No, Maria did. When she fired Scott's gun, she had never shot a gun before, and the recoil hit her in the head. It knocked her out for a few minutes. Maria thought that Austin had been hit, as did everyone who rushed in the door. When they found the pillow, there was such relief. Then everyone had to look for the babies, who were still in the dark closet."

"I have known grown men that didn't have so much forethought. But it sounds as though she has been fighting this battle her whole life. It must have been a relief for everyone," Andrew said.

"Everyone but Sara, she killed a man. Her priest has showed her the places that say she had the right to protect herself and her children, but she does not talk about it," Frances concluded.

"Her uncle knew that she killed his nephew, and he kidnapped her anyway? What was that purpose?" he asked.

"She is, in his eyes, the next one who is fit to be in line to head the family. Even though she is not actually a blood relative, he will name her as the duchess. He will let her mother, brother, and baby sister know tomorrow following the funeral at the news conference. Tommy is not fit, his youngest sister is too young, and both were too close to their father. Saline will not even speak about him, and he will give Sara the choice on worldwide TV. But she will only be identified as his niece rather than her name."

"I believe I may request attending the funeral tomorrow. I am sure Mummy will not mind if it is I who attends rather than her," Charles said. "And perhaps, if you don't mind, Andrew, you may want to accompany the plane to Texas tomorrow. After all, she is a lady and a close friend of one of our noble families."

"I will be happy to," Andrew said.

"Uh, Andrew, have you ever seen a picture of Saline Catherine Victoria Alexander?" Frances asked.

"She is just a teenager, right? Younger than Sara," he said.

"Well, she is blond and a little taller," was all that Frances would say. She thought about how he would react to the most beautiful young lady in the world.

Charles was talking to his mother for a few minutes before he returned.

"Her Majesty suggests that I leave tonight for Germany. I will have to call my people, and she also suggests that the flight wait until the funeral is over tomorrow afternoon at 1:00 pm our time out of respect. It will also give some idea as to what the announcement of a different person who will head the family at his death," Charles said. Frances was always impressed at how her cousin, the queen, would organize things so completely, with so much thought, and process it quickly. She had spent over half of her life as a monarch and had to always be organized, a trait that Charles shared.

"I am going to excuse myself to catch my flight later tonight, so I bid you good night," Charles said. Prince Charles, the Prince of Wales, was considered to be the world's most eligible bachelor as he would be the next king of England.

Still in his mid twenties, he had been raised to be no less than a king. He was a serious man who loved his country. Like his mother, he loved the countryside, especially that in Scotland.

He never liked to hear of violence but was not naive to its existence. He knew many of his relatives both in England and the world leaned toward using violence to get their own way. He would not address anyone with the exception of the duke at the funeral. Part of his duties as a royal prince was to attend the weddings and funerals of other heads of state, which included other royals, the aristocracy and presidents, etc.

Andrew also left to ready himself to leave for a few days; he greatly admired the couple he had met and hoped that when he married, he would be so happy.

Everyone else retired for the night to get some rest for the long day ahead of them.

CHAPTER 12

The following morning started early in Hamburg. It was several hours until the funeral, then there was the family breakfast, talking to reporters immediately thereafter, welcoming important people from around the world who were in Hamburg only for the funeral. At about 11:00 am would be an early lunch for the family and honored guests, then they would be placed in luxury cars for the slow two-mile trip to the church.

The crowds had been forming on the entire route to the church since the previous evening. They estimated that there would likely be half a million people lining the streets.

When Joan and the two Alexander children arrived at the estate, they discovered many things. First was how cold it was. Hamburg was only about one hundred miles south of the North Pole, and it was still the wintertime.

They were led through the courtyard to the centuries old, exceptionally well-preserved palace that had been in the family for generations.

They followed the man directing them until they came to a very large room where they saw the duke sitting behind a huge desk, talking to another man. Both stood when the trio entered. When they were immediately in front of the desk, the duke stepped around it.

He stood and looked them up and down. There had been reporters at the airport when they landed that spoke to them for several minutes. The story of the family of Lord Henry Alexander had arrived at the airport wearing wrinkled, casual, multicolored clothes, disgracing themselves and their uncle.

"Did you not understand that you are not to speak to reporters until following the funeral and that you were to wear suitable clothing for mourning?" he said, seething.

"We just got off a fifteen-hour flight. We decided to buy the clothes here for the funeral, Uncle," Joan said.

"I am not your uncle. You will address me as Your Grace. Thomas, I expected at least you would have respect enough for your father to dress the part. Never mind, I should have expected nothing less," he said.

"Uncle, is there a mall close by? I really would love to go shopping," Sophie asked.

The face of the duke turned deep red. "You are here to attend a funeral, not go shopping. Did you, or did you not bring suitable clothing for the next few days?"

"I don't wear black," Sophie said, turning to look at the room.

"Sophie, you are twelve years old now. You need to learn proper respect. You will wear black," he said, walking directly to her, staring her down, a gesture that her father had done so many times it did not affect her. "You will wear black dress, hat, purse, shoes, and stockings."

"Down, old man. You're not my father," Sophie said but was cut off. Her uncle had slapped her with an open hand, so hard in fact that it made her eyes tear and her ears ring.

"One more word out of any of you and you will be going home on your own. Now sit down," he demanded.

Then he picked up the phone and called his private secretary, Ranulf von Strassen. He entered the room. "Ranulf, it is quite like we thought. They are not respectable. Please have the clothing brought to their chambers. You have thirty minutes to get dressed and be back for a private breakfast with me. Understood? Good," he said, turning his back on them like they were garbage. "And, madam. Control you brats."

Joan thought she would explode but said nothing, thinking about all the good fortune that was fixing to come her way as mother to the next duke of Hamburg.

A few minutes later, they had all changed clothes. Joan, who had been wearing curlers in her long black hair when she had first seen him, had brushed her hair out, fixing it fashionably, then was going back down the stairs. She had looked in the mirror and thought about how beautiful she looked. In one of the small dining rooms, she walked in, wearing the black dress. She thought to herself how he had been a widow for nearly ten years and how he would swoon to her beauty.

"Madam, when this meal is finished, you need to put that hair up. This is a funeral, not a fashion show. Now the three of you, this is my companion, Lady Catherine. You may call her Lady Catherine. We are to be married later this year. My love, this is Thomas, Sophie, and their mother, Mrs. Redding. Please be seated." Catherine sat on his right. When everyone was seated, the duke began to speak. Covered plates were placed in front of each, and tea and coffee were offered. Sophie was given milk and juice.

"I had a chance to talk to Sara on the plane ride over from Texas. She is a true lady. There is not a false heir in her at all. Madam, you and your former husband have spent the last eighteen years lying about her," he said.

"How can you speak of her like that? She is a sorry bastard," Tommy yelled, standing.

The duke did as he had before and slapped him soundly. When Tommy recoiled and attempted to return the blow, he was back-handed for his trouble.

"Sit down, or leave. You say that word again regarding that young woman and you can swim back to the States. I understand that you put Lady Saline in the hospital not long ago, Thomas. Did it make you feel like a man to strike a young woman? Since none of you seem to be hungry, let's do some paperwork," he said.

Here we go. We're about to each be living in wealth for the rest of our lives. But the papers that were thrown on the table one by one mentioned all three of them in various magazine and newspaper articles from around the world.

"This is my personal favorite of yours, madam."

Joan looked down at the paper that had her on the front page with the heading "Prostitute or Whore." "Which is it? Never mind. Thomas, you have been put in the drunk tank so many times I lost count. You have beaten up three girlfriends and put them in the hospital in the last three years, and this is my favorite, 'Sir Thomas's Bastard's Attempt to Buy Silence.' This was likely one of the most shocking and pathetic, Sophie, a full picture of you naked, kissing a man, another man sucking your breast, and I would imagine I know what the third is doing with his face where it is. And by the way, on page 3, it has you laughing on the naked lap of what looks to be a forty-year-old black man, his hands on your breasts, and you laughing. And these are parts of the photographs that were sent from hundreds of different people.

"Ranulf, ask my ministers to step in and then lock the doors, please."

"Yes, Your Grace." He smiled.

"Yes, he has seen these pictures, but as you are a German citizen, my ministers are entitled to see if they can help with them," he said.

Twenty-five men entered the room.

"Gentlemen, I have been referred to as old, so I would like to know if I am interpreting these correctly. This is Lady Sophie Alexander. And I believe this is her a year ago. I believe these two men are sucking on her breasts. And this is on the same day. I am sorry, I forgot to mention the details. Here, Lady Sophie," he said, giving Sophie the small pictures and pulling out hundreds of enlarged photos of her. "Now you notice that she appears to be sucking on his penis. And if we pull out just a little—"

Sophie broke in, "Stop, it was just one night, and I was so ashamed I couldn't tell anyone. I got drunk, and these guys took advantage of me."

"Just a minute here. No, I don't think so, this one has you on your hands and knees, still with a man's penis in your mouth, you are sitting on this one's penis, and he appears to be sucking your breasts. And this completes this set. She is still sucking his penis, sitting with this man's dick in her vagina, and this big black one must have just taken the last hole in your anus," he said.

"Stop, I am only twelve years old. Don't do this to me. Let me go to my room." She cried.

"Sit down, you whore. She may try to say they raped her with just pictures with men in them. So let's see if I am right about this. Is that a beer bottle? If it is she, excuse me, my dear. Please let Lady Catherine out of the room. The rest of these are pretty bad. First, she is taking a drink then putting it in her vagina. Is that her anus again? Then she takes another drink, out of the same bottle. Please pass these around. I just got this this morning. Ranulf, make sure she sits there. Lights please," he said then turned on a movie. "I will let her tell you what is happening here."

The movie started. "Oh, Felix, is that as good as you can do?"

"No, I have lots of friends. But until they get here, I think I can help," the forty-year-old man said. "This is my friend Mr. Broom. But I will have to put my dick in your ass." He does so.

"I want it all." He does. "Eat me and fuck me. Make me hurt. Make my clit bleed. I need more. I am so horny and empty. I have been so bad." She gets on her hands and knees. The man begins to do as requested, then gets a razor strap and begins to whip her. Welts begin to form. "Oh god, I am in love. I am trash, hurt me more. I am having my uncle's baby. He is a duke, hurt me more. I want it. Oh, it feels so good."

"Let's take you to my friends. They are waiting where you told them to." The man walks with her, attached to what appears to be a filthy alley someplace in downtown LA.

"Please stop. Don't show this. I am not staying," she begged her uncle.

"You are staying until it is done," he said.

The man threw her on a Dumpster, and one after one, man after man of every color and different numbers continued.

When it seemed to stop, the true shock came. "Tommy, come show me how they do it in Germany." The skin on her thighs and buttocks threatened to bleed. Then Tommy, Sophie's own brother began. The last picture was Sophie spread-eagle, naked. It was obvious that everyone had been rough. Her fingers felt her own breasts, and she continued to use her fingers to fondle herself. A different man came over and was completely naked. He put his face in her crotch. Sophie started to scream with pleasure. "Please harder, I have been bad." The same man put her on her hands and knees. He entered her anus very roughly, prompting her to scream. "See if you like this." He got the lighter out of his car and went back to Sophie, entering her anus the same way, then took the lighter and put it in her vagina. After a few minutes of her screaming, he roughly turned her over and started chewing on her breasts. "Oh, thank you, baby. You were the best. I was so bad." The man then tied her up, placed the broom stick up her anus, and a beer bottle in her vagina. They took her to the park not far away and left her there for all to see. Then they called the press about Lady Sophie of Hamburg. When the press arrived, they took all the pictures, and Sophie appeared to like it. Then it was over, and the lights came up.

"That was not really Sophie. It was an actress," he said.

"It really wasn't me. It is like he said," she said.

"Ladies, please show us her right thigh," the duke said, handing them a picture. Sophie fought and was restrained. When her thigh was exposed, the bruises from the razor strap were still present, along with a tattoo of a skunk.

"Now what is going to happen is this. Sophie, you are leaving from here following the funeral to a restrictive girl's school, complete with a psychiatrist to straighten you out. And by the way, there are no men there. And your teachers are women from the German authorities. Thomas, you will be entering the German military."

"I have to go back to college," he said.

"You will enter the military for five years, or go to a German prison for twenty. Choose," he said.

"You can't do that to me, you son of a bitch. I will be the next duke," Tommy said.

"Not in our country. If one of them chooses, and only if they choose, that place will go to either Sara or Saline. I know the day this was filmed was the day your father died," he said.

Sophie was crying.

"One word of any of this after you have done your time at my ministers' choosing, and what your father did, and you will never receive a dime. When you get out of the service, you will receive one hundred thousand dollars. If you go to prison, you get nothing. Sophie, your custody goes to me," he said.

"No. Grandma won't let me go," she said through tears.

"Who do you think gave me the film? She found it the day after your dad died. You can say good-bye to her at the funeral. She does not want you. She will be moving to Texas to be closer to the other two girls."

"I will tell everyone I am having your baby," she said.

The ministers, though disgusted, laughed. "You stupid little girl. We never had any children because I am sterile, and if you had picked up anything about me, you would have known that."

"My dad didn't want my body. I would have let him, but he didn't want me. He would—" Sophie said.

The duke put his hand up. "The service will take place, but only because his mother was a decent person. Sophie," he said, kneeling beside her, "someday you will thank me for this. Your mind is not right. I just couldn't see what a horrid man my brother had raised. I pray to God that you will be grateful you got a chance to be happy."

"I hate you. You can't talk that way about my dad. I could have made him love me someday," she said, swinging at him. But rather than being angered, he held her tightly so as she couldn't hurt herself. "Stop looking at me like that. I want my dad."

"Take her upstairs and medicate her and let her rest before the funeral," he said and watched her get dragged from the room. "Don't leave her alone."

How could he have been so blinded as to what was happening? He turned away from the broken young girl who had no idea how damaged she was. Then his gaze hardened. He looked at his remaining visitors at the table. "Thomas Frederick Alexander, you are nearly twenty-one years old. You knew what you did to at least two of your sisters, your blood. You are filth, just as your father before you. I cannot place you in a situation where you defend your people. Not with what I just witnessed. So I ask my ministers to deliver whatever is right and appropriate. Of course, you will attend the funeral, under guard."

"I will be returning home after the funeral. I am an American. You can't hold me against my will," Tommy said, standing.

"You must have been drunk when you took political science, so I will tell you. You were born in the United States to a German. Your blood makes you German, and you can be charged and held here as long as warranted. And you have also been charged in Germany with raping a German minor. You will be treated appropriately. Your passport has been confiscated, and the embassy has been notified. You wanted to be here, so I may have forgotten to say, welcome to Hamburg.

"At last for you, madam. I will give you a choice for after the funeral. You have a couple of choices to make. As I understand it, you were trespassing on private property when you pulled my nephew, a German, from his sister's arms, and though considered an accident, as we see it, you were committing a crime when he died, making his death manslaughter. Or you will leave, never come back, and we will never talk again," he said.

"But I had four of Henry's kids. I raised them," she said. "I don't work. I can't just be sent away with nothing."

Her face reddened. Her eyes became those of a wild animal that was about to strike.

"I don't care if you work or not, but when you return to your farm tomorrow, I would assume that you and your husband are going to need money to live, and for that, you will be needing money, and from what I have heard about you, well, let's just say while you are in the position to make your money, you can take a nap.

"And regarding the four kids, one has been adopted by a family who cherishes her, one is dead, one is being sent to a mental hospital, and the other is going to prison. So if you want credit for something,

I wouldn't try by making yourself a good mother. A cat is a better mother than you ever were.

"But at least it will ease your mind that your daughter with a different father is wealthy beyond anyone's imagination. The people on the ranch where the girls live will fight for them."

"Are you forgetting that it was not I who killed Henry, but his stepdaughter Sara? And there is nothing she could say that could be believed. She ran away from home and stole my two younger children. Have you forgotten that? You have never even talked to her." Joan spat.

"Actually I have. For ten hours on the plane back to Hamburg, we talked. I checked everything she said and talked to the witnesses. She was not lying. She is a perfect lady. You, madam, don't know the meaning of the word," he said.

"Sara is here?" Joan said with her eyes wide. "I want to talk to my daughter and see my grandchild. She has not let me see him yet, and he is a year old. Please let me talk to her. I miss my girls so much."

"Sara is in Europe, but I don't know where. Face facts, Mrs. Redding, they don't want you. You allowed God only knows what to happen to your children. You used your own children. You are far worse than any animal I know of. You may finish your breakfast, if you wish. We leave for the funeral in about thirty minutes. We have things to do," the duke said and he and his ministers exited the room. There were four men who stayed.

"Mom, they are going to send me to prison. You have to help me. I can't go to prison. I will do anything if you won't let them, Mom. I know that you have gotten quite a bit of dad's money hidden. If you get me out of Germany, I will go to work and help you out," Tommy said.

Joan suddenly started laughing, a loud sadistic laugh. "I can't believe that you were so stupid as to have someone film you and Sophie together. Stupidity is obviously something you get from your father. Why could I possibly want you around? It would be like having two Oscars around," Joan said.

"Then I won't stay with you, but don't leave me here. At least you will have one of us who can get you out of trouble if you need us," he reasoned. "Without Dad around, I could be useful."

Joan thought about it and decided he was right. "Let's get out of the funeral. They cannot watch us all the time. And with all the people in the streets, we could just disappear. Surely we could make it to a city with an airport before anyone can find us."

"Okay. Do we go to the funeral?" Tommy asked.

"Yes. Make them think we are scared of them. Then we will take off. Go back to your room and put on different clothes under your clothes. I will do the same."

The two had made their plans and left the room to go to their own rooms. They then returned and waited for the rest of the people and got in the cars and left for the church.

That same morning, Scott had awoken early as usual, Sara awakening shortly thereafter. She was anxious to go home. She just knew that her son would forget her. He had to have grown so much in the last four days.

A knock came on the door, and a lady walked in, carrying a tray and placing it on a table in their room. "Good morning, my lady, sir. I have brought fresh coffee, and breakfast will be served in thirty minutes in the morning room."

"Thank you very much," Scott said.

She smiled then walked toward the door. "Would you like me to help you dress, mam?"

"No, mam. But thank you," Sara said.

After she left the room, Scott leaned over to his wife and kissed her. "Good morning, Lady Sara."

"Good morning, Prince Scott," she returned, smiling.

"Did you sleep well?" he asked, knowing that she slept peacefully all night.

"I did. I think it was my partner beside me." She smiled. "Can you turn the TV on? I want to see if they mention the funeral on TV."

"I didn't think you were interested," he said.

"I didn't get to tell you that at the hospital he was very nice. He didn't know about anything. And he gave something to Saline and me," she said, throwing the cover back and picking up the heavy box. She put it on the bed and sat down in the middle of the bed with it.

Scott was curious and looked at what he had given her.

"He said it belonged to Saline's aunt, his wife that died," she said.

When Sara pulled it out of the box and handed it to Scott, he couldn't believe his eyes. "He realizes now that I am not related to him by blood. And he is going to leave us alone. So I just thought I would give it to Saline. Maybe someday she will want to meet him again."

"Sara, this is real and worth a thousand fortunes. You don't want it at all?" he asked. He thought about how girls always wanted to be princesses.

"No. I have all the fortune I will ever need," she said and gently stroked Scott's cheek.

"I believe that I will get us both some coffee. What do you think?"

"I like being a kept woman," Sara answered and lay back against the pillows.

Scott fixed them both a cup of steaming hot coffee and turned back to Sara, who was staring out the window a million miles away.

"Something wrong?" Scott asked.

"He was nice to me. He wanted me to talk to him, and I yelled at him. Then in the hospital, he said he would not bother me or Saline again. But if I chose, even though I am not German, I had all the qualities to take his place. I should have said I was sorry. He is going to have a long day."

When Scott had heard from Lady Dickerson that Sara was safe and well, he packed a suitcase with things of hers that he thought she may need, including her long cape to fight off the cold and even her camera.

"Let's do something a little different. Get your cape out of the closet."

Sara went to get the heavy cape that she had been given just after they had said their "I dos."

Scott then brushed her hair, letting it flow over her shoulders and down her back. "Now put this on," Scott said, referring to the beautiful tiara from the box. Now, stand over by the window." Sara did as she was told, and Scott picked up her camera. He snapped several pictures of her that made her look like a queen.

"Now, we can have these developed, and we can send him one as a present," Scott said.

"Can we have one made together, do you think?" Sara asked.

"Let me find someone to hold the camera," Scott said, leaving the room and coming back with Andrew.

"Sara, you look very lovely this morning. This will be a very good picture. And one very befitting a couple of your status," Andrew said. After a few more shots, it was time to go to the table.

The TV started to tell about the funeral of the former successor to the Alexander Aristocracy. It showed Tommy, Sophie, and Joan arriving early that morning, walking from the plane with curlers in her hair.

The reporter began telling the family history in detail. Questions as to the arrival of Sara and Saline were also mentioned.

"Is it going to be like this all day long?" Sara asked.

"More than likely."

Sara covered her head with a pillow and slid down in the bed. Scott turned to see what else they were saying for a moment.

"The shooting that took the life of Lord Henry Alexander of Hamburg that happened at the ranch of billionaire oilman John Austin Byers, who currently has custody of Lady Saline Catherine Alexander. Her older sister, Lady Sara Alexander Byers, was abducted four days ago from a grocery store near a small town about thirty minutes from the Byers ranch.

"Authorities are not willing to give any information whatsoever regarding the happenings of the last week. Security was tight on the ranch with several armed men from the ranch who refuse to make any comment to reporters.

"Last night, a spokesman from the Alexander family said that the shooting was a tragic accident, and there were no charges to be pressed.

"When questioned about concerns regarding his niece, the representative said, 'No comment.'"

Scott walked over and turned the TV off. "Sara, come on, baby, you need to get dressed."

"I can't do this, Scott. Does anyone know I am here?" she asked.

"Here in London, yes. But specifically here at Kensington Palace, I don't' know how anyone knew, likely someone saw you when you were leaving the hospital," Scott said. "I have seen no reporters outside, so we will likely be able to leave without being seen. Or that is the hope."

"I don't want all the trouble to start over again. I thought that we were just going to be left alone to our family. And maybe I could start taking some courses so I can be a nurse. But if I can't go to the store, how will I ever go to school?" she said.

"Right now, Sara, it is just because of the funeral that they are taking notice. Next month, or next year, when you would want to start to nursing school, things will likely have settled down. Trust me, I know. When you begin going to college, you disappear into thousands of students. It is the perfect hiding place."

"I hope that I can still be a nurse. It seems like I get started in the right direction and keep getting pushed back.

"On the plane, Scott, I thought he was going to kill me. But he never raised his voice. Then I wondered if he was going to put me in jail because it was I who killed Henry. He said I was the only one he really didn't know.

"Henry had told him that I resisted authority and was spoiled rotten. So I was sent away. I don't really know what opinion he has of me now. Do you think he just thinks I am a bastard and is glad to be rid of me?" Sara asked.

"No, I believe he thinks you to be honest, a perfect lady. And after dealing with your mom, Tommy, and Sophie, I believe he can tell the real thing when he sees it," Scott said.

"Do you think that he would like it if we sent him some flowers to his house and leave him a nice note?" Sara asked.

"I think that would be a perfect thing to do. Let me go and see whom you would talk to, and you had better get dressed for breakfast."

Sara got out of bed again and hurried to dress for the day. Knowing what was expected on a day of mourning, she dressed in a black maternity dress that Frances had provided for her. She found herself nervous, but until it was time to leave, there would only be her, Scott, and Frances. Knowing that she relaxed a little, she turned the TV back on to the same channel and found that not only was the news on, but the news of the day was the funeral of Lord Henry Alexander.

Then she saw a face from her past that she had not even thought about in so many years, her grandma Catherine, Henry's mother, and the woman that Saline was named after. She had been the only adult in California that she had ever been able to rely on. She knew that Sara was not her actual grandchild, but she had always loved her.

Grandma Catherine looked sad as she walked off the plane and got in the car that would take her to the palace. Then she saw another more recent person, Charles, the Prince of Wales, shaking hands with the duke.

"My god," she whispered.

The newscaster who had spoken to him earlier had said that he was there to represent both the Crown, the Dickerson family, and the Byers family, telling the man that currently, Mrs. Byers was indisposed. His words as a gentleman made Sara's absence both expected and acceptable.

"Lady Sara has had a difficult last few days. Most know that she is now expecting her second child and has been told by her physicians to excuse herself with regrets," Charles said.

"Thank you, Charles," she whispered.

"Mam, who are you talking to?" her lady's maid asked as she walked in.

"The TV set," Sara said and smiled. "Prince Charles just told people why I would not be attending the service, and I really appreciate that."

"He flew over last night. Both of the princes enjoyed their time with you and your husband last night," she said and smiled.

"I enjoyed their company as well," Sara said and laughed a little. "I believe it is the first time I have ever met men without running and hiding."

"My lady, you have the sweetest laugh. Are you ready for breakfast?" she asked.

Sara stood and went to follow her.

"You forgot shoes, my lady," she said.

"Oh. At my home, I spent so much time barefoot I forgot," Sara said, blushing. "I said that out loud, didn't I?"

They both got a laugh from her comment. She put low-heeled slippers on, and they walked to the morning room. When they arrived, she saw Scott, Frances, Andrew, and another man she had not met. She walked quickly over to Scott, who was talking to Andrew. She stood a little behind him, and Scott reached around and pulled her to his side.

"I keep telling her that she belongs by my heart, not my backside," Scott said, kissing her hand.

"Good morning," Sara said.

"I do hope that you slept well," Andrew said.

"Quite well, yes," she answered.

"Sara, the prince will be accompanying us home," Scott said.

"Why?" she asked softly.

"Maybe his mother wants to make sure she gets her plane back," Scott said, winking.

"Oh, Scott," she said, taking a step and standing directly in front of him. "Don't say such things." She stomped her right foot like he knew her to do when she tried to make a point.

Scott raised his eyebrows a little, looking down at her. "I have never been scolded by a lady before."

Sara returned his smile and again stood at his side.

Everyone sat down to eat. Talking was kept light. No one mentioned the funeral at the table. When finished, they went to a comfortable room that had the TV on, but it was turned down.

They talked until they saw cars coming from behind some very tall iron gates that had just opened. Before the cars were men on identical horses. One man behind the rest sat his horse and pulled a horse that was saddled, but there was no rider. Sara knew that was representative of a fallen rider being honored. Dozens of cars driving very slowly went down the city street that was lined with thousands of people.

She saw her baby sister sitting rather stone faced beside her uncle. In the following car were her mother and Tommy, and in still another car sat their grandmother with an official-looking man beside her.

Out of respect, cameras were not allowed inside the very large Lutheran Church.

Sara knew that such events in Europe and the UK were very big events that drew officials from nearly every country in the world. And though they were aristocratic rather than nobles, it made no difference.

The casket arrived and was carried in in grand style, with the people following in the cars, exiting the cars and walking inside.

"Keep in mind that Lord Henry and his wife married in this same church twenty-three years ago. Now he returns to be eulogized before being laid to rest," the man on the TV said.

Sara got up from her place beside her husband and went closer to the TV and sat on the floor, much like a child would sit. She watched as the people began to enter the church.

"Lady Sophie Alexander, who has been the subject of a huge scandal in Southern California, enters with her uncle. Lady Sophie appears to be heartbroken as she stoically enters, leaning heavily on her uncle," he said.

"Something is wrong with Sophie," Sara said.

Scott came over and sat beside his wife, who, when watching TV, was generally sitting on the floor, playing with their son.

Andrew joined them, though he sat a couple of feet away. "Were she and your father close?" he asked.

"I hope not. Oh lord, I mean, I don't know," she answered.

"Sara has not seen her sister in six years. They have been living in different states," Scott said.

"Sara, are you comfortable sitting like that?" Frances asked.

"Yes, mam. Lauren used to sit like this all the time in front of the fire."

"But that was back in school. You were little girls," she said.

"I mean, at the ranch, we still sit in front of the fire on the floor. That is why there are always pillows in front of the fireplace," Sara said.

"It would dislocate my knees to sit like that," Frances said, smiling at the sight.

"Why would Momma be there?" she asked.

"Perhaps for your brother and sister?" Frances said.

"Of course," Sara said. "Tommy is with Momma? Look, Scott, that is Grandma Catherine. She was always nice to me."

"There is Charles," Andrew said.

"It is funny to see someone in person and then see them on the TV a few days later," she said.

If not for the fact that Sara was expecting a baby, she appeared to be much younger than her eighteen years.

"Do you remember Lady Caroline, Sara? You and Lauren went to school with her," Frances said.

"Of course, I do. She is so pretty now. She had braces on the last time I saw her. She was a bit of a tomboy then," Sara said.

"Still is," Andrew and Frances said in unison.

Sara smiled at them.

Andrew reached over and picked up Sara's hand. "Your hand is bleeding," he said.

Sara pulled it back a little abruptly and sprung up and left the room. Frances motioned for the men to keep their seats. Scott whispered that he did nothing wrong. "My father did that over two years ago, and she threw a coffee pot full of coffee at him. That is how we met," Scott said.

"Were you angry?" Andrew asked.

"I didn't have time to be. When she turned to run, she ran right into me and fainted," Scott said.

Andrew laughed in earnest. "I believe that is the strangest meeting I have ever heard."

"I had been trying to meet her for two years," Scott said. "She didn't mean to act so abruptly. She considers this day her fault. Lord Henry shot first and grazed her right arm. She likely forgot to dress it this morning."

"I had forgotten about that. It is hard to put that little thing with a gun in her hand," he said.

"She had never picked up a gun before but had seen me shoot a snake one time. Then of course, she watches *Bonanza* every time it is on." Scott smiled. "She still has a bruise under her bangs from the recoil of the colt .45 pistol. It knocked her out. My opinion regarding her having hit him with the wrong hand and having never shot a gun before is that God had to have guided the bullet."

"I believe Frances told us something about that," Andrew said. "But she had to shoot him. Why so guilty?"

"Because she is Sara. When I entered the house, it was the longest thirty feet to her I have ever taken. She had also been shot in the stomach. I thought she was holding our son. It turned out to be a pillow. It took me fifteen minutes to pry the gun out of her hand," Scott explained.

"He shot twice? I thought he was an excellent marksman. And she only shot once?"

"That's the way it happened. She is right handed and had the gun under the bundle she carried and shot with her left hand, a single shot. According to the autopsy, he couldn't have shot after she shot him because the bullet severed his spine."

"But you can't imagine the not knowing if your wife and child are both dead for those seconds," Scott said, shaking his head.

"Her priest even tried to get through that she had only protected herself, her child, and saved her friend's life. But she doesn't talk about it, except maybe with Maria."

"Who is Maria?" Andrew asked.

"Her husband and I went to school together. His father and mine were much like Mark and I. His father worked on the ranch as the foreman, and he owned a good deal of his own land. He died on the ranch of a heart attack, and my father adopted him after that, and we became brothers. Maria is her friend who is also expecting a baby. She saved her life," Scott said.

"Scott. There is a problem. Andrew, please call for a physician," Frances said.

Scott was up and running to his wife's side.

"Frances, what do I tell him?" Andrew asked, obviously concerned.

"She has lost her baby," she said. "Scott also asked if you would call this number and ask if his mother could fly over."

Andrew made the call downstairs, and in minutes, one of the physicians on staff at the palace was there.

Andrew dialed the number given to him by Scott, and a woman immediately answered. He listened to the phone ringing, and then a woman with an accent like Scott's answered.

"Hello, is this Mrs. Byers?" he asked.

"No, this is Maria St. Clair. May I tell her who is calling?"

"Yes, this is Andrew. Scott asked me to call his mother."

"Allison, you have a call. She is on the way. Is Sara okay?" she asked.

"I afraid she has lost her baby," he said, hoping it was okay to tell her.

"Oh no. Allison, Sara lost the baby," Maria said and handed her the phone.

"This is Allison Byers."

"Mrs. Byers, this is Prince Andrew. Apologies, this is Andrew. I am here with your son and daughter-in-law. Scott has asked if you could come to England," he said.

"Of course, I will be there as soon as I can get a flight over," she said.

"If I may, may I make a suggestion?"

"Yes, of course, Andrew," she said.

"Bring her child. I believe it would help her."

"I believe you may be right. Thank you."

"And if I may. The plane that was to take Sara and Scott home can be sent to bring you and whoever would wish to come to

England," he said. "Just let me make a call, and I will let you know what time to meet the plane. Do you mind holding for a moment?"

"Not at all. Who is this?" Allison asked.

"I am Andrew, second son of the queen," he said.

Allison could hear him dialing, then address Mummy, speak a few words, and then was back on the phone.

"The plane will be landing at Dallas Fort Worth in eleven hours. It will leave in just a few minutes," he said.

"Is there room to bring her sister and Maria?" she asked.

"As many people as you would like to bring over, mam. We are at your disposal."

"Will I see you there to thank you?" she asked.

"Yes, I will be here. See you soon."

Hours passed. Scott had come out of the room shortly after the physician arrived. Both lunch and supper had been served and cleared, untouched. Scott went to Sara frequently and found her resigned to the fact it was God's will because she killed a man. She didn't say it aloud, but Scott knew his wife well.

Andrew told Scott what he had suggested, and Scott thanked him.

They sat together as the duke of Hamburg announced that his successor would be one of his nieces, either Sara Alexander Byers or her just younger sister Saline. He was telling the people at the press conference what prompted his decision. He told of Sara's marriage to Texas royalty and that they already had a child and were expecting their second. He was telling the reporters about Saline when a note was given to him. He was silent as he read the note, and his expression changed. He dropped his head, and when he raised it the next time, there were tears in his eyes.

"Excuse me," he said and walked away, past the thousands of people, back inside the church, never saying another word.

The next time he was seen, it was only to get in the car to go home. As the rest of the people got the waiting cars for them, the people lining the streets seemed to move in the direction of the car. As the other people continued to make their way back to the palace, the phone rang. Andrew was closer than Scott, so he picked up.

"Hello," he said simply, on the off chance that the person on the other end had been a reporter.

"Andrew, I slipped a note to His Grace, telling of what has happened to Sara," his older brother told him.

"Is that why he left so abruptly?" Andrew asked.

"Yes. It hit him quite hard. He broke down when he came back into the church. How is she doing? Has she been taken to the hospital?" he asked.

"No. According to the doctor, it was over before he arrived. He has a midwife at her side until she is feeling a little better and can return home," Andrew said.

"Scott's mother should be arriving soon. I hope that will help her. I asked that she bring her little boy along. She is so pale. Her eyes have no sparkle. She has said nothing. According to Scott, she is blaming herself for killing her stepfather."

"I will be leaving here in a couple of hours. I have told His Grace it would likely not be a good idea for him to attempt to visit her. He is largely responsible for the loss of her baby. He has no business putting himself in her life at this point," Charles said.

"Her baby boy."

"What?"

"The baby was a little boy. He didn't have a chance. She does not talk. She stares out the window. She does not cry. Scott is brokenhearted. I can't imagine such a love as they share. It is rare," Andrew said.

"I will see them in the morning. Let them know how sorry I am. And make sure Mummy knows. She has taken a keen interest," Charles said.

"I will. See you tomorrow," he said then hung up the phone.

The following morning, it was cold in London. The plane from Texas arrived at 4:00 am. The passengers were Allison and Maria, of course. Austin was being carried by his grandmother. Saline was also with them, which Allison didn't think was a good idea, but John had told her that unless she wanted to chain her in the basement, she had better come along. John had also come along.

When the plane stopped at the gate reserved for arriving dignitaries and royals, there were two cars that also arrived. Allison, Maria, and Austin got in the first, with John and Saline, with the luggage in the second.

They drove through the quiet streets from Heathrow Airport to Kensington Palace. They were escorted to the suite that the Dickersons frequently stayed in. At the door, Andrew was about to greet the welcome visitors when he saw the most beautiful girl that he had ever seen. He was speechless at the sight of the blue-eyed blonde.

"Where is my sister?" Saline asked forcefully.

"I don't think it is a good idea," was all that Andrew said before Saline landed a clean slug before anyone could stop her. Andrew, not expecting the blow, fell to the ground. John put his arms firmly around his adopted daughter.

Maria was on her knees to make sure that Saline had not injured the man. "Are you okay?" she asked.

"Yes, of course," he answered, rubbing his jaw. "I am Andrew."

John nodded his head, still firmly holding an instantly enraged Saline. "John Byers, son, let me apologize for our daughter. She is so anxious about her sister. Saline, apologize now!" he said, releasing her. "Swing again and you will be put on a plane home. Understand?" he said.

"Yes, sir," she said with her eyes on Andrew. "I want to see my sister."

"Lady Saline, I am Andrew. I am glad to meet you," he said. Only then did he notice that the man that had released the beautiful young woman had a swollen shiner. It didn't take Andrew long to figure out who put it there.

John put his hand out and firmly shook hands with the young prince. He led them to the study where Scott and Lady Dickerson sat. Both were on their feet when they saw that the expected party had arrived.

Everyone greeted everyone. Knowing that Saline's short fuse needed to be assured that her sister was being well cared for. "She was asleep for the first time since the loss of her baby and has only been asleep for a few minutes." Seeing this with her own eyes, Saline went back to the room where everyone was. Allison went into the room where Sara slept and took a seat beside her, as she had done so many times before.

Austin had been handed to his father, both had embraced snuggly. "Mumma," he had said, looking at his daddy's face.

"Mumma is asleep, son. Shh," he said, putting a finger to his lips. Austin repeated the gesture back to his daddy. Then he kissed his dad sloppily and began to explore the room.

Scott asked if Saline had given him the shiner, and John smiled at the thought of his own broken nose a couple of years before.

Fresh coffee and breakfast were brought for the visitors and the people already present. When everyone was seated in the morning room and Austin was happily eating from the lap of his father, conversation began.

Saline knew that Sara would want her to apologize. "Your Royal Highness, I am sorry about slugging you. I have no excuse."

"Evidence to the contrary, my lady. And call me Andrew please," he said and smiled.

"I am Saline Byers, Andrew."

"Son, tell us about Sara," John said.

"The doctor told us that between the trauma of the shooting, being kidnapped, terrorized for eleven hours, and weakened by years of neglect that she has not yet recovered from, he said that it was a miracle that the pregnancy survived the last week. But when she has recovered, she will likely be able to have more children, which is no consolation whatsoever," Scott said with tears in his eyes. "I don't know how I am going to make it. I can only imagine what Sara is feeling. She has said she is sorry so many times I lost count. But she doesn't cry, Daddy. She just stares out the window. When she finally went to sleep, I was glad because at least she is not tormenting herself."

"I touched her hand. I only meant to tell her she was bleeding. I pray that I was not responsible for what happened to her," Andrew said.

Both Scott and John were out of their chairs when Saline's head popped up. "Saline, we have talked about this," John said firmly.

She did not rise because of his words.

"Sis, we were watching the TV. We were all sitting on the floor and Andrew just so happened to notice first. I think she had just thought of what all had happened the last few days from watching the TV. Andrew did nothing inappropriate. Okay?" Scott said.

Saline looked at Andrew, and her anger was lost. "I am sorry. We have always protected each other. She protected me so much growing up. I wouldn't be here without her. And I am sorry for taking it out on you," Saline said.

Andrews's heart went out to the young girl. "Your sister will likely sleep for a little while, Saline. You had a long flight. Would you like to take a walk?" he asked.

"Daddy, may we go for a walk?" she asked, looking up at John's face.

"Of course you can. Just think of what Sara would want, and, Andrew, good luck." John smiled as he rubbed his own eye.

The sun hadn't risen as yet, so Andrew decided to show her more of the palace.

"Your Royal Highness, how did you meet my sister?" she asked.

"Frances is our cousin. She has an apartment here, and we had lunch the first day she was here. We were invited to dine with them," he answered.

"We?"

"My brother Charles and I were both here for a few days. He is currently on his way home from Hamburg. He went to represent the Crown and your family for the funeral. He told His Grace right after he had said that either Sara or you would be the next duchess of Hamburg," he said.

"What? My brother Tommy is supposed to be the next duke. What happened?" she asked, remembering the last time she saw her brother.

"He was unseated as the next in the succession. Neither he nor your younger sister will be considered eligible. He holds you and Sara in very high esteem. I believe he acutely realizes that he is partially responsible for the loss of her baby," he said.

"I didn't know where Sara was for two days. I didn't know what they wanted with her. I was afraid that they would punish her for killing my dad," she said.

"Punish? It was clearly self-defense. He had shot her twice."

"Yes, but you don't know my brother and sister. I don't even know my uncle very well, and Sara…" she trailed off.

"Scott told me. We have had lots of time to talk. Does your sister throw a punch like you do?" he asked.

"Sara will put herself between someone who is going to hurt someone she loves and take the hit. But she rarely hits back. She is not strong and is quite fragile. I don't know what my uncle was thinking when he took her. You don't know how afraid she is of men," Saline said.

"I cannot imagine. She is lovely. I don't see many girls who blush like she does. Conversation here generally consists of stayed topics that are quite boring, and politics. Scott has told me so much of Texas that I will be flying back with you when you return," he said.

"Sara used to tell me about my family. She knew our family tree back five hundred years. Our mother would never tell who Sara's father was, so she could not research herself. She loves English history, horses, dancing, music, all of which she has only been able to do in the last few months because of, well, you know the story," Saline said.

"What grade are you in?" he asked.

"I graduate in May. And I start college in the fall," she said.

"You look a bit young," Andrew said, trying to assess if she was pulling his leg.

"I was moved forward a few grades," she said.

"Did your sister graduate early as well?"

"No. Sara had to quit school so she could work," she said.

"She must have missed being around people her own age."

"Not so much. I don't know what you people over here teach in schools, but it is completely different over there. And she didn't do well in public school," Saline said.

"The work was too difficult?"

"No. Sara is very smart. But when she learned to read, Lord Henry made sure it was in French, not English. And Sara is scared to death of boys. She is better in the last couple of years, but still," Saline explained.

"I heard that she attacked her father-in-law," he said.

Saline stopped walking, and when Andrew looked to see why, he could see that he had said something wrong. "My sister, sir, has never hurt another human being in her life. In case the story got misconstrued, let me tell you that John Byers put a hand on her first and nearly scared her to death. She threw the coffee pot because she was afraid. She shot that son of a bitch father of mine because he had a knife to Maria's neck. If you don't believe me, she had some stitches put in her neck. And that piece of shit deserved worse than he got," she said. "I need to go and see to my sister. You people listen to way too damn much gossip."

"Wait, Saline, please," Andrew said. "I meant no disrespect to your sister. We have all spent the last few days visiting. All of us have enjoyed each other's company." He thought for a moment how the perceptive young girl would interpret the statement.

Saline's intense eyes seemed to soften as she realized that once again, she had overreacted. She dropped her head. "I am sorry, sir. Old habits are hard to break. I thought I had lost Sara forever, and I went crazy when she was taken, and then we heard she was safe. I'm sorry."

Andrew looked at the young girl. Restraint was not something that came naturally to her. He wagered that her new family had taught her to be less impulsive, and no doubt it was a big job. "There is nothing to be sorry about. I should be the one to say I am sorry. I didn't mean disrespect to your sister or you."

Saline took a step toward Andrew and started to walk as they had been; Andrew followed.

"The sun should be rising in a few minutes. Would you like to go to the garden to see?" he asked.

"Yes, that would be nice. I never used to like the country and being outside when we still lived with my mother in Texas. On the farm, there was nothing to do. But when we moved to the ranch,

Riley and Colton began to teach me to fish, ride horses, care for baby animals, and so forth," she said.

"Do you still dislike being outdoors?"

"No. There are not enough hours in a day to get everything that I want to do outside. On days when Riley is not doing something, we always go fishing and generally bring home enough to feed everyone. I even clean and cook the fish."

"Who is Riley?" Andrew asked.

"Scott's younger brother. He goes to SMU now. I don't get to see him so much. He is the world's best brother," she said. "I am still working on Colton. He is as close to hopeless as anyone I have ever seen."

Andrew smiled at what must be sibling rivalry. He was familiar with what happened between brothers and sisters.

"I think you must know everything about me. How about you?" she said.

"I don't have as interesting of a life as you do," he said and opened the outside door. They both walked to the gardens.

"You are a prince. I should think that you have quite an interesting life. Sara has told me that down the line, our German blood crosses with your German blood. She knows the history of my father's family. I think that was just to make up for not having a father of her own," she said. "She loves history. At night at the farm, I was teaching her to read better in English so that she would be able to attend nursing school one day. Her hero in life is Florence Nightingale."

"My mother and brother are very fond of history. Charles has studied history extensively. I am not as enthusiastic about history as they are. In a few months, I hope to do my duty and join the RAF. I want to be a pilot," he said.

"That sounds exciting. They let princes join the army?" she said.

"Absolutely. Charles has already served. But most people view the second in line to the throne as the spare," he said. "I have more options than Charles. His life is quite rigid, as rigid as the queen's."

"You refer to your mom as the queen?" Saline asked.

"Sometimes. I am sure you are aware of royal protocol. It makes things stuffy at times. In public we are to recognize titles. In our private quarters we all call her Mummy," he said.

"What else do you like to do?" she asked.

"When I have been busy for a time, I like to kick my shoes off and turn the TV on and eat popcorn all day," he said.

"I will bet that flies like a lead rock," Saline said, and they both laughed.

Andrew noticed Saline rubbing her arms from the cold. He removed his jacket and pulled it around her shoulders.

"It is a bit cool," he said.

"Thank you. It is very beautiful here. The rising sun is making all the flowers seem to glow. Reminds me of the Robert Frost poem. Do you know the one?" she asked.

" 'Nothing Gold Can Stay' I like the American authors." They both watched the sun continue to rise for a few moments.

Saline started to feel a little mischievous. "I would bet that I can do something that you can't."

"That is a loaded statement," Andrew said, squinting a little.

"I will show you. There is no secret agenda," Saline said, walking back inside and walking over to a simple wooden chair. "Walk to the wall, take three toe-to-heel steps back, bend over until your head touches the wall, and pick up the chair with your elbows out, then stand back up. See?"

"Anyone could do that," Andrew said.

"I will bet you that you can't do it," she said.

"What is the bet? If I win, you have to bow to me every time you see me and bring me whatever I ask for until the end of the day," she said.

"Deal. And if I win, you have to kiss me," he said.

"No matter what level of the financial chain a guy is at, that is always the bet. Deal," she said, and they shook hands.

Andrew knew that he had the bet won and did as he had seen Saline do. He attempted to stand up and failed. A second time he tried so hard he lost his balance.

"I won," she said.

"No. Show me again. This is a trick."

Saline laughed and repeated the same thing she had done previously. Andrew tried a number of times and gave up.

"I have been waited on so many times for that," Saline said and started laughing out loud.

"You little devil," Andrew said.

Saline's eyes got big, and she turned to run, continuing to laugh the entire way. Andrew caught her easily and began to tickle her. He quickly discovered that she was very ticklish.

Saline continued to laugh, as did Andrew until they were both so weak they fell to the ground laughing. Only then did they notice that there were people who had come to the first floor hall to see what the commotion was so early in the morning.

Both stood somewhat soberly, and Saline looked to Andrew, and he bowed from the waist.

Saline laughed again for a moment. "I have never been kissed for that," she said.

She and Andrew walked back upstairs to Lady Dickerson's apartment. When they entered, both looked a little disheveled, but their moods appeared to be a little lighter.

"Is Sara awake yet?" she asked.

"Yes. She woke up a little bit ago. You can go see her if you like," Scott said.

Saline went quickly to the room where her sister was. "Sara, I never thought I would see you again," Saline said, going to her sister and hugging. Then she started to cry. "I am so sorry about the baby, Sara."

"So am I," she said.

Austin, who was on the bed with his mother, put his hand up to his mother, only wanting his mother for himself. Saline sat on the bed beside her, and Austin sat on his mother's lap. Sara pulled him up and hugged him close.

"What happened to Andrew?" Sara asked.

Saline looked over her shoulder, and Andrew bowed.

"Oh no. Saline, I have told you a million times to stop hitting people," Sara said weakly. "You did your chair trick, didn't you?"

"He lost—lock, stock and barrel. Do you know what he bet?" Saline asked.

"A kiss." Sara looked to Andrew. "What has he got to do?"

Andrew walked over to where the two most beautiful women he has ever seen were. He bowed again. "Is there anything you need, Lady Saline?"

"Yes, some breakfast would be lovely," she said.

"Right away," he said. "How are you feeling, Sara?"

"Better, I guess," she answered. "I am sorry, Andrew."

"You have nothing to be sorry for," he said. "It was my fault."

"The doctor assures us it was nobody's fault. I was just a little too busy the last few days. Please don't try to take blame for this."

"I won't if you won't," Andrew said.

Sara closed her eyes, and a tear escaped. She then opened them and looked at Andrew. "Okay," she said with a weak smile.

"Good, then I had better feed you sister," he said and left the room.

"Are you going to be okay, sis?" Saline asked.

"I will be fine. Just a little sad for a while," she said, trying to reassure her sister.

"As we will all be," Maria said.

Sara knew inside herself that no one was likely to be taking care of themselves while she was in that room. "Has anyone eaten yet?"

"No. Breakfast will be served in a few minutes," Lady Dickerson said.

"I would like to go to the dining room to eat. Would that be okay?" she asked.

"Of course," the midwife answered. "But let's take it slow. Shall we?"

"Yes," Sara answered. "Are you hungry, Austin?"

The little tot nodded and hugged his mother again. Maria leaned down and picked him up and handed him to Saline.

"Why don't you take him in there and I will help Sara up," Maria said. Saline didn't answer but did as she was told.

Sara, wearing clothes, appeared in the room with the TV a few minutes later, and Scott went over to her and kissed her cheek. "Are you hungry, baby girl?"

"A little," she said. "When did your dad arrive, Scott?"

"This morning, with the others. He has just been staying in there," Scott said.

John walked over and looked at the young woman that he loved so much and kissed her forehead. "Baby girl, I died a million times when I thought we'd lost you. You're a little pale. Are you sure you want to go to the table?"

"I am sorry," she whispered.

The billionaire rancher and oilman's heart broke. He embraced her in a crushing hug and held her close. No words were exchanged. Sara's arms went around the man who had made her life possible. After a moment, they went to the table, and the entire party of Scott, Sara, Saline, John, Allison, Maria, Frances, and Andrew sat at the table, Little Austin in his grandfather's lap.

Breakfast was served, and one by one, the party began to eat, including Sara, who knew that no one would eat unless she did. Conversations were started among everyone. After a few minutes, Sara began to talk.

"When are we going home?" she asked.

"Likely tomorrow, if you are up to it," Andrew answered.

They heard from a distance the front door of the apartment open. A moment later, Charles entered. He had just returned from Germany.

All but Maria and Allison stood when he entered, and he motioned for them all to keep their seats. John remained standing and extended his hand to the young prince.

"John Byers, Your Royal Highness," he said.

"I am Prince Charles, but Charles is quite all right," he said, looking up at the powerful man. He saw the man's face was swollen and bruised. But he looked to his brother and found that he had a swollen black eye as well.

"Andrew, was there a brawl?"

He didn't answer, but everyone's eyes went to the most beautiful young lady he had ever seen. "You're kidding?" he laughed, prompting Saline to raise from her chair and John to use his left hand and keep her seated.

"Young lady, remember what I said," John said.

"Saline Byers, sir," she said and extended her hand. "This is Maria St. Clair, Allison Byers, and of course, Austin," Saline said a little too sweetly.

"Nice to meet you all," Charles said, shaking Scott's hand and kissing Sara's cheek. "My profound sympathy for your loss," he said to the couple. "Mrs. Byers, Mrs. St. Clair, nice to meet you both."

Charles took a seat at the table and was brought coffee by the server. Before mentioning any happenings regarding the funeral, he would talk to Scott first, so he restricted the conversation to small talk.

"What day is it?" Sara asked.

"It is Saturday. Why do you ask?" John asked.

"What time is our flight tomorrow?"

"Around 4:00 pm. Why?" Scott asked.

"Would we have time to go to church?" she asked.

"There is plenty of time. Are you sure you are up to it?" Maria asked.

"I think so. I went to church after Austin was born," she said.

"Is there someplace you would like to go?" Scott asked.

"St. Paul's Cathedral," she said. "We went there when we were girls."

"You did go there once, didn't you?" Frances remembered.

"It is beautiful there. It is one of the most beautiful places I have ever been," she said.

"I believe that would be completely possible if we entered from the side. There are stairs in the front of the cathedral that may be difficult at present," Charles said.

"Then as long as you are well rested and feeling a little stronger," John said in a paternal manner.

Andrew looked from one sister to the other. One sister was obviously a proper, obedient gentlewoman. She never missed a step regarding what was expected of her. The other was taller, bolder to the point of attacking a split second if she thought her sister was threatened.

Then he paid close attention to man who headed the family. A gentleman, true, but his carriage and demeanor commanded respect. His wife was a lady, in every since of the word, a loving and giving woman. They were people who stood for people who couldn't stand on their own.

"Mr. Byers, I understand that you raise horses, any particular breed?" Charles asked.

"Quarter horses, working stock, it takes a strong animal to do the work that we do in Texas. It also takes instincts that are bred in quarter horses. Recently, I have become interested in Arabians, but that is more of a hobby than a business," John said.

"Maybe we can discuss it over coffee, if you will join me," Charles said.

"It would be my pleasure," John said, standing. "Sara."

"Yes, sir," she said, looking up at him.

"Get some rest this afternoon. Okay?" he said softly.

"Of course," she said.

The two walked down the hall together. "I believe that we have something else to discuss besides horses, do we not, son?" John said, putting a hand on the younger man's shoulder.

"Yes, sir. Unless you would rather I talk to your son regarding her family," he said.

Stopping at the door, John stopped him. "Son, there is nothing that I do not discuss with my son. But let's give him a few minutes to make sure that he has Sara napping, and I will get him here in a manner that leaves no suspicions."

"I believe you have the better idea," he said, and they entered the apartment.

John went to the phone and dialed the number up the hall. "Son, say something about that massive horse of yours, and dismiss yourself to come down here."

"Champ? Why would he be interested in Champ. Yes, I know he is the best. But I am not selling him for any amount. Sure. I'll come down and brag about him. Okay."

John hung up the phone. "He will be here in a minute."

"May I say that I have never met anyone with such a soft touch that is deserving of such respect?" Charles said.

"Then you don't know my son very well. Scott is ten times the man I could ever be," John said.

Scott arrived in the apartment occupied by the Prince of Wales, and let them know that he had to defend his horse's honor.

"Charles, what would you like to tell us?" John asked.

"First, may I say that what you have done for the two beautiful young ladies is beyond what anyone else would have done. But there are some things that I don't believe that you know," Charles said. The pained look on his face told that it was beyond imagination. They all sat, and Charles told of the happenings of the day of the funeral, about how a brother was having an illicit sexual relationship that was documented in California.

Sophie's antics since she was about nine years old were shocking to the point of sickness. She was being sent to an asylum to see if she can be helped.

"Tommy, on the other hand, has fled from the church when the duke was talking to the press and was likely going to attempt to leave Europe for California. He had been placed under arrest for the rape of his minor sister and was to serve a twenty-year term in prison in Germany. For now, he is an international fugitive.

"Joan Redding appeared to have gone with her son to assist him in avoiding going to prison. Their clothes had been found in the church."

When Charles had found out about the loss of Sara's unborn child, he passed a note to the duke. The guilt was evident after reading the note. He did not say another word.

"Their younger sister, what will become of her?" John asked.

"He has sent her to a private girls' school with psychiatrists on staff. According to the people close to him, she was not abused, but rather she pursued her father, and he refused her advances to keep her as second in line to the aristocracy. The girl saw this as her father not loving her, so she began to pursue men in their forties and fifties, several at a time. I believe her uncle actually wants what is best for her. She was so medicated at the funeral she just stared.

"It scares me to think how their sister's problems will affect her sisters. And as Sara and Saline were named as heirs rather than their brother, I would be uneasy about him returning to the United States."

"As would I, but I believe that the ranch will be completely secure, and each of the two girls will never leave alone," John said.

"Though the doctor said that Sara lost our child because it was not meant to be, I believe what she was put through in the last few days led to her miscarriage," Scott said bitterly.

"There is something else that you would likely want to know. His Grace said that until Tommy is found, there will be people watching the entrances to the ranch, and if either of them leaves, they will be followed to further add to security.

"As a public official myself, I know that security and reporters are a bother. At least for the time being, I believe I would not mention the security. If they don't know it is there, I don't believe they will ever notice," Charles said.

"How young is the younger sister?" John asked.

"Her name is Sophie, and she is only twelve years old," Charles added.

"I believe that after church, we should stay invisible. No one is expecting Sara to be in church tomorrow, so it should be pretty safe," Scott said.

"All of your pictures have been on the TV for nearly a week. Ladies Saline and Sara are very distinctive. But maybe by making just a few changes, we can mix in with the rest of the church and not be detected," Charles said.

"Why, are you attending with us?" Scott asked.

"I spoke with the queen, and she has said, with your permission of course, that Andrew and I are to be with you until you are on the plane. At some point in time, Mummy would like to meet all of you. She is out of the country until Friday. You will have plenty of security," he said.

"I don't know if you are aware, but Sara is a lady in Her Majesty's court. She was presented at twelve years old. She has dual citizenship. They are both considered German citizens. Your young charges are complex."

"We will all go to church tomorrow, and then stay here until we leave for the airport," John said. "As royalty, Charles, aren't you very busy people with preset engagements?"

"When there is a death in a political official, we are to attend to the funeral, and many events are canceled out of respect."

"Realistically, do you think that anyone will notice two ladies going to church?" Scott asked.

Charles hated to tell them that they had been on the news and news specials regarding the change in succession. It was a big deal for the people in Europe, not to mention for the economy of Hamburg.

"Very few people should know that she is in London, much less at St. Paul's Cathedral. I believe all will be well," Charles said.

"I believe for now the news about their brother, sister, and mother for another day. Sara is very devout. She was baptized during her school years in this country. And going to church is good therapy for her," Scott said.

John and Charles nodded. All would be well, one way or another, and then they could go home.

CHAPTER 13

Dreams Coming True

Everyone was up the next morning to ready them for church. Black was the traditional color of mourning, but having worn her black dress the day before and never wanting to see it again, Sara pulled a dark navy-blue dress out that Frances told her could be suitable.

Everyone else had chosen dark colors as well to possibly blend in with the other worshippers. Everyone went downstairs to the waiting cars that would take them to church.

After a little fuss and assuring the group she was fine, she wanted to go in the front as to mesh with the other people and not the side that would draw attention to the smaller group. They went up the stairs to the thousand-year-old cathedral, and only a few feet inside, they could see what had been described as looking like heaven. The light streamed in through the rotunda, the picture of which had been caught during World War II as having survived the air raids.

A section of seats at the front side of the cathedral was where the honored guests would sit, fairly normal for England. The choir sang, the opening prayers sung, and sacred scripture taught.

Sara, as always, seemed to immerse herself in the service. The members of the party who were visiting for the first time could hardly believe how long ago the cathedral had been built. It would have humbled any king stepping in for the first time.

"Is there a place in here that I can buy a prayer book? I don't have one of my own as yet," Sara asked.

"There is a gift shop downstairs. We will go there after the service is complete," Andrew said.

Following the service and true to his word, Andrew led them to the downstairs gift shop. The ladies looked around a bit. The men tended to wait outside and look around at all the things to be seen in the crept. Sara found the prayer book she wanted, and it even had all the songs in it. That is the one she decided on. She then picked up a couple of things she thought Austin would like. And in the case in front of them were rosaries. Sara walked out to ask Scott if it would be quite all right if she also got a rosary. Of course, he said yes.

Charles walked in and spoke with the woman who was checking people out.

There was also a beautiful cross with praying hands on it. It was solid gold, and she had never bought anything so expensive. As though reading her mind, Scott walked up behind his wife and said how he loved that necklace on her, and she should get it.

"It is quite expensive, Scott," she said.

"Nothing is too expensive for you," he said.

All the ladies bought books that had pictures to show how beautiful it is to those at home and other things that they liked. When they all checked out, the lady at the counter said thank you.

"You don't want us to pay?" Sara asked.

"It is a gift of the Crown with compliments," she answered.

Everything had gone well for the service. They seemed to have blended well. John, Charles, Scott, and Andrew followed behind the ladies as they walked toward the way that they had come in. Austin had been left back at the apartment with a sitter that had been called.

They made it to the front doors when what seemed like an ocean of reporters came from nowhere, people wondering who had been reported as being there. Advancing through the crowd was difficult. Then the small party halted the men keeping the ladies with them.

"Why were you not at the funeral of your father?"

"When did you arrive in London?" the reporters began to ask question after question.

Sara and Saline were rather obvious when standing side by side. Sara's beauty was unique, but Saline had the looks that would rival any noble or aristocrat in the world.

"Your Grace, will you be taking your father's place in succession?"

"What?" Sara questioned.

"You are not aware that your uncle named you as his namesake?"

"That is news to me. I know nothing about it," Sara said. "And I don't have the title Your Grace."

"Why did the duke leave the podium without saying anything?"

"I don't know," Saline answered.

"Your Royal Highness, how long have you known the Byers family?"

"I have only recently met them," he answered.

"Do you usually attend services with—"

He broke in, "Mrs. Byers has been a member of Her Majesty's court since she was twelve years old. She may be a recent friend to me, but she spent most of her childhood in school here. Now we need to be going. Thank you," he said.

Security that was within the crowd cleared a path for them to retreat. When they were seated in the cars, everyone took a breath.

"Scott, what were they talking about? I saw Tommy and Sophie at the funeral," Sara asked, surprisingly calm.

"Sara, will you trust me to say that it is a better conversation left for a later time? I promise I will tell you everything," Scott said.

"Okay," she said simply.

The party arrived back at the apartment. Charles excused himself and told them how he had enjoyed their company. Andrew stayed with his new friends to accompany them safely back to their home.

Lunch was served, and everyone relaxed before going to the airport.

Heathrow was not terribly busy. The weather was colder than it had been all the previous week. There was no holiday that brought anyone to the airport, so at least when they were in front of the terminal, no one had really taken notice.

Inside the terminal, there were many people, but none of the reporters that had drowned them earlier in the day. The plane was still fueling, and a different pilot was called as the other pilot had returned from Germany earlier.

Sara looked out the picture window at the dreary day. The day looked like she felt inside. The doctor had explained to her about the effect of stress on pregnancy, telling her that she had nothing to do with the loss of her child. Everything that had happened the week prior was more than enough to cause a miscarriage. She knew he was right, and separated it from what had happened to her when she was so young. God had given her so much, and if she had lost the child, she would meet him one day in heaven. Still, she didn't know that her arms could feel so empty.

She turned and saw Austin playing in the arms of Maria. She walked over, and Maria handed him to his mother.

"Are you sure that you are okay, Sara? I feel so guilty," Maria said.

"Don't be silly. If the situation were repeated, I would do no different. He would have killed you. He never loved me, and I loved you at almost the moment we met. You are always there for me, no matter what," Sara said.

"How do you do it?" Maria whispered.

"Do what?"

"You take on so much hurt that looks like it would cripple any mortal being," Maria said. "I know about needing faith, but when the going gets tough—"

Sara gently put her fingers on Maria's lips. "Don't say such things. Lauren always told me growing up that God never closes a door without opening a window. You don't know what you can do, no matter how bad, until you are faced with it. You told me not to get Austin. But I couldn't let him hurt you."

"He could have been bluffing," Maria said.

"He wasn't," Sara said.

"But—" Maria said.

"Maria, I know he wasn't. He had killed before. He killed our nanny in California in front of Saline and me. He always told us the same would happen to us," Sara said.

Maria looked at Sara and knew that even though he was dead, she was still scared to death of him. She reached out and took Sara's hand before she spoke. "But now he is gone and can't hurt you again."

"But his son is just as bad. The things they did to us," Sara said and stopped. "Terror is like a runaway train, Maria. You can't stop it."

A man in a uniform called for the Byers party. The words were loud enough that the people in the terminal turned to see who the Byers party was. Everyone had been seen on TV earlier in the day.

A woman in her fifties came over and said how sorry she was for the young women's loss. Saline didn't know how to respond. Sara thanked the woman and hugged her.

People around them also uttered regrets for the two girls. The door was opened, and Sara, Andrew, and Frances waved to people who were standing, looking at them.

On the plane, Sara put her arms up to receive her son from John. She held him close and closed her eyes. How she thanked God for him. He was perfect.

When everyone was seated and fastened in, the plane pulled away from the terminal and taxied around the tarmac at Heathrow until they were to the outbound runway. After they were in the air, movement began in the cabin of the plane. Saline and Andrew were seated together and talking. John and Allison were seated across a small table from Maria. Scott and Sara were seated together with little Austin. Sara was clinging to him as she had been doing since returning to Kensington Palace. She had not told anyone that she had come to a decision. She was going to do her best to start nursing school.

Austin was big enough. If she left him for a few hours a day, with either family or Maria, she could do her best to make good grades. She had been thinking about when she would start to study to be a nurse, and she had not been to any kind of school since she was fourteen, so she really didn't know how she would do. She knew that she would have to get a lot better at reading, and maybe she could take a reading and math courses in the summer and start nursing school in the fall. It sounded like a good plan. She would be nearly nineteen years old, and if she got her LVN first, she could work toward her RN later.

"Scott, what do you think about me starting to work toward a nursing degree in the fall?" she asked.

"I think that is a very good idea. What schools have nursing programs?"

"Most colleges have nursing courses. You would have to drive anywhere from thirty to fifty miles one way there and back. And someone would have to accompany you in case trouble starts," he answered.

"I hate to put anyone else out by having to stand guard over me. And besides, by the fall, I may be yesterday's news. Or at least, I hope so. Do you think it would be wise to take a reading and math course in the summer?" she asked.

"I think that is also a good idea. You are smart and determined, and I believe that before we fill our house with kids," he said, smiling. He looked at his wife and could tell something is on her mind. "What is it, Sara?"

She sighed and then asked the question. "Do you think it was my fault that we lost our son? I mean, do you think that I killed someone and he was the price that I had to pay?"

"No. Absolutely not," Scott said, just raising his voice enough to where the other passengers and attendants looked in their direction. "Look at the facts." Scott continued in a lower tone. "Henry could have killed Maria, the boys, and you. Think about what he would have done if he had been able to get you himself. Then there is being forcefully kidnapped. Not to mention all the crap that is not being mentioned. I know how traumatized I feel. I can't begin to imagine how it would have been for you."

"Do you think that Uncle Alex or Dr. Quinton would be references for me?"

"Wouldn't surprise me if they'd already written," he said, smiling at her.

"I believe you now have a plan. So next year at this time, you could be in nursing school," he said.

Sara smiled at the thought.

Scott looked at his wife's expression; she seemed to be content at the thought of learning to care for others. Somehow he knew, no matter how difficult, she would do it.

Hours later, the plane landed at DFW. It was late afternoon, and the weather was as they had left it—cool and drizzling rain.

The airport was only a little crowded. The passengers waiting for planes that would let them travel over the Atlantic while they slept.

Riley and Mark had others from the ranch to drive the weary travelers home. And as expected, reporters were waiting when they arrived. Questions were directed toward Sara and Saline regarding the death of Lord Henry. They were so interested in the two sisters that no one noticed that Prince Andrew traveled with them. They spoke only briefly and then continued to the waiting vehicles.

Lauren had also accompanied them to the airport and was happy to see her mother and her friends return. She ran to Sara first. "My god, Sara, I thought you were gone from us again. I am so glad that you are finally back. Did he try to hurt you?" Lauren asked.

"No, nothing like that. He wanted to talk to me, so I guess in Germany, it is okay to kidnap someone to do that. He had been told so many lies from Lord Henry that he didn't know what to believe. So I straightened him out on the plane. As it turned out, he was very nice to me. At the hospital, he gave me something pretty big. I will show it to you later," Sara said.

"Have you seen the papers?" Lauren asked after they were both seated in the car.

"No, not lately," Sara said.

"Here is one, 'Lady Sara Lyn Byers or her sister Saline Catherine Alexander will be the next duchess of Hamburg.'" There were several papers. All had front-page articles.

Sara, holding Austin, slid down into the floor of the large car and covered them up. Austin thought of it as a game and was only too happy to play with his mother. She didn't want any more flash-bulbs going off in her face; people had enough pictures. She stayed in the floor until they were well on the way home.

"Charles asked Mummy to give this to you when you got home," Lauren said, holding a wrapped present. She opened it delicately and saw it was the prayer book she had wanted. It had her name on the front of it in gold. She then opened the inside cover and saw a note from Charles and Andrew. In the book, it said, "Your time in our country was entirely too short. Please keep this number and call if you would like to return, your friends Charles and Andrew."

"That is so sweet. I hope we get to go there again someday. I would really like to go," Sara said. "But right now, I just want to be at home. I want to apply to nursing school, take a reading and math course, and begin nursing school in the fall," Sara said.

"Which college?" Lauren asked.

"Likely Tyler Junior College," Sara said. "Where are you and Saline starting out?"

"University of Texas at Tyler. We will be in Tyler at the same times. We could have lunch together," Lauren said.

"Like our parties in our beds in the middle of the night. I love our parties in the middle of the night," Sara said.

Lauren thought for a minute. "I think you can sit in the seat now."

Sara got into the seat and relaxed for a bit. "I have decided to start to college in the summer just to take reading and math. In the fall, I will be in nursing school. Being an LVN first, because it takes less time, then I will be taking courses toward going to school to be an RN."

"Wow. You have really been thinking about this," Lauren said.

"Think about the things we no longer have to be afraid of any-more. Lord Henry is gone, the duke has said he will leave us alone, and Momma, Sophie, and Tommy are all in Europe for a while. So it sounds like the perfect time to start school," Sara said.

"Sara's right. You and I could take some summer courses as well to get started, until the fall semester starts," Saline said.

"Wow, we will all be in college at the same time. This is going to be great. I can't wait until this summer," Lauren said.

"Saline, have you thought about what you want to do in college?" Sara asked.

"As a matter of fact, I want to go to nursing school as well. I want to get my bachelor's in nursing," Saline said proudly.

"Really? I am so glad. You will make a great nurse," Sara said.

"Think how popular the three of us will be in school. Three ladies. And one of you is to be a duchess one day. A real transatlantic group," Lauren said.

The three of them continued to chatter, all picturing what it would be like to attend college.

"There is another thing we had not thought about—guys—we can meet other guys going to college," Lauren said.

"I am married. I don't want to meet anyone," Sara said.

"I know that. But Saline and I are free as birds," Lauren said.

"I have never even thought of dating. But you are right. But to most guys in college, I will be considered jail bait," Saline said.

"Jail bait? What is jail bait?" Sara asked.

"A minor," Saline said.

"Oh," Sara said. "Well, I don't have to worry at all about anything like that. I am a married adult just there to learn. I can hardly wait."

When the party arrived at the main house, everyone was glad to be home. Andrew, who had never been to the ranch, was glad to be there after the long plane ride.

"Welcome to the ranch, Andrew," John said.

"Glad to be here, sir. I wish it were not going to be such a short visit," Andrew said.

"When you get some of Momma's cooking, you will wish you were here forever," Scott said.

Riley and Colton were out of the house to welcome the rest of the family home.

"Andrew, these are our young boys, Riley and Colton. And this is Mark St. Clair, Maria's husband," John said.

Mark shook hands with Andrew and then turned his attention to his wife.

"It appears you have your own city here," Andrew said.

"We are fairly self-contained. Enough room for plenty of privacy yet friends around if you need them. My son will show you to your room," John said.

"Daddy, Sara and I are going down to our house for a few minutes. I believe she is ready for some rest," Scott said.

"It has been a long time since church this morning," John said.

Sara, Scott, and little Austin drove to their house. When they entered through the kitchen, it was so quiet. Sara went to the nursery and laid Austin down for a nap and then returned to the family room. She stood in the last place that she had ever seen Lord Henry. She tried to shake off the fear she remembered feeling at that time. She turned and went to the kitchen. She put a pan of water on to fix some tea. While the water was heating up, she put her hand on her now-flat tummy. Two weeks before, she was expecting her second child, and now he was gone.

She, Lauren, and Saline talked all the way home about starting to college, but it could not erase the fact that she had lost her baby. She kept expecting to feel his movements, but there was nothing.

While the tea continued to make, she went back to the bedroom and began to unpack the suitcases from the trip. As when she left, she had nothing but the clothes on her back, so everything had to be bought for her in England.

She took the clothes that had been worn and put them into the hamper. The unworn clothes were hung up in the closet. Some she folded and put away. The beautiful maternity dresses that Frances had bought for her were hung toward the back of the closet.

When the suitcases were empty, Sara put them in a closet in the hall. She then went back and finished making the tea. She sat at the bar and took a big drink from her glass. In the UK, that was one thing that they didn't serve—ice tea. In Texas, it didn't make a difference what time of year it was; ice tea was always served. After a few minutes, she walked back to the bedroom to check on Austin, who was sound asleep.

She remembered the box that the duke had given her. She picked it up and looked inside of it. The emerald-and-diamond tiara was beautiful. It was very heavy and appeared to be several hundred years old. The ring that was in the box was lovely as well. Sara had intended on giving the box to Saline. She really didn't want it. She was no longer afraid of the duke or anything like that; she just wanted to forget.

In ten days' time, she had been shot, shot and killed a man, been kidnapped, been hospitalized, met the two princes, lost her baby, and now was home. The thoughts sometimes came so fast that it threatened to drown her.

She picked up the phone and asked if Saline or Lauren would mind watching Austin for a few minutes. It was only a few seconds before both were at her house.

"Are you going to take a nap, Sara?" Saline asked.

"No, I was just going to take a walk and clear my head for a little bit. Are you sure you don't mind listening for Austin?" Sara asked.

"Not at all," Saline answered and continued her talk with Lauren.

"I will be back in a bit," she said and was out the back door. She ran hard to the horse barn and saddled her horse. She had changed into her usual long full skirt and a thick sweater and her riding boots.

The weather was cold, and it looked like it could rain or snow. She had forgotten a heavy coat and hoped that the falling weather would hold off.

When Bunny was saddled, she got into the saddle and started riding hard. She wanted to clear her head. Too much had happened. Bunny seemed to understand what Sara wanted and was only too happy to comply. After about an hour, she decided that Bunny had better walk for a little bit, so they were quite a distance from the house, and it was late evening, and they would be losing daylight before long.

It was so quiet. Not a sound from any place could be heard. After a few minutes of rest, Sara figured she had better start in. She turned Bunny in the direction of the barn and began to canter in that direction. Not long after they started home, it began to rain. Not a soft rain, but a pouring down cold rain. They picked up the pace and began to run the same way that they had left.

By the time that they arrived back at the horse barn, Sara was shivering, and her lips and hands were blue. She started working to get the saddle off Bunny as quickly as she could. She didn't hear when someone walked up behind her.

"Sara!" John yelled. "Did you know that nearly everyone on this ranch is looking for you? You have been gone over three hours. What the hell is wrong with you?" he yelled, taking his coat off and pulling it around her shoulders. "My god, you are half frozen," John said, rubbing her arms to try to generate warmth.

He quickly pulled the saddle off her horse and put her in her stall with fresh hay, then got Sara in the truck and went to the main house.

When they arrived, he turned to her. "I am sorry, baby girl. I didn't mean to yell. All of us have just spent a few days that we thought we lost you. Let's go inside and get warm," he said gently.

Sara didn't move.

"Come on, baby girl, you are going to catch your death," he said gently.

In a soft, almost childlike voice, Sara spoke, "I killed a man, was kidnapped, and lost our baby. I just felt like I needed to run away for a little while. I am so sorry I lost our baby, Poppa. I wanted so much to have another baby." She was crying so hard now. John got back into the pickup and started the engine, turning the heat up. He wrapped his arms around Sara and let her cry.

She had been through so much, and now this. Earlier inside, Allison, Maria, and Saline had been talking about how beautiful Kensington Palace had been, how welcome they had felt in a country they didn't know. Sara had not talked very much at all in the last few days.

John and Allison knew too well the effects of losing a baby. After having done everything right, they had lost their daughter nearly the same way. He remembered that pain like it had just happened.

"Baby girl, listen to Poppa. I know how you are feeling now. The loss is so great it feels like it is going to crush you. And in some ways, you likely wish it would. But you are going to make it through, and we look forward to more grandchildren later. Even if there is never another child, there is one thing we just can't lose right now, and that is you. Austin needs his mother, Scott needs his wife, Saline, Riley, and Colton need their sister, and Momma and I need our baby girl. We love you, Sara. Come inside with me, please," he asked, getting out again, putting his hand up to her. She took it and slid out of the truck.

"I love you too, Poppa. I am so sorry I let everyone down." The statement brought fresh silent tears from her eyes.

They walked in the dining room door, and nearly everyone who had been looking for her was there. "I am sorry." She sniffed and tried to wipe her eyes. "I didn't mean to make everyone worry."

Scott came to his wife and wrapped his arms around her. Then Mark came over for a minute.

"Sara, I didn't get the chance to say thank you for saving my Maria and our son's life," he said, hugging her.

"I think I need to go home to Austin," she said, wanting to get away from everyone.

"He is here. Supper is ready, and we are eating here tonight," Scott said.

"I need to go home to change, Scott. I am soaked," she said.

"Momma, we will be back in a minute," he said. "Come with me, my very wet baby girl."

At their house, Sara got another skirt and sweater and put on. She tried to use a towel to dry her hair and got some of the water out of it. She pulled her boots back on and went to Scott.

"I am sorry, Scott," she said when she approached him.

"Sorry about what?"

"Losing the baby, all the trouble, everyone looking for me," she said.

"None of that was your fault, Sara," he said.

"That is what I keep trying to tell myself," she said.

"It was out of your hands, from the shooting to the kidnapping and everything else. You didn't make this happen. Now I won't hear you saying that. Okay?" he said.

Sara looked at the ground.

"Let's get back to Momma's and show Andrew how Texans cook," Scott said.

"Okay," she said.

A few minutes later, all the family and some of the friends were seated around the very large dining table to welcome everyone home. Nearly every meal now had some kind of soup available if Sara was going to be eating with them. Sara was quiet through the meal, polite when asked questions, but everyone at the table could feel her sadness. No one knew what it must have felt like to take the life of another or the fear of being taken against your will and never knowing when you will see your family again. On top of that, she lost a baby. It was going to take her some time to get to feeling better again, and everyone knew it.

But at the same time, everyone was glad that they had her home and safe. At one time or another, everyone told her that.

"I have never seen so much good food in my life," Andrew said. "What kind of sea food is this? Mountain oysters? I had never eaten them before, and they are about the best thing I have ever eaten," he said and continued to stuff himself.

"Andrew, they are not actually seafood," Riley said.

"They are oysters, and that is seafood," Andrew said.

"Well, they are," Riley stopped for a minute and looked at how many women were at the table. He leaned over and whispered in Andrews's ear. "They are calf nuts."

"They are what?" he said.

"Calf testicles, from when we castrate bulls," John said.

Andrew looked at what was on his fork and thought if he could be kidding. "Are they safe to eat?"

"Of course they are," Allison said. "Half the men at this table are eating them."

"They won't make my first child look like a calf, will they?"

"No," Scott said. And everyone laughed.

"Well, the bulls' loss is definitely my gain," Andrew said.

"Sara, baby, may I request something?" Allison said.

"Anything, Momma," Sara said.

"Would you, Scott, and Austin mind spending the night up here tonight? Just one night with all our children under our roof. When you were taken…" Allison's voice cracked. "Well, I just wanted everyone close tonight, is all."

Sara rose and went to her. "Oh, Momma," she said, hugging her. "When I never thought I would see everyone again, I just knew that I would die."

"So did we, baby girl." Allison continued to cry.

"Mark, Maria, do y'all and the boys think you could stay here tonight as well?" John asked.

"Of course," Mark said. Maria got up and went to Allison and Sara and cried with them.

The moment was touching. Andrew had never seen such a family. Even those not related were treated as extended members of the family. It was impressive for a man as wealthy as this man was to have such deep feelings for the people around him.

When the meal was over, the ladies quickly got the dishes done, and the men went to the huge family room to relax. Maria's two sons and Austin were the entertainment. They were busy trying to pull out every toy in the large toy box in the family room. They played with everything that made noises, bounced, flew, or did anything else.

The adults talked about everything. Lady Dickerson was glad to once again be in Texas but would have to return when Andrew did because her George was not feeling well these days. He had gone to the doctor a few days before and had not heard back as yet. She really wanted to be there when they found out what was wrong.

Sara sat on the floor of the family room, close to the fireplace for warmth. She hoped she had not given herself a cold, out riding on a day like it had been. Lauren joined her after a little bit.

"Was it awful for you, Sara?" Her best friend asked, only wanting to help.

"Which part?" Sara asked.

"I don't know. Can you tell me what happened?" she asked.

Sara looked around, and everyone was talking to someone else. "Two men I didn't even see grabbed me so fast I didn't have time to yell. They put me in a car and put a hood over my head and taped my hands together. They told me that they would not hurt me, but I had to do as I was told. I was terrified. Maria had been with me, and I didn't know what happened to her. They put me in a seat on a plane and took the hood off after the plane took off, and they untied my hands." She started to stare.

"Sara, are you okay?" she asked.

"Oh, yeah, I guess. The duke was seated directly in front of me. He told me that we were going to my father's funeral. He started telling me that he wanted me to be next in line for the head of the aristocracy, but I said no. Then he started telling me he knew from my father what a brat I was in refusing to obey anyone. I told him I did everything that anyone told me to do. And I did it with a smile on my face, because that is how we were trained." Again Sara stared at the flames. She didn't speak for a long time, just stared at the flames and rubbed her arms.

Lauren moved closer to her friend and got a blanket off the couch and wrapped around both of their shoulders. She tried to help Sara warm herself.

"He started telling me what Lord Henry always said about me. And how confused he was because he always spoke to the people at school who said I was an excellent student who would do anything asked of me.

"He started telling me what a disappointment Lord Henry, Tommy, and even Sophie were. He said that they were in the news at least every few days for one reason or another, and they were never for good reasons.

"I found out while I was over there that Tommy filmed Sophie having sex with three men at a time. All colors of men for that matter, even showed Tommy and Sophie having sex. And Sophie is telling them she wants more. He said her reason for doing it was because her father would not do it with her. He said she had to be kept pure.

"Tommy was into drugs, alcohol, and raping underage girls. I couldn't believe what I was hearing. He said you didn't have to look at the news long before either Tommy or Sophie was on it. And as Lord Henry had gotten into so much trouble of late, he would not allow them to head the family. He said that he wanted a member of the family who was responsible, caring, and intelligent. Being married and having children was one thing that also helped. But then he mentioned Saline. She is very, very smart. The only thing is that she is a minor, not married. I couldn't believe he announced it with both Tommy and Sophie standing there. They are going to hate us, and we didn't say yes. But surely to God they would never try to come here," Sara said.

"No, of course they won't. They have seen what can happen. So if they want to live, they will stay away," Lauren said.

"That was what we were watching on TV when I started feeling cramps and lost our little boy. Oh, how Scott must hate me for losing the baby," Sara said.

"Sara, Scott was with you the whole time in England. And he could never hate you. He loves you no matter what," Lauren said.

"Most of me know that. There is just this part here lately that makes me feel so empty. My arms ache because I will never hold our second child.

"Then, after everything on the plane that I said to him, including from when I was twelve and that horrible place, he said he was sorry. I told him everything, how he truly hated me for my mere existence and about being locked into the shoe closet for days at a time, his threats to bury us alive. I told him everything that his nephew had done, not just to Saline and me, but to every young girl whose father happened to work for him. Then he asked me a question," Sara said. She returned to staring at the flames.

"Sara, what was the question?" she asked.

"He asked me if I hated him. I wanted to say yes so much, but I couldn't. I finally told him that my faith in God is what kept me from hating him, that I would not put my soul in danger for choosing to hate him. I told him that this would really make him think I was stupid, that I actually prayed for him. I prayed that he would know God. Maybe if he did, he would have seen how wrong he was and would not be in hell right now," Sara said.

"What did he say?" Lauren asked.

"That was when he said I would be the perfect duchess. I also told him then that I was not German. I was the product of an affair my mother had had with just about any man who showed interest in her. But he said that didn't matter. We had been going after everything for about nine hours in the air, and my chest suddenly began to hurt. I think it had started to hurt earlier that day, but all of a sudden, I couldn't catch my breath, and that is all I can remember. I woke up in the hospital in London. He was there when I woke up, sitting very close by. He thanked me for my honesty and said how difficult it had to be for me to tell him the things I did. He said that as far as he was concerned, I was the next person to take his title after he was gone. He said how sorry he was for what his nephew had put both Saline and I through. And if I ever wanted to talk to him, his private number was in the box. He kissed my cheek, then my hand, and said he would talk to me another time," Sara said. "I thank God for everyone in my life, for Scott and Austin of course, my sister and new family, and for you and your family. I will love all of you always," Sara said.

A knock on the front door brought both of them back to present, then a woman walked in with tears in her eyes. "Saline, Sara, my babies."

Sara and Saline looked up and were immediately on their feet. "Grandma!" Saline screamed. Both girls went to her.

"Grandma, how did you find us?" Saline asked.

"Your new parents gave me directions. I told them I was moving to Texas to get close to my granddaughters and my newest member, my great-grandson," she said.

Sara turned her back and started to cry. She had killed her grandmother's son. Did she know that yet?

"Sara, Grandma knows what happened when Henry died. It was not your fault. None of it, from the time you were born, was your fault. I know you always felt different, but Grandma has always kept her hair the same color as yours, has she not?" Grandma asked.

Sara nodded. "Look at me, honey. Grandma has always loved you."

"I love you too, Grandma. I always have." The two hugged so tight.

"Have you met anyone here yet?" Saline asked.

"No, not yet. I was afraid they would not want me here and took my chances," the girls' grandmother said.

"This is the best daddy in the world, John Byers," Saline said.

"Mr. Byers, I am Catherine Alexander, and I assure you I mean no harm to my granddaughters," she said, shaking his hand.

"It is good to meet you, Mrs. Alexander. Saline has told us an awful lot about you, and you are most welcome here. This is my wife, Allison, and our sons, Scott, Riley, and Colton. And this is our almost-son, Mark, and his wife, Maria. These are the Dickersons, Lord and Lady. Their daughter Lauren is with Sara. They went to school together in Wales." Everyone shook hands at the newest member.

"And this little scut is John Austin Byers the second. He is the toughest cowboy on the ranch," Scott said and handed the happy baby to his great-grandmother.

"He is the most beautiful baby I have ever seen," she said with tears of joy flowing down her face. "Thank the Lord. Thank all of you."

"Please, Mrs. Alexander, join us and meet the others," Allison said.

"Please call me Catherine," she said.

"And I am Allison, and this is John."

"And I am Frances. My husband George is currently home in England. That is our daughter Lauren with Sara." Frances invited.

"And I am just Andrew, Mrs. Alexander," Andrew said, extending a hand.

"You're a little young for first names, so just call me grandma, son." she said.

"Okay, Grandma," Andrew said.

Everyone took seats again and continued talking. Grandma held little Austin for a long time then let him back down to play.

"I am afraid I am being a little silly about what all happened the last couple of weeks. I have asked all the kids to stay here in the main house with us for a night or two. You are more than welcome to stay with us if you like. We have more than enough room," Allison said.

"I would be happy to stay, and thank you for inviting me into your home. And I don't think you are being silly at all." She yawned. "I am sorry, please excuse me for yawning. I think my jet lag is catching up with me."

Saline smiled at a memory.

"What are you smiling at, Saline?" Andrew asked.

"Just remembering. Grandma used to be the only one to try to protect us. She tried to have us taken away so many times. Now she is here. I am just happy. Have you been shown your room yet?" Saline asked.

"Not yet," he answered.

"Well, let's go." Both of them went for the steps. "Momma says you are to stay in the blue room. It is not far from Grandma's room. Here we are," Saline said and opened the door of the oversized room. Like most of the bedrooms in the main house, it had its own bathroom, a sitting area, and a beautiful view from one of three windows. "Look okay?"

"Yeah, it's great. I wish I would spend more time on a place like this," Andrew said.

"Why is that? You don't like being a prince?" Saline asked.

"The photographers, the crowds, the ceremony, the big meals, what's to miss? Seldom at home do I have a moment such as this. For me to date, everyone knows who she is and everything about her, does not make for a long relationship. But here, no one really knows who I am," he said.

"I have an idea, if you want to hear it," Saline said.

"What?" he asked suspiciously.

"Why don't you call your mom and tell her you are discussing the oil business with Scott and Daddy. Make it a business, and maybe you can stay a little longer, besides always being welcome to visit," she said.

"Good idea. But I would have to lie to my mother," he said.

"Then don't. Talk to them about gas, oil, the new refinery, and they will talk to you about it. It won't be a lie. As it is, Daddy will likely send your mom a tanker of oil. He is very generous, and every country always needs oil. And your country was very nice to us at such a sad time. I mean, Charles taking the place of the Crown and the Byers family. We will never forget that," Saline said.

"I believe I will give her a call right now," he said.

He picked up the phone and dialed all the numbers necessary for the country-to-country call. He had asked Saline if she would stay.

"Mummy, how was your trip?" he asked. "Good to hear. I have a question. I am at the Byers ranch in Texas tonight. Believe it or not, I was completely undetected," he said.

He was listening intently to what his mother was saying. "Speaking of that, Mrs. Byers and his eldest son, Scott, Lady Sara's husband, were talking to me about the oil supply in England. They have just opened their own refinery over here, and there is already a tanker being sent to England as thanks for caring for his family."

"Yes, I know. They are the most generous people I have ever met. Charles even liked them. I would like to stay a day of two to find out a little more about the business. What do you think, Mummy?"

"Are you sure? Yes, mam, I will. I will let them know. See you then," he said and hung up the phone.

"Believe it or not, she has given me two weeks to stay here. She also wants me to personally invite your family here to stay at Buckingham Palace as guests of the Crown at their first free moment," he said, smiling.

"Let's tell Momma." Saline jumped up, took his hand, and ran down the hall and took the steps down two at a time.

Sara and Grandma sat in the beautiful room that had been selected for her.

"I am so glad to see you well and happy, Sara. And I am so sorry about the baby. His Grace wanted me to make sure you were aware you are in his prayers," she said.

"He was nice to me after we got everything straightened out. Do you know what is going to happen to Sophie and Tommy?" Sara asked.

Grandma took a breath. "Sophie is being sent to a special girls' school, one that will meet her emotional needs for the next few years. She always considered you and Saline the lucky ones because of what Henry did to you. Her thinking is just not right. Maybe he can help her. I hope so. And Tommy at first had his choice of going into the German military or going to prison for statutory rape. Then His Grace's ministers saw the video that they had made. The military was taken aback, and he is to start his prison term for what he did to Sophie. Sending their uncle that tape was the hardest thing I have ever done. But Sophie needed help, and I could not get around Tommy," she said sadly.

"It is okay, Grandma. Maybe there will be someone there like the ones who found Saline, Jody, and I. Maybe they will love her, and she will be okay," Sara said. Then she remembered Jody.

"Would you like to see Jody's grave?" Sara asked.

"I would."

"You had better put your coat on," Sara said. They went downstairs. "Poppa, it has stopped raining, and Grandma wants to see Jody's grave. May I take her there?"

"Uncle Alex wants to have a look at you, but I will be happy to take her there," he said.

"Thank you, Poppa," she said, kissing his cheek.

"Catherine, are you sure you would rather not wait until morning? It is quite cold out," he asked.

"I don't mind braving a little weather," she said.

So together they walked to the private cemetery. John showed her the specific place where he was buried.

Grandma knelt down and dusted off the headstone. She began to cry. John knelt with her. "Everyone on this ranch loved Jody. When he died, he was happy, not hungry, unafraid, and safe. That is until that morning the kids' mother barged in," John said and put an arm across her shoulders.

"Thank you, John. What you and your Allison have done for those two girls is a miracle. There is something that you must know," she said, standing.

"What is that, Catherine?" he asked.

"After His Grace was given the note from the prince that told of the loss of Sara and Scott's second child, he was so distraught that he lost track of Tommy and his mother. Nobody knows where they are at present. They have quite a large amount of money for which to travel. Either wants to be put in a German prison. So at some point, they will make it back to the States, and I don't know what they will do from there. Tommy had set his sights on being the duke, and to find that His Grace had changed his successor, well, you likely know more of what they are capable of.

"And may I assure you that I want nothing but to be able to visit my grandchildren. I would never attempt to take them. And I would never lay a hand on either of them unless it was in love," she concluded.

"I have no doubt. And I am glad that the girls have someone that they think so much of that is a relative," John said.

"There were so many times that if I had not either come along or been called by either Sara or Saline, they could have died. When Joan was in labor with Sara, Henry left on a long trip to Catalina Island, off the coast of California. He didn't return until she was two weeks old. Her biological father was there for the birth and stayed with her while she was still in the hospital. He looked very much like Sara. He had her eyes and hair. She got his smaller stature. She was always such a pretty quiet little thing. You never really knew if she was around unless you happened to see her. She was never seen in public at all. When she was home for holidays, she and Saline would be together all the time. Those two girls would not let an ocean separate them. They had to develop a way to make sure that each got their letters. Sara would send letters to Saline through me, and Saline would have one of her friends mail her letters to Sara. God only knows the times that in the middle of a cold night, Sara would be outside with nothing on. I would take her for days to weeks at a time.

"There were also times that I would pick up both girls and keep them in a hotel someplace if he was having one of his so-called parties," Grandma said. She put her head down and was shaking it.

"What are these parties you are talking about?" John asked.

"Henry and Joan were very much a part of the party scene when they were together. What would happen is, he would invite a few dozen very high-ranking men over. Tommy and Sophie would be sent away for a few hours. There would usually be little girls of some of the people who worked for Henry. Alcohol and drugs were added to the mix, and he would throw the two girls and any other girls outside and lock the house doors. The men would be drunk or high or perhaps both. The girls would be the entertainment. What is worse is that kids that Saline went to school with would be looking over the walls and taking pictures. Saline attempted suicide at one point.

"When Sara and Saline moved out here, I thought maybe it was for the best. But my son's way of controlling a situation is fear. The man that he bought the farm from wanted a little more than what Henry was offering. He disappeared and has never been heard from."

"Are you talking about Gerald Patterson?" John asked.

"Yes."

"He went missing a few years ago," John said.

"I don't know what happened to him, but I have no doubt the girls do. He likely did whatever he did in front of them to instill fear," she said.

"How could you ever return a child to those people?" John asked.

"I never did. I would take Sara and Saline. I even went as far as New York one time, thinking it would be big enough to hide the girls so he could not get to them. But somehow he always did," Grandma said. "I would never have taken them back."

"After what happened when Sara was twelve, her sister called me and said that Sara was bleeding to death. Henry was not in the house, so I picked up Sara, and Saline followed me. Tommy attempted to stop me. I had no choice but to put Sara down for a moment. When I did, I picked up one of Henry's beer bottles and crashed it hard over his head then continued out with my girls. I took Sara to the hospital over fifty miles away. What they did to her," she said, shaking her head, "you can't imagine. I attempted to take them to my brother-in-law, but as usual, he had people who knew.

"The worst thing that a mother can say regarding their child is that it was the worst thing that they had ever done in having it. Henry's father died when Henry was six. Even at that age, all he could think about is being the duke. His father was the duke, but when he died, his brother became the duke. But Henry was next in line. Having come from that kind of a background, he thought he could get away with anything. I am glad that Sara showed him he couldn't," she said.

John thought when he first found out who this woman was it may not be the best idea to have her on the ranch. But this woman was tough. She had been trying to save these girls their entire life, and it didn't matter what it cost her. She tried. He liked and appreciated this woman.

"One more thing I believe I should trust you with, John. And that is that I have cancer. The best they can give me is a couple of years. And I would like to spend time with the girls and of course our grandson. And I would rather that they not know about this just yet," Catherine said.

"Is there treatment?" he asked.

"Yes, but it does not lead to any better outcome. I have lived my life to try to keep my girls safe, and they are both safe and happy. And now I can at least be part of their lives, if only for a little while, if you will allow me to," she said.

"Of course you are to be involved. Just let us know if you need our help. My brother-in-law is a doctor, and I am sure he could find someone suitable to treat whatever kind of cancer you have," John said.

"We will talk about that another day. For now, I believe I would like to say good night to the girls and my great-grandson, if you don't mind."

"Not at all. It's starting to get a little late," John said. They walked up to the house. Mostly small talk was discussed.

Catherine went to Saline's room first to say good night. "Grandma, I am so glad that you are here. I have missed you so much."

"I had missed my girls as well. Tell me about yourself," she asked.

"Well, I graduate from high school with honors at sixteen and am about to start college in the fall. And I think Sara has me looking into nursing. Or maybe even being a doctor," Saline said. "Someday, I want to marry someone as wonderful as Scott and have lots of children. I just hope that my someday husband does not mind living on the ranch forever. I can't imagine ever living anyplace else. We have been so happy here," Saline said.

"I can see that, baby," Catherine said, taking a seat beside Saline on the bed. "I wish I could have done more when you were younger to protect you girls," she said.

"Grandma, you did everything you could. Remember what he did to nanny for getting too involved? And at least we knew you were there," Saline said.

"I am so glad to be here. I don't even care that it took Henry's death for me to be able to be here. He was never a son to me. He was a bully, not so different from his father. Are the Byers family good to you both?" she asked.

"The best, I love all of them so much. If they wouldn't have taken us when they did, Sara would have died. Momma wouldn't let her take her medicine, and I could tell she was close to death. But Uncle Alex and Dr. Quinton have got her healthy again. Sometimes we both laugh so much we make ourselves hurt. Scott, Riley, and Colton are the most wonderful brothers in the world. Maria is like an older sister to both of us. Momma and Daddy are just the best. They would never hurt either of us.

"Did you know that we all went over to England when Sara got kidnapped by His Grace? We were so afraid. But Lady Dickerson was with Sara, and now His Grace said he would not be bothering us anymore but that we are welcome in Hamburg anytime, and he would very much like it if one of us chose the title. We are so lucky, Grandma, and now you are here," Saline said, hugging her grandmother.

Catherine caught a couple of tears that had escaped her eyes. "You don't have to worry. I live in Texas now and will never leave. I want to be around the two of you and Austin as much as I possibly can. You may even get tired of me."

"Never happen." Saline let out a yawn. "I am sorry. I think the jet lag is starting to catch up with me. Will I see you in the morning?" she asked.

"Just a few doors down. I love you, Saline. I hope you have always known that," she said.

"I have. And I love you too, Grandma. See you in the morning," Saline said and turned over.

Grandma saw Scott in the hallway and asked where his and Sara's room was and if Sara were still awake.

"Let me take you there, Mrs. Alexander," he said.

"Please, just call me Grandma."

"Okay, Grandma, let's see if my wife and son are still awake. Uncle Alex saw her a little while ago and gave her something to help her to sleep. She has had a very long last few days. Then after losing the baby, she is still very weak," Scott said.

"You would have to be the person I would have picked out to marry Sara. The way that you two look at each other is so romantic. Thank you for loving my granddaughter," she said.

"She is a pleasure to love. In many ways, she is still so innocent. She knows of the bad things in this world but is still new to the good things. She is a wonderful wife and mother to our son. But in raising Saline and Jody, she had lots of practice," Scott said. "Here we are, and she is still awake and playing with Austin. Against medical advice, I believe."

"I am sorry Scott. He was awake, and I just had to pick him up. Hi, Grandma. I am glad you are here. Austin, can you say *grandma?*" she asked.

"Nana" was what came out.

"Well, that is a good thing for my great-grandson to call me, Nana. Feels like a good fit. I just came to say good night, my angel. And I will see you in the morning," she said, walking over to where Sara was already in bed.

"I thank God you found us, Grandma. Uh."

"What is it, baby?" Grandma asked.

"Are you sure you don't hate me for killing your son? I would understand if you did," Sara said.

"No, baby, quite the opposite. I thank God that it is he who is dead and not you. Grandma will always love you no matter what." The two embraced and held each other for a moment.

"And if you keep having little bruisers like this, I will love all of them as well. Get you a good night's sleep, my angel, and I will see you in the morning. I love you," she said.

"I love you too, Grandma," Sara said.

"And we love you too, Grandma," Scott said while holding Austin. "Good night."

Catherine turned and went back to the family room in search of the kitchen.

"Catherine?" Allison said.

"I am sorry, hon, I am looking for the kitchen. I usually have a cup of coffee before I go to bed," she said.

"Well, I will show you, and maybe we can talk for a few minutes," she said.

They arrived in the kitchen, and Allison went to the coffeemaker. "I believe we have both had a very long last few days. I am having trouble unwinding myself."

"Thank you," Catherine said with humility.

"Excuse me."

"Thank you for raising my granddaughters. They didn't have many chances when they were young. And now to see them so happy and healthy, I am glad that I lived to see it," Catherine said.

"We love those girls like they were our own. When we thought that we would never see Sara again, I thought it would kill us. Little Austin cried himself to sleep every night. I hope you will want to stay very close to them. You are the only relative who has ever had any kind of feeling for them," Allison said.

"I never want to be far from them again. As long as my son was living and had Sophie with him, I had to stay close by. Now, since she is with my brother-in-law, and he has custody, I hope I still have a chance with Sara and Saline and my only great-grandchild, Austin."

"While you are looking for a place to live, you are most welcome to live here with us. As you can tell, we have plenty of room. There is generally even more room, but since the kidnapping, I asked everyone to stay here tonight for me. Tomorrow, John and Scott will be going back to work. Sara, Scott, and Austin will be going to their house, not far from here. Maria and Mark and their two boys will be going to their house, also not far from here. And Andrew is going to be visiting for a few days before he has to go back to England," Allison explained.

"You have a big group here. I can tell how close everyone seems to be," Catherine said.

"Everyone on this ranch is like family. Then there is the oil company and now the refinery. We are blessed," Allison said.

"When Henry came back from Texas the first time, he had heard of your family and knew where the kids were. His thoughts were to somehow end up with this ranch, thus having everything that you had. That was always the way my son was. Henry always knew that his becoming a duke one day was not as a noble. His family was one of the wealthiest families in Germany. Germany is retrying to be a republic, but the aristocracy still exists in the wealthier lines. They associate with nobles, and they are almost seen as nobles, but they are well-respected wealthy people. His Grace is a very well regarded man by his people. He is moral and decent and good. I wish you would have gotten to meet him under different circumstances. He really believed everything that Henry had told him until the last year. It broke his heart when Sara lost the baby. He very much feels responsible. I hope that one day, only when all of you are ready, perhaps you can meet him again as a person, not a duke," Catherine said.

"I see what you are saying. I understand that most of the misunderstandings were caused by Saline's father and the girls' mother. Maybe when everything settles down somewhat, we can see what the girls think of talking to the uncle," Allison said. "The coffee is ready." Allison poured each of them a cup, and they sat at the table together, still talking.

Allison felt for the woman. She had just lost her son but blamed his death more on his self than anyone else. She had a better understanding of the life that Saline and Sara had had to endure. After a little while, Catherine said that she was starting to feel jet lag beginning to catch up with her and excused herself for the night.

"I will see you for breakfast. Have a good rest," Allison said.

"You do as well," Catherine said back.

Allison was walking to their room and heard voices. She went to the family room and found Saline, Riley, Colton, and Andrew talking much the way you would find a group of teenagers talking.

"Don't y'all stay up too late. Good night," Allison said.

"Night, Mom" came from the room.

When she got to her own room, John was coming out of the shower. "Good evening, my love. I tell you I think my body clock is broke. I can't tell you what time of the day or night it is," he said.

"I think they call that jet lag. I am starting to feel a little of that myself. I got a chance to talk to Catherine. She seems like a wonderful woman," Allison said.

"Yes, she is. She answered a lot of questions that I had but hated to ask the girls about. She tried hard for so many years to get those girls and take them just anyplace, but he always found her. The only remaining question I have is what happened to Sara when she was twelve. I think I have heard just about everybody allude to it, but never say what it was," he said.

Allison sat down on the end of the bed. She took a breath and told her husband what happened to Sara in Los Angeles. "While he was living, it just seemed a little better not to mention it. I was afraid what would happen if you got a hold of him knowing that," she said.

"I would have castrated him before they took him to Peru," he said.

"I think it will do the girls some good having her around for a little while," Allison said.

"The only thing is is that it will only be for a little while," John said.

"Is there something wrong, John? Do you not think she is a good woman?" she questioned.

"I believe that she is a saint of a woman. But she has cancer. She has a year, possibly two, but no more. There were so many things that she told me. Like you, I believe the girls will appreciate her being here," John said.

"Would you mind if she stayed here, in the house? When the time comes, she will need help, and she has no one else," Allison said.

"I was going to suggest that. She is a very nice lady and one that the girls love very much. She is in no way a threat," John said. "And since she is going to be staying here, we can have her sent to MD Anderson Hospital in Houston to see if they can do anything for her."

"One of the things I love about you is that you know how to take charge of a situation."

For the next few days, those who were in the house tended to stay close with the exception of John and Scott. Their work in Dallas kept them all day long most days. In addition to the first night, everyone stayed another three nights until everyone felt secure enough to go back to their own houses again.

Andrew took part in the various things that happened on the ranch. He even went with John and Scott to the oil company and then flew with them to the refinery. He was impressed by the sheer size and enormity of everything that the Byerses stood for.

Then at the ranch, he helped to feed the cattle with the other ranch hands.

Then one Sunday evening, after they had returned from church, Sara, Saline, and Lauren decided to go riding. Andrew asked if they would mind his riding with them, and of course, they didn't. Scott, Riley, and Colton also joined. Allison brought out a set of saddle bags with some snacks in them and gave Sara her medicine.

"All of you have a good time, and be back in time for supper." Everyone agreed and was off. All but Sara rode astride. She rode as always, sidesaddle on Bunny.

Saline was saddled and ready to go first. "Race y'all," she said, turning her horse, and then was out of the barn. Everyone saddled and rode to catch her. Everyone knew their ways around a horse, so the ride was great fun for them all.

Uncle Alex had told Sara that she would have to take it easy for about a month when she had seen him the day after she had returned from England, but she really and truly felt like riding with the best of them. Before long, they were several miles from the house. They stopped to rest the horses at a creek that swells so when it rains that there was no way to cross it.

The horses got a drink and rested there at the creek bank. As beautiful as the day was, it was still under freezing. They also had to keep up with the time because the days were so short.

As the horses rested, they all started talking about one thing or another, then they started playing catch with a ball that was in one of the saddlebags. They were all having a great time when a ball was thrown to Saline and went just a little above her head where she had to jump to catch it. Not realizing how close she was to the side of the rolling creek or how slick the sides were, one second she was catching the ball, the next she was in the frigid water of the fast-moving creek. It only took seconds for everyone to get on their horses and try to get ahead of her so as to be able to get her out. Only one rider didn't go for his horse, but rather jumped into the water and began swimming after Saline. He could see her just ahead of him, screaming for help.

Scott, Riley, Mark, and Colton got about a mile ahead and tied all their ropes from their saddles together. Then Colton got one end and swam across with it. They pulled the rope tight so as to catch the pair. The real hope was that they wouldn't have struck their heads on a rock and knocked themselves out.

When they saw them coming, they could see that Andrew swam while holding an unconscious Saline. He saw the line and reached for it, taking it firmly. With that, the two, plus Colton, were dragged in.

"She has hit her head. I barely caught her before she went under," Andrew said his lips already blue. Scott took his coat off and had Andrew take his off and put Scott's dry blue one on. Sara did the same for her sister. Mark pulled his coat off for Colton.

"Riley, ride back and get Saline's and Andrew's horses and ride for the main house. The rest of us need to ride hard until we get there. Understood?" Scott asked. "Mark, make sure everyone is staying together in back. Andrew, can you ride holding her like that?"

"Not a problem. Let's go," he answered.

The group took off at breakneck speed with the freezing weather being felt by everyone. Sara was so afraid for Saline she didn't think about how cold she was getting.

It took them just over an hour to get to the main house. Everyone came through the kitchen door and into the family room where the fireplaces were lit and hot.

Allison, Grandma, John, Maria, and Frances started getting towels and blankets. Allison called Uncle Alex, who was at his home on the ranch only about ten minutes away.

Sara began undoing the buttons on her sister's shirt and pulled it off her, and then keeping her covered, she got the rest of the wet things off her. She asked if Lauren would get her heavy bathrobe from her room. Lauren was back in a flash.

Colton had gone to his own room and changed out of the wet things.

The rest of the riders who took off their coats were already beginning to cough and sneeze.

When Uncle Alex arrived, he saw a very quiet Saline. She had hit her head and had not come to as yet. The lump was immediately over her right temple. Grandma stayed with Uncle Alex and looked so worried.

"John, I am going to have to take her for a head x-ray. And to see how much water she may have gotten in her lungs," Uncle Alex said.

"I kept her head above water, sir. I don't believe you will find her to have swallowed or aspirated any water," Andrew said.

"Alex, this is Prince Andrew of England, he accompanied us home from London and is staying for a few days," Allison said.

"Good to meet you, son. It looks like you saved her life, but we will know more at the clinic." Alex picked her up, and Grandma was following her out the door, as were Andrew, John, and Allison.

"The rest of you, get warm. Sara, you need to get warm and rest," Uncle Alex said then was out the door.

Everyone did as they were told, all ending up in the kitchen, drinking how coffee to try to warm themselves. They were waiting on the phone to ring, but so far, nothing had happened. Gradually, they moved back to the family room by the fireplace.

Sara and Scott sat as usual in front of the fireplace on the floor and played with Austin. Mark, Riley, and Colton stayed close, and Maria made sure that hot coffee was always ready.

Then the phone rang. "Hello," Mark said, because he was the closest. "How is Saline?" he asked.

"Oh no, will she be okay? Scott, Daddy wants to talk to you," he said, passing the phone to Scott.

"Yes, Daddy," Scott said.

"Scotty son, it looks like she hit a rock pretty hard. She has some bleeding in her brain, and they are sending her to Baylor for further treatment. Andrew is taking it pretty hard, thinking that it was his fault," John said.

"It was no one's fault. The banks were just soft and slippery, and she went in. If not for Andrew, she would have died," Scott answered.

"He has not left her side. He wants to ride on the ambulance to Baylor, and unless we want to restrain him, that we had better let him," John said.

"Uncle Alex says for Sara to rest, but she will want to know what is happening to her sister. But I will leave that up to you. There is really nothing that will be able to be done until she wakes up. Call again when y'all arrive," Scott said.

"Well, Scott, what does Uncle Alex say?" Sara asked.

"They are sending her to Baylor. She has not woken up yet, and they think she may have bleeding in the brain. But they don't know yet," Scott said.

"Can you take me? I don't know the way," she asked.

"Uncle Alex said for you and the rest of us to stay put, and he would call when something changes," Scott said.

"No, Scott, I have to go to her. I have to look out for her," Sara said.

"Baby girl, a week ago you lost our child, you have had a cold since, you are still weak, and Alex said specifically that you needed rest and he would call. So we will take the phone with us, and both of us will go lie down. Right, everyone?" he said, looking at his brothers and Mark, who had been there. Maria took charge from there.

"All of you, look. You have been riding hard in freezing weather, wet in your shirt sleeves. No, go in and lie down. I will bring hot chocolate in a few minutes. That is an order. That includes you, Mark."

With only a second's hesitation, everyone did as they were told.

When Maria brought hot chocolate, she had spiked it with a little cinnamon rum to warm them and, as ordered by Uncle Alex, put the tranquillizers in Sara's drink.

Sara never knew what hit her; she was sound asleep in minutes.

CHAPTER 14

In Dallas, at Baylor, the doctors examined Saline for a couple of hours before they knew anything to tell the family.

John and Allison prayed that all would be well. Grandma knew that she just had to be well, because they had all just come back into one another's lives.

But Andrew was guilt-stricken. He was afraid of how much damage could have been done.

The doctor finally came to talk to them.

"The Byers family," he said.

"We are the Byers family. We are her parents, her brother, and grandmother," Allison said. "How is our daughter?"

"We did a CAT scan on her brain and her neck. Many times neck injuries can happen if one's head it hit hard enough. She has a disc that herniated, but the main thing is that she hit the side of her head and caused a bleed, and we need permission to do brain surgery to stop the bleed. After that, it will just be wait and see. It will take forty-eight hours for the swelling to go down after surgery. The herniated disc will be fixed if and when she wakes up," he said.

"If?" Grandma whispered.

"Can we see her?" John asked.

"Only for a minute, they are prepping her for surgery. The surgery will likely take three to four hours."

The four of them walked to where Saline was. With the exception of the cervical collar and a bruise on the side of her face, she looked to be sleeping. "Saline, baby, Grandma is here. We haven't had enough time together, so you are going to have to wake up. I love you, honey. And Grandma will be here when you wake up," the elderly woman said and began to cry.

"Come on, Catherine. I think you need to sit down," John said.

"Saline, baby, we are all here, you have to come back to us. We don't have anyone to keep Colton in line without you. And we love you so much. All of us do," Allison said through tears.

Andrew took Saline's hand. "Wake up, Saline, and I will stay here so you can boss me around some more," he said before crying.

Allison took the young man in her arms. They cried on each other's shoulders and only left when they came for Saline. They were shown to a waiting room that was empty, and they all got ready for the long wait.

"John, Allison. Would it be okay with you if I called her uncle? Just to keep him informed. He truly does care," Catherine said.

"Yes, of course," John said. "And, Catherine, if he decides to come over here, that is okay as well."

Catherine went to a phone in the waiting room to make the call.

John called the ranch and spoke with Maria, asking about everyone who had gone riding. Maria told about sedating Sara.

"Colt already has a sore throat, as does Mark and Scott. According to Mark, someone threw Saline a ball that went over her head. She caught it, but when she came down, the bank collapsed. Andrew didn't hesitate and jumped into the creek after her. They were all just having a good time, and this happened," Maria said.

"Maria, there may be someone calling from Germany. We let the girls' grandmother call their uncle. Just keep him up to date with how Saline is, if you don't mind," John said.

"I will. When the others get up, do you want them to come to the hospital?" Maria asked.

"All of them got pretty cold and need to take care of each other. Can you also call Alex? He should be back soon and let him have a look at everyone who went riding."

"Yes, sir. I will," Maria said and hung up.

"How is she doing, honey?" Mark asked.

"Saline is having brain surgery. They don't know if she will make it," Maria said and began to cry.

"How is Andrew? He left here soaking wet," Mark asked.

"I didn't think to ask. I will next time I talk to them."

"Allison, would you mind very much going someplace and getting Andrew some warm dry clothes? He is beside himself and doesn't know his way around Dallas," John asked.

"Yes, of course," Allison said. Then she walked to the nurses' station and requested a couple of blankets. She walked over to Andrew. "Andrew, baby, you need to try to get warm. I would hate for your mother to get angry at us for your getting sick."

"Thank you, mam. I will."

Allison pulled out her keys and left to get Andrew some clothes. She couldn't stop thinking about Saline. The thought of losing her was out of the question. She was happier now than she had ever been. She drove to a high-end department store and parked her car and went inside.

Being the mother of three boys, she had no problem finding his size. She picked him out several things and then checked out. She had wanted to keep those she was closest to in the house with her for a couple of days.

"Are you Allison Byers?" a reporter asked.

"Yes, I am, please excuse me," she said.

"Did you attend the funeral last week?"

"No, I was not there for a funeral. Please excuse me," she said.

"What was your whole family doing in London?"

"A private matter that was nobody's business," she said, walking faster.

"Why did the Alexander daughters not attend their father's funeral?"

"Byers, their last name is Byers. There was an illness in the family," Allison answered. She also saw that reporters had blocked her being able to both get into her car and leave. "You son of a bitches have had your fun and caused enough hardship to our family to last a lifetime. Now, I have something that I have to return to urgently," she said, pushing through to her car and getting in.

The reporters stayed all around her car. And no one had moved the van that belonged to some of the reporters. It was in that instant that Allison made a decision that would make them take her more seriously. She put her town car in reverse and backed up right into the van, pushing it nearly twenty feet before she put her car into drive and continued on her way.

When Allison arrived back at the hospital, she took the bags of fresh clothes inside and gave it to Andrew.

"They are just some dry clothes, Andrew. You don't want to catch cold. I didn't know what you normally like to wear, so I got a couple of different things," Allison said.

"Allison, are you all right, hon?" Catherine asked.

"I just had a run-in with some aggressive reporters, is all. I really didn't think about them, so by the time I knew that they were there, it was too late," she said.

"Thank you for the clothes," Andrew said.

"It is the least I could do after you saved our daughter's life. Why don't you go and change and just put the wet clothes in one of the bags?" Allison said.

John reached out and took her hand and pulled her down beside him. "Allison, what else happened?"

About that time, a special new report came on showing Allison trying to work her way through the sea of reporters. "A reporter was injured when Mrs. Byers backed into an NBC van. Mrs. Byers was reportedly acting as though she had been drinking or under the influence of some kind of medication when she backed into the van and left." It showed the entire incident. "Dallas police have not yet been able to locate Mrs. Byers at present to question her regarding the incident in the parking lot."

"I am sorry, John. The reporter parked directly behind me and blocked me in. I just had to get away from them before I said something I shouldn't. I am sorry about the car."

John began to laugh.

"You are not angry at me?" she said.

"I have wanted to do that for over two years. I am completely jealous," he said, hugging his wife. He then called a friend at the police department to let him know what had happened and where they were, if there was a problem. The friend assured him that the entire incident was captured on tape, and there was no problem, and the so-called injury was when a reporter tripped over his own microphone cord.

Andrew had changed and come back into the waiting room with the others. The four of them got a good laugh about running into the news van.

Then the door opened, and the doctor who had operated on Saline entered. It had been nearly four hours since they had taken her back.

"How is our girl?" John asked, standing.

"She is stable. We were able to stop the bleeding. She has not woken up as yet, but it could take a couple of days or longer. We did a CAT scan on her neck after having repaired the bleeding in her brain, and she does indeed have a herniated disc at the level of C4–C5. It will require surgery after she has recovered from the skull fracture. So we will be leaving a cervical collar on her. She did come off the ventilator and is breathing on her own, which is great news. About 60 percent of brain injuries require a ventilator until they can breathe on their own again.

"There could be some problems associated with the area in the brain that was affected. We won't know that until she wakes up. We don't have her on anything to support her blood pressure. She is doing well on her own in regulating her body. She was very cold when she got here. Her body temperature was only eighty-eight degrees. She is now up to about ninety-three degrees. That helped to a degree and kept the brain damage from being worse. She has a warming blanket on for now to get her body temperature up to ninety-eight degrees.

"My opinion as things are, I believe that she will wake up within the next two days, if that helps you at all. I will be staying in the hospital tonight to keep a close eye on her. She will be taken to neuro intensive care in the next few minutes, and you may see her there," the doctor concluded.

"Excuse me doctor, what is your name?" Allison asked.

"Wayne Ligon, I am a neurosurgeon. I have also left word in the ICU that a member of the family may remain at the bedside at all times," he said.

John shook the man's hand and thanked him.

"I have seen in the news of late that the reporters have really given y'all a bad time. In my opinion, reporters take advantage of people entirely too much, and for that, I am sorry," Dr. Ligon said sincerely.

"Then you would have been proud of my Allison about an hour ago. She went to a department store to get some clothes for our son. He is the one who pulled her out of the water. The news van was blocking my Allison in, so she backed her car right into the van and pushed it out of the way," John said.

Everyone began to laugh about Allison's newfound agitation.

"I had seen all of you on the news at various different times for the last couple of years. It is wrong to continue to pester honest people like they have done all of you. May I ask a question?" the doctor asked.

"Of course," John said.

"When did the queen put her son up for adoption?" he asked seriously they broke into a smile. "Don't worry, Your Royal Highness, I have told no one who you are. And you don't look very much like a prince at present. I will keep the secret," he said and started to the door.

"Dr. Ligon?" Catherine said. He turned back to face her. "I am Saline's grandmother. I have only recently come back into the girls' lives. Will we have a chance to get reacquainted?"

"It is my opinion, Your Grace, that she will. Just have a little patience, and I believe you will have your girl back," he said, putting a reassuring hand on her shoulder.

"Thank you so much for all you have done," Catherine said.

"It is my great pleasure," he said and was out the door. "And she is entered in the hospital as a Jane Doe for protection."

Everyone in the room seemed to breathe a sigh of relief. But they all also knew that until she woke up, they would not know how bad the injury was. Each decided to make a phone call home. Allison called her brother; Catherine called her brother in law, only to discover that he was on a plane bound to DFW that should be arriving early in the morning. Looking at the clock, it was only three in the morning. John called the house to let everyone know that things were looking better than before, and Andrew called Buckingham Palace to keep his mother and father apprised of any updates and requested to stay until the incident resolved itself, perhaps another two to three weeks.

"They are wonderful people, Mummy. They have treated me very well, and in talking to the doctor, I was introduced as one of their sons so I would be allowed to visit," Andrew said.

"I got a call from the port today. There is an oil tanker that is to be coming to England as a gift for the English people. We are being sent a gift of badly needed oil?" she asked.

"Yes, Mummy. John and Scott Byers decided, in return for the kindness shown by the English people during their stay at both St. Thomas Hospital and Kensington Palace. Not to mention Charles standing in for their family. It is merely the family's way of saying thank you, and they truly hope you accept," Andrew said.

"Please make sure and thank him for me until I can catch up to one of them. And tell them that the young girl, Saline isn't it, is in our prayers. I wish her a good recovery," his mother said.

"I will tell them, Mummy. Mr. and Mrs. Byers are both right here. Would you like a word?" Andrew asked.

"Yes, if they are up to speaking at present," she said.

"Mr. Byers, the queen wishes to speak with you," Andrew said.

"Thank you, son," he said and gave Andrew's shoulder a pat.

"This is John Byers, of whom am I speaking?" he asked.

"I am the queen. More to the point, I am Elizabeth, Andrew's mother," she said.

"Very good to meet you. You may call me John," he said.

"In private and on the phone, you may call me Elizabeth. How is your family this week?" she asked.

"Sara is still quite weak, but does not like to show it. Our sons are all quite well, although it will not surprise me if all of them have pneumonia from the ride yesterday. Maria, Allison, and I are quite well. But right now, we are very concerned about Saline, our younger girl. She is sixteen. While all of them were riding today, they had stopped about five miles from the main house to water and rest their horses. Saline jumped up to catch a ball that was thrown to her and the bank of the swollen creek caved in. We are in debt to you for Andrew's actions. He jumped into the freezing water and got a hold of Saline. The others rode their horses downstream and one of my other boys swan a rope across the creek. Andrew caught the rope and they pulled them both in. My Allison just went out and got him some dry warm clothes. He considers this his fault because he was the closest to her when it happened. He will not leave the hospital until he finds out if she is okay," John said.

"Dear me, all of you have had a very busy last two weeks. Andrew may stay as long as he can be of use to all of you. He is a good young man," she said.

"Thank you, mam. He is a very good and very brave young man. I will never be able to thank him enough," John said.

"Speaking of thanking him, am I to understand you correctly that you are sending an oil tanker to England?" Elizabeth asked.

"It is the least I could do. The way that the English people treated us like we were royalty helped at such a time. The use of a private plane, Charles having stepped in to represent both the Crown and our family, St. Thomas Hospital, and of course, Kensington Palace—there is no way to thank you enough. I hope you accept our gift, it is the least we could do. It will be doing us a service as well as since opening the refinery, we seem to have more than our share of oil. And if it can help our friends, we are grateful," John said.

"On behalf of the English people, we accept with pleasure. And do keep me informed on how the two young ladies are getting along. Lady Sara was presented at court here when she was but twelve, which makes her English. I like to keep up with all my ladies," she said.

"With respect, little lady, I have to say I don't know very much about court law. I am afraid that business in Texas keeps me from knowing what it means when you say that Sara is one of your ladies," John asked.

The queen knew that John Byers was a well-educated and respected man in business, family, and as a statesman. She also knew that most people did not have common knowledge of a monarchy.

"Sara began school here when she was five years old. It is common, I am afraid, for children in Sara's situation to be educated in boarding school to give them foundation as a young lady. As you know, her uncle is a member of the family in Hamburg. Her uncle is the one who selected Meadow Park in Wales for Sara to attend," she said.

"After Sara had attended school for a few years, my cousin, Lady Dickerson, feared for young Sara's life. She took steps and legally, by the time she was presented at court, she had been adopted by the family. I know of the young girl's family, I am afraid. But all the things that she is are things that are exhibited in so few young ladies in this day and time. Respect, absolute faith in the church, courage enough that at all times she will give her life for another without regret, and I don't know how you will feel about this, devotion to the Crown, and any other authority figure she respects. Her title as a lady is not so much of what she is called as what she is," the queen said.

"And what is that?" John asked.

"All that is good about my country and yours, and if His Grace has his way, he wants her for Germany. And if I may voice an opinion in regards to His Grace," she asked.

"Please do," John asked, wanting all information regarding the duke.

"The duke knows that Sara is obedient to a fault. If he were to pull her into that world, it is one that would crush her. He is a good and decent yet very powerful man. He would groom her into being something she is not. England wants nothing but Sara's happiness and security. England would no more abuse those qualities that she has than you and your family would."

John had heard her words loud and clear. She was worried for Sara as a parent would be for their child. "So if the duke wanted to, say, be a part of the girls' lives, you would say?"

"As an uncle in one of our two countries, not as the duke wanting a successor. He will be able to use her education to his benefit," the monarch said.

"You see things very clearly. I thank you for that. And I pray for the day that we may meet. As I understand it, you have never met Sara," John said.

"Only for a few moments formally, and through my cousin of course. She is only eighteen and only just now happy. She has functioned as an adult her entire life. I believe she has the right to be your 'baby girl.' I believe Charles has heard you refer to her, for a while."

"Thank you, Your Majesty. I believe they want us to visit Saline at present. I hope we talk again," John said.

"As do I. Give my son our love."

"I will," John said.

"Thank you, Mr. Byers."

"Please, little lady, call me John."

The queen was a little amused at his having called her little lady. Most who spoke with her were either tongue-tied in awe, hoping for position. This man was rare and one she would like to have as a friend. "John then, until we speak again."

And the call was ended. John caught up with the rest of the party at the door to Saline's room. He stepped inside to find a very bruised and battered Saline. Part of her hair on one side of her head had to be shaved to allow the neurosurgeon to repair the damage.

Catherine went directly over to her, as did Allison, and picked up her hands. "Darlin' this is Grandma, and I am not leaving here until you talk to me. Please come back to us, baby," she said gently.

Saline began opening her eyes, though slowly.

"That's it, baby. Open your eyes and look at Grandma." Saline's voice was hoarse, but she did manage to say Grandma and Momma.

"You fell in the creek, baby. But Andrew was there, and he jumped in and saved you. You got quite a bump on the head. But now you are going to be fine," Grandma said.

"I have a terrible headache," she said.

"Nurse?" Grandma said. "My granddaughter needs something for a headache. Can you get that please?"

"Immediately," the nurse said and called Dr. Ligon. "Sir, Ms. Byers is awake and talking. She said she has a headache. May I medicate her?"

"Yes, go ahead. Keep me up to date on anything," he said.

"Yes, sir," she said again and hung up the phone.

When she returned, she noted that Saline was talking to all four members in her family. Her speech was clear, so she gave her the medication in her IV. "This will likely put her to sleep," the nurse said.

"The doctor said one of us could stay with her all the time," Allison said.

"Yes, that is true," the nurse said.

"John, why don't you and the others go home and get some rest and I will stay here with Saline. Catherine, I know you need to rest, you as well, Andrew," Allison said.

Everyone nodded.

"I would be happy to stay with her if you like, Mrs. Byers," Andrew said.

"Then you may have the next watch, after you have rested," she said. "Do we all agree?" everyone nodded.

"Then take the car, and I will see you in a few hours," Allison said.

Andrew smiled a little to himself. Allison Byers reminded him very much of his mother. She had a quiet forcefulness that one had to respect, something possessed by one who was married to a powerful man and having dealt with men her entire life. He very, very seldom met any one woman that was entirely like his mother. However, she needed no crown, tiara, or a title to make her who she was.

John went to his wife and hugged her warmly. "Honey, are you sure that you have this?" he asked, hugging her.

"Yes, John. I need to be here when she awakens. I need the first face she sees to be one that she loves. She already knows that she is hurt, but what if she forgets how she got here and thinks about her father? I will just feel good staying with her for a little while. Please take Catherine and Andrew home to rest.

"Could you do me one other favor?" she asked.

"Anything," he answered.

"Have Alex come over and talk to Catherine. I want to know just how to care for her, and she appears a little frail at present," she asked.

"I will. It is a shame that she was not allowed to be around her grandchildren until the end of her life. But maybe we can make the time she has left quality time," she said.

"I am so glad that you married me. I am the luckiest man in the world." He kissed her soundly and said he would see her after a while.

When they left, she sat down beside Saline and took out her sewing. The nurses would come in and check on her, give medications and all the things that could be expected in ICU. Allison stayed out of the way and, from time to time, would talk to the nurses. All the nurses were friendly and helpful.

They had ordered Allison a guest tray so she didn't have to leave to eat.

Saline would awaken from time to time and reach for Allison's hand.

"It's all right baby. Momma is here," she said.

"Am I going to live, Momma?" she asked.

"Of course you are. You are going to be very sore for a while," she said.

"Why can't I move my head?" she asked.

"When you were in the water, you hit your head pretty hard, and it caused a disc to herniate in your neck. After a little time, they will fix that, and you won't have to wear the neck brace again," Allison said.

"I have to be operated on again? How long will I be here?" she asked.

"Just a few days, is all. Then at home you won't be able to do anything heavy for several weeks, until your neck heals," Allison said softly.

Out of the corner of her eye, Allison could see a familiar face standing outside of the room. "I need to go to the bathroom right quick. Do you need me to get you anything from the gift shop?"

"You will be right back, won't you?" she asked.

"Of course I will. I will only be a few minutes," she said and walked out.

Allison walked out of the room to the man who had been looking in.

"Hello, I am Allison Byers. I am Saline's mother," she said.

The man extended his hand, and Allison took the man's hand. "Do you know who I am?"

"Yes. I believe you are Saline's uncle. Catherine told me she had called, and I told her it would be okay if you wanted to visit. Although right now may not be the best time," Allison said.

"No, of course. Can you tell me the nature of her injury?" he asked.

"She fell down a creek bank. With the rains that we have had, the creeks and rivers are pretty swollen. She likely hit her head on something like a rock. She surprised us all by waking up so quickly. But it will be a few days before we know how much damage she may have. She also has a herniated disc in her neck that will have to be fixed in a few days. Andrew, who jumped in to get her, made sure her head stayed out of the water so her lungs are okay," she said.

"When the timing is right, may I see her for a moment?" he asked. "I assure you that I am here alone. I would never try to take her from you."

"I will have to ask Saline. Anything that happens that upsets her causes pressure in her brain. But I will ask. Your Grace, I need something to be understood. If and only if the girls want you in their lives, you may be their uncle. You will do nothing to influence them in regard to Germany. Your family has taken enough of these girls' lives," she said. "Excuse me for a few minutes," Allison said and went back to Saline's room.

"Saline, baby, I need to ask you a question. And it is completely your decision, and no one is going to make you do anything. Okay?" Allison said gently.

"Yes, Momma," she whispered.

"Your uncle heard about your accident, and the first thing he did was get on a plane. He is by himself and would just like to see you for a minute," Allison said.

"What do you think, Momma? Does he want to hurt me or Sara?" she asked.

"No. The only time you ever heard about being hurt by him was from your dad. I believe your uncle is actually quite concerned for you."

"Will you stay with me?" she asked.

"Of course I will."

"Okay. I will see him," Saline said. Allison smiled at her.

She stepped to the door and motioned him in.

"Saline, when Catherine told me about the accident, I got right on a plane to make sure that you would be well," he said.

"How are you, Uncle? I am sorry that my dad made things so unclear between us for so long," Saline said.

"You have nothing to be sorry for. I wish I would have known what the three of you were going through. I would have been here and taken you home and treated you all well," he said and broke down.

"He told us that we didn't matter to you, just Sophie and Tommy. The rest of us were nothing," Saline said.

The duke picked up her hand and kissed it then very gently took her in his arms. Saline's left arm went around his neck.

Allison noticed that her right hand didn't move. She stepped over to the nurse and asked if she had noticed her right hand was not working. The nurse called the doctor.

The duke gently laid Saline back down.

"I promise you that for the rest of both of your lives, if you ever need anything, want to see me, or want to come to Germany, you will be welcome. I never want us to be estranged again," he said.

"I can't speak for Sara, but I would very much like to get to know you a little better. All I know is what my dad told me," Saline said. "He would never allow me to talk to you while we were in Germany."

"I can assure he was quite wrong. I had several hours to get to know your sister. She is a very good and brave young lady. I have no doubt that the two of you would die for anyone you love," he said.

Saline just smiled a little. "I have a headache." She started blinking. "Oh god, my head."

"Nurse, my god, nurse get in here please," he said.

Allison stepped over to her. "Help is on the way, Saline. Try to relax, honey. Help will be here soon."

The nurse came over and gave her something in her IV. "It will take only a second, Saline, and it will be better. Slow down your breathing." Saline did as she was told, and in a few seconds, she was back to sleeping.

"Her blood pressure is up just a little. I will start a drip to keep it down. And I have put in a call to the doctor. He will be here in a few minutes."

The doctor arrived and asked them to step out for a minute, and he would talk to them immediately after he was finished.

Allison and the duke walked out of the room and sat in a nearby waiting room for a minute. "You have done a wonderful job with the girls, Mrs. Byers. They are both well mannered and lovely young ladies," he said.

Allison knew that for him to compliment her was something this man was not accustomed to doing.

"Thank you, we love those girls like they are our own," she said.

"When Sara started telling me about what Lord Henry had done, I began to research her life. It was only after his death that Catherine had sent me a video tape that she had found in Sophie's room then found more of them all over the house, along with pornographic material where Sophie was featured," the duke said.

"So he abused her as well?" Allison said.

"Actually no. That was a problem for her. She wanted what her dad 'gave' to the other girls, and if he didn't want her, she would find someone who did. She was taped with several men at a time and also taped with her brother. And she insisted in the film that she needed to be treated like trash, so it appeared to be filmed in a back alley in Downtown LA. She was started into a private girls' school for the mentally disturbed. I hope with time, help, and as much love as there is, maybe she is still young enough to be saved," he concluded.

"Their brother, Tommy, was to be arrested following the funeral, but I am afraid I got distracted when I got the note saying that Sara had lost the baby. And he and his mother got away. My feeling is they will likely try to come back to the States. I don't know if they will be any trouble to your family and the girls, but I would keep an eye out for him," he said. "My sister-in-law, Catherine, has always tried to see that the children were well cared for, but Henry was as abusive to his mother as well as his children. Even so, she would take Saline and Sara away for a while at a time, only to be caught later. Catherine was diagnosed with lymphoma a few weeks ago. She has a year or two at the most. I have invited her back to Germany with me, but she wants to be where she can see her grandchildren often.

"Again, Mrs. Byers, I am sorry down in my soul for the trouble that I caused the girls and your family. And I will never forgive myself for the loss of Sara's baby."

Allison studied him for a moment. He was a broken man who was speaking from his heart. "Your Grace, my husband is the final authority regarding the ranch, and our son has the final say so about his wife. But consider yourself welcome after you talk to John and to Scott," Allison said. "But understand me, sir. If you ever attempt what you did before, I will kill you myself."

The fierceness of the woman in defense of the two girls was felt. "Thank you, mam, and I look forward to apologizing to your husband and your son. And please, unless we are in a formal situation, please call me Joseph," he said.

"And you may call me Allison."

"And I am John, and this is our son Scott. And of course you know Sara. And this is our very dear friend Andrew. And I have heard what you were saying to my wife. You can see the difficulty we had at first in thinking that your feelings about the girls were the same as your nephews," he said.

Joseph walked over to Sara and Scott. He picked up Sara's hand, kissing the back of it. "Sara, from the bottom of my heart, I am so sorry for causing you to lose your baby," he said.

"Your Grace, there are a number of things that caused me to lose our baby. It is not your burden to carry," she said.

"Thank you." He then shook hands with both Scott and Andrew.

"Momma, may I go in to see Saline?" Sara asked.

"Yes, of course," Allison said, and Sara, with Scott right behind her, walked into the room.

"Saline, I am here," Sara said softly. "I am right here. Are you awake?"

"Sara?" she said. "I am so glad you are here. I am sorry I fell in the creek and caused so much trouble."

"It wasn't any trouble. It was just an accident, and now it is over. You just have to get well, and I will be there the whole time. I love you, sis."

"I love you too. I am going to take a nap, okay?" she said.

"You go ahead and sleep, and I will see you after a while."

John put a heavy hand on the duke's shoulder. "We have to talk."

The duke was taken down the hall into a small room. "What is this about?" Joseph asked.

"The rules, sir," Scott said. "My wife is not your niece in reality. If you want the honor of being included in our family, it will be just that. She takes total responsibility for the death of her stepfather no matter what anyone tries to say to make her feel otherwise. She spent her entire childhood protecting those she loved. She has excused your part in the loss of our son. I am not so forgiving. My daddy has spent the last hours talking to some extremely important people in two countries that will prove to be your true opponents if you were to ever try to take one of the girls again."

"Her Majesty has a message for you as well, Your Grace," Andrew began.

"With respect, Your Royal Highness, friendship to a family does not put the United Kingdom between me and them," Joseph said.

"Hear me, Your Grace, when she was eight, Sara didn't return to the US for two years. In that time, she was adopted by Lord and Lady Dickerson and, as such, was made a member of Her Majesty's court at the age of twelve. It was never disputed by anyone. Your nephew told the Dickerson family when she returned to California that year that Sara had died. Your sister-in-law took the two girls and was taking them to London when Lord Henry found them. They searched for her, but Henry left no clue," Andrew said.

John pulled something from his pocket and looked at it for a moment, then leveled his gaze at the duke. "The morning that we took the three kids, it was raining and about thirty-five degrees outside. Following a night of sleeping in the cold barn, Sara walked to work, a mile up the interstate. This is what she looked like," John said, giving the picture to the duke. "You knew she was not in school, knew that Saline and Jody had not been heard from for over two years. Were they really not all that important to you that you didn't try to find out where they were? Look at the picture, Joseph. Sara had four broken ribs, was so black and blue that you could not touch a place on her." John took a few other pictures from his pocket. "While you were in your nice warm bed, this is where these children had to sleep. You spoke to the other two kids and your nephew at least every couple of weeks.

"So before you become part of the lives of these two fine young women, it will be as their uncle. There is no Germany. No palaces or castles. No ministers and no more news conferences. No big announcements of how one of the girls would be the future of anything more than what they want to do," John said.

"There are people who are willing to accept them," Joseph started.

"I don't care about Germany," John said.

"You leave me no choice," Joseph started.

"No, there is a choice. There is just no Germany. And this is Texas. There is someone always watching, and chances are, they are packing. They belong to me. They are your nieces, not the future of Germany. Or you leave now."

The duke heard the passion and force of what he was saying. He had done his research on the Byers family in the last weeks and months. He had not however seen the pictures before. His hands trembled as one by one he saw what the girls had lived through and this family had saved them from. His heart broke as he thought of two young girls living through such a hellish existence. He thought of his nephew, now dead at his own mother's hand, being raised by his nieces in unimaginable circumstances. Feelings of outrage at his nephew and his wife treating their children in such a way caused a feeling that he had never felt so heavily—shame.

"I am shamed, sir. I assure you. I only want what is best for those girls. And that is all of you. If I had any idea of what, I will live my life for their forgiveness and their trust, and I pray for this. For your friendship," Joseph said and extended his hand.

John could read people well. He took his hand and shook it firmly. "I will pray for that as well."

Weeks passed since the accident on the creek. Saline's recovery was quite slow. She had to relearn to use her right arm again but was doing well.

Joseph had no choice but to accept the terms offered if he wanted to be part of the girls' lives. But after Saline was released from the hospital, he discovered what a blessing it was to be included as family to people, not subjects. When he returned to Germany following staying in Texas for two weeks, he saw things in a different light. He smiled most of the time now in thinking about his nieces and nephew and the entire Byers family.

Saline, after having spending time with her uncle in both the hospital and home, surprised him by handing him a legal document. On the document, it changed Saline's name from Saline Byers, to Saline Catherine Alexander-Byers, in his honor. Complete with formal pictures of both girls wearing his wife's tiara and ring.

Andrew had gone back to England, but he and Saline talked every few days. He promised to come back and visit from time to time and invited Saline to visit as well.

Sara had been accepted into the nursing program in Tyler. Her plans were to become an LVN first and then work toward her RN. Lauren had started school at the University of Texas at Tyler. Most days Sara and Lauren had lunch together. There were no reporters or anyone outside bothering them. The thought of two young women from two very prominent families attending college was far from the reporters' minds.

Riley continued taking his courses at SMU to become an attorney and lived and worked at home the entire time.

Saline had decided to start college in January rather than in the fall to give her a chance to fully recover.

Grandma had moved into the main house at the ranch at John and Allison's insistence. She spent lots of time with Saline and Austin while Sara was in school.

In the summer, when Mark and Maria had their third child, Sara was there at the Country Hospital, helping her to push. The baby was a perfect little girl. They named her Brittany St. Clair.

Nursing school was everything that Sara ever could have hoped for and more. She listened intently in class so she could keep up as her reading skills were still a little slow.

About two months into nursing school, they started taking care of patients. The more she learned, the better she felt about herself. After a couple of more months, she had mastered most of the skills necessary for an LVN to perform. She was doing very well on the written exams due to her ability to remember everything exactly. At night Scott would read from the textbooks. Or even Lauren, Saline, or Grandma. Anyone who had a little free time would help her to study.

Grandma would go to Scott and Sara's house on days that Sara was in school to cook supper and to watch little Austin, who was now running, and not walking. She loved her little great-grandson so much and never in her life thought about being as happy as she now was.

Since the birth of her only child, and not long afterward his father dying, her life had turned into a living hell. Henry had never been a giving child. He wanted everything in life and wanted to do nothing to obtain it.

Even in primary school, he had been kicked out of two private schools because of his tendency toward violence. He had gone to school in Germany for ten years, from the time he was five until he was fifteen. Then he began going to school in Southern California. He had graduated from Berkeley, majoring in international affairs and engineering.

He decided, as at present he was not needing to return to Germany, he would instead make his already sizable fortune even greater and would start a company that designed swimming pools of every kind for the stars. His natural ability at designing the perfect pool for every yard and never making two alike made him independently wealthy. Of course, his house and pool had always to be the biggest and the best. His neighbors were on the Southern California A list. That included stars of TV and the big screen, politicians, big businessmen, and other millionaires and billionaires.

Because of his status as a future duke, he had to have his children educated at the schools chosen by his uncle. His only thing in life that he actually had to do was to produce an heir and a spare.

He threw the best parties to be had in California. He was very well-known in Las Vegas with owners of casinos. People who knew that he was from wealth and position in Europe made his already huge ego even bigger.

Catherine thought about what she could have done to change him, as she had done at least a million times before. There was nothing. Henry's own words were always that he was born to be great and expected nothing but the best.

When his uncle had taken him out of the line of succession, he got desperate. He had to be the duke, even if he had to kill his own children to do it.

Catherine loved being at Scott and Sara's house. Sara, who had always been such a sickly child who was forever afraid both for herself and her sister, was now a living, lovely, and happy young woman who cared for people. Nothing else seemed to matter. Henry could send her away and have a country and an ocean between the two sisters, but they were always close no matter what he did.

She loved to watch Sara dance when she didn't know she was watching. She expressed so much as she moved so gracefully across the floor. From time to time, she still had medical problems, but when she considered how sick she was as a child, it was nothing shy of a miracle that she was here today.

"Grandma, I didn't know that you were standing there. Is Saline okay?" she asked.

"She is getting better every day. Maria has even come up with a hairdo so you can hardly tell that she has ever had surgery. How do you have the energy to dance?" she asked.

"I never dance for very long. Sometimes I just need to unwind. How are you, Grandma?" Sara asked.

"I can hardly wait for my granddaughter to graduate from college in a few weeks. Do you really like nursing school that well?" Catherine asked.

"It is everything I thought it would be," Sara said when they were in the den. "Don't stand there, Grandma," Sara said.

"Is there something wrong?"

"That was where he died. I don't like it when anyone stands there," she said, and Catherine had already moved. "You were always so good to me growing up, and I am so happy you are here. I will never forgive myself for killing Henry," Sara said.

"Hon, you know as well as I do that if you wouldn't have killed him, he would have killed you, or worse. If I would have been brave enough, I would have killed him the first time he ever touched you," she said.

"I was not his, and he knew it. And he never let me forget it," Sara said.

"That is not on you, Sara. Don't ever think of yourself as anything but beautiful and good. You have never been anything but good to anyone. Henry took advantage because he thought of himself as entitled. Your biological father wanted you, but Henry would not let him have you just because he wanted you," Grandma said.

"But maybe if I wouldn't have been born, he would have been better to everyone else," Sara said.

"Let's not talk about him. He would have killed you before I met my great-grandson, and that would have been a huge loss for everyone. What kind of nursing would you like to go into?" Grandma asked, changing the subject.

"I want to take care of people with heart problems, like the people who took care of me did. Remember when you would see me at the hospital and we would sit on the floor and do puzzles? Dr. Quinton helps teach me about reading monitors and listening to heart sounds and feeling for pulses everywhere, and I love it all. I would like to work with him at Baylor for a little while, then I would like to start working at St. Mary's in Tyler. They are building up their heart program, and I can get in from the ground floor," Sara said. "What do you think, Grandma?" she asked.

"After what you went through as a child and as a teenager, I think you would be the very best heart nurse there is, especially with Steve teaching you," Grandma said.

About then, Austin was telling them that his nap was over. Sara started to go get him, but Grandma really wanted to see him. She went in and picked him up and started laughing the way he always did when Grandma was over. She came back to the kitchen with him and got him some juice.

"Are you tired tonight, Grandma?" Sara asked.

"No, why do you ask."

"Scott has been getting off so late here lately, and we have finals coming up soon, and if you could read part of it to me, I believe it would help," Sara said.

"I can always do that."

"Do you mind if we go to the main house for a minute? I have not been up there in a couple of days, and I miss everyone," she said.

"Let's go now, before we have to start supper," Grandma suggested.

Grandma, Sara, and Austin drove down to the main house. Saline was on the phone, likely with Andrew. She also had a friend over. Riley and Colton were in the horse barn, putting the horses to bed for the day. John and Scott were still in Dallas. Maria was at the main house with little Brittney. She was growing and getting prettier every day.

Sara and Scott had recently started trying to have another baby; they also had a baby boy that they were planning to adopt. He was just a few months younger than Austin. His parents had worked for John most of their lives and had no relatives. In their papers, they had said that they wanted Scott and Sara to have him if anything happened to them. Scott was supposed to be bringing him home tonight, and they had kept it a secret because it was to be a surprise for everyone.

"Momma, is everything okay?" she asked. Allison seemed to be a little stressed.

"Uncle Alex is sick. Steve says he needs open-heart surgery because of a bad valve. And he says Alex is going to have to slow way down because of the size of his heart."

"Is he going to be okay?" Sara asked with tears in her eyes.

"Steve believes so, but he refuses to have the surgery until after you graduate in a couple of weeks. He says he needs that time anyway to find another doctor for the clinic and the hospital. He hates not being able to practice as much as he always has, but knows it is for the best," Allison said.

"I can take care of him when I get out. The same way he has always taken care of me. Grandma, did I tell you that Austin was born at home and Uncle Alex delivered him? That was a long afternoon," Sara said.

"I would have thought that they would only deliver in the hospital with your background," Grandma said.

"I didn't know I was in labor all night and day. I thought it was just a bad backache. Then my water broke. It was the sweetest thing you have ever seen. Scott, Lauren, and Maria were in the room, and everyone else was in the family room. There was ice on the road, and we never could have made it to Tyler. So he was born down at our house. But I believe, the next time, I will go to the hospital a little earlier just to be safe," Sara said.

The ladies laughed a little, and the kitchen door opened. John came in first and then Scott holding their newest addition, Brad.

"Who is this?" Allison asked.

"This is Brad. He was Lane and Debra's baby. They left him to Sara and me. So this is our latest son," Scott said. Sara walked over and took the little boy. His hair was dark brown and curly, his eyes were hazel, and he had a beautiful olive complexion.

"He is nearly two, and as Austin is three, they will never know that they are not natural brothers. What do you think, Momma, Grandma? Are you surprised?" Sara asked.

"Both women rushed toward the baby and took turns holding him. Then they put him in the playpen with Austin. Both boys immediately began building a very complex structure out of building blocks.

"We have to go and find Austin a youth bed, and Brad can take Austin's baby bed until he gets a little bigger. He is now 100 percent Brad Douglas Byers."

Saline came into the kitchen where she heard the noise. "Saline, meet your youngest nephew, Brad. He is nearly two," Scott said.

"But how?" she said, picking up the child.

"His parents were killed last week, and they wanted Sara and me to have him in case anything happened to them."

Riley and Colton came in when he was explaining.

"Oh, Sara, I am so happy for you," Maria said.

"We didn't want to tell anyone before we knew for sure, but here he is. Oh, and I think we need to get back to our house. I have meat thawed and ready to cook. Good night, everyone," Sara said.

On the way out, she bumped into Lauren, who seemed to have her head in the clouds. "Why don't you come to our house for supper? I have a surprise for you."

"Okay, I will be down in a minute," she said.

The next weeks took a little more organization on Sara's part, as she was now the mother of two. The entire family fawned over Brad the same way they had Austin. Then finally, the tests were over and graduation completed and Sara was a graduate nurse. She took the state board exam in September of 1980 and passed the first time she took it. She was really a nurse.

Alex had had his operation, and it was decided he would have to retire from the clinic and his practice. But he had found a doctor fresh out of school to take his place. He had been in Vietnam as a paratrooper for over a year and had cashed in his GI bill and became a family practice doctor at the age of thirty-five, older than most who graduated from med school, but a doctor all the same. He was a likeable man and seemed to know his stuff.

After Sara had graduated, she worked with Dr. Quinton for over four months to learn about cardiology. Then she applied at the Country Hospital for a job as a staff nurse.

For the first week, she was to follow a nurse who was about the same age as herself.

Elaine Rogers had been a nurse for well over a year and seemed so much smarter. She showed her how to start an IV, what to do in the ER if someone came in, things that LVNs in large hospitals don't get to do. They were fast friends.

Elaine was the daughter of a Pentecostal pastor and had married her high school sweetheart a year before. Her father had paid for her to go to college.

They had known each other for several months when her husband had to go to an educational lecture on mine safety in Las Vegas. Sara invited her to come to the ranch for supper. She, of course, accepted.

When she pulled up to Scott and Sara's house, she saw two little boys playing in the front yard. "Elaine, these are our little boys, Austin and Brad. And this is my grandma, Catherine Alexander. This is my friend, Elaine Rogers. I invited her to supper as her husband is out of town. My Scott will be home in a little while," Sara said.

As they were talking, the door opened, and Saline and Lauren came in. "Elaine, this is my sister, Saline, and my best friend from school, Lady Lauren Dickerson."

"Lady?" Elaine said.

"We went to private school in Wales and then England," Lauren said. "My father is a member of the House of Lords."

"What about your mother?"

"She is at the main house right now helping Allison make supper," Lauren said. "Momma and Allison want to know if all of you want to eat supper at the main house tonight."

"That sounds good. It was a busy day today. Is that okay, Grandma?" Sara asked.

"Are you kidding? You are turning into a fine cook, but some of the things that Allison makes are just too good for words," Grandma said.

"Elaine, is that okay with you? I can fix something here if you prefer," Sara said.

"I would love to join all of you," Elaine said.

Sara wrote Scott a note telling him they were invited to the main house for supper. Then all of them picked up the boys and went to their vehicles to drive to the main house.

Elaine rode along with Sara. "Sara, who are you?"

"What do you mean?" she asked.

"Well, you cover well, but I can tell you have an English accent, and your friend's father is in the House of Lords. What about her mother?"

Sara paused for a minute. "She is second cousin to the Queen. They are very close," Sara said.

"Wait, let me think. A few years ago in town, there was talk about a young girl who was a something marrying. That is you? You are royalty?" Elaine said.

"No, not royalty, an aristocrat. There is a big difference. And I am not related by blood, my first stepdad was a lord. His uncle is the duke of Hamburg. Saline's father was Lord Henry Alexander. She is Lady Saline Catherine. But we don't use titles. I am married to Scott, and Saline was adopted by his parents. I trust you, Elaine. I have never brought anyone else out here. Please just treat me like Nurse Sara and not that circus of crap," Sara said.

"I won't tell anyone. You have my word. But why are you so opposed to being known as a royal?" Elaine asked.

"Because it is a circus, and I have had enough circus to last a lifetime. Someday I will tell you. But not right now. It is a very long story," Sara said.

"Can I ask a question?" Elaine asked. "Why are you working as a nurse?"

"I always wanted to be a nurse from the time I was a child. And Scott said he would put me through school to be one," Sara said.

"A few years ago, there was a huge wedding in the county seat. Was that you and Scott?" she asked.

"That was us. He has been so good to me. We constantly get followed around by reporters. Just here lately no one has done anything newsworthy," she said. "And I love working at the little Country Hospital. Uncle Alex used to be the doctor there, but he had to retire due to health reasons," she said.

"I remember Dr. Carmichael. He was so sweet. Now we have Dr. Rick Powell. He can be a horse's ass when he wants. Did you know that his wife is a nurse and he will not even let her practice?" Elaine said.

"Why?" Sara asked.

"Because in his way of thinking, if a woman has kids, she needs to stay home and take care of them and the man works," Elaine said.

"I didn't start school until after I had Austin. We are planning on having a big family. We are hoping to have another baby soon," Sara said.

Everyone went in the kitchen door and saw Allison in the kitchen fixing supper. "Hi, Momma," Sara said.

"Hi, baby girl, where are my boys?" she said.

"They are bringing up the rear," Sara said. "Momma, this is Elaine Rogers. She is an LVN at the Country Hospital. Her husband is out of town tonight."

Allison turned around to see a very pretty young woman with hair as dark as a raven's wing, and eyes of the same color. Her skin was like ivory, her smile perfect. Her hair was cut to her shoulders and turned under at the ends. She was a couple of inches shorter than Sara and was quite petite.

"I am glad to meet you, Elaine. You are the first friend that Sara has ever brought home. She is a little shy. Her sister has friends over all the time," Allison said. Then she saw how Sara was blushing and changed the subject.

"Momma, Elaine's husband is out of town tonight, and I asked her to have supper with us, is that okay?" Sara asked.

"Of course it is. Make yourself at home, Elaine," Allison Said.

"Let me take the boys to the family room, and I will help you with supper," Sara said.

"No, hon," Grandma said. "You girls go and visit. You have been at work all day long."

"Yeah, good idea," Saline and Lauren said together, half dragging Sara and Elaine down the hall.

Introductions were made to everyone including Uncle Alex and Dr. Quinton. Sara, Elaine, Saline, and Lauren had their own conversation going on.

"You don't look any older than I do, and you already have two kids. You must have been a baby when you had Austin," Elaine said.

"I was seventeen when he was born. I was supposed to have him in Tyler at St. Mary's, but the backache that I had turned out to be fourteen hours of labor, then my water broke," Sara said.

"That was an exciting day," Lauren said. "I stayed in there with her the whole time."

"Who delivered him?" Elaine asked.

"Uncle Alex," Sara said.

"Your uncle delivered your baby at home?" Elaine questioned.

"He is Scott's uncle. I thought you knew Dr. Carmichael. There were actually two doctors. Dr. Quinton was at the main house," Sara said.

"Where does Dr. Quinton practice?"

"He used to be in Los Angeles, but he moved to Texas when he found out that I was living here. He is my cardiologist," Sara said.

Elaine had so many questions that she wanted to ask, but decided that she would just learn things about her new friend as they came up.

"Austin, stop that," Sara said, getting up from her seat on the floor. She went over to the toddler, who seemed to be into everything at once.

"Am I really the first person Sara has brought here? How long has she lived here?" Elaine asked.

"About four years now," Saline said. "We moved here in April of 1976, and it is nearly the end of 1980. So I guess it is over four years. Don't tell her I am telling you this, but Sara tends to be afraid of most people. Becoming a nurse was her dream, but having to be around people is really stressful for her. But she is better than she used to be."

"How long have she and Scott been married?" Elaine asked.

"Four years in November. They got married the day after her seventeenth birthday. That was a great day—horse-drawn carriages, thousands of people including mayors, senators, and governors. You should look at the pictures," Saline said.

"When was Austin born?" Elaine asked.

"I know what you are thinking, but it is not the way that it is. Yes, Sara was expecting when they got married, but no one knew except her. She didn't want him to marry her for a baby, but because he loved her. She told him at the reception. She didn't even tell me," Saline said.

"When Scott gets home and you see the way that they look at each other, you will know how much they love each other. He fell in love with her two years before they formally met. She fell in love with him when she finally did meet him," Lauren said. "Trust me, I have known Sara for most of her life, and I have never seen her so happy as when Scott is with her."

Sara came back to where they were holding Austin. "I think that two little boys are getting very hungry."

"So is their daddy," said Scott, who was just walking in. He picked up Austin and kissed Sara. They held each other's look for only a few seconds. "And who is this?" he said, looking at Elaine.

"Scott, this is my friend from the hospital, Elaine Rogers. She is an LVN also," Sara said. "She is roping me around."

Everyone looked at her, thinking about what she was trying to say. "Showing you the ropes?" Scott said.

"Showing me the ropes," she said, blushing.

"Are you blushing?" Elaine asked.

"She blushes all the time. Like I said, she is shy," Saline said.

"Suppertime," Allison said, coming in from the kitchen. "Don't let it get cold."

Everyone got up and started moving to the dining room.

When everyone was seated, the meal began along with friendly chatter.

"Riley, what are you studying this week?"

"Litigation. It is like learning to argue legally. I think I have memorized four sets of encyclopedias in the last week." Riley said. Everyone laughed.

"Scott, is everything still running smoothly in the gulf?" John asked.

"So smooth it nearly runs itself," Scott said.

"Sara, I can't believe you brought someone home. I am proud of you, baby girl. Someday I may have to stop calling you that," Scott said.

"Not too soon," she said, looking up at him.

"Elaine, where do you live?" Allison asked.

"Salt Flats. Not too far from the hospital. I have lived there all my life. My father is a pastor, and my mom is a housewife," she said.

"What does your husband do?" John asked.

"He is the night foreman at the salt mine. He has been working there since he was fourteen," she said.

"Sara, I have never seen anyone eat so much soup as you," Elaine said.

"It is something we got used to at school. Every night we had some kind of homemade soup," Lauren said.

"What kind of school did you go to?" Elaine asked.

"It was a private girls' school for members of nobility and aristocracy. It is very different from schools here. I have been attending UT for over a year, and there are still things I need to work to learn," Lauren said.

"What are you going to be?" Elaine asked.

"After two years of college, I finally decided on becoming a doctor, a doctor specializing in oncology," Lauren answered.

"Why oncology?" Elaine asked.

"Lauren had cancer when she was young. If she becomes a doctor, she will have cancer cured in six months," Sara said.

"It could take me a year, but I will cure it," Lauren said.

"Grandma, are you quite all right?" Sara said, noticing her grandmother was pouring sweat and that her lips were turning blue. "Grandma," Sara said, jumping up from her chair, barely catching her before her head hit the floor. Sara put her head on her chest and could tell she wasn't breathing. She gave her two breaths and then checked her pulse. "Uncle Alex, she has no pulse." Sara started CPR. Elaine got on the ground to help Sara.

"Allison, call an ambulance. Steve, what do you think?" Alex said.

"Stop CPR for a moment." Dr. Quinton took his fist and hit her in the middle of her chest then once again checked her pulse. "I have a pulse, but she is still not breathing. Sara, continue mouth to mouth." Sara did as instructed. Dr. Quinton had taught her so much, but she never thought about ever having to perform it on someone she knew.

"Dr. Quinton, what is wrong with Grandma?" Saline asked through tears.

"I don't know yet, honey, but I will do everything that I can to help her," he answered.

John was conflicted. He knew that she didn't have much time left but hadn't told the girls as yet. In the back of his mind, he had hoped that clean air, good food, and happiness would be all the cure that she would need. He prayed that she would regain consciousness so as she could tell them herself. But he knew that if it came to it, he would be the one who had to tell them.

The ambulance arrived about the time that Grandma started to regain consciousness. Oxygen was applied, as well as electrodes to her chest, and an IV was started. Dr. Quinton identified himself as her cardiologist and said that he was riding with her. Alex said he would follow in his own car with Aunt Pauline.

"Sara, honey, you really need to wait here for now. I promise I will call right away when I know something," Dr. Quinton said.

"But she is my grandma. Can Saline go then?" she asked.

"Saline, you coming?" he asked.

"Yes, sir." Saline turned and hugged her sister tight and promised to call soon.

"Get some rest, baby girl. You have a checkup coming up next week. Okay?" Dr. Quinton reminded her.

"We will be following you as well, Steve," John said of him and Allison. Then it seemed like her whole world disappeared.

"Please excuse me a minute," she whispered and walked from the room in the direction of her old room. The room she had when she and Saline had first come there to live. She got on her knees and prayed then lay down on the bed and cried her eyes out.

Back downstairs in the dining room Scott, Riley, Colton, Lauren, and Elaine remained.

"If no one else is going to eat anymore, I will clear the table," Lauren said.

"I will help you, Lauren," Elaine said.

The three brothers also assisted.

"Why was Sara not to go to the hospital with her grandmother?" Elaine asked.

"Sara has a heart condition that causes her problems already, but she is also about six weeks pregnant. She has difficulty carrying babies," Scott said.

"She is only twenty and has two beautiful babies. How much trouble can there be?" Elaine asked.

Scott had heard Sara speak of Elaine as a good friend for the last few weeks since she had started working at the Country Hospital. He hoped he was not making a mistake in telling her a little something so she would understand.

"True, Sara had Austin, but she had to be watched like a hawk by her OB and her cardiologist. Her next pregnancy, she lost after she had been kidnapped and was taken to London. The intension was to take her to her stepfather's funeral, but she began having chest pain and was put in the hospital in London. I had gone over to bring her home, and that afternoon, at over four months pregnant, she lost our second child. Last year she also discovered she was pregnant, but before she had time to make the appointment with her OB, she lost that one as well. Her cardiologist and her OB are concerned about her having a baby right now, especially with her working. I didn't worry about her working as long as she was working where Uncle Alex was going to be close by. But he had to retire recently, and she hasn't gotten another primary doctor as yet. She really does not want a new doctor, especially someone she does not know. If a man were to raise his voice at her, she would quite literally pass out.

"How are the new doctors working out at the Country Hospital?" Scott asked.

"They are all okay. So far, no one has any complaints. Two of them are still a little wet behind the ears. One of them is cocky. He likes to exert his authority," Elaine said.

"Better keep some distance between that one and Sara for the time being," Riley said.

"Sara does a pretty good job avoiding any of the doctors. She does exactly what she is to do and leaves the RNs to deal with the doctors. She is great with patients," Elaine said.

"She is ordered to rest every minute that she is at home. She continues to take her heart medicine, and if she so much as catches a cold, that can be a real complication. But her passion for nursing is so heartfelt that it only could have been a gift from God.

"She has a terrible history, she and Saline both do," Scott concluded.

"They both have histories you could never imagine. Hell is a very real place for them both, because they have literally lived through it. But don't let her know what we have said. We just thought you should know a little so you can watch out for her at work, if you don't mind doing that," Lauren said.

"Of course I will watch after her. We always work the same shifts so that will make it easy. Please let me know if there is anything else I can do to help," Elaine said.

Sara came back to the dining room. Her face was tear streaked, and her nose was running. "I am sorry I left like that. I am better now."

"No harm, we were just doing the dishes. Since everyone is mostly done, why don't we all go down to our house so we can put the boys to bed in a few minutes?" Scott said. Everyone agreed.

When they got to Scott and Sara's house, the house was a little cool, so Scott and Riley added a couple of logs to the diminishing fires.

Sara, Lauren, and Elaine went to give the boys their baths and put them to bed. "Your husband is wonderful. I have never met two people so in love," Elaine said.

"I am very lucky and blessed that we found each other," she said.

After the boys were put to bed for the night, Lauren, Sara, and Elaine returned to the family room.

"Have they called about Grandma yet, Scott?" Sara asked.

"Not yet, baby girl. But you know it takes a while to get to Baylor. Then they have to do all those tests that you have to have when you go to the hospital. It takes a while. You want them to be thorough, right?" Scott said.

"Yes, of course. And Uncle Alex and Dr. Quinton are there. Momma and Daddy and Saline are there, and they will call. They will call," she said. "It is strange."

"What is so strange, baby girl?" Riley asked.

"She is not even my real grandmother, but it never mattered. She loved me, and I love her." Scott held her against his shoulder. "Lord Henry hated me from the second I was born until I killed, until, uh…" She couldn't continue. She never had come to grips with having taken a life.

"It's okay, my angel. She loves you very much. And to her, you are just as much her grandchild as the rest of them." Scott pulled back from her so she would see he was serious. "Sara, I want you to call in for tomorrow. And then I want you to go in and take the medicine Dr. Chambers gave you. And I promise, we all do, when they call, we will come and get you."

"I can't call in, Scott. I will be okay, really," she said.

"Sara you are six weeks pregnant. You don't want to take a chance on losing the baby because you are upset and not getting enough sleep, do you?" Scott asked.

"No, I don't' want to lose our baby," she whispered.

"Now, you go on in and get a bath, and I will get your medicine and a glass of milk."

"Yes, Scott. I will," she said, then turned to go to the bedroom.

"Scott, Doug won't be getting home until tomorrow. May I stay just in case you need a nurse? Unless you would rather I go," Elaine said.

"It would be very helpful if you stayed. I can get you some of Sara's clothes and anything else you may need. Riley, can you show

Elaine to one of the guestrooms please. I am going to make sure Sara is okay and take the phone out of the bedroom," Scott said.

"Please, Scott. Let me," Elaine asked.

She walked into the bathroom and could see the bathtub filling. Sara was sitting at her dressing table, crying. "Sara, go ahead and get a bath so you and the baby can have some rest," Elaine said softly. "I was going to spend the night tonight so you can have your friend here in case you need me. I didn't bring any extra clothes."

"Oh, yes. There are some panties that are still in the package in there if you want to take them," she said. "I won't be in here for long, I am suddenly so tired. I am sorry, Elaine. I didn't mean for this to happen."

Elaine took a seat beside her on the side of the tub. "That is what friends are for. And of course, you didn't know this would happen."

"In my dressing room, there are nightgowns and robes if you need them. You look about my size, and I have plenty of clothes. You are more than welcome to," Sara said.

"Okay. Get you a bath and think of that little life inside of you. If you need me, I am here. I will call in for both of us for tomorrow," Elaine said and left Sara to take a bath.

"Thank you for volunteering to stay with us, Elaine. Usually Momma and Saline are around for a shoulder to cry on. Having both you and Lauren here will help. Do you mind calling in for Sara?" Scott asked.

"I have already called in for both of us. I have a feeling that you know that something is very wrong," Elaine said.

"Her grandmother has cancer. She was only given a year, two years at the most. Grandma asked us not to tell the girls. She wanted to make some happy memories with them and get to see her great-grandchild," Scott said.

"Is there anything I can do to help her?" Elaine asked.

"Not at present. I think after a hot bath and her medicine, she will go to sleep. Then we will see what the morning brings. Can I trust that you will not repeat any of this to anyone?" Scott asked.

"Of course. I would never say or do anything to hurt her. May I ask a question?" she asked.

"Sure," Scott said simply.

"Did I hear her say she killed someone?"

"Yes, you heard right. It was her stepfather, Saline's father. He came to our home and took Maria, one of Sara's friends here on the ranch, hostage and threatened to kill her unless Sara got Austin and went with him to Germany. She wrapped a big pillow in a baby blanket, got my handgun, and put it under the pillow. He let go of Maria and told Sara to come on. She refused, so he started walking to her, holding a gun on her. He shot twice, hitting her in the right arm and hitting the pillow with the other. Sara only shot once, and he was dead before he hit the ground."

"My god."

"She has a very complicated past. But even with that being said, she is a very special lady. The rest of us are going to be waiting up in the den to hear from someone regarding their grandmother. Feel free to join us, or get some sleep. Just make yourself at home. And, Elaine, thanks for being here," Scott said and then walked out of the room.

Elaine got a quick shower and put on the gown and robe provided and went to the den to wait to find out what was happening.

Earlier that week…

At the Country Hospital, one of the new doctors was looking through some charts to get an idea of the caliber of patients he would be seeing in a small town. Richard Powell hadn't gone to a great medical school because he spent his first four years in college mainly concentrating on partying and sleeping with as many women as possible. Then he was drafted to go to Vietnam for a year. Only after he returned from his tour did he know what he wanted to do. He collected his GI bill and was looking for medical school he would attend. But as he had a D average, the only one he could attend was in Mexico City. So when he opened his practice, he was in his midthirties.

He studied family practice and was hoping to get on staff in a big city hospital but was unable to find anything that met his needs.

Then the job at the Country Hospital became available. He had spoken directly to the founder of the Country Hospital, Dr. Alex Carmichael, who also told him that as they spoke, the hospital was being enlarged to three times its size.

He told him that there was only one hospital in the county, and there was plenty of backing to build the hospital any way that he had wanted it. As his last act before he retired, he designed a perfectly functional seventy-bed hospital, with a new lab, a brand-new CAT machine, a big operating room, two rooms for laboring mothers, and a modern delivery room. He made sure also that the hospital now had six telemetry monitors for people who had lesser heart problems. The emergency now had four bays and was much more functional.

The sign outside the hospital and all the stationary called the hospital the Country Hospital, then in small letters under the name, it said "A Carmichael-Byers Partnership."

But now Rick wanted to get a feel for the people in the town where he was to live. The nurses who had worked in the hospital since it had been opened by Dr. Carmichael over thirty years ago told him that looking into patients' records that were not his patients as yet was no way to come into a small town.

Next, when he started seeing the patients, he would tell the patients that he was not Dr. Carmichael and would not run his clinic by getting paid with chickens and eggs. The nurses told him that the people in a small town did not like being talked down to and would be more than happy to go to the next town for care rather than deal with a yappy know-it-all.

They also said reading the private interactions with Alex Carmichael and his patients was unethical and intrusive. But he justified it as what he had to do to take over for a doctor that suddenly abandoned his patients.

When that comment was made, Allison had gone up to the clinic to get Sara's chart from the clinic per her brother's request.

"Just who the hell do you think you are?" Allison yelled. When the nurses heard Allison's voice, they came to stand with her.

"Lady, I am just starting to work in a place that had been abandoned by what used to be the only doctor in town," Rick said. "Who am I addressing?"

451

"Allison Carmichael Byers. Alex is my older brother. And he would still be here if not for his heart. He has been the only doctor in town for most of his adult life. And the people from this town and the surrounding towns loved him. So if I were you, I would shut up. And I need some private files from my brother's desk. So if you don't mind, move," she said.

"This is my desk now, and I would very much appreciate the key."

"I need to get those private files. They are private patients that will continue to be treated by Alex," she said.

"How many files are there?"

"Nine complete medical records, and I will be out of here."

Rick stood up so she could get to the drawer. She opened the drawer and retrieved the records. The chart that was on top said Sara Lyn Byers. Then another that said Saline Catherine Byers. She took a box and placed all the medical charts inside then put a top on it.

"It's all yours," Allison said and walked out. She walked over to radiology and requested some x-ray films, and of course, the people there had no problem in giving them to her. She stood there and talked to a few people for a little bit, and then everyone heard a voice that they had not heard in the last couple of years.

"I am in agony. I need some Demerol and something for my nerves." Joan Redding's voice was very distinctive. At hearing her voice, Allison gladly kept her back to her, so perhaps she would not know who she was.

Rick saw the way that Allison Byers was avoiding the woman that had just come in. When she saw that Joan was not looking at her, she left. She walked out completely undetected by Joan Redding.

Rick walked over to the very loud woman and introduced himself. "Mam, I am Dr. Rick Powell. What seems to be the problem?" he asked.

"I was at work. I am a waitress, and I broke my ankle," she said.

"You seem to be walking and putting weight on it well."

"It was the only way that I could get in here without crawling. I shouldn't even be working. My nerves are too bad, and I had a baby born dead a couple of years ago, and I have not physically gotten over it yet. If my damned daughters would come home rather than live with someone else, I wouldn't be working like this," Joan said.

"What is your name?" Rick asked.

"I am Joan Alexander Redding. I need a shot for the pain," she said.

"Are you here by yourself?"

"Yes. My son of a bitch of a husband is at work, and my son is doing something else," Joan said.

"Is there someone else to drive you home?" Rick asked.

"My daughters if I can get a hold of one of them."

"Give me their number, and I will call and tell them that you need a ride home. If I can't get in touch with someone, I will give you a prescription ,and you can take it when you get home," Rick explained.

Joan began digging through her purse to see if she could find the only number she knew of to get her daughters.

"They are going to do an x-ray, and I will try to get in touch with your daughters," Rick said, walking into the office and picking up the phone. He dialed and waited for someone to pick up.

"Hello," came the voice of a girl in her late teens.

"Hi, this is Dr. Rick Powell. I am at the Country Hospital. I have a Joan Alexander Redding here, and she seems to have either a sprained ankle or perhaps even broken ankle. But I can't give her something for pain until I know that someone can drive her home. Are you her daughter?" he asked.

"At one time I was her daughter, but I haven't seen her in two years," Saline said.

"Do you live close to here?" Rick asked.

"Yes."

"Then perhaps you can give her a ride," he said.

"No. I don't think so," Saline said.

"Do you have a car and a driver's license?" Rick asked.

"Yes to both. But I am not picking her up, and don't call this number again. Good luck," she said and hung up.

Her attitude toward her own mother angered him. He redialed the number again and the same person answered.

"Hello," Saline said.

"Excuse me, miss. What is your name?" Rick demanded.

"Why?"

"Because I like knowing who I am talking to," Rick said.

"Saline. Now that you know that, could you not call back?" she said and hung up.

Now Rick was really mad. He dialed the phone number again. "I don't know who the hell you think this is, but I am a doctor at the Country Hospital, and your mother has a serious injury and I can't give her any medicine unless there is someone to drive her home. She is in pain! Now I insist you come here and get your mother," Rick said.

"Are you listening to me right this second?" Saline asked calmly.

"Yes."

"And what is your name?" she asked.

"Dr. Rick Powell," he said through clinched teeth.

"Well, Dr. Dick Powell. I am not going to come to town for her. But if you go in there and spread her legs, she will give you some and you can take her home. My sister and I do not associate with that trash anymore. If you don't like that tough," Saline said and hung up again.

Rick banged the phone down as hard as he could. He then went to Amy, one of the nurses. "Excuse me, could you please call this number and ask the little bitch who answers the phone to come and get her mother. I have to medicate her," he said.

Amy looked down at the number. "Excuse me, Dr. Powell. I am not calling the good people at this number to do a favor for that trash. You want to talk to them, you talk to them."

"You are a nurse. You have sworn to care for people," Rick said.

"I know what I am, and that crazy bitch is a junkie whose husband broke my arm a few years ago and stole all the narcotics. That is while she was in labor with their dead child. I will take care of every human being I can. But that bitch doesn't qualify," she said and walked back to what she was doing.

"Come back here," Rick yelled. "Come back or you're fired."

"You can't fire me, you pompous ass. I am on the board of directors." He heard other nurses laughing at what Amy had told him.

"Mrs. Redding said she has two daughters. Do you know the second one's number?" he asked.

"Sure. She works here. But she will not come up here either. And those girls' family, that is the family that adopted them, they are people that you don't mess with," Amy said while filling up a medicine cup for a patient.

"Give me her number, and I will try anyway," he said.

"No. I won't give you her number. That woman has put those two girls through enough. I will call and let her know she is here, but she will not come up here. If you feel so sorry for her, you drive her home." Amy dialed Sara's number.

"Hello," Sara answered.

"Sara, this is Amy at the hospital. Your mother is up her and has sprained her ankle and is screaming for Demerol. Dr. Powell would like you or Saline to give her a ride home…That's what I told him. He called Saline at least three times and demanded her to come get her…I will tell him," she said and hung up.

"Sara is forbidden to get anyplace near her, for her own sake. Sorry." Amy went to walk away, but Rick caught her arm.

"Call her back so I can talk to her," he said.

"I have put up with this crap because you are new to this town. Sara has a husband and two small children and is expecting her third. She also has a heart condition that has to be monitored by her cardiologist. Her number is not listed anyplace, and I will not give it to you, not for that trash. Now, I have work to do." Amy pulled her arm free and walked away.

Rick walked down to where Joan Redding was. "Is it broken?" Joan asked.

"Looks like it is just sprained. I will wrap it and give you some medication you will have to get filled," he said.

"I need Demerol. I am in agony."

"There is no one to drive you home, and your daughters refuse to come up here," he said.

"You talked to Sara Lyn and Saline?" she asked.

"I spoke with Saline four different times. The nurse spoke with Sara. Her husband won't let her around you, according to the nurse,"

Rick said. "But you can take this when you get home. That's the best I can do." He finished wrapping her ankle and wrote her prescription and sent her on her way.

CHAPTER 15

At a little after 3:00 am, the phone rang. "Hello," Scott said. Everyone aside from Sara was still awake.

"Son, the girls' grandmother is in pretty bad shape. She likely won't last another twenty-four hours. Is Sara getting some sleep?" his father asked.

"Yes, sir, I gave her something to help her sheep. She has been asleep since about nine," Scott answered.

"I am awake now, Scott. How is Grandma?" she asked.

"Daddy, we will be up there in about an hour," Scott said.

"Baby girl, Grandma is not doing well. Can you come over here and sit with me?" Scott asked.

Sara did as requested.

"When Grandma came here, it was to see you, Saline, and her great-grandbabies. She told Daddy and me that she had been told she only had a year or two at the longest to live. But she didn't want the two of you to know. But she was so happy these last two years. And she was so glad to be here.

"The cancer is making it where she can no longer breathe on her own. Do you want to get dressed and go up to say good-bye?" he asked.

Sara looked up at her husband with big sad eyes and nodded. "I will get dressed," she said and walked to their room.

"Baby girl?" Sara turned back to Scott. "Dress warm, it is pretty cold out there."

Sara just nodded. In her dressing room, she put on her cotton slip first and then her petticoat and her usual full skirt and sweater and then pulled her good boots on. She then halfheartedly brushed her hair.

When she came out of the dressing room, she saw Elaine standing there. She walked over to her friend and gave her a hug. "If you need me to, Sara, I will watch the boys. Or I can go with you. What do you need me to do?" she asked.

"I know it is the middle of the night, but would you mind going with us? Grandma only came back into our lives two years ago. We both love her so much. She had no reason to love me, but she did. Even after I killed her son. I thought she would hate me for that. She didn't blame me," Sara said, taking a seat on the bed. Elaine sat down beside her.

"Sara, we have only known each other for a few months, but there is one thing I do know about you, and that is your reverence for life. I don't have any kids yet, but it has to be the hardest thing in the world to know that your child is so horrible that you believe the world would be better off without them in it. As I understand it, that is how she felt about her son," Elaine said.

"When I was growing up, my father is a pastor, and my mother has never worked. Money was always very tight. I used to daydream about what it would be like to be wealthy and to have people always fawning over you. I had never thought how some people may act if they believe that they are entitled. But you and Saline and every member of the family you belong to now do not act like they are entitled. All of you are warm and caring. Just knowing that about you tells me that you would not have killed someone unless they were threatening you or someone you love. And I know that must have been the way that your grandmother felt as well," Elaine said. She saw the tears that streaked Sara's face. She had gotten through to her.

Elaine reached over and hugged her friend again. Sara sobbed for a few minutes then pulled herself away. "Thank you, Elaine. I would appreciate it very much if you would come with us. With

Momma and Poppa, Scott, Saline, Lauren, and you, it would really help if you were there."

"Have you got something that I could wear? I don't think that I should be wearing a night gown to the hospital," Elaine said.

"Sure, come on in," Sara said, walking into the dressing room.

Elaine looked around the huge dressing room. There were more clothes than you would find in a department store.

"Do you have any more skirts like that and a sweater?" Elaine asked.

"I practically live in these skirts. Don't you need a petticoat?" Sara asked.

"A what?" Elaine asked.

Sara didn't know how to describe it, so she pulled her skirt up a little bit.

"Wow. That is the first time I have ever seen one of them besides in *Gone with the Wind*. Are they warm?" she asked.

"Yeah, they are made of cotton." Sara pulled out a few things so Elaine would have a choice and then gave her some privacy so she could get dressed.

When they were both dressed, they went to the living room. Scott had called Maria to watch the boys. Mark had stayed at their house to watch their three children who were sleeping.

"Are you ready, baby girl?" Scott asked.

"Is it okay if Elaine comes with us?" she asked.

"I rather thought it was understood that she was coming. Riley, can you and Colton stay with Maria?" Scott asked.

"No problem," Riley answered and then hugged Sara warmly.

The nearly hour-long drive was undertaken in near silence. Scott was driving, and Lauren sat in the passenger seat, and Elaine and Sara sat in the backseat.

When they got to the hospital, there were several dozen reporters already there even though it was the middle of the night.

"Oh no!" Sara said.

"What is it?" Elaine asked.

"I believe what Sara is saying is, those reporters may be here for someone else, but chances are, they are here for us," Scott said.

"You haven't told her, Sara?" Lauren asked.

"I didn't see the point. It has been nearly two years since anyone has been interested in us. I went all the way through nursing school without so much as one flashbulb in my face," she said.

"What is everyone talking about? Sara, who are you?" Elaine asked.

"According to those bloodthirsty animals, she is the next duchess of Hamburg," Lauren said.

"You know better than that, Lauren," Sara said.

"But Sara and I are both members of Her Majesty's court in England since we were twelve. Don't worry, Elaine, they can't go into the hospital," Lauren said. "Sara, remember what Mummy said. We have to deal with this kind of thing all the time, so hold your head up."

Sara just nodded.

"You hanging in there, baby girl?" Scott asked.

"Yes. I just want to get to Grandma. We don't have to stop and answer questions, do we?" Sara asked.

"No. When we get out, all of us hold on to each other, and we will plow right through them," Scott said, and everyone agreed. Scott parked the jeep, and the small party got out. They were surrounded in seconds.

Scott, Sara, and Lauren knew exactly what to expect. Elaine was overwhelmed. But with Scott holding her hand firmly on one side and Lauren on the other, she was keeping up.

"Your Grace, have you been in Germany or England?"

Sara didn't answer but put her head on Scott's shoulder with tears beginning to roll down her cheeks.

"No one has heard anything about you in the last couple of years or you, Lady Lauren. Are you visiting with Her Grace?" another said.

"I have been rather busy," Sara said.

"How many children do you have now? Rumor has it you want to have a large family."

"We are expecting our third child," Sara said.

"Now since your uncle has named you as his successor, does that mean you will be moving to Germany?" another asked.

"I have never been to Germany and never plan to go. I have dual citizenship in the United States and in the UK," she said.

"Your Grace, sir."

Scott interrupted at the mention of a title. "I prefer to be called the emperor of Texas," Scott said and winked at the three women with him. All three smiled up at him.

"Lady Lauren, is it true that you are moving to Texas?"

"I have been living in Texas, attending college for over three years," Lauren answered. "You people are not very well informed, are you?"

"Excuse me, who is this with you?"

"A very close friend of the family," Scott answered.

"Your Grace, is it true that you stole the title of the duchess of Hamburg from your brother?" a reporter asked.

"I have never stolen anything in my life, so why would I start now by taking something I don't and have never wanted?" Sara answered.

"Then how do you reply to the fact that your brother was taken out of the line of succession and your uncle has been to visit you in the recent past? Do you think you are better than your brother?" the reporter concluded.

Sara stopped walking and stood with tears now free-falling down her face.

"Are all of you a bunch of idiots, or do you just not think of who you could be hurting with your stupid-ass assumptions? All of you should be ashamed of yourselves. This is a hospital, a place that you are not allowed, so leave us alone," Elaine said.

At that, they all got in the elevator that would take them to the floor where Grandma was. When they arrived, they saw Saline in the waiting room. Sara all but ran to her little sister.

"How is Grandma?" Sara asked.

"She has been asking for you for the last hour. She is dying, Sara. She just came back into our lives, and now she is dying," Saline said, beginning to cry. Sara pulled her into her arms and let her cry.

"I am going to go down and see her. Are you okay for a minute?" she asked.

Saline nodded. Elaine and Lauren stayed with Saline, and Scott and Sara went to see Grandma.

When they got to Grandma's room, they went right in. "Grandma," Sara said.

"Sara, baby, come and sit next to Grandma," she said.

"Why didn't you tell me you were so sick?" Sara asked.

"I was selfish for a little while. While the two of you were growing up, I couldn't always be there for you. Every time that I would be there, you and Saline were always afraid, and even in those times that you were together, you always seemed so alone. Then when I saw you both for the first time together and you were laughing with people who loved you, that was all I ever wanted for the two of you," she said. "I know that you will be sad for a little while, but I am dying a happy woman. I lived to see my babies happy and loved. And I have no doubt I will see you in heaven. I love you, my Sara. I loved you from the first time I ever saw you."

"I will always love you too, Grandma," Sara said through tears and laid her head on Grandma's chest and cried silently. Grandma put her arm around Sara. She stroked her hair and soothed her.

A few hours later, with her granddaughters by her side, their grandmother died a peaceful death.

A stateside funeral was held with Uncle Joseph in attendance. He then traveled back to Hamburg, and she was buried beside her husband as she had wished. As requested, she was laid to rest without fanfare and no press release.

Three days after the funeral, Sara returned to work at the hospital. Assignments were made by the charge nurse. Sara and Elaine talked for a few minutes, and then each went to see about their patients for the shift.

The three new doctors came into the hospital at about the same time to make their own rounds on their patients before going to their offices.

Dr. Powell had heard from Joan Redding at least three times a day regarding her medication, and she told him she was no longer able to work and for him to give her a note explaining that to her boss so she could draw workman's comp. Dr. Powell kept telling her that it was only a sprain and to take a week off. He did, however, refill her pain medication but told her he would not prescribe her anything for her nerves until he knew more about her.

Every time she called, she ranted about the way the world had not treated her fairly. That would prompt him to think about the daughters who refused to see about their mother. And the thought that one was a nurse was disgraceful. He had waited for a Sara Redding to come to work but never found anyone with that last name.

Then he began to think of a last name that he had heard a few times, and then the two charts that he had seen being picked up by Dr. Carmichael's sister. The name Saline was rare. And her sister's name was Sara. There was only one Sara who was a nurse in the hospital. So he decided to confront her. And she was caring for two of his patients.

He saw her name on the assignment board. He looked down the hall and saw her right away. She was at a medication cart, preparing to give medications. He walked directly to her and asked if she was the daughter of Joan Redding.

"I am a nurse in this hospital. That is all you need to be aware of, sir. Excuse me," she said.

Rick put his hand out and took the young woman's arm. "Your mother asked that you come to her side while she needs aid. That puts me in between the two of you."

Sara turned back to face him. "Unhand me," she said softly.

"I had to ask the nurse to call you after your sister refused to come up here. She would not even give me your last name. I believe that Dr. Carmichael may have expected less out of his nurses than I do. I want an explanation and not the ranting of a spoiled child," he said.

Sara took her free hand and slapped him as hard as she could. "Don't propose to lecture me about a situation you don't know anything about."

"Educate me," he said, shaking her arm.

With that, Sara screamed. She screamed so loud that everyone in the hospital heard.

Amy looked in the direction of the scream and immediately saw that Dr. Powell had a hold of Sara's arm. She ran the distance that separated them. "Unhand her," she demanded.

"This has nothing to do with you. I need to know who is taking care of my patients," Rick said.

Another nurse appeared out of the corner of his eye, and the next thing he knew, he was on the floor, gasping for air. "Touch her or any other nurse in this hospital again and I won't smack them. I will cut them off," Elaine said in his face then stood and stepped over him.

"Are you okay, Sara?" Elaine asked.

Sara looked down at the man on the floor and then back at Amy and Elaine. The look on her face was one of amusement, and she began to laugh and turned and walked around the corner of the wall.

Amy and Elaine really didn't know what to think. Curiosity took hold over the man on the floor. When they caught up to Sara, she was trying to cover the fact that she was indeed laughing.

"Sara, are you okay?" Amy asked.

"Yes," she said, trying to contain her amusement. "I have never been defended by a woman before."

Then, all three broke into laughter.

"Oh, Elaine, you were wonderful. I appreciate you both so much," Sara said. The three of them stood together a moment longer then decided that the coast was clear and went back to work.

For the first time, she felt like she could work all day and night without a thought. She knew that it was only relief that she felt but decided to enjoy the moment.

There was someone who didn't feel the relief that was shared by the three nurses. Dr. Powell heard them all begin laughing. He was furious with all of them. Nurses just didn't know what a physician had to know to function in a practice. There was something that he didn't know, so he was going to find out what. He did know that whatever it was, he would not be finding out from any of the people in the hospital. They were all loyal to one another. He did know someone who would be all too thankful to answer his questions.

A week went by, and no incidents occurred. Sara had been to see Dr. Chambers, who told her she could work no more than two days a week. When she saw Dr. Quinton, he concurred. She let Amy know, who was glad to do everything she could to assure she worked no more than two days a week.

After a few more days, Dr. Powell's temper cooled, but he still hadn't forgotten the incident.

The next time that Joan Redding had called, he had insisted that she come to his office so she could follow up on her ankle injury. And as long as she was in the office, getting a history would be something that was expected. So he made an appointment for her.

On the day she came to the office, he had thought of all the things he wanted to know.

"Please have a seat, Mrs. Redding. I need to get your blood pressure," the office nurse said.

Joan did as she was told and waited for the doctor to come in.

When Rick entered, they exchanged the usual pleasantries. "So how is your ankle feeling, Mrs. Redding?" he asked.

"It hurts like a son of a bitch. I haven't been able to go back to work, not that I need to be working anyway," she spat.

"Let's take a look at it, shall we?" he said and examined the slightly swollen ankle. "Does it hurt when I do this?" he asked, moving it slightly.

"Are you trying to kill me? Of course it hurts."

"You could need some physical therapy," he said.

"I don't have any insurance for physical therapy. Just give me a note and some stronger pain medicine," she said.

"Do you have anyone at home who can help you?" he asked.

"My daughters will not answer my calls, and my husband works," she said.

"Is there something wrong between you and your daughters?" he asked.

"They are spoiled, thoughtless girls. My oldest, Sara, took my other daughter and my baby boy away from me. She ran away from home," Joan said.

"Have you tried to talk to her about coming home?" he asked.

"I even went to where she and Saline are living right now and was almost physically thrown off the place. Imagine having your babies calling someone else mom. And those people like to throw their weight around like they own the state. I even tried to take my youngest away from Sara, and he fell. It is not my fault that he died. I just wanted my family back," she said.

"Of course you did. Any mother would. Why would she harbor such ill feelings toward her own mother?"

"Because Sara is a bastard, my former husband, the man that Sara killed, knew that she was not his. You have seen her with that red hair and those green eyes. All of our children have blond hair and blue eyes. She was so defiant that her stepfather sent her to another country to go to school for seven years so as not to lead her half siblings astray. But we moved back here, my husband divorced me, and Sara started to work on Saline." Joan seethed.

Rick let Joan Redding talk until he thought he had a good knowledge of this woman whom the other nurses praised so much.

In his mind, Sara was a spoiled child who had turned her sister against her mother. Now he was ready to have a discussion with this young woman who neglected her family so much.

The following morning at the hospital, the nurses had all gotten report from the preceding shift and were already in the process of caring for their patients. A great number of the patients were elderly and unable to care for themselves, so physically, it would be a heavy day.

Elaine had six patients, three of whom were total care. Sara had six patients, with two of them being total care. Each had decided to assist the other with the total-care patients. They had both started recently talking about taking the courses necessary to become registered nurses.

Both of the young nurses had become popular with the other nurses and patients at the small hospital. Both were eager and loved their work. The fact that they worked well together was an added bonus.

When nurses were needed in the ER, Elaine and Sara were assigned together. Elaine preferred it that way as she could keep an eye on Sara to make sure that she didn't overdo.

It didn't take but a short time before they could read each other's movements as a fluent team. Each began to tell about what had brought them to work at the Country Hospital. Before long, they knew each member of the other's family by name. Each visited the other at their homes and enjoyed each other's company. As they saw it, they were born and raised thousands of miles apart, and both had ended up meeting in a very small town. Elaine's father was a pastor at the Pentecostal church in Salt Flats. She had always lived in the same town and knew the same people. Sara was her first close friend that lived in the country.

Elaine was Sara's first friend who was a nurse. Sara gradually began to tell Elaine bits about her life. As did Sara begin to learn about Elaine. She would listen intently as she described attending school in Salt Flats with her father being a pastor. Whenever they were together, there was no lack of conversation.

When Sara was three and half months pregnant, Elaine used the Doppler to listen the baby's heartbeat. As they listened one day, Elaine was curious about Sara's past at a private girls' school.

"I don't know. We never really thought of titles or royalty. We were just little girls. Lauren and I talked to each other. All of us played. I guess it just wasn't something that we thought about," Sara explained. "Such as, were you more religious because your father is a pastor?"

"No. Of course not. I think that I tried just about anything when I was growing up just to make up for having been born to keep from being known as a preacher's kid," Elaine said.

"I never rebelled or anything like that, but I suppose it is the same sort of thing," Sara said.

"But you are a lady. That had to have been different from here. Here women are either miss or Mrs.," Elaine said.

"Until after I had met Scott, I was not regarded as anything here, except for maybe white trash," Sara said.

"Don't say things like that. You are likely the person I would regard as the farthest thing from trash. And no one from town knows anything about you except that you are Scott Byers's wife and the mother of two beautiful little boys," Elaine said.

They both listened to the baby's heartbeat as though completely entranced.

"Well, like with my other babies, I have to pee right now," Sara said and walked to the door that led to the hall. She walked toward the nurses' station where the ladies room was located. It was just outside the bathroom. She ran into Dr. Powell.

"Excuse me," she said and brushed on by.

"Sara, I was looking for you earlier," he said.

"I can't imagine why. I am not taking patients today," she said.

"I just wanted to tell you how your mother's ankle is healing," he said.

"As I told you before, sir, I don't really care. Just because you are stupid enough to treat her does not mean I am going to care," Sara said and started to walk by him.

"It doesn't matter that she could use your help at home?"

"Not at all. I have given her all that I am going to give her," Sara said. "And my home is where my husband and sons are."

"All she wants is her daughters back at home."

"Saline and I are both adults. I understand that you don't understand saying anything politely, so I will say this straight out. My mother wants nothing but cigarettes, drugs, booze, sex, and money. I have nothing else to give her. If you choose to treat her, fine, but I don't want to hear about it again," Sara said.

"You are awfully cold for someone so young. Did all those years educating with other spoiled brats teach you such disrespect?" he said.

"No. It was the years of being around pushy people like you that would have done that. Now you can leave me alone unless I have a patient of yours," Sara said, literally shoving her way past him.

"Sara, get back here," he yelled. But she kept walking.

"You are never going to learn, are you?" Amy said.

"Learn what? That girl is disrespectful to authority," he said. "I insist that you do something like docking her paychecks for her not respecting. Maybe by taking away part of her paycheck, she will learn to respect a physician's authority."

"I would say that is a case of a pot calling the kettle black. Sara makes nothing working at the hospital. She donates her entire check when she gets paid. I don't know why you insist on inviting trouble. Sara is down to working two days a week. She cannot take a heavy load right now, so there is no reason why you don't just leave her alone. She is a good nurse. That is all you have to think about."

"I don't understand the mentality in small towns. In the city, a nurse knows her place. And how does someone donate her whole paycheck? But here, it is different," he said.

"What is it that a nurse is expected to do? Sara has no reason to speak to her mother. That woman is not even half human. She is married to a man only five years older than her daughter. All they ever did when those two girls lived at home was get drunk or high. She cared nothing for what that husband of hers would try with her daughters. You have made the wrong person in your little drama the bad guy. And as long as Sara works in this hospital, she is under my authority, and I say no one messes with my nurses for their own amusement," Amy said.

"Why don't you tell me the whole story?" he said.

"Because it is none of your business, that's why. This is a small town. Everyone knows everyone. If you want to maintain your practice, I would suggest you respect the people here, or move on." With that, Amy went on about her business.

Rick watched as she walked away. He was now more curious than angry. He had always hated being in the dark. But more often than not, these days, he was in the dark.

At the ranch at night recently, Saline had begun to think about the past. Things that she had tried to put behind her seemed so clear to her now. How she loved her life now. There were people who loved her and looked up to her. Even finishing her sophomore year in college at eighteen, she was way ahead of most people her age. She had people who loved her and that she loved. Even with all that, she had started to feel guilty for feeling happy. The last couple of years since Grandma had come to live at the ranch, she had been so happy to have her there. It was like a family should be.

She had friends at college whom she tended to hang around with and had fun with them. Some had been to the ranch to go riding or fishing or just to study. Most were highly impressed with her lifestyle and wondered what it was like to live such a life. But Saline, much like her sister, insisted that every member of her family worked very hard for what they had.

Saline and Lauren had decided that summer that in the fall, when they returned to school, that as they would both be carrying heavy schedules, they would move to Dallas. Lauren had planned on transferring to University of Texas, Southwest Medical Center in Dallas. Her straight A grade point average in difficult courses were something in a young woman that medical school was looking for.

Saline had decided to attend Texas Women's University, only about a block from where Lauren would be attending.

John had listened as the two young women that he loved so much explained their plans to live in either an apartment or rent a house. Lauren lived on an allowance she received while she attended college.

John and Allison had also set up such a trust for Saline so that when she attended college, she could concentrate on her grades and not have a part-time job. Allison hated to see both of the young women leave home but was comforted by the fact that they were only a little over an hour away. John had thought about it and said that even though they were both adults, he would appreciate it if they could find a house with four bedrooms so as to have someone there to keep an eye on each of them.

He reminded each that even though they had been able to relax in the last few years, they were both considered to be somewhat of celebrities if they were noticed. And to go along with that, Joan Redding was still around, although they had not seen her in the last couple of years. Everyone knew that she had gone to the Country Hospital when she sprained her ankle and had told one of the new doctors a sick, twisted, completely false story.

Both Saline and Lauren agreed to the arrangement, so John had a friend of his in Dallas to find a house fairly close to the schools and large enough for four people. What they had come up with were three houses that were in gated communities, for security purposes. The two girls had a good time looking at the houses, deciding on where they were going to live their first time living away from the ranch. Both were excited at the thought.

Each had decided to remain on the ranch until Sara delivered the baby. She was due toward the end of August, and they didn't start school until September 2.

Sara was pleased that she had got to work until she was just over eight months pregnant. Now she was just waiting for the latest baby Byers to arrive. She had decided to work nightshifts the last four months both for the easier work load and to avoid Dr. Powell. On the nights he was on call, she worked giving meds to patients. On the nights that he was not on call, she worked the ER. She was so glad that the other new doctors didn't regard her like Dr. Powell did. The other two were younger and seemed to appreciate the nursing staff.

Dr. Jeff Middleton was born in the Country Hospital twenty-seven years ago. His entire family lived not far away. Scott already knew him from school from the time they were in grade school.

The other was from Georgia; Dr. Allan Sykes was also in his late twenties. He had married a nurse right after finishing medical school, before his residency. They already had two little girls, but his wife, Lindy, worked in the hospital. He knew that to disrespect any of the nurses would result in more trouble than anyone wanted to deal with.

Sara had come to know everyone who worked in the small hospital. And from there, she began to know people from town, many of which had attended the wedding and/or the reception when she and Scott married. She hated it when she had to stop working a month before her delivery. But this pregnancy had gone so much better than when she was pregnant with Austin. She hadn't had pleurisy or pericarditis since she had been pregnant before she had gone to nursing school. She maintained her weight of 125–130 pounds before she had gotten pregnant and now weighed a little over 145. Dr. Chambers said that he would appreciate it if he got to deliver this baby rather than to find out she had delivered at home due to the ice on the roads. Sara assured him that as it was one hundred degrees outside, that ice likely wouldn't be a problem. He could only smile at her seriousness.

Dr. Quinton and Uncle Alex had both decided to retire, except for a few favorite patients, and they began to work with another doctor from Baylor, who flew all over the world to provide medical services for those in need. Both doctors began to enjoy their time in foreign countries. Sara had asked if after she had the baby and he was a little older, if they would take her to help out. She said that she could help because she was a nurse and spoke French. Many of the places they went were in North Africa or in the Far East. Many who had been taught by missionaries spoke French rather than English.

Both had approved. When Elaine discovered what Sara wanted to do, she asked if they would also let her assist. Elaine knew that it was not something that paid but still wanted the chance to help. Elaine spoke fluent Spanish, for such countries as Central and South America.

Sara knew that Elaine needed a paying job, so she asked if the money that she donated to the hospital could be paid Elaine and for her to be told that the hospital was paying her for her service. But she was never to know where the money was coming from.

As Elaine was able to leave in the summer, she would leave with whoever doctors were going to a week at a time. She loved it. Both Elaine and Sara had received Red Cross training in both first aid and CPR while in nursing school, and Drs. Carmichael and Quinton were excellent teachers. The rural clinics were a little more than shacks with generators to make the lights work.

There were volunteers that helped to dig water wells, teach women about hygiene and birth control, give vaccinations, and deliver babies. From the first time Elaine had gone with the doctors, she was excited for the next time. They would start with no organization at all, and only a day into beginning to help people, everything ran smoothly.

All the medical team was told not to stray outside of the clinic area due to things like competing rebel forces. In Central and South America, both were known for their cocaine that was sent to other places in the world. If the drug cartels felt threatened, they wouldn't ask questions; they would kill people.

On August 24, very early in the morning, Sara told Scott that she thought it may be time to go. Scott was up and dressed in what seemed to be seconds. He called the main house to ask for someone to come down and babysit Austin, five, and Brad, barely four. In ten minutes, Allison, Lauren, and saline were all there and ready for Sara to have the baby. This time, she had not told anyone what she was having, and no one could wait to find out the sex of the baby.

"I will stay with the boys until I know that Maria is up, and then I will be to the hospital with you. Saline, you and Lauren go with them, okay? And I will be up as soon as Maria is awake," Allison said.

"I'm awake. I saw you drive down and decided to check it out. I will stay here until the morning, and Mark will bring the kids over here." Maria walked over and hugged her friend.

Maria was so proud of Sara, and Sara took pride in Maria as well. Immediately following her graduation from nursing school, Maria decided that she would also become a nurse. She knew that she was going to have to take the college courses like Sara and Elaine had begun taking. But Sara told her that she would help her with her three kids, the same way she helped with her two.

At the hospital, Sara had preregistered as requested and was awfully glad that she had. Then, Sara sat in a wheelchair and was taken to a labor room. Allison, Scott, Saline, and Lauren were shown to the waiting room. On the way to the hospital, the contractions were about five minutes apart. Sara kept on telling them that her back didn't hurt, so it may be false labor. But with how she gripped the door handle when she would have a pain said that it was actual labor.

After about an hour, a nurse came to the waiting room to report progress and asked if anyone wanted to see her.

"She is dilated at about seven. The pains are four minutes apart, and her water broke on its own when she was getting into bed. It will likely be another three to four hours, but she is doing fine. And my name is Judy. I will be her nurse today. Please follow me this way," Judy said. "You may visit, but try to keep the visits to only two people at a time," the nice young nurse said. "Sara, how are you feeling since I saw you last?"

"Like it is going to be a very long day," she said.

"Would you like something to help with the pain?" Judy asked.

"Please. At least I don't have the backache this time," Sara answered. "Did someone tell Elaine that I am in labor? I believe she is working today, if you will call the hospital. I promised I would tell her."

"I will go and call her. I will be right back," Scott said.

Allison, filling in as her mother, and Saline decided to stay with Sara for the first little while. Saline had not been in the room while Sara was in labor with Austin because she was so young. She was only fourteen at the time. Now she was nineteen years old and was about to enter nursing school, so she rationalized that she could handle whatever came about.

When Sara would have a pain, she could tell it must have been a lot of pain because at times she would cry out. She picked up her sister's hand and held it the entire time she was in the room.

When Scott had come back from making the call to Elaine, Saline decided to go back to the waiting room. She hated seeing her sister in pain. It just didn't seem fair that she had to hurt so bad to have something she wanted so much. Then she thought about the first time she saw her nephew. He was so beautiful and perfect, and she loved him like he was hers. She took a seat beside Lauren.

"Did she hurt this much having Austin?" Saline asked.

"I believe she hurt more and longer with Austin. Her back had been killing her since the night before. Don't worry, she will be fine. I promise," Lauren said. She picked up Saline's hand and held it.

At the Country Hospital, Elaine had just hung up the phone after talking with Scott. She had to finish the shift before she could go to St. Mary's. Likely, she would have delivered the baby before she got there. She walked over to Amy.

"Just to keep you up to date, Sara is in labor at St. Mary's right now," Elaine said.

"How is she doing?" Amy asked.

"She has been in labor since last evening, and is dilated to a seven right now. It really shouldn't be too long."

"Are you planning on going to visit after work?" Amy asked.

"I am planning on it. Do you want to come along?" she asked.

"I would like that. I will see you at the end of the shift," Elaine said and started walking back to her patients.

Dr. Powell was at the nurses' station when the two nurses were talking. He heard that Sara was having her baby. "Sara is having a baby at St. Mary's? I didn't know she was pregnant. Why is she having her baby in Tyler rather than here?"

"She needs better monitoring that we can provide. She is high risk. But she is doing much better than her first baby," Amy said.

"There are three doctors here, and all of us, deliver babies. So far as monitoring, we have the proper equipment to monitor both mother and child," Rick said.

"Her doctor is Dr. Carmichael, and he said she would have to deliver in a bigger hospital because of past problems she had," Amy said.

"What kind of problems?" Rick asked. "She could come here for treatment one day, and it would help to treat her if I knew something about her."

"That will never happen. Her uncle lives at the ranch, and her cardiologist now lives only about fifteen minutes away. So there is nothing you need to know. Her chart was pulled, so there is nothing here written about her," Amy said.

"Does her mother know she is having her grandchild?" Rick asked.

"Absolutely not. It is not any of her business. And I will turn you in for violating her right to privacy and putting Sara in danger if you mention any of it to that whore," Amy said. "She lost custody of her kids. I am tired of you bringing her up. If you are so stupid to believe someone like her, you deserve what you get."

She picked up one of the charts and began charting on it.

A few hours later, Sara sat up in bed, holding her newest baby boy. He was named Ryan Joseph Byers. His first name was after Allison and Uncle Alex's father who died a few decades before. His middle name was given for Uncle Joseph.

Several members of the Byers family and friends were in the room, along with several flower and balloon bouquets and little-boy-themed gift baskets. The TV was on but turned down.

"Hey look, Uncle Joseph is on the TV. Can someone turn the volume up?" Sara asked. It appeared he was making some announcement.

At that same time, Rick was sitting in his office on a break for lunch. He had closed the office door and turned the TV on to the news while he was eating his lunch.

"Your Grace, when did you find out about your newest heir?" Someone asked.

"I got a call from my niece Saline a couple of hours ago," he said.

"Is it a boy or a girl?"

"It is a healthy baby boy. My third nephew, and I am very, very proud and touched that I got to hear about it so quickly," he said.

"What is the new child considered to be, Your Grace?"

"He is Lord Ryan Joseph Byers. Ryan after his great-grandfather on his father's side, and Joseph after my name. Scott and Sara Lyn, if you are listening, I am so touched," he said with tears in his eyes.

"Was he born in Hamburg?"

"He was born at an undisclosed location to keep their privacy at this happy time," he answered.

"Have you seen him yet?"

"No. It will be a few days before I have the chance to see them," the duke answered.

"Can we assume then that he was born in Texas?"

"You are welcome to assume anything you like. I will confirm nothing. Thank you," he said, walking back up the lawn to the palace.

"There you have it from the horse's mouth. Scott and Sara Lyn Byers are happy to announce the birth of their third child, Ryan Joseph Byers, early this morning at an undisclosed location. Lady Sara Lyn Byers, who may well be the next duchess of Hamburg, is the niece of the duke. A few years ago, following the accidental death of Lord Henry Alexander, who was then the next in line, he named either Lady Sara or her sister Lady Saline as next in line as opposed to their brother Lord Thomas Alexander. No one has ever given a reason for his decision," the reporter said.

Rick was now listening intently to what the reporter said. In his mind, it had to be a huge coincidence, the more he thought about it. He turned off the TV and went up to the hospital to ask Amy if she had seen the news. When he arrived, he heard all the nurses laughing and talking about how happy they were once again. They had all been watching the TV. All of them knew who and what she was and not one had told him.

He had no reason for now why that made him so angry. He went to the small doctors' lounge and found the TV on there also. On the news at that time was a picture of Sara Lyn Byers in a wedding gown following her wedding. The gown that she wore was not one that was seen in a simple country girl. He turned the TV up and listened to what was being said.

"It was a modern-day fairy-tale wedding complete with thousands of people in attendance to cheer the new couple on. Millionaire Texas royalty Scott Byers and German royalty Sara Lyn Alexander married in a beautiful wedding in St. Justin's Episcopal Church on November 5, 1977. The entire town, along with various members from different royal families, attended the wedding, including Lady

Sara's best friend from England, Lady Lauren Dickerson, daughter of Lord and Lady Dickerson. Lady Dickerson is the second cousin of the Queen of England. Both Lady Lauren and Lady Sara have been members of Her Majesty's court since they were twelve. Lady Lauren served as Lady Sara's maid of honor. Governors and mayors from several states, not to mention congressmen and senators, also attended the ceremony.

"The happy couple spent the first hours following their wedding on a lavish reception befitting that of any member of a royal family. The beautiful gown was designed especially for Lady Sara's wedding. Lady Frances Dickerson had loaned the beautiful tiara that she wore, the same tiara that she had worn for her own wedding twenty-seven years ago at Westminster Abbey. Following the I dos, her new husband placed a floor-length burgundy cape over her shoulders to help fight off the cold day before they got in the horse-drawn carriage that would take them to and from their reception.

"Lord and Lady Byers live in East Texas, and Ryan Joseph is their third son. Through her family and friends, Lady Sara is described as a very polite, down-to-earth young woman. And although financially secure on both sides of her family, she has graduated from college while being a wonderful wife and mother and works as a nurse near the Byers family ranch and also works as a member of the Red Cross and Doctors without Borders giving medical aid to people in impoverished parts of the world.

"We will have more on the happy event later tonight." A close-up picture of the smiling couple was shown at the end of the report.

The English accent, things that several people had said about her, the woman who had taken the charts with both Saline and Sara's names on them, and the close-up picture of the green-eyed girl with burgundy hair donning the tiara—Rick sat down for a minute. No mention as to Sara's family was mentioned. A brother was mentioned only briefly. And the only comment made about a father was that he had been killed in an accident. He knew there was one person who would give him answers, but the woman was not at all likable. Perhaps there would be another way. He could go to her house to give her congratulations on the birth of their son. After all, they did work together. He would see if his wife, Amelia, would want to go to her house with him in the next couple of days. Amelia had worked in the hospital a few times, as she was also a nurse. She loved living in the small town and working in the small hospital. He knew that she knew all the nurses in the hospital, and that would make it easy to visit.

Late that evening, Rick arrived home. He went into the kitchen where Amelia was cooking supper. "Good evening, honey. Dinner smells good."

Amelia gave him a questioning look. Rick never gave compliments unless he wanted something. "What is it that you are wanting?" she said.

"I don't want anything. I was just wondering if you wanted to go for a ride with me to congratulate Sara on the birth of her son," he said.

Amelia started laughing at his words. She knew that in the last months, her husband had offended nearly everyone in the hospital with his superior attitude toward them. She got the dishes for the table and began to set the table.

"What are you laughing about? Amy said that Sara had her baby, and I would like to—"

Amelia broke in, "Rick, you saw the news at lunch like you always do, and you discovered that she is not just a nurse in the hospital that you can bully. Now since she is someone more interesting, you want to be in her world."

"That is not true. I just want to do my best to get to know the nurses in the hospital so we can work better together," he said.

"Yeah, and who else are you trying to get to know? I know nobody. But just to be fair, the nurses don't want to get to know you. They all know you to be a horse's ass," she said.

"Does that mean you won't go with me?" he asked.

"No. I won't go with you out there. The Byers family is all nice people. I will not go someplace with you where you plan on making a complete fool out of yourself sucking up to them only because they are wealthy," Amelia said.

"I am not sucking up to anyone. I don't have to. I am a doctor. On the socioeconomic scale, they would be my equal, and that is something that I thought didn't exist in this town," he said.

"Rick, on that scale you speak of, you are not high enough to live in their mailbox. But they are also not people to draw attention to themselves. They are hardworking, honest people who give generously to the community. If you were to walk up to any of them in town, you would never guess they owned a good portion of East Texas," Amelia said.

She knew that Rick had a thing about knowing wealthy people. She had gone to Vanderbilt to get her nursing degree. Her parents were wealthy, and that is how they got to know each other. The two were in Vietnam at the same time. Rick was a private who had been drafted, and Amelia was a captain due to the fact that she had a master's degree in nursing. Rick had been injured, and she was his nurse. He found out she graduated from Vanderbilt and thought her to be from a wealthy family and decided he would one day marry her. It took a couple of years before they did marry. She had never put up with any crap from him, and she wouldn't now.

"You talk like you know them already," he said.

"I have been out there a few times to both Sara's house and the main house," she said and turned to get something out of the cabinet.

"Why didn't you tell me you were going to her house?"

"She changed to working two nights a week so that she didn't have to hear you verbally accosting her," she said. "Her mother is nothing but a lying whore, and you won't stop bringing her up."

"Can't you show me how to get to her house?" he asked.

"No, and it is because I won't. Now I need to put supper on the table, so I have to get the kids," she said.

"Amelia, can you at least tell me how to get there?" he asked.

"No, I won't."

"But why not?" he asked.

"I have only known them for a few months, and I consider them friends. I am not going to take you out there when you have already alienated half of the family," she said. "If you want to go out there, go, but I will not be a part of it. Now supper is ready," she concluded.

Rick went to the table and ate with his wife and their three children. He had to find someone to show him the way to Sara's house. There was no need in trying to get Amelia to show him the way. When she had made up her mind, there was no way to changing it. So he would be making a visit on his own in the next couple of days.

After Sara and little Ryan had come home from the hospital, it was time for Saline and Lauren to move to Dallas before school started. When the last of their things were in the trunk of the cars, they hugged everyone and said they would be home the following weekend.

Saline and Sara had never been apart since she had come home the last time from the UK. They couldn't imagine being apart for several days at a time, but Sara knew that it was time for Saline to spread her wings. They parted with tears and promised they would talk every day. With that, saline and Lauren had gone.

Sara had plenty of things to keep her busy, thus keeping her mind off her sister. Austin had started back to school as a first grader. Brad at five was starting kindergarten. So while the boys were in school, that left her alone with Ryan for several hours a day.

Ryan was a sweet baby, much like his older brothers. And like his oldest brother, Sara was breastfeeding him as well. She felt much better than she ever thought she would, so she did little things around the house while the baby slept. She napped during the day as well to make sure she didn't get any more sleep deprived than she had to. It was while she was napping that the doorbell rang. She sat up on the couch and went to the door. She looked out the peephole and saw Dr. Powell. She couldn't imagine him being there. She had been avoiding him for months.

She decided that she would just simply not answer the door. She turned and walked in the direction of her and Scott's bedroom to check on Ryan. He was still sleeping. So she lay back down on the bed. She decided she didn't want to miss one minute of being Ryan's mom, before it was time to return to work. She sure wouldn't be wasting time on Rickard Powell.

She picked up the remote for the TV and turned it on. The news was on, and as it had been since Ryan was born, they were on the news. She listened to them talk about what they knew versus what they thought they knew. Maria walked in about then.

"Maria, you will never guess who is on the news again," Sara said.

"Again? Oh well, they will get tired of it sooner or later. Did you know that Dr. Richard Powell is at the front door?" she asked.

"Yes, that is why I am in here. I don't want to see him. He keeps talking to Momma and telling me how selfish I am for not taking care of her."

"Do you want to see him?" Maria asked.

"No," Sara answered.

"Then that is what I will tell him. Be right back," Maria said, putting her little girl down to run around in the master bedroom.

Maria got to the door and opened it.

"Can I help you?"

"Yes. I am Dr. Rick Powell, a friend of Sara's from work, and I have come out to congratulate her on the birth of her son," he said.

"Just a minute, let me check something," Maria said, picking up a piece of paper with names on it. "I am sorry, Sara is resting just now. May I take your number and have her give you a call?'

"No. I came all this way to see Sara and won't leave until I have spoken to her. I am sure she will want me to take care of the baby and perhaps herself. So I need to talk to her," Rick said.

He and Maria had words for a couple of minutes before Sara came to the door. "What are you doing at my home, Dr. Powell? I don't have the energy to hear how much I should feel sorry for my mum. As I recall, the last time I saw you, that was all you wanted to talk about," Sara said.

"May I come in?" he asked.

"No. I had a baby a few days ago, and I only visit with friends and family. As you are neither, you need to leave."

"I just wanted to congratulate you on your son, and tell you I would be glad to be his and your physician. You no longer have a doctor, and I am managing all of Dr. Alex Carmichael's patients," Rick said.

"Dr. Powell—"

"Please, call me Rick," he said.

"Dr. Powell, my doctor and our family doctor continues to be Alex Carmichael. I can only conclude that you must have seen the news, and now suddenly I am worthy to be around you. I am not explaining anything to you. I am not interested in my mother, and this is all the visiting I am doing with you. I work at the hospital, not for you." With that, she attempted to politely close the door.

"But, Sara, I would really like to get to know you and your family better," he said.

"Why? You have done nothing but give me a difficult time since I went to work for the hospital," she said.

"I find it completely unusual that a woman that has had three children and does not have to work works anyway," he said.

"Why I work is truly none of your business. And may I add that what we are having is polite conversation like you would have on an elevator. Having just had a baby, I am sure you know, if you actually did pass your boards, that it is not good to keep me standing here for so long. If you want to get to know our family better, go to the *Dallas Morning News* archives. I have to feed my son," Sara said and closed the front door.

Rick stood there for a moment and tried to get his head around what had just taken place. He knew that he could knock again, but she would not answer. He would not be getting any information from her. He got in his car and started to leave. He looked around and saw Sara's jeep parked in the garage not far from the house. There was also a larger vehicle parked in another bay. There was what looked to be a very elaborate horse-drawn carriage and a new pickup truck.

It angered Rick that she had closed the door in his face, but she had just had a baby and her hormones were likely settled back to normal as yet. That thought pacified him somewhat. He drove back down the private fifteen-mile road that was their driveway. All around him, though it was August and dry and hot, were rolling pastures with herds of cattle grazing. There were men out in the pastures that appeared to be feeding the cattle and putting out hay. Then he saw two men on horseback moving at breakneck speed toward something he couldn't see. Although Rick had never been on a horse in his life, with the men running the horses so quick, on such a hot day, it seemed to be that something was wrong. Behind him, in the distance, looking out his rearview mirror, he saw Sara holding a bag of some sort, running toward her jeep. She got in and quickly drove to the same place the horses were heading. Rick turned his car around and found himself driving in the same direction, only to see Sara's jeep driving at breakneck speed back into the pasture. He attempted to follow her in the pasture, but his car could not make it in the pasture. He saw the house where the horses had run. Only, this, like Scott and Sara's house, was a mansion.

Rick waited for a few minutes for the people who had gone to the pasture to come back. When they didn't, he decided to make his way back to town. The day had been wasted, so all he could think about was forgetting about it. Likely, in a few weeks, Sara would be back to work and he would be able to try to forge a friendship with them.

Out in the pasture, about a mile from the house, Mark's horse had stumbled when he and some of the hands were attempting to drive the cattle from the pasture they had been in before, to a different pasture that had more water. The tank the cattle was getting water was low due to the dry summer that had brought with it little rain.

The riders could see Sara's jeep coming across the pasture. When they arrived, Sara jumped out of the passenger-side door and ran to where Mark was on the ground. His horse had fallen on top of him, pinning his leg under the horse and saddle. Mark had also hit his head but was responsive and in a great deal of pain.

"We need to get the horse off him," Sara said.

"We have tried. I had to shoot his horse because of his flailing. Mark's foot is through the stirrup, and we have not been able to get it out while it is under the horse," Scott said.

"Let me take a look," Sara said and got up and walked around the horse and rider. Mark's cries of agony were unnerving. Sara went to the other side of the horse. Mark's leg was through the stirrup, and his ankle was broken. "Scott, give me your knife," Sara said. She then began to make quick work at cutting through cinches and girths. When she was certain that the saddle was no longer held in place, she began to tell the men what she needed them to do. She prayed she was right.

"I cannot stabilize his leg until we get the horse off," Sara said. All the men who were driving the cattle had stayed to help Mark. "Take hold of the horse's legs then on three, pull. Mark, I am sorry, this is going to hurt. But right after, I will splint your leg and get you to the hospital. Okay?"

"Okay, Sara. You don't need to pull. You just had a baby," Mark said.

"Don't worry," Sara said softly. "We will both be okay. I promise."

"Okay," Mark said.

"Okay. Here we go. One, two, three, pull,." Sara said.

There were a dozen ranch hands that pulled the dead horse off Mark's leg. Mark's scream as the weight of the horse was removed was bloodcurdling.

When the horse's body was off Mark, Sara began finding what needed to be done. He had two breaks in his leg, one in the lower fibula, the other in the upper tibia. Farther down in the leg, she appreciated also a break in his lower tibia at the ankle.

"He has a least two breaks in his right leg. Does anyone have something that is long and straight?" Sara asked.

The men around them looked and found one of the sorting sticks that were being carried on a saddle. Working using bandanas to tie Mark's leg to the long sorting stick, Sara was finally sure his leg was stable for the ride to town to the hospital.

The men working together laid down the backseats of the jeep so as he would be lying flat. Sara crawled in beside him. With Scott driving and Riley in the passenger seat, they drove across the pasture, the mile that would take them to one of the access roads that would take them to the county road and to town.

In town, at the Country Hospital, they had gotten a call from the ranch telling them about the accident. Amy and Elaine were working in the ER. Both knew Mark St. Clair from the Byers ranch. Amy had called the MD on call, Rick Powell.

Scott pulled the jeep into the ER bay at the hospital, and he and Riley were immediately out and opening the back end of the jeep. Amy had brought a stretcher when she had seen Scott pulling in. Sara got out of the back end and started telling Amy what had happened and told her about at least two broken bones. Amy and Elaine rolled him into the ER. Amy ordered x-rays of Mark's leg.

Dr. Powell entered the room and asked where the patient was.

"I sent him to have films of his leg," Amy said.

"Without an order?" Dr. Powell asked.

"It is an emergency and obvious. And he is in a good deal of pain. You may want to treat him for that," Amy said.

"I don't take orders from nurses," he said.

"Excuse me. Mark's leg is obviously broken. He really needs something for pain," Scott said.

"And are you a doctor?" Rick asked.

"No. But you don't need to be a doctor to tell you that Mark's leg is broken. I would suggest you get him something for that," Scott answered.

"Who are you to tell me what needs to be done?" he asked.

"I am the owner of the hospital. If you want to be on staff here in fifteen minutes, you will treat him, now!" Scott said.

"Who the hell do you think I am?" Rick yelled.

"Sir, I don't give a damn who you are. As long as you turn your attention to what is happening right now, my wife says he has at least two breaks. I would suggest that you look to that for further commentary, because if you don't, you are fired," Scott said.

Rick was intimidated by the younger man's statements. He turned to go to x-ray to check on the new patient. He walked into the control room, and Sara Byers was standing talking to the technician.

"What are you doing here?" Sara asked.

"I am on call. I could ask you the same thing," Rick said.

"This man is family. He was injured on the ranch. And why are you thirty miles away when you are on call?" she asked.

Rick was angry when her thoughts were said out loud. The technician listened to the conversation taking place. Then a bell rang, signaling that the film should be ready.

"Why are—" Rick started to say.

"Dr. Powell, you have a patient in front of you, and he is in pain. Turn your attention to him," Sara said with fire in her eyes.

"Listen to me, young lady. You are a nurse, and you don't talk to me like that. And—"

"And nothing. I am going back home to our new baby. See to my husband's best friend and brother, or look for new employment," Sara said and walked out.

Sara walked out to where Scott was. She put her head on his chest, and he folded his arms around her. "I can't believe that man is the one on call," she said.

"Why is that?" Scott asked.

"Right before Riley rode up, he was at the house wanting to talk to me," she said.

"What did he want?"

"He said that we needed to get to know one another better and that he would be glad to care for our children and me. I told him I have a doctor, several of them. I told him no thank you, but he kept pushing on the door. I am glad Maria was there," Sara said and then saw Maria walk through the doors. "Maria," Sara yelled.

"Sara, is he alive?" She cried.

"Yes, of course, Maria. He talked to me all the way to town. His leg is broken, and he is in terrible pain. But the doctor should have given him something by now. Who is watching the kids?" Sara asked.

"Allison is staying with all our children at your house," Sara said.

"Can you take me to where he is?" Maria asked.

"Of course I will," she said, taking Maria to where she thought Mark would be. "Here he is."

"Mark, are you okay?" Maria asked, going to her husband.

"I think I am starting to be, honey. They just gave me something that is really great," he said and attempted a smile. "When you finish nursing school, are you going to be as big a badass as Sara is?"

"I don't know. Is that a bad thing or a good thing, to be like my mentor I mean?" Maria asked.

"She is a great nurse. A really great nurse," Mark said.

"I think I am going back home, Mark. You get well soon," Sara said.

"Thanks, Sara. You take it easy," he said.

"I will," she said and walked into the hall.

"Don't think you are getting out of here without answering to me," Rick said. "Do you think that because you may be considered royalty wherever it is that you are from it gives you the right as an LVN to where you can function as a doctor? This is the United States, and our laws are different."

Sara turned and looked at him for a second, then returned to walking toward the doors to the ambulance bays.

Rick followed Sara and had caught her long before she arrived at the door.

"Don't you understand English?" Rick said.

"I understand a few languages actually. And it is none of your business anything about myself personally except that I am a nurse who got her nursing degree in Texas and passed the state board Exam of vocational nursing here in Texas. I owe you no more than that. So leave me alone," Sara said.

"You owe me more than that," he said.

"How in the world do you figure that?" Sara asked.

"I have been caring for your mother for months. She works as a waitress and has to be on her feet several hours a day. I see her every couple of weeks, and she does not have the money to pay me. But she has a close relative who could be helping her out," he said.

"That is none of your business."

"Do the German people not pay enough that you could pay your mother at least to be able to live? Or are you so disrespectful that you don't want to?" Rick said. He could see that comment stirred something in the woman in front of his eyes that he had not expected.

Sara turned around and quickly walked to her jeep and pulled out her purse. She reached inside and pulled something out of it, then returned to where Rick still stood with the same pleased expression on his face.

"For your information, sir, I was born in California. I believe it is still considered the United States. I am married to a man from here in Texas, and we have three children who are also Texans. Rumor has it that you were educated in Mexico City because your grades were too poor to be admitted to a university in the States, and this is the only place that would hire you. And as you seem to have the idea that you need to watch out for my mother, you will need lots of this," Sara said, throwing nearly a thousand dollars in his face. There were people close by who heard the exchange and laughed at the gesture.

"Now go and take care of Mr. St. Clair," Sara said. She turned to walk out the door and got a little dizzy. She put her hand on the wall to steady herself, and Amy and Riley were immediately there.

"You okay, sis?" Riley asked.

"Yes, I just turned a little too fast. I assure you I am fine. Is Scott going to stay here with Mark?" Sara asked.

"Yeah. He can likely get a ride back with Maria and Colton."

"Would you mind giving me a ride home please?" she asked.

"I would rather talk to that jackass first," Riley said.

"He is not worth your time, Riley. He is just one of the new doctors. I threw money at him because he keeps bothering me about Momma. He thinks I am terrible because I am not at her side."

"The man is obviously an idiot. Come on. Let's tell Scott that I am taking you home," he said.

Both Riley and Sara went to the room where Mark was being treated.

"Scott, I was going to take Sara back home. She was a little dizzy a moment ago," Riley said.

"Are you okay, baby girl?" Scott asked, feeling her forehead. "You have a fever. Have you taken your antibiotic as yet today?"

"Not yet. It seems that someone had a horse fall on them," Sara said. "I will when I get home. See you in a bit."

Scott kissed her forehead, and she and Riley left.

Rick watched and listened to the trio as he began to put Mark's cast on.

Amy and Maria stepped out for a second as Mark slept. Then it was just a sleeping Mark, Scott, and Rick in the room.

"You know that she would be a little more streamlined into our culture if you didn't treat her like a child, don't you think?" Rick asked.

"Excuse me, what are you talking about?" Scott asked.

"The way that she speaks and acts speak of someone from another country. What is it Australia, England?"

"She was born in the US. She is as American as apple pie. She was educated from the time she was five in the UK. And she has been married to me for nearly seven years. We now have three sons. I believe that is enough information for now. If she wants you to know more, she will tell you," Scott said. "What is it that you wanted of her at the ranch?"

"Only what I would like of those who work in the hospital, to get to know them better and of course to congratulate you both on your latest son. I assume that, what do they call her, Lady Sara will not be working following her third child," Rick said.

"Your assumptions are wrong. Sara likes to be called by her name, and as long as she wishes to work and her physicians say she is healthy, she may work," Scott said.

"As with his other patients, is Sara not to become my patient?" Rick asked.

"No, for reasons that are of no business of yours. Sara is still the patient of the same doctors who have been taking care of her since she was sixteen. She was sick for the first few years of our marriage, and they got her through it to her present state of good health. She does not like changing physicians, and I will not try to convince her. So the two of you work together, and that is all. And by the way, do not bring up that whore to her again. You are trying to go into an area you don't know a thing about. I am sure that you have dozens of people you will have to get to know as their physician, but that does not include our family. Is that understood?" Scott finished.

"I refuse to understand what it is that so many people think that they are keeping her from. I am only interested in what is best," Rick said. "No one can fault a person for that."

"Sara is special," Scott said.

"We all believe our wives are special. My wife and I have three children as well. I told her that she was not to work following the birth of our second child. I have to hell her from time to time that before she is a nurse, she is my wife and the mother of our children. And I didn't marry her so our children can have a part-time mom," Rick said. "Women need our guidance. Their hormones and emotions get the better of them from time to time."

"Isn't your wife Amelia?" Scott asked.

"Yes. We met in Vietnam. She worked as a nurse in a MASH unit," Rick said.

"As a nurse, she entered as an officer, did she not?" Scott asked.

"She was a captain when we met," Rick said.

"And were you an officer as well?" Scott asked.

"No. I entered the army as a private first class," he said.

"That makes me understand your need to control your environment better. And you are likely a younger son as well. I have met your wife several times when she has come to the ranch. She continues to work part time as well?" Scott asked.

"She works only enough to keep up her nursing license. Two of our children are in school, but one is only four," Rick said. "He needs a mother."

"Sara is the best mother I have ever known. She loves our children. We both want a big family."

"Sara appears to be very young to have school-age children," Rick pointed out. "I read where you are described as a millionaire. You have a father that made a fortune and passed it down?"

"Dr. Powell, I don't know or care where you have gotten you half-baked information. Let me give you the short version of who and what I am. Yes, my father is worth several fortunes. And if he were to give away his empire and start from scratch, he would be a millionaire by week's end. He is just that kind of a man. And he is the most generous man in the world. Anyone who works for us is treated like family.

"I am the eldest son. I graduated with highest honors from high school at the age of sixteen, and with honors from SMU with dual majors in both business and agriculture at twenty. I guess if I would have gone to college and spent my time drinking and whoring such as you, things could have been different. I am the founder of the Byers Oil Refinery on the Texas gulf, etc. That should give you the idea of what I am. Then of course, there is the ranch. Now your curiosity should be somewhat satisfied. Could you please finish with my friend here?" Scott concluded.

"And this man, how is he related to you?" Rick asked.

"I have worked on the ranch since I was born. I was adopted by Scott's parents when I was young. I now own my own ranch and am a geologist. And I receive half of the proceeds of every oil well that I find," Mark said with his eyes still closed. "Sara and Saline are like my little sisters. And I am a wealthy man, so can you get a move on treating me so I may go home?"

"The x-ray showed two breaks. I am nearly finished with the cast. You will have to wear it for three months. Crutches for two weeks, and a walking cast for the rest of the time. I will give you some pain medication. As the bones have been reset, it will feel better than it did when you came in," Rick said.

"So I am released?" Mark asked.

"Yes. You need to return to the clinic in five days to check and see if your leg is healing. Just call for an appointment," Rick said, his thought was to get Mark St. Clair to his office and win him over as his doctor.

"I will need a copy of the films to give to my doctor," Mark said.

"I just assumed you would be following up with me. I can make you an appointment at your convenience," Rick said.

"I know my physician would like to have the films for his records of me. I have had the same doctor since I was a boy. Why would I change?" Mark said. "My wife had all three of our children here, and Dr. Carmichael delivered them all. We both have the utmost confidence in him. There is no insult to you intended."

Rick didn't say another word but rather picked up the chart and walked from the room.

"Well, I guess he is pissed," Mark said.

"Yeah, big time," Scott said. "Let's go home."

"Ready when you are," Mark said and pulled the crutches under his arms and left with Scott.

Sara and Ryan had both grown stronger during the weeks following his birth. At six weeks, he continued to be breastfed and was taking baby food as well.

Rick made two additional trips to the ranch with the excuse that he was there to check on Mark St. Clair. He had gone to Scott and Sara's house both times. The first time, he said he had come there to check on both her and the baby and, of course, Mark. Sara had once again said he had wasted the trip and closed the door in his face. The second time, a week later, she had tried to close the door, and he put his foot in the way.

"I am not leaving without knowing how the two of you are doing," Rick said.

"This is my home, and I don't want or need you here. Move your foot," Sara said.

"I am a doctor, and I am not leaving without an answer. Are you such a child that you don't know concern when you see it?"

"I am not a child. I know a nosey, self-indulgent, second-rate man when I see one. Now leave here before you bite off more trouble than you could possibly be worth," Sara said.

"You need to watch your mouth. I know what you are, and it is not Lady Sara. And I happen to know that you killed your father. What did he do, refuse to let you do anything you like?" Rick asked.

Sara left him standing at the open front door as she left and ran from their room. Rick took that opportunity to walk inside and close the door. He looked to see where she had gone but decided to wait until she came back. It was a few minutes before she came back, and he turned and saw her walking from the direction she had gone in.

"Get out my house now," she said.

"I came out here for something, and I am not leaving until I get it. Now, I don't see the baby, so if you could direct me in the direction where he is."

"I said leave. This is the last time I am telling you. I didn't invite you in. You took that liberty upon yourself. The differences in our positions now are that I am right," Sara said.

Rick stood and began walking slowly toward her.

Sara pulled a gun from behind her and cocked it. "It was my stepfather," she said. Then she put her other hand on the gun to give her stability.

"You can't honestly get me to believe that you are going to shoot me just because I am in your house. You likely don't even know how to shoot a gun," Rick said.

"Then why did you back away? I shot my stepfather because he was asked to leave my home. He was a boar of a man, not so different from you. He decided that he was going to come into my home and take both me and our baby to Germany with him. He held my friend Maria St. Clair at knifepoint and then at gunpoint. Like, the only reason that you think I killed him was because my mother also told you about how I shot him. And I did. Right after he shot me twice. That is well-known. They know that he shot first because the one time that I shot him, he was both paralyzed and dead instantly. Now, you bully your way into my house and like him, you refuse to leave. So, sit down," Sara said.

"Why don't you put that gun down?" Rick said. "I would feel a lot better if you put that gun down."

"If you wanted to feel better, you should never have come here. Now sit down and shut up," she said. Rick did as he was told. "I was born in California. At the age of five, I was sent to the UK to a private and very exclusive girls' school because I was not only a stepchild, I was the child of an affair that my mother had a year after my just older brother was born. I was never told who he was. He used that excuse to abuse me when I was home from school. He also abused my younger sister, his actual daughter, until we moved back here, and he abandoned us as well as our infant baby brother. Our dear mother, the slut that you defend, found her newest husband in the same high school that I was to attend if I had been allowed to go to high school. She married him as soon as her divorce was final. Then I had her and her husband to support. My sister and baby brother had to sleep in a falling-down barn to keep from being raped by him for over two years. Saline and I were beaten and starved by those two for over two years. And when we had been taken from that place by the kindest people that you can ever imagine, she came here months later and attempted to take my baby brother from my arms, his head striking a table. He died of a cerebral hemorrhage two hours later.

"That should be enough for you to leave me alone from now on. And for you to leave here and never come back," Sara said. She had tears of frustration running down her face.

"Sara, I didn't mean to—" Rick started, but then the shot took him completely off guard. He was on the ground before he even thought about it.

"I didn't ask you what you meant. I told you to go," Sara said. Then as Rick started to stand, Sara began to laugh. Only then did Rick realize he had wet his pants. He saw that she was now laughing so hard that she had forgotten about the gun that had previously been aimed at him. He walked toward the door, and she spoke again. "Next time you try to intimidate a woman, put in a catheter in first," she said.

Rick opened the door to several men looking at him, including her father-in-law. "Baby girl, who is this?" John asked.

"Dr. Rick Powell. He forced his way into the house, and I did what you told me to do the next time," she said.

"That stupid bitch tried to kill me, she just missed," Rick said through his humiliation.

"No. She didn't miss. After what happened before, we made sure she knew how to shoot and shoot well. She just replaced the bullets with blanks, and from the looks of you, it scared the piss out of you," John said, and those present began to laugh. Rick fairly ran to his car and flew down the driveway.

"Baby girl, you did well," John said. Sara smiled at him then went back inside and checked on Ryan who was still sleeping.

Sara went to the phone and dialed the hospital and asked for Amy.

"Amy. This is Sara."

"Yeah, Sara. How are you feeling?" she asked.

"I feel wonderful. I need to tell you something. Dr. Powell came out here again and pushed his way into the house," she said.

"Not again. Do you need me to call Amelia?" Amy asked.

"No. I hope she is still speaking to me after today," Sara said.

"What happened?" Amy asked. Sara told her the whole sorted tale of how he had been berating her and Amy began to howl.

"Can you do me a tiny favor, just to see if he is likely to repeat this again?" Sara said.

"Anything, just name it."

"Could you take an envelope and write on the front of it 'To Puddles' Powell'?" Sara asked.

"Absolutely, and as an added bonus, I will spread it around and let you know what happens," Amy said. "I will call you later."

Rick had gone home from Sara's house and changed clothes before he saw his wife so she would not know what had happened.

The following morning, he went to the hospital first as he always did. When he walked in through the ER, however, he thought that the nurses in the ER were smiling and chatting overly much, but then he decided it was likely in his head.

He went to the nurses' desk and picked up the charts on his patients that he had to see before going to the clinic. He asked which nurses were covering his patients today and was given their names.

Elaine had three of his patients. He went down to where she was caring for patients and waited by the medication cart. He noticed that on top of the cart was a urinary catheter kit. He could feel the heat in his face, and without seeing himself in the mirror, he knew he was blushing. The thought made him angry.

Elaine came out of a room to the cart. "Good morning, Dr. Powell," Elaine said with a smile.

"Are you taking care of some of my patients?" he asked.

"Yes, I am. In here is Mrs. Johnson from Blue Bird Nursing Home. She had wet herself and through that they discovered her to have a urinary tract infection. Would you like me to put a catheter in?" Elaine asked.

Rick waited a minute before he answered. "Yes, that would be fine," he answered. She smiled like she knew a secret, picked up the catheter kit, and went to her patient's room.

He rounded and noticed that all the nurses had the same smile as Elaine had when he was talking to her. Maybe it was in his head, because he was actually paying attention to what the nurses were doing. He decided to put it out of his mind and saw all his patients. After he was finished, he went to the doctors' lounge for some fresh coffee. On the message board, there was an envelope. Rick walked to the board to see if it was a note for him. On the envelope, it said, "Dr. Puddles Powell."

Rick jerked the envelope down from the board and opened it to see who had done such a thing. "How did it feel to be afraid? I would learn some self-control. Signed the nurses of the Country Hospital."

Rick stood there for a moment. He could feel that his blood pressure was rising at the thought of all the nurses knowing what happened at Sara Byers's house. He turned toward the door to tell Amy what her nurses had done, only to see her standing a few feet from him.

"Did you know about this?" he blasted.

"I am the one who put it there," she said.

"So that insipid girl told you that she pointed a gun at me and fired?" Rick said.

"That would be impressive had you not been trespassing, threatening, and God only knows what else. You have been told by nearly every nurse in this hospital that you are rude and intrusive. After this, you're going to have to do something to look like an authority figure. And no, we do not tolerate bullying. If you have a problem with a nurse, tell me and I will take care of it," Amy said and left the room.

As angry as Rick was, there was nothing that he could do. He had been on the biggest cattle ranch in East Texas and found himself thinking about what it would be like to live on such a place. The times he had seen Sara, be it driving across the pasture, answering the door, or caring for patients, he had known inside of himself that she was damaged. Sara Lyn Byers was special and had everyone in the hospital and the place she lived on protecting her.

Weeks passed and before she knew it, it was time for Sara to return to work. Ryan, like their other children, was healthy and strong. Both of the older boys were doing well in school, and Allison, along with other women at the ranch, kept the boys while she worked. But unlike before, Sara returned to work only part time. She didn't give a reason why she only wanted part time, but those who knew her well knew that even though she had felt better immediately following Ryan's birth, she had started to tire more easily, and though she was a light sleeper, she appeared to be so tired at bedtime. Ryan would cry, and she wouldn't wake up right away. Scott had suggested that she take a few more weeks, but Sara had told him that she really needed to keep her skills for when she started school to get her RN.

Sara returned so she could work two or three eight-hour shifts per week. As she didn't want a paycheck, it was easy to pretty well make her own hours.

On her first day back, the other nurses had to tell her that they had brought Dr. Powell to his knees with the reference to his incontinent episode at the ranch. Sara smiled about the thought. She received report on her patients for the day and began to make rounds.

She was in deep thought when she was preparing to give her patients their morning medications.

"So after what you did to me, you have the nerve to come back to work here?" Dr. Powell said.

"Good morning, Dr. Powell," Sara said, continuing to get the medications ready for her patient. "Do I have some of your patients?"

"Nice try. I am looking for an apology," he said.

"Then you need to look elsewhere. I am busy. If I am taking care of some of your patients, I will assist you. Otherwise, I need to take care of them," Sara concluded.

"You tried to kill me. You scared the hell out of me," he said.

Sara interrupted his usual complaints about her. "Dr. Powell, I am a nurse in this hospital. I tried to get you to leave my house before you decided to walk in. I did everything I could to keep you from making a fool out of yourself. I am going to say this directly so you know exactly what I mean by it. Leave me alone. Don't come to the ranch or anyplace for that matter to see me. If you need to know about your patients, then ask."

"You don't want to know the things that your mother has said about you?" he asked.

"No, now excuse me," Sara said and walked by him.

"She is struggling to make ends meet," Rick said. "She is waiting tables to make a living. Her husband also works, and your brother's living with her as well."

"Have you finished?" she asked.

"Yes," he answered.

"Good," she said and pushed by him and went into the patient's room.

Rick, however, was not put off so easily. "You are heartless. I have never seen anyone who cared so little for another person, much less their own mother."

Sara got ready to give medications to another patient and completely ignored him. When she turned to go to that patient's room, he took her by the arm.

"What is wrong with you?" Sara asked. "Telling you what I did at the ranch, I thought that you would be human enough to leave the situation alone. The money that I threw at you should keep you in payments for your services to her for a very long time." Sara turned from him for a moment. She put her hand to her chest then lowered it and then turned back to face him. She could feel herself start to sweat. "I will say it again. Leave me alone, or I will file charges."

"She wants to be part of your life and that of her grandchildren's lives," he said.

"Tough," Sara said. Then she put the medication cup on the medication cart. She walked quickly to the ladies' room on the other side of the nurses' station. She went inside and locked the door.

Rick started to knock on the door. When she didn't answer, he started to beat on the door. When she didn't answer, he started to beat on the door. Amy came over and asked Dr. Powell what the problem was.

"I was attempting to have a conversation with your nurse, and she refuses to listen," Rick said.

"The kind of conversation you want to have is completely inappropriate. I believe you have rounds to make, Dr. Powell," Amy said.

"I am going to finish my conversation with this girl," Rick said.

"No. You will not. I am her boss, and I take care of my nurses, the way that Dr. Carmichael used to do. I assure you that he never acted like you have acted since you came to work here," Amy said.

"And how is that?" he asked.

"Like a spoiled child. There is no nurse here who has any remaining respect for you. And all I have to do is suggest you be fired, and it will happen," Amy said. She then turned her attention to the bathroom door. "Sara, it is Amy. Could you open the door for me please?"

When the door didn't open, she asked the housekeeper to open the door. Sara was on the floor. "Help!" she yelled.

People started coming to find out what had happened. "Elaine, call Dr. Carmichael immediately," Amy said.

"No need. I am here. I will take care of her," Rick said.

"No, you won't. Her doctor will be here shortly. Let's get her to the ER. Sara, Sara," Amy said, shaking her gently. "Elaine, see if he can also bring Dr. Quinton."

"Get her on a monitor please. And I will start an IV of normal saline," Amy said to the nurse who was recording the code.

Although told he would not be caring for the young woman, Rick started to take over the situation. When no one seemed to be paying attention to him, he started to raise his voice. "I need to know her history. I cannot treat her without knowing her history," he said.

"We all know her history, and we are acting on the authority of her doctor and her cardiologist," Amy said. With that, she took out her stethoscope and listened to her heart. Then she turned Sara's head to the side and saw the jugular vein was distended. "Tell them to hurry, Elaine. It won't be long before she tamponades."

"She has heart problems?" Rick said. Everyone in the room could see that he was feeling guilty at his verbal attacks of her.

"Rheumatic fever as a child with every complication you can imagine, and some you can't. If you are staying, check her throat," Amy said.

Rick did as he was told. "Her throat is red," he said.

"Strep throat. We have all been here before. Elaine, where was Alex when you spoke to him?" Amy asked.

"He is here in town," Elaine said.

Another nurse said, "No pressure."

"Starting CPR, Elaine, bag. Open IV saline," Amy said.

"Make sure Alex or Dr. Quinton have what they need when they get here," Amy said.

Rick watched as the nurses in the room efficiently ran the cardiac arrest on their friend. Then Alex and Steve came in the room.

"When did you lose pulse?" Dr. Quinton asked.

"Ninety seconds ago," Amy said.

The rapid movements of the famous cardiologist amazed Rick. This doctor was relying completely on the nurse's words, making him feel impotent.

"I will take care of this, Elaine. Could you call Allison please? I don't know where Scott is this morning," Alex said.

"Will do."

Dr. Quinton expertly inserted the four-inch needle into the area around Sara's heart and then began withdrawing enough fluid that was choking her heart. When he had withdrawn enough fluid, he instructed Alex to hold compressions. Sara's heart began to beat. And she began to awaken.

"Let's get a blood pressure. Sara, it is Uncle Steve. Alex is here as well. Don't you think you can move your hand so I know you understand?" Dr. Quinton asked.

Sara did as requested. "Let's get a mask on her please," he asked.

"I am still going to heaven, Uncle Alex. I didn't do anything wrong," she whispered.

"Do you know who is in the room?" Steve asked.

"You, Uncle Alex, Amy, Kathy, Dr. Powell, and Elaine went to call Momma," she whispered.

"She can't possibly know that. Is she guessing?" Rick asked.

Everyone in the room smiled a little. Her blood pressure was coming back up, and she was stabilizing.

"I need to put a drain in, Sara. We have been here before. I am going to give you something so it won't hurt so much, okay?" Steve said.

"I am still going to heaven," she said. She smiled radiantly. Nothing else mattered in that moment.

"You can't possibly put in a pericardial drain here," Rick said.

"Why not?" Dr. Quinton asked.

"Because she needs to see a cardiologist," he said.

"Yes, that is correct. And she has the best right here. I am Dr. Steve Quinton. And who might you be? A new nurse perhaps? Wait, you are not the one who peed his pants, are you?" he said and turned back. "Can someone tell me how this happened?"

"Looks like she has strep throat," Amy said. "And I believe she and Dr. Powell were having another heated discussion."

"Dr. Powell, when you were hired, it was understood that I would keep some of my own patients. Why is it that you feel it necessary to press her? It is not like you don't have enough patients who come to your office," Alex said.

"How do you know that I press her as you call it?" Rick asked.

"In order to treat her effectively, I have to keep up with what is happening. She has been my patient since she was sixteen, and she does not lie," Alex said.

"She just hasn't been caught in a lie. Have you ever thought about that?" Rick asked.

"Step outside, Dr. Powell. Steve, could you join us?"

"Have you got this for a minute, Amy?" Steve asked.

"Yes, of course," she answered.

When the three of them were outside the room, Alex began, "What is your problem with Sara? She is a gifted nurse. She loves her patients and would die to protect anyone she cares about. She cares nothing for herself, and if you heard from that filth that she shot a man in cold blood, you are stupid for believing it. She has had a childhood that would compete with your worst nightmare from Vietnam.

"She does not lie. She may not answer, but if she does, it is the absolute truth."

"Everyone lies. You may not catch her in a lie, but everyone lies," Rick said. "You people treating her like a child or a saint is just wrong and stupid on your own parts. The girl has no regard for her own mother who is living impoverished. Any daughter who would do that is—" Rick didn't get to finish his thoughts. Alex had him up against the wall.

"Listen, you cold-blooded bastard. I was in California, and she was my patient. She was pronounced dead by every doctor that was in that room. What happened in those twelve minutes was something that brought me from not believing to having faith again. I worked in Children's Hospital in Los Angeles. I saw children die from various things. When Sara came back from death, she told me the names; first, middle, and last and the titles of everyone who was in that room. She said exactly what we had done to attempt to bring her back. God spoke to her. Not in a voice like you would understand, but she knew what she was to do in her life. When she was having unimaginable things done to her at home, she continued to have faith. Her stepfather in California did everything to keep her from having faith, but he could not beat, starve, or anything to keep her from having faith. And he tried. In the ninety seconds that the nurses were working on her in there, I would gather that the same thing occurred. For years she thought she would go to hell because she took the life of a man who was going to kill her friend and kidnap Sara and her first child and take them to Germany. He shot twice, one missed and the other hit her in the arm. Then she shot. That single shot paralyzed Lord Henry Alexander and hit his heart. She was shooting with her left hand and had never touched a gun in her life.

"So, I tell you now. Leave her be. She gives hope and faith to everyone she sees. If she has a patient that is dying and is afraid, because of what she tells them, they go peacefully. And I would wager everything I have in this world that she has a Bible in her left pocket. She always does. Knowing what I have told you, you should respect her. If not, that is your problem, not hers," Steve finished.

Alex released his hold on Rick. "There is a very long article in the *New England Journal of Medicine* from the fall of 1968. I would suggest that you read it. Sara is a miracle. Nothing less. Disrespect her or another nurse in this hospital again, and you will be looking for employment elsewhere. I am going to check on my patient," Alex said and walked back into the room.

"Baby girl, you scared me," Alex said.

"I am sorry, Uncle Alex. I didn't think it was strep throat this time. I guess I was wrong. Please don't send me away," Sara said weakly.

"That is up to Steve. He has to put the drain in. Do you want me to stay with you until Scott gets here?" he asked.

"Do you need to be someplace else?" she asked.

"Are you kidding? I'm retired. And we don't leave for another week to go to South America. So I have lots of time," he said.

"It had been so long since I had problems, I thought it was just a cold," Sara said. Alex could see that she had beaded sweat on her face, and her hands and arms were clammy.

"Are you in pain right now?" he asked.

Sara nodded.

"How long have you been in pain?"

"The last couple of days my chest and joints have hurt," she said and turned her head away.

"Amy, could you get the lab down here to draw blood please, and get Sara some Demerol as well," he asked.

"Yes, sir," Amy said and was off.

Elaine came back into the room. "Allison has called Scott at the office, and he is waiting to hear from you. Sara, are you okay? You are my best friend, and it scared me so much that you would die," she said.

"Like they said, we have been here before. I will be fine. Are you going to be my nurse?" she asked.

"If you want me as your nurse, I will be," Elaine said.

"She requested to see her mother earlier," Rick said.

"She asked for Momma. That is Allison. She is the only person she regards as a mother who lives stateside," Elaine said.

"Sara, you asked to see your mother. Who were you talking about?" Alex asked.

"Allison Byers, who else?" she said. "She loves me, and I love her. She wanted a daughter, and I needed a mother. God made sure we found each, remember?"

"I remember, baby girl. She and Maria will be here in a little bit," Alex said.

"Thank you, Uncle Alex," she said before she was asleep.

"Let's get that drain in before she tamponades again," Steve said.

Amy gave her the Demerol in her IV to help with the pain.

An hour later, when everything was done, Sara was taken to a room in the hospital that was reserved for special patients. When they got to the room, Steve picked her up and gently placed her on the bed.

Alex was already at the desk writing his orders on her.

Rick had finished his rounds and writing his orders on his own patients. He was irritated that he was not going to take over as Sara Byers's doctor and decided to let Dr. Carmichael know.

"Dr. Carmichael, I would be more than happy to take over the care of Sara Byers for you, as you are now retired," Rick said.

"Not on your life," Alex said, never stopping what he was doing.

"Don't you think that I would be the better person to care for her as you are family?" Rick said.

"No. I don't."

"I am completely qualified as a physician to care for her," Rick said.

"Dr. Powell, you have shown everyone who knows her that you are a constant irritation. Letting you care for her would be a mistake. What were you trying to prove this morning? It was her first day back at work. How could she have done something so quickly?" he said.

"I wanted an apology for her having shot at me and humiliating me in such a way," Rick said.

"Why were you in her house? Did she invite you in?"

"No. She asked me to leave. I was there both to congratulate her on the arrival of her second son and to tell her about her real mother," Rick said.

"She has three sons. And if you are talking about Joan Redding, she has never been a mother to her or her sister. Scott has said she is not to talk to her mother, and Sara wouldn't go against anything he said. She also has no desire to see Joan Redding. The only reason that she would like to see Sara is for money. And that is not going to happen," Alex said.

"I will talk to her one day when she does not have all of you around," Rick said. "She is a nurse in this hospital, and I like to know who is caring for my patients."

"What is it about her that bothers you? She is good at her job, she is nice, and all the patients love her. Is it that she is from a wealthy family, or that she is regarded as a German aristocrat?" Alex said.

"A title that is not hers to have. She is another man's bastard, not the duke of someplace," Rick said so anyone could hear him.

"Use that word in regards to her again and I will kill you," came a voice that Rick had heard in the recent past.

"And who are you?" Rick asked.

"I am Joseph Thomas Alexander, duke of Hamburg. Sara was named by me as the next in line of succession. So I would watch what I said about her," the duke said.

Alex stood and extended his hand, "Good to see you again, Your Grace." The duke took his hand and shook it.

"Good to see you again, Alex. And how many times do I have to tell you to call me Joseph?" the duke said.

"Yes, so you have, Joseph," Alex said.

"How is my niece? My little baby Sara. Allison called their house and was kind enough to let me know something had happened to her, and I wasted no time getting here. Was it her heart?" he asked.

"It was. Steve is still in the room with her, but she is now stable. I believe we will be keeping her here for now. You know that Steve will likely stay here day and night until she is well," Alex said.

"May I see her?" he asked.

"Yes, of course," Alex said, starting in the direction of her room.

"I am Dr. Richard Powell, by the way," Rick said, extending his hand.

The duke turned around, facing Rick. "So you are," he said, not taking Rick's hand. "Stay away from Lady Sara. You tend toward upsetting her, and she has had enough of that kind of treatment," he said and continued down the hall toward Sara's room.

"She is going to be groggy because of the pain medication," Alex said and explained about the things that were concerning him.

Steve came out of the room and also shook hands the duke. Rick watched the three of them talking like a group of men who knew one another well. He would have loved to have stayed around but knew that he was running late for his patients in his office. So he left, but he would be making lunch rounds as well, and then the other doctors would have left.

CHAPTER 16

Sara's health improved more quickly than it ever had, and she decided to take a few extra weeks just to make sure that all was well and to spend time with all her family. That gave her time to do things around the house, to help Momma making preserves and putting things away for the winter. They even went to cornfields and picked hundreds of ears of corn to shuck, clean, and put into bags for the freezer. At night at the main house, there would be everyone gathered shelling peas for the freezer as well.

Saline and Lauren even loved that time. It was close family time, and everyone had a hand in it. Frances, who had never been involved in such things before she had met the Byers family, had now come to enjoy the late evenings and getting ready for the winter.

When Scott was not at the office, he was busy on the ranch. It was a busy time of the year, and everyone knew what there was to be done.

At times Elaine and Amelia would come to the ranch, and the three of them would ride horses. This day, many of the horses were gone from the barn, so Sara had Elaine ride Bunny, and she rode Scott's horse, Champ. The people from the barn assisted the ladies in saddling the horses and bid them to have a good ride.

"How did you manage to make it here without Dr. Powell following you?" Sara asked.

"I just waited until he had gone to work and called Elaine. It is just too nice a day to spend indoors," Amelia said.

"I agree. I have spent the last weeks doing the things around here I love doing. I decided to wait until next week before I start to work at St. Mary's in Tyler. Uncle Steven thinks that is a good place to start if I am serious about being a heart nurse. I can hardly wait to get started," Sara said.

"How do you stay in the saddle like that? I have seen women ride like that in movies, and I just don't understand it," Amelia said.

"You are welcome to try if you like," Sara said.

"I think I will." The three of them stopped, and Sara and Amelia changed mounts.

"Put one foot in the stirrup and the other around the pommel. You just have to squeeze your thighs together to stay in the saddle. What do you think?" Sara asked.

"How do you get him to go like this?"

"Kick just a little with your left leg, and he will go." Sara watched as she rode a little bit just to get the feel. "What do you think?"

"I feel like such a lady. And you can run like this?" Amelia asked.

"Stop for a second, and I will show you," Sara said, and the two women change horses again. "Watch this," Sara kicked Champ to where he was running, the other two women following her. When she came to a fence, she jumped it. The other two also jumped the fence. The three friends were having a great time, riding and jumping, going through streams, and them just talking.

"I don't think I have ever seen such a bold rider," Amelia said.

"I have been riding since I was a child. Do you want to see what my favorite thing to do is?" she asked.

"Sure."

Sara tied her reins, and when Champ was running, she closed her eyes and held her hands out.

"She is such a beautiful rider," Amelia said in awe.

Elaine then took off running on her mount. She began to jump over piles of rocks and low fences. Sara looked over where she was going and saw a low branch. "Elaine look out!" she screamed but was too far away to be heard. She began to run Champ at full speed to try to get to her friend. Amelia saw the object of Sara's concern and began to run toward her as well.

Elaine never saw what had hit her. The branch caught her in the head and sent her off the back of the horse. On the ground, she never moved.

Sara jumped from the saddle and ran to her friend. "Elaine, Elaine, talk to me. Open your eyes," she said without moving her. "Oh my god. She is breathing. Amelia, do you know the way back to the main house?"

"I don't think I can find it," she answered.

"I will go for help. Don't let her move at all. I will be back as fast as I can," Sara said and jumped on Champ and rode at breakneck speed to get help for her injured friend. Nothing stood in her way, jumping every fence, creek, and pile.

Riley saw the fast-moving rider coming toward the main house. He ran to meet her.

"Sara, what has happened?" he asked.

Sara was trying to catch her breath. Riley pulled her from the saddle. "Elaine got treed. Amelia is with her. It has knocked her completely out. I need to get help to her," Sara said, pleading.

"Mark, Scott, Ray, we need help." In seconds, there were no less than a couple of dozen ranch hands including Mark and Scott.

"We need to call an ambulance. It is very serious," she said. "I need a fresh horse."

"You should stay, baby girl. We will find her," John said.

"No, I have to go to her. I promised Amelia I would be back," Sara said.

In record time, the men got horses, trucks, and anything else they thought they could need. And they were off, Sara leading the way.

When they arrived, they found Elaine still unconscious. "She is still breathing, but she has not responded."

"We need a board, tape, and a truck," Amelia said.

"We have that." Working quickly, they got Elaine on her back and taped her head to the board and immobilized her to avoid any further injury.

"Is Uncle Alex at the clinic right now?" Sara asked.

"He is waiting for her. So let's go." The truck went gently but quickly across the pasture and then to town.

At the hospital, Alex waited for the people from the ranch to arrive. He knew that Elaine was the one who was injured and had not regained consciousness. When he saw the truck driving in and Sara's jeep not far behind, he went to work. They got her into the ER and immediately sent her for a CT scan of her head and her neck.

Having seen people from the Byers ranch arrive, Rick left his clinic to find out what had happened. He immediately saw his wife and Sara crying in each other's arms.

"What the hell happened now?" he demanded. "I demand an answer."

"A riding accident. Elaine is hurt," Amelia said.

"It seems that every time someone gets near you someone gets hurt," Rick said.

Sara, already crying her heart out, ran away.

"That girl needs to learn her place," Rick said.

"How dare you treat her like that? It was just an accident. We had been riding half of the day before that happened. Now I need to go find Sara, and you stay away from her," Amelia said.

"You will do nothing of the sort. She needs to grow up, and you treating her like the rest of that family does is not helping," Rick said, and Amelia immediately pulled away.

"I am looking for my friend. You go back to your busy little life," Amelia said and walked away.

Amelia knew where she would be. In the chapel, Sara sat on the altar and cried her heart out and prayed at the same time. Amelia got on her knees beside Sara, and the two women held hands and prayed for their friend.

Dr. Middleton was on call for the hospital when Elaine came in. He had heard Rick's tantrum when the other two had brought their friend in but had to concentrate on the patient rather than correct his bad behavior. He ordered CT scans of both the neck and head to assess for any damage. He could see Elaine's left arm was broken and quickly set it while she was still unconscious.

Rick walked into the CT scan control room and told Dr. Middleton he would be handling the case.

"Not on your life. Stay away from her," he said.

"She is a friend of mine. I have that right," Rick said.

"No. You are not. I am on call for the hospital, and Elaine is now my patient. I heard what you told your wife and Sara. You will not be involved in any aspect of Elaine's care," he said.

"Who are you to tell me?" Rick started.

"I am not a nurse you can try to order around. Now get out before I throw you out," he said.

Rick retreated, knowing that he was not going to be able to muscle his way into taking care of Elaine.

Elaine began to awaken when the scan was completed. Jeff Middleton walked over to her. "Elaine, can you open your eyes?"

"Sure. Dr. Middleton, what are you doing here?" she asked. "I need to catch up to the others."

"You are in the hospital right now, and they are not far away. What do you remember about today?" he asked and smiled a little at her thinking she was still at the ranch.

"Amelia, Sara, and I were riding. You should have seen Amelia on Sara's saddle," Elaine said. "Why am I here?"

"From what they said, you tried to take out a three-hundred-year-old oak with your head."

"Oh god. Is that why my head hurts? What about Bunny?"

"Was Bunny riding with you?" he asked, thinking it was someone he didn't know.

"Bunny is the horse I was riding. She is Sara's own Arabian that she usually rides. We were jumping things and having a good time," Elaine said.

"That was about two hours ago. Your horse went under a limb and you went off the back. How does everything feel?" he asked, assessing for any further injuries. He was glad when the well-liked young nurse hadn't lost movement or sensation. "You have a concussion, so you will get to spend a couple of days here. And you are not to take that collar off until I clear your neck. Understood?"

"The way my head feels, I am yours to command," Elaine said.

Elaine's husband came into the room with a worried look on his face. "Honey, they said you were unconscious."

"Doggie. I didn't mean to worry you," she said, hugging her husband.

"Is she going to be okay?" he asked.

"She will be fine. She has a concussion, so we will keep her here a couple of days, and she will back riding again," Dr. Middleton said.

Doug noticed that from the time the three women had become friends, they seemed to give energy to one another. Elaine had started to take interest in the things the other two did. Something she had never done before because she thought of herself a leader rather than a follower. Elaine had always done things the absolute safe way. She had never taken any kind of chances whatsoever. It had made their marriage very stable, so to speak. Now Elaine was excited when she woke up in the morning, whether it be to go to work, clean house, or go to the ranch. On Sundays, when they went to church where her father was the pastor, her parents even noticed the change in their youngest child.

Sara and Amelia came back to Elaine in the ER exam room. Their relief was very visible. The three women, along with Doug, visited throughout the afternoon.

Sara began to work at St. Mary's Hospital in Tyler not long after Elaine had recovered from her concussion. Dr. Quinton and Uncle Alex had both given good references, along with Amelia Powell. With the completion of the cardiac center, she started work on the telemetry unit. Within just a few days, she was oriented to the workings of the unit and the patients she would be responsible for. The charge nurse on the unit, Linda, said that she had never seen an LVN with such an advanced knowledge of the heart.

Wearing her signature locks in either a ponytail or a bun on top of her head kept anyone from thinking that she was anything except Nurse Sara. Her patients responded to her gentle touch and kind words.

At lunchtime one day after Sara had been working for six months, Linda saw the young woman sitting, eating lunch in the break room. She had let her hair down and was rubbing the back of her neck while she was reading what looked to be a textbook.

"You have beautiful hair. I don't believe I have ever seen that color before," Linda said.

"Thank you. It is quite heavy when I wear it up all day. I will put it back up before I go back to work," Sara said.

"You have a real gift caring for cardiac patients. Most nurses take a while to learn everything on the telemetry unit," Linda said.

"I had a good teacher before I started here. My cardiologist taught me so much," she said.

"Who is that?" Linda asked.

"Dr. Steven Quinton. He used to be in California, but he moved to Texas a few years ago."

"I have heard that name before. Why does someone so young need a cardiologist?" Linda asked.

"I had rheumatic fever when I was a child," Sara said.

"How does a young English girl see a cardiologist in California?" Linda asked, opening the cabinet and getting a cup for coffee and taking a seat.

"I was born in California. I was just sent to Wales to attend school. I don't seem to be able to lose the accent," Sara said.

"I think it is sweet. I have lived here my entire life and rarely do we hear a different accent," Linda said.

"You should see when we have friends over from the UK. They really enjoy visiting the ranch," Sara said.

"Your family owns a ranch?"

"My husband's family are ranchers, among other things. You should come out sometime. Do you have kids?" Sara asked.

"We have three boys and a girl," Linda said. "Do you have kids as well?"

"We have three boys. The older two have their own ponies and already ride quite well. Our youngest is still a baby," Sara said with a light in her eyes.

Linda had gone to nursing school immediately following high school. She had achieved her bachelor's degree in nursing and married immediately there following. She had never traveled more than one hundred miles from her Tyler home and had never really thought she would like to. Now she was getting to know someone who had been places that she had only just seen in books.

"You don't look old enough to have three children," Linda said.

"I got an early start. I married at seventeen to the most wonderful man in the world. Is your husband from here?" Sara asked.

"Like me, he has lived here his entire life. He is an attorney here in Tyler. And always busy," Linda answered.

"I know that feeling. My Scott has to fly down to the gulf a couple of times a week to check on the refinery. But we are both quite busy, what with work and school. But we are home every night with our children. We are hoping to have a daughter next," Sara said, smiling.

"You are still going to school?" Linda asked.

"Yes, of course. I want to get my RN. My friend Elaine and I are taking classes together. She is smarter that I, but she doesn't mind helping me along. She is an LVN as well," Sara said. "I had better get back to work. I do hope you will bring your family to the ranch one day."

"I will make a point of it."

"Scott and our family are always telling me that I need to be more outgoing and feel free to bring friends home like my sister Saline does. I guess I am just a little shy," Sara said and was out the door.

Linda sat for a moment, thinking about the lovely young woman that worked so well with patients. She was very shy, so much so that this was the first time she had ever really spoken to her since she had begun working on the telemetry unit. Her story had a familiar ring about it. She then remembered having to speak with the unit supervisor and left the break room.

"Debra, I have the new schedule requests for you," she said.

"Thanks, Linda. How are the new people doing?" Debra asked.

"Fair, with the exception of one. Sara Byers is doing exceptionally well," she said. "She said that Dr. Steven Quinton has been training her to work with hearts."

"Really. I knew she listed him as a reference. I wonder if he would want to lecture here. Is Sara happy here? Do the patients like her?" Debra asked.

"She loves it here, and her patients are almost never on the call lights. I have heard her talking to them when they are afraid, and she calms them better than the most experienced nurses I have ever known. Did you know she has three children? She seems so young."

"You know who she is, don't you?" Debra said.

"Not until a few minutes ago. I don't know how I missed it. She always wears her hair up and is so nice to everyone. I never knew that kind of wealth was anything but snobby," Linda said. "She asked me to go to her home with my family to visit."

"I would go. I have heard they have a beautiful ranch about fifty miles from here."

"I believe I will, just out of curiosity," Linda said.

"From what I have observed, she is rather timid. I think you are the only person she talks to here," she said.

Then she went back to work.

Debra looked down the hall a little later and saw Linda and Sara talking. She was taken a little aback when she saw Sara hug Linda. She knew that Linda was not one to break a confidence, so she had faith that Sara's life outside the hospital would remain between them.

A few weeks later, the Byers family had their annual BBQ. As always, everyone was invited. The people from the Country Hospital who were not working were all present, as usual. The atmosphere was casual and inviting.

Linda had done as Sara had invited her before. The first time she had gone to the ranch, she had gone alone. She had met most of Sara's family there and had supper at Scott and Sara's home. She had decided to bring her family to the BBQ this time. As it had turned out, Linda's husband had met the Byers family before on business. There were dozens of children that were playing, swimming, etc., all around them. Someone was always watching the children. She had asked Scott where Sara was and then saw her riding up. Her hair was loose down her back as she, Lauren, and Elaine rode up. She had never seen a woman riding sidesaddle before, but Sara appeared to be at home as such.

"Linda, I am so glad that you made it today," Sara said, sliding from Bunny's back. "This is my friend Elaine Rogers, from the Country Hospital, and Lady Lauren Dickerson. She and my sister are going to school in Dallas now, so I don't get to see them as often."

"Nice to meet you, Linda," Lauren said.

"Same here," Elaine said. "Do you ride horses, Linda?"

"Actually I do. Although it has quite a while since I have."

"Why don't you take my horse, Linda? I need to check on the baby, and I will get another. Oh, do you ride sidesaddle?" Sara asked, blushing.

"Don't worry about it," Elaine said. "I will take Bunny, and she can ride mine."

"I will be back in a few minutes," Sara said, running to the house.

"Was she blushing?"

"She always blushes. Don't worry about it. She is a little shy," Lauren said.

"Is this your first time out here?" Elaine asked as Linda got on the horse.

"No, I have been here a few times. Is that the governor?" Linda asked.

"Yaw, he and John are friends. Are you a little overwhelmed yet?" Lauren asked.

"Not as much as I was the first time. This place is like a dream. And the family is so nice."

"Oh. Here comes Saline and her friend," Lauren said. "When did you arrive, cousin?"

"Just got here, and Saline already has me on a horse," Andrew said.

"Linda this is my cousin Andrew. Andrew, this is Sara's friend from St. Mary's, Linda," Lauren said.

"So nice to meet you, Linda. Sara does not tend toward bringing so many people around. Not like her wild and crazy sister here does," Andrew said.

"Wild, crazy, and still a better rider than you," Saline said and kicked her horse forward. "See you in a little while, Linda," she said over her shoulder with Andrew on her heels riding Champ.

"Prince Andrew? The queen of England's son?" Linda asked.

"Yaw. He and Saline are buddies. He is here for a few days," Elaine said.

"Y'all know the royal family? Wow," Linda said.

Sara came back outside and hugged a man who looked to be middle-aged. Although dressed as the rest of the people who were present, he and the woman who was with him looked a little out of place.

"Linda, this is our uncle Joseph and his wife, Catherine, the duke and duchess of Hamburg," Sara said.

"Very nice to meet you, Linda. Sara has nothing but good things to say about you," Uncle Joseph said, extending his hand to her.

"Sara's uncle is a duke? Pardon me, sir, what do I call you?" she said.

"You may call me Uncle Joseph, young lady. At least here at the ranch. And welcome," he returned.

About then, a very loud voice was heard above the other sounds of people. "Sara. I need to have a word with you," came the voice of Rick Powell.

"Oh lord, why is he here?" Sara said.

"Think nothing of it, my dear. You go with your friends, and I will take care of that windbag," the duke said. He quickly assisted Sara on the back of Elaine's horse.

"Sara, you come back here," Rick said as the three horses and four riders left.

"Dr. Powell, what are you doing here? I believe you are on call at the hospital," the duke said.

"I need to speak with Sara," Rick yelled.

"You start one of your tantrums here today, and you will be escorted off the ranch. Everyone is here to have a good afternoon and not listen to you," the duke said.

"I don't believe I was talking to you, Joe. I am talking to Sara," Rick said.

"It is Your Grace to you, Puddles, and if you attempt to bother my niece, I will make a point of telling those who don't know it already the story of your nickname," Joseph said.

Catherine laughed a little at the thought of the little man making such a fuss. Rick walked away from the couple.

Linda's husband, Tad, was soon visiting with John, Scott, and Mark. All the children were playing with new friends.

The smell of BBQ was in the air, adding to the casual atmosphere of the day.

Amelia and Sara quickly saddled additional horses to join the others. As there was only one saddle like Sara's, she put a Western saddle on another, and both rode out to meet the other women riding. When they caught up, she and Elaine changed horses. Andrew and Saline quickly joined the group, and all spent the afternoon riding.

Rick was furious at having been ignored by Sara. When Amelia had told him the night before that she and the children were going to the BBQ, he had said that she would have to wait until he got someone to cover his place at the hospital so they could go together. When he was unable to get the other two doctors to take his call because they also were attending the BBQ, he decided to go out and make his anger known to Sara. Now he couldn't find Sara or his wife or anyone else for that matter.

Not long after speaking to the duke, he was paged to go to the hospital. He left the ranch to see what was happening at the hospital. He decided that if it were something small, he would return later in the evening.

When Rick arrived at the ER, he heard the voice of the same woman who had become a chronic patient at the clinic.

"When the hell is my doctor going to be here? I am in pain. I need a shot of Demerol," Joan Redding said.

"Mrs. Redding, I am here. What seems to be the problem?" Rick asked.

"I have a migraine headache and have nothing to take for it. I need some Demerol," she said.

"Nurse, get her 25 mg of Demerol IM," Rick said to the nurse.

"You have your codeine tablets at home, Mrs. Redding. Did you try them?" he asked, disgusted at what was obviously a ploy for medication.

"Of course I tried them. Do you think I would let those idiots drive me here if I had not tried them? My nerves are too bad now. My boss says he is going to fire me for taking off," she said.

"I am surprised you are not at the ranch for the BBQ they have every year," Rick said.

"What are you talking about?"

"At the Byers ranch, there are hundreds of people there including their uncle for the annual BBQ. I just thought you would be there," Rick said, knowing that she would not have been invited.

"I need to get this headache under control so I can be there. I had completely forgotten about it," Joan said.

"The duke is there? Mom, we can't go out there," Tommy said.

"You know your sisters will be glad to see you," Joan said as the nurse gave her the injection of the potent narcotic. "Let's just give this a chance to work, and we will be on our way. Can you give me something stronger in case the pain comes back?"

"I will give you the same thing that you take normally," he said.

"What about something for my nerves?" she asked sweetly.

Rick thought for a minute about what to do about the request for something for her nerves and elected to give her a muscle relaxant instead. Almost at the instant he gave her the prescriptions, she and the two men with her were out of the ER.

"Is there anyone else I need to see?" he asked.

"No, Dr. Powell. I think everyone in town is at the Byers ranch," the nurse said, taking the completed paperwork and walking away.

The nurse's comment angered Rick, but he chose to say nothing.

"Joan, you were not invited out to the Byers ranch. Don't you think the law will be there? I don't have any desire to go back to jail again," Oscar said.

"I didn't ask you to go. I will go out there myself. You two can do whatever you want to do. I can hardly wait to surprise your sisters again," Joan said.

Joan dropped off Tommy and Oscar at the farm and made a beeline for the ranch. As she drove onto the ranch, she could tell, the closer she got to the houses, the more activity she saw. There were literally hundreds of people everywhere. She drove past the main house, knowing that the woman who lived there knew what she looked like. She saw several dozen nice brick homes spread around, almost like it was a town. Then she saw the huge mansion about half a mile from the main house.

She knew that could be no one's home but that of her bastard daughter Sara. She and Saline had always talked about what they would consider the perfect house, and this was it. With so many people in and around the house, no one would notice one more. Joan braided her long black hair and twisted it into a bun on top of her head. She pinched her cheeks a little to give her a little more color and looked in the mirror to see that she was presentable. She decided that she would somehow find her daughter's bedroom and change into something else to blend in.

She parked the car with several other vehicles that were already there and went in a side door that appeared to be a kitchen door. She smiled pleasantly to the people she met as she walked through the massive house.

When Joan saw the family room, she couldn't believe her eyes. The huge room with plush carpeting wall to wall had open beam ceiling, and a fireplace was in the middle of the room. And in one corner was the most beautiful cherrywood baby grand piano she had ever seen. Just that room was about half the size of the farmhouse. There were family pictures on all the walls that told of six years of happiness in the life of this family on the ranch. If not for all the people present, Joan would have loved to have torn the pictures from the walls.

On the other side of the large room was a doorway that looked to go to a hallway. Joan walked to the doorway and saw a series of rooms that went in one direction, and the other way was only one door. Joan elected to take the room by itself. She went to the room where the door was open. When she entered, she found the most beautiful room she had ever seen. She and Henry had lived in a beautiful mansion in California, but nothing like this room. The furniture was of the highest quality cherrywood. Unlike the rest of the house, this room was made for a lady. The floral drapes and bed covering were expensive and appeared to be made for that room. The carpet was plush burgundy. There was a sitting area complete with a chaise lounge close to one of the windows. She walked farther over to another door in the room that led to the bathroom, complete with a huge walk-in closet.

Joan could not believe the way Sara seemed to have fallen into the life Joan had always wanted for herself. She then heard a baby close by. She walked to the other door in the bedroom and found a small room that was a nursery for a baby that looked to be about months' old, who appeared to be waking up from a nap. She looked at the child and saw he had thick dark wavy hair and bright-blue eyes. The tot sat up and looked at the strange woman in his room. Although she cared nothing for having another child, this baby was beautiful.

Then Joan heard someone coming up the hall to the bedroom. Joan ducked back into the huge closet.

"Is my Ryan Joseph awake?" she heard her daughter say to the tot. "Momma has been out riding while you were napping. You have a bunch of new friends outside now that are just your size. So let's get you out of that wet diaper." Sara then started to sing to him as she changed him.

Joan then heard the baby begin to laugh and wondered what was causing him to do so.

"Sis, are you in here?" Saline said.

"I am changing Ryan," Sara said.

"Uncle Joseph wants to see his namesake. Better make him cute. I don't think Aunt Catherine has seen him yet," Saline said. "I can't wait until I finish this semester so I can go on more trips to places like Africa. Amy, Uncle Alex, and Uncle Steven are such good teachers on the way over there," Saline said.

"I really want to go this next time as well. There is no need in all of you having the fun without me," Sara said.

"You will have to get your doctors to agree, you know that."

"I know. Well, Ryrie, it is time to go see Uncle Joseph and Aunt Catherine," Sara said, and the two sisters, with the baby, left the room.

Joan found a heavy desk that had the drawers unlocked. She opened one, and there were thousands of dollars in one-hundred-dollar bills. Joan had brought a big purse with her and filled it completely full of money. She also saw a fur coat in the closet that looked like it would be warm for her to wear. As easy as it had been to get around, she decided that she would be putting what she had at present into her car and try for more things to help make her life easier.

Staying several feet from her daughters but watching them just the same, Joan saw Sara take the baby to the duke. The duke picked up the little boy and began to speak to him. Then his wife wanted to play with him as well.

"Go on, Sara, my dear, I will see to Ryan with your uncle," the woman said.

"Thank you, Aunt Catherine. I promise I won't be long," Sara said.

"Have fun, we will be fine," she said again and played for a while.

"Uncle looks so happy when you are with him, so you will have to come here every time you can," Sara said.

"I would love to. It feels like everyone is family."

"We are," Sara said and winked.

Everyone walked out of the master bedroom and went back down to the family room. Joan looked through a few other things where she had found a couple of other things she would take with her when she left the room. One was a necklace that had a very large diamond center stone in it and a Rolex watch that was obviously Scott's. Then she opened a box on a dresser and found several thousand dollars in it. Joan made quick work of putting everything she found into either her clothes or her purse. Then once again, walked out to her car and put everything in the trunk. Damn! This was the life she deserved; she had to get involved in it somehow.

It was getting quite dark, so those who had planned on it decided to go to the pool house and get ready to go swimming. The yard, deck, and patio lights were all turned on. There was a large wading pool for the children and a huge swimming pool, with slides, diving boards, love seats, and a separate hot tub for anyone who wanted to relax.

Picnic tables were everywhere. If a person didn't want to swim, there were tables set up in both houses. There were people who helped cook, but the next minute, that same person would be doing other things.

While in Sara's bathroom, Joan applied makeup to disguise herself. She changed into something she found in Sara's closet. There was no way to wear her pants because she was six inches taller than her eldest daughter. She next selected a skirt that went to her knee and chose a sweater that matched for the most part.

"Sara," Joan said in a whisper. "Help me, Sara."

Sara froze at the words that sounded like it came from the grave. She picked up little Ryan and backed away.

"What are you doing here? You really do need to leave before you find yourself in jail again," Sara said, taking another step back.

"I am sick, Sara. I only have a few months to live. If only I had gone to the doctor sooner. But we both know how that works, don't we?" Joan said and began coughing uncontrollably.

"What is wrong with you?" Sara asked, continuing to back away from her.

"Dr. Powell is still looking for what is wrong," Joan said.

"When you find out, let me know. But for now, you need to leave my house," Sara said.

"If I could just lie down for a few minutes, it would help," Joan said, walking toward Scott and Sara's bed.

"No. If you need to lie down go home. The sheriff is just up the hall, and you will be arrested," Sara said.

About that time, the bedroom door opened, and Austin and Brad came in looking for their mother. "Momma, Mark says he is going to beat you in chess," Brad said.

"Who do you think will win, Brad?" Sara asked.

"You will," the boys said in unison. "You always win."

"Okay, can you, my angels, take Ryan to his uncle? I think he has been wanting him to wake up since I put him here. He really thinks he can finally beat me. I hate to break his heart again," Sara said good-naturedly. Sara left the room to look for Mark.

"Hey, Mark," Scott said. "Rumor has it that you want to challenge Sara to a game of chess?"

"'Bout time. She has everyone thinking I am a baby. Is she ready for a rematch?" Mark asked.

"She is in the family room, ready."

"I can hardly wait," Sara said and was off in that direction.

"You have to be named underling to me," Sara said proudly.

"Only until after this game," Mark said.

The two set up the game at the kitchen counter to start. In no time, they couldn't tell if there were people around them or not as they concentrated too much on the game. People watched, and others wanted to see what was so interesting about the game. Before they knew it, they had been playing over three hours.

"Oh no, not again," John Byers said. "We have hundreds of people here. You two can finish this later." There were people around watching the game since it had begun, but everyone was told it was time to eat.

The meal was casual. Some chose to eat outside, some inside at the counter. Some just walked around while they ate.

"How long have the two of you been playing chess?" Linda asked.

"A few months ago, Mark broke his leg and was stuck inside for several months. Everyone did their best to see to him, but one afternoon, he wound up at being at Scott and Sara's house for the day. Sara taught him to play chess very well. She taught him so well, in fact, that they would have a game that would last hours to days.

"It is your turn, lady smarty-pants," Mark said, obviously thrilled with himself.

All the men within earshot heard when the challenge was made.

Both Sara and Mark sat at the table. Neither made a move for a few minutes, but rather seemed to look at every piece on the board.

Sara broke the stalemate and moved. With that, she got back up and was talking to the women in the kitchen regarding how long until the side dishes to the BBQ would be until it was ready.

Mark, on the other hand, was confused as to why she had made the move she did.

Sara began to help in making sure that there were plenty of tables outside and enough plates and tables as well. After she was done with those tasks, she ran to their room to check on Ryan.

"How is mummy's Ryrie?" Sara said to the baby.

"Mama," He returned and smiled.

"That is right, Mamma. We are going outside so you can play with the other children. Did my big boy have a good nap?" Sara asked and then listened as the little boy babbled.

"I will bet you are likely hungry, Ryan. Something tells me you will get your first rib tonight," Sara said and gasped as she turned around. "Mum, what are you doing here? You are not supposed to be anywhere around me, don't you know that?" Sara said, backing toward the corner of the room, slipping Ryan behind her.

"I just came to see my grandchildren and my daughters, is all. Your children do not know anything about how my life has been since you have left. When I was told there was a BBQ today, I decided to take a chance and see my girls," Joan said and took a seat on the chaise lounge.

"You need to leave, Mum. You have lost all rights to see any of us, and you are trespassing."

"I will leave right after I see my grandchildren. I have that right as a grandmother," Joan said.

"You have no rights whatsoever. We don't belong to you any-more, and that goes for our children as well," Sara said with an edge to her voice that she had never heard from her older daughter before. "This is our home, and you were not invited, so you need to leave immediately. You ever touch my children again and I will kill you," Sara said and held her ground.

"You make like you are someone else's little girl, but it is time to come home now and bring that sister with you. You can leave the brats here," Joan Redding said.

"I am going no place with you. If you need money, get a job, or have one of your male friends to do so for you. Now you have ten seconds to get out of my house or I will scream," Sara said.

"I have seen all the places to have been to in the last years. For a fraction of what you have, you could be rid of me from this moment on," Joan said.

"I will pay you nothing. You did everything in your power to make sure that we lived our life in terror. Now you need to leave before I yell and get half a dozen ranch hands in here," Sara said.

"I will not leave here until I have what I came after, and that is enough money to keep me from having to work from now on," Joan said.

Sara, while holding Ryan, turned her back to her mother. "Get out of my house this minute."

"I want the money and to see my grandchildren," Joan said.

"No," Sara said and stood her ground.

"How would you like all the people here know how you came to be?" Joan seethed.

"They all already know. They all say that Saline and I are not responsible for our mother being a whore and a junkie. We have the most wonderful family in this world who loves us both just for being what we are. Now you need to leave."

Joan could feel her anger rising in her throat. Her daughter was no longer afraid of her. Now she was bold and protective of anyone she loved.

"I will leave when I have what I came here for," Joan said, causing Sara to hold closer to her baby son. "You stupid child, there will never be any place that is completely safe for them," Joan said, and the panicked looked on her daughter's face told her all she needed to know. Now she had her attention and planned on keeping it.

"You will never see my children. You stay away from then. You never wanted me. There is no reason you would want them. I am going out of this room and getting the sheriff. I am quite sure that he will be glad to see you again," Sara said with a tear-streaked face and physically shaking.

"If I have learned anything about this place, it is that it is over thirty minutes to the nearest town." Joan seethed.

"I don't know if you have noticed or not. But there is a very large party going on at present. The sheriff is currently standing by the swimming pool. I am sure he will be glad to see you. And Uncle Joseph is here as well," Sara said.

"You are lying. That son of a bitch would never visit the home of the woman who killed his precious nephew," Joan said.

"Go to the family room. You will find him there. You have just one more time to leave on your own power. It is your last." Sara took that last moment and stepped into Ryan's room and pushed the button. The heavy door was designed for just such instances as this. With she and Ryan safely inside, she called the kitchen to alert whoever answered that Joan Redding was in her and Scott's room and attempted to take her and Ryan.

John, Scott, Andrew, Alex, Riley, Mark, just to name a few, were the first to respond. They found a very angry Joan Redding.

"What the hell are you doing here?" John asked.

"Where is Sara?" Allison asked. "Answer me, you filth."

"Don't get your panties in a knot. She is in that room," Joan said.

"Sara, baby, Poppa is here. Scott is with me. It is safe to come out."

The way these people treated her bastard daughter made her ill. Then Ryan started to cry.

"Daddy, give that bitch to Randy. We have to open this by the floor release. Make sure Uncle Alex is still here." Scott then pulled the lock when Joan was out of sight. As he expected, Sara was on the floor. Ryan was crying by his mother's side.

"Come on, Ryan baby. Let Uncle Alex and Uncle Steven see about Momma," Allison said.

"Yes, mam, Nana," the tot said and kissed his grandmother's cheeks and went to play with the various other children.

Back in the master bedroom, Sara's eyes opened slowly. Then remembering what had just happened, she wanted to know where the children were.

"They are all fine, baby girl. Randy has taken her into custody," John said.

"How did she know she could get here so easily? She was in our room when I arrived. She could have taken Ryan, and we never would have known what happened to him. Where are the children, Scott? I need to see my children," Sara said, attempting to get up to look for them.

"You rest, baby girl. We will go and find them," Mark and Riley said. Within just a few minutes, the three Byers children were in the master bedroom with their mother. Sara trembled as she got each one of their children close to her. When she was feeling a little more secure about the whereabouts of those she loved, she asked about where her mother was.

Scott told her that she was being held in one of the spare bedrooms at the other side of the house.

"Children, Scott, Poppa, and everyone, will you follow me to where my mother is?" Sara asked.

"Are you sure you know what you are doing, Sara?" Uncle Alex asked.

"Absolutely," she said and held Ryan, and the other two followed. Sara took a breath before entering the room.

Joan was seated when she entered.

"Austin, Brad, Ryan, before Auntie Saline and I were adopted by Poppa and Momma, this woman was our momma. She hurt us, starved us, and didn't care about any of us. Remember her face, my angels. She is a very bad woman who hurts anyone she can get her hands on," Sara said.

Austin was the only one who took a step toward the woman, and with all his strength, he slapped her across the face. "You are the evil woman who gives our mommy bad dreams. You need to leave our home and never come back," Austin said and walked back to where his parents were.

"Please take her from here. The charge is trespassing."

The sheriff started walking to the backdoor so as not to interrupt the party any more than had already been done so.

"You spiteful bitch. What brings you to my family's home?" Joseph said.

"Your family. You know Sara is not your family. Don't think I will let it be known to the world when I get out of here," Joan said.

"You are going to jail from here. Assuming that there will be bail, you had better have someone who wants to bail you out. And should your son happen to show himself, he will be taken back to Germany and tried for the rape of his sister," Joseph said. "Get her out of my sight."

"Wait. This is the first time I have gotten to see my grandchildren. Can I have a moment with them?" Joan asked a little too sweetly.

"Kids, do you want to see this woman?" Scott asked.

"No, sir. She hurt Mommy. Come on, guys, let's go and play with our friends," Austin said, taking both Ryan's and Brad's hands and walking down the hallway.

"Don't ever come around me again," Sara said then added, "How did you know that you could come here today?"

"I will give you that information for a price," Joan said.

"What do you want from me for that information?" Sara asked. "Done. Who told you to come to our home while we are entertaining people from everywhere?"

"My doctor knows how desperate I have been to see my children and my grandchildren. I would love to live closer so I can see them every day. I see you have several houses here where I could potentially live so I may see my family every day," Joan said sweetly.

"You crazy bitch. Do you honestly for one second think that you will ever get to be part of our family now? You spent every day of mine and Saline's lives telling us your true feelings. Those feelings will never be known by our children. Now you have seen them. They don't want anything to do with you. So leave and never comeback," Sara said and left the room.

Joan was handcuffed and taken to the country lockup.

"Let's get you kids back where you can play with the other kids," John said.

Sara watched as the children were happily taken away by their grandfather. She walked back to their bedroom and sat on the bed for a moment. Rick had told her to come to the ranch, and she would be there. She had always felt so insulated from the world. But there was a party going on outside, and if she stayed inside too long, people would know something was wrong.

When she stood, she noticed her jewelry box was missing, along with a few other things that were obvious. She walked out to where the cars were parked and remembered the last car she had seen her in. She looked inside and found the things that were missing from their room and then some. Then she walked to Scott.

"Scott, she was robbing us. She took things from our room, and they are in her car," she said.

"I will find one of the deputies. And I want you to have a good time. Agreed?" Scott said.

"Agreed," she said and smiled. She hurried off and went to find her friends.

The rest of the afternoon was wonderful. Sara, Saline, Lauren, Linda, Amelia, and other nurses from other hospitals spent much time visiting and talking about the latest trip to North Africa the following week. As Sara was pregnant, all her doctors said no to her traveling. But Amy, Saline, Lauren, Uncle Alex, and Uncle Steven were some of those that would be going this time. It would be Saline's first time to travel as a nurse. She and Andrew had already made arrangements to meet.

Andrew had told her of his upcoming marriage to Sara Ferguson. She was so happy that her friend was going to be happy.

As the sun started to set, music started, and so did dancing. There were still hundreds of people present, still lots of eating, swimming, and other activities.

Since they had taken an interest working with the Red Cross and Dr. without Borders, many more nurses and doctors had become involved as well. They had so many stories to tell about nursing in other countries.

"I am so jealous of all of you going to Africa next week," Sara said.

"I can't wait. This is my first trip as an actual nurse. I think it is easier to learn by asking the doctors questions," Saline said.

"The next time that you go, I don't care what Rick says. I want in. I am a good nurse and speak three languages, and I know I can be of value," Amelia said.

"Then count on being on the next trip," Sara said. "I know I won't get to go until after the baby is born. Anyone for some swimming?"

The ladies raced to Sara and Scott's bedroom and changed into swimsuits. There were already several people in the huge swimming pool. The children were in a wading pool that was designed for young children.

Everyone looked around from one smiling face to another. There had never been a better time—good food, good fun, and good friends. There was no greater happiness that was known.

It was very late by the time the last of the people from the BBQ had left. Then another two hours to clean up from so many people had been in attendance.

"Sara, would you mind very much if the kids and I stayed tonight?" Amelia asked.

"Sure, no problem," she said.

"I heard that it was Rick who sent your mother out here, and I just really don't want to see him tonight," Amelia said.

"Not a problem. I know you had nothing to do with it and you and the kids are always welcome here. You know that."

Linda approached Sara and thanked her for such a wonderful day. She had been to the ranch several times before but never to one of the BBQs that they had.

A few days later, Scott and Sara were the ones to drive the Red Cross party to the airport.

"Don't worry, sis. I will be back in a few days and tell you everything," Saline said and hugged her sister, as did Amy and Lauren.

"All of you just be careful. I will miss you so much," Sara said.

Uncle Alex and Uncle Steven also hugged Sara and said how they would all take care of one another. When they boarded and the plane took off, only then did Scott and Sara leave to go back to the ranch.

"Don't you have to work today?" Sara asked.

"Yes, but I will take you home first," Scott said.

"Why don't you just ride in with your dad and I will take yours home?" Sara asked.

"Are you sure you are up to it?"

"Of course I am. I am feeling fine," Sara said.

Scott saw the logic in Sara's statement. "Okay. I will see you tonight then."

Sara drove the way home, listening to country music. She had to work the next two days, and then she was off for several days. Sara had always loved the spring of the year. There were berries to pick and preserve, gardens to plant, and the kids.

In North Africa, Andrew's plane was about to take off to return him to London. He and Saline had spent most of the days talking about his upcoming wedding. There had been injections to give to children, and there were people to dig water wells so that there would always be clean water. It had been a very busy week.

"I believe after I gotten most of the dust off me, I will sleep all the way home," Saline said.

"I was rather thinking the same. Will I see you at the wedding?" Andrew asked.

"Of course you will. I can hardly wait. Sarah is a lucky girl," Saline said.

Each kissed the other's cheeks and separated to go to their planes that would take them to their homes.

Lauren took her seat and leaned her head back and closed her eyes for a few minutes. "I am so tired I could sleep for a month."

"I know what you mean," Amy said.

"Are all of you ladies ready to go home?" Uncle Alex asked.

"More than ready," they all said. The weary travelers had had a successful trip and were all looking toward home.

In no time, they were airborne.

At Scott and Sara's house, several of the ladies of the ranch as well as Elaine and Linda were at the house, planning a homecoming party for their loved ones who had left just a week before. The TV was on, more for noise than anything. The children were happily playing in the family room. The women were all close by.

"Please excuse this urgent message from the north part of Africa. The team who travels frequently together crashed in the sea just off the northern coast of Africa. So far, no survivors have been recovered. We are withholding the names until the families have been notified."

"Sara, baby, what is wrong?" Lady Dickerson asked as Sara stared in disbelief at the announcement. "They just said the plane crashed, and there are no survivors."

All the women from around the room were now watching. Allison, Frances, Sara, and Elaine were sitting on the floor in front of the TV.

The phone rang, and Maria answered. "Byers residence."

"Is a member of the Byers family there?"

"Yes. There are also members of the Dickerson family, the Carmichael family, and the Quinton family as well. May I put this on intercom?"

"Yes, of course, I am calling to let you know that various members of your families were on the plane that crashed just over an hour ago. There are divers en route, but word has it that they are expecting no survivors. I am so sorry to deliver this information to you. If we have any further information, may we call again?"

"Yes, please do."

For hours, everyone sat in near silence as they continued to listen to the report. All the women were openly crying their hearts.

Linda went to the kitchen and fixed some tea and some coffee.

Amelia had been taking Amy's place at the hospital when she saw the report at lunchtime. She told the charge nurse she had to go to the Byers ranch and explained about the Red Cross flight. She walked down the hall to where she saw one of the doctors and explained what had happened. She asked if he may want to come out after his rounds were completed and maybe bring something to help them rest at such a time.

"Here is a prescription for Ativan, enough to last until I get there. I will hurry. Did you want me to let your husband know?" he asked.

"No. He would only cause problems, and right now, they don't need that kind of thing. Thank you, Dr. Middleton."

"See you in a bit, Amelia."

When Amelia arrived, there were over a hundred people in the family room, just hoping that someone would be found. John, Scott, and the boys had also arrived and were trying to see to the family.

"Sara, your doctor wants you to take this. He is afraid of you getting so upset that you lose the baby," Linda said and handed the medicine to her with a glass of tea. Amelia and Linda also medicated Maria, Allison, Frances, and Elaine.

Linda, Amelia, and some of the other ladies of the ranch went to the bedrooms and got pillows and put them on the floor where everyone was sitting.

Food and drinks were offered, but no one took but a bite or two. When Dr. Middleton arrived to the heart-wrenching scene, he quickly assessed the needs.

"Momma, Sara, you need to eat just a little. You are carrying a baby," Scott had made her a glass of milk and put the medication that her OB has suggested.

Then the report came that everyone had dreaded coming. "Several hours ago, there was a plane crash north of Africa. Several of the victims have been identified. Dr. Alex Carmichael of Texas. Dr. Steven Quinton, who had recently moved his practice from California to Dallas. Nurse Amy Morgan from Texas. Lady Lauren Dickerson, III, cousin to the queen of England. Lady Saline Alexander Byers, niece to the duke of Hamburg." They went on to name others on the flight.

About that time, Rick was at the hospital for his evening rounds and saw the nurses all crying. He looked at the TV and found the reason for their distress.

"Did no one think to call me?" he demanded.

"No. Dr. Middleton and Amelia went immediately to watch after the people who are affected."

"They are going to need a new doctor as their doctors have all been killed. So I am going over there now," Rick said.

"The charge nurse picked up the phone. "Amelia, this is Carol. Rick is on his way out there and is likely going to say some hurtful, stupid things. You may want to get someone to meet him at the gate."

"Thanks, Carol, I will do just that," Amelia said and walked over to John. "John, I hate to disturb you with so much that has happened, but Rick is on his way over here and has already started saying some really stupid things," Amelia said.

John put a hand on Amelia's shoulder in thanks. Like the rest of the family, John was quite upset. He had lost his brother-in-law, two girls he regarded as daughters, and dear friends. None of them needed Rick Powell's antics. He looked in at the women who remained in front of the TV set. Sara had her head in Allison's lap. Allison stroked her hair, and Sara held her hand. Frances sat on Allison's other side.

"John, I believe that we need to get the ladies away from the TV. They have been there for hours, and I have no doubt they are emotionally and physically exhausted," Jeff said.

"I believe you are right," John said and walked over to where the TV and turned it off. "I think that we all need to get something to eat and get some rest. It is going to be a very long next few days."

"I have made some soup that is ready," Linda said.

Everyone slowly got up and went to the dining table. There was no talking. Encouragement was the only thing that kept everyone eating.

The kitchen door opened, and in walked Rick Powell. No one acknowledged his presence in the least. When after a few minutes no one spoke to him, he decided that he would speak instead.

"It is good that all of you have decided to continue on with your lives," Rick said.

"I beg your pardon," Linda said. "What kind of an insensitive rat bastard are you? This family has just lost several close family and friends, and they are barely coping. You need to keep your stupid mouth shut or leave."

"I am here as their doctor as their doctors are now dead. I thought they could need something medically," Rick said.

"You are no one's doctor here. And Jeff is already here, so feel free to leave," Amelia said.

"I will stay just in case," Rick said.

"If you stay, you will keep your mouth shut," John said.

"I am going to go in and lie down for a little while. Can you call if you hear anything further?" Sara asked.

"I will come with you, if that is okay?" Allison said.

"I was hoping you would say that, Momma," Sara said, and the two women disappeared down the long hall that went to Scott and Sara's room.

Scott got up from his place at the table and went directly to Rick and took a firm hold of his arm. "You need to leave. I never thought you would have the nerve to show up out here again after sending Joan Redding out here. From now on, consider yourself unwelcome to the ranch."

"That woman has the right to see her children and grandchildren. Now she will never see one of them again," Rick said. With that, Scott slugged him and threw him out the door.

"Get off of my land and never come back," Scott said and slammed and locked the door.

Once Rick was gone, and as people finished eating, the TV was turned back on for more news.

It was four days before all the bodies were recovered. As complicated as the recovery was, the funerals for people from three different countries were even more so. It was decided that the funerals of those from the United States would take place first. Then three days following that, Lauren's funeral would take place at Westminster Abbey, and there would be a memorial service in Hamburg for Saline two days following.

Every member of every family and their friends were already spent from emotional exhaustion.

The family decided to have the funerals of Saline, Uncle Alex, Uncle Steven, and Amy as one service since they were all so close.

Scott had talked to Dr. Chambers the night before the funerals to ask if he thought that Sara was up to traveling for all the funerals. The two talked for several minutes and decided that she would likely need to have a cardiologist to travel with her. Dr. Quinton had spoken with one of the cardiologists at the hospital regarding her care if something happened to him. Dr. Eric Dane was a very well respected cardiologist out of Duke University. Dr. Quinton had given him a copy of her medical records.

Scott called him two days before they were to board the plane for England. The two had talked a few times but had never met face-to-face. He didn't really know how long to tell him they would be gone, but would do his best to find out.

Scott told him that they would be taking a diplomatic flight and gave him the gate number and time it would leave.

Even though Rick had been thrown out of Sara and Scott's house, he attended the funeral as his ever present need to be around the powerful family. Amelia had no thoughts about Rick wanting to attend the funeral, so she went to the ranch first.

She went in the kitchen door as she had done since she had first started her friendship with the family. Allison was sitting at the table in the kitchen by herself. Amelia walked over and hugged Allison warmly.

"I wish there was something I could do to help," Amelia said.

"It helps that you are here," Allison said.

"Momma, it is about time for us to get started," Riley said.

"Momma, Charles and Andrew have just arrived," Scott said.

Allison stood and walked over and hugged Andrew and shook hands with Charles. "Thank you both for being here today. Amelia,

I know you have met Andrew when he was here for the BBQ, but I don't think you have met the Prince of Wales, Charles."

"Nice to meet you, Your Royal Highness. Good to see you again, Andrew," Amelia said.

All exchanged pleasantries. Soon everyone was in cars on the way to the funeral home.

Several rows were designated as being reserved for family members. Amelia and Elaine were invited to sit with the family, along with Charles and Andrew.

When Rick saw that Amelia was arriving with the family, he attempted to move to sit with her, but because of increased security, he was not allowed to move once seated. Uncle Joseph had arrived the night before and was beside himself with grief over the loss of his cherished niece. Over the last few years, Joseph had come to know a few things that were important in life. He had always been wealthy and well-known, but until he had his two nieces so close, he had never known the love of a family. Now it was the most important thing in his life.

No one had even mentioned the thought that there would be press coverage. It was a given. Two titled women from different countries on a plane doing humanitarian work. No one answered questions before the funerals began.

Frances, Allison, and Sara were beside themselves with grief, but having been raised in private schools, Frances and Sara maintained an unhealthy control of their emotions. The combined service telling of all the members and their selfless contribution to help others seemed the only way to honor those who spent their last moments of life in one another's company, and it was completely appreciated. It also made the service last longer.

Sara began to feel pressure in her chest before they arrived but didn't want to complain. As they began to file out nearly two hours later, Sara had to steady herself. Then she saw Frances began to slide to the ground but was kept from falling by one of their sons and John. Sara immediately responded to her apparent distress, forgetting about the pressure she had been feeling.

"Frances, do you need to sit down?" John asked.

"If you could just help me to the car, I think I will be fine," she answered.

The men quickly ushered Frances, surrounded by people from their party and personnel from the funeral home. With all the mourners, the reporters were unable to tell that there had been any kind of an incident.

Between the funeral home and the ranch, Frances sobbed her heart out regarding the huge loss in the arms of her husband. By the time they arrived back, she felt a little better.

When they arrived at the main house, Amelia suggested she may want to go to the hospital just to make sure she was well, but Frances said that likely she just needed to lie down for a little while. When Amelia was certain she was feeling the huge loss of the last week, she left the room to let her rest.

The afternoon was full of most of the people from the funeral paying their respects. After several hours on her feet, thanking people for their presence, Sara went upstairs to Saline's old room. She looked at the things that remained on her desk for a few minutes then walked over to the bed, picking up one of Saline's pillows, thinking that breathing in the lingering scent of her sister would make her feel like a part of her remained. When she felt no relief, she fell into the bed and held the pillow to her chest and cried.

About an hour later, Elaine found her friend still crying hard and worried for the effect such extreme emotional distress would have on her now, with her well into her second trimester of pregnancy.

"Sara," Elaine said softly. "I know what you must be feeling, but for your sake and that of your baby, you need to eat something. You haven't eaten all day long."

Suddenly everything took so much effort. Her body ached as though the grief she felt had broken half of the bones in her body. She sat up and took a painful breath.

"I know you are right, Elaine, but I just can't go back down there right now. I know that I should check on Momma and Frances and the boys," she said and her words trailed off.

"Everyone is holding everyone else together right how. But what if something happens to your baby because you haven't eaten? We can take the back stairs to the kitchen and avoid so many people."

Sara managed a sad smile and agreed. "Elaine. Can I tell you something?"

"You can tell me anything."

"I was going to tell Saline first. I am having a little girl. She really wanted a niece," she said and fell into Elaine's arms and sobbed like a child.

John stood at the door to Saline's room when he heard Sara crying. "Baby girl," he said gently. He walked over to where Elaine still held her friend in her arms. "Elaine, I believe Maria has made something for her, Frances, Allison, and yourself, so you can eat upstairs and rest a bit. Would you mind checking that for me?"

"Yes, sir, of course."

"Poppa, I am so sorry," she said.

"You have nothing to be sorry for," he said.

"If things had been different, if you had never known me, so much would be different. Everyone was on that plane fulfilling my dream. I brought everyone together, and now they are gone." Sara sobbed.

The intense sadness in the green orbs spoke to him in volumes.

"Baby girl, listen to Poppa. You had no more than a few days left to live when you came here, and what would Saline have become? She was an angry young girl when she came here. She hated everything and everyone in the world, except you. You lived half a world away, and your love carried her through life. Rather than starving, cold, and alone in the dark, she died with friends. She was happy. When you think of Lauren, think of how glad she was when the two of you found each other again. Alex was my brother for most of my life. We were best of friends. When Steve came here for you, he also gave Alex a few more years with us. They were doing what they loved for people who wouldn't have had a chance to live, as was Amy.

"We have three grandsons and are expecting what I understand to be our granddaughter. I can't imagine how anyone could fault you for the things you have done for this family. You will always be our baby girl, and there is no one in this house who doesn't love you. God brought you to us. I believe that with all my soul, the way that he brought us to you." John hugged her for a moment and kissed her forehead. "Now, go wash your face so all my girls can relax for a few minutes and eat something."

Sara stood and looked at John, who still sat on the side of the bed. She softly put a hand his shoulder. "I love all of you too, Poppa," she said then stopped and searched his face as though someone had whispered something to her. The look on her face, he had never seen before. "I have to save you, Poppa." Then as though she had never said the words, she walked to the bathroom and did as Poppa had told her.

John started to ask her about what she had just said, but he knew that the week had been a nightmare for everyone, and she had to be completely exhausted. He walked down to let Allison and Frances know that they were being brought something to eat in a few minutes.

Before long, Elaine, Amelia, and Maria came upstairs with a pot of hot soup and a fresh garden salad and all the trimmings. The six women had formed a closer bond over the last week and knew that they still had two more funerals to attend in two different countries.

In England, the funeral of a royal was traditionally a state event, much like a wedding, but solemn. Hundreds of thousands of people gathered in the streets of London lined the route from Buckingham Palace to Westminster Abbey. Sara and Saline had gotten up early to watch the royal wedding when Prince Charles had wed the lovely Lady Diana Spencer in St. Paul's Cathedral, with the glass coach, the horses, and the smiling faces of the English people. Lauren had gone to London for a visit to attend the royal wedding and returned in time for school a few weeks later. Although invited, Sara and Saline decided to send their regards with Lauren and watch the event unfold on TV.

Lauren's funeral would not be a happy event. Since her, Sara and Saline had all become so close they tended to be in newspapers if something was newsworthy. And since the wedding, the new princess had kept reporters busy with everything she did. Sara had been sitting on the floor while watching a news report a few days before they wed when Diana had been reduced to tears at a polo match. Sara had tears in her own eyes knowing how the young woman must be feeling. Overnight, she had gone from being a kindergarten teacher to being the future queen and then having Prince William a year later.

Sara wondered if they would be seeing the new princess at the funeral but brushed the thought from her mind because of the sadness she once again felt.

CHAPTER 17

Saline's Promise

Over the next few days, everyone from the family traveled to London first for Lauren's funeral at Westminster Abbey. Next, for her uncle, Sara asked Scott if he would mind traveling on to Hamburg to the memorial service for Saline. He agreed because he thought it would help them all through the difficult time without those that they loved.

Elaine had accompanied the family to London and to Hamburg as a member of the family. Dr. Quinton had spoken to a cardiologist from Tyler a few months before his death. Dr. Eric Dane had graduated from Duke University a few years before. He had specialized in the long-term effects of rheumatic fever.

Steve had been so impressed on his research that he had requested to speak with him regarding a patient of his. Dr. Dane had heard of Dr. Steven Quinton, of course, as one of the foremost authorities on rheumatic fever and mitral valve disease.

He brought with him only the parts of Sara's records that involved her heart. He reasoned that there was no reason for someone she worked with having knowledge of something that didn't pertain to her situation.

He told him about how they had put tetracycline in the chest and pericardial tubes when she was eight, and everything that involved her heart. Dr. Dane was receptive to the older man, hearing everything he was saying and the way he had said it. He knew that there was a reason that he taken not only a medical interest but also a protective role in her life.

Then there was something that might be of interest, and that was about her family being related to the German aristocracy.

When the conversation had ended, Steve had no question that this was the cardiologist he had been looking for in case something happened to him.

Eric arrived at the airport to board the royal flight that would take Lord and Lady Dickerson, the entire Byers family including Mark and Maria St. Clair, Elaine Rogers, and him to London and finally to Germany.

Eric knew Sara from the hospital as a nurse. She was gifted. Patients responded well to her. At first, when she had begun to work on the telemetry unit, if she thought there was something wrong with a patient's progress, she would not stop calling until the doctor would pay attention. At first, the doctors thought her to be an irritation, but one by one began to regard her as having some form of insight.

Sara had called Eric one day three times within a few minutes about his patient because of a feeling she had. He had just said all three times to call if she had figured it out. Five minutes, he had gotten a call that Sara's patient had arrested. Since that time, everyone had listened.

Eric had asked Sara how she knew something was wrong. She answered that she didn't know, that she just knew. He knew that she was only an LVN but was studying to be an RN, so if he saw something educational that may help her in her studies, he made a point of letting her know. The only way he had ever seen her was in a nurse's uniform with her hair in a pony tail. Now in complete contrast, she was dressed in all black, with her hair down.

Scott had called him a couple of days before about possibly accompanying them to Europe for a funeral but had not prepared him for whom he walked into boarding the plane. There were no rows of seats like found on commercial flights, but rather seats like would be found in a living room.

Eric had seen several of the people on the plane he had seen on TV before. John and Scott Byers were seen from time to time regarding their oil company. Lord and Lady Dickerson had also been on the TV several times both of family friends to the Byers family and as being related to the queen.

Scott looked up and saw Dr. Dane standing at the front of the cabin. He walked up to him and shook his hand and introduced himself. It was a few minutes before they took off, so he turned to the pilot, who was standing not far from him.

"Will it be all right if I step off the plane to speak with Dr. Dane for a moment?" he asked.

"Yes, Your Grace. It will be a few minutes before we take off," the pilot said.

"Thank you," Scott said and went out the door of the plane.

"Dr. Dane, I am sorry if this is inconvenient for you," Scott said. "It has been a very long week for us all. Sara is under the care of a cardiologist, but he died a few days ago, along with my uncle, who is her doctor as well."

"Yes. I spoke with Dr. Quinton a few months ago regarding her. He has given me all the information regarding her medical problems. Does she know that he has spoken to me?" he asked.

"I don't believe so. But she does speak very highly of you. And Dr. Quinton was very impressed with you as well. He had no children and has regarded Sara as a daughter," Scott said.

"I got the impression that he cared about her deeply," Eric said. "And please, call me Eric."

"And I am Scott," Scott said and heard a familiar loud voice. "Please forgive what is about to happen. And he said to give you this as well."

Eric turned toward the man who was yelling for Scott to stop. "Rick, we told you that you are not accompanying us anyplace. Now we are about to board."

"I have already bought my ticket. There is no reason for me not to go. I need to know where to go to board. It is a thirteen-hour flight, and I am sure Sara needs me close by," Rick said.

"Rick, I cannot stop you from going to Europe, but it will not be to travel with us," Scott said.

"According to the time that the plane is to leave, this is my flight. American Airlines flight 472, see. Dr. Carmichael and Dr. Quinton are no longer with us, God rest their souls, and Sara needs a physician near who knows a little about her," Rick said. "I have been trying to see her for the last few days since she is my patient now."

"Yes, I heard you were trying to come to our home. Rick, if you are going to London, you had better find your flight. We are about to take off, if you will excuse us," Scott said.

"This is my flight, I believe, I said," Rick said and began to follow Scott.

"This is a diplomatic flight, Rick. You can't get a ticket for it, so if you will excuse us."

"Scott, Sara needs a physician to go with her. I am sure Dr. Quinton would have insisted," Rick said, following Scott.

"Yes, he would have. I have her cardiologist right here. So, go catch your plane," Scott said.

"I am accompanying my patient. You want someone who knows something about Sara, not one who does not even know her."

Eric was irritated at the middle-aged man butting his nose in.

"I have known Sara quite some time, sir. We work together at St. Mary's Hospital in Tyler. And for your information, Dr. Quinton spoke with me personally in my office regarding Sara. There is nothing in her medical chart I don't know.

"Now this family has been through a lot in the last few days. And I need to board and see to my patients before takeoff. If you will excuse us, I believe all three of us have a flight to catch," Eric said.

"I will be boarding this plane with my patient."

At the door of the plane, the pilot made sure that only the right people entered. "Dr. Dane, Your Grace. Excuse me, sir. You are on the wrong plane. You need to step away."

"I am Dr. Richard Powell, and Sara Byers is my patient. I will be boarding to monitor her on the trip to Europe. I insist."

"No, you won't. Please leave before I have you arrested," the pilot said.

"I have a ticket to go to London," Rick said, showing his ticket.

"Then I would suggest that you find the right plane. This is Her Majesty's flight, and only the people who have clearance to board may do so," the pilot said.

"Then I would suggest you call and get me cleared. Mrs. Byers needs me to fly with her," Rick said.

"Step back, sir. If you try to board this plane, you will be arrested," the pilot said and pushed Rick as hard as he could, causing him to lose balance and fall to the ground. A man who was coming up behind him jerked him to his feet.

"Sir, you need to come with me. This plane cannot take off with you in here," the man said and began half dragging Rick back up to where people were happily waving as their family members take off. "My suggestion to you would be to find your flight and board," the man said and walked off.

Rick stood, furious as he saw the plane pull away from the gate. It was indeed not American Airlines. He had planned on taking the same plane as the Byers family had. He had looked up what flights were destined to fly to London that day and used process by elimination to book the flight.

He had never wanted anything to happen to Dr. Carmichael but had been very busy since he and the others on the plane that had crashed had been killed.

Then Amelia had said to him that she had been asked if she wanted to go. She had declined the invitation because of her children but said her prayers were with the entire family.

Rick, on the other hand, had not been asked to go but chose to invite himself as the replacement for Alex Carmichael and Steven Quinton. He was angry that instead of asking him to go as the doctor who knew more about Sara, they invited a cardiologist to go with them. Rick turned and went to the gate that was on his ticket and boarded the crowded plane. When he had bought his ticket, he hadn't noticed that he would be sitting in coach. He told the woman who was seating the passengers that he had wanted a seat in first class for the very long flight but had been told that the plane was sold out and he would have to sit in coach.

He had no idea what hotel the Byers family would be staying in in London, but he knew when and where the funeral would be. He would catch Sara there and speak with her regarding becoming her doctor and then fly with her to Germany as he had planned in the first place.

After the plane was well in the air, Eric undid his seatbelt and walked back to Sara, who was seated looking out the window. She had noticed little since she had gotten on the plane. Eric had heard her mention her beautiful sister several times. He could tell she admired and loved her and could see the pain in her eyes as she looked out the window.

"Sara?" he said.

Sara looked up at him. "Dr. Dane. What are you doing here?" she asked.

"A few months ago, Dr. Quinton asked if I would consider becoming your cardiologist if something happened to him. If that is okay with you, of course," he said. She only continued to look at him. "What do you think?" he asked, turning it into a question.

"Okay," she said simply. "I confess I have not thought about anything lately," she said and looked out the window again.

"I didn't know you were expecting a baby," he said.

"Yes. It is our fourth. I hope that I am not being a bother in your having to travel with us. You are always so busy," she said.

"Not at all. How are you feeling?" he asked.

She only looked at him. Steve had warned him that she would never lie to him, only not answer.

"Are you hurting right now?" he asked.

"I really don't feel anything. My sister, best friend, my boss, and Uncle Alex and Uncle Steven are all gone," she said.

"That is a huge loss, Sara. I can't imagine what I would feel in the same instance. And I don't want to seem overbearing, but I want to make sure you are well," he said.

"Thank you," she whispered. "I promise I will not keep anything from you. I am very glad that you are here. I was afraid that somehow Dr. Powell would be here. He is so overbearing that he makes me afraid. He is not even our doctor. But I know that Scott wanted a doctor with us after what happened before. Have you met my Scott?"

"I have talked to him on the phone before but just met him a little bit ago," he said.

"Would you like to meet the others on the plane?" she asked.

"I am sure I will be meeting them," he said.

"I see that Eric found you, baby girl," Scott said.

"I think I was being rude," Sara said as Scott took his seat back beside her.

"How is that?" he asked.

"I didn't even know he was here," she said, blushing prettily.

"A hanging offense indeed," Scott said.

"Would you mind making sure he knows everyone?" she asked.

"Sure. Come along, Eric," he said, and the two walked toward the front of the cabin. Scott introduced him to his parents and brothers, then Mark and Maria. They talked for a little while.

Next, he introduced Eric to Elaine, who was sitting with Charles and Andrew. He had no idea he would be meeting royalty. They all talked for a few minutes. The Dickersons walked to where they stood and introduced themselves. After talking for a few minutes, they took a seat across from John and Allison.

After a few more minutes of meeting another handful of people who traveled with them, they went back to where Sara was seated.

The first meal was being served to everyone. When he was sure everyone was engrossed in their meal, Eric had to ask a couple of questions.

"I have to say, I spent most of my adult life attending college and then medical school. So I am not up to date on most things.

So I will just ask. How does a family from Texas come to know the royal family?"

"It had nothing to do with Texas," Scott said. "Sara attended school in Wales as a child. Lord and Lady Dickerson's daughter, Lauren, went to school with her. Sara's uncle, the duke of Hamburg, had to fly back yesterday."

"I don't recall which one was their daughter," Eric said. He noticed that Sara put her head back against the seat and looked out the window again.

"She was one of those killed in the plane crash," Scott said.

"Oh. I am so sorry. Like I said, I have spent most of my adult life in school," he said.

"It is okay, Dr. Dane. I haven't slept well in the last few days. I think I will go to lie down for a bit," she said, absentmindedly rubbing her belly.

"Are you really okay, baby girl?" Scott asked.

"I will be," she said. "I will see both of you in a bit."

"I had no idea that she was anything but a lovely young woman, Scott. Her patients love her," he said.

Elaine approached where Scott and Eric sat. "I am going back with her for a few minutes Scott. Okay?"

"Yeah, go ahead, Elaine. Thanks," he said.

"There are beds on the plane?" Eric asked.

"What can I say? When you travel with royalty, it is different," Scott said.

Charles and Andrew came back to join them after Elaine and Sara had left the cabin.

"I suppose this would be the same as borrowing my mum's car," Andrew said. The four men sat and talked for a while.

Elaine came back to the front cabin. Scott got up to see if Sara needed something. "Excuse me for a moment," Scott said.

Elaine took his seat for a minute. Allison then walked back to join Sara.

Allison knew the same sense of loss of her beloved brother Alex. It had been a terrible shock to know that she would never see her big brother again. They had been so close. But he had loved what he and Steve had been doing over the last few years. He had told everyone a million times that he found the reason he became a physician. He had loved practicing in the Country Hospital, but the people in clinics around the world had never had someone to see about their health. He now practiced with people who had never heard of simple things like Tylenol.

Allison laid her head down and silently started to cry. She had always had Alex in her life. When they lost their parents, she still had her big brother. She had never known a loss so profound with the exception of their little girl so long ago. With the service, and having to travel to London for Lauren's funeral, she hadn't had a chance for her emotions to catch up with her. Now, on the long flight, she was feeling everything that she had lost.

"Momma?" Allison heard the soft voice of her daughter-in-law. She turned to see Sara, who had sat on the floor next to her.

"Sara, baby. Are you okay?" she asked.

Sara merely nodded, but her look of thought bore deep into Allison's soul. She then sat on the side of Allison's bunk and pulled Allison into her arms, much like she would have one of her boys. Allison began to cry on Sara's shoulder as Sara and Saline had done in the reverse so many times before. Allison was wounded. Sara knew all too well how she felt. She knew that all you had to do after you lost something was to stand still, and it would hit you, harder and faster than life. Allison cried for nearly an hour before she pulled away, feeling spent and exhausted.

"Sara, I didn't mean to—" she said, but the young woman put her fingers to her lips.

"How many times have I cried on your shoulder? You were there for me when no one else wanted me. You told us time and again that we were worth fighting for. You knew that I was not really what decent people would refer to as pure, but you loved me anyway. I would die for you in a heartbeat without regret if need be. But right now, I am glad that I can be here for you to have a shoulder to cry on.

"When we cry alone in the dark, we lose a little of ourselves. That is something you never get back. Uncle Alex, Amy, Saline,

Uncle Steven, and Lauren were precious to all of us. Why should we have to cry silently alone?"

"I am so glad, so blessed to have you. You have lost so much, and still you are able to walk through life seeing something good in everything. I love you so much," Allison said.

"I love you too, Momma. Sleep now?" Sara asked. "I will be right here with you."

The comfort that the younger woman gave her was warmth that made her feel like she could sleep for a week.

"Then we can watch out for each other," Allison said. With that, both women slept.

While the Byerses and Dickersons were on the flight to London, another few family members were just discovering what had taken place several days before. Joan, Oscar, and Tommy were awakened by a knock on the door of the farmhouse. Joan went to the door to find a reporter who wanted a story about how she felt about the death of her daughter.

"What are you talking about?" Joan said.

"Your daughter Saline was killed in a plane crash a few days ago. You were not aware?" the reporter said.

"No. Those people don't keep me up to date on what happens with my daughters, and I have never even seen my grandchildren," Joan said and turned her back to the reporter at the door. She used her fingernail to poke her eye so she would have tears in them when she turned back around.

"It has been on the news since the accident happened. The Red Cross plane went down in sea above North Africa."

"What was my daughter doing on a Red Cross flight?" Joan yelled.

"Both of your daughters are frequently on flights to various places to offer medical aid with their uncle," the reporter explained.

"The duke of Hamburg is flying around on a mercy flight?" Joan spat back.

"No. Their uncles Dr. Alex Carmichael and Dr. Steven Quinton traveled with them. Both Sara and Saline are nurses now and are revered by those whom they assist."

Joan thought for a moment before she spoke. "I always taught my daughters to care for others, but I never thought they would travel to other countries to do so. That surprises me. Now I have lost my beautiful Saline," she said and turned and appeared to be crying.

"I am so sorry, Mrs. Redding. Is there a better time I could come back?" the reporter said.

"Yes. Give me until tomorrow. This is so hard to process. I didn't even attend her funeral because I work so much," Joan said and closed the door quickly. She watched as the reporter left the property, then turned to tell Tommy and Oscar they had a window of opportunity.

"Saline is dead?" Tommy said. "That means that there is no one left except me and Sophie."

"And with Sophie still in the Looney bin, that leaves you. Your uncle will have to eat his words," Joan said.

"Except that he wanted you to be in jail the last time you saw him," Oscar quipped.

"Things have changed. I look forward to being back in line," Tommy said.

Joan turned on the TV set and tried to find any word about Saline's death. The morning news program could not stop talking about the plane crash that had involved so many countries. Joan also learned that along with Saline, Sara had also lost her friend from the UK, Lady Lauren Dickerson.

"I believe we must be looking more favorable to Sara now that her precious sister and friend are gone. Not to mention your nosey grandmother that died a few years ago. She likely would like to have some blood relatives around her about now," Joan said.

The three of them continued to watch the program and only rarely did anyone see Sara for more than a few seconds. Then the camera stopped with both she and the duke arm in arm, talking, following the funeral. But it was not until they embraced and he opened the car door for his "niece" that the reporter stated that she would be the next one to head the Alexander family.

Tommy yelled and put his fist through the wall. "She is not even related to him, and he knows it. She cannot do this to me," he ranted.

Joan knew she had found a way to enrich her life once again.

The plane touched down in London two hours before the sun rose, making the airport a virtual ghost town except for arriving transatlantic flights. Austin, Brad, and Ryan had slept the entire flight after they had eaten. Now the three were wide awake and ready to move around. Sara leaned down to pick up Ryan and carry him off the plane, but Andrew picked up the tot, remembering years before when she had lost their baby because of the stress she had been under.

Austin and Brad took the offered hands of their grandparents to walk off the plane. There were several cars waiting for the passengers when they arrived, and there was the hearse that was to take Lauren's casket. No one seemed able to move while they watched the attendants load the casket and finally drive away. Then everyone went to the various different cars that were available. As they would only be in London for three days, before traveling on to Germany, the Dickersons urged the party to stay at Kensington Palace. The funeral the following day would be held in Westminster Abbey.

Dr. Eric Dane discovered very early in the journey that he was completely out of his element. His father had been a physician before him, thus he had gone to medical school. So he was considered to be well off. But when he discovered that Sara, the quiet, young LVN, was considered to be part of a royal family was blowing his mind. Not to mention her being part of one of the wealthiest families in Texas. He had spent the entire flight having conversations with two princes, a lord, two ladies, and a family of multimillionaire oilmen/ranchers. He had started out talking to Mark and Maria St. Clair as a means of easing into talking to others only to find that he not only worked for John Byers but was also independently wealthy in his own right.

He had never thought of people of this class as being warm people. In general, he was like most physicians and felt he was at the top of the food chain in the hospital, but now he felt quite foolish.

The sadness in the faces of every person on the plane told of love and deep feelings of loss that no amount of money could ever change. It was a lesson he would remember always.

Elaine had accompanied him to the waiting cars and got in with him.

"Feeling a little uneasy?" she asked.

"You have no idea," he answered.

"I do actually. When Sara and I first met, we were friends from the start. It was only after knowing her for a few months that she asked if I wanted to join her family for supper because my husband was out of town. Have you ever been to the ranch?" she asked.

"No. I have only talked to Scott over the phone."

"It is a town of its own. You can't imagine. That is when I found that Sara was in the line of succession to be an aristocratic duchess in Hamburg. She is to follow her uncle," Elaine said.

"I had no idea," he said. "She is a royal?"

"Not exactly, but Lauren was. They met when they were five years old," Elaine continued to explain things to put Eric a little more at ease with his surroundings.

"We are both studying to become registered nurses. I don't know how Sara does it all with three kids, but she does. On our trips with the Red Cross, we have extra study time in flight, and that helps."

"My wife and I have twin daughters and a son. I know that we are both in our mid thirties. To think that Sara has grade-school kids, she must have been very young when they married," Eric said, knowing that she was currently twenty-four years old.

"They are an ideal couple. Don't think badly of her if she seems distant. She risked her life time and again to save her sister. This week has been very hard on her," Elaine said.

"Does she have other brothers and sisters, or her own parents?" he asked. After his question, he could feel Elaine's eyes on him.

"There is a doctor at the Country Hospital, the hospital built by Dr. Carmichael. This doctor is forever asking questions about

Sara, Saline, and everyone else in the family. He doesn't care so much about her well-being as he does about his position." Elaine paused a moment before she continued, "I can tell your curiosity is not like his."

Eric thought about the man at the airport. "Is that Rick?"

"You know him?"

"No. When Scott and I stepped off the plane, a man named Rick tried to muscle himself onto the plane and was escorted off the skywalk," he said.

"Sounds like Dr. Rick Powell. He muscled himself into Sara's hospital room one time when she had a pericardial drain and scared her by grabbing her hand so badly that she ran to her jeep and drove home. It nearly cost her, her life," Elaine said. "It scares me not having Dr. Carmichael to keep him in line now."

The car stopped, and the door was opened.

"Please don't let anyone know what I have told you. I hope I can trust you," Elaine said in more like a command than a request.

"Don't worry, little one. I don't kiss and tell," he said with a good-natured wink and look that conveyed trust with the two medical professionals. He stepped out of the car and put his hand down to assist Elaine. "Where are we?"

"Kensington Palace. Lord and Lady Dickerson have an apartment here. We will be staying here while we are in London."

"You are not related to these people, are you?" he asked.

"Of course not. I told you that Sara and I met a few years ago."

Over the next few hours, the families were escorted to where they could relax before the noon meal was to be served and the official order for the state funeral for Lady Lauren.

Eric listened as people spoke and responded in a kind that put people at ease. Following the meal, he found Andrew and requested a moment of his time. He really didn't know what his role was as far as being with people he had heard of only on the TV set.

He found the younger man very helpful indeed. Telling him if he chose to attend the funeral, he would be staying with the family members he had traveled with.

"You will likely find things very formal as both Lauren and Sara were both presented at court at the age of twelve. Sara will know her role. As you are not a member of Her Majesty's court, you are not held to the same standard," Andrew explained.

"All the same, I don't want to be a burden for the family now. Tell me please, what I should know?" Eric asked.

"Very well then. In private quarters, you may call us by our names as you have been, but in public, it is Your Royal Highness. Anyone with the title of a lord or lady is referred to as my lord or my lady. Sara is Her Grace and as her husband, Scott, is His Grace."

"I thought Sara was a lady," Eric said.

"She is a lady, but she is also the proximate heir to the aristocracy in Hamburg, so her title is that of a duchess. If you are introduced to anyone with a title, you would nod your head at the neck, thusly." Andrew indicated. "And don't reach for a hand unless it is offered. Should you meet Mummy, her title of course is Your Majesty. You never walk in front of her or show her your back. Chances are, you won't have to worry about any of that. Do you attend church at home?" Andrew asked.

"All Saints' Episcopal in Tyler. Why?" Eric asked.

"Westminster Abbey is the Church of England. It is essentially the same."

"Will it be a large service?"

"Do you watch very much of TV?" Andrew asked.

"I went to college, medical school, and was in private practice by the time I was thirty-one. I suppose I am a little retarded when it comes to the TV lately," Eric said, looking at his toes and thinking of every nurse he had ever given a hard time to.

"Nonsense. Never look at your toes," Andrew said good-naturedly.

"The Byers family knows all this?"

"They didn't until Scott married Sara," Andrew answered.

"How does a Texas oilman's son meet a German duchess?"

"No one knew she was a duchess at that time, not until after the Byers family adopted the three of them," Andrew answered.

"The three of them?"

"Sara, Saline, and their baby brother, Jody," Andrew said.

"There is another brother living with the Byers family?" Eric said.

"No. There was an incident at the ranch. The mother found the kids, and Jody died at three years old as a result. But I wouldn't mention that," Andrew warned.

"I get the feeling that people tend to step out of their comfort zones to try to protect this girl," Eric said.

"Wouldn't you?" Andrew said seriously. "Saline was a very dear friend. She was fifteen when I met her and Sara. We kept in touch since that time. She said that her Uncle Steven gave you Sara's medical records. Have you read them?"

"He told me of her past history of complications of rheumatic fever. But I confess I have not sat down and read the entire file. I hadn't even noticed she was pregnant until I saw her dressed on the plane," Eric said absentmindedly.

"Do you have any of those records, Eric?" Andrew asked. When he saw him nod, he continued. "Maybe you should look at them," Andrew said, standing and patting Eric's shoulder. "You will do well. Have no fear." He gave a reassuring smile then walked from the room.

Andrew heard the door close quietly and knew he was going to look at the medical records.

Eric had been reading for several hours when two knocks came at the door, and the door opened, nearly knocking Eric from his chair as he was so deep in thought.

"Dr. Dane?" came the voice of a uniformed attendant.

"Yes," he answered.

"Dinner is served, if you would like to come with me. It will be served in the formal dining room, sir," the attendant said.

"I will be right with you. May I splash some water on my face?" he asked.

"Of course."

Eric quickly did as he had said and, out of habit, put his suit coat back on. "Am I holding you up?" he asked.

"Of course not, sir. I am here for your convenience. There is no hidden agenda, I assure you," the man said, smiling.

"Will I know everyone who is eating?" he asked.

"His Royal Highness, Prince Andrew, asked that you be seated near him," the man answered.

"Thank God," Eric muttered, causing the attendant to chuckle a little. He was led into a room where several people were talking. Most he knew from the plane. He walked over to where he saw Sara, Elaine, and Maria talking together.

"Good evening, ladies," Eric said.

"Dr. Dane," Sara said. "Did you get to rest a little?"

"Yes. I did. I am afraid I spent most of the flight talking to everyone on the plane, and a nap was just what I needed. And please call me Eric. Did you get some rest as well?" he asked.

"No, she didn't. She has been playing chess with me, and might I add, kicking my bottom," Mark said.

"I told you, you can't beat a well-trained opponent," Sara said proudly.

"I don't know how they play that stupid game. I can feel their brain cells working harder than the worst day in nursing school," Maria said. "They have neither one of them made a move in over an hour."

"Chess? You have been playing chess all afternoon?" Eric asked.

"Since right after lunch. Riley told me I couldn't beat her, and I bet him I could," Mark explained.

"Who is winning?" he asked.

"She is," every one said in unison.

"It has been six hours since lunch, and you have been playing games of chess all this time?" Eric questioned.

"One game," Sara said. "And like I said, when I taught you to play, you will never beat me."

"Okay. You two get on the same side of the fence for a while and stop talking about that game," came the authoritative voice of John

Byers. "Baby girl, didn't I tell you that you have to let the boys win every now and then or they start feeling weak?"

The way that John looked at the young woman he had basically saved the life of was one of pride.

In his studying of her medical file that had been provided by Dr. Steven Quinton, it had knocked the air out of him several times. At five feet six inches tall, she was considered to be average in height, but her bones in her chest had shown signs of healed fractures at different times. And according to the same file, her mother, brothers, and sisters were all at least six feet tall. Then there was a detailed account of Dr. Carmichael's findings when she was sixteen. It had brought tears to his eyes thinking of the one-hundred-pound girl putting herself time and again between her stepfather and her young siblings again and again, starved nearly to death. At that point in the file, there was a handwritten note from Dr. Quinton that if this was not something he was going to be able to consider, to stop reading and return it to him only.

He read that she had again put herself between Maria and her stepfather and had been wounded herself and killed her stepfather. It was then that the knock on the door came.

Andrew could tell from the way that he watched the people around the young woman in the room that he had read about her. And yes, he would be there for her now.

"Come along, baby girl. You need to move around a little bit. Why don't you show Eric how he is to do things around here? He is looking a little shy," John said, kissing her cheek.

"Yes, Poppa," she said and smiled radiantly at him. "Come along, Eric." She put her hand out, and as Andrew had told him, he took hold. "I haven't been very social. I am sorry. How do you know my Scott?" she asked, walking with him.

"I only just met him in person today. Dr. Quinton had told him that if something were to happen to him, he would like if I looked after you. But I leave that to you," he said.

She stopped for a minute. "Me? Why me?" she asked.

"Don't you say who takes care of you?" he asked.

"No, Uncle Alex. But he is not here any…" she trailed off.

"Dr. Quinton asked me, now I am asking you," he said. Her eyes searched his. She missed nothing. Her decisions had made the difference in life and death for her family.

"I promise, I will never hurt you." He felt compelled to say.

"Thank you," she said and continued to walk. "You will do, I suppose." Then of course, she blushed.

They went into a large dining room, larger than the one from lunch. He was introduced to several people and did as Andrew had instructed. Before long, he found himself being shown into a large sitting room with several people who were interested in things he knew.

Once again, Sara was talking to Elaine and Maria while sipping sherry. She was starting to look a little fragile, but then Allison Byers, with Lady Dickerson, joined the ladies, and before long, they were all in deep conversation.

A man in a uniform walked around the room from time to time and offered the men scotch, and the ladies more sherry. There was a TV on a news program on, and Sara saw something that interested her. She excused herself and walked over to the TV and took a seat in front of it. She did as she always had and sat on the floor so as not to turn the TV set's volume up.

Eric looked at the group of women, now minus one member, and looked around the room for her. Austin and Brad had found their mother seated on the floor and joined her. It only took a few minutes before both boys were asleep, leaning on Sara. One of the attendants from the plane came and told Sara she would put them down for her. She kissed both of their cheeks as they walked out of the room.

"Oh no!" Andrew said. "Scott, look!"

"Son of a bitch," he whispered. "Damn that woman to hell," he said, putting down his glass and moved quickly toward the place where his wife stood with her hand to her mouth. Tears of disbelief were already starting to streak her cheeks.

"What is it, Scott?" Eric said. He looked at the screen and saw the headline in bold print: "Sara Alexander Byers Exposed!" "Who is that woman?"

"Sara's mother," Andrew said.

"The one that…" Eric started.

"Yes," Scott said, taking a seat beside his obviously upset yet silent wife. "Baby girl, don't pay any attention to what she is saying." Scott started, but too late.

Sara still held the glass that held the sherry that fell to the floor. At the sound of the fragile glass breaking, several of the other people in the room noticed the TV. Scott reached over and turned it off. Before he turned back, Sara was out of the room.

"What do you need me to do?" Eric asked.

"Pray that bitch is in England so I can kill her," Scott said. "I am sorry for that," Scott said, shaking his head when he saw Riley and Andrew leave the room as well, Colton not far behind them. "Sara was the result of an affair her mother had. If you saw her sisters and brothers, you would be able to see that clearly. But that animal has made it seem like Sara was trying to steal something from her brother in being named as a successor," Scott explained.

"That is ridiculous," Eric said.

"She doesn't see it that way. No one else sees it that way," Scott said.

Eric held up his hand, taking a step closer to Scott. "I read part of her medical file this afternoon," he said.

"Good. You can't know what it is like trying to explain my wife to people."

"Your Grace, you have a phone call," an attendant said, handing Scott the phone.

"Scott Byers." He listened for a moment. "I have to take this. Be right back."

Rick had gone ahead and flown to London in the hope that his own flight would be arriving at about the same time as his own, and he could follow them to the hotel they had selected and checked in. He thought for a moment about how nice it would have been if Amelia had come with him and made a vacation of sorts of it. Then he remembered that this trip was for business only.

When his own plane had landed in the hours before dawn, he saw a plane that had landed, and its passengers were on the tarmac awaiting the arrival of cars he supposed. He could see the Byers family and other members of the party waiting and then turning toward the plane when Lauren's casket was being unloaded and put in a hearse.

Rick saw that Sara had become weak in the knees at one point and put a supportive arm around her waist. The doctor who had accompanied Scott to the plane was quickly there with them. It angered Rick because he rationalized, if he would have been there, he would have taken better care of her.

At the front of the airport, it was easy to get a cab at the early hour. He waited until he saw the cars he had seen on the tarmac and instructed the cabbie to follow them, that they were friends of his.

They drove through the streets of London with a definite destination in mind, with Rick's cab immediately behind them. When at last they stopped for a moment, Rick looked out to see where they were. He saw tall iron gates in front of a huge red brick building.

Rick told the cab driver that he would be right back and walked to the nearest car to him and knocked on the window. The window rolled down to the car that held Elaine and Eric.

"What the hell are you doing here?" Elaine asked.

"As I told Scott earlier, I am here to take care of my patient," Rick said. "Do you know which car she is in?"

"Yes, I do. But I will not tell you. And if you are staying in London, good luck finding a hotel," Elaine said.

"This hotel will work for me," he said.

"No. You will not be staying here. As Sara's new cardiologist, I will be staying here with my patient. This is Kensington Palace as we were invited to stay," Eric said.

Rick was immediately angered. "I will be staying here as well. Where do I check in?"

"Rick, this is not a hotel. People live here. It is a royal residence, and you have to be invited or be a member of Her Majesty's court to stay here. You will not be admitted here, so you had better leave before you get into big trouble," Elaine said. "And in defense of my friends who invited me to be here, you don't need to upset any of them any further."

At that, the iron gates began to open. Rick got back into the cab that was still waiting for him. After the cars entered that had clearance to do so, the gates closed, with Rick still on the outside.

"May I suggest a hotel, sir?" the cab driver asked.

"No. My patient is staying here, and I need to stay with her. Whom do I call to get a room here?" Rick asked.

"This is not a hotel, sir. It is a residence. One of the people who reside here will have to okay you staying here. There are hotels that are close to here if you would like me to take you to one."

Rick looked at the tall iron gates and knew he would not be able to stay at the same place the Byers family was staying. But he would find a place he could stay and then catch the family on their way to the funeral.

"Is there a suitable hotel that is close to here?" Rick demanded.

"Yes, of course. The Kensington Arms is only a couple of blocks away from here," he said, not liking Rick's manner. "I will get you there right away," the cabbie said and drove straight to the hotel. "That will be ninety-seven pounds."

"What? How much is that?" Rick asked.

"Two hundred fifteen dollars. I take both British and American currency," he said.

Rick pulled his wallet from his pocket and retrieved the necessary funds to pay for his ride. Rick pulled his suitcase out and closed the door before he looked at the hotel he would be staying in. When he saw the hotel was little more than a dive, he turned and saw the cab driver had already gone.

He walked into the hotel and requested a room.

"I am sorry, sir. We are sold out due to the funeral tomorrow," the clerk said.

"Is there another hotel close by? I have had a very long flight and am a doctor. Her Grace Sara Lyn Byers is my patient, and I have to find where she is," he said.

"Perhaps one of the larger hotels a few blocks away," the clerk said.

Rick picked up his bags and walked to the waiting cabs. He went to several hotels before he found one that had a room. The hotel was large and only had one open room. Rick had to pay a premium price that he figured was due to the funeral that everyone kept telling him about. The very small room had only a twin bed. His room was on a low floor that overlooked a filthy alleyway. This hotel room was likely the opposite of the place that the Byers family was staying in.

Rick turned on the TV set to see if there was anything said about where the funeral would be. The news not only told about Lauren, but about everyone else who had been on the flight with her.

The more Rick watched, the angrier he got about not being allowed to board the plane with the rest of the party. He remembered the irritating smirk that the cardiologist had on his face when he was being told he would not be allowed on the plane.

He rationalized that all he wanted was to keep the family healthy at the loss of their doctor. The thought that someone beside himself would be allowed to give medical care to that family made him angrier every time he thought about it. The only member of that family he took care of was Joan Redding.

Rick picked up the phone and called home to see if Amelia had been told where the family would be staying and how he could get in touch with them.

"There is no way for you to get hold of them," she said.

"What hotel are they staying in while they are here? I can leave a message for them."

Amelia laughed a little at the thought. "They are staying at Kensington Palace as guests of the queen. I would imagine it will be hard to find a hotel now. Leave them alone, Rick, and come back home. I am tired of you making a fool out of yourself and your family. Be home tomorrow, or you will find the kids and I gone," Amelia said.

"Amelia, you know the only reason that I am here is for the well-being of my patients," Rick explained.

"Not one of them is your patients. You have twenty-four hours to get home or we will be gone," Amelia said and hung up the phone.

566

Rick was angry about Amelia giving him an ultimatum. After the sun came up, he got a cab and had the cabbie take him to Kensington Palace. He thought if he could find someone who would let him go inside, he could find the Byers family.

Rick walked to what appeared to be a guard at the gate and asked him if he could be permitted to enter. He explained about having missed the flight due to an emergency. The man at the gate asked what the name of his patient was and Rick told him. He picked up a phone and called inside and asked about the family.

"Please follow me, sir," the guard said and led him to a side door.

"Are you going to take me to the room the Byers family is in?" he asked.

"No, sir. You will not be seeing them or their family," the man said.

"Then where are you taking me?" Rick asked. "Or if you just let me in, then I can find them."

"Left unaccompanied, you would not be allowed," the man said. Two quick knocks on a downstairs door and the man walked into the room.

"What is your business here?" the younger man asked.

"I am supposed to be traveling with the Byers family. I am the family doctor," Rick lied.

"They have a doctor with them, so obviously you are not part of the party. And as you were not on the flight with them, you are not going to see them. And a word of advice. This family and friends of the family have been through a lot in the last few days, and they do not need to be put though the crap that you are forever starting with them," he said.

"Who are you to tell me I cannot see them? They are American citizens," Rick said.

"I am Prince Andrew, second son to the queen. I speak on her behalf. And you are not wanted or needed here. We all have a busy day tomorrow, and as part of the party, I can tell you we all need rest and solace," Andrew explained. "And Sara is expecting a baby and does not need to have to put up with you."

"Exactly the reason I should be with her."

"You don't seem to understand what I am saying. You will not be seeing the family, and if you try, you will be arrested. The closest you will be to them is on the parade route from Buckingham Palace to Westminster Abbey," Andrew said.

"I plan on attending the funeral," Rick said. "I will meet up with the family when they arrive. From there, I will be seated with them."

"They will be seated in the Royal Box and will not be arriving with others attending the funeral. Security will be tight, and when royalty is involved, nothing is taken to chance," Andrew said.

"Are you telling me I cannot visit a tourist attraction here?" Rick asked.

"I am telling you as long as there is one member of the royal family, one of their friends, or a visiting dignitary, security will be heavy."

"And if Sara said that she wanted me close, would that change anything?' Rick asked.

"Never happen."

"Ask her," Rick demanded.

"No," Andrew said. "When she discovered Dr. Dane was to be traveling with us, she said that she was afraid that you would be coming. She said that you scare her, and that is not tolerated. Please escort Mr. Powell out, and make sure he is photographed and his picture given to security," Andrew said and walked toward the door he came in through.

"Don't you walk away from me until this is resolved," Rick said and walked toward Andrew and was curtly behind him. Immediately Rick was stopped by security.

"This way, Mr. Powell," the security guard said and pushed him through the outside door. Before he knew it, the iron gates were again closed, and he was on the outside. He realized that there would be no way he would be able the see that family. He had no idea why it angered him so much. He had, after all, followed them to England and made himself available to ensure the health of their family.

Not knowing exactly why he did it, he called Joan Redding and asked if she was aware of the death of her daughter. He then turned on the TV to find out what time the funeral would be. As bad as he hated to admit defeat, he knew he would not be able to see the family and called the airline to book a ticket, once again to find, the only ticket available and that he could afford was coach.

Sara sat quietly in the garden outside of Kensington Palace. She thought about her picture being on the news. How could she sit in church for Lauren's funeral following this? She rubbed her chest. She ached to talk to Saline about their mother. She could always make her feel better. She was exhausted from the constant effort of trying to play down the mental and emotional hurt of the past week. Uncle Steven would have seen right through her attempts. She placed a worried hand on the precious life inside her. She had only found out before seeing the plane had crashed that her baby was a girl. She worked to convince herself that Uncle Joseph had known about her father and not caring. He had looked so injured when she had last seen him in London.

A woman stood from a good vantage point behind the younger woman. She saw that she rubbed her chest. She had been called when the news had come on. Her busy schedule had kept her from receiving the visitors for supper, but she came at the insistence of her son.

"Sara, it is very cool out," she said softly so as not to scare the young lady.

Sara heard the faraway voice of her youth. She turned so quickly she lost her balance momentarily but recovered and curtsied. "Your Majesty," she said, rising.

The queen was startled at the emerald eyes she had seen only once before, a little fair child, with long dark red hair.

"You have come home?" the queen asked.

"You know me?" Sara asked.

"I make a point of knowing all my young noble ladies. Please come inside," she said, putting a hand out to her.

"Oh, Your Majesty, you don't really know who I am," Sara said, crying fresh tears. "I am so sorry I have come here and disgraced you."

The queen had never been overly hands-on as most people in her position. But this was a rare exception. She knew her past from her cousin, before she had been received at court fourteen years before.

"You are expecting a baby, are you not?" she asked.

"Yes, Your Majesty, in December," she answered.

Then, taking her hand, she pulled Sara to be at her side. "I do remember you from the parade many years ago. You had a book about a prince that didn't look like Charles. Remember that?"

"Yes, mam," she said.

"I saw you again, Sara Lyn. I asked you to be in my court. Not who you were. My cousin wrote your name as she stood behind you. Lady Sara Lyn Dickerson. No one before or after could ever change that. Now, I have some time. Tell me about yourself," she asked, and the two walked arm in arm back inside.

"Who is that lady with, Sara?" Elaine asked, looking out a window with Maria and the younger Byers boys.

"Mummy," Andrew said. "She said she would be stopping by tonight."

"They know each other?" Maria asked.

"They have met twice before, once in a parade with Lauren, in Wales, and then when Sara became a noblewoman. Mummy knows all her nobles. Sara just got misput for a time," Andrew said. "No woman or man will ever doubt who and what she is again."

Eric saw the group talking and approached. "Have any of you seen Sara? Scott is looking for her."

"Tell Scott she will be back momentarily. She is talking to Mummy," Andrew said.

"And he will know who that is?" Eric asked.

"The queen," Elaine said.

"This is a strange country," he said as he saw the door open and the two together. Everyone went back to find Scott and put his mind at ease.

About an hour later, the queen had finally gotten Sara to speak of herself. Every movement and gesture was that of an exceptionally groomed English woman, intelligent but not boastful. Honest to a fault. She knew exactly what was expected from her. Qualities that she hoped would be in one of the girls her sons would one day marry.

She would be personally rearranging the seating to have her close at hand. She had lost so much; she would make sure she knew she still had someone else who stood for the human spirit she exhibited. Frances had been right from the start.

"Your Majesty," Scott said softly, bowing his head.

"Your Grace," she said and extended her hand to him.

"Not to interrupt, but I believe my wife needs some sleep. Did she tell you she spent the entire afternoon playing a very long chess game?" Scott said then asked.

"Chess. You play chess?" the queen asked.

"When Lauren and I were out of school for over a year when we were both sick, our tutor taught us to play. I was winning," Sara said.

"I play myself from time to time. Well done."

"Thank you, mam," Sara said.

"I will see you tomorrow, my dear," the queen bid, standing.

"Elaine was looking for you, baby girl," Scott said.

Sara excused herself, curtsied, and slipped from the room.

"Your Grace, I understand Sara has medical problems. I saw her rubbing her chest," the queen said. "Were you aware?"

"Not this time. It has been a very emotional week, and we have all been trying to hold ourselves together. And please, in private quarters, I am Scott Byers. I have the cardiologist who is stepping into Dr. Steven Quinton as my wife's doctor."

"Please, Scott. What can we do?" she asked in earnest. "Are you a walker?"

"Yes, Your Majesty. Care to take a turn with a Southern gentleman?" Scott said, extending an arm.

The monarch smiled and took the younger man's arm. They walked and spoke for a few moments. She was impressed at the well-spoken young man. His active listening skills were rare in someone so young. She was well aware of the precious oil tanker that had been sent to England as a gift to the Crown.

She had spoken to John Byers himself and found him a very pleasant man. Their son had married one of her personal nobles. That made them welcome guests at any time. She had offered for them to stay at Buckingham Palace, but Lady Dickerson had respectfully declined due to the fragile young woman that she had just spoken to.

"I understand you are to leave tomorrow following the service," she said.

"Yes, Your Majesty," he said but didn't say that it concerned him.

"If I may make a suggestion that may perhaps change your plans," she asked.

"Of course, mam," he said.

"Don't continue on to Hamburg. Although I understand that the government there has been putting pressure on Sara, I understand she is very distraught and perhaps even ill from the loss of so many that she loved. It is my opinion, my expressed opinion, that it is an unacceptable risk to her and your family. With respect to His Grace, the politics involved are outweighed by the health and happiness of the family. I can send a spokesman for the family," she said.

"You see things very clearly, mam. My father will of course have the final say, but it would be a relief to me for one. I happen to know, especially in regards to the news tonight. She is terrified," Scott said with relief in his voice.

"Then following the funeral tomorrow, you will be moved into Buckingham Palace, where you can rest before continuing back home at your leisure. I will speak to the duke. So until tomorrow," she said.

Scott agreed with the wise woman that reminded him so much of his mother in the way that she handled authority.

"Your Majesty." He nodded, stepping back two steps and allowing her to leave before he turned his back.

He couldn't wait to tell Sara they would not be going to Germany.

Sara hadn't found Eric, so she went and checked on her three sons. She was reading to Brad when Scott entered. He picked up Brad and told Sara he would finish. She kissed the boys and went to bed. Her fatigue apparent, she was asleep before he arrived in their room.

A nightmare, the first she had had in a long time, awakened several people that night. By the time Scott shook her awake, she was flushed.

Eric stood at the door. Allison, Maria, and Elaine were immediately in the room. Unfortunately, she had run into a wall.

For her sake, and for her unborn child, she had to rest. Eric had brought with him what he had thought he might need to help Sara. He had to remember the baby when giving medication, so he switched from giving a Valium-like medication to sleeping medication that was safe for both.

He entered the room again, and Scott held Sara, whose eyes were wild with fear, like a doll. Elaine took the offered injection and gave it to her friend.

"Don't worry, we have been here before," she said to him.

By morning, Sara had slept only fitfully for the remainder of the night.

"We are not going on to Germany," Scott said.

"We have to. Uncle Joseph said we had to out of respect for Saline," she said.

"No. We won't be. And breakfast will be brought in her for you in a bit, baby girl. We won't be losing another child to Germany. Rest for a little bit. Okay?" he asked.

When she agreed so easily, it worried him.

When they left for the funeral, the black seemed to make her appear pale. At the church, she didn't know the seating had been changed, and they had to enter from the side. She sat on the left-hand side of the queen, for the entire world to see. The formal service was difficult for everyone present.

During the service, Scott noticed his wife sat with eyes open but didn't focus. When he put his hand to her, he found she had a high fever. He leaned to look at the queen for guidance. She needed only to wave to an attendant. Eric and the attendant assisted Sara to the side before she collapsed, Eric scooping her up.

"I am her doctor. We need her husband and a ride," he said.

The man returned with Scott, Andrew, and another man who said he was the queen's physician and to follow him. They left quietly, unseen by most in the church, including most of their family. Inside an unmarked yet guarded ambulance, Scott saw her like she had been ten years before.

"She is burning up. I thought she was feverish last night," Scott said.

"Her right lung has collapsed. Has that happened before?" Eric asked.

"No. Not since she was a child."

"Where are we going?" Eric asked.

"Buckingham Palace," the queen's physician said. "We have a facility there. You are a?"

"Specialist in critical care and cardiology," Eric answered.

"We will provide you with what you need for Lady Sara. As a member of Her Majesty's court, we will do everything for her," he said, assisting the man. "We are aware of the child she carries. A midwife will be waiting for us as well. If need be, we will transfer to the hospital. But for now, this will be better." He then leaned to the front of the ambulance. "Tell the officials at the palace all tours are cancelled until further notice, yes now. We will be arriving shortly, and we need no unnecessary people there," he instructed.

When they slowed for the gates to open, the assisting physician said to cover her in case they had not cleared the people. When the doors opened, Eric again picked her up. "Lead the way," he said.

In record time, oxygen was applied, a chest tube placed, and she was on a monitor for both her and the baby, who was fine so far. Only as the lung re-inflated did she groan.

"She will need some Tylenol for the fever. She has had tetracycline in both the pleural space and the pericardium. I will need an echocardiogram, a chest film, and her medical chart from my briefcase back where we were. Damn." He thought of the chart he had not yet read.

"Right here, sir," an attendant said.

"Thank you. Protect the baby for the x-ray please. Sara, can you hear me?" he asked.

"Dr. Dane," she said and was confused.

"Yes. Tell me about your chest," he said.

"It hurts. I can't breathe," she said.

"I am going to help that. Scott is here with us. The baby is fine, but you are sick. Give her two of morphine at a time. Watch her pressure," Eric continued.

For the next two hours, they worked to find the source of lung collapse.

Nurses kept constant checks on everything.

"Your Grace," came a voice from the door. "Could you accompany me for a moment?"

"Go ahead, Scott. I will be here," Eric said.

"Yes," he said.

"Please come with me. Her Majesty would like a word," he said as he walked quickly. He knocked two times quickly on a door at the other end of a long hall. "Your Majesty, His Grace."

"Thank you, Robert."

He left from the room, closing the door.

"Is Sara better?" she asked.

"Hard to say right now. She collapsed just outside of the chapel," he said, walking to the window. He saw thousands of people standing almost in total silence. "Are there always so many people?" he asked.

"A state funeral always draws people from all over the world. But at present, they are here for you," she said.

"Me? I have only been here since yesterday."

"You and your family are by no means unknown. Please sit for a moment. You look dead on your feet," she urged.

A door opened, Prince Phillip and John Byers entered.

"Daddy," he said. The embrace of the two men melted one of the highest-profile couples in the world.

"How is our baby girl?" he asked.

"She is pretty sick, Daddy. Eric is with her and about a dozen other people as well. Where is everyone?" he asked.

"They are downstairs. We are expecting a call," John said. About that time, the phone rang.

"Yes, Your Grace. You will be talking to me," she said.

"Did the Prince of Wales make my position quite clear?" she asked and listened. "I will not change my mind. Her Grace of Hamburg will not be attending services, she and her family have been through enough." Again listening. "Raising your voice does not make me change my position. When you pick up your papers in the morning, they will be reading about Lady Sara Lyn Dickerson-Byers has returned to court here until further notice. Your politics are not important at present."

John walked over and requested the phone. "Thank you, mam. Joseph, we will not be traveling further. You may take that up with your former daughter-in-law and her son. Sara is a citizen of Her Majesty, and you have no standing in this. No further calls are necessary," he said, hanging up. "Beg your pardon, little lady. The man didn't seem to understand plain English. And a man does not talk to a lady like that," he said, removing his diamond buckle Resistol hat.

The room was quiet for a moment.

"Son, you need to go and eat something. I am sure Her Majesty will have them call if something changes," John said.

"Let's all join the rest of the group downstairs. They have no idea what is happening at present," he said.

It was two days before the fever broke. It was then discovered Sara had had scarlet fever a few years before. Eric, in his frustration, kept his promise to her and called his good friend and honors graduate out of Duke University Dr. David Glass.

"David, this is Eric."

"Eric, where the hell are you?" he asked.

"I have a new very complicated patient that you know. Her name is Sara. She is an LVN on telemetry. Great with her patients. More wine-colored hair than I have ever seen before," he described.

"Green eyes. Yeah. She is great with patients with a thoracentesis," he said.

"Yes. She had every complication of rheumatic fever you could imagine. Dr. Steven Quinton was her doctor, who died this past week. He had to instill high doses of tetracycline into both her right pleural space and her pericardium. Even with a chest tube placed, I am not sure I can remove it without collapse. And further, she is five months pregnant with her fourth child," he said.

"Ye ouch. Is she on a ventilator?" he asked.

"No. She is in a lot of pain right now. She has inflammation of both spaces. I know you specialize in cystic fibrosis cases, and the doctor here is unfamiliar with what to do next," he said.

"I will go there, but I still don't know where to go," David said.

"If you can, drive to DFW. Take your passport. I will call you in a moment," Eric said.

"John. I could really use his help. Is there anyway?" Eric asked.

"Give me his name. I have access to the Concorde out of Paris. Tell him it will be there in about seven hours. I will make it worth both of your whiles. She is our life."

Eric looked out the window of the very weak young woman's room. People were gathered in near silence, day and night. He hadn't had time to read newspapers in the last forty-eight hours. Cases like this were why he had become a physician.

"David, are you ready for this?" he asked.

"Yes. Without a doubt."

"Drive to DFW to the transatlantic terminal. The Concorde will be there in about seven hours from Paris. It is going to be refueled, and you will be in London in about thirteen hours from now. Someone will meet you there," Eric said.

"Eric, you are being serious? This isn't one of your little surprises?" David asked. "The Concorde. What hotel are you in? The Ritz?" he chided.

"Buckingham Palace. David, are you alone?"

"Yes."

"You can't even tell your wife this. Pretty little Sara Lyn Byers, is Her Grace, Lady Sara Dickerson Byers of Her Majesty's court. She could be dying," he said.

David raised his voice. "You have been in Buckingham Palace taking care of a junior nurse that cares for the sickest patients? I will be waiting. How long will I be gone?" David asked.

"I don't really know, but on the way stop by the Country Hospital and pick up her films. There is a pain-in-the-ass doctor there named Rick something, another who will try to follow you onto the plane. He is not to know where and what has happened. I have to warn you. This is an international event you are entering. Get some sleep on the plane."

After the next hours, David Glass was on his way to the airport. He watched as the world-famous Concorde arrived, the streamlined jet that would take him to London. There were people coming off the plane toward him.

David looked at the huge plane.

"Dr. Glass?" a woman asked.

David turned to find a woman who had been in the news for the last few days. His mouth fell open as the queen spoke.

A young man stepped forward and introduced himself as Scott Byers. "May I present, Her Majesty, the queen. You will be her guest," Scott said, shaking his hand.

"I believe he has lost his tongue," the queen said and smiled.

"I apologize. I was on call last night and have been running for several hours," David tried to explain.

"Scott Byers," came a voice over every person at the airport. "Where is my patient? Did you realize you had made a mistake? You killed her, didn't you?" Rick Powell yelled. A nice introduction to the shocked physician became a public incident. Riley and Colton were on Rick in seconds. Rick's year as a soldier in Vietnam hadn't prepared him for the attack of the two young men. John, Scott, and security from both countries had to pull the two angered, scared young men off the man on the floor.

"Rick Powell, you clear your belongings from our hospital immediately. You are fired," Allison said.

"I am John Byers of Byers Oil. I am the Byers that's on the contract here at DFW. I want that man arrested immediately. He is promoting an international incident with representatives of the UK. Two airport guards assisted Rick to stand.

"I want those monsters arrested. I have a plane to catch. And unless you have changed what country you are from, you are still an American, and I don't see my patient with you," Rick began again.

Scott took Rick's face in his hand and pulled him to himself. "My wife is sick, likely dying, and the last thing she needs is a sick showoff junior varsity son of a bitch like you. Do you understand me?" he said. No one moved. He took Rick's face and nodded his head for him. "Yes, I understand, Mr. Byers. And I can read your mind. I am sorry, Your Majesty and Byers family members. I will not be any more trouble."

Scott was shaking Rick's head roughly, mimicking his lame attempt to draw attention from the high-stress situation. When Scott released him, Rick stumbled and fell back.

One by one, with the stress still high and needing an outlet, everyone began to laugh. Scott had to sit after a few moments of laughing to catch his breath.

"Momma, Your Majesty. I am sorry. I don't know what got into me. He just struck me as a puppet." Scott laughed.

Riley, who was normally very intense, started laughing at the sight of his brother making a public display. The three brothers and their father sat together for a moment as Rick was escorted out.

"Allison, I assure you he will sleep on the ride back," Prince Phillip said.

"Thank you, Your Royal Highness. Phillip. And you will call me if," she asked.

"We will call you and keep you informed. And someone will always answer the phone. No matter how long it takes," the queen assured. "All will be well." The two women with their own empires clasped hands.

Allison, on impulse, hugged her new friend. "May the Lord bless and keep us safe until we meet again, Elizabeth," she whispered in her ear.

"Amen, Allison." The two women parted.

Pictures were being taken, but no one seemed to care. Soon they were loaded back on the plane. A safety check was done, refueling, and the plane was ready with a new set of pilots to return to England.

John, Allison, Mark, and Maria had to return to the ranch, along with Riley and Colton and of course Scott and Sara's three sons. One last passenger joined them on the flight. Marsha Dane,

Eric's wife, had been invited as a guest. Marsha was a surgical scrub nurse at St. Mary's and knew Sara fairly well.

Marsha actually knew she was something but didn't pry.

Everyone was seated in the living-room-looking seats so as the new members could become more familiar with the international group of people who had come together to save two lives.

After they were at cruising altitude, the queen spoke. "Dr. Glass, I am sorry we didn't get through introductions before the entertainment. Because we will be in proximity, I will tell you about who we are. I am Queen Elizabeth of England, etc. While in private, I am Elizabeth, if you wish. But I am afraid, if we are in public, Your Majesty is proper. My husband here is Prince Phillip. He is Your Royal Highness in public," she said.

David stood. "I am pleased to meet you both." He extended his hand, and it was taken by each of the passengers. "I specialize in the lung, internal medicine, and critical care medicine. I am very familiar with the article regarding Her Grace that he wrote in the fall of 1968. Did you know that Sara was pronounced dead by six physicians for twelve full minutes? The article here chronicles conversations she heard and what happened to her in those moments. If anyone would like to read it, I have it here," he said, placing the article on the table. The queen picked it up.

"Scott, what can you tell me about the last few hours?" David asked.

After he knew what he needed to know, he excused himself to read some of what he needed to know. Eric had copied her medical for his convenience. After about two hours, an attendant came to where he sat alone studying her file.

"Dinner is served, sir. Right this way," he said, and David followed.

"I must say, Daddy rented a nice plane. This is my first trip on the Concorde. David, pull up a seat and get some food in you," Scott said. "I only have a few minutes to eat and then lie down or Her Majesty is going to have me beheaded."

"Then I will try to get some sleep as well. Right after I finish with my lobster tail and my steak. First class, here I come," David said.

David's arrival to Buckingham Palace was appreciated. He was welcomed by everyone. He saw the crowds of people who waited for something.

He was taken to a place that seemed to be a functional hospital of its own. Inside a room were Eric, several nurses, and a very pale Sara Byers.

Eric looked up from his present position. He rose and warmly greeted his friend. "David, thank you for coming. It could all be in vain. I think we are going to lose them both," he said.

"Who is that man beside her?" David asked.

"The archbishop of Canterbury. She asked for her priest. She knows. You are her last chance. Taking the baby is not a consideration for her, by the way, so don't suggest it. She is the most devout person I have ever known," he said.

"Sara, do you know me?" he asked.

"Dr. Glass?" she said.

"What kind of trouble are you causing?" he asked.

"I didn't know I was sick. I didn't realize. It was a long week. I didn't think," she said.

"Okay. We will talk later, but right now, let's get you and your baby well," David said. "Do you remember what Dr. Quinton had to do to save you?" he asked.

"Yes," she said with fear in her eyes.

"Keep in mind it is not as it was before. I will put lidocaine into the medicine, and it will just burn for a moment. I won't hurt you if I don't have to. Okay?" he asked.

"I trust you. Scott." Her eyes got wide.

"I am here, baby girl," he said, taking her hand and kissing her head.

"I am sorry, Scott. I love you so much. Tell the boys how I love them," she said.

Monitors screamed. "We have lost her blood pressure. No pulse," Elaine said, starting compressions.

"No. Sara, no," Scott screamed.

"Scott, step away please. Her drain is not draining. She has tamponaded." Together they began.

In the room was her husband, a queen, two princes, and Lady Dickerson.

"No, not Sara too," she screamed.

For over two hours, she rallied. Her heart would beat for a few minutes, and the next minute she would be gone again.

"It's over," David said. He saw that the baby's heart still beat but knew that without his mother as life support, the heartbeat would slow and it would be gone too.

The room was silent for a moment. No one moved, just watched the heartbeat of the child that would soon be lost.

In another place, a peaceful place where the air felt comforting and the sun had never been so warm before, all around for as far as the eye could see were people who loved her. She was death's newest soul who waited as the souls of the ones she loved came to her.

"Sara," came a familiar voice.

"Saline, I am here," she said.

"I know. But you can't stay," Saline said.

"Sara." Lauren came to her with her own leg again. The light in her eyes were not of those who lived on the world.

"I miss all of you so much. I am expecting a girl. I wanted to tell you first," Sara said.

"You will have a girl. She will be late. You will have her just after midnight—a Christmas present, a special gift," Uncle Alex and Uncle Steven told her. Amy was close by.

"It is peaceful here. I want to stay. I have never lived without you. Saline, I can't make it," Sara said.

"I will always be with you. We all will. But you need to go back. Scott, Momma, Poppa, and the boys need you to be there. Tell Lauren's mom that she left her something in her hidden drawer, and name your daughter after her. Tell them we are waiting here for them. And this is important. Never trust Momma, Tommy, or Sophie. You are not safe if you trust them," Saline said.

"But Sophie is so young," Sara said.

"Her father's and mother's own," Saline said.

"Tell David Glass for me that my death was worth everything as long as he knows I am waiting on him to come back to church. He is my only child and I love him," The man who looked like David Glass said. She knew he had to be David's father.

"Let Allison know she was always my girl, and tell John he was always my brother," Uncle Alex said.

"Sara," Uncle Steve said, coming to her, holding her as a father would. "You were the daughter I always wanted. Your job now beside that family of yours is to take care of those patients that need *you*. You can be their hope through darkness. Show them the way to God, and ask them to make sure they know him. Don't pay heed to Rick Powell. He is not vicious but wants to be in your good graces for all the wrong reasons. Eric Dane and David Glass will help you to do what you promised to do so long ago."

"Will they want to?" she said. "Some people think I am a little nuts when I say such things to them."

"They will both know."

"I am so tired. I want to stay and rest a while. Saline, don't you want me here?" Sara said, already feeling the fatigue of being pulled back.

Saline hugged her sister for a long moment. "Forever and always we will be together. I love you, sis. I know everything you ever did for me," she said and backed away.

"Saline, come back," she said in a voice barely audible. "Saline," she said again with tears down her face.

The room was completely quiet, with the exception of occasional sobs. Nobody moved. The sound of the baby's heartbeat continued on the monitor. "We saw so many people this time and did so much this time. All of us were talking, and we all agreed it felt like the last time. We all knew we were never alone before the crash. Then we were here. Now, go back with all of our love. Everyone needs you at home, Sara. We will have eternity to be together. Our Lord walks yonder. Look at the light."

Sara looked where Uncle Steven told her. Her eyes took in the bright light then it was gone.

She was in pain. Saline and Lauren were gone again.

"Let me stay," she whispered. Tears came from closed eyes.

"Who said that?" Scott asked. Everyone looked around to shaking heads.

"Lauren, let me stay," she whispered hoarsely.

"She is crying. It is coming from her," Scott said. "Sara, open your eyes."

"She is gone, Scott," David said.

"Scott. My Scott," she whispered.

"She lives," the archbishop exclaimed. "She speaks."

The people who were around came to her bedside. David felt her pulse. "Her pulse is strong. The baby's heart never stopped," he said.

"It is a miracle," the archbishop said, kneeling, as did several in the room.

"Sara, baby Sara," Lady Dickerson said.

"Lauren said she left you something in her hidden drawer," she said, coughing, obviously in a great deal of pain. "And our baby girl will be named after her so as to always let us be close."

"You saw my baby?" Frances asked. Sara nodded. "The others?"

"Yes. Dr. Glass," she said.

"Honey, you should rest," he said.

"Your dad said his death was worth it as long as he knows you will find your faith again so he will see you," she said, looking directly into his eyes.

"My, my dad? How did you know?" he asked.

"He just told me. He pushed you out of the way," she said and winced. She touched his hand, then his face. He couldn't stop the tears.

"We will have to talk more later. But to do that, I need to make sure you stay with us," David said.

"Stay with me, Scott," she said as he laid her back.

"I will always be here. They will want me out of the way for a little while, but I won't be far," he said.

"So will I. My chest hurts like it is broke. I am so tired. Can I sleep?" she asked.

"Sleep now, and we will talk later," Eric said. "Is her pressure stable now?"

"Yes, Eric, for the first time in the last two days. Her heart rate is eighty. The baby is doing fine as well," Elaine said.

"Give her some morphine for the ribs we likely cracked please," Eric said. "David, what about what you are thinking?"

"I am thinking now that we should give her something to keep her asleep and instill tetracycline into both the pleural and pericardial spaces so she does not have to dread them later. She is stable, and I believe it is what is going to save her life," David said.

"I think you are right. Let's get it done. What can we use for sleep?" Eric asked.

Dr. Gordon Lawrence, the queen's physician, told them the medication to use. When they were sure she would not awaken, they started to work.

"David, this is Sir Gordon Lawrence, Her Majesty's physician," Eric said. "And do you know Elaine Rogers? She is an LVN and studying to be an RN. She and Sara both are. They also used to go to other countries with the Red Cross themselves."

"We had a lot of fun. Now we won't be able to go anymore," Elaine said.

"Why not?" David asked.

"We lost three nurses and our two doctors and our pilot that carried us," Elaine said.

"I have a plane," Eric said. "Where do you go on those trips?"

"Some to disasters, to places in Africa that are in a famine. Places in South America where children need shots. If a place needed medical care, we went. Sara and I studied on the plane most of the time, and if we had questions, we had two doctors to help us. It is one of the most rewarding things you can imagine," Elaine said.

"We will talk about it," Eric said.

"Don't forget about me. I like to do such things as well," David said.

"May I ask a question, Doctors?" the queen asked. "Is she going to live?"

"Yes, she is. We will not let anything happen to our miracle," David said.

"Will it be quite all right if I tell the people outside that have been praying for her that she lives and will recover with her baby?" the queen asked.

"They have been waiting for word for so long. I believe that it is a good time to tell them," David said.

"Thank you. Scott will come with us just for a few minutes?" the queen asked.

The queen, Prince Phillip, Scott, Andrew, Lord and Lady Dickerson and the archbishop, and Elaine left out of the room.

"I need to let my people know something. Please follow me," she said. They followed her to a balcony on the front of the palace.

First the archbishop spoke, "Just a word about how Lady Sara is. She is a miracle, an honest-to-God miracle. Now Her Majesty would like to speak to you."

"Lady Sara Lyn Byers has rallied for several days, but it gives me great joy that she is going to survive. When she is strong enough, she will come and wave, but it will be a few days," the queen said. The cheers were deafening. And may I introduce Lady Sara's husband, Lord Scott Byers." More cheers came from the happy crowd. The group then went back inside.

Drs. Glass, Dane, and Lawrence did what they had started out to do. They mixed the lidocaine and tetracycline together and first put it into the pleural tube and then clamped the tube.

"Eric, look at this with me. If we put the tetracycline into the pericardial sac, it will become more scarred, and her heart will not have enough room to beat. What about a pericardiotomy?" David said.

"That is surgery. Do you really think she is up to surgery right now?" Eric asked.

"It would end her problems with tamponade. But I don't know about surgery. Let's see if this helps with her lung first," David said. "Eric, have you left this room in the last few days?"

"No, he has not," Elaine said.

"Likely that means you have not left either. I order the two of you to get something to eat and get some sleep. I will be reading her chart in here for a while. That goes for you too, Dr. Lawrence. She will sleep for a time, and all of you need some rest," he said. One by one, everyone filed out of the room.

For a while, David looked at the previous chart. About two hours later, he heard Sara groan. "Scott," she whispered. "My throat and my chest hurt so badly."

"Are you awake, Sara?" David asked.

She opened her eyes. "Dr. Glass. Where is Scott?"

"He is lying down for a little while. Can I help you?" he asked.

Sara tried to sit up. She gasped at the attempt. She had tears in her eyes. "David, it hurts so much. Can you help me sit up? Maybe that will help," she said.

"Sure, I will help you, but we will do it slowly."

So he began to assist her.

"Do you think I can sit in a chair for a minute?" she asked.

"Do you feel strong enough to do that?" he asked.

"I hope so. It will make everyone feel better if it looks like I am getting better," she said.

"It is going to be a long time before you are better. You know that, right?" David said.

"I want to go home," she said.

"Honey," David said, taking a seat beside her, "as it is right now, it looks like it may well be a month before you are well enough to go home. But let's see if you can do well sitting in a chair for a few minutes," he said. "First, let's swing your legs off the side of the bed, slowly." The two worked together, and of course, David did most of the work. "I will be holding you while you slide down to the floor."

"Okay," she said. "I am ready."

David eased Sara to where she stood on the floor for a quick minute while he padded the seat with pillows and warm blankets. "Take a step to the right, another, and now let me ease you into sitting. She sat slowly.

"I am a little dizzy. Will that go away?" she asked. "What happened to your dad? If I may ask."

"A car was driving too fast down a street. I had chased my ball out there and held it up so everyone could see I had it. What I didn't see was the car coming right to me. Dad saw it. He ran and pushed me out of the way. The car was going so fast that it hit my dad and threw him fifteen feet in front of him. But he drove over him anyway and left. I was there alone with my dad. He died a few minutes later," David said.

"I hope you will start back to church so you can see him again someday. He misses you but is so proud of you." Sara tried to take a deep breath. She couldn't.

"I will change your linens while you are out of the bed. Are you okay sitting for a minute?" he asked.

Sara didn't say anything. "Before we leave England, I really would love to attend services with you and your family," he said.

"I would love that. What church have you attended?" she asked.

"I attended the Episcopal Church," he answered.

"Here, it is the Church of England. I would love to go. I was carried out of the funeral. I have disgraced myself," Sara said.

"Nonsense. You were sick. How do you feel sitting up?"

"A little dizzy, but I will get over it. My chest hurts so much," she said. "Can Scott see me in a chair for a minute, just to give him some hope please?" she asked.

David stepped out to go and get Scott. While he was out, Sara made her way to the bathroom, after using the bathroom, her chest hurt even worse. She went back to the chair until Scott arrived.

"I just wanted you to see me out of bed. I even went to the bathroom by myself. Now I feel foolish because I am exhausted," Sara said.

"Let's get you back into bed. Your lips are turning blue. I am going to assist you to stand." She attempted but didn't do very well. "Let's do this," David said and picked her up and laid her in bed. "I will give you something for the pain. We did an awful lot of compressions before, and you will likely have some cracked to broken ribs. Let me get you some morphine. Then I need you to do some deep breathing for me. While you were asleep, I put the tetracycline in your right chest tube and capped it for a while. Is that hurting at all?" David asked,

"No. I can tell I have pericarditis. It hurts so much. I feel like I have glass broken in my chest. My heart hurts very badly. Can I sit up in bed?"

"I will raise the back of the bed for you. I am going to try something completely new for the pericarditis. I am going to insert steroids into the sac. If I am right, it will stop the inflammation. If it does not, you will need a pericardiotomy. Let's get going on this," he said.

David, after telling Sara his plan, went to work. "Can some of you tell me who and what you are please?" he said.

"I am Margaret, a nurse."

"Ellen, nurse."

"Jamie, I am a doctor."

One by one, David was introduced to the people who would be helping him. "Well, I am David Glass. Please call me David. I need some Solu-Cortef to put in the area around her heart. Who will be assisting me?" he asked. And all three of the people he had just met volunteered.

"Now we have to wait and see," David said. He looked at her vital signs, and they were holding.

He sat not far from her and pulled out films and medical records. At sixteen, every rib in her body had either been just broken or healing. He could count at least ninety places where there were thoracenteses done. And there was a huge scar from a long-term chest tube. From the looks of it, that lung could not fully expand. "That tetracycline is really bad stuff," he muttered. It was only he and Sara in the room at that time.

"Dr. Glass, may I have something to drink?" she whispered hoarsely.

"And what will the lady be wanting?" he said, winking.

"Iced tea would be nice. May I ask one more thing?" She attempted to sit up again. David immediately helped her to sit on the side of the bed and let her feet hang over.

"What is this other thing you would like?" he asked.

"You are going to think it is silly. But could you ask my ladies' maid if I can have some soup? Is that okay?" she asked, putting her head down.

"Are you sure you don't want something better than soup?"

"No, sir. I am sure that they make very good soup. Hadn't you better get something to eat as well?" she said.

David opened the door. "Excuse me, young man." Andrew had been walking by. "Would you mind telling whoever needs to know that Sara would like a bowl of soup? And if you could just bring me something to eat as well, I would appreciate it. And who am I speaking with?" David said.

"Prince Andrew. But in the palace, it is just Andrew. I will have something brought up immediately," Andrew said. "Would you mind if I joined the two of you? Her husband and Dr. Dane and Elaine are asleep right now."

"You are a friend of Sara's?"

"Oh yes. But mostly her sister Saline. I was the last person to see her alive. They took the Red Cross flight, and I had to take the royal flight back to London. I will be right back," Andrew said.

David again walked over to Sara. "May I sit in that chair so my Scott will see me getting well? Just to eat, then I think I will take a nap. Is that okay? I am not going to scare anyone if I take a nap?" she asked.

In a few moments, with the help of both David and the nurse, Sara was seated in a reclining chair.

The sweat on her forehead told that just with a small effort, she was both fatigued and in pain. "I am okay. Let me catch up a little," she said, breathless.

"I really think you should go back to bed," David said.

"Please let me try. I know I can do it," she said, trying to catch her breath. She closed her eyes for a minute and caught her breath. She whispered, "Lauren, Saline, help me." She attempted a deep breath time and again and could not catch her breath. "Please help me. I want to sit up." She had begun to sweat with the effort.

"Settle down, baby, let's get some O2 on you. Now breathe easy," David said.

"It hurts so much," she whispered. "My back hurts."

"What part of your back hurts?" David asked, hoping she was merely sore from having stayed in bed for a few days.

"Right here," she pointed, very breathless.

"I think that before supper we need to take care of that," David said.

"Please let me eat with my husband first," she said, becoming ever more breathless every time she spoke.

David knelt down to her eye level. "Honey, you will get to eat with your husband after this is done, but you really need to get back into bed and sit on the side," he said, gently urging her to stand and walk to the bed. "I will talk to Scott, and you can eat afterward," he said.

"This will hurt a lot, yes?" she asked.

"I will do my best, Sara, but yes, it will hurt."

She started to cry. The heaving was not helping her already compromised state. "I am scared. Please don't let Scott be close by. He has been through so much, but nothing like this."

"I won't leave you, baby girl. I am a big boy," Scott said.

Sara didn't have the strength to argue. "Okay," she said, breathless. "When do we start?" she said, trembling.

"Scott, this is going to be painful, having-a-baby painful. There is little that can be done for the pain. Are you sure you are up to it?" David asked.

"David, I have been with her through everything. Holding her hand, wiping the sweat from her face. How can I be anyplace else?"

David nodded. "What about Elaine, can she handle it?" he asked.

"I think she is too exhausted to handle anything. The two of them are best friends. She went to sleep a little bit ago, crying about how many ribs she broke during compressions. What do you need?" Scott asked.

"I need Eric, one nurse, and the supplies that I will request from Dr. Lawrence."

In a few minutes' time, the three doctors and one nurse, plus Scott, were in the room. Sara was assisted to sit at the side of the bed.

First, the tetracycline was drained from both her pericardium and pleural spaces. More would be instilled in a few hours.

An over-the-bed table was put at the side of the bed so Sara would have a place to lean on. "Scott, you need to keep her elbows pulled up like they are now."

"I've got it," Scott said. "I am right here for you, baby girl." When Scott saw the fear in her eyes, he himself became afraid.

The door opened, and Eric and Dr. Lawrence came inside, along with the queen and Prince Andrew. "We will be completely out of the way. But Sara is a noble, and a noble needs one of her own in the room at such a time," the queen said.

"If you are up to it and Sara has no objections. But to respect her modesty, you need to wait on the other side of that wall. When Sara assists me for these procedures, she is strict about maintaining her patients' dignity. I will show her the same respect," David said.

The back of Sara's hospital gown was opened. "I am cold," she said.

"Give us a few minutes and you will be warm again. Scott, put her oxygen mask on and turn the oxygen all the way up," Eric said.

"She has a fever," Scott said.

"We know. This will help. Sara, it is going to get really cold on your back," David told her.

"I am so cold." Her hands were shaking, and her teeth were chattering.

"I am inserting some lidocaine right now, so you will feel a pinch and burn," he said and Sara reacted by sitting up. "Put your head back down, angel. Now you will feel an ache from putting lidocaine deeper," David said.

"I can't do this. Please stop. I can't do this," she cried.

"Hold on to her, Scott. Hold her tight," David said, looking straight into his eyes.

David closed his eyes for a moment, thinking about how many times he and Sara had done exactly the same thing. She was the perfect nurse for such things.

"Here comes the needle, Sara, and I am so sorry for this," David said.

Sara grabbed hold of the over-the-bed table and then Scott's hands. Then she moaned, not wanting to make those present know the pain she was in.

"Jesus, help me." She moaned louder every time the needle was moved.

"It is too thick, Eric. I will need a 12-gauge needle," David said.

Scott knew from messing with cattle the size of needle he was speaking of.

"I am pulling out the needle for a moment, Sara. Try to relax for a few seconds.

Weakened from the pain, Sara didn't have the energy to move.

The queen stood and walked over to where Sara and Scott were. "Don't worry, Sara. It shouldn't be long from now. May I stay close?" she asked of Sara and Scott.

"It is pretty terrible, Your Majesty," Scott said.

"David, in things like this, who is the person who holds the patient?" Scott asked.

"The nurse. But you are good with her and the two of you she respects."

"Okay, Sara, take three deep breaths for me."

She took the first breath and was cut off by pain. She tried the next two times without luck.

"Thank you, those were good attempts. Sara, we are having to use a larger needle this time. This could take a while. Ready?" David said.

"I guess?" was all she said.

"Good enough. Eric, hand me the syringe please," David said. "I am beginning again, and again it will hurt."

He began pushing the very large needle into her back.

Sara began screaming loudly. "Please stop, it is killing me."

"Just wait, Sara," David said.

Sara was shaking so violently that it was affecting needle placement." Scott was holding her tightly.

"Sara, honey, they are trying to help you. They can't stop or they will have to begin again," the queen said.

The needle was pushed deeply into Sara's lung, going through nerves that made Sara feel like they were cutting her in half. Her screams were of agony for two straight hours, and then she passed out.

"David, is she alive?" Scott asked.

"Very much so. The pain just got a little too much for her. It is easier on her this way," David said.

For an additional two hours, David drained the very thick fluid from around Sara's lung. He then sent some to pathology to find the source of the fluid. It was also time to drain the old tetracycline and re-instill more, in both the right lung and the area around the heart.

Sometime during the late evening, Sara awakened, feeling like every bone in her body was broken and ill set. Scott had his head resting on the side of Sara's bed. Sara put her hand on Scott's head.

Scott moved his a little bit before he realized it was Sara's hand that had touched his head. "Hey, baby girl. I thought you would be sleeping for a week," Scott said, stroking her hair.

"You look like you need to sleep for a week. I am sorry, Scott," Sara said.

"What are you sorry for?" Scott asked.

"I didn't realize I was sick. I thought the loss of Saline and every-one," Sara said.

"Don't you ever apologize. We both lost a good part of our family last week. I wouldn't have been able to tell if someone had cut my leg off. Saline is the one person who made you feel safe before we met. You make me feel safe, and I will be here for you forever," Scott said.

After several days with a chest tube and a pericardial tube in place, both David and Eric agreed it was time for them to come out. If she tolerated the tubes being out for a few days, both thought she would make the long flight home.

People continued to remain outside the gates of Buckingham Palace, curious about the young woman who had been in the news so many times recently.

Progress seemed so slow for Sara. She wanted to go home and see her children and her family. She was so grateful to the queen for stepping in so she was not going to Germany. She never wanted to go to Germany.

She was looking out the window one morning at the crowds of people outside, and the queen walked in.

"Sara," she said.

"Yes, mam," she answered.

"You are looking well today. How do you feel?" she asked.

"I am sore all over, but I think I am getting better," she answered.

"May I ask a favor of you?" she asked.

"Of course. Anything you want. You have been so kind to all of us," Sara said, thankful the queen had given her permission not to curtsy.

"As you may have noticed, there are thousands of people that are waiting to find out who has been receiving so much attention here. Would you mind very much stepping on the balcony and waving for a moment or two? It is completely up to you," she asked.

"Of course, mam, but all those people are waiting to see me?" Sara asked.

"Yes, most have been there since the funeral. They just want to see you well," she said.

"Yes, mam, of course I will. For you. Can Scott be there?" Sara asked.

"I am in hopes that all of you will be there. Would this afternoon be too soon?" she asked.

"No, mam. I hope I don't disappointment them," Sara said.

"I assure you. You won't. I suggested to your doctors that you may like to have lunch in the dining room downstairs. Does that sound like something you would like to do?" the queen asked. "I know that everyone would like to see you looking well after the last couple of weeks."

"I would like that very much," Sara said, smiling.

"After we have all eaten, we will go to the balcony, and then you likely need to rest. We don't want anything upsetting that little life inside."

"No, mam," Sara said. The two chatted for a few more minutes, and then Scott and David came back.

"How are you feeling being up?" David asked.

"I think I am okay. What do you think?" she asked.

"I believe you are looking better than I have seen you in a long time," David said. "I don't want you navigating the stairs just yet, and you are going to have to take frequent rests until the baby gets here, so that means no going back to work for a while. And if all goes well, you should be able to go home in a few days," David said. "Now, don't you think you should get dressed for lunch?"

Sara nodded. Elaine came in to help Sara dress. "Thanks for staying, Elaine. I am so glad you have been here."

"Are you kidding? When I haven't been in here with you, I have been exploring the place. There are things here I never dreamed of ever seeing. And getting waited on hand and foot. Is it like this in Germany?" Elaine asked.

"I suppose. I have never been to Germany. Never wanted to go. The last time I was this close to Germany was when our uncle kidnapped me. I was pregnant then as well, and I lost the baby. Very long story," Sara said.

Elaine saw that her friend's eyes were beginning to mist, so she changed the subject.

"Lady Dickerson picked out some beautiful maternity clothes. What color do you want?" Elaine asked.

"What color do you think?"

Elaine picked out a dress that was the same burgundy as her hair. The dress was silk with long cream-colored sleeves. "It is beautiful. Lady Dickerson has some of the most beautiful clothes you have ever seen. The year that Lauren and I were out of school, she always dressed us alike," Sara said.

"Then let's get you into this and show her," Elaine said and helped Sara in getting dressed.

When they were all eating, Sara thought about how good it felt to be up and around even for short periods of time. As she looked around the table, she noticed how different people looked in places that seemed a little foreign.

Scott and Prince Phillip were deep in conversation about something. Elaine and the queen were deep in conversation as well.

"Are you okay, Sara?" Eric asked.

"I am okay. Just off in thought, I guess," she said.

"What are you thinking about?" David asked.

"You will think I am crazy," she said.

"Never happen," David assured her.

"Uncle Steven said the two of you would be in my life," Sara said.

"When did he say that?" Eric asked.

"When I died. He said the two of you would help me keep a promise I made as a child," she said.

"And what promise would that be?" Eric asked.

She took time in answering him. "I promised God that I would take care of the sickest patients in the hospital one day. The way that they took care of me," she said.

"I believe we can help you keep that promise," David said. "Nearly every person at this table was present when your heart stopped and you slipped through our fingers. We were also there when you came back to us. Having witnessed something like that changes the way you see the world. I believe I speak for everyone who was present that we will always be in one another's lives."

After having said that, Sara looked around the table at those present and found them looking to her and nodding. She was at a loss for words. Nothing more need be said.

Not long after that, the people from the table were all walking on the balcony. The ocean of people began to cheer as if on cue—the first formal gathering of the visitors from Texas standing with members of the royal family.

Sara took a cautious step forward and looked into the happy faces of the people before her. People waved, cameras flashed. The others on the balcony waved, so Sara picked up her arm as high as she could and waved, shyly for a few seconds before her arms gave out.

As the queen had said, they only stayed on the balcony for a few moments, after which, Sara was ready for a nap. But rather than being taken to the room she had been in, she went to one of apartments that Scott had been in. Sara took her shoes off, laid down on the king-sized bed, and was asleep in seconds.

That Sunday, the entire party went to church at St. Paul's Cathedral. They sat with the royal family. Both David and Eric marveled at the beauty of the place. As they had a few years before, a few of them went to the gift shop and selected some items.

A few days later, the entire party was ready to fly home. Sara thanked everyone who had cared for her so completely.

The queen offered one of the royal flights, but they had already planned on having the Concorde to bring them home. John Byers had thought it better for Sara and the rest of the party to fly home faster.

When the huge, sleek plane arrived at DFW a few hours later, people couldn't help but to be curious about the arrival. The late-morning arrival found the airport fairly busy. The hope was that before anyone could figure out who was on the plane, the party could be through the airport to the waiting cars.

Elaine had become accustomed to having people taking pictures of them in recent weeks to the point that she would do her best to avoid being in public. She knew that all she would have to do is end her friendship with Sara to stop the interest in her, but she and Sara were more like sisters now than friends.

Sara and Elaine walked side by side and were surrounded by the men. When they reached the waiting vehicles that would take them to the ranch, John, Allison, and others from the ranch greeted them. As always, everyone was glad to have everyone back where they belonged.

At the ranch, Scott and Sara could hardly wait to see the kids, and the kids could not wait until their parents got home. There was no amount of soreness that was going to keep Sara from hugging the boys until she didn't miss them anymore. Everyone constantly reminded her that her activity was limited. Sara would have never gone against anything that she had been told, but in her happiness to be home, she would forget about herself and think only of her children.

For the remainder of the summer, until the older boys started back to school again, there was someone who always seemed to be around every hour or two to help around the house. Austin and Brad were old enough to help in watching Ryan in between times. Still at other times, Austin and Brad would go with the men, and Ryan would be picked up for Sara to be able to nap.

Elaine, Amelia, and Maria were three of the nurses who visited frequently. Then there were nurses from St. Mary's who would go to the ranch to visit their friend.

Linda had been to the ranch several times before the plane crash. She and Sara had become friends, and Linda was an excellent teacher. Sara was a regular sponge when it came to learning about the heart and more advanced nursing knowledge. When she had gotten to Scott and Sara's house, she found several people in the family room around the TV set. Sara was on the floor, sound asleep with her head in the lap of one of the ladies. In that moment, seeing so many people who had lost so many people who were dear to all at once, she realized that money really couldn't buy everything.

At the loss of her brother, Allison felt the loss so acutely she thought she would die from the pain. Alex was several years older than his sister and had always been there for her. Decades before, when they had lost their parents, Alex became big brother and father to his little sister. Allison had felt so alone when he died. She and Sara had gotten even closer in that loss. Sara completely understood exactly how Allison felt.

Frances had spent much of her time stateside awaiting the arrival of the baby. Quite like the boys, Frances was regarded as the Byers children's grandmother. Now, with Sara expecting a daughter, Frances felt a particular closeness to both Allison and Sara.

Dr. Rick Powell had been allowed to visit as well. He had come out a few times with Amelia and posed no threat to anyone. He had offered several times to deliver the baby as Sara might feel better being in the Country Hospital rather than St. Mary's. Without Drs. Carmichael and Quinton to run interference, frequently someone would have to remind him that Sara having the baby anyplace else was not an option.

When John and Allison had returned from England, they had asked Amelia if she wanted to work as a fill-in as the director of nursing for the Country Hospital, taking Amy's place. She had agreed before she even mentioned it to Rick.

She and Rick had some words over it, but in the end, she began to work.

No one could ever replace Amy, but all knew that there had to be a nurse to oversee the workings of the hospital.

After Thanksgiving, when Scott would leave for work, he would take Sara to the main house. Dr. Chambers had said it might not be a bad idea to take the baby by C-section, but Sara said as long as it was not necessary, she didn't want a C-section.

The Sunday following Thanksgiving, Amelia had told Rick she was going to the ranch for a little while. Rick had wanted her to wait until after the football game, but Amelia was hoping the football game would keep him home rather than going with her. It didn't work.

When they got to the ranch, they went first to Scott and Sara's house. No one was there, so they went to the main house.

They arrived in the family room to find most of the family in front of the TV watching the football game. Sara was not in the room.

"Is Sara resting?" Amelia asked,

"Yes, and Eric is also checking on her as well," Allison answered. "Go on up and say hello if you like. Rick, you should likely stay down here."

"I would also like to have a look at her. You can never tell I could be delivering the baby," he said. Amelia had already disappeared to go to see her.

"No!" most of the people in the room said in unison.

"We had a discussion about this when you tried to board a plane that was not there for you. You are not her doctor and will not be her doctor. She could deliver any day and does not need to be upset. You may be her friend as long as there are others present, but nothing else," Scott said.

"You don't seem to understand how important it could be to have a physician so close rather than in Tyler," Rick said but was cut off.

"Dr. Powell, you will not be upsetting my patient. Is that understood? You will also not be seeing her today," Eric said emphatically.

"Not even just to say hello?" Rick questioned.

"Sara is having a bad day today. So, no, you may not," Eric said.

"Don't you think you should ask the young lady?" Rick asked.

"No," Scott said.

"I am her doctor. I say she needs rest and a quiet environment. Even her sons are well versed on how she needs to rest. Upset their momma and they will bite your ankles off," Eric said.

"If two little boys do not upset her, I won't either," Rick said, rising.

"She has three sons. Now stay in here if you want to, but you will not be upsetting our daughter," John Byers said.

Rick sat back down, sulking. "Has it ever occurred to any of you that if you treated Sara more like an adult, it might be better for her?"

"That is a family and physician decision. The family and I have discussed it, along with Sara's other treating doctors, and it is agreed upon. Perhaps you need to learn by your own design. To me, drinking and partying all through college is a behavior you should work on," Eric said. Everyone in the room began to laugh at Eric's remark.

"What I did or didn't do while I was in medical school is not any business of anyone here."

Upstairs, Amelia and Sara were talking. The three boys were watching TV quietly. Every now and then Austin or Brad would ask their mother if they were bothering her, or if she needed something to eat or drink.

"How are you feeling, really?" Amelia asked.

Sara's eyes had never had very much life in them since the death of her friends and family. "Just lonesome, I guess. I am always so tired. My back hurts all the time lately."

"Did I hear you tell him, after trying not to tell him, that your chest is bothering you?" Amelia asked.

Sara didn't answer, just looked out the window.

601

"Sara, I am your friend, talk to me," she said.

Little Austin answered for his mother. "Mommy is sad. She cries because we miss Auntie Saline and the rest of our family," he said sadly. Then he got up on the bed beside his mother and put his hand on hers.

"We all do, sweet boy." The other two boys had also gotten up on the bed and sat with their mother, careful not to fall on her. "But we won't always be sad. You have a little sister that will be here soon. She will make all of us so happy that we will forget about being sad. And all those that we are sad about are in heaven now. Do you think that when they look down on us, they will want us to be sad?"

"No, mam," the intuitive little boy said. He kissed his mother's cheek and put his hand to her face. "I love you, Mommy."

Sara looked down at the little boy who looked so much like his father. She couldn't help but smile at him, remembering the day he was born. She had been given so much since she had Scott and his family. She loved her life that being her husband, children, and what she did. Just on the ranch, she had so many people that cared about her and she cared about. "I love you too, my angel."

Austin smiled back at his mother. "Come on, Brad, let's take Ryan and go play so Mommy can rest. Our little sister in Mommy's tummy is a girl. She is not as strong as a boy like we are, and she needs to rest too."

Austin was a born leader. It didn't take but a few seconds before both of the others kissed their mother's hand and followed their brother.

Amelia smiled at the little boys as they left the room. "Sara, come back to us. I know that it feels like nothing will ever be the same."

"There were three of us. Momma and Poppa adopted three of us," she whispered at nothing in particular."

"I know," she said.

"What if I am not enough?" Sara said and immediately looked away.

The thought that she had spoken something she felt so deeply made Amelia think about what she would say.

"Honey, you are more than enough for anyone," came the voice of Allison, the one person in the world who had lost a sibling that she loved. "Baby girl, that was not the thought that we were getting three for the price of one. It was you who led us to them. It was to them that you were both as sister and a mother. You risked your life a million times, putting yourself between danger and someone you love. You are one of the best mothers I have ever seen. Most women your age want to be housewives and mothers. I know also that a large number of nurses become nurses to put themselves closer to doctors.

"Not you. You made promise after promise in your life, and you have never not kept one. Do you remember when you were asked to step out on the balcony in England?" she asked.

"Yes, mam," Sara whispered.

"That ocean of people had been there for days. They waited and hoped in near silence for all that time, day, and night. It had been announced by the queen that Lady Sara Lyn Dickerson Byers had collapsed at her sister's, the Lady Lauren Dickerson's, funeral. She made you a member of the royal family, as did Frances, on the day you were accepted in court. She is the one who changed your name.

"The queen told the duke that you were a member of her court, that to try to influence her otherwise was best not done. The two of you had ever only talked for a few moments. In a few years, you went from being virtually alone to having people around the world who love you. Not Saline, not Jody, just you. You are likely one of the most loved women in the world. And you will never find a family that loves you more than we do. I know that you miss Saline. Every good mother misses her children, even if they are only three years older than the child," Allison said. "Never have a doubt, Sara. You are never alone again."

Unlike previous pregnancies, Sara had begun to wonder if she was going to be pregnant forever. On Christmas Eve, Scott, Sara, and the rest of the family attended Mass at church. Sara felt the first contraction as they were singing the final hymn. Not far out the front door, her water broke. Scott had told his parents it was time for the baby.

Frances rode to the hospital with Scott and Sara. John and Allison had Mark to take the boys home so Maria could go with them.

By the time they got to the hospital, the labor had progressed quickly. Dr. Chambers had been waiting at the hospital for them.

"Scott, I need permission, if necessary, to do a C-section. I will only do it if I have to. This is a large baby, and with as sick as Sara was earlier in the pregnancy," he said, alluding to her heart.

"I have been telling her that for weeks. She knows that a C-section would be easier, but she insists that the baby will be born early Christmas day. You were not in London when she was pronounced dead by Eric and David. After that, she told us what she had seen in that time. One thing was that she would have the baby late, and it would be born on Christmas day," Scott said.

Knowing part of what happened from both doctors, Dr. Chambers didn't put too much pressure on him to repeat.

"Just know that if, and only if, I think that either she or the baby is in danger, I will do a C-section. Agreed?"

"Agreed," Scott said.

In the next few hours, in addition to Dr. Chambers, David and Eric would pop their heads in. Eric told her that he would really like her to think in terms of having a C-section. She was in hard labor, and many women were easy to convince that a C-section would be the way to go.

He could tell that with the pain of labor, and the relatively short time between contractions, she thought about it, but she would just smile and tell Dr. Dane she was fine.

After midnight, she felt the urge to push. Her blood pressure had risen out of the parameters that had been set for her by all three doctors. Then she was taken to the delivery room. Frances was at her side, telling her it was almost over. Another thirty minutes of pushing and Scott and Sara's first daughter was born. Her weight was nine pounds even.

Eric Dane arrived only seconds after she delivered. Sara's blood pressure fell dramatically, so much so that even lying flat, she was dizzy.

After a short exam, the baby was wrapped in a warm blanket and handed to Frances. The baby girl's eyes were wide open as Frances looked into her eyes.

"Have you picked a name for her?" Frances asked.

"Lauren Catherine," Sara said then turned her head away.

Frances knew the emotions that Sara was feeling. Allison had been right about the maternal feelings that the young woman had for her sister. Sara respected her sister as an equal but looked after her like a mother. It had been an emotional last few months for them both. There were no words to comfort either of them, so Frances sat at Sara's head and held her daughter's namesake quietly.

It was several hours before Sara seemed to stabilize from having their daughter. Scott stayed at Sara's side when she had been taken to a private room on the postpartum unit of the hospital. It was Christmas day, and she had not so much have mentioned what was happening with the boys. To make matters worse, it had begun to rain. Sara stared out the window at the rain and didn't volunteer to say anything. She answered questions politely. She got up on her own and attempted to walk to the bathroom, but because of dizziness, she had to have Scott's assistance.

Meals were brought and removed, untouched. Baby Lauren was brought for feedings and to spend time with her mother. Sara had asked the nurse to leave her in the room but was told that her doctor wanted her to rest between feedings due her weakened state at present.

Eric had been on call for his group on Christmas Day; therefore, he had all but lived in the hospital that day. He had gone in to check on Sara a few times and was worried because she was so despondent. He knew she was having very strong afterpains because she winced with them. He and his wife had three children, and he knew the effect that hormones had on the personality following childbirth. He thanked God for being born a man. But in Sara's case, she had lost so many at once. He didn't care how much a person had; losing so many people in a family could not be imagined. The Byers family was not like most rich people he had ever known. They were warm, caring people who would go out of their way to help others.

Eric had been invited to the ranch several times since they had all returned from England. The people who lived there were as close as family and were treated as such. Knocking on the door was foreign. The people who had lived and worked there were welcome at any time. When he had been there on Thanksgiving weekend, he had taken his wife and children with him. All of them had been welcome. There were several children in both the den and outside, playing while they were there.

He had been there when Dr. Powell and his wife had arrived. Rick Powell had to be one of the pushiest people he had ever known.

Eric rationalized that combined with just having had a baby, exhaustion from carrying a big baby and caring for her family, and depression from the huge loss could cause emotional problems of its own.

As promised, Scott had called the queen when Sara had delivered. He told her about having named their first daughter after Lauren and how happy it had made Frances. Then, when asked about Sara, Scott was not able to be so optimistic. They talked for a few more minutes, and they wished each other a merry Christmas. A few hours later, a huge basket arrived with pink ribbons and a banner that said Baby Lauren. In the basket were several things for both the baby and her mother.

Sara's nurse had seen the beautiful basket and happened to also see whom it was from.

"It must be nice to have such grand friends. Between having a beautiful new baby and such a gift, I would think you would be more upbeat," the nurse said.

Sara looked at her nurse, gave a weak smile, and continued to look out the window.

When she left the room, she went to the nurses' station and found another seated. "If I were Sara Byers, I would be over the moon, what with everything in the world that she has. Have you seen that gift basket she has?"

"Who didn't see it? It is beautiful," the other nurse said.

"Did you know it was sent to her by the royal family in England?"

"You're kidding."

Eric was looking at Sara's chart while the two spoke. "Try not to judge Sara. She has had a very traumatic last few months," he said.

"She appears to be a little spoiled," her nurse, Lindsey, said.

"Do you remember hearing about a plane crash this past summer?" Eric asked.

"Yes, of course," Lindsey said.

"There were five close members of her family that died in that crash. I don't know how she survived the loss. Following that, she was quite ill, and that forced her to be on complete bed rest until she delivered. As I said, unless you have survived something as traumatic, try not to judge," Eric said and walked away.

Scott stepped out when Sara had fallen asleep for a little while. He didn't know how she had stayed awake for most of the day. He was exhausted and knew she had to be. When she hadn't eaten breakfast or lunch, he decided that there was something that he could do. He could provide her the native comfort that had always seemed to work. He let the nurses know he would only be gone a few minutes and gave them his cell phone number if he needed to hurry back.

Joan Redding and Tommy Alexander had been looking for a time when they could talk to the only surviving sibling since Saline had died. Knowing that she would likely attend Mass on Christmas Eve, they waited in the parking lot. When they saw her and her husband not go in the direction to the ranch but to Tyler, they had followed.

It had taken all day on Christmas before that husband of hers had left the room for even a second.

When he did, they decided to visit and give her a little surprise.

They saw the nurse from the nursery take a sleeping baby in a hospital baby bed and go into the room. When she came out, the baby was still there.

Joan walked over to the tiny crib that held the sleeping baby. The pink bunting told her it was a girl. She leaned down and picked the baby girl up, only then realizing that it was her grandchild.

From what the papers had said in the last few weeks, this was her fourth grandchild.

"Sara," she said, devoid of feeling. "Sara, wake up."

Sara woke up and looked over and immediately saw her mother. "Momma, what are you doing here?" she asked. "Please give me my baby."

"This is my first grandchild to actually get to hold. Besides, you look a little pale. I am not sure that you wouldn't drop her. Have you named her yet?" she asked.

"You don't care about her or me. So please hand me my daughter," Sara said.

"You have been a lot of trouble for me these last years. For a very small part of that family's money, I wouldn't have had to work. I could have bought a much better house. But you have done everything in your power to avoid me," Joan said.

"Momma, please. Put the baby down. She is nothing to you. I will do anything, just put her down," Sara begged.

"Really," Joan said. "I have an amount in my head. Oh, and there is always Tommy, who would like to once again be in the line of succession. I am sure that if you were to mention it to his uncle, he would be all too happy to listen to you," Joan said.

"Please hand me my baby. I have my own bank account. I can write you a check."

"And have you put a stop payment on it? No thanks. But you can start off with giving me that pretty little thing on your finger," Joan said about her daughter's engagement ring. "I will even be a good sport and throw in that you can keep the band. Otherwise, do you know how easy it would be just to walk to the fire escape and be out of the hospital before anyone is able to stop me?"

Joan all but ripped her engagement ring off Sara's swollen finger. "I will give you anything, and you give me my baby. Just take it and go," Sara pleaded.

"I wonder if a newborn is as fragile as Jody was," Tommy said.

Sara threw the cover off herself and attempted to stand, falling to her knees with dizziness.

Joan laughed about her daughter having fallen. "So this is what happens to one of the *great* Byers family," she said. "What I would rather have is some money. A Christmas present from my daughter," she said.

"And I would love to be titled again. What do you say to calling Uncle Joseph right now? I am sure he would love to hear about his latest bastard," Tommy said.

Joan blew in the baby's face, causing her to awaken. The baby began to cry.

"Please, Momma. Let me have her. Please don't hurt her. I beg of you," Sara said, crying.

"How about this? I will put her on the bed, and you get dressed and we will take the fire escape and leave," Joan said.

"Anything. Just put her down," Sara said with tears streaking her face.

"I have a better idea. Let's make sure that she keeps her promise and take them both with us," Tommy said. "After what happened at the old man's funeral, not to mention that she is the one who killed him, she goes with us."

"No. We are not going anyplace. I will go with you, but she has to stay," Sara said.

"I don't think you are in the position to fight. Let's go," Tommy said, roughly taking Sara by the arm.

Quite unexpectedly, when Tommy grabbed her, Sara screamed. She screamed hysterically like a mad woman would, Tommy attempting to cover her mouth. Joan put the baby down to help Tommy in keeping her quiet.

Outside of the room, the nurses' station was fairly quiet. Only a handful of patients were present on Christmas Day, so there were even fewer patients. Scott was coming back from picking up something for them to eat when he saw Eric writing on Sara's chart.

"Eric, I took pity on you. I picked you up something to eat that didn't come from the cafeteria," Scott said.

"Oh man, thanks. I appreciate it."

"Least I could do. You have been keeping an eye on my wife all day long," Scott said.

"Have you gone in to see her in the last few minutes?" Scott asked.

"I was going to go in, but her nurse said she was sleeping," Eric answered.

Then, Sara's scream was heard by everyone on the floor. It was obvious where it was coming from. Everyone was drawn toward the sound. When the door was thrown open, they saw Joan Redding and her son attacking Sara.

Both Scott and Eric went to where Sara was, and a nurse went and picked up the now-crying baby, taking her from the room. Tommy fought back with fist swinging. Joan used her fingernails like an animal. Security was called from the nurses' station. It took a few minutes before the two were subdued.

Even after Joan and Tommy were removed from the room, Sara continued to scream at the top of her lungs.

"Baby girl, look at me," Scott said, getting down on the floor beside her. Her eyes stayed wide, unseeing.

Eric left the room. Sara's nurse made sure her IV hadn't gotten pulled out with all the activity.

Scott pulled her to him gently and began to stroke her hair as he had done so many times before. Nightmares were part of the package that was his wife. He knew that her current state of health didn't need anything that spent as much energy as this. She couldn't even stand without help, yet she fought for her baby with the fierceness of a grizzly.

Scott knew the baby was safely back in the locked nursery. Now he had to get Sara safe.

"I am here, baby girl. I am not going anyplace. I went to Red Lobster and got you some clam chowder. Let's get you back to bed, and I will have your nurse to heat it up for you," he said.

"Scott, she really needs to get back in the bed," Eric said. He could see the sweat on her face and knew that having had a baby only hours before, her energy was spent.

"Give me a minute," he said softly. "We have been here before."

Scott continued to talk to Sara, and when she began to respond to him, all in the room were relieved. Scott stood and helped her back to bed.

"Don't worry, baby girl. They won't be coming back," Scott told her.

"She took my ring," she whispered. "She tried to take us both." Was all she could say before the medication took hold, and she was finally sleeping peacefully.

Eric looked to nurse. "Stay in the room with her. Don't leave her alone."

"I have other patients, Doctor. I can't stay in here all the time," the nurse said.

"Two people just tried to kidnap her and her baby. If she wouldn't have screamed, chances are they would have gotten away with it. You stay in here with her, or find me someone who will. Do you know the name of the new wing of the hospital?" he asked.

"Of course. The Byers cardiac wing," she answered while tapping her clipboard.

"She is the Byers cardiac center. Stay here," he said.

Eric left the room and went down the hall where security and Tyler police had Joan Redding and Tommy Alexander.

Scott walked directly over to Joan Redding. Maybe her son went along with her on this, but he had no doubt that she had suggested it.

"You sorry bitch. If I didn't think you would enjoy it, I would beat you to death with my bare hands. I told you before that if you ever came near my wife again, I would kill you," Scott said, pinning her to the wall. "Officers, I would like to press charges against this woman for attempting to kidnap my wife and baby."

"She is my daughter, and that is my grandchild. You cannot arrest me for loving my daughter," Joan said, attempting to get sympathy from the officers.

"There is still a restraining order keeping you from coming within a mile of her and the rest of our family. And," Scott said, reaching for her hand, "this is Sara's engagement ring. Take a look at my wife's hand. It was quite difficult to pry it off."

The Tyler police began to arrest Joan for the attempted kidnapping and violation of a restraining order.

"What about him?" asked the other officer.

"I believe you will find that he will say he has diplomatic immunity. At the same time, however, he is wanted in Germany for rape. I have a phone number you can call for verification. And I will call him myself if you wish to speak with his uncle," Scott said.

"I did not steal that ring. My daughter gave me that ring to sell. She knows that I need money for my bad health. She knows how it hurts me that I cannot see my grandchildren, so she invited me to see my granddaughter while she was here," Joan said.

"When was it that she called?" Scott asked.

"Very early this morning. She waited until you had gone home to call me."

"That is almost funny. I have not left her side until this afternoon. That makes you a lying slut. Take her away please," he said. At that, Joan and Tommy were both taken away.

"Wait," Eric said. "In addition to what my friend has said, I am Sara's doctor. As such, charges need to be pressed for reckless endangerment. Judging from my patient's connections with the British royal family, releasing either one would likely cause some hard feelings with a friend of the United States."

"British!" Joan and Tommy said in unison. "She does not have a drop of British blood in her body. She is a bastard."

With that, Scott moved quickly toward Joan, but Eric stopped him. "My wife, your daughter, was presented in the queen's own court at the age of twelve as Lady Sara Lyn Dickerson. Lady Dickerson filled in her name and title herself. So argue, you slut, with one of the most powerful women in the world." With that, Scott and Eric left and returned to Sara's room. The nurse was still unhappily at her side.

"Eric. You need to get hold of her other doctor and get her released tonight. If by some chance one of those two or her husband happen go get out of jail, Sara and the baby could be in danger."

"Scott, Sara is weak. This was a very hard pregnancy on her. She should be safe here," Eric said.

"This is supposed to be the safest part of the hospital, and those two had no trouble getting in to her. I will not risk it again. I would imagine that I can get one of her friends from home who are nurses to stay close to her," Scott said. "Unless there is another reason to keep her here, I think I need to get her home," Scott said.

"Scott, I don't think Bill is going to let her go less than twenty-four hours since she gave birth. She is not stable. She can't walk by herself. Let's give her until tomorrow to catch her breath. I believe that would be the safest course of action," Eric said.

"Eric, you don't know what her family has done in the past. Her mother is ruthless. She was here, wanting Sara for something," Scott explained.

"If she were to begin to hemorrhage, she would be dead before anyone one could get her to help. I am thinking about what is best for Sara. Besides, they were arrested," Eric said.

"That reminds me," Scott said, walking over to the nurses' station and asking for the phone. He dialed a very long number, and it began to ring. "Joseph. I am going to make your day. Sara has had our daughter. She is beautiful and healthy. But I am calling to let you know that I found your nephew. He and his mother decided they were going to kidnap Sara and the baby from her hospital room."

Scott explained everything to the duke about how a terrified Sara had begun screaming as her only way to defend her child. When the call ended, it was understood that the duke would handle the situation himself.

As promised, the duke arranged for Tommy to be arrested and sent to Germany where he would be standing trial for the rape of his little sister.

Sophie continued to be in the secure psychiatric hospital for girls. Even after several years of counseling, she had not improved to a point that had been hoped. Her moods would be despondent and then combative. Psychiatrists said that she could be requiring to be hospitalized for years to come. The duke prayed they were wrong. He visited her frequently so she always knew there was someone who loved her.

Following the attempt on her and the baby, Sara was moved to the VIP suites for the remainder of her hospital stay with a private nurse close by.

The following morning, when Dr. Chambers made his rounds, Sara asked if she could go home. The boys would not open a single present until their mother got home.

"Do you think you are ready to go home?" he asked.

"I think so. I can walk to the bathroom by myself. I am able to nurse our daughter myself. I am tired, but I felt like that with the boys as well," she said.

Dr. Chambers looked around the room, admiring some of the flowers that had been sent. "It almost looks like a flower shop in here. Rumor has it that you have flowers and gifts from England."

Sara didn't say anything.

"Sara has close friends in London, including the royal family, of which she is considered a member of," Scott said.

"I think, as long as you take it very easy, I will release you today. That is as long as your other treating physicians discharge you as well," he said.

"Thank you. I really miss my boys, and they are anxious to meet their new sister," Sara said.

"You are most welcome, my lady." Dr. Chambers teased. "I hope all of your family has a belated merry Christmas," he said and was off.

When Eric came by, he was not sure about sending Sara home with it being so far away. But he was reassured by the fact that there were so many nurses close by. He detected a slight fever, likely related to her having just had a baby. But he was taking no chances.

"If I release you, this is the way it is going to be. First, you need to take it slow. That includes doing nothing outside of the house for the next two weeks. Taking your antibiotic until you finish it. Drinking plenty of fluids, and eating plenty as well," Eric said. Then the door opened, and David came in to see her as well.

"How is my favorite Jane Doe getting along?" David asked.

Sara was looking out the window.

"I think she is ready to go home to the ranch," Scott said.

"Do you feel up to going home today, Sara?" he asked.

"I think so," was all she said. "It is easier to rest at home because of the noise here."

"You have been through so much in the last few months. Are you sure you don't need to be here another day or two?" David asked tenderly.

"I want to go home today if I can," she whispered.

"Promise me that if you start to feel any kind of bad, you will call. Or, Scott, if you think she feels bad, call. You have all my numbers," David said.

"We will. And thank you for everything," Scott said, then followed them out the door. Once outside, he asked a few questions and again said he would see them later.

CHAPTER 18

Following the birth of baby Lauren, everyone breathed a sigh of relief. After she was two months old, Sara began to work a couple of days a week.

She and Elaine were taking two night-school courses a week on the two days a week that Sara worked in Tyler. Somewhere between having a new baby, a toddler at home as well as two school-age children, working, going to school, and being a housewife made Sara seem in constant motion. When people would ask how she managed with what all she had going, Sara would always just tell people that it was all in the planning of a thing. Scott knew that on the days that she did work, he had David and Eric to help keep an eye on her. From time to time, one or the other would make a comment if she appeared fatigued. She had regular checkups with both to assure that her good health continued.

On the days that she worked and went to school, Scott and the children would have supper at the main house. The other days in the week, she was home with the children, doing her best to be the perfect housewife.

She loved teaching Austin and Brad to ride their ponies. Scott already started to look for Austin a suitable horse as Austin was growing and was quite literally outgrowing his pony. During the spring and summer, at least a couple of times a week, Allison would come over and watch the children while Scott and Sara would go riding. It was something that had brought them closer together when they were getting to know each other. Scott frequently thought of that first time when Sara was sixteen and they rode Champ together to the horse barn. She sat in front of him, sideways. She never ceased to amaze him.

Elaine frequently came out to the ranch either to study with Sara or to ride horses. She was happy to go to the ranch because she knew Sara didn't like spending too much time away from the kids. She had actually thought about going to work at St. Mary's in Tyler rather staying at the Country Hospital. Amelia assured her that if she wanted to try working there, she would keep her place open in case she didn't like working or driving to Tyler. She knew that Sara was right about how much more experience she could get in Tyler.

Rick tried to go with Amelia to the ranch every time she went out. Allison frequently invited her out to go shopping, make preserves, etc. Rick had been given one last chance to keep his job. Part of what he had to agree to was to never go to Scott and Sara's house alone; on his days he was on call, he had to be no more than ten miles from the hospital; and to treat the nurses at the hospital with respect. The final thing was in regard to Joan Redding, which was that Rick was not to mention her name to anyone from the ranch.

Rick, who had always been a control freak, hated the thought that it was now him that was being controlled. He knew that if he were to get fired from the Country Hospital, he would have to work in a hospital ER in someplace like Parkland Hospital in Dallas, a place where he would be paid a salary rather than having his own patients. He had been to the ranch with Amelia several times and tried to find a moment when he could catch Sara alone. The few times that he had caught her alone, she would either walk away or ignore him.

Knowing someone who was in the news and that had friends and family who were considered to be royalty, that was something he had to be a part of. He knew that if she were his patient, he would then be pursued by reporters, and other people of the same status would want him as their doctor.

Joan Redding had been put in jail following her attempt to take Sara and baby Lauren from the hospital. Their plan in kidnapping them was to collect ransom from the Byers family. If one of them were to get caught, the other would be there with the bail. As it happened, Tommy was deported to Germany to stand trial for rape. Joan was remanded to the county lockup for six months then was to be released, awaiting her trial for attempted kidnapping. When Joan had not been to his office the first month, he counted his lucky stars for her absence. The second month, he suspected something was amiss. He dialed the sheriff's department to see if he could find out where she was and was surprised to find she had been locked up for two months. He found out how to visit his patient and told one of the deputies that he was under his care and needed to see his patient. The deputy called and had Joan brought to a visitors' room.

"Mrs. Redding, nice to see you again. How have you been?" he asked.

"How the hell do you think I am doing? They have me caged like an animal. My son was sent to Germany forever, and my husband, I cannot trust with the money I have hidden. I have no other family except Sara. And that family protects her from her own mother.

"When you told me about the BBQ, I finally saw one of the children. He was the most beautiful child I have ever seen. Fortunately, he looks nothing like his mother," Joan said viciously.

"Yes, I have seen Ryan Joseph. He is a beautiful boy, and he does very much look like Scott," Rick said.

"She named that child after the duke? Likely in an attempt to stay in his good graces. And with her precious Saline dead and Tommy on his way to prison, not to mention Sophie in the nuthouse."

"Who is Sophie?" Rick interrupted.

"She is my youngest daughter. She is in a nuthouse somewhere in Hamburg. It has been over five years since I have seen her as I am no longer allowed to visit there." Joan spat. "I would imagine that he does not know that Sara is a bastard. Not a drop of German blood in her body."

"Does she know who her actual father is?" Rick asked.

"I never got around to telling her." Joan laughed. "Sara belongs to my first husband. She even has a brother that she doesn't know about. One does not know about the other one. But I give them this. Her father and brother have the same eyes and hair color as she does."

Rick could not believe what he was hearing. This woman was evil. She made his skin crawl.

"My first husband and I married when I was fifteen. James was twenty-three, and I was pregnant with my son Adam. It was 'Marry me or go to prison.' When she was born, James Sterling said he would take his daughter. I told him that it would cost him. He even paid me one hundred thousand dollars for her. I took the money and kept Sara. I even tormented him by telling him about how Henry loved having sex with her from the time she was four, how he loved to beat her at the same time. Then when he started sharing her with his friends and finally when she was twelve, she was pregnant with Henry's child, but we fixed that in taking her to a butcher and getting rid of the child. She was five months pregnant at the time," Joan bragged.

"You knew what your husband was doing to her?" Rick asked.

"And Saline. Saline was just too pretty for him to keep his hands off her. James Sterling even called, begging time and again and even sent more money so he could have his daughter. Then when we moved out here, he didn't realize that he was within two hundred miles of his daughter. If he knew she was in Texas, he would go to her."

"Is her father still living?" Rick asked in a whisper.

"He was when I talked to him a few months ago. He and that first boy of his still live in Bryan. Adam does not know he has a sister," Joan said.

"How about you? Is there anything medically speaking that you are in need of?" Rick asked, wanting to spend as little time as he had to with the woman.

"I am having a nervous breakdown with all the noise in here. And my back is killing me. And keep in mind a couple of years ago my baby was born dead," she said.

"That was nine years ago," Rick said.

"It was still my baby I lost. And my son Jody and now Saline. I just don't know how much more I can take," she said.

Rick had no doubt that this woman was pathological. "I will leave prescriptions with the people here that will help you some. I have to go to my clinic now," Rick concluded. When he was leaving, he wondered about the information that he had just learned about.

Rick thought about it on the drive back to the clinic. He decided to get the phone number of Sara's biological father. When he arrived at the clinic, he called the number given to him.

"Hello," a woman said.

"Is this the home of James Sterling?" he asked.

"Yes, it is. May I tell him who is calling?" the woman said.

"I would rather not give my name. But I do have some very important information to give him."

"Mr. Sterling, you have a call," she said.

"Thank you, I will take it. This is James Sterling. Can I help you?" he asked.

"Mr. Sterling, did you know that you have a daughter living not far from you?" Rick asked.

"Sara lives in Texas?" Mr. Sterling asked.

"She is married to Scott Byers at the family's ranch about 180 miles from you. She has lived in Texas since she was fourteen."

"Are you sure of this information? Is Sara well and happy?" he asked, anxious for any information.

"Sara is the girl who has been in the news for the last few years. She now has four children, three boys and a girl," Rick said.

"Four kids? She is only twenty-four years old."

"When she was expecting her last one, she nearly died. If it had been my child, she would have taken better care of herself," Rick said and gave him directions to the ranch and to Byers Oil and Gas. "Her husband is Scott Byers. I just thought you and your son would want to know where your daughter and sister is," Rick said and hung up the phone. Now he would see what happened.

James Sterling hung up the phone and must have appeared a little pale. His son came into the room and went to where he was sitting. He had no idea if the information was true, and if it were true, if it would be front-page news without letting his son know.

"Daddy, are you okay?" Adam asked.

"Son, I have something to tell you, and I pray you will not hate me for it," James said. "Your mother that you know and love was not the woman who gave birth to you," he began and told him the long sorted story about how their lives came to be.

Adam was a soft-spoken, honest man that believed his father to be what he wanted to someday be. He couldn't imagine, so he listened intently as his father spoke.

"Daddy, there is no blame here. I love Momma and could not ask for someone who would be a better mother."

"Son, there is something more. Something I am so ashamed of. She has had five children, two who are now dead. One is in a mental hospital in Hamburg, and the other in prison for raping a minor. The minor is the girl in the mental hospital. She was nine the first time they began having sex. Those are your half siblings."

"And the other one?" Adam asked.

"The young lady that has been in the news so much in the last few years," James said.

"Princess Diana?" Adam asked.

"No. Her Grace, Lady Sara Lyn Byers. She is my and my former wife's daughter, and I am her father."

As his father explained the hellish life that the young woman had lived to that point, he told Adam about the abuse she had endured, how she and her sister had been starved nearly to death, and lastly about what had happened when Sara was twelve.

"And you knew what she was being put through and did nothing? Daddy, what kind of a man are you? You knew about everything, and she is my sister and you knew. Where is she now?" Adam asked with tears of frustration streaming down his face.

"Her in-laws own Byers Oil and Gas in Dallas. They also have the largest ranch in East Texas," James said.

"What is her husband's name, and are they good people?" Adam asked in almost a whisper.

"They are the kindest people in the world. His name is Scott Byers."

"I need some space," Adam said as he walked out the door.

Several hours later at the ranch, Sara, Maria, Elaine, and Allison were in the kitchen of the main house when the doorbell rang. Sara was still laughing at something Elaine had said when she opened the door.

Sara looked up at the man who was several inches taller the she was. But his wine-colored hair and his emerald green eyes were distinctive; it was like looking at a picture of herself in male form. Adam's reaction was similar to Sara's. He couldn't believe his eyes. But he didn't have time to study her completely before her eyes rolled back and she fell into his arms.

"Help, is someone in there?" Adam yelled while now holding a very unconscious Sara.

The three women came as soon as they heard the call for help. Their reaction when they saw Adam was complete shock.

Allison was the first to recover her tongue. "Who are you?" she asked.

"I am Adam Sterling. Is there a place I can lay her down?" he asked. "I will tell you everything. I promise."

"Yes, of course," Allison said and motioned him to follow. They went upstairs to Sara's old room, and Adam put her down on the bed.

"Let me have a quick look at her," Allison felt Sara's pulse and found it to be very slow. "How are you related to Sara?"

"May I ask your name?" he asked.

"Oh, I am sorry. I am Allison Byers," she said.

Elaine and Maria were also in the room.

"I just discovered about six hours ago that I am Sara's brother. I never knew she existed until then," he said. "My dad told me he has always known about her. He said he tried so hard to get Joan to give Sara to him, but she decided that since he wanted her so badly, it would cost him if he really wanted her," Adam said.

"How did your dad find out she was married and living on the ranch?" Allison asked.

"Someone had told him today, but I don't know who it would have been. He said that until today, he lost track of her when she was fourteen. He tried to find her, but it was like she had never existed."

"That has a familiar ring to it. Her cardiologist was told that she had died. The family in England that she spent time with also was told she had died. Did he tell you how he found out she was in Texas?" she asked.

"No. I left before he could. He told me what he knew was happening to Sara," Adam whispered. "Can we talk where she can't hear us?"

Adam, Allison, and Elaine walked down the hall and left Maria with Sara.

"He knew about the abuse, all the way back when she was four years old. He told me everything, including sending her money to try to buy Sara back. And that Sara is his daughter," Adam explained. "With all he told me, I had to come immediately and see if she is okay."

Allison could see that the young man's interest was Sara's well-being. "Sara has had a terrible childhood. Did you know that at one time or another, every rib had been broken? Sara has a real bad heart problem, and her mother would not let her take the medication that kept her heart beating normally. The day that she came here to live, she had been working with four broken ribs for over three weeks, and she was near death. She is five feet six inches tall and weighed only one hundred pounds. Can you wait here for a moment?"

"No problem," Adam answered.

Allison went to their bedroom and retrieved the pictures Alex had taken years before, also pictures of the tack room at Joan Redding's farm. She took them back down the hall and gave them to Adam.

"The things you see in those pictures speak volumes. Sara gave up her childhood to provide her brother and sister a chance." Allison explained and watched the man in front of her grow pale with each picture.

Adam whispered to Allison, "I promise I am not here to hurt her."

Allison smiled at him, nodding.

The three of them walked back to where Sara and Maria were. "Baby girl, it is okay. This is Adam Sterling, and you may have noticed that he has your hair and eyes. He would like to talk to you about it if that is okay."

Elaine whispered to Adam while Allison talked to Sara. "Sara is terrified of men. If your intentions regarding her are good, so be it. But don't hurt her."

Adam appreciated how much these ladies protected Sara. He walked over to her and asked if he could sit down. Sara nodded.

"I am not here to hurt you, Sara. I only just a few hours ago learned that you are my sister. My, I mean, our dad only just told me about seven hours ago. He told me how you came to be and that you had not had a good childhood."

"Baby girl, you need to breathe," came a male voice from behind Adam. "I am Scott Byers. I am Sara's husband. When my wife is afraid, she tends to hold her breath, which prompts her to faint. Please explain to all of us," Scott said, taking a seat by his wife. He looked from Sara to Adam and back. There was no question; these two were brother and sister.

"My dad got a call from someone who told him that Sara was alive, living here in Texas. We live in Bryan." Adam started and told them everything he had found out from his dad. "I know it was the phone call that bothered him because he was pale after he got off the phone. He said the man didn't give his name."

"Why was your first instinct to drive all the way here?" John asked.

"With all that my father told me, I just had to make sure she is safe. Nothing else. This was as big a shock to y'all as it was to me. But if you don't want me here, I will understand," Adam said.

"It is okay with me if you stay a little while. What do y'all think?" Sara asked.

"Would you like to stay for supper, Adam?" Allison asked.

"If it does not put anyone out, or make her afraid, I would love to," Adam said. "Are you sure, Sara? I swear I will never do anything to hurt you or those you love."

Adam felt her eyes bore into him, making him feel like she could see his soul. He could not get over seeing himself in female form.

"I can't get over how much we look alike," he said.

"Neither can I. Have you talked to your dad since you came here?" Sara asked.

"No. He knew you were being hurt, Sara. He could have stepped in at any time," he answered.

"He could have been afraid of what Lord Henry would do. He has killed people before. Lord Henry had diplomatic immunity and knew he would never be held on any kind of charges," Sara said as she stood and went to the window. "Try not to be too hard on him. He didn't really know me, and he is your dad."

Adam's father knew what she had been through. Adam, having seen the pictures of the cruelty she had been through, was not going to be so easy to forget.

Sara and Adam heard fast-moving footsteps coming, and three little boys came running toward their mother. She kneeled down and put her arms around them, hugging and kissing each. She sat on the floor for a moment and listened to the details of their day. "I have someone for you to meet, guys. This is my older brother, Adam. That makes you his nephews. Can you say hello to him?"

Austin, as always, was the first to greet him. He put his hand out and said, "I am Austin Byers, Uncle Adam."

Adam smiled at the little boy and shook hands with him. "Nice to meet you."

"These are my brothers, Brad and Ryan," he said.

"Good to meet you, boys," Adam said. "Sara, they are all just beautiful."

"Our sister, Lauren, is napping."

"And I had better get her up so she will sleep tonight," Sara said and left the room.

"Come along, Adam," John said and put a heavy hand on his shoulder. The pair walked slowly. "Sara has had a terrible life before she came here. Try not to talk about that part of her life."

"Yes, sir. What happened in her past is not what I had in mind. It is more the future I am concerned with."

"Good. But keep this in mind. If you hurt our girl, you will be sorry."

Adam looked at the man making the statement. The intensity in his eyes spoke volumes. "Sir, I swear that the only reason I came here was to see she was okay. It was my first response. My dad told me that you are good people, and I believe that. But with him being her dad, I just don't know how he could have left her with those people."

"Sara has absolute faith, son. Two times in her young life, Sara has been pronounced dead. Two times, by several medical professionals each time. She does not hate," John said.

"Not even."

"No one. She takes care of the sickest patients in the hospital and has traveled to foreign underdeveloped countries to help the people there. And she is devoutly religious, so I would not be swearing too much to her. When Sara first came here, she was near death and spent the first few years trying to get healthy. Everyone who meets her say that they are better for having known her," John said.

"Poppa, look who is awake," Sara said, holding baby Lauren.

Adam looked at the baby girl, who had her mother's hair and her father's blue eyes.

"Is my little cousin awake?" came a very British accent. Andrew said, taking Lauren from Sara.

"Andrew, this is Adam Sterling. And Adam, this is Prince Andrew from England. And for safety reasons, we would prefer if that was something you didn't tell everyone," John said.

Everyone was in the dining room for supper. Adam watched as fifteen persons had seats at the dining table.

"For anyone who does not know, this is Adam Sterling from Bryan." Over the course of the meal, everyone got to know Adam a little better. The only question that remained was how Adam's father had discovered that Sara now lived on the ranch. No one at the table questioned whether or not Adam was related to Sara because of the hair and eye color.

Adam had so many questions. He didn't want to be intrusive but took a chance. "I can't help but ask. How is it that you have a prince at your table?"

"That is a long story. But it started when Sara became a member of Mummy's court when she was twelve. We lost track of Sara for about six years, but when we found her again, we have kept in touch," Andrew said.

"What am I supposed to call you?" Adam asked.

"Andrew in private, but if you were in public, I am afraid it would be Your Royal Highness. Just like Scott and Sara, you would refer to as my lord and my lady, or in Germany, it would be Your Grace," Andrew said.

"Don't worry, Adam, if you are around much, you will get used to it. We stayed in Buckingham Palace for nearly a month last year, and you get educated very fast over there," Elaine said.

"Excuse me," Sara said and got up from the table.

There was silence in the room for a few seconds, then Scott got up and went where he thought Sara would be.

"Is she okay?" Adam asked.

"Mommy gets sad since our family died," Austin said.

"I didn't mean to pry. I am sorry," Adam said.

"You did nothing wrong. Last year we lost her younger sister and best friend, Saline; her doctor and my brother, Alex; her cardiologist that moved here to be closer to her, Steve Quinton; her best friend since she was five, Lady Lauren Dickerson; and our good friend Amy, who was the director of nurses in her first job as a nurse. They had gone to North Africa with the Red Cross. Sara couldn't go because she was expecting baby Lauren.

"Sara basically raised Saline. They were the closest two sisters you have ever seen. And might I add, they were likely as different as two sisters could be," Allison said.

"I have a lot to learn," Adam said.

"Allison, this was a great meal as always. Can I help you clean up?" Andrew asked.

"Oh, not necessary, Andrew baby," Allison said as she rose to clear the table. Riley's girlfriend and Elaine were happy to help clear the table with Allison. The men went to the family room with the exception of Andrew, who asked if Adam would walk with him. The two left the kitchen and went outside.

Scott had no idea where Sara had gone. He had been to the stables and her old room without any luck. He saw Adam accompanied by Andrew, who appeared to be in deep conversation.

"Have y'all seen Sara?" he asked.

"You haven't found her?" Andrew asked.

"I looked in the usual places, and I was fixing to go look at our house," Scott said. Together the three of them got into Scott's truck and drove the half mile and got out.

Andrew had been answering the questions that Adam had within reason, trying to give him a little background regarding the complicated woman that was both his friend and Adam's sister. When Adam pulled out the pictures that Allison had given him earlier, his outrage regarding the inhuman treatment of two young girls was apparent.

"I have seen them," Andrew said. "All of us have. Lord Henry Alexander was an animal, and his wife is just as bad." Andrew thought back to that first time they had met in London. The child that his friends had lost in their first meeting was tragic. "One might think that letting people closest to Sara view the photos would violate her privacy. I assure that is not the way of it. Seeing how completely savage they were to both Sara and Saline has resulted in those close protecting them."

The three men walked in the kitchen door in search of Sara. The lights were on, so Scott knew that she was indeed home. Scott walked to the master bedroom only to find it empty. The other two also began looking in different places in the nearly sixteen-thousand-square-foot house. Adam heard music from a very large room that was void of furniture, save a couple of stray chairs. The powerful music from the *Phantom of the Opera* was playing very loudly, and

Sara had pulled off her boots and put on her ballet slippers. Her fluid movements had him transfixed.

Scott and Andrew soon found him and watched as well. When the music stopped, the three who watched her applauded. Sara was startled just a bit but quickly recovered and walked over to them. They all broke into conversation and went to the family room. After a little while, Sara asked Scott if he minded going to the main house to get the children and tell Elaine where she was. As Doug was out of town, and Elaine had a few days off, she had come to the ranch to spend a couple of nights and study with Sara.

"Would it be okay if I stayed and we could talk a few minutes?" Adam asked.

"Up to you, baby girl," Scott said.

"That is fine," she said simply. "We will be fine."

When Scott and Andrew had left, Adam moved closer to Sara so the two could talk.

"You have a beautiful home, Sara."

"Thank you. I think Scott must have paid attention to everything I ever said I wanted in a house when we were building it. We want a big family," she said.

Adam paid attention when she talked and noted that she had a British accent. "How does a little girl who was raised in California and moves to Texas have a British accent?" he asked.

"Lord Henry knew that I was not his child. He always referred to me as the bastard and told my half siblings to do the same. He hated me from the moment I was born. When I was five, he put me on a plane and sent me to a private school in Wales. That is where I met my best friend, Lady Lauren Dickerson. We went through a lot together in the seven years that I was in school there. I nearly died when I was eight with rheumatic fever and was still recovering when Lauren had cancer. Her parents took us both out of school for a year and had us taught by tutors. We lived in their estate near Bath in England," Sara said, smiling at the memory.

"Were you happy there?" he asked.

"Oh yes. If my sister Saline had been there, it would have been perfect. I didn't get to go home for two years, and I missed her terribly, and she began to write me letters that scared me. But that doesn't really matter now.

"I have told you about myself. What about you? Are you married, or do you have children?" Sara asked.

"I am not married yet and so I don't have any kids yet," Adam answered. "Since I graduated from college, I have worked in my dad's bank with him. I stay so busy all the time I don't get out and socialize much."

"I am going to get a glass of tea. Would you like one as well?" she asked.

"Sounds good," Adam answered.

Adam followed Sara into the kitchen. Conversation continued to flow between the two siblings who had just met. Before long, Scott and Andrew came back with Elaine and the children. Sara and Elaine began the busy night routine of getting Austin and Brad ready for bed so when it was time, all they had to do is go to bed to be up early for school. Then they got Ryan and Lauren bathed and put to bed.

When the kids were ready for bed, they went to the family room where the men were talking.

"Andrew, when do you have to leave?" Adam asked, making conversation.

"Day after tomorrow. I have to be in England for a reception the following day. It is always so nice when I come here and just be another guy. Are you going to be staying here for a few days?" he asked.

"Oh no. I have to drive back home tonight," Adam said.

"Nonsense," Scott said. "Why don't you stay here tonight and get a fresh start in the morning."

"Are you sure?" Adam asked.

"Sure. We have plenty of room. It will just give us a little longer to get to know one another. What do you think, baby girl?" Scott asked.

Sara smiled. "That would be nice."

Rick got home later than usual following his visit to the county jail and, following that, to the hospital and finally the long afternoon at the clinic. He walked in the front door of their home and saw the kids playing in the living room and watching TV. He walked into the kitchen and saw Amelia.

"How is the most wonderful wife in the world?" he asked, a little bit too cheerful.

"I am fine. You have been in a good mood all day long. What are you not telling me?" Amelia asked.

"Why does something have to be wrong? I am just in a good mood. How is everything at the hospital?" he asked.

"Everything is great. The next schedule is out, and everyone got the times they requested. That is usually something that takes an act of God."

"I am glad to hear that. What is for supper?" Rick asked.

"Pork chops."

"Sounds great. I think I will get a shower before it is done," Rick said and walked into the kitchen, kissing his wife on the cheek.

Amelia watched as he walked down the hallway toward their bedroom. When she heard the shower start, she picked up the phone and called Rick's office manager and discovered that Rick had been out of the office for two hours starting at 10:30. No one asked where he went. She then called the ranch and spoke to Allison.

"Did anything strange happen today?" she asked.

"As a matter of fact, yes. You have no idea how strange," Allison said.

"I will be there in a few minutes," Amelia said and turned off the stove and told the children that supper was ready when Daddy got out of the shower.

Amelia drove quickly to the ranch to find out if Rick's mood was because of something he did. When she arrived, Allison said they needed to go to Scott and Sara's house.

When they arrived, Allison asked what the reason was for her call.

"When Rick got home, he seemed a little too pleased with himself. It was like he had a secret and didn't want anyone on to know what he had done. Every time he gets like this, I usually find the reason for it," Amelia said and got out of the car.

When they got to the family room, a man stood up with the same hair and eyes that Sara had. He looked to be about eight to ten years older, too young for a father, likely a brother.

"Amelia, this is Adam Sterling, evidently Sara's brother," Scott said.

"The two of you look like you could be twins," Amelia said. "How did you come to be here?"

"My father told me today that I have a sister. Before that, I knew nothing about her. I had to see that she was okay after everything he told me about her. I promise my presence here is pure. I would never hurt her," Adam said before Sara was back in the room.

Amelia smiled at the man. "I am Amelia Powell. I am the director of nurses at the Country Hospital," she said and put her hand out. Adam took it.

"Very nice to meet you, Mrs. Powell," he said.

"Please, call me Amelia."

"Amelia, when did you get here?" Sara asked.

"I just got here. Allison and I had something to talk about regarding work," she said, hugging her friend.

"Did you meet Adam? He is…" she couldn't finish.

"We have met," she finished.

"Why don't we get our business taken care of? Come along, my dear," Allison said. The two went back to Allison's car and began to piece together the happenings of the day.

"Who could Rick have talked to to receive the information he wanted?" Amelia asked out loud and finally came up with the only person who could have told him. "Joan Redding," they said in unison.

"I will call the county lockup and find out if he is signed in," Allison said and started the car and drove to the main house.

About twenty minutes later, it was confirmed that Rick had paid a visit to Joan Redding that day and stayed about an hour. They then called Adam's father, and he was glad to know that both Adam and Sara were well and safe.

"It appears that Rick's little plan may have backfired," Allison said. "He is a warm, young man and appears genuinely concerned over Sara's well-being. The boys even like him. And the two look so much alike it is uncanny. When Sara answered the door, she fainted."

"What do you say we make Rick aware that his dreams have come true?" Amelia said, and both women smiled.

Rick had no idea where Amelia had gone, so he and the kids went ahead and ate their supper. A little while later, Amelia's parents came to visit the kids and Amelia.

The phone rang a little while after they got there. "Rick, I am at the main house on the ranch. Sara has collapsed after a vicious man came here," Amelia said.

"I am on the way," Rick said and ran out the door. He was smiling on the inside. thinking that he finally had his chance. He was driving as fast as he could and was even pulled over, but the officer let him go when he said he had to hurry.

Rick arrived at the main house and ran to the front door and entered. "Where is she?" he asked.

"Who is that?" a polite young woman asked.

"Who are you?"

"I am Brittany Beaumont, Riley's soon-to-be wife."

"Where is Sara? She needs me," he said.

"Right this way," the girl said and led him to the family room. When he got there, all of the men in the family were present. Allison, Amelia, Maria, and Elaine were also present.

"Where is Sara? Amelia said she needs my professional help. I told you this day would come." Rick said.

"Not to worry, Rick. Dr. Dane just so happened to come to visit right after Amelia spoke to you." John said.

"Where is she? She is my patient now."

"No, Rick, she is not and never will be." Scott said. "We spoke to the people at the jail a little while ago. They said that you and Joan Redding had a good long visit today. Then there was a call to James Sterling from you. That prompted Adam Sterling to make the four-hour drive from Bryan to see his sister."

"I need to see my patient. Amelia said she needed me," Rick said.

"Well, I don't," Sara said.

Rick turned to see her standing, arm in arm with a man who had Sara's hair and eyes. He was taller than she was, and several years older, but there was no mistaking that Adam Sterling was Sara's brother. Sara walked up to Rick and stared him down, then she slapped him so hard that it made his ears ring. "I don't know what your intentions were Rick, but if I were dying, I would not want you for a doctor. You have as a patient the only member of my family you will ever have. I know she has filled your head with a couple of facts, and you made up the rest, and you are so stupid you believed her."

"She told me everything about you, Sara. You are not pure and sweet. Anything but that according to her, seducing your stepdad. I couldn't believe my ears. And then persuading your sister to run away from home, leaving your poor mother in poverty and in ill health," Rick said.

Sara was shaking her head at hearing the words coming from Rick's mouth. "Rick, why do you want me as your patient so desperately? Did you think that by repeating Joan Redding's lies I would see the error of my ways and quit working as a nurse and become your patient so you could call a news conference every time I had an appointment?"

"All I have ever wanted for you is for your family to treat you like an adult and not a spoiled child. You have three children and need to take care of them, and if you worked, it needs to be where you will be looked after.

"And have you told your brother that you killed your stepfather so you could have his place as a duchess?" Rick spat out.

"That is enough. Poppa, Scott, can I get you to do something for me?" she demanded.

"You know you can," Scott said.

"Could you call the sheriff's department and have Joan Redding taken to the farm with several deputies? Tell him that we will all meet them there. And we will need flashlights and shovels," she said. "And if someone would, drag him over there as well."

"Come along, Rick. We are all going for a ride," Mark and Riley said.

"I am not going anywhere," Rick said.

"Yes, you are. Your constant interference ends tonight," John said. "Now move."

A half hour later, everyone with the exception of Maria and the children were at Joan Redding's farm. Joan was wearing handcuffs and being guarded by two deputies after attempting to kidnap Sara the day baby Lauren had been born.

"What the hell are all these people doing on my property? And why is she here? Did you get homesick?" Then she saw Adam. She couldn't believe her eyes. Sara and Adam were standing arm in arm. Never in a million years when she had told that doctor about who Sara's father and brother were did she see this happening.

"What did you do, you idiot?" she said to Rick. Rick stood, shaking his head for her not to say more.

"What is this about, Sara?" Randy said.

"A means to an end. Follow me," she said and walked to the back door of the farm.

"So help me, Sara, I will kill you," Joan said.

Sara could feel goose bumps and fear rising, so she pulled her cape tighter around her. "Rick, as you're the person who put this crap in motion, you can do the honors." Those close to her knew that for all her bold behavior, it was only to mask the terror she had to be feeling on the inside.

"I am not going to dig in the dirt," Rick said.

"You will do as the lady said," Riley said, being the only person who knew what was about to be revealed.

"Sara, that is not something that you want to do," Joan said again.

"Riley. Would you please read for me?" she asked.

Riley looked from Sara to Scott to his father, the look asking a question that Sara merely nodded to. "I can't run and hide any longer," she whispered, half pleading. Riley knew she was right, and though honored by her trust, he felt the pain that she must have felt for so long.

Point by agonizing point, Riley read the document that had been told to him by the two sisters. "Acts of torture of every kind—

physical, emotional and psychological—locked in closets and storage containers after having been beaten, raped, and abused by Henry and Joan Alexander; beaten but never raped by Oscar Redding, but only because they defended themselves and were able to stop him together."

"My sister would never be able to have children because of her own parents. Saline was born with both aristocratic and royal blood. We were both raised as royals. But only a few knew what was happening to us or even cared." She looked lovingly to Lord and Lady Dickerson. "I was adopted by Her Majesty's own cousin and her husband, here present. Both royals. Their daughter was my best friend, and she and Prince Andrew were dear friends until her death, and is frequently a guest in our home." Sara stopped only to draw breath and continued.

"And we still consider you ours, my baby," Lord George Dickerson said, not attempting to hide the emotion he was feeling.

"And yes, they knew what they were getting. A bastard. The result of my mother's whoring ways." Sara walked over to Rick. "You have pursued me like an animal does its prey. You accuse me of seducing my stepfather. Tell me, would you? As you say, I am a lesser human. Do they teach five-year-old girls to seduce a man in the schools here? I was raised in the UK, and they didn't teach us that. Because that is about how old I was the first time he and his friends used me as their party toy." She then looked to Scott and the rest of her family who knew what she was about to say.

"You never asked why I was never returned to school when I was twelve," she whispered to him and looked to Joan Redding, who was shaking her head silently, threatening her. "I was expecting Lord Henry Alexander's child—" she was interrupted by Frances.

"We begged her not to return. She could have the child, and we would care for both of them with all the love and protection that could be offered. But at twelve, she received a letter from her sister. She had emergency surgery from having nearly hemorrhaged to death. Lady Saline Alexander was nine years old. That cost her her womb. They took Sara to a butcher, who terminated the pregnancy in what can only be described as horrific circumstances in a place where there were rats that were present. The child lived a few minutes. And when we called and searched for the girls for over two years…"

"Another set of strangers found us," Sara said and looked to John and Allison. The love she felt for them and the Dickersons as parents was untold. "They saved us. And as a wedding present, Scott found them, and all of us are now family." She then looked to Rick again. "Tell me, Rick, was your own daughter taught to seduce you?" She waited only a second. "I didn't think so. Being a person with a title is a life of service. Be that serving as a queen, all the way down to a nurse. We know what we are supposed to do. No different from our family's business. There is no nurse here that is not aware of that, your wife included. As you recall, she never had to work either. But she chose to care for you boys in a field hospital. Even the ones who were not able to avoid the draft.

"Do you think I pursued my husband?" she smiled, thinking about their first official meeting.

"She ran right into my arms immediately before she collapsed. I had been trying to ask her out for over two years, who, even after being beaten so badly, was and is still the most beautiful thing in my world," Scott said.

"And even as the second son of a queen, a prince in my own right. As with her sister, and every member of her family at the ranch, we are there for her," Andrew said.

"And we are here for her as well," Randy said, tipping his hat.

"And at the hospital and wherever she is, she is and will always be our patient," Eric said.

"I don't understand any of you." His frustration was clear. "What is her hold? Why do you take her word as fact?"

With lightning speed and unseen action, Allison stepped forward, using her fist in a very uncharacteristic manner, into Rick's face, obviously breaking his nose. "You worthless son of a bitch. A strange set of circumstances surround the loss of that child," Allison said.

"On that very day, we lost our daughter," John said. "And nearly lost my Allison. When Sara went to work in my café, we took a keen interest because of a good friend of ours who told us what was happening to those girls. We planned to legally remove them from that whore. And Sara Lyn became our baby girl."

When they were two feet down, one of the deputies said that there appeared to be something rolled up in a carpet. Sara began to feel sick. The only person she had ever told about what was buried at the back door was Maria.

"Excuse me please," Sara said. She walked away from the crowd of people who were now interested in what was buried by the back door. She walked to the barn. She didn't know why she felt so compelled to do so, but she pulled the tin back and crawled inside. She reached on the small shelf and found the flashlight was still there, and surprisingly, it still worked. The tack room was exactly like it had been the last time she saw it. The little cooler was no longer there, but anything could have happened to it.

The dirt floor, the small pile of hay covered by an old blanket, and some of the old clothes left over from years ago. She picked up the other blazer that she had. It was worn and much too small for her now, but it had been taken care of so she would have clothes. She picked up a couple of things of Saline's and Jody's. She remembered the fear that they had to live with for so long—all the wild animals, cold, hungry, and so completely alone. The tiny tack room had been the place where they felt safe to be, but it was anything but safe. There were spiders, wasps, skunks, and snakes that they had to watch out for. Then there was the ever-present fear that Oscar would find out where they were.

"Sara," Scott said as he watched his wife, who was now kneeling as she looked at the meager belongings that meant so much at the time. He knew that she had not heard him as he crawled into the tack room.

"I am sorry, Scott. I didn't hear you come in," she said. She acted almost ashamed that Scott had married her, knowing she had spent two years sleeping in such a place. Scott knew that displaced shame was something that children of abuse too often felt.

"When we first moved here, Lord Henry had been told that the man selling the farm had changed his mind. So he took Saline and me with him to talk to that man. He didn't let him get two words out before he shot him in the face. Saline and I had that man's blood and brains all over us. Then Lord Henry told us to start digging a hole using our hands to bury him. That man was not far from where we were digging. It took him a few minutes to die. Listening to that poor man trying to breathe was sickening. He told Saline and me to remember what he had just done. If either she or I ever told anyone about anything he had done, we would be lying beside him. Momma always made sure we remembered it. He rolled that man up in the piece of carpet and pushed him in the hole and covered him up.

"How could anyone believe that Saline or myself could ever want to seduce him? I know that he is dead, and has been for seven years. But except for Maria, I have never been able to tell anyone about it until now. Am I going to have to leave so that Rick Powell will leave the rest of you alone?" she said and started to cry.

Adam had been completely silent, but he listened to what Sara, his sister Sara, had been saying. How he hated his father for keeping everything from him. How he also hated his birth mother for all she had done. How could anyone treat children the way this woman had?

"Baby girl, I can tell you that I would never let you leave. You have done nothing wrong. Rick is just an insecure man that tries to make himself feel bigger by bullying those weaker than he is. And if you ever left me, I would not stop looking until I found you. I love you, baby girl. I can't live without you," Scott concluded.

"I can't live without you either. And I should have told you about that poor man earlier, but I was afraid," she said. "And I hope you are not angry about what I told everyone." She looked at her empty hands and shook her head. "For a moment, when he arrived and began his latest rant, and to say how my sister and I could possibly pursue him, he reminded me of him. But I didn't want to hide or run away any longer. Everyone has protected me here for so long. Everyone has literally changed their lives to make sure Saline, Jody, and I were safe," she said, taking a painful breath and continuing. "That woman tried to take our baby daughter and myself, and Rick tries to rationalize her behavior. I just couldn't run any longer. As difficult as it is to live with, there was nothing that we could have done except what we did, and that was to survive. Running, hiding, holding on to each other no matter what. The filth that no amount of soap, water, and scrubbing could take away." Then regardless of what all had happened to her and Saline, a weight seemed to be lifting for the first time in her life. "Only an undying, unconditional love of a family that only seems to grow in size and strength every minute. From rancher to royal, no one has ever lied, hurt, or walked away. Everyone kept every promise they ever made. You have always said I was a little slow. It has just taken me nine years to stand on my own two feet," she said and blushed.

"Baby girl, we needed you. All three of you, maybe more than you needed us. We no longer have to stay in hotels but rather stay with friends and family in castles and palaces. We knew that because of your past, you may never understand how loved and needed you are. And that we thank God for you in our lives," Scott said, gently embracing his wife and kissing her forehead.

"Why don't we go see what Rick has to say about all this? I wish I would have brought a camera to take a picture of him digging in the dirt," Scott said. "Let's get you out of here and get you warm."

"I feel bad for Amelia. I can't believe he is making such a ninny out of himself. I know it must be humiliating for her."

"She and Rick have already had words about it. Momma took her back to the ranch, and her parents are going to bring the kids to the main house for a couple of days. When Amelia saw that what he was digging up was a body, she told him that if he ever said another negative word about you and our family, she was filing for divorce."

"Sara, I have a few questions about what you know about this," Randy said.

"I know," she said, looking at her mother not ten feet away from her.

Joan knew the brave look that she gave was completely different to how she was feeling. So all she had to do was stare her down.

"That is the man who owned this place before Lord Henry and my mother bought it. When he tried to tell him he had changed his mind on the sale of the land, Lord Henry shot him in the face," she said.

"Were you the only one present when this happened?" Randy asked.

"No, my sister Saline was there and Momma," Sara said, never looking up from the ground.

"She is making it all up. You can't trust a girl who kidnaps her sister and brother," Joan said.

"I never kidnapped, seduced, or lied. The fact is that if you had never brought Oscar home, I would have worked and never complained," Sara said.

"She is lying. That man and Sara were found by her father, and in the heat of the moment, Henry shot him," Joan lied. "And without Saline here to confirm or deny, it is her word against mine."

"That is where you are wrong, Momma. Both Saline and I had papers as you heard being read earlier, regarding what happened if something should happen to one of us. Riley, if you don't mind handing the copy to the sheriff. And, Sheriff Oakley, if you don't mind reading the part regarding this out loud, I would appreciate it," Sara said, looking as though she wanted to run.

Sara and Saline had asked when Riley had become an attorney if there was something they could put into writing in case something happened to one of them, that the surviving sister would be able to say what had happened in their childhood up to that time. Horrors that even the Byers family didn't even know. Quite like his older brother and their father, Riley never told a secret. He had taken a great load off his two adopted sisters to lessen their pain just a little.

The late evening grew colder with every word that was spoken. At first Sara looked to her mother to see what she was doing while Riley was telling of her life of misdeeds. Joan changed from being merely angry to breaking free of those that kept her standing between them to having her hands wrapped around Sara's throat.

"You bitch!" she screamed, throwing Sara to the ground, continuing to choke her.

The noisy commotion woke Oscar from his drug-induced stupor, and he came outside, prepared to run if he felt like he was to be taken to jail again.

Even with all the people struggling to pull her off Sara, it took about three minutes to remove her hands and to shackle her.

The attack had left Sara struggling for breath. Rick began to walk toward her and was quickly halted.

"She needs my help. Can't you people see that?" he said.

"She needs nothing from you, Rick Powell. We know who it was who called Adam's father today. You had gone to the jail to get more information from that whore," John Byers said.

Sara was coughing, struggling to catch her breath. Eric was immediately at her side. "Look at me, Sara, and try to breathe. Look at me."

As expected, the terror of having been attacked so suddenly made her want to flee, but first she had to be able to breathe. When she tried to speak, her voice was hoarse and barely audible.

"Don't try to talk, just catch your breath," Scott said.

"She asked them to call her doctor because she was not feeling well," Rick said.

"According to the people at the county lockup, she had an unannounced visit from you. The visit lasted for more than an hour. And immediately after that, you called her former husband and told him where Sara was."

"No. No one had to steal your children from you. We came and got two of them, and the other had nearly died because of you and your husband. It took them a long time to believe that someone could love them, want them, and go through the fires of hell to keep them. I am the one she calls Momma. There are two other women who consider her their daughter, and neither one is you," Allison said.

"And if you look to an older reality, my husband and I adopted Sara Lyn Dickerson when she was nine and had been living in England for nearly three years without any visits from her so-called family, or trips home. Our family suffered cruelly when you told us she had died. We searched the world over for nearly two years and could not find her. Then to think about everything you put Sara and Saline through, along with baby Jody, I pray the laws here are severe. However, I have spoken to some people back in England, and there is a case that can be made for the kidnapping of our adoptive daughter. All of us love her, and then there is you. You want her for what you can get," Frances said with pride.

"Well, Mrs. Redding, we have some new charges to apply to you. A body in your backyard and everything else means you could be staying with us for some time to come," Randy said.

"Wait. I want a moment with my daughter, alone. She won't be pressing any charges against me," Joan said.

"No," Scott said simply.

"You have no right to speak for her. She is a grown woman. Why—" was all that Rick could say before John grabbed him by the upper arm in a vice-like grip and began to drag him to the barn.

"What the hell do you want to tell me here that you couldn't have told me in front of the rest of them?" Rick asked before the tin of the small tack room was pulled back and he was shoved into the darkness and dirt floor and very cold room.

Rick strained his eyes to see in the darkness and raised to stand only to hit his head on the rack that was historically used to put saddles on. "Damn it! Are you nuts? First you make me dig up a body, then pull me from someone who needs care, and now you assault me and throw me in this pigpen."

"It would serve you right to make you spend a few days in this room," John, said turning on a flashlight. "Do you see how the hay is piled up a little? Inside that small chest are the only clothes they had to wear. Recall if you will how cold it can be in the winter."

"What does that have to do with you pushing me into this filth-infested place?"

"Think about how wet, dry, and cold it was and they had no coats, not even a raincoat. Or the heat that was made even hotter without any airflow in this room. Did you know that the last weeks that they lived in here, they were starving to death in every sense of the word. I have discovered that during your time in Vietnam, you were less than a good soldier. As a matter of fact, rumor has it that your injury could have been self-inflicted, but with nothing proven so close to the end of your tour, you were gladly sent home," John Byers said with a little smirk.

"Who have you been talking to?" he asked, standing.

"You only had to live under those circumstances for less than a year. Think about having your entire life terrified and no end in sight.

This is where the children lived for over two years. Sara continued to have faith, and it was that faith that sustained the three of them.

"The morning that they came to live at the ranch, Sara had been beaten black and blue with multiple broken bones. But she had to get money for her brother and sister, so she walked to work, in the cold rain, wearing only the very worn school uniform. She had no coat, and it is a mile to where she worked at a little café," John said.

"Once again, that is what you were told."

"Wrong, you filth. That is what the manager herself told us. I own that café. I saw her day in, day out. Waiting for just a chance that there was someone who knew them who hadn't discovered how badly they were treated. They had no one.

"You say that we treat Sara like a child. Most of that is true. But she was a warm, strong-minded, smart young woman. She was nobody's baby girl. My brother-in-law referred to her as a child of the wilderness. She has had all the responsibility in her young life. Before us, no one even acknowledged them. All they needed was a chance, and we have given it to them and got back more than anyone could have ever given us. Even a simpleminded second-rate physician who beats his chest at his own greatness. The only reason that you have been able to practice at the country hospital is because of her. This time, I will tell you with absolute certainty that your privileges have been suspended from the hospital. You have your clinic to practice out of, but if someone needs to be hospitalized, you will have to go through one of the other doctors until further notice. No exceptions."

"In all fairness to me," Rick bellowed.

"When did you ever think about fairness to her? From the time you started working here, you have been on her back. True, you have not been nice to a single employee, but she never does anything right according to you. To that end, she quit the hospital and began working in Tyler. You go to the ranch and yell in front of our guests here, follow us to and from the airport, just to name a few things. Most people who dislike a person avoid that person, but instead, you make a point of keeping track of her so you can taunt."

"I only want for her what is best," Rick said.

"Good, then we understand each other perfectly. Leave her alone. I don't care what you do with that whore, but no one wants to hear anything regarding her," John concluded. "And just to let you know, Sara's grandmother offered to tell her who her father is. She declined wanting to know," John said.

"Why wouldn't a girl like that not want to know who her father was?" Rick asked.

"Her words to her grandmother at the supper table in our home were, she didn't want to know. She already had a father," John said. Remembering those words made him swell with pride.

"Could it be as, Mrs. Redding said, that Sara wanted the title so badly that she killed her stepfather?" Rick asked.

John had held back his contempt for this man for long enough. "Give me your coat."

"It is only twenty-five degrees. I will not give you my coat," Rick said.

John struck Rick hard in the jaw. "Your coat and suit jacket. That would be now."

Rick took off his coat and suit coat, feeling a chill that went to the bone.

"Hope you have eaten," John said, exiting the tack room. "See you in the morning."

"You can't be serious. It is freezing, and I haven't eaten since this morning."

"I am very serious. See what it was like for those children. You have the same things that they had for two years. There is bunting for a bed of hay, a flashlight that works somewhat, but I would watch your battery usage," John said.

"I am not an animal. You can't treat me like one. The law is here, and I will file charges," Rick said, his fear rising.

John laughed a little as he exited the tack room and replaced the tin. It didn't take Rick but a moment to begin to yell for someone to help him. The cold wind was easily felt. He hadn't thought about being hungry until John Byers mentioned it.

When no one responded to his calls for help after what he thought had to be hours, he sat down on the cold floor. After the second hour, he began to try to exit by means of the tin but found that something had been placed in front of it. After a little while, he took the ragged blanket and tried to warm himself, then after a time, he began to hear the scratching of creatures, likely rats or perhaps even skunks. Rick had never lived in the country because of such things. After a time of fighting the creatures of the night, the cold, and not knowing how long he was to be kept in the tack room, he fell asleep.

Outside the tack room, the officers of the sheriff's department took Joan Redding back into custody. In addition to the charges that had been brought against her were now charges of attempted murder of her daughter and the possibility of charges against her for the killing of the man that had been uncovered. The medical examiner in Dallas would determine if what Sara had described was true.

Oscar, who had come outside only briefly, went back inside due to not wanting to risk going back to the county lockup.

John, suspecting some form of repercussions from the evening, asked if Scott would mind staying at the main house rather than waking the children and taking them home. Allison had requested it of them, and Scott agreed it may be a good idea.

When they arrived home, Sara went to check on the children and then to the kitchen. The weather called for possible snow that night and the cold crept through her like a knife. She decided to make some hot chocolate and put a pan on the stove. She even made sure and made enough for everyone. While she was waiting for it to cook, she heard someone walk into the kitchen. She turned and saw Andrew.

"Andrew, I am making hot chocolate, if you want some," she said, obviously a little ill at ease.

"Thanks, I think I will," Andrew said, taking a seat at the table. Sara poured them each a mug of hot chocolate. "You were awfully quiet on the way home."

"Do you think I was wrong?" she asked, looking at her cup.

"No. I think that it was long overdue. Your mother is a monster and needs to be held accountable for her actions," Andrew answered.

But as he had seen with his friend before, there was the guilt that she had lived with her entire life. "She is locked away now, Sara. She can't hurt you anymore." Right away he could tell his words were no more than white noise to the young woman. Although the same age, like most of the people around her, he knew that she had never actually had a childhood. Anyone could see the child in her that was still afraid and needed to be protected.

Sara stood a little abruptly and asked that Andrew let everyone know she had made hot chocolate, that she was going up to bed. She had never taken the warm cape off and pulled it tightly around her as if she had never come in from the cold.

Andrew now thought of her as his friend, of course, but through Frances as his cousin. Maybe not in the bloodlines that made her a royal, but with the selfless heart that made her a lady. "Sleep well," Andrew said simply. Then he took the cup of hot chocolate and went to the family room with the others.

Adam was invited as well. Everyone in the family thought it best for him to stay for a few reasons: first, because of the late hour and the long drive home, and second, the thought of getting to know him a little better seemed like a good idea. The third was even more practical, and that was the roads that were already cold would likely freeze, and there would be ice.

He agreed to stay and had been shown where his room would be. He then returned to the family room. John and Riley were not present, but everyone was. There was only one topic of conversation, and that was centered on the happenings at Joan Redding's farm.

"I thought I had seen and heard of every horror that the girls had gone through since they came here. I just never imagined," Allison said, and her voice broke. "No wonder they were so afraid."

Frances, who sat beside her, picked up her hand and gave it a squeeze. "Because Henry was German, he could never have been held accountable, but not so for his former wife. I pray they put that animal away for the rest of her life."

"I cannot believe Rick could stoop so low as to visit her so he could get information he could use. He is no better than a drug dealer. I am so sorry for all this," Amelia said.

"It is not your fault, Amelia. You have tried and tried to reason with him, and he just doesn't listen. Perhaps he sees her differently now," Allison said.

"Besides, I believe that he will be a little empathetic in the morning. Daddy is letting him spend the night in the tack room," Scott said.

"The one that?" Amelia asked.

"The vary one. He put something in the way to get out so he would not be able to get out. Randy left one of his deputies there, so there is no danger to him. He and Riley took his car to the farm so he will have a way home in the morning," Scott said. "But he does not know that."

Amelia smiled a little on the inside, thinking about the spoiled city boy being left in the cold, dark tack room.

"I never should have come here," Adam said.

"Nonsense, Adam. That whore would have eventually found a way to use her information. You had no way of knowing that you had a sister until your father told you. And your first response was not that of someone who was just curious, but that of someone who cared enough to see that she was finally safe," Allison said.

Andrew had told the family what she had said about having fixed hot chocolate. Everyone continued to talk. Allison and Frances got up and came back with several cups of hot chocolate.

John and Riley came back about an hour later. It was well after midnight, and everyone was beginning to talk about going to bed when they heard the first hysterical screams. The entire room was immediately on their feet going to Scott and Sara's room. Scott was the first to arrive to his wife's cries. He was quickly across the room on floor with Sara, her eyes unseeing and wide, not responding.

"Sara, wake up. Wake up, baby girl," he said, taking her into his arms.

"Come on, Scott will take care of her," Allison said.

"But she is still screaming. She is scared to death," Adam said.

"No. She is terrified. Her demons are real. They haunt her," Elaine said.

"A few years ago, Saline said terror is like a runaway train—you can't stop it," Andrew said. "The first time I ever heard her screams was at Kensington Palace, she said that to me. Her words and Sara's screams I still can hear at night sometimes."

"I know what I am going to do," Adam said in a fierce voice as he headed for the door. A heavy hand fell on Adam's shoulder.

"You're not going anywhere right now, son," John said.

"Why not? That bitch deserves killing. So does my father," Adam yelled.

"She deserves much worse than that. But if you go after her, it will keep you from getting to know your sister further. Is that what you want?" John said.

Adam saw the reason in what he was saying. "I am sorry, sir. I didn't realize what I was going to do."

John walked over to a bar that was in the family room and poured Adam scotch to try to help him settle. Both sat and listened for nearly an hour.

One by one the rest of the family decided to return to the family room rather than going to bed, to stay in the family room in case they were needed. Elaine stayed in the room with Scott and Sara.

"The last time we were all sitting around this quiet was when Sara had Austin," Frances said.

"All of you went to the hospital when Sara had their first child?" Adam asked.

"Oh no," Frances said and smiled a little. "She had a backache the night before and didn't realize it was labor pains. Our daughter, Sara's adopted sister Lauren, was sitting with her. Then her water broke."

"As it happened, the hospital was fifty miles away, and the roads were icy, and no one wanted to take a chance of her delivering on the side of the road," Allison said. "My brother, who died last year, was up here at the main house, as was her cardiologist."

"Not long after we got her to bed, she needed to push. For almost two hours, that is what she did. We all alternated between watching the clock and doing busy work. All the ladies went to the kitchen and started fixing food," Frances said.

"Then we heard the cry," John said. "John Austin Byers, my namesake, was born. He weighed over nine pounds. Scott, Lauren, and Maria were also in the room. When Scott brought him out to us…" John's voice broke, and tears were in his eyes.

"I have always been a royal. I also married a royal. Our daughter and Sara met the first day of school in Wales. When they were eight, both of them nearly died so many times. We even pulled them both out of school and had them tutored at our home in Bath. I don't think either of them would have made it without each other. Every time she went home for school breaks, she would return to us and be black and blue. She had nightmares much like what you heard. We wanted for her to stay with us and to adopt her, but Sara felt that she was the only thing that kept her sister safe," Frances said and then put her head down and began to cry. Allison held her.

Everyone continued to talk and then again heard the same screaming, but this time, before part of them got upstairs, the scream was cut short. She had run into the door facing and was then on the ground. She sat up before anyone got to her.

"Sara, are you okay?" Scott got to her and asked.

"I think so. Why is everyone here? Where are the kids?" she asked, obviously a little confused.

"Momma asked us to stay last night. The kids are still asleep down the hall and are fine," Scott said.

She looked up and saw the family, along with Elaine and Amelia, then looked down at the floor. "I am so sorry," she said, then started to cry.

Adam walked back down to the family room. Suddenly the room felt so cold. He walked over to the fireplace and put a couple of logs on the fire them took the poker and stirred the fire a little to bring it back to life.

Andrew had come back into the room and walked over to Adam. "Need a refill?"

"Yeah. That would be good. Thanks," Adam said. "I am going to be her brother. That woman is the lowest human life form that I have ever seen."

"Then the most important thing you need to know about your sister is that she cares nothing about herself. She would and has spent a lifetime putting herself between those she loves and harm. That is why anyone who knows her, from a ranch hand to the queen, does their best to protect her. She does not know that every time she leaves here alone, there is someone following her to make sure she is safe. There is no one here that does not feel that way about her.

"Last year when the family was in London, all of us had lost family and friends in the plane crash and were in mourning for them. Sara had become very sick but was hurting so much from the loss that she didn't realize it," Andrew said and cleared his throat. "She collapsed during Lady Lauren's funeral and was taken to Buckingham Palace to a medical facility there. Sara's heart stopped and, after two hours trying to get her back, was pronounced dead. The baby's heart never stopped beating. Several of us here were in that room. Scott, Elaine, two of her doctors, Frances, and even the archbishop of Canterbury when she came back to us. What Sara Lyn Byers experienced in those minutes shook all of us to the bone."

Adam didn't know at what point he made up his mind that he could never be so far away from his sister again. He could get work anywhere. And working for his father, knowing how she had been treated, was not an option. He didn't get to be there the first twenty-five years of her life, but he would be there from that point on.

The rest of that Friday night was not as dramatic, but it was only because Sara was willing herself to stay awake. Scott had asked John if he would mind calling either David or Eric to see if they could come to check on her or they would bring her to them. David had said he would be there within the hour.

As he said, David was there in less than an hour. He knew that they had never called him to come out, and there had to be something major going on for them to call. The moment he saw Adam, he knew that things had just gotten complicated.

"David, this is Adam Sterling, Sara's brother," Allison said. "Neither of them knew the other existed. And, Adam, this is one of Sara's doctors, and a good friend, David Glass."

The two shook hands. "I can tell you are thinking the same thing that we were when we first saw him. They share the same mother and father. And they live in Bryan. As soon as Adam heard about Sara's life, he drove straight here," Allison said.

"I assure you that I did not come here with anything but good intentions. I would never do anything to hurt her." Adam felt compelled to say.

"We know," Allison said. At that, David went upstairs to Scott and Sara's room, the same room they always used when staying at the main house. He could only imagine how this sudden new knowledge came about, but there was question as to them being brother and sister.

"How is my superstar nurse feeling?" he asked.

"I had a cold last week," she said.

He could see that one side of her face was swelling a little from running into the door facing of the large bedroom.

"It sounds more like you had the flu to me," David said, taking a seat beside her on the bed and picking up her hand. "Has your chest begun to hurt at all?"

Adam, Allison, and Amelia had come upstairs when David had.

Sara's eyes darted around the room and settled on Scott. She whispered, "Please don't leave."

"I am not going anywhere, baby girl. You know that," Scott said and gently kissed her forehead. "Can you answer David for me?"

Nobody knew what to think about her frame of mind. "It was just cold in the tack room last night. I was afraid it was going to rain on us. It is my turn to stay awake. Saline needs her sleep."

David looked at Scott. As if reading his mind, he answered, "She has been like this since about three. She is running a little fever, and she is splinting."

"Not to mention wanting to get a jug of milk and go to the barn with Saline and Jody," Elaine said.

Sara spoke again. Her voice was still hoarse from Joan Redding's attack. "Could you take it to them for me?" she asked Elaine.

"Sure, I will be right back," Elaine said, never leaving the room.

"Uncle Alex said I may have cracked some ribs when I fell. But I will be quite well." She began to speak in French for a little while. Sara was not combative at all, so David listened to her chest, hearing the friction rub in the right side and over the heart. At that, David asked for Scott to step out of the room with him. Amelia went to Sara's side.

"How hard did she hit her head? And what all happened yesterday?" David asked.

"She hit that door facing hard. It didn't knock her out. It woke her up from the nightmare. David, it is one of those things you had to see. She just told the sheriff where to dig, not what was there. Her stepdad used the man selling the house as a means to keep the girls in line. He shot the man in the face just a few feet from them then told them to dig a hole with their hands.

"But the look on her face was as if she was trying to determine if what she remembered was real. The things that she and Saline told Riley were beyond all comprehension," Scott explained. "Her mother was there with sheriff's deputies, but she managed to break away from the deputies and put a firm stranglehold on Sara's neck. The bruises are already apparent."

Riley walked over and handed him a copy that he would likely be wise to keep.

"Why don't we go downstairs and talk for a moment?" David said, not wanting Sara to listen for now.

"I will stay up here with Amelia, if that is all right," Andrew said.

Adam was so moved by the family that no doubt loved his sister with every fiber of their being. He listened to all that David had to say and was included in the conversation when appropriate.

Upstairs, Andrew sat with Amelia. "Sara, do you know who I am?" he asked.

He could see her struggling to think. "Andrew."

"That is correct, and Mummy sends her regards," Andrew said. "Remember when Saline popped me in the nose?"

"You and Poppa, yes?" she asked. "Do you know our friend Amelia? She is such a good nurse, me and Elaine want to be like her one day."

"We met a few months ago. The three of you could rule the world," Andrew said.

"Oh no, don't say such things. Your mummy has that task. She sent her regards. Do you know if Saline passed her boards? I don't think I am getting enough sleep. I can't remember if she told me," Sara asked, then stood to walk to the bathroom, a little unsteady.

"I will be right out I promise," she said. Amelia walked quietly over to the closed bathroom door. She didn't hear anything such as falling so she just waited. When the door opened, she saw Sara in the more direct lighting, and her color was a little dusky, so she picked up her hand and noticed they were cyanotic. Likely, between hitting her head, having a cold, and being violently choked about three minutes was causing the confusion.

"Andrew, could you go and tell David I think I have put some pieces together," she asked.

"Will do," he said, leaving the room.

In Bryan, James Sterling waited on into the night for word from Adam. He had never stayed away without calling. By morning, Mr. Sterling decided he would see if he had gone in search of his sister. It didn't take long once he got to Dallas and to Byers Oil. He was given the address of the ranch and even good directions on how to get there. He was an hour away from seeing the daughter that he had known about for over twenty-five years.

It was a little past noon when he arrived at the main house. He found his palms sweating at the thought of meeting the young lady who Joan had used to torment him with.

When the door opened, a man who looked to be about thirty answered. "Can I help you?" Mark said.

"I am looking for my son, Adam Sterling. Am I at the right house?" he asked.

"He was here until a couple of hours ago. He accompanied the family with his sister to the hospital," Mark said.

"What happened to Sara?" he asked.

"What did you think was going to happen when you told him you had lied to him his entire life? Last night he heard from the horse's mouth what happened to her, her entire life. Or should I say what you allowed to happen?" Mark asked.

"Her mother was sent money to help care for all the children, not just Sara," James answered.

"And you know your former wife to care so much about her children, after all, Adam was the first that she abandoned. When your daughter was born the bastard daughter of a monster, did you think he would embrace the situation?" Mark asked.

"That was twenty-five years ago. Sara is a grown woman now. From what I understand, she is happy and well cared for now."

"Mr. Sterling, the morning Sara came here to live, I was here. I was in the café that she walked one mile up the interstate to work. She had been beaten so badly that it would have put the toughest ranch hand down for weeks, but she had to feed her brother and sister. Four broken ribs were only part of her injuries. When she collapsed in Scott's arms, she was near death. All one hundred pounds of her. When he put her into my arms to immediately take home to our mother, he got in his truck and went to Joan Redding's farm. He picked up the siblings and also took them to the ranch, where anyone who meets Sara has nothing but a desire to protect her," Mark said, almost in a whisper, closing his eyes to the memory.

"You have to understand, I was raising a son who didn't know that he had a younger sister. He didn't know that the woman he calls mom was not his mother. I am the president of the bank and the owner of Sterling Industries. If I had done differently from what I did, my wife would have known about my infidelity. I would have to explain to my son who was only eight years old when she was born, and I would have lost my standing in the bank. Can't you see it was what I thought best for the most people?" James Sterling said. "I really need to explain this to my son."

"Adam has gone with part of the family to the hospital with Sara. He said if I heard from you to tell you to go to hell," Mark said with an easy confidence.

"My son needs to come home. He is an officer in the bank and has a duty," Sterling said.

"He has seen what the president of the bank does with his responsibilities and is following his example. Now I will tell you, you are to leave this ranch. Leave Sara and Adam alone. They want no part of you or Joan Redding," Mark said.

"I am a powerful man and can cause you a great deal of trouble. I would suggest you let me know where my son is," he said.

"I am right here," a very exhausted Adam Sterling came up behind Mark. "Thanks, Mark. Like my new brother-in-law just told you, Daddy, I no longer want to have anything to do with you."

"Son, you have a job and responsibilities at home," James said.

"Do you know what my responsibility is now? My sister. My nephews and niece. You said nothing about the four beautiful grandchildren that you have. My half sister Saline died a few months ago," Adam said.

"According to her mother, she lies for her own purposes," James said.

Adam moved toward the man with lightning speed, knocking his father back out the door into the yard. "She does not lie. Her nightmares are traumatic. You can feel her terror. Last night she hit her head and now has a concussion. That slut, all of us watched as she attempted to strangle her own daughter. Last night, I saw where she lived for two years."

"That was when she was a child. She is a grown woman. You would give up the life you have for a sister you don't know?" his father yelled while dusting himself off.

"You are the one I never knew. Sara has the purest heart of any human being I have ever met, and so help me God if something happens, because of you and your whore you will pay," Adam said. "How do you think your customers will feel about the bank if they find out the things I have discovered in the last twenty-four hours?"

There was another set of ears that was listening to what was being said. Then all at once, there was an eight-year-old boy who was using his hands, feet, and teeth to combat the man who had caused his mother so much pain.

"No, Austin," Mark and Adam said, but the boy's fury was not so easily spent. Mark reached down and picked up the young boy.

"Austin, is this what Mommy would want you to do?" Mark said. The young boy was now crying tears of frustration and fear for his mother. Mark hugged him tightly for comfort.

"No, Uncle Mark," he said and sobbed. "But I hate him."

"Go in and wash your face," Mark said and hugged the little boy who, wanted to be a man and protect his mother.

"Yes, sir," he said and did as he was told.

"Sara is only twenty-five. That cannot possibly be her child."

"That is her and Scott's first child. I was there when he was born at their house when she was seventeen," Mark said. "I believe you were told to leave. So I would suggest you do so," Mark said and closed the door.

James Sterling was not a man to give up on something because he was told to. He had never had Adam to raise his voice to him in protest. Sara had touched something deep within him. He got in his car and thought about where the closest hospital would be. He knew there was a small hospital in town, but likely Tyler was a better choice. There were two big hospitals there. So that is where he would look. If he could find her, he could reason with her. She could talk to Adam.

He drove to the first hospital in Tyler and immediately saw that there was a wing called the Byers-Quinton Memorial Cardiac Center at St. Mary's Hospital. He parked his Mercedes-Benz in the pay parking lot and walked inside. As with most hospitals, it was not as full as during the week. He went to the main desk and found Sara's room number upstairs.

He took the elevator to the sixth floor and walked to the room where Sara was supposed to be. He slowly opened the door and saw the sleeping young woman that looked so much like his son. Both had their mother's high cheekbones, but had his hair. He had not yet seen her eyes but had been told they were the same green as Adam's were. She looked even younger than her twenty-five years.

No one else was in the room, so he stepped inside the room and closed the door. He thought about the little boy who had stood up for his mother. He had never given much thought to the idea of being a grandfather. But as Sara was his daughter, that meant the young boy was indeed his grandson. Then there were the three that he had not seen as yet. And as an added bonus, she was married to one of the wealthiest families in Texas. Like most bankers, he had a healthy respect for bottom lines.

The only thing that worried him was his wife. She had no idea that he had been unfaithful to her early in their marriage and through that conceived a daughter; that had been twenty-five years ago. However, it was partly due to her family that he held his present position.

At fifteen years old, Joan had been the most beautiful, exotic woman he had ever met. She looked to be well beyond her age at that time. When she became pregnant, she had then told him her age and of course he had no choice but to marry her or go to jail. She was tall and stately, and when they attended social occasions, she turned heads. Taking care of her son was not something she liked to do, so Adam spent most of his time with nannies. When he began to hear rumors about the time Joan was spending with other men, he didn't want to believe it. When he caught her in their bed with a man, he filed for divorce. He had married his present wife only two months later on the rebound.

He found Amanda to be a somewhat cold woman, saying from the beginning that she never wanted children. But James had Adam, and he was enough. Then when Adam was seven, he ran into Joan again; their affair resulted in Sara Lyn. Now he had found that he had grandchildren that he lived only a few hours from, and he wanted to get to know them.

Sara's eyes opened, and she thought she was dreaming. "Who are you?" she asked, moving toward the far side of the bed.

"Sara, I am Adam's father. And as it turns out, your father as well," he said, walking toward her.

"No. I have a father who wants me. Please leave," she said and began to cough painfully.

James hurried to her side when he saw her distress. "I am not here to hurt you," he said, touching her arm.

Although having difficulty catching her breath, she got out of bed on the other side farthest from James. Her oxygen pulled from her face.

"Please, honey. You are going to hurt yourself. I just want to talk. I didn't know you were in Texas, or I would have come to see you years ago," he said, trying to put her at ease. "I have met one of your children when I was at the ranch. Your brother-in-law Mark said his name is Austin, and he is eight years old. He is a beautiful boy. I look forward to meeting and getting to know all my grandchildren."

"No. Where is Austin now?" she asked.

"I was coming down here so I left him at the ranch with his uncle," he said, avoiding most of the truth. "Please get back into bed," he said, walking around the bed toward her.

"Stay away from me. I don't want you near me. Stay away from our family," she said, continuing to back away from him. She was already having trouble breathing from having been choked by her mother. With the oxygen pulled off, she was beginning to have serious distress. She was backing into a corner, and the thought of him being so close to the children had her terrified.

"I am your father, Sara. Joan said you were spoiled, but I at least thought you would want to meet me," he said.

"My grandmother offered to let me know who you were years ago. I didn't want to know," Sara said. "Get out of here."

"But I am your father. And I love you and want to get to know my grandchildren."

"Stop saying that. A father wouldn't have left me to be raised in a house with a monster and a mother who is no better than an animal," she said, attempting to catch her breath. "I have two sets of parents who love and want me and took me, Saline, and Jody from that life we were living. You threw money at the problem. I never saw you anyplace. I was in school in the UK for over seven years and you were never there."

"What if I had gotten there and they were visiting? What then?" James asked.

"Neither of them was ever in the UK, not even on layovers on the way to Hamburg. You didn't want me, Mr. Sterling, any more than they did," Sara said.

"I paid your mother hundreds of thousands of dollars to either get you away from her or take care of you," he said. James, on impulse, reached out and put his hand on Sara's arm.

Sudden terror overtook Sara. She pushed James back and ran past him and out the door, pulling her IV out in the process. James paused only a moment before he went out the door in search of his newfound daughter but saw no sign of her in any direction. When he tried to think of a place that she would go, he realized how little he knew about her. He suddenly felt ashamed of himself for his lack of involvement in her life. He was her father, however, and no one could tell him to stay out of her life. He began to look for places that she could have gone.

Downstairs, in the chapel, Sara walked to the front and sat down then knelt in prayer. She was wearing a long gown with no robe. She was barefooted because she left the room in a panic. She couldn't believe yet another nightmare had come into her life.

After a few minutes in prayer, she took a seat and looked at the beautiful chapel. It was a peaceful place where even nightmares didn't seem so bad. Her face was pale with tear streaks that she didn't seem to notice.

Coming into the chapel from the front was the priest. He looked at the woman who was so deep in thought. He also noticed that she was not wearing a robe or shoes, and there was a bloody place on her sleeve.

There had been a silent alarm to watch for her, so Father Ron walked over and phoned upstairs that she was in the chapel and was okay. He then slowly walked to the young woman and took a seat beside her.

"You look lost," he said.

"Maybe a little," she said, never turning to look at the concerned priest.

"Can you tell me a little about it?" he asked.

"No. It is not worth telling," she said, shaking her head.

Father Ron saw fresh tears beginning to fall. She began to rub her arms as though she was cold. The priest removed his cape from around his neck and placed it around her shoulders.

"Thank you," Sara said and smiled for a second. "I never wanted such a complicated life. I make things difficult for my family with all the baggage that follows me wherever I go."

"I am Father Ron. May I ask your name?"

"Sara Lyn Byers. I work here part time on the telemetry floor," she answered.

"I believe I have seen you around here. But you wear your hair up when you work."

"That is correct," Sara said and took a breath. "Although lately I don't work very much."

"You look like you came down here in a hurry," he said, looking at the sleeve of her gown that was bloody.

"I didn't realize I had pulled it out," she said.

"Did something frighten you?" he asked.

"I had to get away. I can't take any more of people like him. He backed me in a corner then touched me. He wouldn't back away," she said, trembling with her words.

Father Ron could tell the young woman was terrified. Terrified of the man that must have been in her hospital room, yet he was sitting next to her and had put his cape around her shoulders and she had remained calm. The man in her room had been a real threat to her.

"He has seen my children today. I have to be at home to protect my children," she said.

"Where are your children right now?" he asked.

"They are at the ranch with our family," she said.

"Why don't we call and let your family know that he was here. I would imagine they will keep him from ever seeing them again," he said. He wrote down the phone number she had given him and asked that she stay put until her returned. She agreed.

First he called upstairs to the nurses' station asking if she could place an order of protection on the young woman including changing her room number and her name so people could not find her in the hospital. With a bit of resistance, the nurse agreed.

He then called the Byers ranch, and a young man answered.

"Hello, this is Father Ron O'Bryan. I am the priest from St. Mary's Hospital," he said.

"Yes, Father, is there something wrong?" the young man asked. "This is Sara's brother-in-law, Mark St. Clair."

"I believe there may be a big problem, Mr. St. Clair," he said and began to tell him what Sara had just told him.

The priest peeked out and saw Sara still sat where she said she would stay. He saw also that she was holding her chest.

"I believe I need to get her back to her room, but for the moment, I believe she is okay. I will stay with her until some family is here," he said.

"The family may have stepped out for a moment, but they are in the hospital. We never leave her alone very long when she is not here," Mark said.

"I have seen the news today. I cannot imagine how she would be feeling." Again he looked to see if Sara was still seated, and she was. He also saw a man approaching her. "There is a man walking toward her." He described the man to Mark.

"That sounds like Scott Byers, her husband. See if she is calmed when he approaches," Mark said.

Scott slowly walked to his wife and appeared relieved to find her. When he sat down beside, her she fell into his arms.

"I believe she will be well now. Please let her family know about the man she was talking about for me," the priest asked.

"Thank you for taking the time with her," Mark said, and the call ended.

Father Ron walked back to where Sara and Scott sat. "I see you have been found," he said.

Scott stood and extended his hand. "Yes. I am Scott Byers." The two shook hands. "Thank you for taking the times with Sara. She said you loaned her your cape because she was cold."

"We are known for the multiple layers of clothes we wear. I just loaned her one," he said with a smile.

Scott took the cape and gave it back to him and put his coat around Sara's shoulders. "What do you say we go back to your room?"

"What if he is still there? Can't I just stay here?" she said, obviously short of breath. She had sweat on her forehead from the effort of breathing and the pain of pleurisy.

"Baby girl, I never order you to do anything, but I am now. We have to go back. But I will be with you. I promise."

Sara looked at the floor and nodded. Her chest hurt, and she knew it would feel better to lie down and splint herself. They started to walk toward her hospital room, slowly. Sara, feeling like any moment she would melt into the floor, had to will herself to keep putting one foot in front of the other.

But try as she would, she felt herself becoming weak and clammy. The world began to spin, and she knew she was going to faint.

Scott had anticipated that she would not make it to her room and took her in his strong arms as soon as she started to fall. Before he had taken five steps, she was out cold.

James Sterling had gone to the cafeteria, the lobby, and the gift shop in search of his newfound daughter. He could tell by seeing her only for a few moments that she really needed to be lying down and being cared for. He would wait a little while and let her thoughts catch up and try to talk to her again. James looked down the hall and saw Scott Byers holding Sara. He hurried down the hall to where he saw Scott standing.

"Excuse me, young man. I am this girl's father," he said.

Scott eyed the man up and down. "No doubt she may carry your DNA, but you are in no way her father. I have to see to my wife."

"I have come so as I may be able to get to know my daughter better," James said.

"That is something that is not up to you," Scott said.

"I have waited all this time."

"So a little more time will not kill you. You do not come in this room or anyplace else that my wife may be," Scott said and went into the hospital room, followed closely by the chaplain.

In the room, it only took a few moments before Sara began to arouse once placed back on the bed. Her nurse came in the room and restarted her IV that had been pulled out.

After a few minutes of remaining silent, Sara spoke with perfect clarity. "Scott, did that man come back?"

"He is outside, baby girl. I told him he was not coming in here uninvited," Scott said.

"Is anyone else here besides you?" she asked.

"Momma, Andrew, and Elaine are right over there," Scott said, gesturing toward the other side of the room.

"Could you ask that man to come in for a moment then?" she asked.

"Are you sure you are up to that, Sara." Elaine asked.

"As long as all of you stay here, I will be fine."

Allison walked over to the door and asked James Sterling to come into the room. He immediately walked quickly toward her but was stopped by Scott.

"Don't get so close. And don't touch her again," the priest said.

"I believe I have waited long enough and paid enough to be allowed to meet my daughter," he said.

"According to Adam, you have known about me since my conception, and this is the first time you have made an attempt to see me," Sara said.

"I am your father. Your blood relative. I have come to meet you and my grandchildren," he said.

"According to Adam, you told him you have always known about me. You knew what was happening to me my entire life and only yesterday decided to act on it," Sara said and stopped when a cough overtook her. With most of her wanting to pull the cover over her head and cry from physical and emotional pain, she continued to speak when she had caught her breath. "I don't want you here. I don't want to get to know you. You are not to come near our children. Is that clear enough for you to understand?"

James was taken completely off guard by the young woman's statement. It angered him that she was not so much as going to give him a chance to be her father and made him that much more determined to be a part of her life.

"Your mother has always said that you were willful and selfish. Adam is usually more sensible in his thoughts. I don't know what it is that you have said to make him turn against me," James said. "But you are my daughter and your children are my grandchildren. I am going to be a part of your lives."

"No. You are a stranger to us. We don't want you here. Please leave and never come back, Mr. Sterling," Sara said and turned her head away from him.

"You heard the lady. You are upsetting her, and she does not need that right now. Why don't you go and visit your former wife? You will find her in jail," Scott said.

"I don't think you understood what I said. I am here to get to know my daughter. I have that right," he said, taking another step forward. "Those kids are my grandkids."

"I have no desire to meet you, Mr. Sterling. When Grandma Catherine offered to let me know who my father was, I told her the same thing I will tell you. I have a father. No, he is not my blood, but he wanted me enough to take me and my brother and sister from the hell we were living in. You did nothing," Sara said.

"I gave your mother money time and again."

"And you knew the kind of woman that Joan Redding was and is. If you really thought that she would care for anyone with the exception of herself, then congratulations. You are the stupidest human being I have ever met," Sara said. "Now leave and never come near any of us again." She then turned on her side, facing away from James Sterling. She would not let him see the tears that now fell over her cheeks.

Allison went up to the head of her bed and picked up Sara's hand, kissing the back of it. "You heard what our daughter said. Now leave. From what Adam has told us, you have a situation of your own to take care of," Allison said. "He phoned your wife and let her know where you are. Now leave."

The door opened, and Sara's nurse walked in with a nurse's aide.

"Sara, we are here to take you to your new room," she said.

"This is one of the people who do not need to know where she is going. This is the second time he has been in her room," Scott said.

"Well then, let's call security," she said and picked up the phone.

"This is my daughter. I have a right to know where she is going to be," James said. "Look at me, young lady."

Sara closed her eyes tighter, as though she could will James Sterling to simply disappear.

"Get out," she said without looking back at him. Then Scott took two long steps toward him and shoved him toward the door.

"You heard the lady. Get out, Mr. Sterling," Scott said.

"Not without talking to my daughter."

Scott grabbed him by the collar and pulled him to the door and into the hallway. "You don't have a daughter here. Are you deaf? She wants nothing to do with a man who allowed her to be tortured for her entire childhood. That is final. She is my wife, and you are not to come near her again. Our children have nothing to do with you. So why don't you go back to hole you crawled out of and spend some more time with Joan Redding and Rick Powell," Scott said and went back to his wife.

It only took two days before Sara was able to return home. In the hospital, she had gotten the rest she needed to let her body heal. On the day she was to return, she was feeling as strong as she had ever felt. Her thoughts went back to the night she confronted both her mother and Rick Powell. True, she had been scared to death when she had Riley to read the documents written by both herself and Saline. Though her written word read by her adoptive brother were not the same as having her there, she felt her sister in spirit more than she had since all the family had lost so many of those they loved. The man who had been buried at the back door of the farm was only remembered by her mother and herself. She wondered several times if it was something she imagined. But the body of the poor man Lord Henry had killed had proved she and Saline were right.

Weeks passed and the cold winter turned to the promising warmth and colors of spring. Between the intense red of the crimson clover and the blue bonnets, it was as though an artist had painted the rolling pastures of the East Texas countryside.

Scott woke up one morning knowing it was time to start working the cattle on the ranch. It was going to be a beautiful day, and it was a time of year all the men looked forward to. The only thing putting a little uncertainty was his father.

In early spring, John had the flu and just couldn't seem to get over it. Normally, Uncle Alex would have treated him usually, and John had not gone to a new doctor as yet. Scott had worried when John had opted to go to the office rather than work cattle.

Allison had been terribly worried as he had sat up the last few nights in the chair having difficulty breathing. When he had decided to go to the office that morning, Allison was worried. John was not a man to run a fever for very long, nor one to stay down for very long. She had tried to talk him out of going to Dallas and rather opting to go to the doctor. He promised he would go the following day.

When Allison had gone to Scott and Sara's house to see the children, Sara could see how worried she was. She wanted desperately to do something to ease her mind, and she came up with a plan. She would suddenly remember something she had to do and ask if Allison could watch the children. As the older two were still in school, it would only be Ryan and baby Lauren. Of course, Allison said yes. Sara dressed quickly and started the hour drive to Dallas to Byers Oil.

Sara arrived and took the private elevator to the fiftieth floor where John would likely be in his office. When she arrived, John was sitting in his chair behind his desk with his head resting on the back, breathing heavily. His lips were blue. Common sense told her that what he had was not a cold. Sara walked to the father she had come to know and love dearly and got on her knees in front of him. She prayed she had the right words to tell him.

"Poppa, please come with me now. We have to go to the hospital," she pleaded.

"I will go tomorrow, baby girl. I am too tired to go just now," he said, panting.

Getting down on her knees Sara put her hands on both of his cheeks.

"Poppa, if you don't, there is no tomorrow. Please, Poppa, we all need you," she said with tears free-flowing down her cheeks.

John looked down into her face and knew she would not deceive him to get her way.

Sara knew that she had him for a moment. She took his hand, and he stood and followed her to the elevator and down to her waiting jeep. Sara then drove from downtown to Baylor, where Saline had gone when she had fallen in the creek years before.

Once in the ER, Sara told the lady at the desk that her father-in-law, John Byers, needed to be seen immediately, that he was in heart failure.

"I will sign him in, and it could be a little while, and—" was all the admitting clerk could say.

"I am a nurse. My father-in-law's name in on one of these buildings, and he needs to be seen, now!" she demanded.

The clerk looked at the somewhat younger woman and got up from her small desk. "I will see if someone can see you."

Sara looked back and saw John slip from his chair into the floor. "I need help," she screamed. John was not breathing, so Sara immediately started resuscitating him. It was not long until the double doors opened and she had help, but she refused to leave his side, reciting orders from when she had worked with Dr. Quinton. "Please, Poppa, don't leave us," she would say.

John was quickly taken from the triage room to the cardiac catheterization lab, then to emergency open-heart surgery for a collapsed aortic valve.

She stood outside the double doors of the surgical suites, alone. Then she realized that all this had taken place without even seconds to call the ranch and let anyone know where she was. She had to collect herself for a moment to call the ranch and tell Allison what had happened. She turned to find the waiting room and bumped into a familiar face.

"Don't we know each other?" he said politely.

"Did you care for my sister when she fell in the drink?" she said in her fading yet still present soft English accent.

"Creek, but good effort," the man said. "Wayne Ligon, I am a neurosurgeon. Do you have someone here, Mrs. Byers?"

"Yes. Yes, I do. My, huh, father-in-law, he…uh…" she was trying to say.

"Why don't we sit down for a minute?" he said.

"No, please. I have to call my family. They have no idea he is here," she said.

"Can you tell me what happened?" he asked.

"He has been sick, and I went to his office and begged him to come with me here. His aortic valve. I thought it was his aortic valve. I told the doctor in the ER what I thought, and he called the cath lab, and he came here. But I couldn't go in there like I could the cath lab," she said.

"Tell you what. Why don't you go and wash your face and give me the number, and I will call his wife and let her know what you just told me. Then I will go back and see how things are going," he said and smiled at the young woman whom he had no idea loved her father-in-law very much.

"Are you sure you don't mind? I don't know what to tell her," she said.

"I am free as a bird right now. So you go on and come back and maybe I can give you the heads-up," he said.

"Oh no. It is his heart," she said. Then realized she had misunderstood. "Excuse me."

He watched the young lady hurry off to the ladies' room and picked up the phone. He remembered the Alexander sisters well, because although they were likely the closest sisters he had ever met, he had followed up on his patient for just over two years following the accident, with regular checkups. He had performed a single-level fusion on the herniated disc, and she was as good as new. He had since watched them on the news from time to time and kept up with them. He heard the phone ringing and was picked up after the second ring.

"Hello?" a woman said.

"Mrs. Byers?" he asked.

"Yes. This is Allison Byers."

"This is Dr. Wayne Ligon at Baylor. I am calling for Sara regarding your husband," he said.

"Oh dear God, Dr. Ligon, is my husband all right?" she cried.

"Yes, he is, but I am afraid he is in emergency surgery for a valve replacement in his heart. I happened to bump into Sara in the hallway just after he went in," he explained. "She is quite upset, so I told her that as I knew y'all, I would call, and she really needed to catch her breath," he said.

"I didn't realize she had gone to check on John. Maybe I should have," she said. "I will be right there."

"I will stay close until you get here," he said.

"Thank you so much. Sara went to check on him, because she knew I was worried. I thought she was going to the grocery store. I pray this is not too much for her," Allison said.

"I will be here when you get here. I will watch out for her, so take your time and be safe," he said, and they ended the phone call.

The surgeon then went into the operating room to check on John.

Bob Carney was a very successful heart surgeon who just so happened to be a friend of Dr. Ligon.

"Bob, how's he doing?" he asked.

"Wayne, what are you doing? Changing professions?" Dr. Carney teased.

"No, I am still all brain and no heart. John Byers is a supporter of the hospital and also the father of a patient of mine. She is here alone, and I thought I would stick around until her family got here," he answered.

"The redhead?" Bob asked.

"That's her. Sara is her name," Wayne answered.

"She saved his life. His heart is enlarged, and his aortic valve was gone. I don't know how he survived this long. What is she, a med student?" he asked.

"Actually, I believe she is a nurse," Wayne answered.

"A nurse. I was taking orders from an RN?"

"No. She is an LVN. But would it help your overabundant ego to tell you she was the personal student of Dr. Steven Quinton for four months following graduating?" Wayne said and waited for his reaction.

"Quinton. I know him. Tragic what happened to him last year," Bob said.

"Is Mr. Byers going to pull through, near as you can tell?" Bob asked.

"Give me an hour and ask again. I will know if his heart is strong enough to come off pump," Bob said. "And, Wayne. Tell Mrs. Byers I will put her through med school anytime she is ready."

"Will do," Wayne said and walked back to where he had last seen Sara. He saw her looking at the double doors, eyes wide, tears streaming down her face. He knew some of the family history from what Saline had told him.

When he approached her, she was not actually looking at him, but looking for the doctor who had taken John Byers back.

"Dr. Ligon. I am sorry," she said, startled when he walked up to her.

"He is on pump," he said, referring to the part of the surgery where the heart is stopped so it can be opened and the delicate part of the operation may be done. "Are you aware of what that means?"

"Yes, sir. Is his heart greatly enlarged?" she asked.

"Yes, honey, I am afraid it is," he said and saw Sara take a quick short breath. "But you know as well as I that there are medications that will help. Let's try to think good thoughts for when your family arrives."

Sara nodded to his words.

"Why don't we go down here and wait?" he said and led her to a small private waiting room rather than the very crowded waiting room. "Dr. Carney said they would call when he comes off pump. That will tell us a lot."

"I haven't gotten a chance to tell you and your family how terribly sorry I was at the death of so many that you loved last year. The world lost when that place crashed," Dr. Ligon said.

"Thank you. It seems now like it was so long ago, and it has only been a year," Sara said. "I was supposed to go with them on the trip to Africa, but I was pregnant, and my doctor said I could not go."

"That must have been very hard. I don't want to imagine what all of you must have gone through," he said.

"When we heard it on the TV, I had several ladies at my house. We were all, including Lady Dickerson, on the floor in front of the TV until all the bodies were recovered. Then there were the funerals stateside a week later. The following day, we left for London and Lauren's funeral. She is a member of the royal family, so it was a matter of state." Sara stopped a moment. "It was a month before we got home. People saw us on the TV at Buckingham Palace and thought how lucky we were."

"Sometimes we have to separate very sad with something good," he said.

"I know," she said as the phone in the small waiting room rang. Sara picked up immediately. "This is Sara Byers," she said.

"Mrs. Byers," she heard the nurse said. "Your father has made it off pump and is currently stable. The doctor is closing, and he should be out in about a half hour," she said.

Sara thanked her and replaced the phone on the cradle. "Poppa is off pump and currently stable."

On impulse, Bob reached out and hugged the brave, obviously relieved young woman, and she hugged him back.

"Oh, Dr. Ligon, you have been with me for hours. Isn't there someplace you should be?"

"I was actually on my way home. And I was glad to stay with you. Not often I am in the presence of royalty," he said and smiled.

The door opened, and Allison and all the boys, including Mark, hurried in.

"Maria is with the children. Have you heard anything?" Allison asked.

"He is stable and should be out of surgery in under an hour," Sara said.

Everyone breathed a sigh of relief. Soon John was in the intensive care unit on the eighth floor. Sara stayed in the room with John as the doctor spoke with Allison and her sons.

"I thank you so much for saving my husband, Dr. Carney. He has never been sick like this before," Allison said.

"You should thank her. He went down in the ER waiting room, and she called for help. She said he needed a cardiologist. She started CPR and continued it until we got him back. I thought she was in medical school and was actually shocked to discover she was an LVN. I would love to recommend her for a place in medical school," he said.

Scott smiled at the thought of what Sara would say to a comment like that. "I appreciate the thought, but she is dedicated to a life in nursing. Thank you for listening to her."

"One question. What if she had been wrong?" Dr. Carney asked, almost knowing the answer.

When Scott failed to answer verbally, only smiling, he had his answer.

When they had finished talking to the doctor, they went to see John. They found Sara sound asleep in the chair at John's bedside.

"Is my husband doing well?" Allison asked the nurse.

"He is doing very well. He already has his breathing tube out and is in only a small amount of pain. He is awake if you would like to visit. My name is Missy. I will be his nurse until in the morning," the nurse said.

"Thank you," Allison said.

"Daddy," Colton said.

"Hi, son," John said.

"Daddy, we were worried," he returned.

"No more than I was, I assure you. I didn't think I was going to make it," John said. "That is some girl you have there, Scotty. Might want to take her home. I believe you will likely find she is expecting again."

"How do you know?" Scott said at the news.

"She went to sleep while we were talking," John said and started coughing. Sara was immediately on her feet.

"Hold your chest, Poppa," she said, putting a hand on his chest.

When he had caught his breath, he thanked her. "You had better get some rest, baby girl. You are making me a new grandchild," he said.

"How did you know?" she said. "I have to take care of you."

"For now, we will let Missy do that. I am here because of you, and I am going to stay here," he said.

"Okay. Thank you, Poppa. But I will see you tomorrow," she said.

Allison reached out and hugged the younger woman. "Thank you, baby girl. Thank you a million times," she whispered. "I will see you later."

"I will see you tomorrow, Daddy," Scott said. He took Sara's hand, and they left the others to visit.

When they got as far as the desk, Sara approached Missy. "Thank you for all your help. Please take care of Poppa," Sara said with tears in her eyes.

Missy had been an RN in the unit for several years. She rose and hugged Sara that she would. "I have one condition."

"What is that?" Sara asked.

Missy whispered in her ear, "Next time you're in England, send me a post card here to the hospital. I would love to hang it up and make everyone wonder whom I know there," she said, and both women had a good laugh out of it.

When they were in Sara's jeep, Scott decided since it was so late, he would find a nice place to take his little wife to eat. It was a special occasion indeed. His father now was no longer dying, and he was going to be a father again. They went to Reunion Tower in downtown and were quickly seated.

"When did you find out we are expecting again?" he asked.

"I was going to tell you after y'all finished working cattle in a couple of weeks. I didn't want you working with cattle and distracted," she answered.

"I have been distracted since the first time I ever saw you. I worry a little because you had a bad time last year."

"We all did. But I have been feeling good for months, and I promise to take care. And I have a name picked out if it is a boy. Chase," she said.

"I like that. How did you come up with it?" he asked.

"It is Adam's middle name. I don't care about ever seeing his father again, but I am glad there is a blood relative of mine that is at least normal and wants nothing from me."

"So am I," Scott answered. The two ate supper and then sat together, looking over the city lights of Dallas and the surrounding area. When she went to the ladies' room, he called Maria at the ranch to see if she would mind watching the children that night. When she agreed, Scott called the Hyatt and made reservations.

"I have a surprise for you. How about if we stay in Dallas tonight, at a hotel?" Scott said.

"We have never stayed in a hotel," she said.

"Well then, I think we should try it out. It does get old staying at those old hovels of our family and friends," Scott said and winked at her. Sara blushed of course, and the two left.

In the hotel, they were shown to the bridal suite. They lay in each other's arms and made love again and again through the night and awakened early to visit John.

He looked so much better than he had even twelve hours before. His nurse said that he would be moving to a private suite in the VIP unit. He stayed ahead of everything he was to have done. He leaned on his daughter-in-law's arm as he walked in the halls, squeezed her hand when the chest tubes came out, and did deep breathing when his nurse, Missy, asked him to.

For years, John had seen Sara through many trips to the hospital. He had been afraid to go to a hospital because he didn't want to take the chance of dying in one. Unlike him, she showed no fear in a hospital, be it as a patient or working in one.

After a few days in the hospital, it was time for John to return home. Dr. Carney went over his medications with both Sara and Allison. He told what to watch for and when to bring him back for a checkup.

"Don't worry, he will be here," Sara said. Allison beamed at her little daughter. "If that is okay, Momma and Poppa," and of course, she blushed.

"I am sorry, I hope I didn't overstep my bounds," she whispered then fled from the room. She had been paying no attention as to where she was going. The stress of the last few days had been so heavy.

All she could think of was, "What if she had made a mistake?" She stopped her thoughts. Poppa was going to be fine, and she had done the right thing. She had to find her way back to Poppa's room so he could be discharged. She actually couldn't wait until she got home and could lie down for a little while before the children got home.

Sara arrived back at John's room just in time for the nurse to have the wheelchair ready to take him to the waiting car out front. Allison drove, and John got in the passenger seat. Sara got in the backseat for the long ride home.

It had been a very long last week for everyone in the family. The turtle hull and part of the backseat was full of flowers. John was a little sore but could tell he was healing. For weeks he had felt like his time was running out, but now he watched the familiar drive home—the farms and pastures, the farmers out in the pastures working their land. Just a week ago, he thought he had seen his last day. In his office, he had wished he had never driven to Dallas that day. All he could think about the entire time he was there was his Allison.

His Allison, he thought. He looked at his wife behind the wheel of the car, her chestnut hair and eyes always warm and giving. She still had the same beautiful face that he fell in love with over thirty-five years before. She lived the life that he brought her to on the ranch, never complaining, always there. Even in the harder times when they first married, she always had that smiled that made him want to keep going. When they lost their baby daughter, they both thought they would never survive the grief, but their love for each other helped make the other strong.

"Have I told you how much I love you lately?" he asked, looking at her adoringly.

"I don't believe you have. But I am available right now if you would like to," she said, smiling.

"I have been thinking about this all week long. Why not, in a couple of weeks, the two of us get away for a week or two?" John said. "We have never gotten away together, unless it was work of course."

"Sounds good to me. But, John, you only just had a major operation. You will likely not be strong enough for months," Allison answered.

"I am sore right now, but aside from that, I feel better than I have in months. And of course, the obvious benefit that it would keep me out of the office and out of the pasture a little longer," he said and smiled. "We could go to Hawaii, or you always talked about seeing Alaska. Or even go to England and be a tourist. You have said you would love to go there just to see the sights. We could plan it for just after the BBQ."

"I am going to hold you to that," Allison said. "And in mind, I have a witness here."

"To be a witness, she would have to be awake," John said, and Allison saw Sara leaning her head back against the headrest, sound asleep. Both of them got a good laugh out of that, and they then spent the rest of the drive home planning their adventure in a few weeks.

The weeks passed, and John was quickly back to feeling like his old self again. And soon it was once again time for the annual BBQ at the ranch. Invitations were sent out weeks in advance.

Sara had invited the people she worked with from the hospital, including David and Eric and their families. Elaine and Amelia and their families were also invited. Amelia made a point of saying that if Rick was going to the BBQ to start problems, he was just to stay home.

Andrew and his new wife, Sarah, would be coming. It was Sarah's first time to be at the ranch. The young couple would be spending a couple of nights at Scott and Sara's house. The young couple arrived the day before the BBQ. Andrew was always a welcome guest at the ranch. Sara had watched the royal wedding on TV, at Westminster Abbey.

Between Allison, Sara, Elaine, Maria, and Amelia, John was well looked after. Every day he was feeling better and better.

By the day of the BBQ, John was looking forward to seeing friends and family and putting to rest any worries that he had not fully recovered.

Adam could not believe how many people he had seen on the news were all present at one place. When Andrew and his new wife arrived at the ranch, it amazed Adam how easily his little sister interacted with people whom he now knew to be quite famous. She then saw someone out of his line of sight and began to run in that direction. Adam moved to see who she was rushing toward and saw an older man and woman. The man embraced Sara and kissed both cheeks. She then turned and shook hands with the woman.

Adam saw that she placed her hand on her tummy, a gesture that he knew women expecting did unconsciously.

Sara waved to Adam to join her and was introduced to the duke and duchess of Hamburg.

"Adam, I have heard much about you in the last months. I am sorry it has taken me so long to come for a visit," Uncle Joseph said, extending a hand. "And my wife, Catherine."

"Sir, mam. I have heard a lot about you as well. Good to meet you both," Adam said, really not sure how he was to address Sara's uncle.

"Please, call me Uncle Joseph. I have found since finding my nieces I prefer to be known as an uncle and husband rather than a duke," Joseph told the Adam.

The two and Catherine began discussing various things they had in common, and Sara began talking to other people at the BBQ.

After a little while, Scott looked around at all the people he saw. He knew all the hundreds of people who were present at the annual event. He looked around and saw the only person he was looking for. She was sitting with all four of their children in her lap and around her. Austin and Brad were involved in trying to impress their mother with a basketball, and Ryan was trying to get time on his mother's lap. Baby Lauren was laughing happily.

"Hey, pretty lady. How about going for a ride?" Scott said as he rode up on Champ.

"On one horse?" she said and smiled.

"I don't know. I married a tiny skinny thing with knobby knees, not a pregnant woman who is as big as my horse," Scott teased.

"You still want to ride with me looking like this?" she said and blushed.

"Even more than I did the first time."

"But the children," Sara said.

"Where is that little grand niece of mine?" came from Uncle Joseph.

"Do you mind watching them for me for a little bit?" Sara asked.

"I came over here to see all the children. And I believe John and Allison are on their way over here as well. Go on, my baby, have a nice time," Uncle Joseph said and kissed her cheek.

Sara handed baby Lauren to Uncle Joseph, and little Ryan took his hand. "See you in a bit," she said.

A few seconds later, the happy couple was cantering away on Champ. They rode over a small hill, making them out of sight to the guests.

"Do you think we can make a quick stop?" she asked as they passed the cemetery.

Scott stopped and dismounted, helping Sara down as well. They walked over to Saline's grave. Sara knelt down and brushed some leaves from the base of Saline's gravestone. "Would you think I was crazy if I told you something?" she asked.

Scott looked at his wife's face and assured her he would not. She began to tell him what she experienced in the moments the year previous, when her heart stopped. Scott took a seat beside Sara as she told him of what she had been told and what she remembered.

Scott listened, transfixed at what she said. He remembered that day like it had only just happened. Her heart had stopped, but their daughter's heart, baby Lauren's heart, never did. When he heard her voice several minutes later, he knew it was a miracle. Now her words gave him goose bumps. He knew her words where what she had seen and felt. He saw everyone in that room stare in awe as she returned to them. She had never spoken of what had happened during that time other than messages given to specific people. The others in the room, a queen and a prince, doctors, nurses, Lady Dickerson, and even the archbishop listened to the messages but asked nothing.

No one had wanted to press her on anything with her being considered fragile for over a week. Scott listened in wonder as she attempted to describe what she had experienced.

"Oh, I have kept you too long here. We had better get back to our guests," Sara said.

"Maybe we can take up where we are later," Scott said, smiling.

"Bet on it, baby," Sara said and returned a radiant smile.

Scott then helped Sara back on Champ and mounted behind her. "I guess the three of us shall return."

John had decided that since he had been given a second chance at life, he would give others a second chance as well. And as there had been no further mishaps regarding Rick, he would give him one last shot at being on staff at the hospital. There would be a specific contract for him to sign, and hopefully he would be happy with his position.

"Rick," John said when he saw him. "What do you think of our little get-together?"

"I only just arrived a few minutes ago with Amelia and the kids. I believe the kids went to go swimming and Amelia is riding horses with Elaine and a red-haired woman I have never met," Rick said when he got over the shock of John Byers speaking to him.

"That is Prince Andrew's new wife, Sarah. They are the duke and duchess of York now. Your grace would be how to address until they tell you otherwise. Do you have a moment for business?" he asked.

"Yes, of course," Rick said.

"We have decided that if you would care to be on staff at the hospital once again, it would be acceptable. There would be a contract, of course. And all would be contingent upon your actions."

"I would very much like to be on staff again. I believe it was unfair to take me off staff over a personal matter in the first place," Rick said.

"You are well aware of the things that got you taken off staff a few months ago and almost cost you your wife. I will not go through all that again. As you likely know, I had a near miss a few weeks ago. Strange as it sounds, just before leaving for London, Sara said she had to save me. I didn't question it. We were all feeling a little shell-shocked. As I have been given a chance to live again, I am giving you that same opportunity. A yes or no is all that is needed," John said.

Rick was irritated by not being on staff to admit his patients. It had hurt his practice. "Of course, I would like to go back to being at the hospital. And I actually did not know you had a brush with death."

"Good regarding your status. I will have the contract made up for you to sign this week. I know Amelia will be pleased. Enjoy yourself, Rick," John said and was off.

Rick watched as he spoke with several people at a time, important people that he had only ever seen on the news. He would not waste being back on staff again. Being around people like this was the reason he had become a physician in the first place. He saw Scott and Sara arrive back at the main house on horseback. While they still sat on horseback, several people approached them, talking about different things.

A man Rick didn't know reached up to assist Sara off the front of the saddle. Then Scott got off and tied his horse to the fence. Rick made his way over to Sara to speak with her briefly. But the same man who helped her off the horse was still with her.

"Sara," he said. "I didn't realize you were pregnant again. When are you due?" he asked.

"Just after the first of the year. How are you, Dr. Powell?" she asked.

"I am very well. I just thought I would tell you I was asked to be on staff at the hospital again by your father-in-law," he said.

"Yes, I know. We all talked about it. Oh, and this is our dear friend Dr. Eric Dane. He is my cardiologist since Uncle Steven died. Eric, this is Dr. Rick Powell from here in Salt Flats," she said. "I will be accompanying Dr. Dane to the Country Hospital every couple of weeks to have a cardiology clinic, so they don't have to go all the way to Tyler. If you will excuse me, I believe I have been ordered to go to our room and rest," she said and was off for the kitchen door of the main house.

"Have you known Sara long?" Rick asked.

"I have worked with her in Tyler since she went to work at St. Mary's a few years ago. She is very gifted," Eric answered. "The cardio clinic was her idea. I am surprised no one had ever thought of it before."

"When did you become her cardiologist?" Rick asked. "I mean, when you have known her as long as I have, she does not respond to suggestion easily."

"Dr. Quinton asked that if something happened to him, I would care for her. She has been my patient just over a year," he said. "Her patients love her."

"I always thought that after a woman has children, they really need to stay at home to raise them. It doesn't seem right to me," Rick said.

"Dr. Powell, my wife is a nurse as well. We have three children, and she works in the OR full time. She has no trouble raising children and working. And quite like Sara, she gets a joy from giving of herself to people in need. That you can't buy for any amount," Eric said.

"My wife had not worked in a few years and began to work in the Country Hospital part time at first. Now she is full time as the

DON. I still believe it would be better for her to spend more time as a wife and mother," Rick said.

"Does that also apply to your being a father? I know how much time I spend as a doctor. But if I didn't work, there would be no food on the table. That, and we live in a day when it is starting to take more than one paycheck in most cases. I prefer to think that my children are better off seeing their mother as an intelligent woman who also works and does not just spend her time as a country club queen. But I can see that if a man is insecure with himself, he would be threatened. And as far as Sara goes, it was she who approached me about the need for a heart specialist to identify patients early about possible heart problems. Now if you will excuse me, I have some friends I would like to speak with," Eric said and started walked away.

"It seems like, as her physician, you would tell her that with a heart problem it is ill advised to have more children," Rick said, obviously attempting to illicit a response. "Or maybe they don't teach that in the medical school you attended."

Eric walked back to Rick and gave an easy smile. In a private setting, he would have loved to have slugged him, but he would never sink to his level as he wanted him to.

"Dr. Powell. I have several advanced degrees in cardiology from Duke, specializing in rheumatic fever and its complications. Dr. Quinton became the ranking expert in that area, and therefore asked me to care for Sara if anything happened to him. Sara Lyn is someone you will never understand. She does not hate, dislike, or backstab anyone, and that includes you. And if you were to get looking into it, she likely is the reason you can again admit patients of your own. She knows her limitations better than anyone, so my telling her she cannot have any more children would be redundant. Because in her words, she is leaving it up to God to pick the number of children she has. The only number that she can control is the number she fosters that came from backgrounds she is intimately familiar with. She loves children, all children, unconditionally.

"You, sir, are a little man who wants to become a part of this family as a means of being near money and power. But I can save you the trouble," Eric said.

"And how is that?" Rick asked. "I mean, you seem to have a lock on that, obviously."

"Everyone here knows you to be a social climber. You are interested in no person, just as using them to get what you want," Eric said and took two steps forward so he was right in Rick's face. "You seem to have more in common with Joan Redding than you know," he said and walked away. He heard Rick calling after him again but didn't respond.

"Looks like you made a friend," Scott said, approaching Eric.

"He is choking on bile about now. I told him he was just like Joan Redding," Eric said, laughing. The two walked in the direction of the main house.

Rick watched the people all around him, some within just a few feet, others out in the pasture on horseback. There was only a very small handful of people that he knew, and those he knew he did not know well. As he looked from person to person, there was no one he knew well enough to even start a conversation. For the present time, Amelia was nowhere to be found.

About an hour later, the side door on the main house opened and out came Sara and her three boys. All four were laughing about something. They ran into a redheaded woman, and she and Sara began talking, the boys running someplace. He made his way over to where the two women were engrossed in conversation.

"Good evening, Sara," he said.

"Dr. Powell. Enjoying yourself?" she said.

"Yes, I am," he answered.

"Is there something you need?" she asked. "There are several hundred more interesting and definitely more powerful people here than I am."

"Is it a crime to stand here and talk to you?" he asked. "We have not spoken in some time."

"We just spoke a little while ago when Scott and I rode up. Had you forgot? And we have someplace to be right now, so if you will excuse us," she said.

"You have not introduced us," he said.

"This is the duchess of York. You would refer to her as Your Grace. Sarah, this is Dr. Rick Powell," Sara said.

"Nice to meet you, Sarah," he said.

The new duchess could see tension in her new friend's face. Clearly, it was caused by the bore of a man that stood before them. So she took Sara's arm in hers and, without answering him, began to walk away.

"Just keep walking, no matter what he says," she said.

"He addressed you that way on purpose. He thinks he is entitled because he is a doctor," Sara said.

Austin lagged behind the others for a moment. "Leave my momma alone. You make her sad," the young boy said with the authority of a grown man.

"It is not very nice when children tell grown-ups what to do. No matter how rich their daddies may be," Rick said. "I hope you listen before you become spoiled like your mother."

Austin was immediately angered; he kicked Rick in the shin as hard as he could with his cowboy boots on. Rick immediately buckled from the sudden assault. "My momma would never do that, so I did," Austin said.

The people standing close by laughed at the young boy's words. Austin turned to catch up to the others. Rick stood and thought about going after the young boy but decided to let it go to get himself out of sight of those who were laughing.

As the evening went on, he continued to walk among the invited guests. Some had already left the ranch. Those that remained had returned the horses to the stable and were closer to one house or the other.

Rick walked around to see if he could find someone he knew. Of course, Elaine, Amelia, Maria, and Sara were together. There were several other women the same age as they were, also talking together in the swimming pool at Scott and Sara's house. The children were in the wading pool, or the shallow end of big pool. All were having a good time. The children were laughing and playing. The ladies were talking and swimming all at the same time.

"Amelia," Rick said from a few feet away.

"Yes, Rick," she answered.

"We likely need to be leaving. Since I am back on staff again, I have call tomorrow," he said.

"Allison has invited me to go shopping tomorrow, so the kids and I will be staying at the main house tonight," she said.

"You need to be coming home," he said. "The kids need to sleep in their own beds. School is starting in a couple of weeks, and they need to start getting used to going to bed on time."

"Allison and I have been planning on going shopping tomorrow for a couple of weeks. I have school clothes to buy, and she has to buy some vacation clothes for her and John," she said. "So go on home, and I will see you tomorrow," she said and went back to swimming.

Amelia's attitude the last several months angered Rick. Since that night at Joan Redding's farm, she had laid down the law about his attitude toward women in general. If she was to stay with him, things had to change. He had even threatened for them to move away from Salt Flats, but she quickly told him that she and the kids would be staying. She had a full-time job and friends that she cherished now. As angry as he had gotten at times, he knew he had been given his last second chance.

He looked back down to talk to Amelia further, and she had already resumed swimming with her friends, only looking for her for a moment before he decided to say good night to the children before he left. When he reached the county road that would take him back to town, a pickup truck with the back full of teenagers came speeding from the night. There was no time to react; the pickup hit his car without ever having braked. Rick could immediately feel pain engulf his entire body. He knew his left leg was broken in at least two places. His back burned in agony, along with ribs he also knew had to be broken. Then the most horrifying thing was that he was pinned. There was no way to get out of the twisted carnage of metal.

In the pickup, the four passengers in the cab had been thrown along with the other seven teenagers in the back. All seemed to become airborne and fly into the night.

Two of the ranch hands saw the wreck happen, and knowing there was a couple of doctors and several nurses, along with the sheriff, one of them called the main house and Scott and Sara's house. Help was on the way, but would it be in time?

Hours later all Rick could remember was a bad dream of a terrible accident that scared him so bad he couldn't move. In the dream, he heard people around him, saw flashes of familiar faces, and the smell of carnage burning not far from him. He was being pulled, and then, a mind-searing pain. He attempted to cry out, but he had no voice whatsoever. Then to his horror, he couldn't move his hands. All he had was his eyes. Would they open? When they did open, he sent a heartfelt message to God, thanking him for that.

Rick began to move his head little by little, until he could finally make out his surroundings. He could see multiple machines around him, and his line of sight finally landed on someone seated. Amelia. He thought, then damned himself for not being able to see the beautiful face of his wife without his glasses.

"Rick, you are finally awake." He heard the voice that was not his wife's. The gentle hands placed his glasses on so he could see. "Can you understand me?" she asked.

Rick nodded then was shocked to see that the woman who sat beside him was Sara Byers. The woman he had taunted for years was now the woman seeing to him.

"I know if I couldn't see it would scare me, and I have never seen you not wearing your glasses. Is that better?" she asked.

Rick nodded.

"Amelia was burned when she tried to help get you out of the car. She is okay and will likely be released from the hospital tomorrow. She has been down here once but was ordered to go back and rest. I will get your nurse," she said with a smile and turned to walk away. Rick grabbed her hand.

Rick's eyes were pleading.

"Don't worry. You will be well in a few weeks." She called his nurse from the doorway. "Oh and, David. He is finally awake."

It seemed like he had only blinked, and there was a nurse and a doctor in front of him. "Dr. Powell, would you like to get that tube out?" David asked.

Rick nodded.

"First, I am going to tell you, you are going to be in intensive care for some time. You may not be able to handle having the breathing tube out, but I would like to see if you can before we have to put a trach in."

Rick nodded, somewhat struck at what he said. His hands were untied, and he was given instructions as to what to do when the tube came out. When it came out, his throat was immediately sore. He attempted to speak but was unable. He coughed painfully.

"Don't try to talk yet. I will tell you what happened so you won't have to speak just yet. About eight days ago, you were in a bad accident just outside the gates of the Byers ranch. You were one of the lucky ones. There were several killed, and several died since. It took some time to get you out of your car. Your left arm and leg are both broken in several places; you had four broken ribs, a small hemorrhage in your brain that required surgery, and a liver laceration, to name a few of your injuries. Amelia was burned on her right arm and back but is doing well and should go home tomorrow. You will be with us for quite a while. ICU for at least two more weeks until you get your chest tubes out and are able to start PT, then you are looking at about a month after that before you are released," David said. "I am Dr. Glass. I am your critical care doctor and your pulmonologist while you are here. You also have a thoracic surgeon and an orthopedic surgeon and a neurosurgeon. I will get you something for your throat, and likely you will need something else for pain. I will see you in a while," David said.

"Dr. Glass," Rick managed to say. "Who was it who put my glasses on me?"

"That was Sara Byers," he answered. "She has taken care of you a few times."

"Is she still here? I want to thank her," Rick said as a tear escaped his eye.

"She has been ordered to go home. She has been spending several hours a day up here. She and Elaine both. That was the only way they could manage to keep Amelia in her bed," he said. "You get some rest now."

Rick tried to absorb all of what the doctor had tried to tell him. He attempted to move again but found the pain too bad to even move slightly.

"Dr. Powell, I need for you to take several breaths for me," the nurse said.

Rick attempted to take a breath, but it was met by pain.

"I know it hurts, but you are going to have to take deep breaths if you don't want that breathing tube placed again," the nurse said.

The thought of not being able to talk again terrified him. His attempts were much better even through the pain it caused. That was the beginning of what would prove to be an experience that would change his life forever.

CHAPTER 19

New Beginnings
Epilogue

For the first few days, Rick mostly slept between times he was medicated for pain. Physical therapy came in three times a day and began to move him around and even got him up to the chair a couple of times a day. He would protest of course and get verbally abusive, but the therapists didn't appear to have good use of their ears.

The problem that really got to him was the nurses. On the very day that he got the breathing tube out, his nurse came and told him it was time for his enema. He told the nurse that it was impossible for his bowels to move as he had been without food for days because he had a breathing tube. But the experienced ICU nurse told him that regardless of what he said, he had been getting NG feedings since he had been in the unit that first day. Rick attempted to resist the stern nurses trying to do something so humiliating, but due to his injuries, he was unable to give much resistance. His humiliation was compounded when he was placed on a bedpan and the nurse came back and cleaned him after he was finished.

The times when he was exposed and someone would walk in the room without knocking angered him. He would be informed that the person entering was a doctor, nurse, or therapist.

Elaine would come to visit every now and then, usually just to bring Amelia as she was unable to drive herself as yet. Amelia's parents would also occasionally come, but there was no one else. He wondered, with his status as a doctor in a small town, why he didn't have more people visit. With so much spare time, his question was answered. He had actually befriended no one. He spent so much time acting superior to people he considered to be his inferiors and chasing people whose lives he wanted to be a part of that he had made no friends. The fact was finally hitting home, and then the depression set in. When that depression began to slow his healing, Dr. Glass had to bring it up.

"Rick, I am going to transfer you to a medical floor in the morning, but I need to know if you are going to be able to do what is necessary to get well," he asked.

"I don't think I am ready to move out of ICU yet. I can't walk yet. I am in constant pain, and what if I need something?" Rick said.

"You call your nurse on the call light. You are hemodynamically stable. And you need to be in a place you can continue your recovery more aggressively. You will have a cast on your arm and leg for some time to come, but none of that requires any more time in ICU. We have all discussed it, and you will be transferred in the morning. You have been in the unit for over three weeks. It is time to move you," David said.

"Whatever you say, but I think you are wrong," he said and turned to face the wall. "Was it not you who told me it was Sara who was sitting beside me when I woke up?"

"Yes. She, Elaine, and Maria stayed with you most of the first week so Amelia wouldn't worry. She will be better able to visit now that visiting time is longer than a few minutes three times a day."

"I have only seen Elaine and Maria when they bring Amelia up here. And Sara has not been back at all. I would have thought that some members of the Byers family would visit since I am on staff at the hospital they own," Rick said.

"You have always acted negatively toward the entire family, especially Sara. Could you really expect her to come up here on her own?" David said, turning his back as he made the comment.

"She works here, doesn't she? I thought as she appeared to be sitting here in this room for some time, maybe she would just pop her head in to say hello," Rick said.

"And maybe she likes you better when you can't talk. Did you ever think about that?" David said a little too short.

"Something is wrong with her. What is it? She is expecting a baby, is that it?"

"Sara Lyn is my patient, and I owe you no explanation. If I were you and wanted something besides outstanding medical treatment, I would concentrate on getting yourself better. I will see you upstairs tomorrow," David said and left the room.

David walked outside the unit to the young nurse waiting to see if Rick took the bait.

"Did it work, Dr. Glass?" Sara asked.

"I believe it has. I gave him something to want to get out of the unit for. A phone," David said and smiled. "How about you, little girl? Is that swelling I am seeing in your ankles?"

"I just worked eight hours and thinking of a brilliant thing to make Dr. Powell want to get better. Not to mention I am nearly seven months pregnant. A little swelling in the ankles is a small price to pay," she said and rubbed her head.

David noticed, like her feet, her hands were also swollen. "A headache?"

"A little. I am tired," she answered and began to walk away.

"Hey. How long have you had a headache?" he asked.

"I am tired, Dr. Glass. That's all," she answered.

"Do you have to work tomorrow?"

"Yes, sir. Then I am off for two days. I am trying to get all the experience I can before the baby is born. I am supposed to graduate in May, and I really need every minute I can get working," she said.

"Yes, I know, honey. And I will be there when you do. Why don't we see what your blood pressure is, and if it is okay, you can go home and put your feet up for a while and rest. If it is high, we really need to call and let Dr. Chambers know."

She nodded, looking down at her feet. "Come on. Don't look so serious."

The two walked to an empty room, and David took her blood pressure. When he saw what it was, he was concerned.

"Sara. How long have you been having these headaches?" David asked softly.

"The last two weeks at the end of the day. But I get home and take two Tylenols and rest, and they go away. I just thought it was a little stress. This is the first time I have had my hands to swell. I promise. I just want to go home and lie down," she said.

"Your blood pressure is 132/90. It is not terrible, but a few more points and it is something to worry about. Are you sure you should continue to work?" David asked.

"Yes. I mean, I work in the safest place in the world, a hospital surrounded by doctors and nurses. I work no more than eight-hour shifts. Just a little longer. I really love what I do, and the nurses I work with are the best teachers," Sara pleaded.

"I am going to let Bill know about the swelling and what your blood pressure is. And keep in mind, I want your blood pressure checked two times a shift by Linda. That way, no one else knows. And one of us will be by during each shift that you work. Okay?" David said.

"Yes, sir. I think I really need to go home now. I am very tired," she said.

"Okay. I will drive you home."

"David, it is fifty miles to the ranch. I know I am taking you out of your way. I can drive," she said and then was unable to cover a yawn. "I will drive straight home now."

"Okay. I will see you tomorrow."

Sara smiled at him then kissed his cheek. "I will see you tomorrow," she said and walked to the jeep for the long drive home.

As she drove home, she thought about her life. She was the luckiest woman in the world. Although still feeling the profound loss the year before, she knew that all those that she had loved and lost were safe with God for all eternity. She had come through the darkest times in her life and had kept the faith that had never let her down.

There would always be times of uncertainty such as when John had been so sick or the irritations of the world such as Rick Powell. But Amelia was her friend, and as such, she would put up with his spoiled child antics to stay close to her friend. And although Rick had not intended on it happening the way it did, he had brought Adam into their lives, and what a blessing he had been to all of them.

God had known the despair the three children had been through, and he had rewarded their faith by handpicking a family for them. She had a family that she cherished, friends that were nearly as close as her family, and the career that she had always wanted. She could feel little Steven Chase kicked her in the ribs as he always did that time of the day, letting her know it was suppertime. She smiled to herself. She had picked his middle name after Adam's middle name, and Scott had picked the first name after Dr. Quinton's first name. She drove to her parking place near the kitchen door and saw Scott walk out to meet her.

"Hey, pretty lady, what are you smiling about?" he asked.

Sara walked over and hugged her husband close. "Just thinking about how lucky I am," she said and smiled up radiantly at him.

"David called and told me I am to baby you tonight. So I called the pizza place, and there is a pizza on the way out here for supper. Then, a hot bath, and I thought about rubbing your feet for a little while," he said.

"Sounds heavenly." she said and heard the kids running to see their momma. She kissed all three boys and went in to baby Lauren's playpen and kissed her chubby little face. She was just nearly walking. It didn't seem possible she was nearly a year old.

After the pizza arrived and the children were bathed and in bed, Scott and Sara sat before the fireplace in the master bedroom in each other's arms on the floor. They talked about everything, from work to the kids to all the things they wanted to do with their second decade together.

"You know. I never in a million years ever thought about being married, having a bunch of children, and having a refinery that I was the one who thought of before I was thirty years old. That is something people in their fifties achieve," Scott said.

"What can I say? I married an exceptional man," Sara said and smiled.

"You are great for my ego. Don't ever think that I could have done any of that without you," Scott said.

"Nonsense. You would have gotten it done faster if I hadn't gotten in your life as early as I did. I am such a lucky girl to have a family and friends that love me and that I love. I am so blessed," Sara said, and her voice broke, and she closed her eyes and raised her hands to hold her head.

"Sara, is something wrong," Scott asked, thinking it was the hormones of pregnancy that caused her distress.

"My head," she said in a whisper. "My head is killing me, Scott," she said again. "Call Dr. Chambers."

Sara had never requested anyone to call a doctor for her. Scott knew this was not normal. He was up in a flash, calling Dr. Chambers. When he could not reach him, he dialed David's number.

"David, this is Scott, something is happening to Sara. We were talking, and she suddenly had a blinding headache," Scott explained.

"She is becoming toxic, Scott. Get her to the hospital in town immediately and have the doctor there to start an IV and a nurse to travel to St. Mary's with her. I will get a hold of Bill," David said.

"We will be up there in a few minutes," Scott said.

He then called his parents to watch the children and picked up his wife and carried her to the jeep.

When they arrived, he again picked up Sara and took her inside. She was now groaning from the headache.

"Help!" he yelled when he went in the Country Hospital's ER.

Immediately there were two nurses and Dr. Middleton as well.

"What is the problem, Scott?" Jeff Middleton asked.

"Her doctor in Tyler said to stop here and start an IV and give her something for the blood pressure and to continue on to St. Mary's. Do you have a nurse you can spare?" Scott asked.

"I will find one. Sara, are you having any contractions?"

"No, my head hurts so much. My feet feel funny," she said in a whisper.

Jeff looked at her feet and noticed she had profound edema. "I am going to give you something for the blood pressure and something for the headache. That should make the ride to Tyler much easier for you."

"Whatever you say," she whispered.

Within a short time, Sara was ready for transport, and thanks to the potent narcotic and medication for her blood pressure.

"She has stabilized, Scott. She and the baby are both doing fine right now. She will be to St. Mary's shortly, and I have no doubt she will be fine," Dr. Middleton said. "I would feel better if she were going on a helicopter, but ground ambulance will be fine."

"Would it be better by air?" Scott asked.

"Yes. It only takes about ten minutes to get from here to Tyler, and the ride is usually better."

"I will make you a deal," Scott said, picking up the phone. "I will provide the transportation, and you provide the nurse."

"You've got it," the doctor said.

"A couple of years before, after we started the refinery on the gulf, it took several hours to drive back and forth. So we invested in a helicopter. My brother Mark learned to fly it," Scott said and then talked into the phone to Mark.

The doctor made sure the clerk turned on the landing lights. When Dr. Carmichael had the hospital enlarged, he included room to make sure in case of emergencies, a helicopter could land, a decision that had saved precious time for critical patients in recent years.

"I have no doubt. She will be well," he said.

"I know she will as well," Scott said, putting a very thankful hand on his shoulder before they left for Tyler.

Everything seemed to be moving in slow motion. Since two days before when she arrived at St. Mary's, Sara had been put on bed rest. With their other children, she had been told to always take it easy, but bed rest was torture. She was glad that she was still able to get up to the bathroom.

She had told the doctor she would do as she had been told at home, but at least for a few days, he wanted to monitor her in the hospital. Family and friends came by, and that helped to pass the time. Adam asked if she minded his visits, which of course she didn't. After only a few days, it was like they had always known each other.

Adam loved their visits, but knew to not press too hard.

Adam had indeed found a home at the ranch. For a time, he lived at the main house. After only a few weeks, he had gone to work for Byers Oil. His insight and education made him an asset from the start. When he had mentioned finding an apartment to rent in town, John had offered him a house on the ranch that had belonged to one of the hands until he had bought his own farm not far off the ranch but continued to work for the family. Adam accepted the offer and moved in after buying furniture.

Adam continued to have his own money from his years of being an officer at the bank. He moved all his funds to a bank closer to his new home so as to more efficiently utilize his funds. For the first time in his life, he felt himself becoming his own man.

From time to time, his father would call and even came out to the ranch one time. James Sterling saw Adam at his new house and even saw Sara riding Bunny with two of their sons also with her on their own ponies, but even though Sara saw that it was him, she did not approach as he and Adam talked. Adam merely told his father that he needed time and asked that James leave him and Sara alone.

Adam learned about both families, both his sister's family and the Byers family, and was treated as one of the family rather than an outsider. There were no secrets. If he asked a question, it was answered. Always before, his father had told him there were things he didn't need to know, setting him up as an outsider.

At the hospital, Sara talked to Adam about life before. But talk centered on her, Saline, and Jody.

"I hate being in the hospital for so long. I am starting to feel like a beached whale. I am getting so fat," Sara said.

"You don't look fat, you look gorgeous. Keep in mind, this is not forever. Before long, you will be holding your newest son," Adam said.

"I know. But I am used to being so active. I miss our home, our children. Last year at this time, when I was expecting Lauren, I had to take it easy from the time we returned from London. I guess if I survived that, I can do this as well. Besides, Dr. Chambers said I may be returning home before Thanksgiving as long as I do as I have in the hospital. At least I won't have to drag an IV pole around with me," Sara said, resting her head on her pillow.

Elaine walked in the room and had a look like she was going to explode.

"How is my almost sister and nephew doing today?" she asked.

"Okay, I guess. What do you know?" Sara asked.

"I had better be getting on, Sara. I will see you tomorrow," Adam said and kissed his sister's cheek.

"See you tomorrow, Adam," she said and smiled. Adam put his hand lightly on Sara's very pregnant belly then walked out.

"I have some news that I was not expecting and I want to tell you first," Elaine said.

"Besides that you will be graduating before I do because I am laid up," Sara said.

"Nope, we will be graduating together because I am pregnant and will have to have time off in the spring," Elaine said, sitting on the end of Sara's bed.

Both women squealed in delight, hugging each other enthusiastically.

"What does Doug say?" Sara asked.

"I just came from the doctor. You are the first to know. Dr. Chambers will be delivering for me. I can't believe I was four months pregnant and just finding out," she said.

"Wow. You are nearly halfway," Sara said, scooting over in the hospital bed. Elaine lay down on the bed beside her as they did frequently when studying. Sara put a hand on her belly.

"Our babies are only going to be about three months apart. I can't believe it." Then she looked at the bag Elaine had brought for her. "You brought me lunch from Jason's?"

"For both of us. We are both eating for more than ourselves. And mine is twins," Elaine said, pulling the tray table over to them. The two women continued to talk until they finished eating. Both seemed to drift off to sleep for an afternoon nap.

Not far from Sara's room, Rick Powell was continuing to recover from his injuries. On this day, he was to walk in the hall with physical therapy. He told them he wouldn't walk in a hospital where he could be seen by others. But in the end, he began his walk in the hall.

He was moved to the VIP floor because of his complaining when moved to the orthopedic floor. He continued to complain, but his complaints began to fall on deaf ears. Then, he looked up and saw the last name Byers on the door of one of the rooms. He pushed the door open and saw that the hospital room was much nicer than his private room. He also saw Sara and Elaine peacefully asleep.

"How long have you been here?" he said loudly. The physical therapist tried to get him out of the room.

"A week. You are not supposed to be here," Sara said, waking up a little.

"I am just a few doors down. There is no reason friends can't check in on one another," Rick said, leaning heavily on his walker.

"She is not supposed to get excited, so you need to leave," Elaine said, getting off the bed and standing.

"You are even starting to dress like her," Rick said, referring to the long full skirt. But there was something different about her.

Sara began to hold her head tightly. "Please leave, Dr. Powell," she whispered.

The nurse came in the room and said that Sara's heart rate was way too high in the last few minutes. The nurse began to take her blood pressure. "You are going to have to leave, sir."

The therapist pulled Rick back into the hall. "You are a real piece of work, sir. Let's keep walking for a while. Maybe you can work off some of your problems."

"It does not matter that I am a friend of the family and I just discovered she is here?"

"No. She is here for the same reason as you. To get better. Upsetting a hospitalized pregnant woman is not a good idea," the therapist said. Just about that time, the nurse from Sara's room left in a hurry.

"I need to go back in there. She may need a doctor, and that is what I am," Rick insisted.

"No. You are a patient. The nurse will take care of her, now I need you to walk," the therapist said, picking up the pace, wanting to get Rick as far from Sara's room as possible.

When they arrived back to his room, Rick suddenly remembered the differences in his and Sara's hospital rooms.

"I also want to know why a nurse rates a nicer hospital room than a physician," he ranted.

"Could be because her family's name is on the new cardiac wing of this hospital. You may rate higher in your own mind, but until you build something like a cardiac wing, you don't," the therapist cited.

"I will be talking to your supervisor."

"Good luck with that. Since you have been here, all the therapists have asked not to care for you. As the supervisor, that leaves me," she said and walked from the room.

Rick sat in the chair the therapist had left him in. He was angry. Every time he thought he was gaining ground with the Byers family and becoming part of the world he had always wished to be a part of, something happened. Now, just a few feet away was the difference that wealth made. He just had to understand the difference a junior nurse made.

Rick then used the walker to pull himself up and made his way back up the hall. When he arrived at Sara's room and was about to walk in, he heard his name called from behind him.

"I wouldn't do that," Eric said.

"I can't even say hello?"

"No. Your hello a few minutes ago has caused premature contractions, and I won't risk her losing her baby because you want to prove you can get to her," Eric said, leaning back in his chair.

"What, is she afraid of someone seeing her in her current state and stopping to gloat? I am a doctor," Rick said but was cut off.

"And she is a nurse. And I am not talking about modesty. I am talking about the fact that she is afraid of you. If modesty were in question, I would think that would be a problem more with you than her," Eric said.

"What are you talking about?"

"Think about it, Rick. You were in the unit for a month. You had ICU nurses around the clock. For several shifts before you were extubated, Sara took care of you, gave you your meds, treatments, and bathed you. She may even have given you a few enemas," Eric said.

"She is an LVN. As such, she does not work in the intensive care," Rick said with gritted teeth. The thought of a nurse he knew seeing him is such a way and touching him so personally! He could feel himself begin to blush.

"She is studying to be an RN, and not far from it. Now I am telling you, you are not going in her room. She is preeclamptic. Her blood pressure when you went in was up to 248/170. I assume that you know what can happen with that," Eric said.

"I also saw Elaine in there. Suppose you tell her I would like to talk to her then," Rick said.

"Elaine is four months pregnant with twins and needs as much rest as she can get. And they were doing that until you went barging in. And it is an order now. You may not visit. Period. Is that plain enough English for you?" Eric said.

There was nothing Rick could say. Entering a private room on a high-secure, VIP unit could cause him problems. He used the walker and went back to his room and sat back in the chair. His anger remained.

Weeks passed and soon it was Thanksgiving. Friends and family gathered at the main house for the huge meal provided by all the women of the ranch and friends from off the ranch.

Sara was still on bed rest, but at least she had company. Elaine was now five and a half months pregnant and was on bed rest as well. Allison invited her and Doug to spend Thanksgiving on the ranch, and Doug accepted since Elaine was not going to be able to cook. In addition to her bed rest, Elaine had been diagnosed with gestational diabetes. She had to control her sugar intake until the twins were born. Elaine joined Sara in she and Scott's room at the main house while the other ladies fixed the meal for the hundreds of people that would attend.

Allison knew that both of the girls wanted to be helpful, so they put them to doing things like peeling potatoes and carrots and such. Both peeled and chatted happily.

Another change that had come about since the accident was that when she was discharged from the hospital, Amelia needed to be looked after. The burns she had received when attempting to extricate Rick from his car were to both arms and her back. As Amelia was seen as close as family now and was always there when needed, John and Allison offered her and the children to either live at the main house or to live in one of the brick houses that were nearby. With everything that had happened, Amelia accepted the kind offer. And as the children all went to the same school, there was always someone to take them to school.

Amelia did such things as making the schedules and other paperwork that were her job at the Country Hospital at home. It gave her something to do. And between worrying about Rick and her own physical pain, she needed the diversion. She was unable to drive as yet, and in general, if she had to go someplace, one of the ladies could drive her.

Rick had been told he would be able to go home from the rehab hospital the week after Thanksgiving. Until that time, he had no idea that Amelia and the kids were living at the ranch.

The weather had turned cold, so while the women fixed their meal, the men were feeding the cattle. Most of the children welcomed going to feed with the men. Baby Lauren of course stayed at home with the women. Elaine and Sara had been ordered to stay off their feet in the family room. The TV was turned on to *It's a Wonderful Life*. After a time, Sara got off the couch and took a pillow and lay down on her side of the floor. Baby Lauren soon came in and saw her mother on the floor and lay down with her mother and was sound asleep in no time.

Elaine could not believe the fatigue she was feeling but closed her eyes for only a moment and, like her friend, was asleep in no time.

After about an hour, the phone rang. Elaine, being the closest to the phone, answered.

"Hello," she said.

"Who is this?" the voice came.

"This is Elaine, who is this?" Elaine said.

"This is Dr. Powell. Why are you there?" he asked.

"I was invited, and it is really none of your business," Elaine said.

"I am looking for my wife," he said.

"If I see her, I will tell her you are looking for her," Elaine said and hung up the phone. Within seconds, the phone rang again.

Once again, Elaine answered.

"I need to speak with my wife," Rick said.

"She is in the kitchen and is busy. I will tell her you called," Elaine said.

"Why don't you go and tell her I am on the phone?" Rick said.

"Because I am on bed rest and am only to get up to the bathroom. I will tell her you called," Elaine said.

"It is Thanksgiving Day. I would have thought that she and our kids would be coming down here rather than out having a good time with friends," Rick said.

"It just so happens, Dr. Powell, that in that same accident that you were hurt in, your wife had severe injuries of her own. The second and third degree burns on her back and left arm left her needing help the last few weeks. She is still unable to drive, so she has been living here at the ranch with the children since she came home from the hospital. All of us have been helping her recover. She is in terrible pain a great deal of the time."

"She was not in the accident," Rick said.

"No. But you were. Your car caught fire, and she would not leave you to burn, so she worked to get you out at her own expense. She was what was between you and the fire. And later this afternoon, she and the children are planning on visiting you. Besides, next week you will be returning home from the rehab hospital, and she and the kids will be moving back to y'all's house," Elaine said.

"Who says we will be moving back to our house? I still need assistance, and from what you say, so does Amelia. I would be okay in staying at the ranch until we are both firmly back on our feet," Rick said, seeing an opportunity to be physically closer to the Byers family.

"Amelia and Allison have already begun airing the house out and have bought fresh groceries. By the time you get home, everything will be pretty much the way it was. Not to mention there will be no reason for you not to go back to the clinic. So were I you, I would be resting up. Next week is a busy week. And I will tell Amelia you called," Elaine said and hung up the phone.

A while later, Allison went to the family room to get the girls for lunch. Sara, Elaine, and baby Lauren were still fast asleep, but Allison could hear Sara moaning in her sleep.

Allison leaned down beside her daughter-in-law and gently shook her. "Sara, baby. Are you okay?" she asked.

"My head hurts a little, Momma. Can I sleep a little while longer?" she asked.

"Why don't I check your blood pressure first?" Allison said and got the blood pressure cuff. She pumped the cuff up and didn't like at all what she saw.

Allison got up and walked to the dining room and saw Adam coming in the back door with Riley. "Adam, I need you to pick up Sara for me and get her to my car. Riley, I need you to go and find your brother. I am taking Sara to St. Mary's. Her blood pressure is way too high, and she is not acting right."

Adam was immediately in the family room and picked up a blanket and picked up his sister, taking care to set baby Lauren beside Elaine. "I will send Maria in," Adam said.

"Call me," Elaine said.

"You know I will," Adam said.

A couple of hours later, Scott, John, Frances, and Elaine had arrived. Maria and the other ladies took over Thanksgiving dinner.

Within five minutes from the hospital, she started to seize. Dr. Chambers said he would have to do an emergency C-section. "There are risks, however, because of how high her blood pressure is, and there is the anesthesia. But I assure you I will do my best."

"Thank you," was all Allison could say.

In only a few minutes, the baby was born and, although a few weeks early, was healthy. He had a full head of black wavy hair, much like Ryan's had been when he was born. Steven Chase Byers weighed in at eight pounds even.

Sara was quite another matter. Between the seizure and the anesthesia for the crash C-section, she was waking up very slowly. Her blood pressure had begun to normalize following the delivery of the placenta. Dr. Chambers told the family to give her a few hours and hopefully she would begin to awaken after her body had time to catch up.

Scott walked directly over to Sara and picked up her hand.

"You need your rest, baby girl. But I want you to know Chase is here. He is perfect. He has lots of hair that looks like yours. I am not going anywhere," Scott said, then softly kissed her forehead.

By the following morning, Sara did indeed awaken. Although fuzzy about the last several hours, she was relieved to know everything was okay.

The following morning, Scott still sat at her side. As the Thanksgiving holiday had the company closed until Monday, he had time to spend with his family.

Sara was sitting up in bed, letting baby Chase nurse from her breast. Scott looked into his wife's face as she nursed the newest Byers tot. Her face had a peace about it when she nursed her children. The rest of the world seemed to float away.

Her trance broke for a moment, and she noticed Scott looking at her with what could only be described as a loving look on his face. "What are you thinking about?" she asked.

"You. How beautiful you are," Scott answered.

"I don't think I have brushed my hair since before he was born. I am sure I must be a beauty queen," she answered.

"You are never more lovely to me than what you are nursing a baby. I cannot imagine giving so much of yourself," Scott said, half dreamy.

"It is one of the perks of having been born a woman," she said, lovingly stroking her hand over the baby's head.

"Bill and Eric both believe that you will be going home today. Do you feel like you are ready to care for five children at the ripe old age of twenty-six?" Scott teased.

She laid her head on the pillow before she spoke. "I can't believe how tired I am."

"You are recovering from an emergency C-section. Could that be it?" Scott asked.

"Probably. I can't explain it, but my joints and bones hurt like they want a complete nap," she said.

"Did you feel like that with the other kids?"

"No. This is new," she said as the door opened and David walked in.

"Maybe you have caught a cold," he said.

"Could be. Am I going home today?" Sara asked.

David put his hand to Sara's forehead and noticed it was a little warm. "You are a little warm, Sara."

"I just had a baby five days ago, a C-section at that. A little fever is normal," she said.

"What about what you were telling Scott when I walked in?" David asked.

"My joints ache a little. I could be catching a cold. But my chest doesn't hurt or anything like that. I am just a little tired," she said. "I think I will do better at home."

"How far have you been able to walk?" David asked.

"I have been up here in the room without a problem," Sara said.

"Let's see how you do walking in the halls a little, and if that goes okay, then you can go home this afternoon. How does that sound?" David said.

"Okay," Sara answered.

"Well then. I will be back after lunch and see how you are doing," David said and was off.

"Baby girl, I need to be in Dallas for a meeting in a couple of hours," Scott said.

"Go ahead, Scott. Elaine has a doctor's appointment today, and likely she won't mind giving us a lift home," Sara said and smiled up at her husband.

With that, they said a quick good-bye, and they would see each other at home.

When Scott had left, Sara reached for her robe and slippers and decided to attempt to walk in the hall. She pulled the brush through her thick hair and pushed it back over her shoulders and opened the door. She looked in the hall, and there was no one to be seen. Staying close to the wall, she began her walk. It was strange walking around knowing she had staples holding her lower abdomen together. She had taken care of women who had had C-sections before, who described the experience as horribly painful. She supposed that somewhere between having several babies, chest tubes, pericardial tubes, not to mention the broken bones from when she was a child, a carefully made incision was just a little soreness. Sara also knew that to get rid of the soreness, you had to move, so with that in mind, she decided how far she was going to go, making sure to remember that she also had to walk back.

All was going well and she was nearly to the nurses' station when an afterpains overtook her and she had to clutch both her abdomen and the rail in the hall.

Sara's nurse seemed to come out of no place to assist her.

"It is good to see you up and about, Sara," Linda said.

"When did you start working on this floor?" Sara asked, wondering why her mentor would be working in the part of the hospital where she was.

"I had to get you well quickly so you can come back to work. We all miss you very much," Linda said.

"I miss all of you as well," Sara answered. "I feel so much better than I did the last few weeks."

"I thought you had a C-section."

"I did. But the last few weeks, I have been so swollen and my head hurt. Then the constant bed rest. You can only rest so much before it starts to be anything but rest," Sara said.

"You had better get all the rest you can now. When you go home, it will be to five children. And the holiday season is here," Linda said.

"Three of the kids are in school. And very seldom do I go through a day alone," Sara said.

"You will need help after this baby. You won't be able to pick up anything besides the baby for six weeks. That includes baby Lauren," Linda said.

"I know. She is walking now, and I don't pick her up very much," Sara said.

"Good. It likely wouldn't be a bad idea for you to stay at your in-laws' house for a little while," Linda said.

Sara didn't have time to answer before the two friends were interrupted.

"I figured you would be at the ranch with my wife and kids," Rick said from behind them.

Sara and Linda turned and saw Rick Powell standing with a walker.

"I had a baby a few days ago, Dr. Powell. I will be going home this afternoon. And yes, Amelia and the kids have been staying in one of the houses. She needed to have people close by to help her," Sara said.

"We just live a short distance from the hospital, and I am sure someone could have changed her dressings had she gone there. Or even Elaine could have gone to our house. She didn't need to pick up and leave our home for weeks."

"Elaine is on bed rest. And Amelia is a close friend of our family. We wanted to help in any way we could. Not to mention the fact that the nurses at the hospital are not your slaves. And since all the kids go to the same school, there was no conflict. I really need to get back to my room, Linda," Sara said.

"Since my wife and kids are settled in on the ranch, and I am going to be recovering for some time, there should be no hurrying her moving back to our house," Rick said.

"Amelia is ready to go home, I believe. But you would have to talk to her. I really need to get back to my room," she said and began walking to her room.

Rick continued to talk and used his walker to try to keep up with Sara and Linda but was unable to do so. The two women were quickly around the corner and to Sara's room before he could follow further.

To be able to stay with Amelia on the Byers ranch would be a dream come true. He would be close enough to befriend the family, not to mention the people who were frequently visiting for one reason or another. That thought was very pleasing. Yes, living on the ranch for even a very short time would be a great thing for him. The door opened from the hall and in walked Dr. Glass.

"Good morning, Rick. Good to see you up and about. Are you about ready to return home?" he asked.

"Of course not. It will be at least a week before I can make the ride home physically. And Amelia will have to talk to the visiting nurses to try to find me a sitter," Rick started, but then David interrupted.

"Rick, you have been in the hospital long enough to where your incisions have healed. Your casts have been off for a few days. To make a long story short, with the exception of some soreness that you will likely have for some time to come, your recovery is all but complete. You are ready to begin your life as a doctor to your patients again," David said.

"Are you nuts? It will take me weeks of physical therapy to get to where I can care for my patients. I will need assistance at home at least a few weeks until I can get some strength built up again," Rick said.

"If you would have done like most patients and returned home a month ago, that would be the case. But as you have been putting off going home for that long, now you are ready to return to work," David said and proceeded to write in Rick's chart.

"Give me one more week to prepare. Then perhaps I will be able to gradually ease into the clinic hours."

"All right, Rick. If that is what you need. I will be sending one of the psychiatrists from here in the hospital to visit with you for a few days. Actually, every nurse, doctor, and physical therapist has suggested the same thing. Maybe that will address some of the issues that you are having in returning home," David said.

"I don't need a shrink," Rick said angrily.

"Then, you will be released this afternoon. You will have a follow-up appointment in a couple of weeks. Better call your wife for a ride."

Rick thought for a moment. "Sara said she is to return home this afternoon. I will get a ride with her."

"Absolutely not!" David said, standing.

"I thought it made perfect sense. My wife has been staying on the Byers ranch," Rick said. The thought of going "home" to the ranch caused him to smile a little.

"I am well aware of that. By the time you are home, Amelia and the kids will be completely settled back in your home again. Complete with the house being aired out, clean clothes, and fresh groceries.

"Sara does not need to ride an hour's drive listening to your complaining about everyone and everything. Unlike you, she has missed not seeing her children and family for four days. You will not be 'carpooling' home and interfering with the family's happiness at this time," David said.

"I can at least ask her," Rick said.

"I will personally sit here in this room until she has left the floor before I will allow that. Does it not matter to someone like you that your continual attempts to push yourself into her life remind her of her stepfather? From what I understand, you have a lot of the same qualities, and he terrified her," David said. "Oh, and I called Amelia before I came in here to tell her you will need a ride home. She is on her way, and before you try to offer her a ride, Elaine is already in the room to give her a ride as Scott is on the gulf until this evening." David stood and walked to the door. "Now I am going to see my patient before she is discharged. You have a nice afternoon, Rick," David said and was out the door.

Rick fell back in his chair, taken aback at the thought of returning to work in the clinic so "soon." In his last nearly ten years of being a physician, sure there had been patients who didn't want to be released from the hospital or didn't want to be released to return to work. But he was not one of those. He thought about Joan Redding and all her so called injuries but tried not to think of that woman.

Rick turned on the call light for the nurse.

"Can I help you, sir?" came the voice.

"Yes. I need for you to page one of my other doctors please," Rick said.

"I will be down in a minute," the voice returned.

A few seconds later, Rick's nurse was in the room, with his chart.

"Dr. Glass has released you to go home as soon as your wife gets here this afternoon," the nurse said.

"That is why I wanted to speak with one of my other doctors. I believe they will agree I am not ready to return home just yet," Rick said.

"Dr. Glass is the last of your doctors to release you. The others have signed off your case. They had left directions, as well as medications that you are to take," the nurse said, going through the chart.

Rick yelled in the young nurse's face, "That is what I am trying to tell you, you stupid cow. I am not ready to go home yet!"

The nurse looked calmly up at her patient. He had been very verbally abusive to anyone who had cared for him. "And why is that?" she asked.

"I still have to use a walker and take pain medicine from all the broken bones and operations I have had," Rick said.

"My suggestion to you then would be to be released as ordered and go to a different hospital and see if they will give you what you want, because you are released from this one. There is nothing physically that you need from a hospital. You need to increase your activity and begin to work again. Otherwise, you will be as miserable as you are now for the rest of your life. Here are your directions from your doctors, your appointments. Let me know when your family gets here to pick you up, and I will wheel you down," the nurse said and left the room.

Rick was left speechless until the nurse was too far away to call back. He then got his walker and stood and walked to the door. Down the hall he could hear people talking. He looked down to see Sara in a wheelchair, with her newest baby in her arms, her nurse pushing the chair and Elaine carrying her bag, walking beside her.

Elaine's pregnancy was very apparent. The three women talked happily as they came up the hall.

"I thought you were on bed rest, Elaine," Rick said when he got closer to them.

"I am. I had a doctor's appointment today and said I would stop and pick up Sara and the baby on my way home. Now if you will excuse us," Elaine said.

"I am to go home today as well," he said.

"Good. I know it will be good for the kids to have their daddy home," Elaine said.

"It would save Amelia a drive up here if you could give me a ride," he said.

"I am not going into town today. I am staying with Sara this weekend as Doug is out of town. But I know Amelia is looking forward to picking you up," Elaine added.

"That and Elaine does not need to spend so much time on her feet. I am lucky she could pick us up," Sara said.

"It would be nice if we could ride and catch up a little," Rick started.

"No. There is no catching up. If you want to leave before Amelia gets here, take a cab," Sara said.

Rick attempted to catch up to the small party and tripped and fell to the floor. The elevator doors opened, and her nurse pushed the wheelchair on, Elaine close on their heels.

When they were in the car and on their way home, the two women would once again breathe easy. "I was afraid he was going to follow us to the car," Sara said.

"I hope he didn't break anything when he fell. I feel for the nurses if he did," Elaine said then giggled a little bit.

Sara also thought about his little display. "Do you think he will feel foolish or blame it on us?" she said, smiling.

"Oh, blame it on us. You know he will," Elaine answered.

"Do you mind if we drive thru the Taco Place on the way home? I am craving a combo burrito and a diet Pepsi," Sara said.

"I am craving everything else on their menu," Elaine answered. The two picked up their food and chatted as they drove to the ranch. When they arrived and Chase had been nursed, both took a well-deserved nap.

Back at the hospital, Rick had been assisted to once again stand up, and only after trying every way possible to stay in the hospital, he was driven home by a very embarrassed Amelia.

When they arrived, Amelia got out of the car and walked into the house to start supper. Rick kept waiting for her to return to assist him into the house. When she did not return, Rick began to honk the horn. When she still didn't return and it began to get dark, Rick got the walker out of the backseat and made his way up to the house.

"What the hell do you mean leaving me in the car?" Rick thundered.

"Exactly what did you want me to do, give you a piggyback ride?" Amelia said. "You are recovered as much as anyone can do for you, the rest you have to do yourself."

"I still walk with a walker."

"You had no trouble making it into the house," Amelia said and walked over to the counter and took a handful of bills and threw them at Rick. "You start back to work at the clinic on Monday. In the last weeks, I have heard you say how pitiful you are to anyone close to you.

"You are educated, have a family who loves you, and still you want the world to feel sorry for you. And why? I have spent the last few years trying to figure out what it is that you want. Well, it comes down to this. I am tired of waiting around for you to be happy. I will not allow our children to live under the roof of a spoiled child any longer. Our sons are not going to grow up to see women as inferior human beings or our daughter to think she is not to do anything but see to the needs of a man.

"You decide tonight. If you don't, the kids and I will be moving out for good tomorrow. I have hurt for you long enough," Amelia finished then turned back toward fixing supper.

Rick had never heard her so angry. Then he thought about saying something back but then thought better of it. He would have to wait and talk with her later, sometime before he was to return to the clinic on Monday. He had to make her understand that in his role as a doctor, he could not let his patients see him getting around with a walker.

In the county lockup, Joan Redding had been told she would be released on probation the following Monday. She had requested for the officers to let her doctor know that she needed her medication, but thus far, the doctor had not visited. Lack of her drugs had made the days, and especially the nights, very long. But she already had an appointment with Dr. Powell for Monday morning.

She leaned back on her bunk and thought about the last night she had seen the Byers family, and everyone else for that matter. They had caused her so many problems. But she would find a way to get close to her daughter, and thus more money than she had ever dreamed of.

Since finding out about being released from jail, Joan had not been able to reach Oscar. It had been over a month since his last visit. He said he was working just to be able to afford cigarette money and that the lights had been turned off by the electric company, but he had contacted his father who paid the bill and got them turned back on. He still had the same job as he had been working for about three years at the last visit. He had asked Joan where she was hiding some money that he knew she had put back. Or if not the money, maybe some of the drugs. Joan had lied and told him that she was completely out and would do her best to get released so she could once again begin working.

On Friday morning, Joan still had been unable to get a hold of her husband, so a sheriff's deputy elected to take her to her farm, just a couple of miles away. When they pulled into the driveway, both could tell that something was not quite right. It had been raining for the last couple of days, and the car had the door open. The mailbox was full to overflowing, and there was a smell coming from the house when the car doors were opened.

Joan got out of the car and walked briskly to porch and into the house, the deputy right on her heels. As Joan went from room to room, she finally found Oscar Redding, dead. He had been dead for at least a week and still had the needle hanging out of his arm.

The shock and smell in the bedroom caused Joan to first scream out and then to throw up. She continued to scream so much that the deputy called an ambulance. He also called the sheriff and, of course, someone to pronounce death so Oscar Redding could be removed.

Joan was taken to the Country Hospital, and tranquilizers were given. Some of the nurses remembered her from years before when she had given birth to her dead son, screaming for more and more pain medication. But all sympathized at having found her husband in the condition that she had.

The sheriff called both Oscar's parents regarding his death and what their wishes were, and then Randy called Scott at his office to let him know what had taken place.

"Scott, this is Randy. I have some bad news."

"Oh dear god, what have those people done now?" Scott asked.

"Joan Redding was released from the county lockup today. The deputy had to take her home because Oscar wouldn't pick up the phone. Come to find out, he didn't pick up the phone because he has been dead for about a month," Randy explained.

"How?" Scott asked.

"Drug overdose. The needle was still in what was left of his arm. I know Sara and the baby are coming home today, but you may want to let her know before the news gets around. You know how things are in this county."

"Especially after what happened last year with that man being buried there. Where is that woman now?" Scott asked.

"She is at the Country Hospital. She got hysterical when they found him. She is medicated right now. Just thought you should know," Randy said.

"I appreciate that, Randy. When she returns home, she will be alone to my knowledge," Scott said. "Is there someone who can be called that could do some cleanup of Oscar's remains? I would be happy to foot the bill for that. Otherwise, Sara is likely going to want to do it."

"Yeah, we have people that we call for things like that. The windows were left open because of the smell. I don't think any burglar will want to break in the place right now. I will call for someone to go out there tomorrow morning before she is released from the hospital," Randy said.

"I would also like to give her some startup money. Could I also do that through you so she won't think she can come out here and get any more?" Scott asked.

"Considering what all that woman has done to your family, that is very generous of you. I will figure out something to tell her as to where the money came from.

"Oh, I almost forgot. I found something when we were trying to collect all the drugs from around her house.

"I found several dozen journals that are Sara's. I don't know why Joan Redding would have so many of Sara's journals hidden away, but I thought that Sara may want them.

"I could tell on that night last year she rather questioned whether her memories were real or not. These may help. But I will leave that to you," Randy answered.

"What is in them?" Scott asked.

"Good buddy, I have a teenage daughter. You never read a girl's journal," Randy said.

"I never thought about that, and it is actually not as generous as it is protecting our family from her coming out here demanding money. I hope I am not asking too much by putting you in the middle. And I appreciate your getting those journals."

"Not at all. And congratulations on the baby. Say hi to Sara for me," Randy said and hung up the phone. He watched as Oscar Redding was removed from the farmhouse. Everyone close by was wearing masks to cover the smell of the decomposing corpse, made even worse from the years of heavy drug use.

The news of Oscar's death didn't come as a big surprise to anyone at the ranch. He had so many close calls that it was almost expected.

Sara had a house full of children that occupied her mind. Although there was always someone popping in to help her and Elaine, still she loved giving her attention to all their children.

On Saturday morning, John and Riley picked up the three older boys to take them to see the cattle auction for the day. The boys always loved to watch the cattle going through the ring.

As Elaine was on bed rest, she could watch little Lauren in her playpen when Sara was tending to baby Chase.

Sunday morning, Sara arose early, looking forward to church services as they were already in the second week of Advent. Normally, Elaine attended at the church where her father was the pastor, but as Doug was working so much overtime and needed his rest, Elaine had been attending services with Sara.

Sara went to her closet and picked out one of her maternity dresses as her belly was still tender from the C-section she had the week prior.

Elaine couldn't believe how big she was getting. The year before, she wondered if she and Doug would ever be having a baby after so many disappointments. Now it felt like she had been pregnant with the twins forever, and she still had six weeks to go. She picked out the maternity dress she would wear to church and got dressed. She felt a little discomfort in her belly that took her off guard. Dr. Chambers told her that she would likely be having Braxton-Hicks contractions during the last weeks of her pregnancy, and not to worry with them unless they became regular. He had also told her that she would likely not carry the twins until her due date.

She pulled on her dress and sat down at the dresser to put on her makeup and do her hair. When she finished, she walked up the hallway and through the den to the kitchen to see if Sara or Scott were up as yet. She found Sara in the kitchen making breakfast.

"Good morning, Sara. Did Chase let you sleep last night?" she asked.

"A little, how about you?" she asked, referring to the twins.

"Not much. I kept thinking about chocolate chip cookies. I know I am not to have much sugar, but at least dreams won't make your blood sugar got up," Elaine said.

Sara stopped a moment with her hand on her abdomen and took a couple of slow breaths.

"Are you okay?" Elaine asked.

"Yeah, I am fine now. I am still having the worst afterpains. I guess I had better take something or people in church will think I am going into labor again," Sara said and got up and left the room. She walked to their bathroom and got the bottle of Tylenol No. 3 Dr. Chambers had given her. She didn't like the idea of taking pain medicine while she was still nursing Chase, but the doctor had assured her that it would not hurt the baby, other than possibly make his nap more pleasant.

"Good morning, pretty lady." She heard the voice of her husband.

"Good morning, sir," Sara answered and smiled.

"What are you doing up so early? I thought you would want to catch up on some sleep," Scott asked.

"I have been up for a little bit. I have to get ready for church. I can't wait to show everyone our baby son."

"Are you sure you are up to it?" Scott asked.

"Of course. Elaine is already up and getting ready. I know exactly how she feels right now. Like she will be pregnant for the rest of her life. I rather look like I am still pregnant. I can't believe how much weight I gained this time," Sara answered.

"I think you look beautiful," Scott said and walked closer to her and kissed her in good morning.

"So now you like your women chubby?"

Scott started shaking his head at her. "You are the only woman that I look at, and you are anything but chubby. You are perfect."

Sara smiled at him, then in a strangely sedate voice, she asked, "Is it a sin to be this happy?"

Scott shook his head. "If you were not this happy, I would be failing to do my job," he said and kissed her forehead. "I guess we had both finish getting dressed."

Sara turned her attention toward getting ready for church. By the time she and Elaine were ready, several family members were there to accompany them to church.

Fortunately for the family, no one really expected Sara or Elaine to be going off the ranch at this time. They were completely undetected by any press and completely welcomed back by their friends at church. Following the service, the family and Elaine only spent a few minutes before excusing themselves to do as they had both been told: to go home and rest.

Doug had gone to the ranch to spend some quality time with Elaine. Only to get to spend a couple of days a week with his wife made his longing for her unbearable. He had a surprise for her this week, however; he had three days off.

"Doug," Elaine said, walking in the kitchen door directly over to him. The two hugged each other longingly. Doug then put his hands on either side of her very pregnant belly.

"How are my little running backs treating their momma this week?" he asked, kissing his wife.

"The way they have been moving this week, I think at least one is a kicker," she answered.

"That will do too," he said. "And how are you and the newest Byers' son doing, Sara?"

"We are both fine. Getting around a little slow, but getting there," she answered, going to the refrigerator to see what all Allison had made and put there for her.

About that time, Riley came in and told both couples and the children that they were having lunch at the main house so they could spend the rest of the afternoon relaxing rather than cleaning up dishes.

"Would it bother anyone if I took my little bride home? I have three days in a row off, and it would be nice to have her all to myself before the babies get here," Doug asked, smiling.

"Three whole days off!" she exclaimed. "It seems like years since we have been at home together," she said again, kissing her husband.

"I guess I don't have to ask if you would like to come home with me," Doug said, smiling.

At that, Elaine went to her room and got some of her clothes to take home. Doug asked if she would still be an invited guest to come back on Wednesday. Both Scott and Sara assured him that she would.

The following morning, as usual, Amelia was up early to get the kids ready for school so she could leave for the hospital.

Rick also got up and was dressed by the time Amelia was to leave for the hospital. As he had not driven as yet, he said he would be riding with his wife.

Amelia knew that Rick was stewing regarding her threat, so she didn't try to force a conversation with him but rather enjoyed the silence.

When they arrived at the hospital, Rick picked up a cane that he decided to use rather than the walker. As he had been out of the office for several months, he didn't expect to have any of his patients admitted. When he did see his name in the rack of charts, he picked up the chart to discover it was Joan Redding.

"Good to see you up and around, Rick. I even have one of your patients that should be discharged today," Dr. Middleton said.

"What is she here for?" Rick asked, dreading seeing the woman.

"She was in jail from last year until Friday. When she didn't have a ride home, one of the deputies drove her to her farm. We found her husband there, dead," Jeff said.

"What happened to him?" Rick asked.

"Overdose," Jeff answered.

"That is what the autopsy showed?" Rick said sarcastically.

"No, an autopsy was not called for. The needle was still in his arm. Ole Oscar had been there for at least a few days. Mrs. Redding got hysterical, so the deputy brought her up here. She was pretty wigged out when she got here."

"Has any of her family come to visit?" Rick asked.

"So far as I know, she has no other family here. And before you start to bite off more than you can chew, Sara knows she is here but will not be visiting," Jeff said. "And with you being her doctor, I turn her care back over to you. I have not rounded on her today. From what the nurses say of last night, she wants more meds and a carton of cigarettes. Oh, and her car keys are in the lockup, if you decide to discharge her."

Rick picked up her chart and made his way down to her room. Before he arrived, he could hear her voice making demands of the nursing staff.

"Good morning, Mrs. Redding. It has been a while. How are you feeling?" he asked.

"I am in a hospital, so things are not worth a damn. Aside from my obvious health problems, my husband of ten years was murdered while I was in the county jail. Now I don't even know how I will get home, much less how I will survive with my husband dead. There is no way possible I can work in my physical shape. That, and I am a nervous wreck. I can't even get these people to give me a cigarette," Joan ranted.

Rick began to listen to her heart and lungs with his stethoscope. "What kind of physical problems have you been having?" he asked.

"I got daily beatings in jail. All those bitches were jealous of my looks and my younger husband. Then there were the guards who abused me severely," Joan lied. "I told those crazy bastards that I was disabled, and they still made me have to pick up trash on the side of the road, wash the sides of building, and pull weeds, just to name a few things. I am in agony from my back pain and headaches. Now I am having panic attacks since I found my husband," she said. She looked at Rick and saw the disinterest on his face. All at once she grabbed her chest, "Oh my god, I am dying," she screamed.

"What is wrong, Mrs. Redding?" Rick asked.

"My chest is killing me," she yelled.

"On a scale of 1 to 10, 10 being the worst pain you have ever known, what would you rate it?" Rick asked.

"A 10, I am dying," she screamed.

Rick pushed the call light and requested the nurse to bring some nitroglycerin and an EKG machine. For the next few minutes, Joan Redding was given nitroglycerin for possible angina-type heart pain. An EKG was done, which showed no changes; and finally, when nothing seemed to work, Rick requested morphine. When after the first dose she stopped yelling, Rick told the nurse to get labs drawn on her and to apply oxygen. Although he knew that she was likely putting on a show for all to see, he decided to come down on the side of caution and had her moved to a telemetry bed for twenty-four hours, and if there were no further episodes, she would be discharged in the morning. He explained his plan to her and asked if she could think of anything else she needed.

"If I have pain again, Demerol works much better for me. Usually between 75 to 100 mg. And I need some cigarettes. I have not been able to smoke for two days because there is no one to bring me any. Have you seen my daughter? Surely she knows what a hard weekend I have had and hasn't come to check on me. Could you call her for me please," she said a little too sweetly.

"You have a phone beside your bed. If you want to call her, you do it. But I will tell you that she will not be coming up here anytime soon," Rick said, somewhat irritated.

"It is greatly because of her that I have no one else in the world to turn to," Joan started but was interrupted.

"Sara had her latest son by emergency C-section just after Thanksgiving. She just got to go home on Friday afternoon. She will be doing no driving or heavy activity for a few weeks. But as I recall, the last time you saw each other, you attempted to kill her. It took four men to get your hands from around her throat. I have no doubt that you have her phone number. And I will see you on rounds at noon," Rick said and was out of the room. He went straight to the nurses' station to make new orders. He wrote her orders very specifically. He knew from her history she would do her best to stay as long as possible and to take any narcotics she thought she could possibly get her hands on.

Rick made a mental note to make sure and check her cardiac enzymes over the next twenty-four hours to rule out any actual heart problems. Then he wrote orders that were specific to what kinds of complaints she could possibly have. Then he ordered physical therapy so she would at least be up and about somewhat. And lastly, he ordered no smoking. If she was going to give heart symptoms, he would treat her like a heart patient. That meant no smoking, no salt, no fried foods, and telemetry monitoring.

It was Rick's hope that she would find the changes so rigid that she would want to be discharged. When he finished, he handed the chart to the nurse and left to go down to the clinic. He was quite surprised to find the clinic waiting room nearly full.

He went to his office to see if there were any messages that needed attention, then began to see his patients. It was the middle of the cold and flu season, so along with his scheduled patients, he had several that came without appointments.

A couple of hours into his busy morning, Rick's nurse saw that he was getting around without his cane, with only a slight limp. She said nothing but did call Amelia at the hospital to let her know how things were going.

Joan Redding continued to complain of various different kinds of pain she was having. If one kind didn't earn her a shot of Demerol, then she always had chest pain to fall back on. Joan Redding knew that it was only a temporary thing, but she liked the thought of being waited on at the moment. That was until she discovered that she only could receive morphine, not Demerol, for only chest pain. Anything else, she was given Tylenol No. 3.

Joan thought about what she would do when she was released from the hospital. She hated working. Before she went to the county jail, she had been working at a cap factory with about one hundred women that lived in the area. Most were uneducated and were married and had a dozen kids. They never wanted anything more out of life than what they had and were completely happy. Joan was never one of them.

She may have to work for a little while, but she would find her a man who would give her everything she wanted. She had done it with two out of three of her marriages, and she would do it again. Her most pressing problem at hand was being able to stay in the hospital for a few days.

Joan then picked up the phone and dialed Sara's number. She heard the phone begin to ring on the other side.

"Hello," a man's voice said.

"Who is this I am speaking with?" Joan asked.

"This is Adam. Who is this?" Adam asked.

"I need to speak to my daughter," she said.

"Is this Joan Redding?"

"Yes, and I need to speak to Sara," she said again.

"She is not speaking to you. She has only just returned home from having her son over the weekend and needs her sleep. You are not supposed to be calling this number," Adam said, then hung up the phone but had not walked away from the phone before she called again.

"Hello," he said again.

"Look, Adam, I have no way of getting home, and I need a ride," she said.

"Sara just had surgery last week and is unable to drive just yet. And did I mention the five children she has?" Adam said.

"Surely she could just drive me home. That wouldn't take too much out of her," Joan said, half demanding.

"I believe that you will find that they have your car and car keys there at the hospital for after you are discharged. So that takes care of the problem. Is that all?" Adam said.

"No. I am all alone in the world now. I need to be able to talk to my daughter. And I am surprised that you have not wanted to talk to me. I am, after all, your mother too," Joan said.

"I know everything I need to know about you. There will be no reunion. You have hurt her enough. Can't you just leave her alone?" Adam said.

"She is the only relative that I have left. I was just in jail for over a year because of her. I have nothing to pay my bills with or buy my prescriptions or food with," Joan said.

"Sounds like you need to find yourself a job like most people do, not bother my sister like you have done in the past," Adam said.

"She is my daughter. She has my grandchildren."

"And you don't care about one any more than the other," Adam said and then hung up the phone. After only seconds, the phone rang again. Adam picked it up and left it off the receiver. He then picked up his car keys and went out the back door and to his car.

Joan continued to attempt to call Sara's number, but it remained busy. She was irritated, so she called her nurse and told her that she was having severe pain, and her nerves were a mess.

A few minutes later, a nurse came into the room. "My name is Courtney, and I will be your nurse today. Where are you having pain?" she asked. The young nurse's perkiness irritated Joan somewhat. "What is that?" she said, looking at all the meds in the cup.

"Good question. I like my patients to know what they are taking, and this gives me a chance to let you know what you are taking. These two are for your nerves," Courtney explained. "I just can't imagine coming home and someone whom I loved for so long is dead," the young nurse said to her patient.

"It was the most horrible thing I have ever seen. I was looking for him, and then he was gone." Using her finger she, scratched the corner of her eye, causing her eyes to moisten.

"I am sorry to have upset you, Mrs. Redding. Perhaps the medication will help just a little," Courtney said, hoping she was right. She had been working the night that Mrs. Redding had been brought in and felt as she would have for anyone who had been through something so horrendous. But there were also things that she knew about Joan Alexander Redding. She had gone to school for two years with her daughter when she had first started in middle school. Saline Alexander was beautiful but was not one to boast or brag or draw attention to herself.

Courtney would see the bruises that Saline tried to cover. Girls envied, and boys ogled her figure. All Saline wanted to do was get her schoolwork done well and be on the bus to be home to care for her little brother and help her sister get a little rest. But Courtney needed to forget about the past when it came to her chosen profession. She would treat her with all the compassion, kindness, and professionalism she could. After giving her her medication, she said she would give her a little time for the medication to take effect and get her to feeling better. When only twenty minutes later she began to complain about severe pain in her back, Courtney brought her her Tylenol No. 3 tablets. Joan took the tablets and threw the container at her.

"How the hell am I supposed to recover when you don't give me anything that is going to control this pain or my nerves?" she screamed.

"Mrs. Redding, I am giving you what the doctor ordered. If it does not help in the next thirty or so minutes, I can give you something different. But you need to let it work," Courtney said.

Joan then picked up her water pitcher and threw it in the general direction of Courtney, screaming like an animal.

The doctors from their clinics had come up to the hospital for their lunch breaks and thought there was someone insane who was running the halls. One other person was there and went directly to the second floor and was not surprised to find it was indeed Joan Redding, his so-called mother. There were about a dozen people who worked in the hospital to try to settle her down. She was throwing everything she could get her hands on, spitting at anyone who got close and scratching and fighting like an animal.

"Madam, stop this instant!" Adam said at the top of his voice.

Everyone in the room including Joan fell mute.

"For the love of God, woman, there are people here trying to recover. Have some compassion for them," he said.

"Who are you to tell me what to do?" Joan seethed.

"As ashamed as I am to say it, I am your son. Why are you acting like you have lost your mind?" he asked.

"They are not treating me with the right medicine. I just lost my husband. They won't give me my cigarettes. I have very poor health and a family that is too selfish to care," Joan said.

"I believe I just heard your nurse say that she had given you medication for your nerves and for pain. And this is a hospital, and you are not supposed to smoke. If you want to smoke, get well, get out of here, and puff away. But until then try, just try to act human," Adam said, obviously angry.

The others from the room had filed out, leaving only Joan and Adam. "Why are you here?" she asked.

"Two reasons. First, I have five thousand in cash with no strings attached to get you started until you can find you a job and get back on your feet again."

"And the second?" Joan asked, looking at the envelope with the money in it.

"The second is that you leave Sara, myself, and all of our family alone. They want nothing to do with you, and neither do I. My father could, I don't know, I leave that between you and him," Adam said.

"If you want to pay me to stay away ,it will take an awful lot more than that," she said.

"Then you will get nothing. Your car is out front, brought by the sheriff's deputy, and the nurse will give you the key when you are discharged," Adam said.

"Make it fifty thousand, and we will be talking business," she said. With that, Adam turned to walk out of the room, and she called him back. "Give me the money," she said.

"First, you sign this. It agrees that you will leave us alone, and for that, you get the money."

Joan jerked the pen from her elder son's hand and signed the paper. He gave her the envelope then was out of the room.

While he was walking up the hall, still angry at what had taken place, a gentle hand was on his arm. He reacted just a little too abruptly.

"I am sorry. I didn't mean to frighten you. I am Adam Sterling," he said and smiled.

"I am Courtney Hyde, her nurse today. I was so afraid of her. Thank you for being there," she said shyly.

"I am sorry she is the way she is. She is an evil woman deep down in her very soul," Adam said. "I wouldn't turn my back on her."

"Isn't she your mother?" Courtney asked.

"She had me when she was fifteen. A few months later, she left me with my father. At that time they were married. She then married the nephew of a German duke. She provided him an heir. Then had another affair with my father, and through that, Sara came into the world. But that is likely more than you ever wanted to know about our little soap opera," Adam said and, as Sara usually did, blushed.

Courtney smiled a little at him, and then completely out of character, she asked a question, "Are you dating anyone, Adam?"

"What? Oh no. Here lately I am still trying to be a cowboy, brother, uncle, and work for the oil company. But if you would like to, I would love to have you to Sara's home for supper tonight. It will be just family. If someone were not cooking, she would be trying to do it all. But she just had a C-section a few days ago and is still weak," Adam said.

"I am an only child, so there are really not family get-togethers I have ever been to. Are you sure no one will mind?" she asked.

"You would be surprised at who all shows up from time to time," Adam said and smiled. "You will be my first date since I moved here from Bryan. Can I pick you up at six? Is that okay?"

"Yeah. That will give me a chance to take a shower and look more human rather than someone who has been dodging things all day. Speaking of which, I need to call her doctor. See you tonight," she said and gave him directions to her house. Adam tried to think about the last time he had met someone and dated, but like Sara, Courtney was a nurse and was levelheaded.

Courtney called Rick at the clinic and informed him of her outburst, about her screaming and throwing things at anyone whom she saw.

Rick was already tired of her. He could not release her for at least twenty-four hours because of her complaints of chest pain.

"Let's give her what she wants this time so at least she will act human. Give her Demerol 50 and Phenergan 25 IV. That should work for a little while. I will see her in a little while," he said.

The nurse took the order and went to give her the injection that hopefully would settle her down.

Courtney arrived in Joan Redding's room after knocking loud enough so she would be heard. "Mrs. Redding, I have an injection of Demerol for your pain."

"Finally. I was about to call my daughter and tell her how bad the care is that I am getting. And you are not to allow my son back in here. He has me so nervous that my nerves are just shot," Joan yelled.

"I apologize for what you perceive as poor nursing. The doctor was just slow in calling me back for a narcotic. May I see your arm please?" Courtney asked.

"I thought you would give it in my ass."

"I am putting it directly in your IV. It was to work immediately then."

"Oh," Joan said. She got back in her bed and prepared for the enjoyment that comes with the strong narcotic. Before finishing the injection, Joan was asleep.

Later, after his day was finished at the clinic, Rick was tempted not to make evening rounds. But if he did that, he would be seen as weak and feeble. That wasn't going to happen. So he walked in the hospital's back door as he had always done and still only had one patient—Joan Redding. He walked down to her room and found her sleeping.

"Mrs. Redding," he said quietly. "Are you asleep?"

"No," Joan said, slurring.

"Did the Demerol help?" he asked.

"I was in so much pain that I could barely tell I got it. I think the pain in my chest is going to kill me. And I have not had a cigarette in nearly a week," Joan said.

"I need you to hear me. You have a choice to make. You say your chest is hurting, and I will call the ambulance right now to take you to a larger hospital. If not, you go home in the morning," Rick said while writing on her chart.

"What do you mean? I just lost my husband, and I can't make it on my own," she screamed.

"Mrs. Redding, this is not a methadone clinic or a psych hospital. And if you are having real problems with your heart, you need to be somewhere where it can be treated," Rick said.

"But I have no one left. I don't have a job, and who will hire me knowing I have spent a year in jail? I need to be here just a little longer until I get over the loss of my husband," Joan said, trying her best to work up some tears.

"Those are not medical problems, Mrs. Redding. You are a middle-aged woman, and if you have never been on your own, maybe it is time. There will be no more Demerol, and you will be released or transferred in the morning," Rick said, leaning down and rubbing the front of his still-healing leg. "I just got out of the hospital myself on Friday. I am going home to be with my family. Have a good night."

Outside of Joan Redding's room, Amelia stood and listened when she heard Rick's voice. His last few statements to the evil woman in front of him warmed her heart nearly to tears. She had her husband back. When he walked out, she went to him.

Rick looked at his wife, his beautiful wife. How nice it was to sleep with her by his side after the long months in the hospital. He put his arms across her shoulder and pulled her to him.

"Hey, pretty lady. Let's go home," he said.

Amelia didn't speak, but the tears of happiness that rolled down her cheeks said all that needed to be said. He handed the chart to the charge nurse and bid her a good night, and the two walked hand in hand to the car.

As the weeks passed before Christmas, there were several shopping parties that went out for brief trips with Sara and Elaine. The weeks before Christmas, a blue northern came through and turned the tanks to ice.

Scott, John, Riley, Mark, and Adam had spent much time in Dallas at the oil company. Scott and Mark had to fly down to the gulf to the refinery to see to the business there and give the employees there their Christmas bonuses. On that night, the wind howled, and sleet came down heavy enough to where Mark didn't want to risk flying back that night. They decided to stay at a hotel and get an early start in the morning.

The ranch hands were out using sledgehammers to break through the ice for the cattle. It was then that Colton, now twenty-two years old, slipped on the ice and crashed through the ice into the tank. It took about fifteen minutes for the other hands to get him out of the water. His arm had broken in the fall, and his body temperature hand fallen. They drove quickly to Scott and Sara's house, knowing that she could help with his arm so they could get to the hospital. Allison, of course, rode with them.

Elaine was the first one to see the young man who was in a lot of pain and shivering from the cold.

"Get his clothes off, and I will get some blankets. His arm is broken. I will try to get it splinted so it won't be so painful," she said. Elaine then turned to walk down the hall to the linen closet and grabbed blankets. When she turned to take the blankets, she felt a pain in her abdomen. It lasted only a few minutes, and she thought she may have just turned too fast. After all, she still had six weeks to go.

Sara had come to where Colton was in the family room by the fireplace. She had brought Scott's heavy bathrobe for him to wear, and some thick wool socks. Both nurses hurried so Colton could go to the hospital. Elaine splinted his arm, and he was ready to go. In the span of only a few minutes that seemed like hours, the two nurses did what they would have done in the ER. Both sat and caught their breath.

When the party was about ten minutes from the hospital, it started to sleet on them. They had to slow to a crawl to drive as safely as possible. When they arrived, they found that the ER was already busy because of the roads. When Colton was taken immediately to have x-rays done, Allison and the others breathed a sigh of relief.

Back at the ranch, the blue northern that had blown through caused breaks in the power lines. Sara got some candles and lit them, then got some glass coal oil lanterns she had bought when they had first married. She and Saline had one for the tack room to use as light so Saline could see well enough to study.

Maria had been watching the kids for the day; that left only Sara, Elaine, and Chase at her house. Sara heard Elaine in the family room cry out and hurried to find out what was happening. Elaine was in front of the fireplace. The terrified look on her face shook Sara to the bone.

"Sara, my water broke," Elaine said, panic beginning to take hold.

"It is okay. Have you started having labor pains?" she asked.

"I have had some pains earlier, but I am not due yet," Elaine answered.

"Not to make you mad, but are you sure your water broke?" Sara asked.

"Of course I am. I thought I was peeing, but I couldn't make it stop," Elaine returned. "Oh god."

Elaine's hands going to her very pregnant belly told her all she needed to know. "Okay, we have practiced this. You need to breathe through it."

"I am trying," she cried. "Oh god, Sara, it hurts."

When the contraction stopped, Sara thought about what to do. The roads were covered in ice, the family was gone from the main house, the men were still in the fields, and the lights were off. She went to the phone and dialed Maria's number, only to discover that the phones didn't work. It was a half mile to the closest house, but she could not leave Elaine and baby Chase alone. The three of them were on their own.

Sara caught her breath and looked to her friend. "Elaine, until Maria brings the kids home, we are on our own. The first thing we need to do is make sure the cord has not come out and see how far you are dilated," she said.

"Okay," Elaine said.

"I have one of Uncle Alex's medical bags here, so I will at least have gloves. Do you want to go to your room, or stay in here?"

"I think we have better stay in here for the light and to stay warm," Elaine answered and added, "Dr. Chambers said the babies were in perfect position my last checkup."

"That is great. But let's not get ahead of ourselves. I will be right back." Sara ran and got the medical bag that had been at their house since the place crash, and she had never even wanted to touch it. Now she grabbed it and ran back.

Once again, Elaine cried out.

"Elaine it has only been four minutes," Sara said.

"I know, but this one was worse," Elaine said.

"Let me get you some pillows from the couch so you can lie down in front of the fire, and I will see where we are," Sara said. "We have both done this before, so between both of us and Mother Nature, we will be fine."

As the two moved to do what was necessary, as they had done together in the ER countless times, Sara also made sure the baby was warm enough and where she could easily work between him and Elaine.

When she checked her friend's progress, she was relieved to find the cord had not prolapsed, but she was over seven centimeters dilated. She then got her stethoscope and listened to both babies and found them to both be fine. Over the next hour, Elaine's progress was progressing, but Chase had awakened. Elaine said she was okay for a bit and to feed her own baby now rather than later. It took only twenty minutes to feed, burp, and change the baby, and he was happily back to sleep.

But ten minutes after he was asleep, she had to push. Sara knew from experience that no matter what she was told during that time, nature took over and a woman had to push. To get as much light as she could with the fire, lanterns, and candles, they both prepared for Elaine's first baby to arrive. Sara prayed to God that she would know what to do.

"The baby is crowning, Elaine. It should be here in just a couple of minutes. Next time I will count for you so you know how long to push."

As Sara had said, a couple of minutes later, Elaine had given birth to a four- to five-pound baby boy. Using the instruments from the medical bag, she clamped the cord in two place and cut between them. When he cried, the two women also cried tears of relief.

"You have a son, and he is perfect," she said, holding him so Elaine could see. Sara wrapped him in two thick baby blankets and placed him beside Elaine. While Elaine took in the view of her new son, Sara took care of the first placenta and awaited the arrival of the second.

Outside, with the four other Byers children in tow, Maria entered the kitchen door and thought she could hear more than one baby cry. She told the children to stay in the kitchen for a minute while she checked to see if all was well.

"Sara, Elaine, is everything okay?" she asked right before she saw that Sara had delivered both babies.

"It is now. Come look, Maria," Elaine said, exhausted but thrilled.

"Elaine, he is beautiful. Are you okay?" Maria asked.

"She is fine. She did this like a pro," Sara said.

Maria went back to the kitchen and got the other children and took them around where Elaine was. She told the older boys to get ready for bed and that they could sleep in by the fireplace in their parents' room so they would be warm. Then she hurried back to the family room.

Elaine began to feel the strong labor pains just a few minutes after Maria had arrived back in the room.

"Oh god, I can't do this again so soon," Elaine said.

"You can do it, Elaine. I have delivered twins before, and every mother says the same thing," Maria said.

"Why don't you take the second one, Maria, and I will help Elaine to push," Sara said.

For the next little while, Sara gave encouragement, and Maria monitored the progress of labor and finally the delivery. Elaine now had a daughter. When everything was done and the three infants were seen to, the three close friends couldn't believe the night they had had.

"Remember when Austin was born here? It seems that when a baby is due, this is the place to come," Maria said.

"At least then we had two doctors that were here," Sara said. "This time there were just nurses."

"None of us is just a nurse. We have all been educating ourselves further, and each of us has delivered babies before the doctor arrived. We are exceptional nurses," Maria said. "And I am also a lay midwife."

All three women laughed quietly so as not to awaken the children.

"Maria, could you see if the tele is working as yet?" Sara asked as she checked.

Maria picked up the phone in the hallway and got a dial tone. "It's working now, Sara. I am going to call the hospital to see how Colton is doing."

The phone at the hospital was picked up after the second ring by the unit secretary. "The Country Hospital, can I help you?"

"Hi. This is Maria St. Clair. Would a member of the Byers family happen to be there?" she asked.

"Oh, hi, Maria. Yeah, they are still here," she said. "Can you hold?"

"Sure," Maria answered and waited.

"This is Allison Byers," she answered.

"Hey, Allison. Is Colton okay?" Maria asked.

"Oh yeah. His arm was broken in only one place, and Dr. Powell has set it. He would just like him to get warm before he lets him leave," Allison said. "Is everything okay at home?"

"I think that is a matter of interpretation, one of those good news, bad news things. Which would you like first?" Maria asked.

Allison had known Maria all her life. She knew if there were something life threatening, she would have said that first and not drawn it out.

"How about the bad news?"

"The lights and phone were off for several hours because of the storm. We only just got the phone working, and the lights came back on about an hour ago. We have an awful lot of snow and ice on the ground, and most of the hands are just now starting to trickle in," Maria said.

"That all sounds like good news," Allison said, relieved.

"Right after y'all left, the lights went out. And not long after that, Elaine's water broke, and she went into labor," Maria said.

"Elaine is in labor. Oh my god, she is expecting twins. I will see if I can get someone to get an ambulance out there as soon as possible," Allison exclaimed, not realizing that everyone in the ER heard her. "Dr. Powell, is Colton stable enough for you to pull away? Elaine is in labor."

Rick snapped off his gloves.

"Get Ray to take you home, Mom. I am fine," Colton said with his teeth still chattering.

"Allison, don't worry. Elaine had a healthy baby boy and baby girl about a couple of hours ago. The phone just came back on," Maria said.

"Oh thank the Lord," Allison said, obviously relieved. "But who…"

"Sara delivered the first one just seconds before I brought the children home. Then I delivered the second. They are a little small, but both of them are beautiful, and Elaine is exhausted and sore, but stable," Maria said.

"Y'all delivered both babies by yourselves! But we just left there a few hours ago," Allison said.

"You two delivered Elaine's babies? Someone needs to get over there fast," Rick said.

"It is okay, Dr. Powell. Maria said that both of the babies are okay. Elaine has already gotten up to the bathroom, and both babies are perfect," Allison said.

"Thank God," Rick said. "Please congratulate her for me."

"I will," Allison said then spoke to Maria further. "What is Elaine doing now?"

"Sara was checking her and asked if the phone was back to working. Here she is," Maria said and passed the phone to Sara.

"Hello," Sara said.

"Baby girl, is everything all right there?"

"I believe so, Momma. Uncle Alex's medical bag that has been here since before the plane crash had what I needed. Her water broke, and then everything started to go so fast. How is Colton?" she asked.

"His arm is set, and he is still being warmed up. But he is fine. Are Elaine and the babies really okay?"

"Yes, I believe they all three are fine. The babies, a boy and a girl, weigh between four to five pounds. Is one of the doctors there with Colton that I could talk to for a minute?" Sara asked.

"Yes. Dr. Powell is here," she answered. "Do you want me to put the phone on speaker so you are talking to both of us?"

"Yes, Momma, please," Sara said. She heard the clicks as Allison switched the phone over to speakerphone. "Hello."

"Yes, Sara, I am here. Is everyone all right?" Rick asked.

"Let me ask you. Elaine's water broke at eighteen hundred hours, and she began to have contractions shortly thereafter. Her vital signs remained stable to slightly elevated throughout. Immediately following the rupture of the membranes, I checked and she was seven centimeters dilated, and there was no prolapse of the cords. I was able to listen and obtain fetal heart rates of both babies every fifteen minutes. About two hours later, she needed to push, and her baby boy was born with no difficulty, and he cried spontaneously. I clamped the cord in two places and cut the cord. I noted two veins and an artery. I estimate him to weigh between four and five pounds. I wrapped him in blankets and laid him down beside Elaine. The placenta was then delivered with no difficulty, and it was only twenty minutes later that she needed to push for the second baby. I have both placentas for her OB. Both appear as Shultz," Sara continued to give him a very detailed account of the delivery of Elaine's baby girl and followed on to tell him about Elaine as well.

Rick thought to himself how ashamed he was of himself for listening to the ranting of a crazy woman about how cruel her eldest daughter had been in "kidnapping" of her younger two children when Sara had been only sixteen. Sara and Saline had saved each other and their baby brother countless times just as he had always been told by countless people.

When she had finished with the assessment, he thought it sounded like she was crying. "Are you all right Sara? Remember you just had a baby a few weeks ago and also need to think of yourself. And it sounds like you did as good a job with Elaine and the babies as could have been done in any hospital. Are they still doing well?" he asked.

"Yes, sir. Elaine is having only a minimal amount of vaginal drainage, and there was no tearing," Sara said.

"You did very well, Sara. I am proud of you," he said. The other end of the phone was quiet for a moment. "Are you still there?"

"I am here," she said, sniffing a little.

"One of us will be out in a little while just to make sure all is well, if that is okay with you. It would be too risky for you to try to drive her to Tyler or even here. And it could take a little time to get there with the roads iced. Will that be all right?" Rick asked.

"Yes, of course. Thank you, Dr. Powell, I was really hoping that you would say that," she said.

"I will see you in a little bit," Rick said, and the call was ended. He handed the phone back to Allison.

Rick or Allison said a word for a few moments, so Colton took that opportunity to break the silence. "Man, a boy and a girl. Elaine won't know if she is coming or going. Do y'all think she is okay?" he asked.

"It sounds like they all are," Rick said and then saw that Colton's temperature was only a couple of points from normal. "Colton, I am going to give you a choice. You can stay the night up here or go home and stay good and warm for the next few hours."

"Home sounds good," he answered.

And with that, Rick wrote him a prescription for pain and told him when to return to the clinic for a follow-up visit.

Allison had left the room and came back in while Colton was being given discharge instructions. Rick had asked the nurse with him to give him pain medication before he left because of the long drive home.

"I hear Elaine had the twins out at the Byers ranch. I will be happy to cover your call if you wanted to follow through with them," Dr. Middleton said.

"I would really appreciate that," Rick returned, then added, "Thank you."

Rick wondered what had happened to all the people suddenly becoming so accommodating. He thought about how things were before he had been in the accident. He had stayed angry with these people all the time, and why? He remembered his first year at the Country Hospital, always making his presence well-known and demanded respect. And not just respect, but respect as he saw it.

He was the doctor to a good percent of the people in town. Yet he did his best to put himself above the town. The statement he had always made about him being a doctor had a hollow ring to it now. He had not spent his off time at home with his family, but rather trying to be involved in the lives of anyone from upper-middle class to the wealthy. That was how he had planned to get what he wanted out of life. Then, suddenly, as if it had lain dormant in the back of his mind since he came here, he thought, had he ever given a compliment to anyone? Or ever offered a smile of encouragement to his patients? Or even worse, had he treated his wife, his nurse Amelia from Vietnam, whom he loved more than anyone in the world, differently since she had started to work as the DON? It was like he had awakened from a dream where he was the bad guy who caused people around him pain. He hated good people thinking about him that way. But he had always rated people on a socioeconomic level. He had spent his entire adult life thinking that way. Now he was only beginning to understand what a terrible mistake he had made.

"Let's get going. It is going to take a while to get home with the roads being as icy as they are," Mark said.

"I will be behind you in a few minutes to check on Elaine and the babies," Rick said.

"Thank you, Dr. Powell. We will see you at Scott and Sara's house," Allison said as they walked out the ER doors.

At the ranch, the Byers and St. Clair children were in the master bedroom. The TV was turned on but was turned down very low. Most of the children now slept, the others beginning to get sleepy.

Maria was warming some chicken and dumplings that Allison had made and put in the refrigerator to help a little with the two young mothers. The children and Maria had eaten before they had arrived. Having had such an eventful evening, Sara and Elaine had not eaten. When it was hot, Maria had made a tray for the two of them, complete with bread, dessert, and a pitcher of tea and three glasses.

"Maria, you are a lifesaver," Sara said. "I didn't realize how hungry I was."

"Now that I have a normal-sized stomach, I am going to make up for lost time," Elaine said, accepting the steaming hot soup.

The three friends talked as they ate and drank. Either Sara or Maria would get up every few minutes to check on the sleeping children down the hall, although the older children were old enough to watch the little ones. With the exception of baby Lauren, the other children had been out feeding the cattle that day and were exhausted.

"What time are Mark and Scott supposed to be home?" Elaine asked.

"Likely not until tomorrow. Mark can't fly when there is bad weather," Maria answered.

"Why don't we move to our room so we can be closer to the children? That way, we won't be getting up and down so much," Sara said.

"Good idea. Do you think you can walk that far, Elaine?"

"You bet. I have to get up to the bathroom again anyway. If y'all can just get me in the right direction. What about the babies?" Elaine asked.

"I will take Chase down, and we will come back and get Maria, and I can get the twins," Sara said.

When the three ladies and the three babies were moved down the hall, everyone relaxed.

"I think that being the only mother and nurse who has not had a baby in the last month, I can safely say that the two who have need to get some rest. You have three kids who will be wanting to eat in the next little while," Maria said with sarcastic authority.

"And I believe that as a woman who has been watching seven very active children for the last few hours, that you need to put your feet up for a while yourself," Sara said.

"Well, I believe that all three of us could use a little nap," Elaine said, and the three of them laughed softly so as not to awaken the children who were in sleeping bags around the room.

Chase started to fuss a little, so Sara went in the nursery and picked him up and walked over to the chaise lounge to nurse him. Before she had finished the first side, Elaine and Maria had joined the children and were asleep on Scott and Sara's bed. When she changed Chase to the other side, she pulled up a blanket at the foot of the chaise and covered them both comfortably as he began to nurse. She was thinking how nice it was to feel so warm and secure when both she and the baby fell asleep.

A few hours later, just out of midnight, the back kitchen door opened, and the familiar warmth of Scott and Sara's house was a very welcome feeling. Andrew had planned on staying at the ranch only a couple of days before heading back England, to his mother's Sandringham Estate, for the Christmas holiday. Having left three days early due to what was to be some rough weather when he was north of the equator and able to manage to get in before the bad weather hit, he would be spending four days with the Byers family before he returned.

He found several lights on in the front of the house, which was unusual. He added some logs to the fireplace in the family room before he went to Scott and Sara's room to let them know he was not an intruder. As he suspected, the lights were on as well as the TV, but what he didn't expect was all the children asleep in their sleeping bags. He saw Sara asleep on the chaise, and Maria and Elaine asleep on the bed.

Maria opened her eyes and saw him standing in the doorway, looking somewhat puzzled.

"Andrew. I didn't know you would be here," she said and walked over and hugged him in greetings.

"I didn't expect to be here early either," he said. "Where is everyone?"

"Scott and Mark got stuck on the gulf because of the ice. Most of the men were in the pastures until late, breaking ice on the stock tanks. Allison and Ray took Colton to the hospital because he broke his arm. They are on the way home, but it is slow driving," Maria said softly before walking over and picking up little Chase from his mother's arms.

"We have had a very busy night," Maria said and began to tell of all the happenings. She placed Chase in his cradle, knowing his mother would awaken quickly to his cries.

One by one, the family and friends began to arrive not long after Andrew had. Rick was the only person who didn't get to arrive. The ice storm had caused several accidents on the highways around town. The ER from the time the Byers left was busy. Dr. Middleton apologized to Rick but said he could use the assistance.

Rick, who just a few days before was depressed because of the accident, being hospitalized, and of course, Joan Redding, felt truly needed and appreciated. And moreover, he could honestly empathize with the people from the accident. He asked Allison if she would mind very much calling when she knew something more about Elaine. Allison assured him that she would and thanked him.

While writing on a chart in the ER, he thought of all the years of college, med school, and residency. But in the last few months is when he gotten the education that he needed to not only take care of his patients but also care for them as people.

The following morning, Doug, Scott, and Mark were the last ones to arrive. They had no idea that Elaine had had the twins and that Sara had delivered them.

Sara had paged Dr. Chambers, and he called back just a few seconds later. He thought it best for the time being to keep Elaine at the ranch because of the ice. He said if something happened, he could send the helicopter to pick her and the babies up. But Sara told him that they had a helicopter and pilot there at the ranch. He felt confident that Elaine would be fine and asked Sara to call him later if needed.

Allison put breakfast for everyone on the table, and everyone, including Elaine, went to the table to eat. Elaine and Doug then took the twins down to Elaine's room so she could rest and feed them.

When they had a moment to talk briefly, John and Allison looked around the family room at all the smiling faces: Mark and Maria and their three children, who had stayed for a while so all the kids could play; Adam, the one sibling of Sara's that everyone knew they could count on; Riley, who teased Colton about his broken arm and his drunken behavior because of the pain medication; Scott, who suggested it to be a good time to put up the Christmas tree so all the children could decorate it together.

The last decade of their lives had changed so drastically, but the love they all had for one another had not. John put his arms around his wife and pulled her close so as to watch the excited children help their daddies and uncles put the tree up and get the lights on it before they turned the children loose with the ornaments.

John had told the ranch hands and his four sons that they would start feeding the cattle and checking the stock tanks for ice at about noon. He saw Scott, Adam, and Mark talking in a huddle and decided to see what they were talking about.

"Boys, it looks like you are hatching a plan about something," John said.

"I was telling Scott that I went to see Mrs. Redding at the hospital," Adam said. "I hope this won't get back to Sara, but I brought her an envelope with money in it. I told her it was hers if she promised to never attempt to see any of us again."

"I wish I would have known," Scott said.

"Why is that? Do you not approve?" Adam asked.

"I did the same thing, but I did it through Randy. And I asked Randy if he could get someone to clean that mess up," Scott said.

And as it turned out, all four of them had done the same thing. All of them laughed at themselves. But at least that would keep her going for a little while.

Scott looked over and saw Sara feeding little Chase. Baby Lauren and little Ryan sat close to their mother by the fireplace. Scott decided to join them.

"I can't believe I am jealous of Chase," Scott whispered in Sara's ear. She returned a radiant smile at him. She was so happy.

"I thank God for you, Scott," she said.

"And I thank him for you. I am so proud of you delivering the twins today. Were you afraid?" he asked.

"Terrified. But Elaine was a pro," Sara answered.

"Strange. That is what Elaine said about you," Scott said and kissed her softly. Then they just sat and watched the children and the tree and all the smiling faces of those they loved. God had truly blessed them all.

Joan Redding had arrived home to find it much different than it had been just a few days earlier. She hadn't looked forward to cleaning the stench of Oscar out of the house. She had to appreciate Oscar. His death had helped her financially. Those men and her eldest son had given her fifteen thousand dollars that would keep for a little while. Who knew? She could likely get more out of that family Sara belonged to if she put her mind to it.

One day, she would find that right person to help her, and she would have that entire bastard bitch daughter had. Rage turned to madness in that moment, and she threw her head back and laughed. Yes. Her day would come.

End of Book One

About the Author

Missy Jo Priest has had her share of adventures in her life. Those adventures appear in part in this book. She and her husband married young and continue to prove marriage is a cherished institution after nearly thirty-eight years. They have three grown children and five grandchildren. Missy is a registered nurse with extra training and education in critical care, emergency care, forensic science, and legal consulting. Her husband, Dusty, is a fifth-generation cattle rancher in East Texas. Mrs. Priest spends her days helping her husband, attending church, riding horses, and writing children's stories for her grandchildren. Her life in East Texas is the backdrop for Child of the Wilderness, which is her first book.

CPSIA information can be obtained at www.ICGtesting.com
Printed in the USA
LVOW10s0242210116

471666LV00001B/58/P